Heartbreak Trail © MCMXCIV by VeraLee Wiggins.
Martha My Own © MCMXCIV by VeraLee Wiggins.
Abram My Love © MCMXCIV by VeraLee Wiggins.
A New Love © MCMXCVI by VeraLee Wiggins.

ISBN 0-7394-1246-9

Published by Barbour Publishing, Inc., P.O. Box 719, Uhrichsville, Ohio 44683
http://www.barbourbooks.com

Cover art by Dick Bobnick.

Member of the
Evangelical Christian
Publishers Association

Printed in the United States of America.

NORTHWEST

*Four Inspirational Love Stories
from the Rugged and Unspoiled
Northwest Territory*

VeraLee Wiggins

BARBOUR
PUBLISHING, IN
Uhrichsville, Ohio

VeraLee Wiggins
is the author of **Heartsong Presents'** most requested series of historical romances. Originally known as the "Forerunners" series, *Northwest* compiles four timeless stories of best friends Rachel and Martha, their lives, their loves, and their marriages.

VeraLee was often voted among the top favorite **Heartsong Presents** authors, and in 1998, she was placed in Heartsong's Hall of Fame. But among her greatest accomplishments were being a wife, mother, and author before retiring to her heavenly home in 1995.

HEARTBREAK TRAIL

For my most special husband in the world,
I appreciate your faithful, caring, gentle way.
Encouraging, but not pushing; helping, but not forcing,
And always being there, no matter what my need.
I love you more than words can say, Sweetie Pie.

Chapter 1

March 1, 1859

P apa," Rachel Butler wailed, her blue eyes flashing. As she shook her head in emphasis, tendrils of red hair fell from her neat braid and then curled around her plump face. "You don't seriously expect me to go all the way to Oregon! Out there, if the Indians don't get you, the wolves will. Besides I'm all registered to start Illinois College this fall. Please, Papa, take me home!"

"Ha!" Papa said. "You'll learn more in six months on the Oregon Trail than you would in four years of college."

Eighteen-year-old Rachel Butler was an only child who'd had a good life in her home in Quincy, Illinois. Nathan Butler, her father, had earned plenty of money for his family in his successful blacksmith shop.

"It'll take all summer to get to Oregon, Papa, if we don't die on the way. It's not fair to make me miss college because of your senile whim."

Tall, graying Nathan Butler, with his clear blue eyes, wide upturned lips, and ramrod-straight, trim, muscular body, looked anything but senile. Just having bought three covered wagons, he displayed undiluted excitement. No one in the world could be kinder than this man who'd always been her champion. But forcing her to go to Oregon in a covered wagon? How could he do that to her?

His soft eyes met her angry ones, unflinching. Then they crinkled into a smile. "We're going, Rachel, so why don't you decide to have fun? Don't you know we're making history? Now, go get your mother and let's find the cattle market. We need about fifteen yoke of oxen."

Rachel didn't rush going for her mama, but found her in a fancy dress shop. BOUTIQUE ELEGANTE—INDEPENDENCE, MISSOURI, the sign above the door said. "Come on," Rachel said quietly, "Papa wants us to help him buy a million oxen."

"Why in the world would he expect us to do that?" Mama asked, hurrying to the shop's door where she almost collided with her husband who'd come seeking her.

His eyes expressed joy at seeing his two "lassies," as he called Alma and

7

Rachel. "What would you be doing in such a fancy place just before starting on the Oregon Trail?"

Alma looked surprised. "Looking for things that won't be available in the wild country."

Nate laughed out loud. "Come on, woman, you won't need anything like those dresses where we're going. Let's go buy some oxen. Should we buy a saddle horse for each of us, too? I'd like to take some milk cows along and a few chickens. I'll bet no one has cows or chickens in Oregon yet."

In the next few days Nate bought the stock he'd suggested plus bolts of sheeting, linsey-woolsey, and denim for men's clothing. Then Nate asked to see the best walking shoes they had.

With disdain Rachel tried on the heavy high-top shoes. "I can't wear these things, Papa," she wailed. "I'd never let anyone see me in them."

"Are they comfortable?" Papa asked.

"Yes, but what good will that do if I don't wear them?"

He nodded with a small smile. "You'll wear them. We'll take three pairs," he said to the storekeeper. While Rachel fussed, he bought three pairs of shoes for Alma and three for himself.

Then Rachel didn't like the warm mittens he bought for each of them. "At least they don't have to be that ugly gray-brown color," she said. "Why can't they be bright?"

"I don't see any others," Papa said. "Wrap them up," he instructed the man.

Then they bought staples: flour, dried beans, dried apples, coffee, sides of bacon, sugar, salt, and baking powder. He bought some potatoes and fresh meat to use the first few days. He added a dutch oven for baking over the fire, some simple pots, and the cheapest of dishes and silverware.

Back at the wagons, Papa put in things he'd brought from home: books, a family Bible, a dictionary, an arithmetic text, a grammar book, some charts, maps, old letters, and diplomas of graduation.

He put some heavy blacksmithing tools into one of the wagons, the only cargo that that wagon carried. In another wagon he put a double-sized featherbed on the wagon floor for him and Alma, two comfortable chairs, plus some of the other things. Rachel's wagon contained one cozy chair, a single-sized featherbed, and the rest of the things they had to take.

"Everything's ready," Papa said, his voice ringing with excitement. "But I have one more thing to do."

Rachel watched with wonder as Papa tore the floorboards from one of the wagons, pushed in a big pouch of money, and replaced the boards. "There," he said, triumphantly, "no one would ever know there's a false floor in that wagon. Would you have known, Rachel?"

She shook her head. "Who cares about false floors anyway?"

He grinned. "You'd better care, lassie! I just put all our extra money in there. Plenty to buy everything we need to get started in Oregon. We'll be leaving in a couple of days, I hope. You know this train we're joining is all Christian, don't you?"

Rachel shrugged. "I know, Papa. You've told me that before. But I couldn't care less. It isn't like joining a church. We'll just be traveling together for safety. We probably won't even meet the people in the other wagons."

Nate got to his feet and jumped down from the wagon. "You want me to give up on you, Rachel? Let you have a terrible time on this whole trip? Well, I just might do that." He walked over to a group of men standing around talking.

The next day, while Papa and the other men elected a train captain and decided on the rules for the wagon train, Rachel and Mama went on a last walk around town. They found a beautiful green ball gown that set off Rachel's red hair to perfection. "I must have it, Mama," Rachel said, spinning around. "You know I won't find one this perfect in Oregon. Their gowns will probably be made from flour sacks. I doubt they've ever heard of satin."

Mama sighed. "I know, love, but Papa told me we can't buy anything more. He says we have to load lightly so the oxen can pull the wagons two thousand miles."

Rachel stomped her slippered foot, but she took off the gown. Then the two had a long, leisurely dinner at a nice restaurant and returned to the maze of wagons and people. Oxen and cows bawled, horses nickered, people yelled, and children cried. The barnyard smell didn't add much to Rachel's serenity, either.

Somehow Papa spotted them and hurried to them. "Everything's all set," he said. "We leave in the morning at sunrise."

He led them to their wagons and talked to them as he fastened a box containing five chickens to the back of Rachel's wagon. "Now we'll not only have milk, cream, and butter," he said, "but we'll have eggs to go with our bacon." He stopped talking and peered at his lassies. "Can't you be a little excited?" he asked.

Alma patted his forearm. "I'm getting excited, dear. It's going to be fun."

Rachel didn't answer.

Nate took them out for supper. "The last time we eat in a restaurant until we reach Oregon," he said, as though bragging.

"How did the meeting go, dear?" Alma asked, putting a dainty bite of white bread into her mouth.

A huge smile spread across Nate's face. "Just fine," he said. "We elected Charles Ransom for captain. He'll be good. Hasn't been over the trail but he's read all he can get hold of. And we decided to use the Ten Commandments for our laws. Ransom said we'd be here the rest of our lives trying to get up as good a set of laws as the Creator gave us." He picked up his knife and fork, cut a bite from his steak, and put it into his mouth. "Oh, yes," he said after eating a few more bites, "Ransom had a bunch of copies of the Latter-day Saint's Emigrants' Guidebook, by Clayton. He said it's by far the best guidebook out, so I bought one."

Rachel swallowed her bite of salad. "Who needs a guidebook, Papa? You said the trail is well marked."

Nate laid down his fork and nodded. "Yes. Well, the book doesn't just show where the trail is. It tells about things like camping spots where there's water, grass, and wood, how far we've come and still have to go. And lots of other things we'll need to know. Say, did you know some of the men are riding horses? No wagons?" He thought a second and smiled. "One's riding a cow. This oughtta be some journey, lassie."

When they returned to their wagons, Captain Ransom stood at the next wagon in line, inspecting its load. "You can't haul this much in one wagon," he told the man. "Them's tried allays wear out their oxen and end up leavin' the stuff beside the road anyways. Better save your animals and lighten the load now."

He left that wagon and approached the Butler wagons. After looking them over, he turned to Nate. "You done good, Butler. You'll get there with as many belongings as anyone, anyways. Might even get there with all your oxen." He started to walk away, then turned back. "For identification, this here wagon train'll be called the Ransom Train."

Papa saluted. "Sounds good to me."

The captain started away but turned back again. "I notice you got a herd of cattle. Got anyone to drive them?"

"Nope. Never gave it a thought."

The grizzled man grinned. "Better give it a couple." He motioned with his thumb over his shoulder. "Some men over there are hopin' to work their way on the Trail." With that, he walked away.

As soon as the captain left, the man in the next wagon approached. "Wha'd the old windbag say to you? Thinks he's God already."

Papa looked at Rachel and winked. "He's purty good. Watchin' out for the animals and all. What you got in that wagon anyway? Seems to have set him off right good."

The man stuck his hand out to Papa. "Thurman Tate. Come'n see what you think."

Rachel followed Papa and Tate to the wagon. She peered inside at a heavy iron cookstove, a big chiffonier, and a heavy dresser. It looked heavenly to her. She'd wanted desperately to bring her beautiful piano but Papa wouldn't hear of it. "Want to kill the oxen?" he'd asked knowing how much Rachel loved animals. They'd ended up leaving the piano, as well as her small dog and two cats with her grandmother.

"Ransom's right," Papa told Tate. "You'll kill your animals and lose the stuff, too. Better unload it here whilst you can get somethin' out of it."

"Never," Tate said. "My wife needs that stuff." He gazed at the oxen a moment. "Them's strong animals, ain't they?"

Nate looked the oxen over. "They're strong all right, but they have a two-thousand-mile pull ahead of them. Better give them every advantage you can." He took Rachel's arm and headed back toward his wagon. "Good luck, neighbor," he called, but he got no response.

When Rachel climbed back into her wagon, she saw Papa a ways away, talking to a group of men. Probably hiring someone to herd the cattle to Oregon. She lay down on her soft featherbed, thinking. Is there any way at all we can stop Papa from this insane idea? If we really go, we'll probably all die before we get there.

—⁂—

The next morning, March fifteenth, men shouting, oxen bawling, and the smoke and the smell of bacon and coffee cooking awakened Rachel early—very early. She hustled into her clothes and climbed down from her wagon. Mama handed her a plate of pancakes, bacon, and eggs, smothered in syrup, and a cup of coffee, black and steaming.

In an hour the wagon masters had yoked the oxen and lined up the wagons in the order they'd travel; the next day, the wagon at the head of the line would move to the back. Rachel climbed into her chair in her wagon. Lots of people milled around on the ground preparing to walk. The atmosphere seemed gala, almost like a big celebration. Well, she'd see how all those silly people felt in a few days. Maybe by then they'd realize what they were getting into.

When the young man beside Rachel's oxen started them moving, Rachel felt herself jarred, jerked, and jolted. The chickens on the back of her wagon must have felt the same way, for they all started squawking.

Twenty-seven wagons, sixty people, a dozen horse riders, and one cow rider began the long ordeal.

Before an hour had passed, Rachel developed a headache as well as a painful back, bottom, and several other body parts. After a few hours, she wondered how she was going to stand such pain every day for six months. Papa had had some crazy ideas in his life, like the time he'd brought home a guitar for her, knowing full well that the piano was her instrument. Well, after she got over the shock and took some guitar lessons, she had found that she enjoyed it a lot. In fact, her guitar lay tucked among some bedding in her wagon.

But he'd really done it now. Mama must be in agony, too. Then she remembered Mama walking with some women from other wagons. Mama had invited her to walk with them but she wasn't about to walk. Riding was bad enough!

At nooning time Rachel sat on the tongue of the wagon while Mama cooked some potatoes and bacon for lunch. "Here you are," Mama said, cheerfully handing Rachel a heavily laden plate. "That should give you energy for the afternoon."

"Don't you start, too," Rachel growled, shoving in a bite of bacon-flavored potatoes. "Papa's ruined my life. If you switch to his side I won't have anyone left."

Mama tried to put her arm over Rachel's shoulders, but Rachel shook it off. "I didn't realize there were sides," Mama said, "but we're on our way so we may as well enjoy it."

"I'm not having fun," Rachel said, "and I'm smart enough to know it. Why don't you go eat so I can at least enjoy my food?"

Rachel thought she'd never survive until evening but she did, hurting in every joint, bone, and muscle. When they stopped for the night, she gingerly climbed down and sat on the wagon's tongue again.

"Come help me with supper," Mama called. "Moving around will make your bones feel better."

Rachel refused. Sitting on the tongue she wondered how she got into this mess and how far they'd go before discovering how dumb it was. Then, hearing squawking, she remembered the poor chickens. Were they the only ones besides her who had sense enough to abhor this trip? She got some cracked corn and water for them and went back to the wagon's tongue feeling a little better.

"Come eat, Rachel," Papa called. "We have fresh butter for our hot biscuits. The churning can worked, and Mama's fixed up a grand supper." Rachel still felt grumpy but ate a good meal.

—m—

The next morning, Mama awakened Rachel at dawn to eat breakfast. After she finished, Rachel struggled back into the wagon. How could riding in a wagon possibly make a person so horribly sore? How could a bunch of people and animals possibly make so much noise? How could Papa possibly have forced her into this ridiculous pilgrimage?

As Rachel sat there feeling sorry for herself, she saw movement out of the corner of her eye and looked to the left. A dark-haired young girl ran up beside her wagon. A medium-sized black, gray, and white dog trotted beside her. "Come on down and walk," the girl called. "It's lots easier."

"Why should I walk?" Rachel snapped. "It wasn't my idea to come on this idiotic trek." Rachel watched the girl's shoulders slump and her run slow to a walk.

"Okay. Good-bye then," the girl called and ran ahead, probably finding someone else to walk with her.

Rachel's conscience bothered her a little for being so rude to the girl, who was just trying to be friendly. But why should she care? She couldn't walk with every inch of her hurting so badly, could she? Wondering if she could live through the rest of the afternoon, she changed her position for the five-hundredth time.

Just when she thought she'd scream in agony, she saw a man riding on the back of a small Jersey cow. He looked unstable hanging onto his belongings with one hand while trying to control the cow with the other. The cow looked as if it were about to fall down under the man's weight, which was obviously too much for her.

When Rachel's wagon moved ahead of the cow, she realized the man and his cow were falling behind. She leaned forward to watch him when suddenly the cow dropped her rear end sharply. The man tumbled off backwards, his arms pinwheeling in the air. Rid of her burden, the cow took off running with the man ten feet behind her, screaming.

Rachel almost laughed until she remembered where she was and how unhappy she was. How could she even think of laughing out here on this horrendous trail? How could she endure the pain any longer?

Then the dark-haired girl appeared beside the wagon again. This time she had a small blond boy with her as well as the dog. "Come on," she called merrily, apparently having forgotten Rachel's rudeness of the morning. "It's fun to walk," she continued. "I'm walking all the way to Oregon." She giggled happily as if she were having lots of fun. She indicated her dog. "Josephine has to walk. Papa told me that before he let me bring her." She giggled again and shrugged. "So, I have to walk with her. Come on. Even my little brother will walk a lot. Maybe halfway. One reason we walk is that this trip is purely hard on the oxen. Every step we take makes it easier on them."

Rachel hated to give in. After all she couldn't think of a single reason why she should walk. She came on this trip under duress and should make it as easy on herself as possible. On the other hand, she liked animals better than people. So if it would make it easier on the oxen. . .besides, her behind was killing her.

After glancing at the dark-haired girl's cumbersome shoes, she reached into a box and pulled out a pair of her ugly new shoes and put them on. Then she climbed down as the oxen lumbered along with the wagon. No sooner had her feet touched ground than the shaggy dog ran and laid her big head against Rachel's side, stealing her heart. She patted the dog's dirty fur. "Nice girl," Rachel said softly. "Oh, you're so sweet, and you like me, don't you?"

The dog raised her head and looked deep into Rachel's eyes then gave her one lick on the hand. "I love your dog," Rachel heard herself say. Now why did she do that? Just because she'd climbed out of the wagon hadn't meant she wanted to be the little waif's friend.

"She likes you too," the dark-haired girl said. "She doesn't take to everyone like that. You must be a special person. I'm Martha Lawford. This is my little brother, Willie, and that's Josie you're petting."

Rachel stiffly told Martha her name.

"Oh, aren't you thrilled to get to go to Oregon?" Martha asked, excitement making her voice ring. "I'm just having so much fun already. I can tell it's going to be a good trip."

"Don't be too sure," Rachel grunted.

"But I'm not going to Oregon," Martha said, ignoring Rachel's negative comment. "We're stopping in Walla Walla Valley, in Washington Territory. That's about three hundred miles before Oregon City. Oh, Rachel, I can't wait to see it. My brother, Jackson, says it's God's Garden of Eden on earth."

"I've heard the same thing about the Willamette Valley," Rachel said. "As far as I'm concerned, Quincy, Illinois, fits the description just fine."

As the girls continued talking and walking along, the man who'd been riding the cow tore past them still screeching at the cow that was no longer in sight. The girls looked at each other and burst into wild laughter. "I hope he never finds her," Rachel said. "I saw him riding her, and she about collapsed under his weight. It was awful."

Rachel walked with Martha again the next day and found it much better than trying to ride. At the end of the third day of travel, the train camped on the Missouri-Kansas border. A festive air emanated from the camp.

"What's all the laughing about?" Rachel asked her mother.

"Everyone thinks we're leaving civilization," Mama said, wearing a happy smile. "I don't exactly know why, as Kansas has been a U.S. territory for five years."

Nevertheless, after the meals were finished and cleaned up, someone brought out one of those new-fangled instruments called an accordion, and someone else a violin. Before long, lively music brought the plains to life. Soon, a square dance was being called and danced. Many people stood around, singing the mood-elevating songs.

"Why don't you take your guitar out there and play?" Papa asked.

Rachel wasn't about to enter into such foolishness. Why, they didn't even have a floor under their feet. Just grass and dust. What was there to sing about, anyway? She sat on her usual seat, the wagon's tongue, to wait for the crowd to settle down and to just think. One of the chickens had died that day while they traveled; the others looked bad. Papa had said they should eat them. He might be right.

"I say, you look lonely," a young man said. "Gotta git up and work out the kinks. Wanna go out there with me?" Not waiting for an answer, he squatted on his heels near Rachel. "I'm Martha Lawford's brother, Jackson."

Why this? Didn't she have enough to put up with? The young man looked clean but his clothes had been mended in several places. Rachel jumped to her feet, elaborately dusting off her long skirt. "I'm afraid I'm tired, Mr. Lawford. If you'll excuse me, I think I'll try to get some sleep, if that's possible with all the racket around here." Then she hopped into the wagon, leaving Mr. Lawford sitting there, alone.

Chapter 2

R achel almost laughed at the man's look of surprise.
"Well, good night, Miss Butler," Jackson Lawford called into the
wagon. "I'm sure we'll see each other again."
She heard him plodding across the ground. There. She'd been rude to
both Martha and her brother. But what did it matter? They'd never see each
other again after this summer. But already she couldn't help liking Martha a
lot. Maybe she shouldn't have been rude to Jackson. She could have let him
know, without being rude, that she wasn't interested. *Oh well, what's done is
done.*

The next day, Mark Piling's wagon broke an axle. The slight, rough-
sounding man with tobacco-stained teeth, was angry and used words that
indicated to Rachel he'd forgotten at least temporarily that he was a Christian.
No one seemed to know what to do, so Nate Butler hauled out his tools.

"Better call nooning," Nate told Charles Ransom, who was trying to
calm the irate Mark Piling. "This'll take awhile."

Several young men crowded around Nate, helping however they could.
"Looks to me as how that axle was near broke before we started on this here
trip," a tall thin man said.

They finished the job in a little less than five hours. "Thanks, fellows,"
Nate said. "That's the quickest I ever fixed an axle."

Mark Piling didn't thank anyone. "Sandy!" he yelled at his wife, "why
aren't you in the wagon and ready to go? I notice you're always in the wagon,
sick, when it's time to do a little work." He emphasized the word "sick" as
though he doubted it. "Get that boy into the wagon right now. You're holding up the whole train."

The thin, pale woman adjusted the baby in her arms and climbed into
the wagon with no help from her husband. "Petey," she called weakly, "come
on now. We're starting again." A moment later, a little boy showed up from
somewhere and silently climbed into the wagon beside his mother and sister.

As the wagons began to move, Rachel, walking with Martha, Martha's
little brother Willie, and Josie, moved close to Martha. "I see everyone isn't
all that pleasant on this wonderful 'Christian' wagon train."

Martha laughed quietly. "He prob'ly felt purely awful holding up the

16

train. It's hard for some people to put others out." She grinned at Rachel. "He may truly be the nicest person we could ever meet."

Rachel grunted. Why couldn't Martha have agreed with her? Maybe she didn't like Martha so much after all. She might be a goody two shoes.

Later that afternoon Rachel noticed the man who'd been riding the cow coming toward them from the front of the train, his gray hair flying, mud and dust decorating his torn overalls. "Where's your cow?" she asked impishly.

"Ain't seen that critter for over twenty-four hours now," he ground out. "She'd better stay outa my sight, too. She might make a big barbecue for this here train."

Rachel couldn't stop pestering the man. "How come you're going the wrong way?" she asked. "It's far enough to Oregon without going backwards part way."

"I ain't dumb enough to walk all that way," he grumbled. "I'm goin' back to Independence afore I git any farther away." He jerked his head forward and, with a determined stride, started off toward the back of the train.

"I wish I could go with you," Rachel called after him, but he didn't miss a step. "Guess that means I don't get to go," she muttered.

The next day they came to a stream with a rickety bridge over it. As the first wagon, which happened to be Rachel's that day, approached the bridge, two tall Indians dressed in buckskins and moccasins came to meet the men driving the oxen. The Indians' long black hair hung in single braids down their backs.

"Twenty-five cents to cross," one of them said.

"Not me," Rachel said. "That bridge'll fall down if a wagon tries to cross."

Nate, driving the wagon behind her, came up to see what was going on. When told, he asked the Indians if the water was deep. They assured him it was. Nate pulled out seventy-five cents for his three wagons and they made it across without incident. Soon, the rest of the train crossed too, one wagon at a time.

All except Mark Piling. "I ain't gonna pay them savages nothing," he grumbled. "I'll just walk my critters across."

"Better not," Nate said. "They said the water's deep."

Piling didn't bother to answer but drove his animals to the water and began lashing them when they refused to go in. Finally, after losing several strips of hide to the whip, they gingerly stepped into the stream. When they faltered, he whipped them again until they walked into water up to their bellies. Suddenly, the wagon began to sink.

"Help!" Piling yelled.

Immediately, Nate Butler ran into the river. Upon reaching the oxen, he took hold of their yokes and pulled. "Come on," he said. "You can do it. Come on, boys, pull!" The valiant animals gave it all they had, but the wagon didn't move. Several more men, in water to their waists, positioned themselves behind and beside the wagon. "This thing's goin' deeper in the mud every second," one yelled. "We'd best hurry." On the count of three, the men in the back shoved the wagon, those on the sides lifted, while four in the front pulled with the oxen. Their concerted effort unmired the wagon, and it then rolled on with the men pushing and pulling with the oxen. In a little more than an hour, the wagon rolled up on the far bank, none the worse for wear. Several men dropped to the grass, gasping for breath.

"Well, I done it," Piling said. "Glad I din't help make them savages rich."

Rachel, who'd been watching the excitement from the bank with Martha, jerked to face her friend. "Did you hear what he said? And not a single man answered him. How come?"

Martha laughed a merry little tinkle. "Because this is a Christian train. Didn't you know?"

Rachel nodded her head. "I know. But what does that have to do with anything?"

"God doesn't want us all to go around saying mean things to each other. Instead, we have to forgive people like Mark Piling."

You might, Rachel thought. *But I'm staying clear of that cowboy. I don't like him. I won't forgive him either.*

As the wagon train continued, Martha and Rachel had only to stroll to keep up with the slow-moving oxen. Even Willie kept up with no trouble for several hours at a time. And Josie ran circles around everyone.

That day they made camp at noon so everyone could prepare for the Sabbath rest tomorrow. When Rachel fed and watered the chickens, she discovered another dead one. This trip was even harder on the chickens than on her. She felt bad to have them dying. After all they didn't ask to be stuck into a crate and hauled on the bumpy wagon. She dug a hole with Papa's shovel and buried the dead hen.

"Want to learn how to make cakes in the dutch oven?" Mama asked when Rachel returned. "It's a big pot you put over the fire, sort of like an oven. Then you put your cake pan or biscuits into it to bake."

Rachel shook her red head. "No. I don't even know how to make cakes in a real oven. And I don't care to." She walked off to find Martha. But her friend was busy doing her family's washing. Josie greeted Rachel as though she hadn't seen her for days. Rachel sat down in the grass and petted the dog for a while, then wandered back to her own wagon.

When she got back, she found Mama doing their washing in cold water from the stream they camped beside. She noticed Mama looked a little tired, but she didn't offer to help, and Mama didn't ask.

Papa found her sitting on the ground and sat beside her. "The chickens don't look good," he said.

"No."

"They're going to die one at a time, you know."

"I know. Oh, Papa, why did we come on this foolish thing?"

"We came because it was the thing to do. Thousands have made this trip already, Rachel, and are starting new lives in Oregon. One day you'll be glad you came. But, back to the chickens. I think the kindest thing we can do is to prepare them for tomorrow's dinner."

Rachel reluctantly agreed, so that's what he did. At least the chickens were through suffering.

That night a good-looking young man went from wagon to wagon inviting everyone to an evening worship service. When the Butlers arrived, they sat on the grass along with everyone else.

Then the young man stood before the group. Rachel noticed first his broad shoulders and muscular body. Then she saw how tall he stood, well over six feet. His closely clipped dark beard and mustache complemented his longish dark hair and eyes to perfection. She'd never seen a more handsome man anywhere, not even in the big church in Quincy.

"Hello," he said loudly enough for everyone to hear. "I'm James Richards. I believe I'm the only minister on the train, so I'll be taking the responsibility of keeping you close to the Lord on this hard trip. Let's begin with some singing."

With his strong baritone voice, he led them in a dozen happy hymns. Soon, nearly everyone joined and the group truly "made a joyful noise unto the Lord." Rachel enjoyed the singing and gladly joined in. Then the young minister preached a short sermon about serving the Lord no matter where you are. "Remember," the handsome young man said, "Daniel served God from the lion's den, and Shadrach, Meshach, and Abednego served from the fiery furnace. I have no doubt we'll think we're in one or the other before we finish this emigration, but we can serve the Lord no matter what's happening or where we are." He closed the meeting with another song and a prayer.

As Rachel walked away, she saw people flocking around Pastor Richards. She wouldn't have minded flocking a little herself. As she lay in her bed that night she decided the trip just possibly might not be so bad after all. Finally, she fell asleep.

—⁂—

Men shouting, oxen bawling, smoke from camp fires, and children crying jerked Rachel from a sound sleep at dawn the next morning. What was this, anyway? She'd expected to sleep late this morning. It was the Sabbath, wasn't it? She turned over on her feather mattress and hoped to fall asleep again, but it wasn't to be. Too many loud voices, too much clattering and banging around. Finally, she struggled from her warm nest, pulled on her clothes, and jumped to the ground to see what was happening.

"The good Lord'll be pleased if you rest with us," Captain Ransom told someone she didn't recognize. "You know the fourth commandment, don't you? Besides, the animals'll fare better with a rest day each week. This trip ain't gonna be easy. Think it over, brother. The good Lord knew what He was doin' when He made the rules for us to live by."

"Well, we're goin'," the strange man said.

"Didn't you know this was a Christian train when you joined?" Ransom asked.

"Shore, but no one said it was fanatical. Might's well save your breath, Captain. We're goin'."

After more noise and confusion, the camp became deathly still, but Rachel couldn't fall back to sleep. She lay in bed nearly an hour before jumping up, wide awake.

Mama squatted beside the campfire, cooking breakfast. After greeting Rachel, she hurried to tell her news. "Six wagons left this morning. That leaves twenty-one. Think we'll make it all right?"

Rachel dropped to the ground beside Mama. "Of course. Who needs those people anyway? Who needs anyone?"

Mama smiled sweetly. "I'm sure we all need each other a lot, Rachel. What makes you so caustic this morning?"

"I don't care if everyone leaves, Mama. I really don't. But I do care that those idiots woke me at dawn on the one day I planned to sleep late. I was counting on catching up on my sleep. This is the day of rest isn't it?"

After breakfast the minister gathered his flock again and had a nice long hymn sing, then a prayer meeting in which everyone who wanted to, prayed. Then he preached a sermon about God, living within us wherever we are.

The man impressed Rachel but she disagreed with his message. "I give God credit for being smart," she told Martha as they walked back to their wagons. "And He'd never be dumb enough to come on a fool's trip like this."

Martha looked at her with twinkling eyes. "Don't you know the Lord says in His sacred Word that He'll live in us if we belong to Him. Don't you believe that, Rachel? If you do, you have to know He's with us everywhere, even out here in the prairie."

Whether God was here wasn't high on Rachel's list of things to worry about, so she didn't.

That day the entire wagon train put their food together for a giant potluck dinner. While they ate, Rachel got a chance to see most of the young people on the train. She felt delightfully surprised to learn there were many more young men than women, even though they looked and talked like yokels. If she'd gone to college she'd have had the cream of the crop from which to choose.

She discovered a skinny woman named Tamara was Pastor Richards's sister. Unimpressive, the mousy little thing looked like the pastor's shadow, letting him do most of her thinking for her. Rachel felt she and Tamara had nothing in common, but what did it matter? She'd probably never see her again—on the Trail or later.

Soon after the meal, Pastor Richards came over to where Rachel and Martha relaxed on the grass. He folded his long frame and gracefully dropped to the ground beside them.

"How's the weather down here?" he asked. "I've been noticing how comfortable you two looked all afternoon. Now I get to find out for myself."

"Oh, Pastor Richards," Rachel gushed, "I'm so glad you stopped to see us. I never have heard a better speaker than you. And what a beautiful singing voice. How did we ever get so lucky as to have you on this wagon train?"

"Thank you," he said casually. Then he turned his attention to Martha. "How did you feel about the services?"

She thought a moment. "Well, I purely loved the singing. And I'd never get through a day if God didn't live in my heart. We need Him more out here in the wild than we ever did at home."

He nodded. "Right you are. And how are you enjoying the traveling? Haven't I seen you walking?"

"Oh, yes. My dog, Josie, and I are walking all the way. Now Rachel walks with us, and it's lots more fun."

He talked to Martha a few more minutes then hopped to his feet. "So nice talking to you ladies," he said. "And I'm especially glad you're enjoying the journey so much. I'm sure we'll be meeting again. I must get back to my sister. She's shy, so she depends on me a lot. Good-bye."

As he walked off, Rachel felt herself getting angry. Very angry. She hopped to her feet too and leaned over the still-sitting Martha.

"Singing is one of my very favorite things to do," she said in an exact imitation of Martha's bell-like voice. "Why didn't you just get up and hug him?" she yelled at her friend, her only friend. "How could you make those cow eyes at him when you knew I was interested in him? How could you do that to me, Martha? How could you?"

21

Chapter 3

Martha's eyes opened wide. Then she got up. "I'm purely sorry, Rachel. I didn't know you were interested in Pastor Richards. And I didn't know I was making cow eyes at him." She stopped and giggled. "Truly, Rachel, I don't even know what cow eyes are, and besides I don't have the slightest interest in the man. Really, I don't."

Rachel felt chastened. If Martha had returned her anger she could have stayed mad. "Well," she muttered, "I'm not interested in him either. I just didn't want you making a fool of yourself."

Martha tinkled out another laugh. "Thanks, Rachel. I purely don't want to make a fool of myself."

A young girl approached them so they turned their attention to her. "Hello," she said hesitantly. "I'm Julia Tate. I bin watching you walking together havin' fun. I wondered if you'd mind if I walked with you sometime."

"We'd love to have you," Martha said instantly. "You just find us in the morning and join us."

Rachel didn't say anything, but she wished Martha hadn't invited the kid. What made it worse, Martha sounded as if she had meant it. "How old are you?" Rachel asked.

"Sixteen," Julia replied. "How old are you?"

"I'm eighteen," Rachel said. "And Martha's seventeen. We've both finished high school." She hoped the girl would get the message that they were older. Then she remembered Thurman Tate. "You must be Thurman Tate's daughter," she said. "How are your oxen getting along with that horrendous load they have to pull?"

Julia looked perplexed. "All right, I guess. I don't pay much attention to them. Were they sick or something?"

"No. Your father just refused the captain's orders to leave some heavy things in Independence."

Martha looked uncomfortable. "Well, you just come and walk with us tomorrow, Julia."

The girl left, and Martha turned her attention back to Rachel. "We have to be kind to everyone," she said quietly. "Whatever we do for anyone, we're doing it for our Lord Jesus, you know."

Later that afternoon Rachel sat with her parents in their wagon, reading Scripture together, something she considered necessary but extremely boring.

"Hello," a young man's voice called from the outside. "Mr. Butler, could I talk to you a minute?"

Papa hopped to his feet, then down to the ground. Rachel sat quietly and listened.

"I just discovered we have an extra cow," the young man said, "and I don't know what to do with it."

A silence told Rachel that Papa didn't know either. All at once she remembered the man who'd been riding a cow. She jumped down beside her father. "I might know, Papa," she said. "Could we go see it?"

Sure enough, she recognized the cow as the one the man planned to ride to Oregon. "It belongs to the man who was going to Oregon on cowback," she said. "I saw him fall off her and try to catch her. I also saw him heading back to Independence on foot."

"Well," Nathan Butler said, "I guess it don't matter all that much, Ernie. Why don't you just leave her with ours for now."

———⟨∭⟩———

The next morning, Martha and Rachel hadn't been walking an hour before Julia caught up with them. "What did you think of the preacher?" Rachel asked. "Handsome man, isn't he?"

Julia smiled shyly. "I guess. But he's too elegant for me. I like plain men better." She giggled. "But I like all men a lot."

A silly, man-crazy girl! Rachel wondered how she'd put up with her all day, every day. Maybe Julia would get tired and go back to her own wagon.

That afternoon a small dirty boy ran up to them from somewhere behind. "My name's Petey Piling," he said, puffing breathlessly. "Mama's sick, and Papa told me to stay away so I won't bother them. Can I walk with you?"

Martha reached for his grimy hand. "Of course. You just walk right here between Willie and me. You two boys will have lots of fun together."

Ugh! Rachel bet Martha would welcome the most vile animal in the world. Why was she like that anyway? With the three big girls, the two little boys, and Josie, they had quite a group. Well, Rachel wasn't giving up her place to anyone.

The little boys started running around and yelling. Josie followed, yapping all the way. Martha acted as if she didn't hear a thing. "Can't you stop that racket?" Rachel asked.

Martha stopped talking and listened. Then she nodded. "They're all right," she said merrily. "We'll worry about them when someone starts crying."

Rachel felt like asking Martha if she planned to have any sanity left when they reached their destination, but she didn't. As she wished for some quiet, a small dirt clod hit her in the back. Spinning around, she saw a look of surprise and fright on the two small faces.

"He didn't mean to hit you," Willie said. "Honest. Petey threw it at me, and you just went and got in the way."

"It's all right," Martha said. "I'll brush her off. You all just go on and play." She moved to Rachel's side, brushed her off thoroughly, and finished with a few loving pats.

Only those pats kept Rachel's mouth shut and even then it wasn't easy. If she were in charge of those boys they'd be seen and not heard.

The next morning Rachel felt put out with the world in general and the extra people walking with them in particular. The boys had gotten cranky after a few miles, but Martha didn't scold them. She started teaching them little songs. Afraid to say anything to Martha about the crowd she'd gathered around them, Rachel began on her favorite subject. "If God loved us even a little bit, we wouldn't be on this horrible journey."

"Not true, my friend," Martha said merrily. "God definitely wants us on this trip. There must be trappers or Indians we'll be telling about God's great love. For that matter there are people on this wagon train who don't know God. Like Mark Piling."

"If that's what we're going for I may start back right away," Rachel said. "I can think of a lot of boring things to do, but that tops the list."

The boys and Julia walked with Martha and Rachel every day, and no matter what they did, Martha never became impatient.

One afternoon, Petey and Willie grew wilder than usual, tearing around and yelling at the top of their lungs; Josie was at their heels, adding her barking to the uproar. Just when Rachel thought she'd lose her sanity, Willie fell down. Petey fell over the top of him and into a mud puddle, thoroughly coating himself with the messy stuff.

"I can't walk in these clothes," the little boy wailed. He looked up into Martha's blue eyes. "Can I take them off, Martha? Can I?"

Martha winked at Rachel. "I'm not sure you should do that, Petey," she said. "But we'll take you to your wagon for fresh clothes. How will that be?"

Petey hung his head as though he'd rather just take off the clothes. But he didn't say anything. Martha took his hand and also Willie's. "Come on, girls," she said to Rachel and Julia. "Let's find the Piling wagon."

Just about the time they found Petey's wagon the train stopped for the night. As they approached him, Mark Piling looked out of sorts. "Petey fell into a mud puddle," Martha said, laughing. "We brought him home for clean clothes."

24

Mr. Piling punched one of his oxen in the nose as he unyoked it; the ox grunted. Rachel stiffened and would have yelled at him if Martha hadn't poked her in the ribs. "I ain't got time to waste with you hoity-toity wimin," he snarled. "I'm too busy taking care of my sick wife. So go on back where you came from. How could I have clean clothes for anyone? What do you think I am, some kind of a nanny?" He turned toward the wagon. "Get down here and make a fire," he yelled into the wagon. "I'm hungry. I ain't laid in bed all day like you. Hurry up, woman!"

A moment later Sandy Piling's pale face appeared at the front of the wagon. She didn't speak to anyone but climbed down and looked around on the ground as though wondering what she could make a fire from.

"Want me to find you something to make a fire?" Martha asked.

"Get out of here before I take a whip to you!" Piling shouted, moving toward the girls. Petey, who'd been standing with Martha, flitted out of his father's way as if used to moving quickly. Rachel didn't need a second invitation. She took off like a deer, back to her own wagon.

"Wait for me," Julia yelled from somewhere behind, but Rachel wasn't stopping for anyone. She put one foot in front of the other as fast as they'd go until she reached the Butler wagons where Mama squatted before a snapping campfire.

"What ever is after you, a bear?" Mama asked with a warm smile. Rachel waited until she caught her breath. "You said it just right, Mama," she finally got out. "Do you remember Mark Piling? He's the meanest man I've ever seen in my entire life. He really is. I hate him a whole lot."

"No, you don't," Mama said. "You don't even know him. Tell me, what did he do to an animal?" She dumped some potatoes into bacon grease in a hot skillet. "This is the last of the potatoes until we find some to buy."

Just like Mama. She knew Rachel got upset when anyone abused an animal. But he did! "He did, Mama, but I got so mad at him later, I forgot all about it. He doubled up his fist and punched an ox in the face as hard as he could. But that's not all. He made his wife get out of the wagon to cook supper, and she's real sick. Then he threatened to use a whip on us. You should have seen Petey get out of there. He's used to Mr. Piling hurting him, Mama."

Mama had stopped her meal preparations to listen to Rachel's wild story. "That's awful. What did you girls do to get him so riled up, love?" She picked up her bowl and started mixing the biscuits again.

"You know Petey walks with us all the time. Well, he fell into a puddle and wanted his clothes off really bad, so we took him to their wagon for clean clothes."

Mama had been shaping biscuits while Rachel talked. Now she put them into the dutch oven and laid it over the coals. "Sounds as if you didn't do a whole lot. The man's probably concerned about his wife. I've been hearing she's quite ill."

Strange way to show concern, Rachel thought. Well, she'd stay out of Mark Piling's way. Poor little Petey! He couldn't stay away all the time. But she could—and would.

"Would you take them some milk and cream?" Mama asked as she poured some of each into bottles and capped them.

Rachel shook her head. "Mama! I just told you he threatened us with a whip. I'm not going over there for anything. Ever again."

"Can you stir the potatoes in a few minutes then?" Mama asked. Without waiting for an answer, she strode off toward the Piling wagon.

She returned a few minutes later, shaking her auburn head. "You're right, Rachel, he isn't very nice. But he accepted the milk and cream for his sick wife. Maybe it'll help her get well."

—∿∿—

The next day, the train reached the Kansas River and camped at noon to prepare for the Sabbath.

Mama carried the tubs to the river and washed the family's clothes. She didn't ask Rachel to help, and Rachel didn't offer. Down the river a ways, Martha worked over a scrub board; Rachel wandered over to talk to her. "How come you're doing your family's clothes?" she asked.

Martha looked up, her face red from exertion. "Oh, hello, Rachel," she said with a welcoming smile. "I'm doing the washing to help Mama. While I'm washing she's doing the baking for tomorrow. Haven't you heard that many hands make light work?"

Rachel thought about that as she wandered back to where Mama worked. When Mama looked up, her face was red from the hard work. Rachel felt a strong love tug at her heart. "Why don't you let me do that?" she asked. "You go back to camp and start the baking."

Mama looked relieved and, thanking Rachel, headed back to the wagons.

When Rachel finished an hour later and had the clothes all hanging on the small bushes bordering the river, she ambled over to see why Martha wasn't finished yet.

"Well," Martha said, "I did finish our wash, but I'm doing the Pilings' right now."

Indignation turned Rachel's face red. "How could you be so dumb, Martha? Mr. Piling doesn't deserve to have one piece of his washing done for him."

Martha nodded, picked a little sock from the water, and scrubbed it on the board. "I know," Martha agreed. "But I'm not doing it for Mr. Piling. I'm doing it for Mrs. Piling and she purely needs all the help she can get."

—⁓—

On March twenty-seventh, the Sabbath, Pastor Richards preached, and the women put another potluck meal together. Julia joined Martha and Rachel for the meal. When the girls had nearly finished their plates, two young men came and squatted near them in the grass. "Good afternoon," the tall, skinny one said. "I'm Andy Shackleford. I hope you girls are enjoying the Sabbath rest."

"Oh, we surely are," Martha said. "And the good food. I believe I counted seven kinds of cake. God takes care of us even out here in the wild country. I'm Martha Lawford, and these are my friends, Julia Tate and Rachel Butler."

"And this is Ernie Cox. I believe he works for your father, Miss Butler."

"Oh." One of the oxen drivers or herders. She didn't know, or care. She'd walk away from these yokels, if it weren't for Martha. She couldn't do that to her special friend.

"Hello, Mr. Cox and Mr. Shackleford," Julia's young voice said. "We're glad to make yer acqu...acqui...we're glad to meet ya."

The two young men hardly gave Julia or Rachel a glance as they talked animatedly to Martha. Finally, they reluctantly left.

"I thought they'd never go," Rachel said. "I expected any minute that you'd be inviting them to walk with us. You're way too friendly with people, you know."

Martha looked surprised. "I didn't know you could be too friendly with people, Rachel." She thought a moment and then broke into merry laughter. "Unless you make cow eyes at them."

That evening several people on the train heard strange sounds and knew for sure Indians were sneaking up on them. Captain Ransom called the people together and warned them. "Everyone better be watchin' every minute," he said. "Else you mayn't have another minute."

When Ransom finished, a young man moved in front of the people. "Hello," he said with a friendly smile. He stood over six-feet tall and looked lean but well muscled. His blondish hair hung over his ears but his closely trimmed darker beard and mustache looked dashing. "I'm Dan Barlow," he said. "I was just thinking what strange creatures we are. I wonder how many of you know that in 1825 the government took all the Indians' property and gave them Kansas for theirs. Now look what's happening," he said. "Here we are, invading their property by the thousands. I wonder what we'd do if thousands of people started taking our country from us?"

He stepped back into the crowd as quietly as he'd come.

Rachel sat up and took notice of Dan Barlow. That man makes sense, she told herself. I'm keeping my eye on him. Not too bad looking, either.

Another man stepped to the front. Middle-aged, the man looked kindly and round. "I'm George Rahn," he said. "I hope we all agree with our kind brother. I do. But I'm still afraid of the Indians, so I suggest we watch carefully."

Chapter 4

Rachel fell asleep that night, frightened almost to death. She knew for sure she'd wake up with a tomahawk in her skull.

But the sun shone brightly the next morning and everything looked normal. Before they finished breakfast, George Rahn came around, laughing and joking. "I've been to nearly every wagon," he said, "and everyone seems to be all right and wearing his hair this morning."

That day Willie and Petey got into more trouble than usual. Willie's father had made him a little white horse from sticks and polished it up nice and smooth. Petey wanted the horse in the worst way and tried off and on all day to take it from Willie. Both boys ended up crying many times.

Rachel wished Martha would spank them both or at least give them a sound scolding. But Martha thought up some trail games. "Let's see what those white clouds look like," she said one time. "I see a sheep."

"I see a man with white hair," Willie said. "I think it's Jesus."

"I see a big white horse," Petey said just before lunging at Willie's horse again.

Finally, Martha stopped Petey and held him by the shoulders. "Petey, it's not nice to take things from other people," she said in her kind voice. "If you'll be really good the rest of the day I'll try to get Papa to make you a horse tonight."

A sun-laden smile covered Petey's face, and he didn't cause any more trouble.

That night one of the horse riders, Stan Latham, appeared at the Butler camp just before supper. Mama was baking biscuits and stirring bacon in a skillet. "You look beautiful tonight, ma'am," he said to Mrs. Butler. "And your culinary skills must approximate your beauty. The food smells totally aromatic."

Rachel felt like vomiting. But Papa only smiled and invited the man to eat with them. Mama kept the man's plate filled.

"Did you observe my herd of twenty-one of the east's finest horses?" he asked. "I'm planning to breed the best horses in the west and earn mountains of money. I'm sure horses will be badly needed there."

"I noticed your horses," Nate said. "Good looking bunch. Lots of luck."

During the meal Stan let slip a few words that Rachel wasn't accustomed to hearing.

After he left, Rachel scolded Papa for inviting such a dirty, sloppy, loud, and uncouth man to eat with them. "You wouldn't have let me associate with his kind in Quincy," she said. "Or were you fooled by his big words?"

Nate shook his head. "Not fooled, Rachel. But the man was hungry."

—m—

The next day, Willie held two smooth wooden horses. The moment Petey joined them, he held out the new one. Petey could hardly talk over his excitement. "I don't have any other toys," he said. "I like it." Martha had to keep after the boys who only wanted to get down on the ground and play with their horses. "Come on or we'll get left behind," she called. The boys would jump up, run a ways ahead of the girls, and flop onto the ground again for another few minutes of play.

That afternoon, clouds started gathering in the sky, hiding the sun. As the hours passed, it grew darker and more threatening. "Looks like rain," Martha said. Rachel hugged herself.

"I bet a thunderstorm's coming," Julia said. "I'm skeered of lightning and thunder."

"Thunder never hurt anyone," Rachel said. "Thunder tells you the lightning missed you."

About four o'clock, the first flash streaked across the sky to the west; thunder followed a little later. In a few minutes, the flashes grew brighter and the thunder followed, quicker and louder.

Josie crept along beside Martha, obviously frightened. The cattle began lowing, and the horses grew nervous. Then the rain came. At first, infrequent big drops, then they grew smaller and came faster. Within ten minutes, a cold, drenching rain poured over them.

"We'd better get into the wagons," Julia said, moving toward Rachel's.

"No," Martha said. "We won't melt any more than the animals will. We shouldn't make it harder on the oxen." Julia came back, and the girls walked in the downpour. Josie, obviously delighted that the loud racket had stopped, ran and jumped and spun in the rain. Soon, the girls were soaked through, and their feet were wet and muddy.

Then Rachel noticed the oxen struggling to pull the wagons. The wheels sank six inches into the mud. Several wagons stopped, and drivers began yelling and then using their whips. The oxen pushed hard on their yokes, but the wagons didn't move. The whips sang through the air, then cracked on the animals' backs. The drivers' yells grew louder; the oxen's bawling made a terrible roar, but the wagons didn't move.

Suddenly, Rachel snapped. She ran to her own driver. "Stop abusing those animals!" she screamed into his face. "Can't you see they're trying their best? The wagons are stuck too hard." She stopped long enough to take in a few breaths of wet air. "You're supposed to be Christian on this wagon train, so start acting like one or I'll grab that whip and use it on you!" She ran the length of the train, screaming the same words at every driver.

By the time she'd said it twenty times the drivers began to see she was right. No matter how hard the men whipped, no matter how hard the animals strained at their yokes, they simply couldn't pull the wagons through the mire. The men unloaded each wagons in the pouring rain. With water streaming down their faces, they put branches under each wagon's wheels and pried each wagon onto the branches until it came unmired. Then, struggling, the oxen moved the empty wagons. Corralling the wagons, they made camp for the night.

The rain stopped as suddenly as it began. Rachel huddled away from the wagons and cried. She couldn't help it. How could anyone mistreat animals so horribly? Blood ran from the oxen's backs. Rachel cried for the animals, then she cried for herself. Whatever on earth was she doing in this awful place? Heartbreak Trail. That's what it was.

Hearing more bawling, she looked back where Thurman Tate still whipped his oxen. Wait! She didn't see his things beside the trail. He hadn't unloaded! She ran right to him, grabbed the whip from his surprised hands, and dashed back to Captain Ransom. "That Tate man is still whipping his animals," she puffed, "and he didn't even unload."

Ransom nodded and headed toward Tate. Rachel threw the whip as hard as she could, about eight feet, and followed the captain. "I thought we all understood we had to unload," Ransom said quietly to Tate.

Tate replied with an oath. "Ain't no one'd help me," he finally got around to saying. "I can't do it alone, so them oxen'll just have to work harder." He looked at Rachel, standing a ways back. "You better get that there wild woman under control if you know what's good for her."

"I'll find someone to help you," the captain said, hurrying away. "Come on, Miss Butler," he said when he passed Rachel. "You'd better stay away from that man."

Rachel helped Mama make a fire with wet wood, then they cooked supper on a sizzling, smoky fire. As they ate, she noticed about ten men approach Tate and unload a heavy cookstove, a large chiffonier, and other things from his wagon. Then the oxen managed to pull the wagon from the mud and into the circle.

After the Butler family finished eating, Rachel stood by the fire, drying her clothes. She and her parents dried their featherbeds and quilts, holding them before the fire, turning them every few minutes.

A young man approached the fire, one of the men who had helped Tate unload his heavy stuff. Rachel noticed several patches on his clothes and holes that needed mending. He wasn't all that clean either. "Hello," he said to Rachel. "I just wanted to tell you I'm elated to find someone brave enough to stand up for the helpless animals. I wish I'd done it, but I didn't and you did. Even a big ox is helpless when a man starts on him, and I agree it's time we considered their feelings, too. Thanks again, Miss Butler." He walked off into the night.

Rachel thought about him after she climbed into her featherbed. The man was a mess, but he cared about animals. She'd thought maybe she was the only one in the whole world who did.

The next morning the sun shone brightly and the people dried their belongings before they started. The same young men who'd unloaded Tate's wagon reloaded it. Rachel heard some of them asking Tate if he wouldn't like to leave the cookstove there to save his oxen. "Never!" he said. "Them oxen are just lazy. After getting away with what they did yesterday they'll be worse now."

The next morning Rachel grumbled to Martha about Tate and what an awful man he was. "I hate that man," Rachel said. "I really hate him. I hate Heartbreak Trail, too."

"It's hard all right," Martha said. Then she giggled. "I was purely surprised to hear you yelling at all those men. But the men may be kinder to their animals now."

"I feel just like you, Rachel," Julia said. "Those oxen feel pain just like we do, and it's cruel to whip them when they can't work any harder."

For the first time ever, Rachel felt kindly toward Julia. When she thought about Julia's father, she could hardly talk to Julia. Now she knew Julia wasn't just a young copy of Tate. Come to think of it, she'd noticed that the girl's parents never checked on her or seemed to care where she was. Julia and Petey were somewhat alike. No one cared about either of them. She really did have something for which to be thankful. Both her mama and papa loved her dearly and would do anything in the world for her.

April third was the Sabbath and Pastor Richards led the group in singing again and preached a fitting sermon. Then he acted as if Martha were of utmost importance to him, and Rachel hated every minute of it.

The next day they'd traveled a few hours when one of the horse riders reported a large band of Indians ahead. Captain Ransom stopped the train, calling a meeting of the men to decide if they should corral the wagons or keep going. They decided to keep going, with weapons loaded and ready.

When they reached the Indians riding spotted ponies, they discovered they wore complete war outfits, including feathers, and held large bows in their hands. Rachel, her heart racing, the saliva dry in her mouth, marched with Martha, their heads high. The stench of the Indians, combined with her terror, made Rachel physically ill. It seemed as if those columns of Indians and ponies would never end but the savages looked dead ahead, never glancing in the direction of the wagon train. Someone counted fifteen hundred Indians.

After they passed, Rachel felt such relief that she got silly; so did Martha and Julia. They laughed at everything and nothing. "What's funny?" Petey kept asking, but the girls just laughed some more.

Day after day they traveled on. Rachel appreciated and loved Martha more every day. She still wished Julia and Petey and even Willie didn't have to be there all the time, but she grew somewhat used to them. After all, where else could they be?

Julia kept talking about a man she'd seen. "He's tall and blond," she said. "You have to see him."

"Show him to us next time you see him," Rachel said.

One afternoon, Martha acted strange, and Rachel wondered what had happened. Maybe she'd seen a man, too. The preacher acted as if Martha were the only girl on the train, but she didn't seem to return the feeling. Maybe she'd seen someone else. Finally, Martha told her. "I'm purely embarrassed to tell you, but my brother Jackson shot a rabbit this morning and Mama asked me to dress it. I've never done such a thing, but I'm going to do it if it kills me."

"Why would you be embarrassed?" Rachel asked. "I've never even touched a dead animal, let alone fixed it to eat."

Martha heaved a relieved sigh. "Maybe you'd like to watch me fix it," she offered as if she could use the moral support.

That evening Rachel watched but didn't help. She couldn't figure out how such a horrible looking mess could turn into something so delicious.

The next evening, as the men corralled the wagons and unyoked the oxen, Tate's animals didn't move fast enough to suit him so his whip whistled as he used it on their backs. The animals bawled as Tate yelled and whipped hide from their backs. Some nearby oxen stampeded, running over several men and into the circled wagons. When they got everything under control, they found Andy Shackleford, Dan Barlow, and another man hurt and two oxen badly cut up.

The young man who'd thanked Rachel for standing up for the oxen came with a black bag. First he checked the men and told them they had no broken bones but were badly bruised and needed to take it easy for a few days. Then he got some stuff out of his bag and began sewing up the oxen. Several men held the animals but the young man doing the sewing kept talking kindly to them. They seemed to understand and stood still. Rachel had never seen anyone so quietly kind to both men and animals. Different from most of the people around for sure. Come to think about it, she hadn't heard him spit out any filthy words either.

The next morning she asked Martha about the man.

"Don't you know who that was?" Martha asked. "He's Dr. Thomas Dorland, a brand-new doctor. I heard someone say he's planning to make a difference in the lives of the pioneers. He's one of the horse riders."

"You mean he doesn't have a wagon?"

Martha giggled. "No wagon. Everything he has, including his medical supplies, is in that bag behind his saddle."

Rachel shook her head. "I don't understand how he can live like that." Then she thought of herself and giggled. "But I don't understand how I'm living like this either."

At dusk that evening a small group of Indians approached the wagon train. The men loaded their guns and stood watch. Rachel didn't have a gun, but she watched the approaching group too, counting five ponies and five men. But when they neared the train, one looked like a woman.

A white woman at that, bareheaded with faded brown hair. When they reached the first wagon, ten men surrounded the Indians, their guns pointed at the ground. The woman jumped from her pony to the ground. "Don't look so scared," she said loudly. "We're friends." She took her pony's reins and handed them to the closest Indian. The Indians turned the ponies and headed back the way they'd come.

The woman, as big as most men, grinned. "Well? You got room for one more?"

"What's going on?" Captain Ransom asked quietly.

"Hello," the woman stuck out a hand, "I'm Deborah Petty, genuine white woman, nothing to fear."

Ransom shook her hand.

"I went mushroom picking yesterday and somehow got lost. Before I found my train, three white snakes got me. They weren't about to help me back to my train so I started screaming my head off." She laughed loudly. "Imagine how I felt when four redskins charged up. I figured we'd all lose our scalps and thought it might be worth losing mine just to see those white savages lose theirs."

"I see you're still wearing your hair," George Rahn said with a grin.

The woman laughed. "Yes, and so are my captors. The Indians scared them plenty but didn't harm them. Anyway, when they saw this wagon train

34

they brought me here and that's the story. They fed me and kept me last night, so my opinion of what color savages are has changed a bit."

Mrs. Ransom put her arms around the big woman and held her close. "You can share our wagon, Deborah. We'll work it out. But what about your train? Do you have a husband on it?"

"Naw. I'm all alone in the world. If you got room for me, one train's as good as the next." She laughed nervously. "You can see I'm plenty big. I like to work, so I can earn my room and board."

—⁘—

As the days wore on, it seemed to Rachel that the mornings were getting colder rather than warmer. She kept putting on more clothes every morning and still froze. "I'm going to have to help more with the cooking," she told Mama, "so I can hang around the fire." She'd been helping some lately and found she didn't mind at all.

The train came to Big Blue River and found no bridge or ferry. The river wasn't wide but was about three feet deep. The men led the oxen in pulling the wagons cross and the women rode horseback. Rachel hung back almost to the last. Already freezing, she wasn't eager to get wet. Finally, Papa told her she had to go. He and Mama rode their geldings and Rachel her mare. "Tuck your dress up as the water comes up," Papa said, "and you won't get wet."

"Somebody might see me," Rachel wailed.

Papa shrugged. "Do as you please."

Lifting her dress modestly over her knees, Rachel gritted her teeth as Ginger, her horse, stepped into the water. She leaned forward and patted the horse's sleek neck. "It'll be cold for you too, baby," she said softly. But the horse didn't seem to mind the water. After a bit Rachel decided the water would come only a little above her knees so she tried to get used to the cold. When they passed the middle, Rachel heaved a sigh. Papa said everything looks harder than it is and this hadn't been all that bad.

Just at that moment, Ginger dropped from under Rachel.

With no time to prepare, Rachel found herself in the cold water, gasping as she took in a big swallow. Burdened with all her clothes, she couldn't seem to get herself above the water.

Briefly, she heard men and women yelling, then forgot all about anyone else as she tried to swim. But she couldn't catch her breath; she just couldn't.

Chapter 5

The next thing Rachel knew was that she felt herself choking and that she still couldn't pull in any breath. Opening her eyes, she found herself lying on her stomach on some grass. Then something pressed on her back and water poured into her mouth from her throat. She choked some more.

"Cough hard," a soft male voice said. "Try hard, Miss Butler. Just keep trying to breathe. You're all right now."

She didn't know who spoke and felt too tired to look. Then the pressure started on her back again and some more water came into her mouth. After a little while she could breathe, though it hurt and made a raspy sound.

Then someone turned her over. She looked into the soft eyes of Dr. Dorland. He smiled at her. "You gave us a scare, but you just need to breathe and cough awhile now."

Suddenly, Papa dropped to his knees beside her, gathering her to him. "My lassie," he said brokenly, "we'd have lost you if this young man hadn't pulled you out."

"Young man?" Rachel looked around but saw only Dr. Dorland.

"Yes," Papa said. "Dr. Dorland swam out and pulled you to safety."

"What happened?" Rachel rasped.

"Ginger stepped into a hole and went under. But you're both all right."

Dr. Dorland, who'd been on his knees beside Rachel, got to his feet. "I might as well go find my horse now if you don't need me any more. Don't hesitate to call me if you feel anxious about anything."

Rachel tried to sit up. Papa helped her. Mama knelt down beside her and hugged her. "I love you, child."

Rachel soon walked to the wagon that had been corralled with the others. She didn't feel too terrible except she still coughed some. Mama made some bean soup that went down easily. Rachel began to feel stronger.

———m———

During the night of April ninth, a cold wind arose, and Rachel felt chilled right into her bones. She didn't get up for breakfast, but Mama brought her some hot oatmeal with cream. It tasted better than almost anything Rachel had ever eaten in her life.

The fierce north wind forced Pastor Richards to cancel the Sabbath's preaching service and potluck dinner. People huddled in their wagons or around their fires, trying to keep warm. Papa read some Bible chapters to Mama and Rachel then said they'd pray together.

"I'm not praying," Rachel said. "If the Lord loved us even a tiny bit we wouldn't be out here in the middle of nowhere."

"That's enough, Rachel," Papa said sternly. "God didn't force you to come on the Trail. I did. You can be mad at me or yell at me or refuse to talk to me. But you're to stop blaspheming God at once. Do you understand?"

Rachel nodded, almost ashamed of her outburst. Almost.

The following week, the train crossed first the Big Sandy River, then the Little Sandy and followed it for several days. The weather improved; Rachel's spirits lifted, too.

One day she noticed the oxen's necks were bleeding from the pressure of the yokes. Rachel felt so sorry for the animals she went off by herself and cried again. Why did the animals suffer so for men's stupidity? Rachel wouldn't consider making the oxen pull her weight in the wagon now. Besides, she enjoyed walking with Martha. Sometimes though, she wished Martha weren't so perfect. Then she realized that that's why she loved her friend and why everyone else did, too.

One day, Willie and Petey seemed extra cranky. Every afternoon the boys took a nap in the Lawford wagon, but it wasn't nooning time yet. Rachel wished it were.

Martha never lost patience with the two little boys. Never. This day she got them into a game thanking God for blessings. The boys, each trying to think of more blessings than the other, forgot to fuss. When they finally grew tired of this game, Julia got them started naming the animals God has waiting for them in heaven. The boys liked that game almost as well as Martha's and searched their minds for animals until nooning time.

The train reached the Little Blue River and traveled along it for several days. Rachel helped Mama with the cooking and cleaning up now. The green willow sticks, their only fuel, put out a pungent smoke that always got into Rachel's eyes. "Smoke follows beauty, you know," Papa said, winking at his only child. "It couldn't find anyone prettier than my two lassies."

· "So how do you explain the bugs?" Rachel asked. "They get into everything, even the food we're cooking."

Mama smiled and stirred the biscuit mix. "One thing the Trail's teaching us is not to be so picky. We just have to take the bugs out of the food before we eat it."

Rachel knew that. But she hated it.

They camped early on Saturday to prepare for the Sabbath. Rachel and Martha did their families' washings then Martha washed Mrs. Piling's things. The poor woman didn't seem to be getting any better.

Mama and Rachel made several kinds of cakes with their supply of milk and cream. The cows' milk supply had dwindled but they still gave enough to share with several families.

With the warmer, calmer weather they would have preaching and a potluck dinner. They made do without eggs and no one seemed to notice. They fixed a big pot of baked beans in the dutch oven for the meal.

Rachel hated to admit it even to herself, but she looked forward to the next day, especially for the chance to see Pastor Richards.

That evening, several men came to see Papa, telling him they'd dallied enough on the Sabbath and that they should all get together and tell Captain Ransom they wanted to get going.

"I wouldn't think of it," Papa said. "The oxen have sore necks, sore feet, and they're losing weight. They need the day to catch up. Trust the good Lord to know what's best, brothers."

The next morning, about the time the preaching began, Rachel saw some women carrying tubs to the river. What were they doing? Not washing on the Sabbath! Then they heard the men pounding on the wagons and saw two of them heading out with their guns.

Rachel, who couldn't care less about the Sabbath, felt shock ripple through her body. No one ever worked on the Sabbath! After sitting in shock for a while, not hearing a word Pastor Richards said, she began giggling to herself. What was she expecting? The Lord to send fire from heaven to consume the Sabbath breakers?

She turned her attention back to the preaching. The reverend was telling the people that Christ's children find ways to serve Him, even in the wilderness. The working field is still there, only smaller. She wondered if she could help Martha a little more with the children. Julia did. If they both helped, it would unburden Martha a lot.

After dinner Rachel went to the minister. "Would helping take care of children be the kind of ministering you meant?"

His smile was sincere. "It certainly would. And it would help you as much as the children's mother." Someone else crowded in to ask the man a question so Rachel went back to her seat. A lot of good that did. She got to talk to him for about two minutes.

A little later the pastor found Martha, and Rachel watched them talking and laughing together for some time. A lot more than two minutes!

"Ah, there you are," Jackson Lawford said, squatting beside Rachel. "Where you been hiding out? Did you make any of the grub I ate?"

"I'm afraid I wouldn't know," Rachel said in a cold voice. "I have better things to do than watch whose food you eat."

Jackson didn't hang around long, exactly what Rachel wanted. She wanted to be alone in case the Reverend wanted to come talk to her. But he didn't. At one point she caught Dr. Dorland watching her, but when their eyes met, he turned away.

—⁓—

The next day they left the Little Blue River to enter the Platte River Valley, so level you could see seven miles. "Look," Petey said, "the grass is getting greener every day."

"Yes," Martha told him with a smile. "I'll bet the oxen like that, don't you?"

"Can we pick some and take it to them?" Willie asked.

"Not now," Rachel said. "The oxen are working. Why don't you wait until almost nooning time, then pick a big bunch for them? I'll help you."

One day Jackson told Martha they were seeing antelopes but couldn't get close enough to shoot.

"Good," Rachel said. "They're too beautiful to shoot."

"You don't mean that," Jackson said. "We're all in desperate need of meat."

Rachel thought that over. Almost all the meat they'd had on the trail was dried side meat. But she still didn't want them to kill the antelope.

The next day three men rode to meet the train. When they reached the wagons, they asked Captain Ransom if the people needed meat. When assured they did, the men gave them four skinned and gutted antelopes.

"How do you happen to have all this extra meat?" Rachel heard Ransom ask the men.

"We found the herd and knew someone would need meat," they answered. "Meat's been scarce lately so we just got it while we could."

"Much obliged," Nate said. "Where you fellows headed?"

"Salt Lake City," one of the men replied.

Pastor Richards seemed to come alive at the name of the town. "You must be Mormons," he said softly.

"That we are," the last man said. "And we'd best be on our way. You folks enjoy the meat."

"I have your trail guidebook," Nate said. "In fact, most of us have a copy. I don't know how we'd have gotten along without it."

One of the men pulled a battered copy from a deep pocket. "We use it, too," he said with a pleased smile. The men saluted, turned their horses, and took off down the trail ahead of the Ransom Train.

As the train lumbered along, some stopped wagons appeared on the Trail in front of them.

"They must be having trouble," Martha said. "I hope it isn't sickness."

But when they reached the wagons it seemed the train was having internal strife.

"Can we help you follow?" Captain Ransom asked one of the sullen looking men.

The men, having a severe disagreement, didn't even hear Ransom speaking.

Rachel, Martha, Julia, and the boys moved close enough to listen.

The men argued whether to continue or go back. "We're already out of food," someone said, "and we're not halfway yet. If we continue, we're sure to starve."

"That's your problem," a loud voice answered. "You knew it was a long way when we left. Let's go on," he said to the others gathered around. The people seemed about evenly divided in their desire to return to Independence or continue on.

After bickering another fifteen minutes, one of those who wanted to continue on turned to Ransom. "Maybe those with guts enough to go on can join your train," he said to the captain.

"You can join us if you're Christian and if you can keep up," Ransom said.

"We'll make them oxen keep up," the man said. Ransom extended his hand. The other man grasped it and they shook.

Hearing the conversation, Rachel didn't like the men. They didn't care a thing about their animals and wouldn't hesitate to mistreat them. She wished they hadn't joined the train. But they didn't treat their animals any differently than their own people treated theirs.

One day she noticed again their own oxen's raw and bleeding necks. The animals' tongues hung from their mouths as if they didn't have strength to hold them up. Many of the animals limped badly. Rachel's heart felt as if it would break as the drivers forced them on. She ran and threw her arms around one of the bleeding necks. "I'm so sorry," she whispered, tears running dusty trails down her cheeks.

"Get out of there!" the driver yelled. "You're in the way."

Rachel dropped her arms and turned to the driver. "You don't even care about these animals!" she screamed. "I hate every one of you. You're worse than animals. Why should the animals have to suffer so much for man's stupidity?" A moment later she covered her face with her arms and moved back beside Martha.

Martha stopped walking and crushed Rachel in a big hug. "I'm sorry for them too," she whispered into Rachel's ear. "But no one knows what to do.

Whether we go on or go back to Independence, we can't do it without the oxen." She pushed Rachel back so they could see each other. Tears ran in muddy streams down her face, too. "What can we do?" she whispered.

Rachel shook her head. She didn't know, but she couldn't bear what they were doing. The rest of the day all five walkers remained quiet.

On Sunday, April twenty-fourth, Rachel once again awakened to men's rough voices at dawn. Why couldn't people catch on that this was a rest day? The only day they got to sleep late. She turned over and pulled the pillow over her head. She still heard the commotion so she jumped out of her featherbed, dressed, and then dropped over the side of her wagon.

The new men had Captain Ransom surrounded. "We didn't bargain for setting around all day," one of them said. "We gotta get going or we'll be caught in the mountains in the winter."

"I told you this is a Christian train," Ransom replied calmly. "We figure we and our animals need the rest." He motioned west with his thumb. "If you don't agree, nobody's holding you here. Just meander on down the trail."

"You tryin' to get rid of us?" one of the men bellowed.

"Nope," Ransom said. "Ain't tryin' to hold you here, neither."

"Who crowned you king and lord of everythin'?" one yelled.

Two others came at Ransom with their fists flying. Ransom barely had time to look surprised before receiving several hard blows to his face that put him on the ground, dazed.

Chapter 6

D aniel Barlow, evidently hearing the fracas, came roaring into the midst of the trouble, punching both men's faces with hard staccato strikes. The two turned on Barlow who could barely handle both. As the men pounded each other, Captain Ransom struggled to his feet. "Stop it!" he shouted, "or you'll all leave this train immediately." The fists continued flying, most ending with a low thud and groans.

Ransom thrust himself into the middle of the brawl still yelling at the top of his voice for them to stop. For some reason they all stopped and stood staring at the brave man.

Someone called Dr. Dorland, who arrived with his little black satchel. On examining the men he found all three cut up enough to need stitches. Rachel moved up almost beside him as he cleaned the wounds and gently stitched them up, all the while talking quietly to the men. Not a word of recrimination, just fixing them the best he could. He was a real doctor, worthy of the title.

Dan Barlow thanked Dr. Dorland several times for his help; the other men said nothing. After the doctor finished, they yoked up their oxen, packed their wagons, and left the train.

The camp seemed exceptionally quiet as the remaining people built fires and prepared breakfasts.

"Wasn't Dr. Dorland wonderful?" Rachel asked her parents. "I've never seen anyone so quiet yet so kind. He's very dedicated."

Mama and Papa agreed, then they all hurried to the preaching service.

Pastor Richards spoke about doing to others as we would have them do to us. "If everyone lived that way," he said, "there would be no more trouble between people—ever." Afterwards, Rachel made it a point to tell him she appreciated his talk and how much she agreed with him. "Thank you," he said with an appreciative smile. "You have no idea how much it helps a pastor to know how his congregation feels about his sermons." By that time several people crowded around, distracting him with their silly comments. Rachel stomped off feeling rejected. She hurried home to help Mama with the food for the potluck dinner.

As usual, Martha, Julia, and Rachel ate on a quilt on their own little spot of ground. They'd barely sat down when Julia started going on about Dan Barlow.

"Wasn't that brave of him to protect Captain Ransom?" she asked. "He'd have beat them both up if the captain hadn't stopped him."

Rachel laughed at the younger girl. "I thought it was pretty dumb," she said. "One against two is never good."

Just then Dan stopped beside them. "Did I hear my name used in vain?"

"I hope not," Rachel said. "I just said two against one is bad."

"I think you were brave," Julia said. "Do you feel all right now?"

"Mind if I sit down?" he asked, settling on the ground near them. "I feel fine. That's one good doc we have. I say we're a lucky train."

"I do, too," Martha said. "We've needed a doctor several times and who knows how many more times we may yet?"

Soon Pastor Richards joined them, seating himself beside Dan. He seemed to direct most of his comments toward Martha.

"You have quite a varied congregation," Rachel said. "Have you found out if everyone is really Christian?"

"I'm not a judge," he said. "If people say they're Christians, they are." He continued his discussion with Martha about caring for two little boys on the trail.

As the little group talked, Rachel felt someone looking at her and raised her eyes to a group of men standing nearby. Sure enough, she met Dr. Dorland's soft gray eyes. He turned away so quickly his sun-streaked hair flipped across his face. What a kind, gentle face. But why was he watching her?

—∿∿—

The next day, the wagon train reached Fort Kearney. Rachel had been looking forward to this because she expected a glimpse of civilization. But it wasn't to be. The frame houses of the four officers looked passable but the rest were made of sunburned brick. The fort, fences, and outbuildings were made from dirt cut into blocks and stacked up. They called it adobe. Fort Kearney was set up by the government to guard the Oregon Trail. Papa's Mormon guidebook said the fort was 319 miles from Independence, too far to turn back.

Fort Kearney disappointed Rachel a lot; and the officers looked more like fur trappers than government men.

After passing the fort, the train reached the Platte River and followed it. Several men in rough boats tried to navigate the wide but shallow river.

"What are you doing?" Julia called as they walked past.

"Trying to catch some fish," one young man said. "We run aground fifty times each day and spend half our time on sandbars." He grinned as if he didn't mind as much as he might.

As they walked along the river, other men called to the girls and Julia always answered. "Don't you know young ladies don't talk to strange men?" Rachel scolded.

Martha laughed. "I don't think it hurts anything, Rachel. There's enough of us here to protect her. It's kind of fun to hear what they're doing, don't you think?"

A strange, unearthly racket interrupted, and the girls looked down the trail toward the sound. A huge line of Indians pressed toward them, some walking, some on ponies. The Indians screamed, howled, and made war whoops that nearly broke Rachel's eardrums. Suddenly, she felt ready to run back home, on foot, all by herself.

But as they neared the Indians, she saw several men carrying a body on their shoulders. The dead man wore a complete headdress and war paint, making it look pathetically fierce. The girls laughed hysterically with relief, knowing the Indians didn't mean them any harm. Besides that, the Indians were making so much noise they'd never hear the girls' talking and laughing. Finally, the Indians passed.

"I wonder if that poor man knew our Saviour," Martha wondered out loud.

Julia and Rachel burst into laughter again. "Tell me, how could he?" Rachel asked.

Martha nodded. "Probably not. That's why we're here, Rachel, to share our wonderful God with them and everyone else."

"Spare me," Rachel said. "I'm not sharing anything with anyone." But inwardly she admired Martha and envied her unwavering faith.

The next day they came to the south fork of the Platte River where they had to cross. The river was half a mile wide but very shallow. "The problem," the men explained, "is the quicksand in spots."

Making sure the animals had all they wanted to drink so they wouldn't stop during the ford, the men hooked several wagons together with eight to ten yoke of oxen for each wagon. The oxen drivers worked with their own animals while other men swam and waded, digging out the wagons as necessary.

The girls and little boys stood on the bank and watched. Andy Shackleford, Dan Barlow, Tom Dorland, Stan Latham, and Ernie Cox worked in the water.

"Who's that big fellow beside Andy?" Julia asked.

Rachel and Martha burst into laughter. "That's not a fellow," Rachel said. "That's Debbie Petty, the woman the Indians brought to the train."

"Well, she's working like a man," Julia said. "I wish I could help."

"Go ahead," Rachel said.

"No, you don't," Martha said. "Debbie's bigger and stronger than most women. You'll just be satisfied to watch. Understand?"

As they watched, the string of wagons stopped and the men flew into action, pushing, lifting, shoving, and shouting. Using a shovel, Debbie frantically pawed mud from around the sinking wagon wheels. At the same time the drivers urged the oxen to pull even harder. When the wagons began moving again, the watching people cheered loudly.

Finally, the last wagon emerged from the water and Captain Ransom called corralling.

As Rachel helped Mama fix supper, she wished Pastor Richards would come calling. He was so good-looking, educated, and always clean. Come to think of it, she never saw him except on Sabbaths. She wondered where he kept himself and what he did during the week.

That night Rachel awakened feeling something on her face. She brushed her hand across it and felt bugs. Lots of bugs! Jumping from her bed in the dark she brushed over her face, arms, chest, and back. They seemed to be everywhere. She tried to sweep her bed clean with her hand but, being in the dark, she felt unsure.

After blindly cleaning herself and her bed several times, she gingerly climbed back under the covers and fell asleep almost at once. Some time later, she awakened again with bugs marching across her face. Jumping up, she went through the wild sweeping off of the bugs from the bed and herself and fell asleep again, exhausted.

Several more times the bugs, walking across her face, awakened her. Each time she fell asleep more exhausted than the last time. Finally, dawn broke and the train began to awaken.

That day everyone laughed and joked about the dor-bugs as they called them. Rachel didn't say a word, but she found nothing funny about the insects, even though assured they don't bite.

"They come out of a hole in the ground," Julia said. "My dad told me they won't hurt you. They just run across your face fifty times. He says we'll get used to them and sleep right through."

Not me, Rachel thought. *Never!*

At least the dor-bugs came out only at night. Many other kinds of bugs swarmed over them during the whole day from dawn to dusk. Sometimes they bit, sometimes they didn't, but red welts covered most everyone's body, especially the children.

Just before serving the beans, Mama scooped the bugs from them. Even so, Rachel always had to spoon out many bugs while she ate. As she did, she remembered how she hated the trail. Most of the time she didn't think about it anymore. Just sometimes.

At Plum Creek the horse riders spotted a single buffalo ahead, the first one they'd seen. Some of the men rode out after it and two hours later they returned, many of them with parts of the buffalo hanging over their horses.

That evening they had another of their rare celebrations with music and dancing. The people ate all the meat they could hold. The next day they jerked the rest of the meat before moving on.

As they traveled, the sand began deepening until it became hard to walk on. The oxen strained to pull the wagons even on flat ground. Wildflowers, starting to bloom on the prairie, sent out a fragrance that brightened the day.

One day they met a wagon with four rough-looking men walking beside it. "We've been up and down this trail," they said. "It gets lots worse. The oxen won't be able to pull the wagons. You won't even be able to walk in the deep hot sand. Your oxen will all die on this trail, and most of you will, too."

"Don't put too much stock in what those men said," Captain Ransom told them after the men left. "Something made them bitter."

Nevertheless, Rachel, Julia, and Martha trembled, remembering what the men had said. The little boys didn't play or fuss as usual either.

That night they camped on the north fork of the Platte River, two miles short of Ash Hollow, 504 miles from Independence, the guidebook said.

Martha and Rachel discovered an empty little cabin near the trail. Inside they found hundreds of letters addressed to nearly everywhere in the world.

"Why would people leave them here?" Martha asked.

Rachel shook her head. "I don't know. Maybe they thought someone would see their letter and would take it to the address on the envelope." As they looked through the envelopes, a noise outside caused them to drop to the floor.

"Shh," Rachel said. "Maybe they won't see us."

When the door creaked open and two men walked in, Rachel thought her heart would beat through her chest. But when the men's voices reached her ears, she recognized them! Andy Shackleford and Dan Barlow.

About that time Martha laughed and scrambled to her feet. "You nearly scared the daylights out of us."

Rachel crawled from her hiding place. "You caught us. What are you going to do with us?"

Andy laughed. "Do you know it's getting dark? We're going to see you safely back to your wagons. How's that?"

The next morning Rachel didn't waste any time telling Julia that Martha and she spent some time in a log cabin with Andy and Dan.

"How come you didn't take me?" Julia cried. "You knew I'd want to go."

"Because we didn't know we'd see them," Martha said sweetly. "We just found the cabin at the same time they did. We didn't even spend time with them. We went right back to our wagons. That's all there was to it."

That day the sand and dust grew deeper, spilling over Rachel's high-top shoes. The dust rose until it caused her eyes to burn and water; soon, they were sore and inflamed. Willie and Petey became cross and fretful. Martha, unmindful of her own discomfort, soothed the little ones the best she could.

Rachel noticed the oxen stumbling blindly along, their eyes nearly closed against the blowing dust. She ran and dipped her handkerchief into the river and tried to clean one of her oxen's eyes. The ox tried to jerk its head away from her hand.

"Get out of there!" the driver yelled at her. "You tryin' to get hurt? Or just gettin' in the way?"

Rachel withdrew, knowing by now it didn't help to argue with the drivers.

The train camped early due to the dust. After Martha and Rachel finished their washings and other work, they explored and found many different kinds of flowers, including wild orchids: dainty, pinkish flowers hiding in the shade of larger bushes, broken branches, or whatever.

Several kinds of butterflies flitted among the flowers—huge yellow-and-black ones, small brightly colored ones, and everything in between. As she watched the beautiful creatures fluttering through the air, Tom Dorland appeared.

Chapter 7

K ind of pretty, aren't they?" Tom asked quietly.
"Yes," Rachel whispered. "I love them."
Stepping a few feet away, he broke a twig and carried it to Rachel.
"Here's one that's fresh out of its chrysalis. Let's watch it." He carefully transferred the yellow-and-black creature with crumpled wings to Rachel's finger where it clung. "It's a tiger swallowtail," he said. "And no, it isn't crippled. That's the way they look at first."

They didn't talk any more as they watched it beat its wings up and down, up and down. Gradually, the wings grew fuller and less crumpled. Then, the little hooks at the bottoms of its huge wings straightened and took on many colors—pinks, blues, lavenders.

"It's beautiful," she whispered softly, holding her hand perfectly still.

"Shh," he whispered. "It's about ready to fly."

As they watched, it lifted its big wings one more time and fluttered into the sky. Rachel didn't want the experience to end.

She turned to the doctor. "Thank you, Dr. Dorland. That was the most beautiful thing I've ever seen in my entire life. And I'd have never seen it if you hadn't happened to be here."

"I enjoyed it, too," he said, turning away. "Thanks for sharing the moment."

After he left, Rachel lost interest in continuing her investigation. On her way back to her wagon, she brushed several metallic-looking green beetles from her clothes. As dusk neared, sand flies and mosquitoes swarmed from the river, biting her face and hands.

—⁓—

On Sunday, May first, the morning wind and dust died down in the afternoon so Pastor Richards invited everyone to a hymn sing and preaching service. Rachel enjoyed watching the man who always looked as if he lived in Independence rather than on Heartbreak Trail. She didn't necessarily admit it even to herself but she enjoyed the songs, too. A few people played instruments, and everyone else sang with whole hearts. Although Papa had asked several times, Rachel left her guitar in the wagon.

48

Pastor Richards told the people in his sermon that faith is the most important thing for a Christian. "We must spend time in the Word," he said, "and pray until our faith grows so strong it cannot fail."

Afterward, Rachel told him she agreed with him that faith was an all-important necessity to a Christian. "I work on my faith all the time," she gushed.

He gave her a brilliant smile. "Please, don't work on it," he advised. "Just spend a lot of time reading His Word and communicating with Him in prayer." As usual, people crowded between them.

Later, the people all brought their suppers together for a potluck meal. Pastor Richards joined the girls, sitting near them on the bare ground.

"I'm so glad you joined us," Rachel said eagerly. "I've been wanting to discuss a theological problem with you." She searched frantically for something she could bring up that would interest the young minister.

He held up a big hand. "No deep talks today," he said smiling to soften his words. "I'm here to relax." Then, he turned to Martha. "Still planning to walk all the way to Oregon?"

She laughed. "We all are, Rachel, Julia, and me. Even the little boys walk all the time, except for when they nap."

Pastor Richards laughed with her. "How are the shoes holding up?"

Dan Barlow appeared and sat down beside Pastor Richards. "This looks like the most interesting conversation around. Mind if I join you?"

Jackson Lawford folded his long frame down beside the other men. "Needing a little protection, sis?"

Rachel sighed heavily. With so many people, Pastor Richards would never notice her. She got to her feet, her empty plate still in her hand. "If you'll excuse me, I should go check on my folks. Nice to see you all."

One more wasted Sabbath, she thought as she ambled toward her wagon. Well, maybe Pastor Richards would see now that she wasn't chasing him. As she thought about it she wondered if he hadn't given his best smiles to Julia today.

The next morning Rachel had nearly finished breakfast when she heard Martha screaming, "Help, someone help, quick!"

Rachel ran back to the Lawford wagon about the time a dozen other people reached the site of Martha's cries. Martha stood beside Josie, who lay on the ground.

"Papa!" Martha screamed. "Josie's hurt. Really bad."

Rachel ran and knelt beside the trembling dog. Then she saw. Through Josie's torn-out stomach she saw the dog's intestines, nearly falling out. She lifted her eyes to Martha. "What happened?"

Martha couldn't answer but shrugged.

Just then Tom Dorland appeared. "What happened?"

"She doesn't know," Rachel answered softly.

Mr. Lawford appeared with a gun in his hand. Leaning over the dog, he talked softly to her. "I'm sorry, Josie," he murmured, "but you're hurt so badly we can't fix you." He lifted the gun and Rachel turned away.

"Don't do it!" Tom Dorland said in a trembling voice. "Please don't do it, Mr. Lawford."

Mr. Lawford lowered the gun and looked into the young doctor's eyes. "Nothin' else to do," he said. "Coyotes got her. She's ripped clean apart." He raised the gun again.

"Let me try to fix her," Tom pleaded. "I don't know if I can save her, and she'll have a lot of pain, but she might make it."

Mr. Lawford looked at Martha. She nodded. "Yes, I want to save her, Papa. I love Josie."

"I know you do. But it's cruel to put her through the pain when she could die painlessly. She'll die anyway, you know."

Martha shot Tom a pleading look. "Please try, Dr. Dorland. Please save my dog."

The young man swallowed loudly, blinking the moisture from his eyes. "I'll do my best," he choked out. He swallowed again, squared his shoulders, and spoke. "Will someone please take Miss Lawford away for an hour? And I'll need someone else to help me."

Suddenly, Rachel wanted desperately to help Josie. "I'll do it," she said, standing straight and swallowing her tears. "I love Josie more than anyone else. . .except Martha. She'll like having me with her."

"All right," Tom said, opening his case. "We'll have to disinfect the wound with alcohol, and it'll burn like fire. Can you hold her?"

Josie lay almost still while Rachel whispered into her ear and Tom poured whiskey over and around her intestines. The pitiful moans caused tears to roll down Rachel's cheeks, but she kept up her soft talk and held on tightly.

"Now I'm ready to sew her up," the serious-voiced young doctor said. "How about a man taking Miss Butler's place. Rachel. . .Miss Butler, you help me with the stitching and keep talking to Josie. It really helps. It could make the difference whether she lives or dies."

Andy Shackleford held Josie still while Rachel held the wound closed and talked to Josie until she thought her throat would close up. "Good girl, Josie. Just lie still so the doctor can make you well. I know he's hurting you, baby, but he has to put you back together." Over and over and over.

"Well, I think we're finished," Tom finally said. "You're a fine assistant, Miss Butler." His voice still shook.

Rachel felt so weak she sat on the tongue of the wagon to catch her breath. As she rested, she heard Tom's soft voice.

"Our Dear Father in heaven," he said, barely above a whisper. "We thank You for loving each of us, as well as all Your creation. We just tried to save this special dog's life, Father. We've done the best we know how. We can sew flesh together, but we can't heal, so we're asking You. We ask in Jesus' name and thank You for hearing and answering our prayers. Amen." He turned to the waiting people. "Josie will have to ride in a wagon for some time."

The doctor walked off quietly, bag in hand. He said nothing and no one spoke to him. The enormous lump in Rachel's throat stopped her from saying anything to anyone.

Rachel's father moved to Josie's side. "She can ride in our wagon."

Mr. Lawford very gently lifted Josie up into his arms. "She'll ride in ours," he said. He laid the dog on Martha's featherbed. "Martha will have to find a new place to sleep," he said tenderly to Rachel. "She won't mind."

When Rachel's strength returned, she ran after Martha and her mother. "Josie's all right so far," she told Martha.

The next day Josie still lived and rode in the wagon. Rachel remembered how bumpy it was and wished she could help Josie somehow.

Dr. Dorland joined them for a few minutes that day. "Josie must have plenty of food now," he told Martha. "You feed her all you can spare, and I'll bring her something when I can."

As they walked along the road, they saw several more graves and lots of dead animals.

—⁂—

Two days later, they reached the trail that led to Chimney Rock, three miles off the Trail. The train stopped so those who wanted could go see the huge rock formation up close, though it was plainly visible from the Trail.

Dan approached them on his large gelding. "Someone want to ride with me?"

"No," Rachel said with finality. "A horse is never supposed to carry more than ten percent of its own weight. That means one person per horse. We'll ride my family's three horses."

"You're right," Dan said. "But we'll be going only a little way, and we'll go slowly."

"We'll ride my family's horses," Rachel said. The three girls rode the horses, leaving the little boys with the older Lawfords.

As they neared Chimney Rock, Dan estimated it to be about 250 feet high, with the chimney on top measuring about 75 feet. The young people climbed up 275 feet and engraved their names in the soft stone, among the myriads of others who'd gone before.

"Look! Indians!" Andy Shackleford yelled as they climbed down the structure. Rachel raised her eyes to see a dozen Indians, each on a spotted pony, moving toward them. No one had any weapons so they just waited.

"Maybe we should make a break for the wagons," Pastor Richards said.

"No Indians have hurt us yet," Dan said. "I doubt they'll be starting now."

When the Indians reached them, Rachel saw they were young, even younger than she. The Indians smiled and pointed to their bows and quivers of arrows. Then they motioned to the train's young people as if pulling back bowstrings.

"They want us to shoot," Tom Dorland murmured. In a little while the red youth and white youth engaged in a shooting contest, which the experienced Indians easily won. Waving and smiling, the young Indians rode off the way they'd come.

The young people of the wagon train headed back to the wagons in good spirits, their opinions of Indians up about 500 percent. As the merry group neared the wagon train, they came upon a herd of buffalo a mile wide by the Platte River. Of one accord they all stayed back, fearing the huge animals would stampede and run over them. The buffalo ignored the people on horses, giving them a good chance to enjoy the magnificent creatures.

Later that day Tom Dorland brought Josie a small, skinned animal. "I'll try to do this often," he told Martha.

The next day they reached Scott's Bluff, 596 miles from home, with many 500 foot-tall bluffs. The crystal clear sky opened up the landscape until it looked as if you could see forever.

"The guidebook says you can see 300 miles," Papa said.

"I'm sure I can see that far," Martha said laughing. "What about you boys?"

"I can see all the way to Heaven," Willie said.

Petey gave Willie a big push, sending him sprawling. "No you can't. That's straight up in the sky."

Tears trickled down Willie's face, then a sob burst from his throat. Martha gathered him into her arms and carried him a while.

"You're a bad boy," Rachel said to Petey. "You made Willie cry. Don't you know he's smaller than you?"

Martha soon had Willie laughing and set him down. She dropped an arm over Petey's shoulder. "You didn't mean to hurt Willie, did you?" she asked the small boy. He leaned against her, putting his cheek on her arm.

One evening a high wind arose, bringing heavy rain. Before long the wagons were in danger of being blown over.

"Call the boys!" Debbie Petty yelled and right away Tom Dorland,

Dan Barlow, Andy Shackleford, George Rahn, Nate Butler, and George Lawford showed up. "Let's fasten all the wagons together," Debbie yelled into the wind.

"Good idea," Nate Butler replied. Working quickly in the wind and rain, they fastened them together so they couldn't tip over.

"Good," Tom Dorland screamed into the wind. "But that won't keep the contents dry. I guess everyone's on his own now."

Rachel's wagon leaked, but it was better than being in the rain. And it felt so much better having the wagons more secure.

The next morning the sun shone brightly and wildflowers bloomed everywhere. After everyone dried the contents of their wagons, they marched onward. And saw more graves.

The train traveled among the gigantic bluffs for several days.

"At least they protect us from the wind," Rachel said to Martha while looking up at the mountainous bluffs around them.

One day as they walked, Josie whined from Martha's wagon. "She wants to walk," Martha said. "She's been begging for several days. Think she should?"

Rachel ran to the head of the wagon line to find Dr. Dorland. "Josie wants to walk," she said. "Can she?"

"For one hour," he said. "You might also tell Miss Lawford that I'm planning to take out the stitches tonight."

Mr. Lawford lifted the dog down and Josie obviously enjoyed herself though walking gingerly. Later, when Martha's father put her back into the wagon, she barked her disapproval.

That evening Tom Dorland stopped by Rachel's wagon. "Come help me take out Josie's stitches," he said. "It wouldn't be fair if I didn't ask you," he added, "as this is the fun part."

When Martha brought Josie out to Tom, the dog began trembling hard. She squatted low and her tail dropped to the ground.

Tom knelt beside her and put his arms around her, talking softly. "I hurt you badly last time, didn't I, girl? I don't blame you for being afraid." He smiled. "But I'm not going to hurt you at all this time." He raised his eyes to Rachel. "Come and hold her."

Rachel dropped to the ground and turned Josie over so her stomach was exposed. She could hardly believe how much better the dog looked. Hardly any swelling, hardly any redness, and the wound itself under the stitches looked dry and black. "It's all right," she whispered to the still-trembling dog. "We're going to be very careful with you, Josie, and make you all well." She couldn't believe the love she felt for the shaggy dog.

She talked to Josie as Tom worked swiftly but gently. "There you go," he said about two minutes later. He petted the big head. "Doesn't that feel better? Now it won't pull anymore, Josie." He lifted his head to Rachel. "Thanks, Miss Butler. Someday you're going to be a nurse." Then he got to his feet and turned to Martha, who'd been standing near, watch ing fearfully.

"She's just fine, Miss I awford. Much better than I could have hoped. She's a good patient, too. Did you notice she didn't flinch once?"

Martha shook her head. "No, but I'll never be able to tell you how much Josie and I appreciate what you did. I love her so much, Dr. Dorland."

He laughed quietly. "Call me Tom. And I can see how much you love her. But don't thank me. I can't heal anyone or anything. God does His miracle every time any wound heals, no matter how small. In Josie's case it was a big miracle. God created animals, too, and He loves them even more than you do. She'd have never made it without His special care. Did you ever think of that?"

Martha's smile held a beautiful radiance. Rachel felt jealousy rise in her throat. "I didn't think of it," Martha answered, "but now that I do, I know you're right." She raised her beautiful blue eyes to the cloudless sky. "Thank You, Father. Thank You so much for loving and healing Josie. I love You."

Tom's eyes softened. "You really do, don't you?" He turned back to Rachel. "Thanks again for the help, Miss Butler." He picked up his black case and headed off among the wagons.

Martha's eyes still radiated love. "Isn't he wonderful?" she said quietly.

"Yes," Rachel agreed. "He's a good doctor." Sometimes she wished she had the faith of these two good people.

The next day they met more turnarounds, as they called the men returning from the Trail.

"There's so many dead animals ahead you won't be able to go on," one of the dirty, tattered men said. "They're in the Trail, beside the Trail, and even all through the streams. The smell makes you sick and the water'll kill you."

True to the men's word, each day rotting carcasses became more prevalent, and the smell truly made Rachel sick. She could hardly face food. One day she happened to take a look at her body and discovered that all the plumpness had disappeared. She looked hard and lean. Smiling, she decided not everything on Heartbreak Trail was bad. Not quite everything.

A few days later they crossed over the Laramie River on a shaky bridge that the Indians had made. They charged two dollars per wagon, which everyone paid rather than ford the river. When the train made camp to prepare for the Sabbath, Indians swarmed everywhere, most of them dressed in white men's tattered clothing. A few wore buckskins. All wore soft moccasins.

Rachel and Martha always did their families' washings now. "Want to help me do Sandy Piling's?" Martha always asked. Rachel usually said no, but this time she took half and they finished it in another hour.

—⁓—

May fifteenth was the Sabbath. Pastor Richards conducted a moving hymn sing early in the morning. With his lovely voice and pleasant way of getting everyone into the spirit, the music bathed the prairie in happy and joyful sound. Rachel felt herself growing close to God and she had no intention of doing that.

Then he preached about how much God loves each person. "He loves us much more than any earthly parents ever loved their own child," he said. "God actually loves us as much as He loves His precious only Son. We know because He allowed his Son to die for our sins, so we could live with Him forever."

Rachel had always heard about "God so loved the world," but she'd never really thought about how much God loved her.

At dinner time Julia, Martha, and Rachel found their own little spot to spread their blanket to enjoy the meal together. Not that there was any special food. Everyone brought beans fixed one way or another, and people had made cakes or dried-apple pies the best they could. But they enjoyed relaxing together.

As the girls filled their plates, Petey ran to them. "Can I eat with you, Martha?" he asked. "I'll be good."

Martha pulled him close. "Of course you can, Petey. Do you have a dish and spoon?" He ran back after them.

When the girls returned to their blanket, they discovered another one a few feet from theirs. "Shall we go somewhere else?" Rachel asked.

"No," Martha said. "Maybe God wants us to meet some new friends today. There are many people on the train we don't know."

Dan Barlow appeared with a huge plate of food and sat down on the blanket. Rachel checked Julia's face and found excitement all over it. That girl really liked Dan.

Chapter 8

Before Dan looked in the girls' direction, Pastor Richards, Tom Dorland, and Andy Shackleford arrived with heaping plates and dropped to the blanket. "Ah," the preacher said. "Does this feel good, or does this feel good?"

"It feels good," Tom said. Then his eyes happened on the girls. "Hey, fellows!" he said with excitement. "Look who followed us here." The others looked the ten feet to the girls and showed surprise, too.

A big laugh burst from Rachel's throat. "You didn't even notice our quilt, did you?"

"No," Dan said. "Was it there?" He shook his light-colored head. "No. Why don't you girls just admit you couldn't resist eating with us?"

"I admit it," Julia said, laughing too. "We put our blanket here so we could eat with you."

Dan moved over a little and patted the quilt beside him. His clear eyes drilled into Julia's. "Is that a fact? In that case, why don't you prove it? Come over here and sit with me. Please?"

Julia picked up her plate, marched over, and sat beside Dan, then smiled a "see what I did" smile at Rachel and Martha.

Half a second later Pastor Richards heaved his six-foot-plus frame to his feet, carefully lifted his overflowing plate, and headed toward the girls' blanket. At last! Rachel had been waiting a long time for this. She moved over slightly to make room for him. But he walked around the blanket and dropped to the quilt beside Martha. For a moment Rachel thought she'd cry, but she swallowed twice and hid her disappointment. Just then Andy Shackleford dropped beside her.

"Well, here I am, odd man out," Dr. Dorland said.

Immediately, Petey got up and carefully carried his half-filled plate to the men's quilt and sat beside the doctor. "I'll be with you," Petey said. "Willie's eating with his mama and papa so I don't have anyone, either."

Tom patted Petey's shoulder. "We'll get along fine, won't we, Petey? Pretty soon we'll go back and get some cake or pie."

Later in the afternoon the talk turned to God and how they could know His will for them.

"God doesn't care for any of us," Rachel said loudly. "Would a God Who cares let His people go through what's been happening to us? Not to mention the animals. How could He let the animals suffer and die when they didn't do anything to deserve it? And little kids! God doesn't care!" When she finally stopped, the silence went on forever. She wanted to demand that the preacher answer her accusations, but she refused to talk to him because he chose to sit with Martha.

Rachel had cast such a pall over the group that they soon broke up and went to their separate wagons. Later that night Rachel wondered if she'd made a major mistake. A minister might want a real Christian for a good friend. . .or especially for a wife.

The next day they reached Fort Laramie, 650 miles from home, the second fort set up to guard the Oregon Trail. The fort looked nearly like Fort Kearney, big, ugly, and adobe. Beyond the fort lay a little city of neat white houses. Rachel would have liked to walk among the houses and feel a tiny bit civilized, but Captain Ransom hurried them on.

As they bought provisions, the officer told Nate and others that '59 was the largest migration ever known. "Over thirteen hundred wagons have been past here already," he said, "and twelve hundred head of herded cattle."

When they returned to their wagons, Nate laughed. "Did you hear the man say thirteen hundred wagons are ahead of us?" he said to Alma and Rachel. "And we thought we were in one of the earliest trains."

They hadn't gone far when the wagon ruts grew deeper. They'd seen deep ruts, but nothing like these. Pretty soon word filtered down the wagon line that this place was called Register Cliffs and had the deepest ruts on the entire Trail. Cliffs on each side of the Trail got taller as they traveled. The wagons had to go single file because of the cliffs, and the ruts soon reached the middle of the oxen's bodies.

Rachel began to feel crowded as she, Martha, Julia, Petey, and Willie walked single file beside the wagons. When Dan Barlow came along, he and Julia messed around until the others left them. Soon, Petey and Willie got cross and so did Rachel. The cliffs on each side made Rachel feel as if she were in a small world and couldn't get her breath.

"This is the worst ever," Rachel complained to Martha. "I can't stand this anymore."

"It isn't so bad," Martha answered. "It's a lot better than the deep sand. The oxen had bad trouble in that."

Rachel knew Martha was right, but she didn't say it out loud. "Well, it's always too hot or too cold," she said, "and too dusty or windy. Or something else."

"But this isn't so bad," Martha insisted. "The oxen are doing all right, and the temperature is comfortable."

"Why do you always have to be so perfect?" Rachel snapped. "Do you have any idea how tiresome that gets?"

Martha crumpled a little. "No," she said in a tiny voice. "I was just trying to cheer you up. I want you to know God loves you, Rachel, and is taking care of you."

"God doesn't love me! He doesn't love you either. You just keep saying that to keep your courage up."

After a short silence Martha spoke in a tiny voice. "Do you believe there is a God, Rachel?"

That surprised Rachel a lot. She couldn't deny she believed that. She nodded.

"Do you believe the Bible is God's Word? And that it is true?"

Rachel bowed her head. "Yes," she mumbled.

Martha looked as if she'd just been given a fine gift. "If you believe the Bible's true," she said, "you have to believe God loves you. It says He loves you as much as if you were His only child. Remember, Pastor Richards said God loves you more than you can love your own children. That means He loves you much more than your father and mother love you. Many times more, Rachel. Did you know He loves you so much He cries when you reject Him?"

Rachel couldn't answer Martha anymore, but her friend's words hung in her mind. God loved her more than her parents? Papa had brought her on this long Heartbreak Trail against her wishes but she knew both her parents loved her with all their hearts. She was everything to her parents. And God loved her more than that?

That night, as she lay on her comfortable featherbed, she thought about it some more. God loved her many times more than her parents did. Martha had said that was because He loved sinlessly, a perfect love, and her folk's love was a selfish love. All human love is selfish, because all have sinned.

As she lay there she felt love for Him grow in her heart until she could hardly contain it all. She felt happier than she could ever remember feeling in her whole entire life.

The next day she asked Martha some questions. "I've gone to church all my life," she said, "but I don't have any idea how to know Jesus as you do."

"It's purely easy," Martha said. "Just tell Him how much you love Him, and that you want to love Him more. Thank Him for dying to pay for everything you've ever done wrong, tell Him you want to become His child, and ask Him to forgive your sins. That's it, Rachel. That's all there is to it." Martha choked on the last two short sentences, as though she were about to burst into tears.

"Aren't you glad I want to do this?" Rachel asked.

Martha hugged Rachel. "I'm so happy I'm crying," she blubbered against Rachel's cheek. "Now, do it."

"I love You, God," Rachel cried. "I love You because You love me so much, enough to die for me. Thank You for loving me so much. Thank You for dying for my sins. Please, God, I want to belong to You! Forgive my sins and teach me how to be Your child." She stopped and sniffed. Then she coughed. "I love You, God," she sobbed.

"I love Him, too," Petey said. "Can I be His child?"

"Me too," Willie echoed. "I love Jesus, too."

Martha stopped right there in that narrow alley between the high cliffs and hugged them both. "You're both His very own little boys," she said to them. "You must always remember that, no matter what. All right?"

"Let's sing," Rachel suggested. So the little boy voices joined the girls' as familiar hymns rang out from their hearts.

The wagon train soon camped along Horseshoe Creek, not getting very far due to the ruts, cliffs, and bluffs. They found plenty of grass and water for the animals and wood for the fires.

As they traveled, they saw more and more graves as well as animal carcasses along the trail. They also met turnarounds nearly every day. They all told of the same dire future for the wagon train.

By the time they reached the Laramie Mountains with snow on the mountain tops, the sun was scorching.

"I'm hot," Willie said one day. "I need a drink, Martha. Please, get me a drink."

"I can't, Willie. We have to wait until we stop tonight."

"I can't wait. I'm thirsty now."

"So am I," Petey said. "My throat hurts."

"Why don't we pretend we're in a nice, cool lake, swimming," Rachel said. "The water comes to our shoulders so we just lie down and start kicking our legs and stroking with our hands. Are you getting too cold, Willie?"

Willie laughed with delight at the game. "Not yet," he said. "I want to swim some more."

"All right," Rachel said. "Just be careful you don't go out too far. It might get deep."

Both boys got into the game until they forgot all about being hot and thirsty.

The next day when the boys napped, Rachel wanted desperately to do something for God. "Martha," she said. "How can I let God know how much I love Him? I just want to show Him."

"You showed Him yesterday," she said. "When you took the boys swimming you showed God your love. The Bible says, if you do something nice for anyone, even the least, it's as if you did it for the Lord. So just look around. There are lots of people on the train who need help. And helping them will make you feel better than you ever have. It's really doing it for Him, Rachel."

Rachel watched but didn't see anything special she could do.

The next afternoon the train stopped for some reason. A few minutes later, Rachel heard a woman crying loudly. When Rachel went to see what was wrong, she found Tom Dorland talking softly to Tamara Richards. As he talked, Rachel realized a snake had just bitten the woman. The doctor kept reassuring the terrified woman, but he didn't do anything. *Why doesn't he get to it?* Rachel wondered. *The woman will die if he doesn't do something.*

Suddenly, Rachel had a strong feeling that she should help the preacher's sister. She walked up to them. "May I help you, doctor?" she asked.

Relief washed over his face when he looked up. "Please do," he said. "I just prayed for someone to come, and He sent you." He showed her how to loosen the tourniquet he'd placed on the woman's swollen arm. "I'll tell you when," he said. "In the meantime I have to incise the wounds. Will you hold the arm still for me?"

When they finished the grisly job, Rachel cradled Tamara's head in her arms for a moment. "I'm sorry we hurt you," she whispered. "But now you're going to get well."

Tom thanked Rachel and told her he'd be calling on her again. "You really should be a nurse," he added with a sincere smile.

Rachel, in a rosy glow, hurried back to her wagon. Martha had been right. She felt better then she ever had.

The wagon train resumed its journey and, after awhile, they came to a ferry. But, since the river didn't look deep, they decided to ford it. As they forced the animals into the river, though the animals refused to cross. After many of the animals refused several times, the people paid the money and ferried everything across—wagons, animals, and people.

"I ain't lettin' these critters tell me what to do," Mark Piling said, wielding his whip. He drove his animals into the water many times, but each time they turned back. Finally, he spurred his horse into the water, too, and whipped the oxen pulling the wagon, ripping strips of flesh from their bodies. His screaming and the oxen's loud bawling got the attention of the entire wagon train, which gathered on the other side of the river to watch.

"Let them go back," Nate yelled. "I'll pay your ferry, Piling. Don't force them across."

If Piling heard, he didn't respond. Finally, the bleeding oxen struggled out of the water, the wagon bumping up the river bank behind them. He drove them on about thirty feet, then turned back to drive his stock across. He had one milk cow, twelve horses, and four more oxen.

Forcing them all into the water together, he continued using the whip harshly on their backs. The horse he rode tried desperately to turn back too, but Piling spurred him until he screamed. This time when the animals reached the current, the cow spun in a complete circle, then, at the mercy of the cruel water, washed downstream, sometimes her head out of the water, sometimes her feet out. Two of the horses lost control, and the river swept them away, too. When the other horses and oxen made it across, they climbed wearily out on the other side. Piling followed them on his horse, pushing it to go faster. They nearly made it to the edge when an undercurrent swept his mount's feet out from under it, spilling the man into the stream. The horse disappeared downstream in the frothy water. Piling managed to stay on top of the water but hurtled downstream until he disappeared.

"Well, so much for that," Captain Ransom said. "Who's gonna tell his woman?"

Chapter 9

No one offered to tell Sandra Piling that the river had swept her husband away.

"Shall we?" Martha whispered into Rachel's ear. "We probably know her better than anyone. . .from doing her washing."

Everything in Rachel shouted for her to get out of there before Martha talked her into doing something she'd be sorry about. "Let's go," she heard a strained voice say, then recognized it to be her own. How could she do this? She'd just caught herself thinking that it served the horrible man right. He'd caused the death of several helpless animals. Why shouldn't he die, too? She shook her head. That wasn't good thinking. God would never have her think that way. *Help me, God,* she prayed as she followed Martha.

The Piling wagon was only a few feet away. Maybe Mrs. Piling had heard the commotion and already knew. Rachel jumped up onto the wagon behind Martha.

"Are you all right, Mrs. Piling?" Martha asked in her soft sweet voice.

Mrs. Piling sat up in her rough bed on the floor of the wagon. "Yes. Is something wrong?"

Tears reddened Martha's eyes. She nodded and took the woman's hand. "Yes. The river just swept your husband away. I'm afraid he's gone, Mrs. Piling."

The frail woman smiled. "Thank you, dear. Now, don't worry about me. I'm all right." Rachel thought for sure she saw relief in the woman's face. No, she must have imagined it.

"Can we do anything for you?" Martha asked.

The woman thought a moment. "I'll need a little time to get organized," she said. "Do you think I can drive the oxen?"

Martha's dark head swung back and forth. "Driving's a hard job, Mrs. Piling. A sick person could never do it. The men will think of something."

"Let me try before you get anyone else. I think I can do it."

"All right. We'll camp here tonight so you can get yourself together."

As the girls hurried back to their wagons, Rachel voiced to Martha her thoughts about Mrs. Piling showing relief at her husband's death.

"Don't even think such things," Martha scolded, "let alone say them."

Captain Ransom gladly made camp. "You be sure to see what we can do for her," he told Martha and Rachel.

The two girls returned to the Piling wagon just before dark. Rachel brought some fresh milk and cream that was getting more dear every day. The cows had cut from thirty gallons a day to about six. They found Mrs. Piling up and caring for her children.

"Would you like us to take the children for tonight?" Martha asked.

The woman's eyes, looking brighter than Rachel had ever seen them, looked up from the fire she cooked over. "Oh no," she said in a strong clear voice. "We're doing just fine. We'll stay together, but thanks anyway." She handed Petey a plate of bacon and pancakes swimming in brown syrup.

As they approached their own wagons again, Rachel didn't say a word, but she'd never seen Sandy Piling look so strong and happy. She wasn't imagining it, either.

A little later Tom Dorland stopped at Rachel's wagon. "Could you go with me to see Sandra Piling?" he asked. "In her condition a blow like this could be very hard on her." Rachel kept quiet but gladly went.

Tom listened to the woman's heart and lungs and did some other things, then smiled broadly. "You're doing just fine, Mrs. Piling. Just fine. If you get anxious or feel bad, don't hesitate to call me. Please accept our condolences. We're so very sorry."

As Tom walked Rachel back to her wagon, she hoped he'd say something. Sandra's relief had been as plain as the rising sun. But he didn't mention Mrs. Piling at all.

Early the next morning Rachel took a pot of oatmeal with cream floating on it to the Piling wagon. Rachel dropped the oatmeal and nearly fainted when Mark Piling himself jumped down from the wagon and met her belligerently. "My family don't need your charity," he snapped when he saw the pot.

Rachel didn't say a word, just grabbed her empty oatmeal pot and ran for her parents' wagon. "Mama, Mama!" she called. When her mother appeared, she continued. "Mark Piling's back. Oh Mama, why couldn't he stay dead?"

"Rachel!" Mama cried in distress. "I thought you were doing so well and now this! How could you say such a thing, young lady? And are you sure he's back? That he didn't drown?"

"He didn't, Mama, and he's as mean as ever." Then Rachel couldn't help it. She told her mother how happy Sandy had been when she thought her husband dead. "She got right out of bed, Mama, and she was all well."

"I've heard about situations like that, Rachel. She might be better off without him, but he doesn't have to die."

Word soon got around that Piling was alive and as nasty as ever. Rachel wanted to go see Sandra Piling to see how she was now, but her mean husband kept people away as he always had.

"Are you happy your daddy's back?" she couldn't help asking Petey that morning. The little boy hung his head and wouldn't answer

That day they traveled in a continuous line of wagon trains; where one ended the next began. And the dust was terrible. Sometimes they couldn't see their own oxen. Everyone's eyes burned as they choked on the terrible dry stuff.

Late in the afternoon word came to Rachel that Andy Shackleford was sick, possibly with cholera. The Ransoms had taken him into their wagon.

That night there was nothing to burn but sagebrush. It burned fast, not putting out much heat, and the smell sickened Rachel's stomach.

The train stayed encamped the next day as Tom Dorland didn't think Andy should bounce around in a wagon.

That afternoon, several cows got into some quicksand by the river. Tom, Dan, Nate, George Lawford, George Rahn, Debbie Petty, and three other men ran to the scene with ropes. Tom, being the lightest, ran to the cattle and fastened them together. Then the men pulled on the ropes while Tom urged the animals to struggle. It looked as if they'd go down. Rachel wanted to run and help but she didn't. Finally, the valiant animals started to move. The men cheered and pulled harder. Within an hour they had them all out. Every one.

The next day they stayed encamped again. Andy seemed a bit better, but one of Thurman Tate's oxen died. Someone discovered rabbits and sage hens in and around the sagebrush. Jackson Lawford and others went out and brought back enough for several meals for their families.

As Martha and Rachel cleaned their meat, they saw a man go hunting without a gun.

"I ain't got one," he answered when they asked him about it. "But I'll catch something anyways." He soon found a rabbit and chased it all around the camp and through sagebrush. He ran until he dropped, exhausted.

Although Martha and Rachel laughed at his antics, they gave him two cleaned sage hens.

—⚹—

On Sunday, May twenty-second, Rachel got to sleep later but still wasn't ready to awaken when Captain Ransom came around.

"We have to move on," he told everyone. "The cattle have eaten all the grass, and they need all they can get."

"How's Andy?"

"Not good. I hate to move him, but we have to care for the cattle, too."

They left the Platte for the last time and camped near Willow Springs. After supper Rachel saw Tom Dorland head for Ransom's wagon. "May I help you with Andy?" she asked.

He shook his head. "I'd rather you stayed away. I'm sure it's cholera, and somehow it gets around. No need for you to chance getting it."

"What about you?"

The doctor shrugged. "Someone has to take care of him. But truthfully, there isn't much a person can do for cholera."

As Rachel walked away, she looked back and saw Tom praying over Andy. A black dread covered her. Andy might die. What a horrible thought! Andy really might die!

Later, Tom asked Rachel to help him dress Tamara Richards's snakebite wounds. The woman looked good, and her wounds were healing nicely.

The next day they saw the Sweetwater Mountains, with ice and snow glistening on the peaks. When Petey and Willie complained about being too hot, Rachel showed them the cool tops of the mountains.

"The white on them is ice and snow," she said. "We'll pretend the cold is down here." She shivered and hugged her arms to her chest. "Brrrr. I'm cold," she whined. "Willie, would you run and get me a sweater, please?"

"No," Petey interrupted, thrilled with the game. "You have to be cold because you don't have a sweater."

"All right. I guess I'll get warm next summer when the sun comes out."

The sight of the cool mountaintops kept the boys cool the rest of the day.

"You're getting good with the boys," Martha told her. "You're really helping 'the least of these,' Rachel."

Rachel laughed happily. "I've discovered you're right. It feels good to help and be kind to people."

One day they met a small train of four wagons. "You're going the wrong way," Julia called when they met.

The oxen driver stopped his wagon. "You're right," he called back. "We're taking seventeen children back to civilization. Indians massacred all the adults in their train and left the children."

Rachel could hardly bear to listen anymore. What was in store for them? Would they ever get to Oregon? Were the same Indians lying in wait for them?

—⟶⟵—

On Sunday, May twenty-ninth, before the preaching service began, Dan took Julia from Martha and Rachel and found a place for them to sit. Afterward, the group put their food together as usual. The girls had barely started filling their plates when Pastor Richards came and asked Martha to eat with him.

"We'd be glad to, wouldn't we, Rachel?"

Rachel's first inclination was to stick her nose in the air and flounce away, but better sense told her this would be an opportunity to impress the minister. So she held her tongue.

Pastor Richards gave his attention so completely to Martha that he barely knew Rachel was there. "Did you like my sermon today?" he asked her.

"Oh, yes," Martha said. "I always love to hear about our Lord."

"I mean the wording, and the way I delivered it."

"Oh, dear," Martha wailed, "I listened so hard to what you said about my Jesus I forgot to notice how you said it."

"Oh. Well, did you enjoy my song leading?"

"The only thing I like better than singing to our God is praying to Him," she said with a silvery laugh.

"I see. Well, did I look presentable?"

Martha laughed heartily at that. "You always look nice, Reverend. How you do it, I can't guess. Everyone else looks like a strong gale just dropped them."

He laughed in appreciation. "I thought it was a minister's duty to look presentable at all times. Do you like the way I wear my hair?"

By this time Rachel began to wonder if the pastor's charm included his good looks and nothing else. She'd never heard anyone so vain in her life. Then her conscience told her she was having a bad case of sour grapes. Maybe. Oh, but he was good looking. She felt like laughing out loud as Martha struggled for diplomatic answers to the man's inane questions.

"I don't notice hair," Martha said softly. "I notice willing workers in an emergency, people out helping others, and I especially enjoy being with people who love to talk about our Lord."

Rachel smiled to herself when Pastor Richards had the grace to blush. Martha's words probably hurt him a lot. Everything she'd mentioned, he lacked. After gulping a few breaths of air, the minister smiled. "Well, know what I enjoy? I enjoy being with you. Know why? Because you're sweet and dear, and one hundred percent honest even if it hurts." He squirmed a moment before continuing. "Now, how about you two lovely ladies going for a little walk with me?"

"I'd like that," Martha said, "but I promised Mama I'd take care of Willie while she takes a nap."

The fine-looking head turned Rachel's way. Suddenly, she didn't yearn to be with him as much as she had. But she couldn't be sure. "I'd enjoy that," she said.

They walked through the sagebrush away from the wagon train, causing several rabbits to scurry away.

"If it weren't the Sabbath I'd get you some meat," he said to Rachel.

"I'm glad it's Sabbath then," she said. "Don't you feel bad having to hurt innocent animals?"

He jerked his eyes open in surprise. "I hadn't thought about it," he said.

"You hadn't? Don't you know they get scared and feel pain just like we do? And when you shoot an animal it may leave a nest of babies to starve."

He slowed to a stroll as he considered Rachel's words. Finally, he shook his head. "No, I don't think so. They aren't smart enough to be scared and I doubt they feel much, either."

"Why do you suppose they run so fast from men?"

He looked perplexed. "I don't know." Then a smile reached from his full lips to his dark, deep-fringed eyes. Rachel's heart nearly missed a beat as she took in the tall, extremely handsome man. "But," the minister continued, "don't confuse me with the facts, all right? You could ruin one of my greatest pleasures—eating."

By unspoken agreement they turned back toward the wagons. "How would you like to think up a subject for me to preach about next week?" he asked as they walked.

"I'd like that," she said quickly before he changed his mind. "And I have the subject already. I'd like for you to tell the people exactly how to accept our Lord Jesus' great sacrifice for us and be saved."

His dark eyebrows lifted ever so slightly. "Everyone already knows that."

"Don't be so sure. You should teach that every few months forever."

By this time, they'd reached the wagons. "Thanks for walking with me," he said. "I'll give your suggestion some thought."

Later in the afternoon, Tom came to Rachel's wagon. "I wondered if you could go with me to check Tamara Richards one more time. I'm sure she's fine but I need to be sure, for her sake as well as mine."

The woman's wounds were almost healed, but she was glad to see Tom and Rachel. "My brother James doesn't stay around much," she said, "and I get lonely."

"There's someone who could really use a friend," Tom said as they walked back to the Butler wagons.

Tom didn't stop long enough to tell her how to go about the good deed he'd suggested. Rachel wondered how she could befriend Tamara Richards—or if she wanted to.

The next day they passed Alkali Lake, an evil-smelling body of water many miles long. The water had an ugly, whitish cast, but the hot, thirsty animals tried hard to reach it. The drivers held them back, for the guidebook said the water was poisonous. The many dead animals lying along the trail reminded everyone to restrain their animals, no matter what. Graves grew more numerous each day, too. The trail was definitely taking its toll.

Soon, they came to Independence Rock, 815 miles from Independence. The huge granite rock, 500 feet long, 200 feet wide, and 250 feet tall stood alone in the Sweetwater Valley. Rachel, Martha, and Julia all grabbed knives, planning to carve their names in the Rock but soon learned that granite wasn't soft like Chimney Rock had been. The many names on the rock hadn't been carved in but painted on. They gave up and ran to catch up with the train.

Later that afternoon Tom Dorland stopped the train to tell them Andy Shackleford had died. Pastor Richards spoke a few words, then they buried him right in the trail. Rachel thought that was awful, but when the wagons started running over the grave she burst into tears.

Chapter 10

W e run the wagons over the grave so animals or Indians won't recognize the grave and dig it up," Tom, who'd come up behind her,
explained. "It looks awful but it's for protection."

Rachel felt black depression after Andy died. Why did the people and
animals keep dying? And for nothing! Right now she hated Heartbreak
Trail more than she could say.

Martha talked to her all the rest of the day. "You feel God's love for you
don't you?" she asked quietly.

Rachel nodded and swiped at her running nose with the back of her
hand. "I thought I did."

"Don't allow yourself to doubt His love. Not for a minute, even when
hard things come. We can't hope to understand everything, but we can trust
and love. Then He'll help us through. Here's something else to think about.
God loves Andy more than we did. Even more than his mother and father
did. Many times more, so we just have to trust Him to make good come
from bad."

After some time Rachel started to feel better. She needed to feel better
for the little boys' sakes anyway. She started a game with them, and by the
time they camped, she felt His love again. Although she felt sad for Andy,
she truly knew God loved and cared for him forever.

They forded the Sweetwater River the next morning. The river was
cold and clear, sixty feet wide and three feet deep. The stifling hot weather
tempted the girls to wade across.

"Think we can?" Martha asked in response to Rachel's suggestion.

"The book says it's three feet deep," Rachel said. "We'll have to carry
the boys partway, but we can do that."

All the walkers in the train ended up wading across and having a wonderful time doing it. It cooled them for several hours.

A few days later they started up the Rocky Mountains on good but
steep roads. Another of Mark Piling's oxen gave out; they left it lying on the
ground.

"Who's going to take care of it?" Petey asked.

Rachel shuddered. "We'll pray for God to help it get well," she told him, and they did. Rachel left the ox, hoping desperately that God would heal it.

Soon the roads became insufferably dusty. As a result, everyone's eyes became inflamed and sore. Some people had goggles to wear over their eyes, others wore veils. Martha and Rachel had only linen handkerchiefs, so they tied them around their faces and also the little boys' faces.

Later the same day, Rachel had an idea. "Martha!" she said, "I'm going to cover our oxen's eyes with thin handkerchiefs." But when she tried, the oxen didn't understand she was trying to help them and neither did the drivers. They yelled for her to get out of the way and not to come back, tomorrow, or the next day, or ever!

A few days later Thurman Tate came past the walking girls, herding a brown cow in front of him. "See what I found," he said proudly. "I can add her to my others and have a herd."

"Does it give milk?" Willie asked.

Tate laughed. "I don't know yet. The thing won't let me get close enough to find out. But I'll get her tamed and breed her in Oregon. First thing you know, I'll have a whole herd of Jerseys."

On Sunday morning, June fifth, Rachel felt the fierce winds as she lay in bed. The top of the wagon snapped so hard she feared it would tear off the wagon and the cold reached through her many quilts right to her bones. When she finally crawled out of bed, she discovered the wind had brought thick dust with it.

Mama and Rachel had a tough time getting a fire going, and, when it finally caught, the smoke and dust burned her throat all the way down. How could she endure this for the rest of the summer?

Before they had breakfast ready, two men came to talk to Papa. "Why should we stay here?" one of them asked him. "Let's get out of this foul weather."

"I'm not the man to talk to," Papa said. "Go see Captain Ransom, but we agreed to rest on the Sabbath, you know. Maybe we should have faith that the Lord will still the storm. He can, you know."

"Yeah," the man said as they walked away. "But I ain't seen Him doin' it."

About an hour later three wagons left the circle, leaving seventeen wagons and forty-one people.

Thurman Tate came along, looking for his cow. "I guess the wind spooked her," he said. "But I'll find her. I guarantee I'll get her, dead or alive."

The wind and dust continued so strongly that the preaching services and potluck dinner were canceled. So Rachel ate and slept; she hadn't realized how tired she'd become. Later in the day the wind and dust died down, the sky cleared, and the sun peeked through, giving the travelers a hint of the heat it could still pour onto them.

That evening Tate went looking for his cow again. "I'll get her, you just wait and see," he told Rachel's father. Later, they heard the report of a gun and figured he'd found the cow. Now at least he'd have meat. But Tate came back herding the badly limping cow. "I got her," he yelled at Nate. "Had to shoot her a little, but it cooled her down."

"Papa, make him kill her quick," Rachel said, as the cow staggered along in front of Tate.

"Better kill the poor thing and get it over with," Papa called to Tate.

"I ain't killin' her yet, Butler. We'll need the meat more later."

"But that's horrible," Rachel yelled. "Can't you imagine how you'd feel if you were all shot up and someone forced you to go on walking?"

Tate laughed. "I didn't force her to run off."

That night the wind came up again. The wagon rocked until Rachel wondered if it would tip over. The top snapped loudly, almost sounding like the report of guns. Rachel finally asked God to help her sleep, and He did.

The next morning, all of them lightened their loads some more. They broke up trunks for wood and threw out extra axles, shovels, chains, and other things beside the Trail. As the drivers forced their tired oxen on, Rachel, Martha, Julia, Petey, and Willie noticed deserted wagons and carts as well as furniture lining the road. Dead animals lay on and around the castoffs.

Rachel and Martha watched Thurman Tate's oxen stumbling along. When they faltered too much he laid the whip on their backs. He'd tied the cow to the wagon and she staggered along the best she could, bawling at nearly every step.

Rachel went to find Tom Dorland as he felt sympathy for animals more than anyone she knew.

"I'll talk to him," Tom said when Rachel told him about Tate's animals. "But I doubt he'll listen. I haven't heard him listen to anyone yet."

He rode up to Tate's wagon. "Your oxen are looking bad," he said. "Want some help dumping your stuff?"

"Them oxen are all right!" Tate yelled. "Why don't you go put a bandage on your mouth?"

"How about letting me treat the cow then? I might be able to make her more comfortable. She'd heal up faster, too."

"That cow's going to be meat in a week or so, so don't worry about her. You take care of your horse and I'll take care of my livestock."

Tom kept beside the Tate wagon as it moved slowly along. "Well, if you need some help, be sure to ask." Touching his heels to his horse's sides he moved ahead.

Rachel stomped along, fuming. "Did you hear that?" she asked Martha. " 'Most everyone in the train heard it," Martha said. "Calm down, Rachel. You have to learn to accept things you can't change."

———⋙———

Two days later, the wagon train reached South Pass. Captain Ransom called the men to a meeting. Thirty minutes later, just as Alma and Rachel had dinner ready, Nate returned with Stan Latham. After they asked God to bless the food and also them, they filled their plates.

"This is where Sublette cutoff leaves the main trail," Nate explained. "It's supposed to save four days travel, but there's a fifty-mile stretch with no food or water for the animals."

Rachel turned her back on him and dipped a biscuit into her beans. "What did you decide, Papa?"

Nate grinned through a mouthful of beans. "Well, most of us decided to stay on the main trail. Our animals are gettin' thin and worn. We decided it'd be too hard on them."

"Good for you, dear," Alma said. "You made the right decision."

"But that's not the end of the story. Tate's taking the cutoff. Said he'd wait for us at the other end."

"Oh, Papa, his oxen are worse than anyone's. And you know about his cow."

"I know. But we can't tell the man what to do."

But later that night Tate fixed part of the problem himself. Rachel heard a gunshot a half-hour before Tate appeared. "Want some beef?" he asked. "Just butchered the old cow. Figured she wouldn't make it through the cutoff."

"You figured right," Nate said. "Your oxen won't make it either. Better dump the heavy stuff and then take the regular trail."

Tate said a few words that didn't harmonize too well with his Christian claims. "Do you want some beef or not?" he added.

"I suppose we could use some," Nate said after a little thought.

"Come and get it then," Tate said, marching off. "Seems like people would appreciate some meat way out here," he mumbled.

"I don't want any of his meat," Rachel said. "I won't eat it either."

Nate glanced at Alma who shook her head. "Go tell him then," he told Rachel.

She didn't have to be told twice. She took off running in the direction he'd taken. She caught him at the Lawford wagon. Dr. Dorland was there, too.

"We're not interested in eating that poor creature," Martha was telling

Tate. "I don't understand how anyone could treat one of God's creatures the way you've done that cow."

Dr. Dorland took up the conversation. "Only a man with absolutely no feeling in his heart could do it. I feel for your family. But about the cow. The meat is infected from her wounds and not fit to eat. I hope no one takes any, Tate, for their sake."

"Well, forget I asked. I shoulda just eaten it all myself." He hiked on down the row of wagons, not stopping at any more.

The next day the Tates stayed to jerk the meat. "We'll still beat you by three days," he told Captain Ransom. "We'll just wait for you and rest."

"I forgot to tell you girls one more thing," Nate said when Rachel returned. "There's another cutoff being built. It won't be finished until fall, but it'll cut off one hundred miles and it has more water than the Trail." He sighed. "Won't do us any good, but it'll be a godsend to next year's emigration. It's called Lander's Cutoff."

The next day the train discovered that even on the main trail water was in short supply. They found none all day, not even at their camp. The Butler herd of cows' milk had dwindled from thirty gallons a day to less than one between them all, less than a cup apiece.

The next day, about noon, they reached Green River. The drivers couldn't hold back their parched oxen, which pulled the wagons into the river. They camped beside the river so the animals could get their fill of grass and water.

An Indian trading post dominated the spot beside the river. Rachel saw Pastor Richards trade some fishing lures for several pairs of soft white deerskin moccasins.

The three girls and the little boys ran around looking at the colorful flowers.

"Look, Rachel," Willie said. "What are these red things?"

Rachel looked and discovered wild strawberries. Strawberries! Real strawberries! The girls grabbed pans and picked all they could find.

Petey looked longingly at Martha's pan filled with the red treats. "I wish I was your little boy," he said.

"You can't be my little boy because you already have a mama," Martha said, hugging him, "but you can have half of my berries. Think your mama would like that?"

Petey's brown eyes sparkled with starry sunshine. "Thank you, Martha. I love you."

Rachel gave Martha part of her berries; Martha's family, after all, had more people to feed than her family did. Still, Rachel took home enough of the juicy red fruit for each family member to have a nice dish of them.

—ഝ—

It was too cold and windy again for preaching on Sunday, June twelfth, so Rachel had a nice day of rest. In the afternoon, the wind died down and Pastor Richards came by her wagon looking as if he'd just stepped from a bath into clean, freshly pressed clothes.

"How about a walk?" he asked.

Rather than hurt him, she tucked up her hair and went. Leading her to all of the train's young women, he invited them to his own wagon.

"What a nice surprise," Tamara said. "I love company."

Pastor Richards got out the moccasins and gave each girl a pair, including Tamara.

"How beautiful," Rachel said, turning hers over and over to see every bead and thread.

"You're welcome," the pastor said. "I wanted you all to have a reason to remember me."

Rachel knew she'd remember Pastor Richards with only friendship in her heart. How could she have thought she felt more?

The next day the oxen started another long hard week. Rachel, Martha, Julia, Petey, and Willie walked together as always. Rachel hardly noticed when it happened, but she now enjoyed the boys and missed them during their nap time.

A bunch of turnarounds told them that five men had been massacred by the Indians a little ways ahead.

"I don't believe them," Martha said. "They're just trying to impress people. And scare them."

Later, they came upon five graves, side-by-side. "Well, so much for what you don't believe," Rachel told Martha. "These are the graves the men told us about."

Finally, they reached the west end of Sublette Cutoff, the road Tate had taken. Not finding Tate waiting for them, they made camp and settled down for the night. That evening, the Tates showed up, wishing they'd stayed with the group.

"We lost two more oxen," Tate said. "And a cow. We can't take our wagon on as we don't have nothin' to pull it."

"I could help you make it into a cart," Nate Butler said. "Maybe your animals could pull it that way."

"No, you aren't," Tate's wife shrilled. "I have to have the things in that wagon."

"Shut up!" Tate said. "I bin listenin' to you too long."

"Then we'll have to keep the half with the cookstove and the dressers."

She glared at Nate. "Do you have any idea how much those things cost?" Then she shook her head, answering her own question. "No, I'm sure you wouldn't."

"Ma'am," Nate said, "do you have any idea how much them oxen are worth or where you'll get some more?"

"Make it into a cart," Tate said. "Don't pay no 'tention to her."

It took all that evening and the following day, but by the next day a light, sleek, two-wheeled cart was ready to go. The cookstove and dressers joined the many other abandoned items beside the road.

As the train moved the next morning, Rachel noticed the Tate items. "How can they live with themselves," she said to Martha, "when they killed and tortured several animals by forcing them to haul that stuff up and down the hills. Now it's by the Trail."

Martha shook her dark head. "What a waste of life."

As they walked and talked, Rachel got brave enough to ask Martha what she thought of Pastor Richards.

"I think he's a good man trying to work for God," Martha answered.

But Rachel wasn't satisfied. "I know he's a good man, but I want to know how you feel about him personally. You know what I mean."

Martha smiled her sweet smile. "You mean do I more than like him? Well, I'll tell you the truth. I'm purely not romantically interested in any man, anywhere." She grinned impishly. "He's all yours, Rachel. Or yours, Julia."

"I don't want him," Rachel said. "I may have thought I did once but I know better now. I simply don't want him. He's all yours, Julia."

Julia giggled. "Well, thanks. But what am I going to do with two men? For the whole trip I've liked Dan Barlow a whole lot. But if you don't like the Reverend anymore, Rachel, who is it you do like?"

Chapter 11

Rachel almost stopped walking as she sucked in her breath. She'd always "liked" someone since she'd been in eighth grade. But who now? She picked up her pace as she thought. "Well," she finally said. "I thought I liked the Reverend just because he's so handsome and tall and clean. Especially clean."

"Did you ever notice how he stays clean?" Julia asked, her eyes twinkling. "He never does a lick of work. Never. Not a lick. I'd rather have a real man."

Rachel laughed. "I told you I discovered I don't care for Pastor Richards that way. But you've put a claim on Dan Barlow, so I can't have him."

Julia laughed happily. Obviously they'd finally found a subject entirely to her liking. "I hope you can't," she said giggling, "but I'm not sure. But who do you like now, Rachel?"

Rachel swung her red head back and forth. "There isn't anyone else."

That afternoon while Petey and Willie napped, the Ransom Train caught up with another train, stopped in the trail. As they walked past the stopped train the girls noticed people standing around in groups. One man stood between two others as if they were restraining him.

The Ransom Train stopped; Martha and Rachel hurried to watch.

"Howdy," Captain Ransom said. "We interruptin' somethin'?"

"We're havin' ourselves a little trial," a white-haired man said. "Wanna watch?"

"Yes, please," the girls whispered to each other. None had ever seen a trial.

They soon learned that the man had stolen a horse from some Indians, who had probably stolen it from a white man. After he'd been declared guilty, the "judge" told the jury they should determine the man's punishment. About twenty minutes later the jury foreman announced that the man should be "hanged by the neck until dead."

Captain Ransom turned on his heel and rushed back to his own train. "Let's get going," he yelled.

As they walked away, Rachel saw someone hoist the criminal onto the back of a big horse. Someone else climbed into a tree and tied a rope to a low branch, dropping the other end of the rope that was then secured around the man's neck.

"What's going to happen?" Julia asked.

"Someone's going to hit that horse really hard and make him jump out from under the man and he'll be 'hanged until dead,' " George Lawford said.

The girls hurried on looking straight ahead, not caring to see what happened next.

"What if he didn't do it?" Martha asked.

"Better hope he did," Rachel said. " 'Cause he's paying for it anyway."

A few hours later they nooned at Soda Springs, nine or ten sparkling, boiling, bubbling springs of clear water. Someone discovered that by adding a little acid like vinegar to the water it made a good drink. Rachel and Mama tried it. *Not that good,* Rachel thought, *but something different.*

"I'll bet it would be good in biscuits," Mama said. Papa brought a small pail of the water and never had Rachel seen Mama's biscuits rise so high. Mama put some water into jars to take with them.

A quarter of a mile farther they found Steamboat Springs with warm milky water. The train camped there and the women did their washings, the first in hot water since they left Independence. Martha and Rachel did their families' washing, then Mrs. Piling's. The woman hadn't gotten better since Mr. Piling returned from the dead. In fact, as the days passed, she seemed worse.

After the girls finished Mrs. Piling's laundry, they did the wash of several of the horse riders and for Mr. and Mrs. Pitman, an old couple who seemed to be in nearly as bad condition as the oxen. They were considerably older than the fifty-year age limit advised for the vigorous journey, but they'd insisted on coming.

Later that afternoon, as Martha and Rachel returned from doing all the washing, they met Dr. Dorland with a small bloody animal in his hand. Josie's nose twitched as she hurried to Tom.

"I got a gopher for Josie," he said. "Thought she'd be needing another one."

Martha grimaced, then reached for the horrible looking bit of flesh. But Tom drew it back.

"No need for you to touch it," he said. "I'll just give it to Josie." She gladly accepted the bloody morsel, biting it twice before swallowing it whole. Tom laughed and nodded. "I'll keep watching for food for her." He hurried away, wiping his hands on his pants as he went.

The dust continued to plague the travelers and the oxen. Not only did it get into man's and animal's eyes but it piled over shoe tops, making it extremely difficult to walk. Rachel, Martha, Julia, Petey, and Willie wore thin linen handkerchiefs over their eyes and noses.

Rachel noticed the oxen's eyes ran thick with yellowish stuff as they limped along on sore feet. After several failed attempts to help them, she'd learned that she couldn't do anything. But one day Tom Dorland happened by on his mare so she called him over.

"We have to do something for the oxen's eyes," she said. "They're just awful."

His smile faded into a solemn concerned look. "I've noticed," he said. "Not only yours, but all the oxen in the train. It's too hard on them."

"Well, what can we do about it?"

He shook his light head. "The only thing I know would be to stop traveling until the dust dies down. But as far as I can tell, it plans to fly forever."

Disappointment temporarily made Rachel forget she was a brand new Christian and that whatever she said "to the least of these" she said to Jesus.

"Are you going to just let them suffer then? Just say we can't do anything? Not get the train stopped?" Her voice grew louder as she continued. "I thought you cared, Tom Dorland, but you're just like the rest. You're not made of fit material to be a doctor!"

Tom watched her fume for another moment before he grinned. "I'm not an animal doctor," he said softly. "But I do care. I cared about Andy Shackleford, too, but I couldn't help him either." He touched his heels to his horse's sides and trotted off to the front of the line.

—⁓—

One evening they camped by a busy little creek of delightfully cool water where grass grew abundantly. Martha, Julia, and Rachel waded along the creek, enjoying the ice cold water on their feet.

"Look!" Julia shouted, "berries!"

Rachel climbed out of the creek in a hurry and found serviceberries growing thickly on low vines. By that time Martha had pulled herself away from the creek, too, and the girls ran back to the wagons for containers. They filled every pot and pan they could get hold of.

"What'll we do with them?" Martha asked Mrs. Lawford.

Martha's mother was sweet and round, always ready to help the young people. "Well," she said, "we can't take them with us." After thinking a moment, she clapped her hands. "I know. Why don't you make some pies, cobblers, fruit cakes, and whatever you can think up and invite the horse riders to help you eat them?"

So the girls did. Each took some berries and cooked everything she could think of with what she had to cook with. Then Julia ran to invite everyone who wanted to come. Soon, people arrived from all around the wagon circle.

"It smells good," Pastor Richards said with an exaggerated sniff. "When do we get to eat?"

Stan Latham arrived with his tin plate and a dirty looking fork. Tom Dorland came next, wearing a wide smile. Dan Barlow came with Tom, both looking as if they anticipated something special. Jackson Lawford trotted into the group, eagerly looking at the treats.

Then Tamara Richards came with her hand through a tall thin man's arm. She looked almost like a real person, Rachel thought. She smiled, her eyes sparkled, and she walked with energy. "I'd like you to meet my friend, Evan Mann," she said almost as if showing off a prize race horse.

"Where'd he come from?" Rachel blurted out. "I thought I'd seen everyone on the train."

"He stays with his wagon and oxen most of the time," Tamara said. She laughed quietly into the man's eyes. "He's shy, but I've been sending him some food, and my brother James shot a few ducks for him, so we got acquainted."

"Good afternoon, Evan Mann," Rachel said, extending her hand. As the man accepted and shook her hand, she recognized him. He was the man who'd tried to catch a rabbit! Rachel tried not to show her recognition and hoped that Martha wouldn't either. It could embarrass the man to be reminded of that hilarious run through the sagebrush.

Julia served Dan first, then herself. They went off somewhere to eat, leaving Rachel and Martha to serve the others. There was plenty of food for everyone who came, and several had seconds. Stan Latham alone had thirds.

—⁂—

Pastor Richards led an inspiring collection of songs and preached his usual stirring sermon on June twelfth. Then the group ate lunch together. Rachel felt rather detached since she'd lost interest in the young minister. The silly young men running after the girls meant nothing to her anymore, and she wondered how she could have been so enthralled with all of it only a few days ago.

The next morning Rachel happened to be near when the handlers yoked up the oxen for the day's travel. For the first time the oxen tried their best to avoid the yokes. But with a few strong words and two men working together, they forced the heavy yokes onto the oxen's raw necks and shoulders. When the rough wood hit their sores, the animals bawled a moment then quieted as if willing to do what must be done.

Rachel forced back the tears that tried to come into her eyes, then ran around the still-circled wagons to Captain Ransom's wagon.

"Mr. Ransom, you have to stop the wagon train so the oxen can get better," she cried.

The man rose from the box he'd been sitting on. "What's happened, Rachel? Are you all right?"

"No, I'm not. And neither are our oxen. They didn't want the yokes rubbing on their sore necks this morning. They're limping on sore feet and they're getting thinner every day. You have to help me, Captain Ransom."

He shook his thick gray hair. "You're right, girlie. Them oxen need weeks to recuperate. So do some of our people."

Rachel felt a moment's relief, but the man continued.

"Thing is, we don't have time. We're already behind our schedule. Gotta get to Oregon City afore the snow flies. We get caught in the mountains, we'll all die, animals and all." He moved to her, put his arm around her shoulders, and pulled her close. "So we gotta keep movin'. I allays tell the men to treat their animals right, though."

Rachel thanked the man for listening and stumbled back toward her own wagon. At least she knew how it was.

Two days later, just after the wagons corralled, Dan Barlow came to Rachel's wagon. "Miss Lawford," he said quietly, "your father wants you at your wagon right away." Turning his eyes to Julia, he smiled. "See you tonight." Touching his heels to his gelding, he rode ahead.

Martha looked curious. "Strange," she said. "Papa's never called me before. I hope everything's all right. Guess I'd better go find out."

"Want me to come, too?" Rachel asked, staying by Martha's side. "Maybe Julia would watch the boys until we get back."

"I'd love to," Julia said, her eyes still full of stars from her encounter with Dan. "You just go on and do whatever you need to. I'll take good care of them."

When they neared the Lawford wagon, Tom Dorland jumped to the ground and met them a few feet away. "I'm sorry to have to tell you, Miss Lawford, but your mother's sick."

Martha's face lost every semblance of color. "What is it?"

He shook his head. "I can't be sure but it looks bad." He drew in a long breath. "Could be cholera," he murmured.

"No." Martha didn't say more or move a muscle.

But Rachel drew in a long breath and bolted for the wagon, slowing only to jump into it. Mr. Lawford sat on a box near his wife who looked still and small in her featherbed. Rachel knelt by the woman and took her hand. "Mrs. Lawford," she said. "I'm here to pray with you."

Mrs. Lawford opened her eyes. "Bless you, dear."

"Oh dear heavenly Father," Rachel began, "we thank You for Your great love for us and giving Your precious only Son to die for us. Oh, Lord, You know how Mrs. Lawford loves You and what a wonderful influence she is on everyone. Please, dear Lord, make her well right away. We all need her so badly. I pray these things in Jesus' precious name, and thank You for hearing and answering my prayer."

Rachel opened her eyes and looked down at Martha's mother, almost expecting to see her get up and start gathering sticks for the supper's fire.

But sweat ran from the woman's unusually red cheeks. She reached a hand to Rachel. "Thank you dear, for that lovely prayer. I'm sure He'll have me up in a day or so."

Rachel, on her knees, leaned down and kissed the hot cheek. "Of course He will," she whispered. "Now you sleep for a while and don't worry. We'll take good care of Willie."

"I know," the sick woman said, her eyelashes falling against her cheeks.

Rachel jumped to the ground where Martha and Tom still talked. Tom smiled at her. "Got yourself all exposed, did you?"

Rachel hadn't given that possibility a thought. Well, if there was anything to be exposed to, she probably had. "I might have," she admitted.

"I'll be back in a couple of hours," he told Martha.

Martha didn't talk much. "We'll keep Willie tonight," Rachel said. "And I'll come over later to see what Tom says."

On being told that his mama was sick, Willie agreed to stay with Rachel. After the supper things were cleaned up and put away, Rachel hurried to the Lawford wagon. Martha met her outside and told her Tom was certain her mama had cholera.

"I'm going to help take care of her and make her well," Rachel said. "I'll be over in the morning."

The next morning Captain Ransom called a day's stop for the train to give Mrs. Lawford a chance to recover.

The woman had worsened during the night, Rachel learned when she arrived at Martha's wagon. "You go do something or rest," she told her dear friend.

Mr. Lawford sat on his wooden box in the wagon, looking heartbroken. "Don't you worry, Mr. Lawford," Rachel said. "We'll have her on her feet in no time. You just sit here and watch and listen if you want."

First she wet washrags in cold water and put them on Mrs. Lawford's hot forehead.

"That feels so good," the woman whispered. "Please, don't stop."

"I won't," she told the weak woman. "I'm going to be here and keep them on you all day."

She applied the cold compresses and read the Gospel of John to the Lawfords most of the day. Both listened quietly to every word. But every time she stopped to cool the washrag, Mr. Lawford asked how his wife was now.

Tom came by a little later. "I don't know if you're helping her physically, but you're doing them both a world of good," he told Rachel. "As you read, you're giving them something positive to think about, and the wet cloths certainly do make her feel better." He smiled a gentle smile. "Since you already got yourself exposed, I'll just say keep up the good work."

At noon Rachel stopped and made some rabbit broth from a rabbit Jackson Lawford had brought and cleaned. After giving Mr. Lawford a bowl and spooning some into Mrs. Lawford's mouth, she went back to reading and applying the cold compresses.

"What have you been doing today?" Rachel asked when Martha finally appeared at the wagon.

"I've been doing people's washing," she said. "I had a feeling I'd be busy when washing day came, so I got it done today. How's my mama?"

"I don't know," Rachel said. "She's not talking as much as she was this morning."

Rachel ran back to her own wagon just in time for supper. Willie and Julia had gathered sticks for the fire and Mama had biscuits and side meat cooking.

Willie slept in Rachel's wagon again and morning came quickly. After breakfast, Rachel hurried to the Lawford wagon again. Martha ran to meet her.

"Papa's sick, too," Martha whispered. "They're both awfully sick."

Both girls worked all day caring for Martha's parents. Both seemed too sick to listen to reading, but Rachel did it anyway, just in case. Rachel cared mostly for Mrs. Lawford, and Martha took care of her father. At noon, both girls fixed broth for Martha's parents.

"Papa thinks I'm Mama," Martha whispered. "Oh, Rachel, I'm afraid they aren't going to get well."

"Yes, they are," Rachel snapped. "God will make them well."

Chapter 12

Tom Dorland came by several times that day and left looking sadder each time. One time Rachel found him kneeling beside Mrs. Lawford, his hand on her forehead, praying earnestly for her and Mr. Lawford.

That night Rachel stayed with Martha to help. Mrs. Lawford died early in the morning. Mr. Lawford didn't know. He died that afternoon.

Pastor Richards said a few words, prayed for Martha, Jackson, and Willie, then they buried Mr. and Mrs. Lawford in the trail. The emigrants yoked up to continue on and many wagons ran over the graves, trying to hide them from Indians and animals. And the wagon train moved forward. Always forward. Relentlessly forward.

Jackson guided the Lawford oxen who seemed nearly as broken as he. They could hardly walk, and Jackson could barely hold his head erect.

Martha, Rachel, Julia, Petey, and Willie walked with Jackson. Rachel thought she couldn't bear losing the Lawfords. They had been good to her, even when she hadn't been all that nice to anyone.

"Why didn't God heal them?" she kept asking Martha. "We prayed so hard. Even Tom prayed."

"We can't understand everything," Martha said, "but just keep on trusting Him, Rachel. He knows the beginning from the end."

Those words didn't satisfy Rachel. "What's the use praying if He doesn't answer?" she asked bitterly.

Martha remained calm. "I'm not sure. Maybe we'll go through some horrible hardships that would have been harder for them than to die quickly and peacefully. This may have been the best way. No, I said that wrong. This was the best way. God loved them much more than we did, and He wanted the best for them even more than we did. But He knows all. And don't forget that death isn't the end, Rachel. There's a beautiful home in a beautiful world waiting for them. . .and for us. Please don't lose your faith."

As the days passed, Rachel thought about the things Martha had said. Finally, they made sense to her. She felt better and God's sweet peace returned to her heart.

One day they neared Fort Hall, 1,300 miles from Independence.

Abandoned wagons, household goods, and dead animals grew thicker around them. As they drew close to the large fort, Jackson called Martha to him. Rachel moved closer, too, as they walked along the dusty trail.

"Have you noticed the oxen can barely walk?" he asked.

Martha nodded. "I've noticed, Jackson. It's really sad, but what can we do?"

He gave her a long look. "They're giving out, Martha. See them stumbling? Almost blindly? They're going to die within two days. We'll have to leave them at Fort Hall. With rest and some good food they might recover. Otherwise, they're dead."

"Leave them, Martha," Rachel cried. "Give them a chance to live."

"But what will we do?" Martha asked. "We don't have extra oxen like you."

"Martha!" Jackson said. "Either we leave them and hope for the best, or they're dead. They can't help us if they're dead."

"Leave them," Rachel repeated. "We have extra oxen. I'll get Papa to put some on your wagon."

So that's what they did. The fresh oxen pulled with a strength that the Lawford animals hadn't had for weeks.

The day after they left the oxen, Jackson called Martha to him again as they walked. "I keep thinking I need to go back on the Trail and meet Aunt Mandy and Uncle Cleve," he said. "They deserve to know what happened."

"No, Jackson," Martha pleaded. "You have to care for the oxen while I watch Willie."

He walked a while then continued. "I have to, don't you see? I just have to, Martha. Someone will help you with the oxen."

Martha begged and pleaded with Jackson, but she couldn't change his mind.

The next morning he gathered his clothes, a little food, and climbed onto his horse. "As soon as I tell them what happened I'll come right back," he said. "I won't be gone more than a few days, so wish me well."

"I'll try," Martha said in a small voice. "But you shouldn't be doing this. The oxen are your responsibility."

"I'll tell you what I think," Rachel said. "I think you're not even a man—just a big baby. Don't you think Martha hurts as much as you? And poor little Willie. How's he going to feel when you run off?"

"Sorry," Jackson mumbled. "It's something I have to do." He touched his horse's sides with his heels and took off trotting, back the way they'd come.

—⚏—

On Sunday, July third, the warm sunny weather lifted Rachel's spirits. And she hadn't heard a single mosquito during the night! Could it be that they were through with that plague?

Pastor Richards preached a stirring sermon on having faith when it seems all reason for faith is gone. "Faith isn't faith," he said, "when all goes well. Faith is believing when all looks dark and your prayers don't seem to be heard. That's real faith. And our Lord will help you with this faith if you only ask."

The people shared the noon meal so they could all be together on their day of rest.

As Martha, Willie, Rachel, and Julia filled their plates, Pastor Richards approached, this time giving Rachel his attention.

"Would you lovely young ladies mind if a tired old preacher joined you for dinner?" he asked.

Before Rachel had a chance to panic, Stan Latham crowded between Pastor Richards and her.

"You look uncommonly lovely today, Miss Butler," he said in his oily, smooth voice. "I'd like the privilege of sharing the meal with you."

Suddenly, she looked longingly at Pastor Richards. At least she could eat with him sitting there. She'd almost for sure throw up if the filthy Stan Latham were in sight. What could she do?

Before she answered, another oh-so-welcome voice broke the stillness —Tom Dorland.

"Oh, Miss Butler, there you are," Tom said. "I need your help right away. . .if you have time. I need to medicate a couple of bad eyes and can't do it alone."

Rachel jumped to her feet before Tom finished. "I'm ready," she said, heaving a huge sigh of relief. "Let's go."

As they walked away from the dinner, Rachel felt a stab of remorse for having left Martha at the mercy of Stan Latham. "Where is this person who needs treatment?" she asked.

Tom grinned. His eyes had a lovely glow that Rachel hadn't seen before. Come to think of it she had never noticed his eyes at all. The soft look must come from his close relationship with God. "Did I say it was a person?" he asked. "I had in mind treating your oxen's eyes with some boric acid. It might make them feel better."

Rachel stopped in her tracks. "What's going on, Dr. Dorland? I tried hard to get you to help those oxen and you refused. What's changed?"

They reached Rachel's wagon where Tom had stashed the medicine. "Well, I mixed up this stuff and decided to try it," he said. "If you still want to, that is." Then they took the medicine and went searching for the oxen but couldn't find them.

"They're somewhere gorging on grass," Rachel said. "Wouldn't it be better to do it while they're yoked?"

He nodded. "I think you're right." He grinned mischievously again. "So, should we go get something to eat?"

Rachel laughed and headed back toward the dinner. "Well, I'm glad you thought about the oxen and got me away from Stan Latham. I panicked when that pig showed up."

"Oh, one more thing," Tom said as they neared the crowd of people. "When we finish eating, I have to take some food to the Pitmans. If you help me, we can do it in one trip."

As they reached the rest of the people, Rachel agreed to help. Pastor Richards and Stan Latham still sat with Martha and Julia. Dan Barlow was there, too, sitting close to Julia. Tom and Rachel filled their plates and joined them.

Rachel faced away from Stan Latham and pretended he wasn't there.

Later, Rachel and Tom carried a nice meal to the Pitmans, who thanked them profusely. As they walked back to Rachel's wagon, she thought about the old couple.

"Will the Pitmans get cholera and die?"

He shook his head. "We can hope and pray they won't."

When they reached Rachel's wagon, Tom seemed reluctant to leave. They talked a little about Martha, how brave she was, left all alone with Willie, the wagon, and the oxen.

The next day they traveled on. Soon, the sun became scorching.

"The dust comes over my shoes," Willie complained, "and it hurts."

"I know," Martha told him tenderly. "It comes over mine, too. Try to put your feet straight down when you step."

He couldn't, so Martha carried him awhile. "It's hot on my feet, too," she told the little boy. "Can you walk now?"

He walked awhile, then she carried him again, all the time keeping the oxen going. Petey managed to keep going on his own.

Early in the afternoon they came to Fall River, which they had to ford. The deep river with steep banks looked impassable.

"How can we go across that?" Petey asked.

"I don't know," Martha said. "Shall we sit here and watch?"

Soon, they saw the men putting secure ropes around a wagon, then tying the ropes to five yoke of oxen. With men guiding both the wagon and the oxen, they let the wagon down the steep cliff. They lowered all the wagons the same way.

Then the same weary oxen pulled the wagons across the deep swift stream. The men made it as safe as possible by hooking several wagons together and doing the same with the oxen. At near dusk, the last wagon emerged from the river, and Captain Ransom called corralling time.

The next morning the road turned into a big rock pile. Big rocks, little rocks, smooth rocks, sharp rocks. So many rocks that when the oxen stepped onto one it rolled onto the others, causing the weary animals to stumble and nearly fall. The girls had the same problem.

The sun beat down so hot that Rachel saw little heat waves coming off the oxen and felt herself wavering, too. She couldn't see one bush or even any sagebrush anywhere to shade people or animals from the burning sun. They nooned at a place where they found a little patch of grass but it wasn't nearly large enough to satisfy the famished animals.

"Why did you stop here?" Rachel yelled at Captain Ransom. "Can't you see the animals need more food?"

"I've heard about enough out of you, young lady!" Ransom shouted back. "Just where am I supposed to find grass, anyway?"

"There must be some if you'd just look harder," Rachel yelled, then burst into tears. Why did she act so mean, anyway? Ransom had never been unkind before. She voiced her worries to Martha.

"He's doing his best," Martha said. "It's the heat that's causing people to lose control. Just ask God to help you be kind."

While Rachel and her mother fixed dinner, Rachel heard people yelling at each other from other wagons and decided Martha was right. The heat made people crazy.

Just before dinner was ready, Papa left the area and Mama asked Rachel to find him. She ran all over looking for him, finally finding him with Captain Ransom.

"I've been looking all over for you," she said much louder than necessary. "Why do you run off just when dinner's ready?"

"I'm not your child," he yelled. "I'll go where I want whenever I want if it's all the same with you."

Rachel wheeled around to run back to the wagon and ran into Tom Dorland. "Why do you have to sneak up on me all the time?" she yelled at him. "You could at least let a person know you're coming."

He opened his mouth, closed it and remained silent a moment. "I'm sorry," he finally said. "I didn't intend to sneak up on you." His voice remained sweet and calm.

Embarrassed at being so unkind, Rachel turned her back on him and tore back to her wagon where she realized she wasn't representing God very well. No, she wasn't representing Him at all. "Please forgive me, Father," she whispered. "I'm sorry to be so terrible. I hope You won't give up on me." Immediately, she had a strong feeling that she should ask Captain Ransom, Tom Dorland, and Papa to forgive her. But she was much too hot to find all of them right now.

Each day was the same. Scorching heat, burning dust, and people yelling at each other. All except Tom and Martha. Those two stayed nice no matter what.

—⚶—

On July tenth, every creature needed the rest so badly and the sun stayed so hot that many didn't turn out for Pastor Richards's service or the potluck dinner afterward. Rachel attended though, so Martha wouldn't be alone. They didn't even have their plates filled when Pastor Richards joined them. Speaking especially to Rachel, he talked about his sermon, the singing, his hard-to-keep-pressed clothing, and his absent parishioners.

She tried to listen patiently, wondering how she'd ever thought he might be the man for her. About the time they finished eating, Tom, who hadn't eaten with the group, arrived with another small dead animal for Josie.

The next morning the train started early and traveled hard. Rachel thought her feet would burn up, even through her shoes. The dust on the ground burned so hot she couldn't keep her hand on it. Finally, after what seemed like forever, the train stopped to camp at Salmon Falls. Tepees, ponies, and Indians swarmed everywhere. One Indian brought a thirty-five-pound salmon to swap for old clothes. Several families traded clothes for the Indian's huge fish.

The Indian gave the fish to Papa, then looked the clothes over. He seemed pleased until he found a long rip in one shirt. With hand motions he requested a needle and thread that someone provided. Then, he sat on his heels and went to work on the tear. A few minutes later, he handed the needle back, nodding and wearing a wide smile. Rachel signed for him to hold up the shirt for her to see. Surprised, she discovered the Indian had used some skill in repairing the shirt.

The next day as they traveled, carcasses became so thick they almost blocked the Trail. The overpowering stench seemed more than the emigrants could bear. And graves became so numerous Rachel lost count.

When they stopped that evening, one of Thurman Tate's oxen dropped dead in the yoke. The other's legs gave way and it couldn't get up. The next morning the ox still couldn't get up so Tate had to leave it there. He also had to leave the cart. Several families took a few of the Tates' clothes but all their oxen were too worn-out to carry much more, so the rest of the Tates' belongings were left alongside the trail.

"I wish someone would tell that man how much misery and death his greediness has caused innocent animals," Rachel groused.

The train continued all day with no grass or water for the oxen. At five o'clock that afternoon they reached the river and, in their eagerness for water, the oxen pulled the wagons into the river again.

So desperately did the animals need the nourishment that the guides went off the trail, looking for grass. The train was stopped any time someone found grass.

The next day the train came to a good camp at Glenn's Ferry at Three Island Crossing, 1,398 miles from home. As the people prepared for the Sabbath and Rachel and Martha washed clothes, Rachel told Martha they'd never see civilization again.

—ᗰᗰ—

On Sunday, July seventeenth, people came from all around to hear the preaching and share the meal. Since no one had much food anymore, the potlucks consisted mostly of beans, biscuits, and dried-apple pies. Fewer and fewer people came to the dinners.

The next morning everyone repacked and threw away anything they could live without. They'd done this so many times that Rachel wondered how there could be anything left. But more items edged the road each time. When everyone was ready, the people lined up to be ferried across the river. All except Mark Piling.

"I ain't makin' those cutthroats rich," he said. "I'll just get myself across and save the money."

"Better not," Nate Butler said. "They say the river's ruthless here."

"Who says?" Piling asked scornfully. "The men who run the ferry?"

Rachel, Martha, Julia, Petey, and Willie sat on the river bank to watch Piling ford the river.

But Mr. Piling came after Petey. "You get yourself over to our wagon!" he bellowed at the trembling little boy. "Fergot you even had a family, din't you?" As Petey skittered past his father, Piling reached out a hand and cuffed the back of Petey's head, knocking him, face first, into the dust. "Get up!" Piling yelled. "Get into that wagon and make sure the water don't get too high." Petey scrambled to his feet, tears running down his dirty face, and raced ahead of Mr. Piling to the wagon.

Piling hooked his oxen to the wagon and started them into the river. The animals balked several times, and Piling rewarded them with hard lashes from the whip. Eventually, they made it to the first island. Then, with more lashing, the oxen reached the second island. They'd nearly made it across.

"It's going to be all right now," Julia breathed.

But, just as she spoke, a swift undercurrent snatched the wagon, tipping it over. Mr. Piling, who'd been in the river with the oxen, grabbed his wife as she tumbled from the wagon. Mrs. Piling held tightly to the baby, but Petey whirled past them and on down the river.

Chapter 13

M artha screamed and bolted toward the river. Rachel caught her just in time to stop her from plunging in after Petey. Mr. Piling held on tight to his wife and baby, watching Petey spin and whirl down the river until he disappeared from sight.

A moment later, the oxen became tangled in the harness and cumbersome yoke and couldn't keep their heads above the water. One of them managed to let out a loud bawl as they careened down the river, over and under the wagon. Soon, the wagon's contents littered the surface of the river and parts of the wagon bounced on the water until they lined the far bank.

"Go get him!" Martha screamed to anyone who might be listening. "Go get Petey! He's in the river!"

No one plunged into the river, but many people ran down the banks looking for the little boy.

Rachel had to restrain Martha again. As Martha screamed and struggled, Rachel thanked God she was bigger and stronger than Martha. Rachel had never seen Martha upset before, let alone in a horrible state like this.

"You can't go into the river hoping to find Petey," Rachel said quietly. "You'd only drown yourself." Martha continued to struggle with all her strength. "Martha," Rachel said a little louder, "you have Willie to care for. Remember, Martha?"

Finally, Martha wilted in Rachel's arms, her strength gone. "They aren't going to save him," she murmured over and over and over. Finally, she quieted.

The men looked for Petey all that night and until noon the next day. Early in the afternoon Pastor Richards held a short service for Petey after which wagon train moved on.

The Rahns took in Mr. and Mrs. Piling and the baby. The Pilings had nothing left for anyone to haul. Rachel walked to a spot where she could see Mrs. Piling. She looked like a snow-white dead person with no expression at all.

The train traveled five miles to a good camp at Wickahoney Creek. Rachel stayed with Martha that night. Poor, confused Willie stayed with Rachel's parents. Martha, who had been so brave when her parents died, went completely to pieces now. She cried and moaned all night; in the rare moments she slept, she called out for the little boy. Rachel cradled her in her arms and held her tightly.

Pastor Richards came to Martha but she turned him away. "Rachel's taking care of me," she said. "I don't need anyone else. No one cares anyway, not even God."

Rachel, realizing their roles had been reversed, reminded Martha that God loved Petey even more than they did and that He was crying with them. "Petey'll wake up with Jesus in the most beautiful home he's ever had," she promised. "Jesus will love him and never hurt him. Mark Piling hurt Petey, Martha. Hadn't you noticed how Petey kept away from his father? And how he hurt him that last day? Maybe God took Petey away from his father to protect him from more pain and suffering."

After several days of crying and listening to Rachel explain how God let this happen to save Petey from his abusive father, Martha seemed to accept Petey's death. She clung to Willie and didn't mention Petey anymore, though her white face told of her continued suffering.

"I want you to remember one thing," Rachel told Martha as they trudged along beside the oxen one day. "You gave Petey more happiness than he'd ever known. I know you did. And you taught him to love Jesus. Day after day you taught him of Jesus' love for him. That's something for you to rejoice about. We both know how much Petey loved Jesus, don't we?"

Martha smiled tremulously and nodded. "We purely do. Thank you, Rachel for being so good for me right now. You've become a real Christian."

But, inside, Rachel wasn't sure about that. She felt so furious with Piling she thought she couldn't handle having him around anymore. One day she told Martha how she felt about the man. "I wish he'd died instead of Petey!" she said. "Mrs. Piling would have been glad, too. I know she would."

Martha took her eyes from the oxen and hugged Rachel. "I know how you feel," she said. "But we can't feel that way. Remember the Lord's Prayer says God will forgive us as we forgive others. Let's ask God to help us forgive Mr. Piling. Let's pray for God to touch Mr. Piling's heart, too." So the girls prayed right then and there.

Still, Rachel couldn't stop thinking about Mr. Piling, and her thoughts weren't good.

—⟋⟍—

One day Captain Ransom stopped the train when a little girl, Jennie, fell in front of a wagon and an ox walked on her. Tom Dorland sent someone after Rachel to help him.

"You have to hold her still while I pull her leg into place," he said in his kind but firm voice.

Rachel held the child, murmuring encouragement into her ear, doubting the girl heard over all her screaming.

"There," Tom said a while later. And, in the middle of a sob, the little girl stopped crying. Rachel looked up with a question in her eyes. Tom smiled. "The bone snapped into place," he explained. "I'm sorry I had to hurt you," he told the little girl. "I won't hurt you anymore." Then he instructed Rachel how to help him put the splint on the leg in the most comfortable way. An hour later they finished; Rachel felt as if she'd been running all day.

"You're the best helper I've ever had," Tom said, his eyes showing his appreciation. "You really must consider going into medicine."

Rachel laughed quietly. "I'll do that," she said. "I'll enter the first medical school I find in Oregon City." Then she thought of Piling. "May I talk to you a minute?" she asked.

"Sure. I'll carry Jennie back to her parents first. Then we can walk for a little while."

When they finally stood where no one could hear them, Rachel felt shy to be talking to Tom like this. He was so good, he probably never had a negative thought about anyone. But she'd brought him here and she would share her thoughts. "I can't stop thinking about Mr. Piling," she said softly. "I can't stand the man, Tom, and I don't think he should be allowed to stay on the train. Could you ask the captain to put him off?"

Tom looked surprised for just a second then cleared his face of expression. "I wonder if you've thought this through," he finally said. "If Ransom puts Piling off the train, his wife and baby will go, too. And those poor people have had it rough enough already, don't you think?"

True enough, Rachel hadn't intended for the wife and baby to go, but they probably would.

Tom smiled kindly at Rachel. "I understand how you feel and I suspect most of the people on the train feel the same way. But we're a Christian group, remember?"

A few days later they met four more turnarounds. "You oughta go back while you can," they said. "It's nothin' but desert fer a long ways. By then it'll be winter and you'll never git through the Blues. Them mountains is killers. They kill the oxen and people just the same."

The men from the Ransom Train huddled around the four trying to decide how much the men knew and how much they surmised. "We must be almost through the desert," Dan Barlow said. "The Mormon guidebook says—"

Suddenly, one of the turnarounds pointed a finger at Dan. "I know you," he yelled. Then he turned to the others. "You'uns know who you got on this here train? That cur's a horse thief. I seen him escape just before he got hisself hanged. 'Twas in Illinois, it was. Ran right through the crowd, grabbed the sheriff's own horse, and escaped. In broad daylight, he did. Get a rope, boys. Let's finish the job."

"Just hold on here," Captain Ransom said quietly. "This here's my son and he's been with me all his life. Never set foot in no state but Missouri. Musta been someone else. Come on, let's get this thing movin'.'"

"Hey," the accuser yelled, "I know that face for sure. He's the man. Get him, boys. 'Tain't right for a man to flout the law." The other three men converged on Dan, who made no effort to protect himself.

Stan Latham turned to Tom Dorland and Nate Butler. "Grab your guns," Stan said. Almost instantly, a dozen men had guns, all aimed at the turnarounds.

"Turn the man loose," Nate demanded. "We don't want a war over this, but you can't come in here and abduct the captain's son."

The turnarounds released Dan, backed to their horses, mounted, and galloped away, cursing loudly.

After the men were nearly out of sight, Dan turned to Ransom. "I'm the man, Captain. I stole a horse when I was nineteen, old enough to know better. I thank you all for defending me but I'm ready to pay for my crime now."

Captain Ransom shook his wiry gray hair. "The Dan Barlow on this train always pulls his weight and then some. He's had plenty of opportunities to help himself to things but never has. He's allays thinking of the other guy. No, the Dan Barlow on this train isn't a taker but a giver." He looked around at the circle of men then back to Dan. "The Dan Barlow on this train is a genyooine born again Christian and I don't want to hear you or no one else say or even think anything foul about this here Dan. Is that clear?" No one said a word, but some flickering smiles met Ransom's stern command.

The train started to move again and, as always, Rachel and Julia walked with Martha and her borrowed oxen, helping her as they could, and especially entertaining Willie, who kept asking for Petey.

"Wasn't that exciting?" Julia asked, referring to the encounter with the turnarounds.

"A little too exciting," Rachel said. "Someone could have gotten hurt."

"But isn't Dan brave? And isn't the captain wonderful? Imagine him claiming Dan for his son."

"That was because he knows Dan's a really sincere Christian now," Martha said, "a new person in Christ. He'd never have done that if Dan was the same man who stole the horse."

"Have you decided to go on to Oregon City?" Rachel asked Martha for the millionth time.

"I purely can't," Martha said. "Jackson and my aunt and uncle and cousin will come looking for Willie and me there. And Josie, of course."

"Jackson doesn't deserve to find you," Rachel snapped. "He should spend the rest of his life looking for you." She pointed at the oxen and the wagon, then down at Willie. "Look what he left."

Martha nodded. "He shouldn't have done that. Sometimes I still get mad at him for it, but he's kin, Rachel. So are my aunt and uncle. They're all Willie and I have left."

"You have me. And I love you more than all of them put together."

Martha smiled but shook her head. "I love you, too. I'd rather go on with you, Rachel. I purely would. But I have to stop. I have to."

Later that afternoon the Trail ran so close to a ten-foot embankment beside the river there was barely room for the oxen driver to walk beside the animals.

Tom Dorland appeared on foot. "You'd better let me take the oxen for a while" he said to Martha. "If they balk just a little they'll push you right off the cliff into the river."

"These oxen are just like Josie," Martha said. "They wouldn't hurt me for anything."

Tom reached for the small walking stick Martha carried. He grinned. "Where's your whip?"

She smiled back at him. "I don't need a whip with these nice boys. Once in a while I guide them a little with the stick, but I haven't had to hurt them even once."

"Okay, I'll use the stick for a cane, all right?"

Martha heaved a sigh of relief as she fell back with Rachel, Julia, and Willie, behind the wagon. She started singing Jesus songs with Willie right away, and the girls joined in. After a while Rachel noticed a strong, clear tenor harmonizing with them—Tom.

Tom walked with the oxen until stopping time that afternoon, then unyoked them and took them off to pasture.

Martha and Willie stayed with their wagon to eat their meal, and Rachel ran back to hers where she found Mama trying to get some sagebrush to burn.

"The trouble is," Mama said, puffing from her efforts, "when it catches, it burns so quickly it puts out hardly any heat."

Between Mama and Rachel they finally got the fire going and made biscuits. By now their supplies were low, the cows had long since given up trying to make milk, so the meals grew simpler and simpler. Every now and then Papa shot a bird or rabbit and that made a big difference. The biscuits were only flour, baking powder, salt, and water. They had side meat with them and sometimes beans, but not tonight. They felt lucky to get enough heat to cook the biscuits and side meat.

"When we reach a trading post, we'll replenish our supplies," Papa said. "That shouldn't be too long."

It was even a shorter time than Papa thought. They camped about where the Owyhee River joins the Snake, three miles from Fort Boise.

On July twenty-fourth, Sunday, the group had their usual singing meeting and preaching but so many Indians, trappers, soldiers, and emigrants, came and went that it didn't feel very restful to Rachel.

The next day, about midmorning, the train reached Fort Boise. The fort was a replica of Fort Hall, made from adobe bricks like all the other forts, but was much smaller. They traveled along the Snake River where a few patches of grass grew. The train still stopped for the grass but thankfully it wasn't quite so rare anymore. They'd seen no trees or even shrubs between Fort Hall and Fort Boise, but at least now they seemed to be through the desert.

Rachel's father bought much-needed supplies at the fort, as did others who still had money left.

As a group walked away from the fort, a whiskered old man told them to be careful about drinking cold water. "Lots of people have died from exactly that," he said.

After they'd gotten away from the man, Tom leaned toward Rachel. "I think that man is miles off. The only time we shouldn't drink water is when it's contaminated. The Good Lord gave us water for cleansing the body, inside and out, and history will prove me right."

Rachel believed him. Come to think of it, she'd probably believe anything he said.

"Let me take the oxen a while," Rachel said one day to Martha who never complained about being tired, or anything else.

"I can do it," Martha said. "They're so good it isn't very hard."

"Get out of my way," Rachel said in play. "They're my oxen and I'll lead them part time." After that Rachel led the oxen half of each day. Julia watched Willie part of the time, and Tom and Dan took a turn with the oxen several times a week.

One day they stayed in camp until two o'clock to let the cattle feed. That day they left the Snake River for the last time and, before the day ended, reached Burnt River where they expected to have plenty of water and grass for the animals. They seemed to be out of the desert.

—◠◡◠—

July thirty-first, Sunday, the train enjoyed a good rest without throngs of people running around and through their camp. Rachel truly enjoyed the uninterrupted singing and sermon that day. The minister talked again about God's unfathomable love for us. How He loves each of us much, much more than we love our children.

Rachel carried the message in her heart and felt better every time she thought about it.

The group put their food together even though it was a pitiful thing to call a potluck. Martha, though, didn't come, so Rachel went looking for her.

"I couldn't come," Martha explained. "All we have to eat is Trail Bread, without most of the things that make it Trail Bread." She laughed. "It's just flour, salt, and water. But Willie eats it and so does Josie."

"Well, you come anyway," Rachel said. "I'll get Mama to fry some extra side meat for you to bring."

As the meal began, Stan Latham showed up and asked Julia Tate if he could join her for the meal. When Rachel saw the cornered look in the younger girl's eyes she thought she might grab Julia's hand and run anywhere. But Tom Dorland happened by and told Latham his horses were leaving the area. Latham hurried off to check his animals, Tom beside him.

Pastor Richards asked Rachel if he could eat with her. Rachel said of course, and called Martha to join them. Julia ate with them, too.

Later that afternoon Tom showed up and asked Rachel to help him. "I need to check Sandra Piling," he explained. "She's failed a lot on the trip."

After checking the woman over, Tom talked to Mr. Piling. "She seems to be failing quickly. You'd better keep her in bed and feed her the best food you can beg, borrow, or shoot."

"Who's gonna fix all that wonderful food if Sandra's in bed?" Mr. Piling asked.

Chapter 14

A look of surprise flitted across Tom's face then disappeared. "I thought you'd cook for your family," he said, "but if you can't or don't have time, I'd be glad to do it for you."

Rachel almost laughed when Tom offered to cook. But Mr. Piling didn't. "Ain't got 'nough food for you," he groused.

"Oh, I'll eat before I come," Tom said. "I won't eat your food."

Piling didn't say any more, so Tom and Rachel headed back to Rachel's wagon. When they got there she turned to thank him for walking her home, and caught a strange but gentle look in his eyes.

"So," he said with a chuckle, "I caught you laughing at the thought of my cooking, didn't I?"

"I hope not," she said with a giggle of her own.

"Well, I did, and I'll have you know I can cook anything. . .as long as it's boiled potatoes. Alas, I haven't seen a potato for months."

The next morning the wagons creaked as tired oxen plodded along with sore feet and necks, almost too weak to pull the wagons. Rachel watched Martha gently urge her animals along, while hearing the sound of whips and anguished bawls, together with rough male voices yelling at their oxen. She told herself that Martha probably got more out of her animals than the cruel men did.

Vultures blackened the carcasses on and beside the trail. As the wagon train passed, the huge birds rose into the air screaming their displeasure at having their meals interrupted, then waited impatiently nearby until the train passed and they could continue their feast.

Late in the afternoon the train came upon a man with a baby in his left arm. The other arm hung bloody and useless; blood covered his clothes, too.

"Dorland!" Captain Ransom yelled, stopping the train. "What's going on?" he asked the man.

"Well, sir, my wife died about a week ago. Two days later, two of my oxen died and the others couldn't pull the wagon, so I left them. I took my horse and four mules and started out, but before long, Indians attacked and took the animals." The man grimaced. "They like horses and mules a lot better then oxen. I'm thankin' the good Lord they didn't hurt the baby."

Tom appeared about then, looking to Rachel like the most beautiful person in the entire world. The man who helped everyone. He glanced through the faces until he found her. "I'll need you," he said softly.

After Mama took the baby, Rachel helped Tom clean the man's wounds with whiskey. The brave man stiffened but didn't utter a sound. Then, she held the man's arm as Tom stitched the wound. When he finished, he looked at Rachel. "Seventy-five stitches," he said smiling. "Looks pretty neat, doesn't it?" Then she helped him put the man's arm in a sling.

The thought passed through Rachel's mind that whoever married Tom Dorland would have to share him with the world. How awful!

Then she realized his compassion had a lot to do with why she loved him. She loved Tom? Yes! She loved him! She loved Dr. Tom Dorland! All she could ever want would be to help him help the world. . .all the time. . . forever. No doubt about it, she loved this man she'd been helping all along the trail. But, suddenly she felt shy, as if she had to get away from him.

"Are we through now?" she asked quietly.

"Yes, for now. Thanks, Rachel. You're always a big help."

"The man and his baby will be sleeping in your wagon," Papa told her when they stopped that night. "There was no other place for them. You can sleep in ours."

Rachel surprised herself and her father by not minding. She'd be just fine with her parents.

The next morning they passed through miles and miles of prairie where the grass had been burned off, leaving a black, stinking mess.

"That's the Indians' way of stopping the white man," Julia said. "Dan told me the Indians are trying to starve our cattle so we'll go back where we came from."

"I wonder how far it goes," Martha said. "We thought our animals would have plenty to eat now." But the cattle went all day without grass.

That night they camped by Powder River with plenty of grass and water. As the girls inspected their campsite, they discovered the river was alive with salmon.

When they spread the news, many men brought their guns to shoot some fish for supper, a dream come true for the weary travelers. The men all tried but no one could hit the fish. Finally, Tom looked up at the watching girls and flashed a smile. Rachel's heart melted into a small puddle in her chest. But he didn't give her any special looks or seem to notice.

"I'm going to shoot under the fish," he called. "We'll see what happens." He hit the fish, pulled it out, and the men crowded around. "Just shoot a few inches under the fish," he said. The men thinned out one by one, as they each shot a couple of the large creatures and hauled them off toward home.

To go with the fish, Mama made biscuits that she'd wrapped in clay and buried in the coals. Rachel invited Martha and Willie to enjoy the feast with them.

After they finished, Rachel took half of a fish to Tom to share with the Pilings. Trembling at the thought of meeting him, Rachel nearly turned back but forced herself on. The Pilings needed the food.

Tom's welcoming smile showed no change. He couldn't tell that she loved him. She'd thought a sign, *Rachel's in Love with Tom,* might be emblazoned on her forehead.

As they delivered the large piece of fish to the Pilings, all Rachel could think about was her love for Tom. Tom, who stood about five feet, nine inches tall, was slim, blond, and boyish looking and was exactly opposite from the dream man she'd carried in her mind all these years. Oh, but he was exactly her dream. She forced the personal thoughts from her mind so she could be casual with him. Mark Piling didn't even thank them for the food, but Sandra did.

As they walked back to the Butler wagon, Tom told Rachel to tell Martha to thoroughly cook some salmon and feed it to Josie. Rachel cooked a large fish and took half of it to Josie, who wolfed it down as if it were half a slice of bread, her tail thrashing the air wildly. When Josie finished, she leaned against Rachel and gave her hand a few sloppy kisses. "I love you, too, Josie," Rachel whispered to the shaggy dog.

Rachel took the other half of the big fish to the Pitmans, the older couple who were doing better now. Through tears, they thanked Rachel for her thoughtfulness. Rachel walked away completely happy. Martha was right. . . nothing satisfied more than helping other people and dogs.

Back at the wagon, she stopped to relax and she realized how cold the evening had become. What a change from the burning heat they'd endured for the last few weeks.

The next day the girls found themselves walking on rock piles again. Rocks on rocks on rocks. The oxen struggled valiantly to pull the wagons over the rough terrain and the walkers tried to keep their feet under them. Finally, the Grande Ronde Valley opened up before them, a large, lush, green valley with the river meandering through it.

—⁂—

On August seventh, a Sunday, the train was camped at a shady, tree-covered spot along the Grande Ronde, the most perfect camping place in the world. But the valley was alive with emigrants, cattle, Indians, and ponies.

Someone said the Indians were Nez Percé and Cayuse, all friendly, well clad, and clean.

Everyone wanted to sell something, or buy or beg something. Pastor Richards gathered his flock and tried preaching, but so many people and animals milling around made concentration impossible and forced him to stop. He substituted a long hymn sing that everyone enjoyed, even those coming and going.

After the service, an Indian approached Rachel, Martha, Julia, and Willie, motioning that he wanted to trade a pony. But what did he want to trade it for? He pointed at each of the girls, then the pony, who was fat, brown-and-white spotted, and pretty.

Papa came to them. "What's going on?" he asked.

"He wants to trade the pony," Rachel said, "but we can't figure what he wants to trade it for."

Looking at the Indian, Nate motioned to the pony. The Indian's eyes shifted to the girls and he pointed at Rachel, then Martha, then Julia, and back to the pony.

Nate started laughing and shook his head no. "He wants to trade it for you three girls or one of you. I'm not sure which." Nate shook his head no again, and put his arms around all three girls. "Mine," he said, pointing to the girls then himself.

The Indian nodded as if he understood, smiled a toothy grin, and walked off. Thanking Nate profusely, the girls followed him back to his wagon.

The next day they started into the Blue Mountains where thick groves of yellow pines adorned the hills, a real treat after the weeks of wallowing in the desert. But the steep hills weren't a treat for anyone, animal or man. Many of the trees carried scars from the chains that the earlier emigrants had used to brake the wagons on the steep descents.

The oxen began the struggle up the hills, deep moans coming from their throats, their feet so sore they stumbled on every step. Their tongues hung from the sides of their mouths and their eyes had the look of wounded animals. Every muscle of their gaunt bodies strained almost to the breaking point, trying to get the wagons up the cruel hills.

"I don't know if they can make it," Rachel said, tears streaming from her eyes.

"They'll make it," Martha choked out past her tears. "Let's pray for them."

"Dear Father in heaven, I know you love the animals more than we do," Rachel began, speaking through her tears. "I know it's a sin to force them to work so hard. But please, Father, help them do the job without injuring themselves."

"Thank you for all your mercies," Martha continued. "Could You just give them the strength to do this hard job? One more thing, Father. Please help them not to have so much pain. It's not their fault they're in such a hard place. And forgive us for abusing them. We don't know what to do. Thank You, Lord for helping us. We love You, Father. We ask these special favors in Jesus' name and thank You so much for hearing and answering our prayers."

"Amen," both their voices said together.

Chapter 15

Rachel watched, hoping to see the oxen pulling easier and limping less. "I think they're better, don't you?" she asked Martha.

"Yes," Martha said, "but we still have to help them all we can." She looked down at her little brother who clung tightly to her hand. "All of us must keep praying all the time. Can you do that, Willie?" The shaggy blond head nodded.

The oxen still limped and moaned as they pulled the wagon up the hill, but both Rachel and Martha thought they were doing it better.

As they neared the top of the first hill, Tom rode by on his mare. Rachel's heart beat so loudly she feared he'd hear it. "When you get to the top, wait for the men to help you," he said.

"We don't need help," Martha said. "We're doing just fine."

He laughed softly. "I'm sure you are, but we're helping all the wagons down. The hills are too steep. So just wait your turn, all right?"

The girls waited at the top even though they considered it time wasted.

When the men came, they brought a huge ox dragging a tree. "All right," Dan Barlow said. "Start your wagon down. Then stop so we can hook the tree to it."

Martha obeyed instructions. "The limbs on this tree will put a hard drag on the wagon, acting as a brake so your wagon won't run over your oxen," George Rahn said. "Just hold your animals back hard. Can you do that?"

Martha nodded; Rachel wondered if she was as sure as she acted. When the men had the tree secured to the wagon, they yelled for Martha to take the oxen down easy.

Rachel could hardly take her eyes from Tom who, with several others, grabbed the top of the pine tree, holding it back. He looked so beautiful and strong and good. How could she have ever thought he was scrawny and plain and dirty?

The wagon began descending the hill with Martha beside it talking softly to the oxen. The men pulled hard on the tree and the oxen walked slowly down the steep hill. "Stop!" someone yelled. Martha stopped the oxen until the men had everything under control. They repeated these steps several more times. A half-hour later, the wagon stood firmly at the bottom and the men led their big ox down to pull the tree back up so they could help the next wagon down.

They repeated the process of struggling up the hill then waiting for help to get down. "At least the oxen get to rest while we wait," Martha said.

The wagon train spent the following days going up and down hills, slowly increasing the distance from Independence, slowly nearing their new home in Oregon City.

One evening, after the train corralled, the men unyoked the oxen and led them out to feed. Rachel and Martha looked around. Majestic, dark green evergreens stood against the bright blue sky, grass grew rampantly, and a clear stream bubbled past.

Dan Barlow joined the group from somewhere with a deer draped over his horse's rump. "I have another one waiting across the ravine," he said, easing the deer to the ground. In half an hour he returned with the other.

Rachel and Martha, along with the other women, washed clothes in icy water; every little while, Rachel had to warm her hands in the folds of her frock. Never in her life had she been so cold. Not only her hands, but her body as well. The girls washed the Pilings' clothes, the horsemen's, and the Pitmans'—though Mrs. Pitman insisted she could do it herself.

That night, the train feasted on roast meat but no one mentioned singing or dancing, for a good night's sleep sounded better than anything.

—⚒—

The next day was Sunday, August the fourteenth. The camp at the top of the mountain caught all the early sunshine to warm the people from the cold night. After everyone enjoyed a hearty breakfast of meat, Pastor Richards led the group in a long hymn sing to warm them up, then he preached a sermon about the glories God is preparing for those who love Him.

"It's right to appreciate the beauty God has given us here," he said. "But it's only a shadow of things to come." As he talked about beauty, several bald eagles soared overhead, a regal sight. When he finished, he held out his hands to stop the people from leaving. "We have a special treat coming up right after this service," he said, wearing his widest smile. "I hope you'll all stay for our wagon train's first marriage. My beautiful sister, Tamara Richards, a schoolteacher, is being married to Evan Mann, a beginning attorney, and a fine man. I'm going to be proud to introduce him as my brother-in-law." He looked behind the group. "They're here now," he said, reaching his hand forward. "Come to the front, please, Tamara and Evan." He performed a simple but meaningful ceremony, ending by asking the people to all join in the Lord's Prayer.

Everyone crowded around the new couple, congratulating them and wishing them the best.

The men had put a third deer on the barbecue early that morning, and soon the group enjoyed still another feast of nature's bounty in honor of the new couple. The women made biscuits to go with the meat, and after Tamara and Evan were served, everyone had plenty.

Watching, Rachel could tell that Tamara wasn't entirely comfortable being the main attraction. Probably couldn't wait to get back alone. . .well, alone with her new husband.

The next day the wagon train started down the hills of the Blue Mountains for the last time. Rachel felt almost happier than she ever had.

The men still helped the wagons down and the oxen still struggled as they climbed the steep hills but each descent went a little lower. Soon, they'd be down to the prairie again.

During this time, Rachel worked so hard she barely had time to think of Tom except while he helped the wagon descend. But when she fell into her bed at night she thought of him, and dreamed of him, and prayed for him. That's all she knew to do.

They reached the valley on Saturday and camped to prepare for the Sabbath again, everyone feeling festive to be on the prairie.

—◊◊◊—

The next day was Sunday, August twenty-first. The people rested, feeling they'd put in a good week's work. Rachel listened to Pastor Richards's stirring sermon with interest. He preached sermons that touched her heart every time and she had to admit he was a wonderfully dedicated man. But, she loved Tom. . .she definitely loved Tom. How could she not have known it long ago? And how could she get him to notice her?

The next day, as they descended lower into the valley, they saw majestic Mount Hood, 150 miles away. Soon, they'd pass only a few miles from that rugged, snow-capped mountain.

One day they passed a Cayuse town where the Indians raised corn, potatoes, peas, and other vegetables to sell to the travelers. Nate Butler bought some corn and potatoes, and others bought what they could afford.

For the next two days, they traveled on smooth, level roads, enjoying the comparatively easy traveling. Martha, Rachel, Julia, and Willie laughed, sang, told stories, and played games, something they hadn't done since before Petey died.

One day, Rachel saw a lone wagon ahead and showed Martha. "Why would it be alone out here? And with no oxen?"

Martha laughed. "I can answer that," she said. "If it weren't for your good father, I'd be sitting somewhere with just my wagon, too."

When they approached, they found a young mother with three small children sitting on the ground beside the wagon.

Captain Ransom stopped the train. "Are you all right?" he called.

She got up and hurried to him. "No," she said. "I have a husband in the wagon who's too sick to sit up."

"Where are your animals?" Ransom asked.

"We were using oxen that belonged to a wealthy man who wouldn't let any of us ride in the wagon. When my husband got sick, he took his oxen and left us here with the wagon."

"I don't know what we can do," Ransom said. "We've been picking up people all the way. I think we'll have to talk." He walked past the wagons, calling the men from them.

Rachel, who made sure she got in on 'most everything, couldn't think of an excuse to follow the men so she stayed with Martha.

A half-hour later, Ransom returned. "We'll try to take you folks," he said, "but we can't take the wagon. The Rahns will take your husband, and Butler said he'll crowd you and the children into one of his wagons."

Dr. Dorland wiggled a finger at Rachel, then grabbed his medical bag. Together, they checked the family over.

"Everyone seems healthy," he said, "except the father, and I'm sure he doesn't have cholera. He'll be well in a few days."

The Ransoms gathered the small amount of food they found in the wagon and put it into their own.

When the train nooned, Papa told Mama and Rachel that he'd had to leave his blacksmith tools to take in the new family.

"How awful," Rachel said. "After you've hauled them this far."

Papa smiled sweetly. "People are more important than tools, lassie. The good Lord will provide some more tools."

The next day high winds and dust hindered the travel but they reached the Umatilla River by noon. They camped to prepare for the Sabbath and also to avoid the ill weather as much as possible.

While Rachel ate dinner with Mama and Papa, he asked her to help him a little later. "There are provisions available here," he said. "But, with all the people we've been feeding and taking into our wagons, I'll need more money." He winked at Rachel. "Could you help me get it from our bank?"

For just a second, Rachel didn't understand. Then she remembered. He'd put a big pouch of money under the false floor of one of the wagons. "I'll help you, Papa. Just call me when you're ready."

After they finished their meal, Papa told Rachel they'd pull the wagon away from the others so no one would know what they were doing. When they'd moved about a hundred feet west of the train, Papa asked Rachel to watch and tell him if anyone started toward them. Then he went to work with a screwdriver and hammer.

Rachel watched the people, listening to the many screeches and squawks as Papa pulled out the nails and lifted the false floor.

"It's gone!" Nate exclaimed. "The money's not here." After a long silence, he sighed. "I must have brought over the wrong wagon," he said. "But that floor looks as if it's been torn up before."

"You said the other wagons don't have false floors, Papa."

He nodded. Then she watched as he tore off more floorboards and double-checked to make sure the bag of money hadn't slid into a dark corner. When he looked up, his eyes met hers. She'd never seen Papa so stricken. Never, not even when she'd acted so terrible about coming.

"It's gone, Rachel," he said. "Someone took it. We're just like all the others on this train. . .almost broke."

Rachel's stomach constricted until it hurt. "Maybe you're looking in the wrong wagon," she said hopefully. "Why don't we check the others?"

He nodded. "All right, but the money's gone. Someone got it while we were away from the wagons sometime or another."

Papa checked the other wagons and found they didn't have false floors. Someone had taken the money. Almost all the money they had! "It'll be a miracle if we have enough money to get to Oregon City now," he whispered hoarsely. "Let alone having any to get started there."

"You'd better tell Captain Ransom," Rachel whispered into his ear. "What are you going to tell Mama?"

Papa looked into her eyes, his still showing shock. "I'm telling her the truth, what else?" he asked. He motioned for her to follow. "Come, let's tell Ransom."

The grizzly haired and whiskered man stood in silence after Nate explained what had happened. "I don't rightly know what to do," the kind captain said. "We both know you'll never see that money again." He looked off into the blue sky. "We don't even know whether it was our own people or someone else," he mused.

"Whoever took it knew it was there," Rachel said. "We haven't been away from the wagon long at any time. Someone had to go right to the spot and get the money in a hurry."

Ransom nodded. "Right. It was a slick one. Want me to try to bluff the guilty man into giving it back? I'm afraid that kind don't bluff."

As they walked back to their wagons, Rachel felt devastated. No doubt about it, this was Heartbreak Trail. No! Money lacked a lot of being everything. God saw the person steal the money and allowed it. Why? Maybe the person's family was starving. Maybe the Butler family would grow closer to

God without money. Maybe God had some special blessing in store for them. Maybe He just allowed this to happen for no special reason. But Rachel didn't believe that for a minute. God loved her family much more than they loved each other so there was a purpose in all this. And they'd be all right.

She dropped back and walked beside Papa. "It's all right, Papa," she said softly. "God just showed me we'll be all right."

Nate reached an arm down, dropped it over her shoulder, and smiled. "Know what, lassie?" he asked. "He just showed me the same thing. He'll care for our needs."

—⁓—

Then it was Sunday, August twenty-eighth. Indians roamed back and forth, Pastor Richards started his hymn sing, and many of the Indians joined them. After the singing, Pastor Richards preached a basic sermon about God's love and sacrifice for all.

"Thank Him for loving you so much," he told them, "and tell Him you love Him, too, and want to belong to Him. He'll come right into your heart and live with you forever."

Rachel watched the Indians and prayed for them as they listened with rapt attention.

That afternoon, when Rachel took food to the Piling family, she found Tom there. "What are you doing?" she asked.

He grinned as he turned pink. "I'm cooking," he said. "Remember I said I would?" Rachel remembered, but she hadn't taken it seriously. Setting her food down, she helped him finish the meal. Serving it onto plates, they gave one to Sandra for her and Judith, and handed one to Mr. Piling.

Piling took the food but didn't thank them for it or speak. He just glowered at them as if they'd intruded.

Rachel felt surprised when his rudeness didn't upset her. She didn't feel hurt or mad. Nothing. Just concern for Sandy and her baby. *Thank You, Lord. You're changing me from a self-centered hothead into a human being. Thank You again, God. I love You.*

"Does he always treat you like this?" she whispered to Tom.

Tom nodded. "He's pretty good today. Must be because you're here. Let's clean up and get out of here."

"Is Martha still going to Walla Walla Valley?" he asked on the way back.

Rachel nodded. "I can't bear it, Tom. I just can't let her go. Help me talk to her, will you?"

He grinned and nodded. "Sure. But she won't listen to me. You're her closest friend."

"I've said all the words I know. She won't listen."

Again, Rachel begged Martha to go to Oregon City, but she wouldn't consider it. "My family will be looking for me," she said, her usual reply.

The next day Nate prepared to take one of his wagons to Walla Walla Valley to leave with Martha but bring back the oxen he'd lent her. "Try once more to talk her into going on with us," he told Rachel, and Rachel begged her not to go. While Rachel was begging, Rachel's mother, Alma, came up. "If you go," she said in a soft loving voice, "I can't let Willie leave with you."

"He has to come with me," Martha cried. "He and Josie are all I have. He has to stay with me."

"How much food do you have?" Alma asked kindly.

"Almost none," Martha admitted. "Just a pint of flour. But my family will be in the Walla Walla Valley nearly as soon as I will."

Tom had arrived and stood beside Rachel. "We can't know that, Martha," he said. "They may not come until spring. Or not at all. We aren't even sure they ever started, are we?"

Martha stared at him with wide eyes. "They planned to come within a week after we left."

Alma wrapped Martha in her arms and held her tightly. "Please, stay with us. You might starve to death if you go."

Martha shook her dark head. "I purely have to go, Mrs. Butler. My aunt and uncle and my cousin and brother will be there. What will they do if I'm not there?"

"But they have each other," Tom said. "You're going to be all alone."

Martha looked serious. A dull red rimmed her eyes. "I have to go."

Alma nodded. "We'll give you a gallon of flour. That's all we dare let go of now that we don't have money. We're taking Willie. Either you can come after him or we'll bring him back next spring."

Martha didn't argue but dropped her head in defeat.

Julia hugged Martha tightly but couldn't talk. Dan Barlow, standing nearby, put his arm around Julia. "Now, don't you be worrying about Miss Tate," he told Martha. "I plan to keep her safe. And happy, too. So you just take care of yourself and Josie."

Pastor Richards made a passionate plea for Martha to go on with them to Oregon City, insinuating he'd make sure she was cared for. She shook her head.

The other Butler wagons would rest at the Umatilla River until the Butlers returned. Captain Ransom hadn't decided whether the train would wait or continue on.

Right after nooning, Martha led her oxen off toward Walla Walla Valley. Rachel walked with Martha, and Papa drove their oxen. The sun shone brightly, prairie grass, though half-dried, grew everywhere.

On the second day they met some Indians with lots of potatoes, wanting to trade. Nate traded one of his shirts for a dozen nice big potatoes. Before the sun set, they reached their destination, Steptoeville, in Walla Walla Valley.

As they approached, only a few, eight to be exact, rough buildings, four on each side of a Nez Percé trail, met their eyes. Several dirty tepees huddled on the north side of the trail behind the shacks.

About a quarter-mile away, past the rickety buildings, a group of even smaller and more destitute shacks sprawled, obviously deserted.

"Doesn't look much like the Garden of Eden to me," Rachel said. "Oh, Martha, I'm sorry. Please, come with us to Oregon City."

Chapter 16

Martha laughed shakily. "You're purely right, Rachel. It doesn't look as beautiful as I expected." Then she pointed south and east. "But look at the mountains. They're pretty enough."

Nate looked, too. "Say," he said, "I think those are the Blue Mountains. We just came over some of them."

The little group parked the wagon at the west end of the Indian trail and unyoked the oxen. A small stream to the north provided plenty of water for the animals as they began grazing on the grass.

The girls prepared a meal with the potatoes, side meat, and biscuits—a feast fit for kings, Rachel said.

—⁓—

On Sunday, September fourth, Rachel and Martha decided this was the quiet Sabbath for which they had been waiting. Entirely too quiet, they agreed before the day ended. Rachel and Papa spent the entire day trying to talk Martha into going back with them, but she couldn't be persuaded.

Early the next morning, Papa gave Martha two of the remaining four potatoes and yoked up the oxen. Rachel's heart hurt so badly she couldn't talk, not even to beg Martha once more to come.

As they returned the way they'd come, Rachel looked back to see Martha kneeling beside Josie, hugging the dog tightly, and waving as hard as she could.

Rachel sobbed until she could barely walk. She ended up crying all the way back. Would she ever again see her dearest friend in the world? Her friend who taught her to love and serve Jesus. Her friend who taught her how to love and be kind. *Please be with Martha,* she cried silently. *Take good care of her, Father. She has no money and so little food. Send someone to help her right away. Oh, thank You, God. I love You so much.*

When they reached the Umatilla River again, they discovered the wagon train had gone on. But two of the horse riders and Tom had waited. Now they had three wagons and about a dozen people in their group.

As Tom ran to greet Rachel, her first thought was of her eyes, red from crying. When Tom reached her, he stopped, and Rachel could see the struggle in his mind. He wanted to hug her! She knew he did.

His arms moved nervously as he stepped from one foot to the other. Finally, he forced himself to settle down. "Welcome back!" he said heartily. "We missed you a lot."

Rachel swallowed. In her wildest dreams she hadn't expected Tom to show this much enthusiasm for her return. "Thank you," she said. "Your welcome makes me feel better. It hurt me so much to leave Martha in that desolate place."

Willie spotted Rachel and came running to her. "Where's Martha?" he asked, tugging on her long calico skirt. "I want Martha now."

Rachel knelt and hugged the little boy. "Martha couldn't come right now," she said, holding him close. "She asked me to take care of you until she can have you with her. She loves you a lot, Willie, and will come after you as soon as she can. Can you be happy with us until then?"

He nodded and returned her hug. Poor little boy. First, he lost his parents, then his brother, next his best friend, and now his sister. Rachel gave him an extra tight hug. She'd have to be mother, father, sister, and friend to Willie while he was with them.

The next few days Rachel tried hard to keep Willie happy. She had nothing else to do or anyone else to be with, so she didn't mind. Rather, she enjoyed his company as they walked, sang Jesus songs, and played games.

The small company camped early on Saturday to prepare for the Sabbath. After Rachel and Mama did the wash for everyone, they made a pie with the last of the dried apples. "At least we'll have a decent Sabbath," Mama said.

—⁂—

On Sunday, September eleventh, the sun shone brightly even though October would soon be upon them. The whole group ate together, since the Butlers were the only ones with wagons and cooking things.

Since there was no preacher, Tom led the group in a hymn sing. The dozen people made a joyful noise unto the Lord. In fact, Rachel thought they sounded all right. After the singing, Nate read some praise chapters from Psalms.

Later, after lunch, Tom asked Rachel to walk with him. He lead her to a quiet place, overlooking the valley.

"Beautiful," Rachel said. "This looks a lot more like the Garden of Eden than where Martha is."

"You may not have seen the best of the Walla Walla Valley," he said.

She laughed softly. "I hope not. What I saw wasn't very nice. But you know what? I asked God to send someone to help her right away, and I know He did. I have His peace to assure me. It makes all the difference."

"You've changed a lot since we started on the Trail," he said quietly. "Do you realize that?"

She nodded. "Yes. That's because God found me, even on Heartbreak Trail. He's with us no matter where we go, did you know that? No matter how foolish we are or what dumb things we do, He's there to help us. Isn't that remarkable? If I were God, I wouldn't be that good."

He laughed. "You would, Rachel, because you'd be God. Perfect, long-suffering, complete love. I've learned to appreciate you a lot on this long, painful trip. You've been irreplaceable, helping with my work. I can't thank you enough for that."

"I enjoyed it, Tom. A lot. You may be right, saying I should be a nurse."

"I don't want to lose you, Rachel. I want you to go on helping me."

"I will. If you stay around. I'd really enjoy that." Rachel giggled. "I purely would, as Martha would say."

Tom swallowed loudly. "I didn't exactly mean just with my medicine," he said in a choked voice. "I've loved you for a long time, Rachel. I want to marry you when we catch up with Pastor Richards. . .or another preacher."

Rachel couldn't answer. Were her dreams coming true? Out here, on Heartbreak Trail? Where she'd seen nothing but death and disaster? She tried to swallow the lump in her throat. Then she sniffled.

"Is there someone else?" he asked quietly. "Maybe back in Quincy?"

She swallowed again. And sniffed again. "No," she whimpered. "I've never loved anyone but you. Never. I've loved you for a long time, too. Why didn't you tell me sooner?"

He smiled tenderly. "Well, I noticed you the first thing. I'd never seen such beautiful hair in my life. And your eyes, Rachel. They're something to take away a man's breath. You caught my attention right away but," his eyes twinkled, "somehow I got the idea you were spoiled. And that you didn't care all that much about God. The life I have to offer a woman will be hard; I need a woman with lots of faith, one who isn't afraid to work."

Rachel laughed into his eyes. "So, I wasn't good enough for you."

He shook his sunshiny hair. "No, you just weren't right for me. But I couldn't quit watching you, and admiring you from a distance. And I ended up watching you grow."

They talked a while then ambled back to the wagons, where they found Nate.

"I have something important to ask you," Tom said. Rachel could see concern in Tom's eyes.

"Well, sit here on the wagon's tongue," Nate said. "I'll do my best to give you a good answer."

Tom stood. "Rachel and I have just discovered we love each other," he began.

Alma burst into laughter. "Why didn't you ask me? I could have told you a long time ago."

Tom smiled. "Well, we learned that we've cared for each other for some time, all right." He turned his attention back to Nate. "I'm asking for your blessing, sir, as I'd like nothing more than to marry Rachel and spend my life caring for her and making her happy."

Nate jumped up from the wagon hitch he'd been sitting on and extended his hand to Tom. "Welcome, Tom," he said happily. "I can't say this is a complete surprise. Not with Alma whispering in my ear. But you're exactly like the son I never had. I'd be honored to have you marry my only daughter."

Alma rushed out and hugged Tom. "Willie, can you give Tom a hug, too?" she asked when she released him. "He's going to be even more special to us now." Willie hugged Tom, always glad to get another hug.

After everyone quieted, Tom asked Rachel to walk with him again. When they found the same quiet place, Tom pulled her into his arms. "Everyone's been hugging but us," he whispered into her hair. "I love you, my flaming-haired princess, and want to never be separated from you again, not even for one day." His arm gently circled her waist as he pulled her closer, tipped up her face, and kissed her parted lips ever so gently.

Rachel returned the kiss that sent tremors through her entire body. A moment later she pulled away, discovering she'd never felt so lightheaded in her life. . .or so happy. She pulled his lips back to hers. "I'm dizzy," she whispered, "but kiss me again. I love you an awful lot."

The next day they traveled on, Rachel walking with Willie. She tried to sing all the songs and play all the games Martha had. The little boy seemed happy, but he clung to her with quiet desperation.

Tom came around several times each day and every night he helped Rachel clean up after the meal. Then they walked and talked and dreamed.

One day at noon they reached the mighty Columbia River. Standing on the banks of the river she'd read about, sang about, and heard about all her life, Rachel felt small and insignificant. What was she? A fly compared to this river, and even less compared to the universe God had created. How could He care about anything so small as her? *Oh, but I'm glad You do, Lord. Thank You for loving me, even more than the mighty things You've made. Thank You, Lord. I love You, too.*

The group nooned on the bank of the river and traded some old clothes to Indians for a huge salmon, then headed for the Deschutes River, where they camped.

—⊗—

On October second, Rachel and Tom spent the cold and rainy day together in one of the Butler wagons with her folks, making plans and trying to keep warm.

The next day they reached The Dalles, 1,820 miles from Independence, about one hundred miles from Oregon City. The Dalles was almost the climax of the journey, the place where they had to decide whether to go by boat on the river or to take the Barlow Road over the Cascade Mountains. The Cascades were said to be even steeper and more dangerous than the Blue Mountains.

Rachel felt disappointed in The Dalles. She'd hoped she'd finally reach civilization there, but the town consisted of only a few houses; she'd call them shacks.

"I know we need food," Papa said as they walked around a little, "but I have to find out how much it's going to cost us to get over the Cascades before I spend anything."

Nate, Tom, and Rachel walked down to the docks, where boats constantly loaded for the trip downriver. A man, obviously a traveler, spoke to them.

"Howdy," Nate said. "We're wondering what's the best way to get to Oregon City."

The man laughed out loud. "You and everyone else," he said. "Well, I'll tell you the best way. Put everthin' you got on boats, even your livestock. 'Course, I can't afford that, so I'm tearin' up my wagon an' shippin' it and all my goods and my wimmin folks. Me and my hired man're gonna drive the cattle over Barlow Road." He shook his head, sending his wild gray hair into a worse mess than before. "By the time the cattle git here they ain't got the stren'th to walk over, let alone haul wagons over."

Nate asked how much it cost to send a wagon and goods. Satisfied by the man's response, he smiled and extended his hand. "That's just what I'm going to do, too. Sounds like a good compromise."

The man shook Nate's hand aggressively. "Best bet," he said. "But if yore gonna go over the Road, best not to even ride yore horses. I heerd of several good saddle horses not making it neither. Just lead the horses and don't push none of the stock."

Nate thanked the man again and headed for the shipping office, where he booked passage for three wagons, the contents, and two women.

"I'm not going by boat, Papa," Rachel said. "Tom will take care of me if I walk. Who'll help us when the boat sinks?"

Alma seconded the motion, so they all worked together to get the wagons and barrels of goods ready to ship, then planned their own trip over the Cascades.

"We can buy some food now," Nate said. "Let's find some."

Before they found any food they stumbled across an overgrown potato patch. "Looks as if no one plans to dig these spuds," Tom said. "Why don't we check on them?"

When they found the owner, he said he hadn't planned to dig them. "If you'll do the work, I'll let 'em go for five dollars a hunnert."

"I don't think we can haul them over the mountains," Alma told Nate.

"Why couldn't we divide them among all the horses?" Tom asked. "Potatoes sound good about now."

They dug two hundred pounds of the potatoes and decided they'd better stop before they had the animals loaded too heavily.

"Are we going to buy other things to eat?" Rachel asked.

Nate shook his head. "Someone might shoot something. Otherwise, we'll eat potatoes until we reach Oregon City." He gave her a quick squeeze. "Things are different for us since we lost our money, lassie."

"Potatoes will be fine," Rachel said. The others agreed so they packed the saddlebags with potatoes, a big skillet, side meat grease, dishes, and silver, and started over the mountains.

The road seemed to be mostly cleared of trees and the biggest rocks, but the ascents and descents were even steeper than those in the Blue Mountains.

"I'm so thankful the animals aren't pulling wagons," Rachel said.

"So am I," Tom, who was walking with her, said. "And I for one will try to keep anyone from pushing the animals." He looked up the hill beside the road, where the trees grew so closely together that a man would have trouble walking between them. "Do you realize the first people over had to clear away trees as they went?"

Rachel prayed silently for God to help them all, people and animals, over the brutal road. Carcasses of oxen, cows, and horses lay at the edge, testifying starkly to the still unmerciful road.

"I'm thankful to God for being so good to us so far," Nate said. "Do you realize we still have all of our original animals, plus the one that joined our herd?" His eyes turned soft as he looked at Rachel. "Mama and I talked last night and decided to give half our animals to you and Tom when we reach Oregon City. That's half of thirteen cows, three saddle horses, and thirty oxen."

Rachel hugged her father, then her mother. "Thank you both. That's enough for a good start. We'll take good care of them as you have."

That night Alma and Rachel fried enough potatoes to fill up all the people traveling with them. Everyone enjoyed the change the potatoes brought.

For the next two days the weather stayed warm and dry, though the evenings turned downright cold. The group slept, wrapped in blankets, under the stars.

One of the young men went ahead and brought back some rabbits to go with the fried potatoes. They all agreed they were eating like kings.

Then it clouded up and rained. Everyone got soaked, and so did their blankets. Fortunately, lots of tree branches lay near the edge of the road, so that night they made a roaring fire and tried to dry their clothes and blankets.

"It's hard," Rachel complained. "The fire's so hot I can't stand close enough to dry the blankets." The blankets finally dried, but as soon as they put them on the ground the wet seeped into them again.

The next morning Rachel got up, sore and chilled, to help Mama cook potatoes again.

When they started walking, the road was wet and slippery; the animals picked their way carefully. The oxen and horses, shod, fared better than the loose cattle.

Tom and Rachel walked carefully, each leading a horse. Rachel felt tired before nooning time and couldn't wait for the rest. As the group struggled up the hill, Tom's horse's foot struck a slick rock and slipped, knocking Tom's feet out from under him.

Although quick, Tom couldn't catch his balance. He fell to the ground, hitting his head on a sharp stone and cutting his forehead. Blood gushed from the wound as Tom lay dazed, uncaring.

Chapter 17

Grab something and shove it against the wound!" Mama yelled. Rachel snatched the hem of her skirt, turned the worst mud inside, folded the fabric a few times, and shoved it into the jagged cut in his forehead.

Tom stirred and opened his eyes. "I'm all right," he said, evidently reading fear in the faces gathered around him. "Head wounds bleed profusely." He looked at Rachel, kneeling next to him and still pressing the hem of her skirt into the wound. "You'll have to sew it up, Rachel."

An enormous lump dropped into her stomach. She couldn't do that! She shook her head. "I'll hold my skirt against it all day, but I can't sew you up. You know I can't, Tom."

He grinned, emphasizing his white face. "Sure you can. You've watched me enough times."

"I can't, Tom." How could he ask her to do something like that, anyway? He'd gone to school a long time to learn how to be a doctor. Now he expected her to be one with no training at all! Then she noticed blood oozing through the skirt she held against his head. "Are you going to bleed to death?" she whispered.

He smiled wearily. "No, I won't bleed to death. But if you don't stitch it up, I'll have a bad scar. Looking at my face will scare you so much you'll run away and refuse to marry me."

She shook her head. It finally sank into her head that Tom couldn't sew up his own wound. None of this group knew anything about medicine. Almost for sure she knew more than any of the others after having helped Tom for the last six months. "Will you tell me what to do?" she whimpered.

A look of relief crossed his face. "Exactly," he said. "Get my bag off my horse." She did. "Now, find the pouch that says needle and thread. Put the thread through the needle just as if you were going to do some embroidery. Then, pour some of the whiskey over it."

Rachel did everything he told her, feeling shaky with all the eyes watching. After pouring whiskey over the needle and thread, she knew the next step—cleaning his wound. She held up the bottle and showed Tom.

He nodded, giving her a small smile. "I get to find out how it feels, don't I?"

She turned his head so the whiskey wouldn't run into his eyes, then slowly poured it across the wound. Watching his arm and neck muscles tighten, she knew it hurt. "I'm sorry," she whispered and touched his lips with hers before remembering the dozen people watching.

His arms reached gently around her, pulling her closer. "Thanks," he whispered against her lips. "That helped a lot." Then he lay back on the ground again sighing. "I guess I'm not very strong right now," he said. "Better get me fixed up."

"All right, Tom, but you have to help me."

With his eyes closed, he instructed her. "Close the wound with your left hand," he said almost in a whisper, "and stitch with the other. Be sure to get the thread through all the layers of the skin."

A picture appeared in Rachel's mind of Tom working on Josie, so much more horrible. She saw him bringing the skin together over the dog's intestines, pushing the needle through the thick layer of skin, then pulling the skin together and stitching again.

She knew exactly how to do it. But it would hurt him! No matter, it had to be done. "All right," she said softly. "Relax. I can do it." She followed the picture in her mind, step by step, until she put the last stitch in and secured the thread.

Tom hadn't said a word and barely flinched while she worked.

"I'm all through," she said when he didn't stir. She leaned down to his ear. "Know what happened?" she asked, then answered her own question. "I did a perfect job," she said. "God showed me how to do it, step by step. In pictures, Tom. He showed me in pictures."

Tom opened his eyes but obviously didn't share her enthusiasm at that point. "Good girl. I knew He would." He quieted and rested a few minutes, then opened his eyes and found Rachel again. "Know why He showed you?" he asked.

Rachel nodded, her eyes dewy from the strain but still thrilled with what had happened. "Because you needed help and there wasn't anyone else."

He nodded, his eyes closed. "That, too," he agreed quietly. "But He showed you because you're walking that close to Him now. If you weren't, you wouldn't have heard Him."

Papa built a big fire and Mama cooked up several more skillets of potatoes, which everyone ate with relish—except Tom who didn't feel hungry.

"I wish you could eat," Rachel told him, sitting close. "I'm hungrier than I've ever been in my life." She giggled. "I didn't realize how much energy it takes to sew people up."

By evening Tom ate like a hungry ranch hand and by the next morning he walked as well as any of the little company.

—ᴍ—

Sunday, October ninth, was cloudy and dry but not too cold. So, Tom led the small company of believers in all the songs they could remember. When they finished, Nate read some Psalms, then offered a prayer of praise and thanksgiving for caring for them on the long hard trip and bringing them safely to God's Garden of Eden on earth.

When he started to dismiss them, Rachel stopped him. "I have something to say," she said, running to the front. "I just wanted to tell you something God did for me," she said, facing the group breathlessly. "I'd helped Tom sew up several animals and people, but I didn't remember how to do it. But when I started to sew Tom's wound, God showed me, step by step, how to do it. He did such a fine job that the wound is looking good already and Tom isn't in pain. It made me think of something He wants to do for us. If we'll read the Bible faithfully, He'll bring it to our minds when we need it. Isn't that fantastic?"

Several people said, "Amen" or "Yes, Lord."

Suddenly, Rachel didn't know what to say. "I guess that's all," she finally said. "I just thought it was so special I wanted to share it."

Nate Butler started them early the next morning, as all were getting excited about arriving in Oregon City. No one knew exactly when it would be but they all knew it would be soon. . .very soon.

Two days later, they reached the summit. A rough sign stated the fact in black hand-painted letters, surely one of the most beautiful sights Rachel had ever seen.

That night the group celebrated with a small deer one of the men had shot. They built a spit, placing a strong green log over two crossed logs, and hung the cleaned animal by its hooves until it turned brown with juices oozing out all over the carcass. The meat and potatoes made a meal they all ate with relish.

The next morning they started down the rugged mountains.

"Down is always easier than up, isn't it?" Rachel asked Tom.

He grinned. "Always," he agreed, "unless there's a wagon behind the animals trying to run over them. Then I'm not sure."

As he talked, Rachel noticed how well his forehead was healing. Not a bit of redness remained, the swelling had gone from the wound, and it looked almost insignificant. Rachel touched the spot. "How does it feel now?" she asked.

He snatched her to him. "You look beautiful, like my own healing angel, like my dearest gift from God, like my reason for living." He released her and looked into her eyes. "That was what you asked, wasn't it?"

She shook her head, laughing into his eyes. "I asked how your wound. . . you know what I asked. So tell me."

"It's all well. I've kept track of it with my fingers. It's smooth, no puffiness or drawing at the stitches. Nothing. It isn't even sore anymore." He stopped and looked to his left, then to his right. "Don't let the word get around, though. I'll lose all my patients to my associate. . . ," his eyes softened as they looked into hers, "my wife," he finished. "One of these days I'll be asking my doctor to remove the stitches."

Alarm bolted through her chest, then quieted. "That's easy, isn't it?"

He nodded. "Simple as pulling a tree down a mountain." Then he laughed. "Yes, it's easy. It'll take about five minutes with no pain or strain."

Nate kept the group moving slowly, though all, even the animals, were eager to reach the bottom of the mountain. "We don't need any accidents now," he said. "So far we're all still here, man and animal alike. But just think how close we came to losing one of us. If Tom had broken a leg we'd have had to shoot him."

As they traveled, Rachel kept her eyes west. Sometime soon the mountains would drop behind them and Oregon City would spread out before them. "What do you think it'll look like?" she asked Tom. "Will it be a nice, thriving city?"

Tom shook his head. "I think it'll look pretty primitive. Some log cabins, a few rough stores. I think there'll be lots of farming and cattle but nothing you'd consider a city."

She clung to his arm. "I can't wait to get there." Her eyes rose to his. "Know why?"

He smiled, his eyes filled with love. "No, but I know why I'm eager."

"Is it so we can find a minister?" she asked softly.

"You guessed it the first time," he said with joy. "You can't know how happy I am that you didn't say you wanted some big department stores or fancy restaurants."

She laughed, a happy sound that gladdened all hearts that heard it. Her eyes twinkled with mischief. "I'm sure some great stores and restaurants would have been my first wish if someone hadn't taken all our money. Now I have to settle for you, Dr. Thomas Dorland." She laughed again. "What a let down."

All that day they came down hills then went back up, though not as far up as down. The entire group was caught up in a sort of holiday atmosphere for their destination lay almost within their grasp, and that was reason enough to be excited.

When they started the next day, Rachel knew for sure that it would be the day, but no Oregon City popped into view between the mountains, and they had to camp one more night on the road.

"I just checked the animals," Tom said, later that night. "They're surprisingly well considering what they've been through. No doubt they'll all make it now."

Late the next afternoon, Rachel thought the mountains were beginning to thin out. But, once again, they camped under the stars, cold but dry stars.

The next day, Rachel and Tom talked so much and so fast that someone else spotted the city before she did.

"There she is!" someone yelled at the top of his voice. "Laid out like a picture between them mountains."

The beautiful sight, plus the thrill of seeing the end of their journey, wrenched Rachel's breath from her throat. A huge valley lay beyond the craggy mountains. White frame houses, each surrounded by acres and acres of farmland, barns, and corrals, looked exactly like Rachel had hoped.

Nate pulled the Mormon guidebook from his pocket. "This thing says we're 1,930 miles from Independence."

"Does it say we're five miles from our new home, the Garden of Eden?" Rachel asked.

He shook his head, joy displayed over his face. "No, but that's about it."

No one wanted to stop for nooning, so they continued on. The descent soon leveled out and the highly excited little company walked as if they'd just begun the long trek rather than ending it.

Rachel felt so much joy she didn't know if she could contain it. Here, before her, was her new home. . .her new home with her new husband. She thanked God that He'd impressed Papa to force her to come on Heartbreak Trail.

It had taken a lot for God to get her attention. Maybe she'd have never come to know Him if she'd stayed in Quincy where everything always went right. Sometimes it takes pain to draw people to Him. Heartbreak Trail had done it for Rachel. How could she have ever gotten along for so long without her dear heavenly Father?

She'd wanted to stay in Quincy to find the cream of the crop, but God had the very very best waiting for her on the wagon train. And when she was ready, He brought Tom to her. Not when she acted like a baby, but when she grew up!

Thank You, God. Please take charge of my life forever. I love You!

MARTHA
MY OWN

For Michael and Julie.
May God bless you both forever.
I love you with all my heart,
But He loves you much, much more.

Chapter 1

S poradic tears dampened Martha Ann Lawford's cheeks as she gazed east while leaning against the corner of her covered wagon. The wagon, battered from its long trip west, huddled alone on the north side of a Nez Percé Indian trail.

Immediately before her, eight rough buildings lined the trail, four on each side, forming a sort of dusty street. Behind the buildings on either side, large and small native weeds grew among the drying grass across the prairie. Several dirty, light-colored tepees marred the view north of the street, and the three or four shacks on the south did little to improve the view. The few trees in evidence bordered the several rivers and creeks that flowed into and through Steptoeville, Walla Walla Valley, Washington Territory, her new home.

The brilliant sun shining on the snow-capped Blue Mountains forced Martha to shut out the clutter of shacks before her and allowed her to feel better. Surely God had something good planned for her after the long horrible trip she'd just endured.

She shuddered, remembering the terror of crossing those innocent-looking hills only ten days ago. They had dragged trees behind the wagons to keep them from careening down the steep hillsides, destroying the wagons, and killing the oxen.

I trust You, Lord, but I don't understand why You let our trip west turn into such a disaster. She straightened her shoulders. Keeping her mind and body busy might prevent her from dwelling on the tragedy that had left her alone in a strange place.

"Come on, Josie," she said to her dog, "let's stroll down the street and see what those shacks are." The eight buildings she referred to stood about a hundred feet apart and looked nothing like the fine homes and businesses she'd left in Missouri six long months ago. Some of the buildings were constructed of slab, some of logs. Others consisted of rough boards nailed together in a haphazard fashion. Some had glass windows, but most of the windows were made from some translucent material Martha didn't recognize.

Josie, though her ribs and protruding backbone poked almost through her long, matted, black, gray, and white fur, jumped with excitement at the thought of a new adventure.

Martha stepped into the dusty street that snaked under the rickety buildings; there were no sidewalks. A small sign in front of the first building on the north side of the street invited one and all to come in to find warm food and lodging. "They mean people with money," she explained to Josie before noticing her mangy-looking dog tearing up and down the street, raising a large cloud of dust. "Josie!" she called. "You get back here. Now." The dog dropped her tail and scurried back to Martha.

Next they passed a saloon, quickly, for Martha didn't want to be seen near the place. Slowing a few feet past the odious building, she giggled. Who did she think might see her or care what she did in this nearly unpopulated place?

A sign on the next rough wooden building announced it to be a trader's oasis; the roughly painted sign on the small building after that read: RACKETT'S TIN SHOP.

Then she came to a small stream separating the street from a barracks type of place with many buildings. Martha stood at the edge of the creek wondering why the buildings were deserted and what they had been. Then her eyes dropped to the brook before her, gurgling praises to God as it rushed over the smooth rocks. It looked shallow and had two small islands in the middle. After a moment she crossed to the other side of the street to check out the four buildings on the south side: an unoccupied store of some kind, then Chapman and Shaffer's Meat Market, another saloon, and a general store. Two saloons seemed a bit much to Martha, considering that the entire town consisted of only these eight shacks.

As she hurried past the second saloon, the front door opened and a wild looking, middle-aged man came pouring out, almost as if propelled by some unseen force, perchance the barkeep's boot? The man gathered himself together, slapped his worn hat back onto his matted gray hair, and started to leave. Then, noticing Martha, he stopped in midstride, a grin splitting his thin lips. His squinty eyes took her in from head to toes.

"Well, whadda we got here?" he asked. "I ain't seen you around, blue eyes. You b'long to someone?"

Suddenly frightened, Martha turned away, but before she could take the first step, his long fingers wound around her arm and jerked her back.

"Why'd a young thing like you walk away when I'm atalkin'?" he asked, his voice thick with alcohol. Before Martha could move, his other arm reached around her, and she found her face within inches of the foul-smelling man's.

"Josie!" she yelled at the top of her voice, before noticing the dog halfway down the short street, rolling in the dust. "Help, Josie!" she screamed, knowing the man could haul her away before the dog reached her.

Suddenly, the saloon door crashed open again and a taller, younger man emerged almost as quickly as the first man had. "Stop, Abe," the older man hollered as a fist landed somewhere on his person. Raising his hands, he tapped the new arrival's chest in an ineffectual attempt at self-defense. "Stop!" he screamed as a fist slammed into his face. "You ain't got no call to do that." A moment later, Martha's assailant lay in the dust, rubbing the side of his face, a large bruise showing already, and blood running from his mouth.

Finally, Josie arrived barking wildly and growling deep in her throat. Perceiving the man still on his feet to be the enemy, she hit him hard in the chest with her front feet, knocking him backward into the dust beside Martha's would-be assailant. Hopping instantly to his feet, the man dusted off the back of his denim pants. Martha noticed how tall, muscular, and tanned he looked.

In spite of her fear, Martha couldn't hold back a tiny nervous giggle. "No, Josie," she said softly, "you're too late." The dog stood beside her and looked at the men, the fur on her spiny backbone standing erect, a deep growl still rumbling in her throat.

The man who'd administered the beating stood over the downed man. "You'd better get out of here, Slick, before I lose my temper," he said softly. "And if you ever bother a woman again, I'll make you wish you were dead." The tall man had a clean, honest look about him, but suddenly Martha felt afraid of everyone.

"I didn't mean no harm," the man, Slick, whined. "I was just tryin' to meet the lady." He scrambled to his feet, grabbed his hat again, and lurched off down the street, rubbing his face with one hand and his back with the other.

"Thank you, sir," Martha said, edging away from the man. If she could get back to her wagon she'd be content to stay there the rest of the day. Maybe forever. What kind of a place had she been dropped into, anyway?

But the man stuck out a big brown paw. "I'm Abram Noble," he said. "Mighty glad to make your acquaintance. Sorry about that fellow. Luckily you won't find many like him around here." He kept the big hand out there forever.

Finally, she allowed him to shake her small hand for a fraction of a second before she withdrew it. "I'm Martha Lawford," she said in a husky voice. "I certainly do thank you, and I'll feel much obliged if there aren't any more around like him."

She turned and started back toward her wagon, only to hear his foot-steps behind, then beside her. "Where are you staying, Miss Lawford?" he asked with a familiarity that frightened her all over again. Should she tell him? That wagon with the battered cloth top offered little in the way of protection.

"I'm staying near town," she answered, realizing they'd be at the wagon in minutes. Where could she go to lead him off the track?

He grinned, keeping almost in step with her. "Where near town?" he asked. "I hope you aren't camping alone on the bank of one of the rivers."

She stopped and held a hand to him again. She had to get rid of him now. "No, I'm not. I'm perfectly all right. Thanks for seeing me this far, Mr. Noble. I'll probably see you around town." She turned, lifted her skirt a lit-tle, and began striding northwest across the dried grass, away from her wagon, thinking that maybe he'd go back now and she could return to it.

But less than a minute later, he walked beside her again. "I have a bad feelin' about you," he said in an easy, friendly way. "Why don't you just show me where you're staying so I won't worry any more?"

She liked the man's looks. His clear, dark eyes, his thin, straight nose, and his square jaw, together with his heavy mop of light brown hair, gave him an upright, honest, and pleasant-looking appearance. She liked his voice, too, and his manner. But he sure knew how to stick like oatmeal to a pan on an overheated fire. She raised her eyes to meet his and shrugged. "I don't seem to have a choice." She pointed to the covered wagon almost behind them now, and south. "That's my house," she said, turning toward it. They reached it almost immediately. Josie crawled under the wagon into the shade and lay there, watching the pair.

"You can't stay in this thing," Mr. Noble said, stretching his neck to look inside. "It don't offer any protection a' tall. Not from four-legged ani-mals or two." He turned and pointed toward the buildings from which they'd just come. "I'm stayin' at Martin's Boardinghouse. You'd best get a room there, too."

She didn't have to tell him she didn't have money, did she?

After a moment he went on. "What you doing out here alone? Where's your people? And your oxen?"

Martha gave a long, loud sigh. She hadn't realized it but she really needed to talk to someone. "Are you purely sure you want to hear?"

"I asked, didn't I?" He sat on the tongue of the wagon. "Let's get com-fortable. I have a feeling it's not a pretty story."

"You're right, sir," Martha said, easing down to the makeshift seat. "My older brother, Jackson, got out of the army last year and, ever since, he's talked of nothing else but moving to Walla Walla Valley. Said it was like the

Garden of Eden. He wouldn't stop talking, so finally our family decided to come. Mama's brother and his wife and son decided to come, too. We planned to all come together but my aunt and uncle had a last-minute delay in collecting the money from their farm. We'd already sold our place and all our stuff. Everything we owned was in the wagon, so we couldn't wait for them. We'd hoped they'd catch up with us on the Oregon Trail. They should be along within a week.

"Our family. . .my parents, two brothers, and I started west last March with a wagon train from Missouri." She shook her head, remembering. "It seems a long time ago, and the trip was so hard." She raised her eyes to his. "I can't tell you how awful that trip was. But my parents made it almost here before they—" she took a deep breath, willing herself not to break down in front of this stranger, "died of cholera." She stopped and dropped her head. *Why, Lord? I still love You and trust You. . .but why did they have to die? I loved them so much. And needed them desperately.* Raising her head resolutely, she continued. "We ran out of food right after that, and my oxen were so worn-out we had to leave them at Fort Hall.

"One of the families had extra oxen so they pulled me this far. They wanted me to go on with them, but I have to wait here for my aunt and uncle." Her eyes burned, so she shut them tight. "I have to wait for them, Mr. Noble," she continued a moment later. "They're all the family I have left. Finally, the Butler family gave me some flour and left me here, but they took my baby brother, William. Said I'd have all I could do to take care of myself until my aunt and uncle come. We'll get him next summer."

Swallowing loudly, Martha closed her eyes tightly again. She'd never felt so alone in her entire life. If Josie would just come out from under the wagon, she'd give her a big hug.

Martha straightened her shoulders and smiled at the man, Mr. Noble. When she met his gaze, his red-rimmed eyes looked almost ready to cry, too.

His Adam's apple jerked up and down. "I guess that's about what I expected. What about your other brother? He die, too?"

She shook her dark head. "When we left the oxen at Fort Hall, he decided to go back and make sure our aunt and uncle were all right." She shook her head again. "I wish he hadn't. I need him more than they do."

They sat together in silence, each deep in private thoughts. She wondered why she'd told this stranger all her troubles. Now he knew her total vulnerability.

Finally, he met her gaze. "You don't have any money, right?"

She nodded. "But I can work. Maybe I could work at the boarding-house. I know how to clean, and I can cook a little."

He dropped his eyes. "That's another sad story. The man got hurt bad

so his wife and four daughters run the place. I think they're pretty broke."
He leaned forward, his elbows on his knees, his chin in his hands, thinking.
"You don't happen to play the piano, do you?"

She laughed out loud. As if anyone in this little town would pay her for
playing. "As a matter of fact, I do," she said. "Is someone at the boardinghouse looking for a pianist?"

He shook his light brown head. "No. But there are two saloons. I'll bet
I could talk one of them into hiring you. You could wait tables when you
aren't playing."

"Sorry, I don't set foot into saloons, Mr. Noble. Don't you know they're
the devil's playground?"

Chapter 2

Abram Noble enjoyed the feel of the cold water on his face and arms as he washed up for supper; it really brought a man to life. But he kept thinking of the girl at the covered wagon.

He continued thinking of her as he ate the steaming meal Mrs. Martin and her daughters had prepared. Potatoes fried with onions in bacon grease, boiled turnips, some kind of meat. *Roast horse,* he thought to himself, trying to chew it. Boiled cabbage, tea, and bread and butter finished out the meal. He'd been there only three days but twice they'd served various kinds of melons. He'd enjoyed that all right.

He hardly heard the other men laughing and talking about how the strange girl had affected his brain. True, he could hardly force his thoughts from her.

In his mind he saw her long, dark hair braided into a crown too heavy for her nicely-shaped head. Enormous, bright blue eyes shone from her heart-shaped face with its ivory complexion. Average height, but small-boned, she looked young, very young. All together, she made a picture that Abe couldn't get out of his mind for even five minutes. Too bad her dress and sunbonnet were so worn and faded; they were not the proper clothes for a girl like Miss Lawford.

What would become of her? He'd gladly rent a room for her but he could tell from their encounter that she'd never accept help. No telling what could happen to her out there alone.

When he finished supper, his feet hit the dusty path. Clearly visible from the boardinghouse, the wagon sat on the north side of the trail only about a hundred yards west.

Nearing the wagon he noticed the girl had a small fire going and some kind of pot over the low flames. "Hello, Miss Lawford," he called in order not to startle her with his sudden appearance. "Thought I'd better make sure you're all right before—"

Josie the dog interrupted, bursting from beneath the wagon with the roar of a tornado. Abe, remembering his earlier encounter with the animal, jumped back and forgot what he'd intended to say and almost about Miss Lawford altogether.

131

"Josie, girl! Stop!" the young woman commanded. The dog quieted immediately but planted herself between Abe and her mistress.

Abe felt a letdown. Why couldn't the dog have slept through his visit?

The girl returned her attention to the pot on the fire. It looked like white dough in the bottom, almost like a pancake but not quite. She scraped the stuff from the bottom, turned it over, and took the pot off the fire.

She smiled at him. "I'd offer you a chair if I had one." Then she brightened. "I have two boxes that I can empty real easy and we can sit on them." She jumped up from her position beside the fire where she'd been sitting on her heels. "I'll be right back," she said, hopping lightly to the frame of the wagon and disappearing under its white canopy. She appeared a moment later and dropped the boxes gently to the ground, before jumping down behind them. "Sit down and relax, Mr. Noble. These are dynamite boxes we packed food in."

She returned the pot to the fire. "I have to finish cooking our supper because I don't have many buffalo chips left. When it's finished, I can talk for a while." As Abe watched, she poured another batch of the pasty stuff into the pot and watched it carefully until she scraped it loose from the bottom and turned it over. A few minutes later she took it out of the pot and put more in. Then she cooked two more from the remaining paste.

"There," she said, plopping onto one of the boxes. "We can eat later. It won't matter if they're cold."

"Would you mind telling me what you just cooked?" Abe asked.

Miss Lawford smiled and dipped her head a bit. "Why, Mr. Noble, haven't you seen trail bread? I make it from flour and water." She shrugged. "It's supposed to have other things in it but flour's all we have." Josie whined and tried to snoot Miss Lawford's hand toward the bread. The dog's pitiful cries made Abe's heart ache for the half-starved animal.

The frail girl shrugged and fed one of the breads to the dog who took it in one gulp. "Sorry," she said. "We each get only a couple of these twice a day and you can see Josie's eager."

"Is that all you got to eat?"

Miss Lawford nodded, her face turning an attractive pink. "We're mighty thankful to have that, Mr. Noble. Our food was completely gone. No one on the wagon train had much either, but they gave me enough flour to last a week. . .until my aunt and uncle come."

Abe felt almost sick to think of this lovely girl trying to care for herself and her dog. And both of them nearly starving. "I got a gun," he said. "I could get you some meat. Rabbits, or something."

She perked up a moment, then settled down. "Only if you have too much for yourself," she said. "I have a gun too, but I'm afraid to shoot it."

Josie put her front feet into Miss Lawford's lap, who got up and fed Josie another piece of trail bread. It disappeared pitifully fast. Then she gave the dog one more, leaving only one small piece.

"I have a plan," she told Abe, her delicate face showing excitement. "Why couldn't I do washing for the men in the boardinghouse? Or wherever they live. I could do it right on the banks of that little creek down past the buildings." She pointed east, down the street. "How are people getting their things washed now?"

Abe, only in town three days himself, hadn't given that problem a thought yet. He shook his head. "I'm not sure, but I'll find out. That would be hard work."

Her laugh sounded like birds singing. "I'm not afraid of hard work, Mr. Noble. I washed clothes for several of the people in the wagon train. I spent most of my Saturday afternoons washing clothes. It wasn't easy but it was something I could do to help. One person was sick, one old and weak, some didn't even have wagons." She sighed then pulled her shoulders back. "My only problem right now is that I don't have any tallow to make soap."

He laughed. "I can buy you some soap right there in that first building on the right. It's a general store and sells most anything a man needs."

She stiffened. "I couldn't let you do that, Mr. Noble. Josie and I aren't your responsibility."

The idea didn't sound half bad to Abe. Never had he met anyone who made him feel so responsible. But he had to be careful not to frighten her away. "Maybe I could loan you the soap and you could repay me or do some of my clothes for free. Would that work?"

"Yes. It sounds good. Thank you, Mr. Noble. You really are, aren't you?"

"I really am what?"

"Noble." They laughed together. When they finished, she cast a questioning glance his way. "You know all about me, but I know nothing about you, sir. That hardly seems fair."

She wanted to know about him? She'd opened up enough to ask? Well, he'd best not keep the lady waiting! "I hail from Iowa and have two parents and two sisters. I been in the army for the last six years. Got sent west to fight the Indians and that's what I been doing. Me and my company chased some Indian tribes past here a couple times and I noticed what a right purty valley it was. I sure understand how your brother felt.

"I tried to file a donation claim several years ago but they weren't allowing settlers in yet because of the Indian wars. No matter where I went, I kept remembering this little valley where the rivers meet. Well, finally the army turned me loose and the government opened the valley to settlers, so here I am. I'm looking for a piece of land I can't live without, so I can put a claim on it."

A look of pure bliss crossed Miss Lawford's face. "That's exactly what I'd like to do, too," she said.

At first Abe felt excitement at the possibility of having her for a neighbor. Then he remembered a man had to be twenty-one years old to make a claim. This slip of a girl couldn't be a day over fifteen. He wasn't sure whether women could make claims, anyway. "How old are you?" he asked quietly.

"I'm seventeen," she replied. "How old are you, sir?"

He laughed. After all, fair was fair. "I'm an old man," he said. "I'll celebrate my twenty-fifth birthday in December."

She nodded. "And what do you plan to do with this claim you're getting?"

He thought a moment. "Well, farm it, I guess, and run some cattle. Maybe some sheep and a few chickens. Plant me some fruit trees. I guess that ought to about do it."

"Oh, Mr. Noble, it sounds heavenly. I'm going to do it, too. First, I have to earn some money washing clothes to buy food for Josie and me, then I'm going to get a donation claim, too. I really am."

As dusk began to drop her curtain over them, Abe noticed mosquitoes. "I hope you will, Miss Lawford, but for now, how about letting me lend you enough money to get a room in the boardinghouse? I don't want you out here. You got no protection a' tall."

A smile curved her lips. "What do you call the hurricane that met you, Mr. Noble? Josie would die to protect me. I'd better stay right here until my aunt and uncle come. It may not be a palace, but it's free."

"You heard about the Indians?"

Her face blanched and her right hand flew to her throat. "What about the Indians?"

He smiled. "I never heard about them hurting anyone, but they walk right into people's houses and demand food. Everyone I know's given them something to eat and they leave. They stink like nothing you've ever smelled because they smear fish fat all over them. They think it keeps 'em warm. They scare people a lot, but as far as I know they don't hurt anyone."

"Oh, but I don't have anything to feed them. I'm nearly out of flour, too. That's why I have to wash clothes."

He smiled grimly. "You'll give them something to eat, Miss Lawford, even if it's your last bite." Seeing her dismay he tried to think of something with which to cheer her. "They probably won't come here anyway, seeing you don't have a proper house."

"I hope not. I really hope not, Mr. Noble. That would purely frighten me to death."

After a little while he left, walking slowly back to the boardinghouse.

"You be sure to bring me your dirty clothes, Mr. Noble," Martha called.

"I will," he yelled back, waving. Before going inside the boardinghouse, he went around back to the corral to make sure his faithful mare, Charity, had plenty of hay, and to give her her evening oats. He brushed and curried the rich bay horse. Stroking Charity's darker mane, he felt pride in the shiny plump animal. "I can't wait for you to see her, Charity," he murmured. "I hope you like her as good as I do." After a few more strokes with the brush, he put her in her comfortable stall in the stable and hurried to his own room and bed.

As he lay in bed, he thought about Miss Lawford again. His horse had more to eat and a better place to sleep than the girl and her dog. Somehow that didn't seem right.

But he smiled in the dark, remembering his visit. He had several things to do in the morning. Besides his own donation claim to check out, he had to find out about Miss Lawford's situation. And before he did that he'd better check around to see who needed clothes washed.

"Be with her, God, and protect her. You might be with me, too. I'd be thankin' You a long time if You'd help me get to know her better." He fell into a sound sleep.

Chapter 3

Martha watched Mr. Noble striding away from her wagon until he went around the boardinghouse and was out of sight. "Well," she told Josie. "I think he'll really help me get started washing clothes. Maybe I'll make enough to buy you all the food you need." She hugged the dog's big head. Josie returned the caress with two swipes of her tongue across Martha's cheek. "Just you wait," Martha continued. "Things'll soon be better. I promise." She turned to the cold trail bread. Knowing she needed the strength the bread offered, she had a hard time getting out her next words. "We'll start right now. I already gave you three of the breads, but you're still hungrier than I. Here, you can have half of this last one." The dog didn't wait for a second invitation but gobbled the offered food.

Martha sat back down on the box and tried to make her piece last as long as possible. She chewed each tiny bite thirty-two times as her mother had taught her, and tried to think about something besides the food. The only other thing she could think about was the washing she might have to do and the strength she would need to do it. She took another tiny bite. As she chewed, three men approached the wagon from the west. Where had they come from? The street and people were the other way. Even the tepees were east and north. Becoming uneasy, she wondered who they could be and what they wanted.

Then she recognized Indians! She sat with her heart in her throat, terrified. *Protect me, Father. Make them be friendly.* When a deep growl rumbled from inside Josie, she reached an arm around her faithful dog's neck.

They stopped within ten feet of Martha, stared into her eyes, and waited. An almost unbearable stench, arriving with the Indians, made Martha's stomach lurch. She didn't know what to say or do. Would they even understand her language?

The three walked over to the tiny fire, and looked into the empty pot. One of them began motions as if eating. "Food," he said. He seemed to be the oldest of the three and wore buckskins. Soft moccasins covered his feet. The other two wore white man's clothes, worn and dirty overalls with ragged long-sleeved shirts. But like the older man, they wore soft deerskin moccasins. Long, matted, black hair hung down their backs.

The old Indian caught her attention again, then repeated his request for food. Or was it an order?

Mr. Noble had warned her they'd want food. But she had so little! What would she do when it was gone?

"Food!" the Indian said again. The three surrounded her as she sat on the box and Josie's rumble grew louder. Mr. Noble had told her to feed them even if it was her last bite.

"You be good, Josie," she warned the dog. Scrambling to her feet, her knees shaking, she tossed four more buffalo chips onto the fire, poured two cups of her precious flour into the bowl and added water. When thoroughly mixed, she dropped spoonfuls onto the bottom of the pot.

The Indians looked friendlier as they watched her fixing the trail bread. They said something to each other then they all sat down beside the box she'd abandoned.

After turning the bread twice, she scooped it from the pot, cooled it a moment, and handed each Indian a piece. They nodded deeply, saying something unintelligible. "You're welcome," she said, smiling. This wasn't nearly as bad as she'd feared—except she could ill afford losing the flour.

As each man took a bite, his expression changed to surprise then anger. All three jumped to their feet and started saying something to Martha at the same time. It didn't take her long to decide they didn't like the trail bread and wanted something else—now!

"I don't have anything else," she said, knowing they wouldn't understand her. "That's all my dog and I have to eat," she went on.

They caught the word "dog" and one of them gestured toward Josie, making motions of eating again. Martha dropped to her knees, reaching her arms around her friend. "No, no," she said. She kissed Josie's dusty face. "I love my dog. I'd never eat her."

After a few moments of talking together, the Indians tossed the trail bread to Josie, who wolfed it down. Then they left without another word. Martha watched them, wondering to which tepee they'd go, but soon they became specks on the western horizon. She dropped to the box, breathing hard.

She started laughing with relief, then couldn't stop. Realizing she'd become hysterical, she forced herself to take deep breaths until she regained control. Then she thought about their rejection of her food and used all her willpower not to start laughing again. "Well, Josie, at least they won't be back to bother us anymore. That's something, isn't it?" Their terrible stink still lingered heavily in the air, so she took Josie for a walk down the street to the creek. After her meeting with the Indians, the buildings with people in them seemed to offer a modicum of protection.

A half-hour later she returned to find the air around the wagon fresh again so she washed the pot and bowl. She lay down in her wagon bed and thanked God for making the Indians friendly. "Thank You for my new friend, Mr. Noble. Protect me from everyone and everything and help me get along without my parents." She hesitated as a few tears rolled down her cheeks. "Help me not to miss baby William so much. I know he's better off with Rachel and her mama and papa, but I miss him. I love You, God. Good night." She hardly noticed the growling of her stomach and tried not to think about the wasted food. Well, the food wasn't wasted. Maybe Josie's backbone wouldn't stick out quite so far now. Tomorrow would be a better day. She fell asleep listening to mosquitoes buzzing around her head.

—⁂—

Martha wakened early the next morning, feeling the warm sun shining through the white wagon top. She tried hard not to think about the Indians. Thinking how different it would be if her folks were here, she reminded herself that they'd want her to get up and get going.

After carrying back the second bucket of water from the creek (she'd bathed with the first one), she mixed up a batch of trail bread. Josie stood beside her, watching every move she made until movement from the street attracted her attention. She exploded into excited barks.

"Good morning, Miss Lawford," Mr. Noble said. "I have a fresh rabbit for you. Am I too late?"

Martha's stomach made an extra loud growl, and Josie showed intense interest in the dressed animal hanging from the man's hand. "Oh, thank you, Mr. Noble, sir," she said, reaching for it. She wasted no time before washing it, cutting it into pieces, and dropping it into a kettle of water. "This certainly will be a treat," she said. "I thank you more than you know, sir." Josie whined and her sad eyes met Martha's. "Would you mind if I share it with Josie?" Martha asked hesitantly.

"I'd be disappointed if you didn't."

Martha wondered if she should invite Mr. Noble to eat, too, but that would be getting far too familiar at this point. He seemed to be a nice man all right, but she mustn't encourage any man's friendship right now. What did she know about men?

"I'll be back in awhile," the man said, interrupting her thoughts. "I'll go see if I can find anyone who needs some washing done. I'll bring back a bar of soap, too."

Martha and Josie each had two pieces of trail bread while they waited for the savory smelling rabbit to finish cooking. "We're going to be so stuffed we won't be able to walk to the creek," she told her dog. But they had no trouble eating the entire rabbit. After they finished, Martha sat on her wooden box, thinking. Not all that long ago she'd have insisted her rabbit be rolled in flour or cornmeal and fried in deep fat with lots of salt. But never had anything, including rabbit, tasted better than this one, boiled in water with nothing else. She had a feeling that Josie, who had eaten two-thirds of the fresh meat, could have had even more.

Well, she might as well try to figure a way to wash clothes. "Come on, Josie," she called, heading east toward the creek. She arrived in five minutes, having met not a soul on the walk.

She walked down to the water and squatted. Maybe she could dig a hole in the shallow water by removing rocks. Grabbing stones by the hand-ful, she tossed them downstream. Soon, she had a deep enough spot to dip from or to soak clothes in. She'd roiled the water, but it would soon settle back down.

She looked around. Not a single twig or branch with which to make a fire. If there had ever been any, someone had beaten her to them. She couldn't use her buffalo chips. They were almost gone, too, and she'd never get any more of them. Sitting on the rocks on the creek bank, Martha enjoyed the warm sun on her back. She looked around again. At least she could dry the clothes on the small bushes scattered along the bank. Maybe she could soak the clothes overnight with lots of soap, then wash them in cold water.

"Come, Josie," she called, gathering up her skirts. Maybe she could beat the dog back to the wagon if she really raced. She took off.

Laughing over her shoulder at her surprised dog, Martha nearly ran into a girl about her own age. The girl's frightened shout stopped Martha within touching distance. Martha stepped back a few feet and gazed into the girl's blazing blue eyes. Much shorter then Martha, she looked nice enough, but her round face expressed indignation at being nearly run down directly in front of the boardinghouse—her own home. The girl wore a coarse gown of an indescribable color, maybe light brownish-gray, and a matching sun-bonnet. Her eyes looked as though they'd burst into flame any minute. She looked up and down the street then back at Martha.

"What were you running from?" she finally demanded.

Martha laughed. "Nothing. I just felt like racing with my dog."

The girl stared at Martha, as though trying to figure her out. "Who are you? Where are you staying?"

Remembering her manners, Martha extended her hand to the girl. "I'm Martha Lawford, and I'm really not staying anywhere yet. My aunt and uncle will be coming on the next wagon train. I guess I'll just stay in my wagon until they get here." As she explained she pointed west to her wagon, its dirty white top contrasting boldly with the deep blue sky and the nearly dried grass in the foreground.

The girl's mouth turned into a round O. "You're the one Mr. Noble was telling us about. Well, I'm Nellie Martin. Mama and us girls do the boarders' washing. Ain't many other people 'round."

Martha's mouth went dry. "What about the people who run the stores?" she asked. "Do they all live here?"

Nellie nodded her red head. "Most of our boarders own or work at the trading post. We do their washing. A lot of the others live in the back of their stores. They ain't married, and I don't know how they git their washin' done."

At that news Martha felt life flow through her body again. She'd have plenty of people to wash for—if she could just get the clothes clean. "How long have you been here?" she asked. "Do you like it?"

Nellie gazed off toward the Blue Mountains, her fingers curving as she mentally counted. "About eight months," she finally said. "That's when settlers were first allowed in. Mama wanted to own the first boarding-house. We all worked in a boardinghouse in The Dalles after Papa got his leg smashed off cutting logs. Mama said she could do better than Mrs. Adamson, so we came."

Martha needed to get started washing clothes, but it had been several days since she'd seen another girl. She hoped Nellie would become her friend.

"Come in and meet Mama and my sisters," Nellie said. "She'd tan my hide if I didn't bring you in. There's only one other woman in the village that I know about."

"Oh, you look so young," Mrs. Martin said. "I hear you've been left all alone in the world. Can I do anything for you, my dear?"

"Would you have work I could do? I know how to clean, and I can cook simple food."

A sad look crossed the woman's face. "I'd like to, but we barely get enough money from the men to buy food. One of these days things will be different. But if you don't have anything to eat, you just come eat with us. We eat breakfast at six o'clock, dinner at twelve sharp, and supper at six o'clock in the evening. You just come any time, hon."

Martha didn't refuse but she knew she'd have to be *really* hungry to take advantage of the woman's kind offer. Besides, what about Josie? She couldn't eat somewhere and forget her best friend. She almost smiled thinking what Mrs. Martin would say if she asked for food for her dog.

After a few more minutes, Martha managed to get away and ran back to the wagon where Josie waited in the shade. The sun stood almost overhead and Martha felt hungry, but she couldn't think of food until evening. She'd just gather up her tubs and carry them down to the creek. Maybe someone would see what she was doing and offer her some work. If not, she could wash her own things. As she hurried around, Josie announced the arrival of Mr. Noble.

He carried a bunch of clothes, a long-sleeved shirt on the outside with the sleeves and tails tied together to form a bundle. "I found some work for you," he said. Then he pulled a large yellow bar from his back pocket. "Soap, too." His grin looked completely satisfied. "I see you're getting ready. Come on. I'll help you carry the things over to the creek."

"Oh, I can do that, Mr. Noble. It won't matter if I make several trips. I have nothing else to do, anyway." She hopped up into the wagon. "I think I have some paper in here," she called. "I'll just write down the price of the soap." A moment later she jumped lightly to the ground, a piece of dirty, torn paper and a stub of a pencil in her hand. She looked expectantly at Mr. Noble. He grinned. "Well, how much is the soap?" she asked.

"Fifty cents. Is that too much?"

She laughed. "Whatever you paid is the price, Mr. Noble. I won't complain." She wrote *Expenses* at the top and under that she added: *Soap–$.50.*

"Now I feel like a businesswoman," she said, shoving the paper and pencil under the edge of the wagon canopy. Picking up two nested tubs, she started off. Mr. Noble grabbed the clothes and the large bucket, and followed her. "Don't worry about the money, Mr. Noble," she said as they hurried down the street. "I'll pay you as soon as I can."

"Forget the money," he said. "I thought you agreed to wash my clothes in exchange for the soap."

When they both had dropped their burdens on the clean stones beside the creek, they sat with their backs to the sun. "How you going to heat the water?" he asked.

She shook her head. "I couldn't find anything to make a fire. Think I could soak them overnight in lots of soap and wash them tomorrow in cold water?"

A smile tugged at the left side of his mouth before he shrugged. "I've never washed clothes. You wash them, and I'll take them back."

Deciding she might as well get the clothes soaking, she rubbed the bar of soap vigorously, trying to make some suds. A few bubbles floated to the top so she continued rubbing until her arms gave out. Puffing, she sat down in the warm sun to rest.

Mr. Noble reached for the soap bar. "Here, let me help with that," he said with a smile. "I'll bet I can work up some suds." Before Martha could object, he grabbed the bar and worked it over. He looked at her, puffing and laughing. "How's that? Think it's ready for the clothes?"

She untied the shirt sleeves and started lifting the clothes into the water. Whew! The stink made her glad they were outdoors. And glad she'd forgotten to bring her own things. She dropped in two pairs of heavy overalls, so filthy they felt stiff, one of which someone had obviously wiped his hand on after blowing his nose onto the ground. She'd never put her clothes into the same water with this filth! She wasn't sure she could put her hands into it. Then she shoved in two unwieldy and equally filthy shirts, followed by a pair of badly stained and malodorous long johns. After she had all the clothes shoved into the water, she pushed them around and around, up and down. She hadn't thought about how seldom these men's clothes got washed. Or what a miserable job it would be. How would she ever get the clothes clean again? Or her hands? If she could find a stout stick she could use that to shove the things around. But there wasn't one stick of any kind anywhere.

Mr. Noble struggled to his feet. "I'll go on back," he said. "I guess you'll leave these things here tonight?"

She nodded, holding her filthy hands away from her body. "They'll be safe, won't they?"

He laughed out loud. "If anyone started taking those grimy clothes, he'd think again. I've never seen anything safer than that stuff." He gave her a salute and headed west toward the boardinghouse.

She sat enjoying the warm sun for a while, then shoved the clothes around again. The cold water seemed to be doing something. At least it looked almost black. Maybe she should dump it and get clean water. "Thank You, God for helping me get the clothes to wash. I'm sorry I acted like a baby, but I'm purely thankful for having clothes to wash. I love You, Father." Before she added the "amen," she heard a man shouting and cursing. Then Josie appeared, sliding down the creek bank with something bloody in her mouth.

Slick, the man who'd attacked Martha that first day, appeared a moment later with a thick stick in his hand. "Get that dog," he yelled. "It stole my meat and I'm killin' it." Josie splashed across the creek and tore off through the grass, the man following at a much slower pace. About the time Slick stepped from the water onto the other side, his boots dripping, Josie dashed back across to Martha where she then stopped to shake off her excess water. Martha snatched the bloody meat from Josie's mouth. "No!" she said. "Bad dog!" She pointed down the street to the wagon. "Go home, Josie," she commanded. "Go!" The dog took off, looking much less exuberant than she had with the meat in her mouth. Martha wanted nothing more than to give it back to her skinny dog, but she had to make peace somehow.

She met Slick as he stepped from the water. "Here's your meat," she said. "Not even hurt."

He looked at her in surprise, then slapped the meat from her hand to the ground. "You! I shoulda knowed you'd be back causin' more trouble. Well, I ain't eatin' after no dog. Pay for the meat or I'll kill the dog. Take yer pick, girlie."

Martha knew she was dealing with a dangerous man. And for all she knew he might be quoting the law of the land out here in the wild country. "I'll wash your clothes free, Mr. . .uh. . . I'll do more than enough to pay for your meat."

"Whadda I want my clothes washed fer? Ain't no wimmin out here no how. Just gimme the money and I'll go back to the meat shop."

Not having any money and not knowing what to say, she bent over the tub of dirty clothes and stirred them around.

"Ya ain't got no money, have ya?" he yelled at her. "I know ya ain't." He looked around. "Where'd that dog go, anyway? I'm goin' after the thievin' mutt right now." He bumbled unsteadily off down the street, as if he might have been at the saloon before the meat market.

Chapter 4

A be Noble cleaned himself up a little, then decided to go see what was happening at the saloon. Stepping through the front door of the boardinghouse to the dusty street, he heard a rough voice yelling. Sounded like Slick. Remembering Miss Lawford at the creek, he sprinted in that direction. As he neared, Slick lurched off across the street toward Galbraith's Saloon. Abe slowed to a fast walk and continued to the creek.

Miss Lawford leaned over her tub with her back to him. "What's wrong with Slick?" Abe called.

When the girl turned around, she brushed a tear off her face, then quickly faced the tub again, jerking the clothes around.

He stepped down beside her. "Slick been bothering you again?" he asked, fearing to hear the answer. She remained silent. "What did Slick do?" he asked louder than necessary.

He heard a tiny sniff. She jammed the clothes up and down. Then, "Nothing, yet. He's going to kill Josie."

Then he noticed the meat lying on the ground. "Where'd this come from?" he asked, turning it over with the toe of his boot.

Miss Lawford kept stirring the clothes in the black water. She hiccuped loudly, then drew in a deep breath. "Josie took it from Mr. . .uh. . . Slick."

"Why didn't you give it back?"

Another hiccup. "He. . .he. . .doesn't like eating after a dog."

Abe began laughing. He couldn't help it. Easing himself down to the warm rocks, his back to the sun, he laughed some more.

Finally, Miss Lawford turned to face him. "It isn't funny, sir. My dog didn't mean to do anything wrong. She's been hungry for so long she'd eat anything she could get."

Abe made a determined effort to calm his hilarity. When he had himself under control, he moved to her side. "I know. It just struck my funny bone to think of that old coot eating after a dog." He chuckled again, then managed to stop. "Josie should be the one who wouldn't eat after him, wouldn't you think?" he asked, still grinning.

"I don't know, sir. But I can't let him hurt Josie."

He nodded. "Right. I'll go have me a little talk with Slick. He won't hurt your dog, Miss Lawford. Don't you worry." He almost flinched, watching her soft hands reaching into that grimy water. "Want me to help you get fresh water before I go talk to Slick?" he asked. "I'll make more suds for you, too."

She shook her head. "I can do it, Mr. Noble. Please go tell that man he can't hurt Josie. Please?"

"But I hate to see you working so hard." He took her other tub, filled it with water, then spun the soap bar between his hands until he worked up some suds. He smiled at the appreciation showing in her bright blue eyes. "I'd offer to transfer those dirty clothes but I know you wouldn't let me. So I'm off to talk to the town drunk." He walked a little way before a thought struck him. "Be sure to take that meat home for Josie," he called. Then he strode off to Chapman and Shaffer's Meat Market.

"Seen Slick lately?" he asked.

"Yeah," Will Shaffer growled, "he stoled one of my best roasts about an hour ago."

Abe burst into laughter again. He couldn't remember when his life had been so riotous. "I could return that roast if you want it," he said. He pointed toward the creek. "It's lying out there on the creek bank, quite a lot worse for wear." Then he told the man how Slick had lost the roast and threatened Miss Lawford's dog.

"You just tell the young woman to let her dog have it," Shaffer said. "How was that rabbit you bought this morning? Tough?"

Abe shook his head. "Just fine, Will. Never ate better in my life. You got another one?"

"I got a couple. Want one?"

"Yeah, I'll take 'em both." Abe took the rabbits, wrapped in rough brown paper, and headed toward Galbraith's Saloon. Stepping inside, he waved to a couple of men, then, not seeing Slick, crossed the street to Ball and Stone. He hadn't been in that saloon before, but it seemed a likely place to find the man he sought. Slick sat at the bar not far from the door. Abe slid onto the stool beside the smaller man.

"What'll it be?" the barkeep asked.

"How about a bacon sandwich?" Abe asked.

"Comin' up."

Abe turned to Slick. "Heard you lost a little meat this afternoon."

"Yeah! I'm gonna git that dog. Show that high falutin' dame, too."

Abe shoved one of the rabbits down the bar to Slick. "You aren't going to do one thing to that dog, Slick. Remember what happened the other day when you bothered Miss Lawford? Well, that'll seem like a Sunday school picnic compared to what I'll do to you if you so much as touch either her or her dog. Don't push me, Slick. Sometimes I go off like a loaded gun."

Taking his newly arrived bacon sandwich, he hopped off the stool, grabbed the remaining rabbit, and headed for the door. "I hear the city's takin' stiffer measures against thieves, Slick. Better watch it."

"Haw!" Slick snorted. "The way I hear it the town's brand new police force, Sheriff Jackson, ain't even got a gun. Who's doin' all this stiffer measure stuff?"

Abe stepped out of the saloon and drew a deep breath of fresh air. Looking east and not seeing Miss Lawford, he turned west. He dropped the brown paper from the rabbit, making a mental note to pick it up on his way back. Miss Lawford would never accept the rabbit if it came in brown paper. That would smack of charity. Maybe he'd get the rabbit there in time to save her precious trail bread. That stuff didn't look too good, but it must be edible.

As he neared the covered wagon, a small spiral of smoke cut into the blue sky. Then the dog burst from beneath the wagon and came after him as if he were the devil in disguise. Miss Lawford called Josie back.

"Good evening," Abe called when he could be heard. Then he held out the rabbit. "I got lucky again," he said. "This may be the last one in the county though." He hadn't lied, he told himself proudly. He had gotten lucky and it might be the last one for all he knew.

She accepted the rabbit graciously with profuse thanks. "You surely didn't need to dress it out for me, Mr. Noble. That's one thing I learned on the Trail."

When she turned those blue eyes on him, he felt himself melting like bacon grease in the hot sun. He didn't mention it to Miss Lawford, but he'd have shaved that rabbit, hair by hair, and cut it into bite-sized pieces if he thought it would please her.

She washed the rabbit, cut it up, and dropped it into a kettle of water as she had this morning. "Won't you sit down, Mr. Noble?" she invited after he stood for a few minutes.

After they rested a moment she turned worried eyes to him. "Is that awful man going to hurt Josie?"

He shook his head. "I guarantee he won't hurt you or your dog, Miss Lawford. I just wish I could be sure about every other man in the county."

They visited a while, she telling him about the Indians' visit.

"You mean they just walked off without eating?" he asked.

She giggled. "That's what they did. At first they didn't like it but they soon decided they'd rather have no food than trail bread. They won't bother me again, do you think?"

Abe didn't feel all that sure about the Indians. He didn't know much about them, except they stank and walked into people's houses, expecting

146

to be fed. Everyone he'd known had fed them. He shook his head. "I do not know."

She smiled. "I think they've had more than enough of me. Oh yes, I met Nellie Martin, too." She went on to tell how she almost ran over the girl in her race with Josie. "I hope she'll be my friend. Being all alone, I purely need a friend."

"I'm sure she needs one, too," he said. Then he told how Slick appropriated the meat Josie took from him. "You gave it back to her, didn't you?" he asked.

She nodded. "I did, because she's so terribly thin. I hope it won't encourage her to do something like that again."

"It won't." Abe couldn't help noticing how thin Miss Lawford appeared to be, too. Her worn blue dress hung loosely, even at the waist. Then he remembered something. "I checked into the donation claims today."

Miss Lawford sprang from her box. Then she sat down again, but with excitement in her eyes and voice. "How many acres can you get? Can a woman get a claim, too? Tell me about it, Mr. Noble. I purely want one of those donation claims."

"Well, the news isn't all good. The claim for a single person is one hundred sixty acres, for a married couple, three hundred twenty. Yes, a woman can make a claim but a ma. . .anyone must be twenty-one unless they're married to someone who is."

Miss Lawford looked crushed for a moment, then relaxed. "I'll just have to stay with my uncle until I'm old enough," she said with resignation. "But you just wait, Mr. Noble. I'm having a farm of my own."

Abe smiled. "I believe you Miss Lawford. I just wish you could get started right away." *What if they're all taken before you turn twenty-one?* he thought. *Four years is a long time.* Wisely, he said nothing to discourage her.

When Abe finally got into bed that night, Miss Lawford's bright eyes, sensitive mouth, dark hair, and thin body kept watching him while he tried to fall asleep.

"Lord," he said aloud. "You watch over that little girl, hear? I worry about her out there alone." He grinned. "But then You care a whole lot more for her than I do, don't You? I guess I can trust You to watch over her. I'll watch over her all I can, too, God."

He'd never in his life seen such a lovely, unspoiled girl. What he'd give to have her on the next farm beside his. What he'd give to have her on his own farm! He finally fell asleep, but Miss Lawford invaded even his dreams.

Chapter 5

Martha shared the rabbit with Josie, even after the dog had eaten Slick's entire roast. Due to Mr. Noble's lengthy visit, the rabbit had cooked so long it nearly fell off the bones. Martha didn't care, neither did Josie. In fact the dog chewed the softened bones and swallowed them.

After supper Martha and Josie sprinted down the dusty street to the creek where Martha gave the dirty clothes a hundred pushes, shoves, and stirs. The water looked as black as it had before Mr. Noble had changed it, but she felt far too tired to get clean water again. Walking back to the wagon, she decided to get up early in the morning so she could finish the clothes and they could start drying.

Was this to be her life from now on? She hadn't realized how distasteful the work would be, but who was she, who needed the work so desperately, to complain? What would she do when the weather cooled? Well, she'd just thank the Lord for letting her do it until Aunt Mandy and Uncle Cleve came. They'd never think of letting her do such awful work after they got here anyway. *Bless them, Lord, as they travel. Keep them safe and hurry their steps. Bless Jackson, too, and William.* Her breath came evenly and she made little sleeping sounds before she managed to tack an Amen onto the end.

The sun shining on the worn canopy of Martha's wagon warmed her and awakened her early. "Thank You, Father," Martha prayed out loud, "for the beautiful warm day. Thank You for keeping us safe through the night, too. I love You, Father. I purely love You more than my lips can say." Josie lay on her rug on the floor of the wagon beside Martha's featherbed, which also lay on the floor. When Josie's long tongue gave her an early morning kiss, she bounded from the bed.

"Come on, Josie," she said. "Time to get moving. We have lots to do this morning. Should we go finish the clothes and let them be drying while we eat breakfast?" Josie wagged her plumy tail and Martha took that for a definite yes. She used the last of the water to wash up, then dressed in clean clothes. Maybe if she didn't get more washing she'd do her own this morning, too. Her things would be simple after what she'd been through trying to clean those filthy things in her tubs.

"Come on, Josie," Martha called, taking off down the middle of the dusty street. "I'll beat you to the creek!" Although Martha had a headstart, Josie easily beat her.

Sliding down the short bank to the creek, Martha thought it looked strange. Clean and empty. Then she knew. The clothes, tubs, pail, and everything were gone! "Where can they be?" she asked Josie in shock. "They were here last night, weren't they?" She looked up and down the creek bank. This was the spot. Wasn't it? Then she noticed the hole she'd dug to dip from. And the yellow bar of soap. This was the place all right.

Somebody had stolen her things! Including someone else's clothes! What kind of trouble was she in now? She didn't have any tubs anymore! Nor her big bucket! She sank to the clean, round stones. After huddling there for a half-hour, too stunned to cry, she scrambled to her feet and turned her face heavenward. "What did I do to deserve this, Lord?" she cried out loud. "I thought You promised to be with us always. Where were You? And what am I supposed to do now?" Her strength gone, she dropped to the smooth stones again, but this time she curled into a small ball. Josie sat down, leaned against Martha, and proceeded to wash her upturned ear.

After awhile, Martha reached around the big dog and pulled her close. "Oh, Josie, what would I do without you?" she asked, rubbing her pet behind the ears. As she fondled the dog, her internal tumult quieted, and she began to put this last blow into perspective. Yes, it was bad. She needed those tubs and bucket. And she had no idea what would happen when the men learned their clothes were gone. But this was nothing compared to what she'd already been through. She'd suffered the most severe blow a young person could sustain—losing Mama and Papa. And Petey, the little boy she'd cared for all the way from Independence. *Why? Why, Lord? If You'll just tell me what I'm doing wrong, I'll quit.* As she lay quietly thinking, Josie suddenly jumped away and began barking, her fur bristling.

"I thought I'd find you here," Mr. Noble said, sliding down and dropping to a sitting position beside her. "What's going on? You didn't sleep down here, did you?"

Martha popped into a sitting position. "No, but you can see we should have. Sit down, Josie. He won't bother us."

Mr. Noble looked wide-eyed at Martha, then glanced around. Finally, he nodded as if understanding her pain. "What happened to your things?"

She shrugged. He didn't respond. "The coyotes got them?" she asked with a tremulous smile.

His sympathetic chuckle rewarded her bravado. "How long have you been here?" he asked.

"We got here about sunrise."

He sat quietly a moment, then stood up. "We know who did it, of course."

"We do?"

"I threatened to hurt Slick bad if he bothered you or your dog. He thinks he can get away with this, but he can't." He stood quietly a moment. "Come on, you may as well go back to your wagon." They walked back together. When they reached the wagon, Mr. Noble showed Martha a dressed duck he'd shoved onto the wagon floor. "You go ahead and do whatever you planned. I'll see you later," he added, hurrying away.

"Thanks for the duck," she mumbled so softly he might not have heard. Do whatever she'd planned? If she didn't feel so awful, she'd laugh at that. Well, at least she didn't have to touch those filthy clothes anymore. She probably should be thankful for that. Maybe those men would never figure out who lost their clothes. That was another laugh. Didn't she just have lots to laugh about today?

She cut up the duck, then remembered she needed water. In ten minutes she returned with the small drinking bucket filled to the brim. She washed the pieces of meat, put them in the kettle with a little water, and sat down to do some more thinking.

"Hello, there," a cheery voice called. "I came to visit." Martha looked up to find Nellie Martin almost beside her. Suddenly, she felt lighter.

"Hi," she returned, pointing to the two wooden boxes. "Sit down, Nellie. I'm glad to see you." Then she noticed something in Nellie's hands.

Martha's new friend handed her a piece of chocolate cake on a small, chipped, blue-bordered plate, then sat down. "Mama thought you might like this. Thought you might not have a way to bake." She took in the fire with the kettle over it. "Guess she was right."

"Thank her for me, Nellie. We'll really enjoy the cake."

"We?"

Oops. "I'll enjoy it, Nellie. I'm used to saying 'we' to my dog."

Nellie looked around some more. "Want to take a walk? Oh, I guess you're fixing something to eat. I'd better go." She stood up.

Martha stood up, too, but feeling lightheaded, sat back down. "I guess we'd better eat now, but could we take a walk afterwards?"

Nellie thought she could and, after promising to come back later, left.

"Well, Josie," Martha said, "let's dig in. Thanks to Mr. Noble our flour is holding out pretty well." Martha had heard you shouldn't give dogs fowl bones as they're sharp and brittle, but she had no idea how she'd keep them from Josie. The dog ate half the duck and all the bones. Then they divided the cake. Martha got impatient when Josie swallowed her half of the cake without chewing it even once. "I may as well have eaten it all," she grumbled. "You didn't even taste it."

—⁂—

About midafternoon, Nellie came back so the girls walked north to the creek. "Mill Creek carries a lot more water in the winter," Nellie said as they tossed small stones into the tiny stream. "Let's take off our shoes and wade."

Mill Creek. So that's what it is, Martha thought.

They both took off their shoes and stockings, held their skirts up, and waded up and down the creek, slipping on the slick rocks. Josie ran in and out of the water, exploring the dried grass, weeds, and all the delicious smells on both sides of the small stream.

"It feels nice and cool," Nellie said just before her feet went out from under her. "It's cold," she screamed, laughing, making no effort to regain her feet.

The girls spent an hour playing in the water, Martha being careful not to fall. How would she ever wash her clothes now? She wanted to tell Nellie about her latest calamity, but for some reason she kept it to herself.

After they finished, they sat in the sun, drying, for another hour. The sun felt so good, and a delicious smell, almost like ripe berries, wafted around the girls.

"What are those buildings on the other side of the creek?" Martha asked as they rested.

"Oh, you mean on past the street? That's old Fort Walla Walla where the soldiers lived during the Indian wars. In '57 they moved a couple of miles west of the street. The soldiers are still there to put down any Indian uprising. They're just not as close as they used to be."

"I see. What's going to happen to the buildings?"

Nellie shook her red head. "I don't know. Maybe someone will take them in a donation land claim." Jumping to her feet she tried to brush the wrinkles from her dress. "The sun's getting low. I'd better get back to help with supper. You can't even tell I've been wet, can you?" she asked, spinning around merrily.

Martha raised her eyebrows. "I'll bet your mother can tell," she said with an impish grin. "Will you be in big trouble?"

Nellie cocked her head, then shrugged. "She never looks at me so she won't know. But she'll notice if I don't get back to help with supper."

They hurried back, Nellie to the boardinghouse, and Martha to her covered wagon. As Martha watched her new friend disappear into the

151

boardinghouse, she marveled at how much she'd enjoyed the day in spite of her ever increasing troubles. Maybe she'd see Nellie a lot. A good friend would make life much more bearable, even if it wouldn't bring back the missing clothes and tubs.

The sun leaned far into the west and Martha's stomach told her it was time to eat. She fixed a batch of trail bread, making a little extra as they hadn't been using it all the time lately. As she and Josie ate, she wondered if Mr. Noble had found Slick. Hopefully he had, and the missing clothes and utensils as well.

Martha's walk to Mill Creek with Nellie that afternoon had honed her curiosity, so she decided to walk south now. She'd seen some buildings in that direction and felt that she might as well investigate. Walking some distance, she discovered a few shacks widely spaced. Maybe these people had taken donation claims but she feared to venture too close. She'd ask Mr. Noble about the crude buildings the next time she saw him.

She didn't have to wait as long as she'd expected because as she neared her wagon his long frame unfolded from one of the boxes by the fire pit. "Hello," he called. "I began to think you'd grown disillusioned with our little town and left."

She laughed. "And how would I go about doing that?" She watched him a moment as he sat back down, apparently with nothing in particular to say. "Did you find my things?" she asked.

His lips stiffened into a straight line as he shook his head. "Slick's not in town today. First time since I been here."

She almost felt glad. "Well! That proves he did it."

"Not for sure. But he did it all right. Those clothes weren't worth stealing. And no one else has it in for you."

Martha leaned forward on her box. "What about the clothes, Mr. Noble? Will they throw me in jail?"

His dark eyes sparkled. "This town don't have a jail. Wouldn't put you in one if they did." Still grinning, he shook his head. "I don't know what'll happen when they find out. The local sheriff don't have any deputies or help." He chuckled. "It's rumored he don't even have a gun. I guess it's up to the fellers who lost the clothes. You got nothing they could take and no money to pay so I guess you're all right." He stood up. "I'd better be gettin' back to my room." He stretched and looked at the western sky. "About to get dark, too." He took a few steps away from the wagon and turned back. "You just get a good sleep and don't worry none," he said. "I'll probably see you tomorrow."

Martha watched him, almost silhouetted by now, until he disappeared, not through the door, but around the boardinghouse. "Wonder what he goes

152

around there for?" she asked Josie. Receiving one thrash of the dog's tail for an answer, she continued. "Think he's getting tired of us?" she asked. "He seemed pretty quiet this evening." She hugged the big soft head to herself. "We can't blame him. We're causing him a lot of trouble."

Something caused Josie to give a little start. Martha released her. "All right, it's not us that's causing the trouble. It's just me. C'mon, let's go to bed."

—⁓—

Martha lay in bed, swatting at mosquitoes, when she heard men's voices. Josie bristled and a growl formed deep in her throat. Martha held the dog tight, whispering "Shhhhh" in her ear as the men stood outside the wagon, talking.

"Think she's in there?" one voice asked.

"Shore. Where else could she be?"

"Let's wake her up. She's the purtiest thing in town."

The other man snorted loudly. "Ain't a lot a wimmin to choose from, Len. But we ain't wakin' nobody up. Next time we'll just git ourselves here earlier and let the lady decide for herself which of us she likes."

Martha hardly dared breathe until the footsteps died away. Even then she feared to slap at the buzzing insects. *Please, Lord,* she pleaded silently into the darkness, *protect me until Aunt Mandy and Uncle Cleve get here. I'm getting purely scared.* She lay stiffly, controlling her breathing, for over an hour. Finally, she fell asleep holding Josie close.

Chapter 6

As Abram Noble poured oats into Charity's manger box, he thought about Miss Lawford. How could she stay so sweet and calm in the face of her problems? When he was alone, her delicate face laughed into his thoughts more often than he cared to admit. Never had he seen such bright color and depth in anyone's eyes, such utterly rich dark hair, and thin straight body. She looked young. Several years younger than her age. But that might be to her advantage right now. Few men would bother a young girl.

Charity's soft nicker interrupted his thoughts. "You want more?" he asked. "You realize I haven't ridden you once in the last week? You aren't burning up much oats that way." He forked a couple of scoops of hay into the manger. The mare nibbled contentedly while Abe closed the gate and went to his room.

———

The next morning, after breakfast, he headed to the Ball and Stone Saloon. After ordering a cup of coffee, he asked about Slick.

"Ain't seen him fer a couple o' days," the bartender said. "That's the way I like it."

Abe nodded. "Yep. Me, too, but I gotta see him. Know where he hangs out?"

The man didn't, so Abe left. He crossed the street and went into Galbraith's. Not seeing Slick, he ordered another cup of coffee. "Seen Slick around?" he asked, sipping the strong hot brew.

The man wiped the shiny board-top of the bar and shook his head. "Not for a couple o' days. Hope he's left the country."

Abe chuckled. "Well, I do and I don't. I gotta see him first. After that he don't have anything I want." He finished his coffee and headed off toward Miss Lawford's wagon. He stopped, turned around, and then headed back to the meat market. If those kinfolk didn't hurry up, that girl would be destitute. He'd help where he could. He surely did believe she'd starve before she'd take charity. Let her dog starve, too? Now that seemed a different matter. She thought more of that dog than most men did their wives.

"Why don't you just keep the paper?" he asked Chapman when the man started to wrap the rabbit.

The rustic-appearing man laughed out loud. "Abe, I took you for a man who wanted to keep things kinda clean. Losin' my knack of judgin' people, I guess." He carefully laid the paper aside for later use.

Abe couldn't help telling the man his problem with Miss Lawford. "So you see if I brought it all wrapped up, she'd refuse it right off. I don't rightly know what'll happen to that girl if her kinfolk don't get here before the snow flies."

The man winked at Abe. "You'll just have to take care of her, Abe. Now ain't that an awful pass to come to?"

Less than five minutes later, Abe walked into Miss Lawford's camp. "Did you find him?" she asked right off.

He shook his head. "Not yet, but I will. He can't get along without his booze forever." He held out the rabbit. "Guess I'm too late for your breakfast."

"Yes, but I'll put it in some water and we'll have it for supper." She flashed him a radiant smile. "I can't thank you enough, Mr. Noble. Your extra meat helps us so much." She looked into his eyes. "It *is* extra, isn't it?"

He assured her he'd had all he could eat for breakfast.

She nodded. "Good. Oh, yes, Mr. Noble. I have something I've been wanting to ask you." She pointed south and east of them. "Do you know what's going on out there? I saw some buildings. Think they could be people getting donation claims?"

He nodded thoughtfully. He needed to get busy and find the perfect spot for his claim. Why had he been dillydallying, anyway? He didn't know what, but something seemed to keep him from moving ahead with his longed-for plans. Well, yes, he did too know what. He kept trying to figure a way to get Miss Lawford on the claim next to his. It looked impossible though. She lacked a lot of years of being old enough.

Miss Lawford's voice brought Abe to the present. "Is there any way I could find out about the shacks?"

"We could go ask them."

Her face colored. "Oh, I didn't mean that. I'd be afraid to bother anyone."

He got up. "I'm not. I'll go get Charity and we'll have ourselves a little ride. She's been needing some exercise, anyway. Might be interesting." He hurried away, forgetting to say good-bye.

—⚬⚬—

The mare nickered when Abe entered the barn as if glad to see him. "Well, you're goin' to get to see a little of the country around here," he told her as he threw the saddle over her back and cinched it up. "Think you're up to a heavy load for a while?" he asked, gently inserting the bit between her teeth. Charity nuzzled his neck as he took the reins and led her out the door. Outside, he swung into the saddle as if he were used to it. And he was. He and Charity had ridden lots of miles together when he'd been in the army. He patted the shiny neck as they turned toward the wagon.

He wouldn't mind at all sitting close to Miss Lawford for a little while. He patted Charity again. "I'll be careful not to overload you, though," he whispered softly.

Then Miss Lawford and Josie ran to meet them. "He has a horse, Josie, a beautiful horse," he heard her say as they ran.

"Whoa," Abe said softly, taking the slack from the reins. When Charity stopped, he slid off. "Ready, Miss Lawford? I'll help you aboard."

Martha looked at the trim horse. "What about you, sir?" she asked.

"I'm riding, too. I wouldn't do it if you weren't so tiny, even though everyone else treats their horses that way. A horse shouldn't carry more than ten percent of its own weight. I've seen three people pile onto a horse, then force it to gallop. I've seen horses with bad swaybacks, too. I've even seen people force horses to run until they died." He stopped with a jerk. "Well, I didn't mean to get going on that," he said, puffing. "We'll just take good care of Charity here."

Miss Lawford moved back a few feet. "I can walk," she said. "Josie and I'll just walk along beside you."

"No. Charity won't mind for a little while. We won't run her and we won't go very far."

"Sure?"

"Sure. Get over here." He settled her behind the saddle, then easily swung himself up, doubling his leg as it cleared the saddle, so it didn't bump Miss Lawford. He handled the reins gently and Charity turned south. "You just put your arms around me," he said. "I got stirrups to hold me and you don't."

"We could have all walked. It isn't far at all." Miss Lawford reached her thin arms around him but Abe could barely feel her. She must be reluctant to be so close. And to touch him.

He nodded. "You just hang on tight, Miss Lawford. You could crack a bone if you fell off. I know we could have walked and enjoyed it." He grinned and wiped his forehead. "I don't know why but a horse gives a man a little authority." He leaned forward and stroked the sleek neck. "You'll be all right, won't you, girl?" He looked east and pointed. "You mean those buildings there?"

"Yes. And a few more."

Turning the mare eastward, they walked straight to one of the ramshackle buildings, Josie running and frolicking alongside. "Whoa," Abe said softly, pulling his leg awkwardly back so he wouldn't kick Miss Lawford as he slid off then helped her down. She took hold of Josie's collar.

A man, who'd been digging with a shovel, looked up. "I c'n do somethin' for you folks?" he asked.

"Yes, sir," Abe answered. "We're interested in a donation claim and wondered if that's what you have here."

The man pushed the shovel into the ground with his foot and let it stand. "Shore is." He spun around looking at the vast expanse of dried grass and tall weeds. "Ain't it a beaut though? Got me three hundred twenty acres. A year from now I'll be harvesting wheat or somethin'."

"I guess I'll have to be satisfied with one hundred sixty acres," Abe said. "But that's a lot, too."

The man glanced at Abe, then Martha, and shook his head. "You can get the same as me and my woman if you hurry. Who knows what they'll do next year?"

Abe and the man talked a few minutes discussing the steps involved in taking a donation claim, then Abe said they should be getting back.

When they reached some distance from the man's place, Abe turned the horse toward another shack south and off to the west. Charity walked sedately to the shanty and Abe climbed off. Miss Lawford slid off before he could help her, called Josie, and held her collar. A woman opened the door with a child on each side, hanging onto her skirt. "You'uns want somethin'?" she asked in a trembly voice that sounded fearful.

"We just stopped to say hello," Abe answered, hoping he sounded harmless. "I'm hoping to get a donation claim, and we're just talking to people, finding out what we can."

The woman nodded, pushing back the strands of grayish hair that had fallen loose. "That's what we got here. Rube isn't here. He could tell you about it better'n I can."

"That's all right. How can you tell where your property ends?"

The woman finally smiled. "It goes on a long ways. Three hundred twenty acres we got ourselves here."

Abe cast a glance at Miss Lawford. "Thanks for taking the time to talk to us. Maybe we'll be neighbors one of these days."

After another short ride they stopped at a raggedy tent and dismounted.

"Looks pretty quiet," Miss Lawford murmured. "I wonder if anyone's around." She took Josie's collar. For the first time the dog pulled against her and growled. Martha's hand tightened on the collar.

Just then a matted gray head poked through the canvas doorway.

"Whatcha want?" he asked.

Abe almost choked when he recognized Slick's thin voice. "We came to see you, Slick. Better come out."

After a long wait the filthy man pushed the canvas door aside and stepped out. Miss Lawford stepped back ten feet; Abe almost did, too. How the man could stand to be in a small, unventilated tent with himself, Abe couldn't imagine.

"Where are the things you took from the creek?" Abe asked.

Slick blinked. "What things you talkin' about?" he asked.

"You know what I'm talking about, Slick." Abe's voice didn't sound so harmless anymore. "You bring them out or I'm coming in after them."

Slick backed up a few feet. "I don't know what you're talking about, boy, but you got the wrong man. I been right here tryin' to git over the flu for almost a week."

Abe shoved the canvas tent door apart with both hands and stepped inside. It took a moment for his eyes to adjust, and the smell turned his stomach. Dirty clothes covered a filthy looking sleeping bag. Several tin dishes lay scattered over the dirt floor. Then he saw the tubs and bucket. Stacked neatly inside each other, they appeared to be the cleanest articles in the smelly tent. Abe grabbed them up and carried them outside. Setting them down, he backed off and took several deep breaths. "How do you stand yourself and that tent?" he asked. "That smell's enough to knock a good man down."

Slick pointed at the tubs and bucket. "What you doin' with them things?"

"We're taking them. They belong to Miss Lawford. Where's the clothes, Slick? She'll be in trouble if she doesn't return the clothes."

Slick snatched at the utensils. "Them's mine and you ain't takin 'em nowhere," he whined.

Abe met Miss Lawford's eyes. "Are they yours?"

She stepped over and looked at each one separately. "Each of my three is different, and these're just like mine. Strange he'd have three exactly like mine." She shrugged. "But I don't know."

Abe nodded. "Yep. A little too much coincidence. Look here, Slick, are you ready to stop messing with Miss Lawford? I'm about to send you out of town faster than you came in. No one in this town would cry, neither." He picked up the bucket and stack of tubs and set them down beside Charity. "Come on, Miss Lawford, let's get you up there." A moment later he picked up the things again, swung into the saddle and held the large pieces of equipment to his side. "Come on, Charity, just a little farther."

As the horse moved away, Josie, growling deep in her throat, jumped two feet toward Slick. Slick screamed. Before Abe could move, Miss Lawford hit the ground and threw herself onto the big dog.

"Josie, stop," she said, grasping the dog's collar. Josie yielded to Martha's touch, calming down. "You go on, Mr. Noble," she called. "I'll have to bring Josie."

Abe wheeled Charity around between Slick and the girl. "All right," he said softly. "You go on. I'll be right behind you." He turned to Slick, whose eyes still bulged half out of his head. "I'm not warning you again," he told the man. "This is it. Next time you cause either of us any trouble you're out of here. Come on, Charity, let's go find some air we can breathe." He turned the already prancing horse and took off at a gallop after Martha.

Chapter 7

Early the next morning, Abe brought Martha another rabbit. "Josie and I can't thank you enough," she said. "Where you getting them, anyway? I watched last night and didn't see a thing."

Abe smiled. "You think they'd come out with Josie there?"

She nodded as she cut up the meat and put it into the kettle to boil.

"Say," he said, "I found the perfect place for a claim. How'd you like to see it one of these days? It's just a little ways. You can ride Charity and I'll walk with Josie."

"Mr. Noble, why don't we both walk? I'd enjoy it. If you have that much time, that is."

"We'll see. Charity would enjoy having you ride her, though. Do you like to ride?"

Martha nodded enthusiastically. "I love to ride. But not when I make the horse's owner walk."

Abe hurried back to town. Martha took the rabbit from the water, cooled it, and divided it with Josie. After they finished she let Josie drink the cooled juice the rabbit had been cooked in. The dog licked the kettle so clean that Martha couldn't find a drop on it.

She'd just finished washing the dishes and kettle when two men rode up. The brown-and-white spotted horses they rode hardly compared with Mr. Noble's sleek bay mare.

"You the girl who's washing our clothes?" the dark whiskery one asked. Neither man dismounted.

Suddenly, Martha felt so lightheaded she had to sit on one of the boxes. Why hadn't she prepared for this meeting? It had to happen. *Help me, Lord. Show me what to say and don't let them get mad at me.* The men didn't really look mean, but everyone around looked tough. Then she noticed their filthy clothes. They owned the clothes all right. Their overalls looked just as filthy as the ones she'd lost. But what could she say? Well, Mama had always taught her the truth was the easiest and best.

She cleared her throat and hung tightly to Josie's collar. "Yes sir, I am."

The dark-haired man nodded. "Any idea when they'll be ready? Folks around here don't have too many clothes."

160

Her mother's voice spoke plainly into her ear. *Tell the man the truth, Martha!* She nodded. *Yes, Mama. You're right.* "I'm afraid I have real bad news about your clothes, sir."

The younger fellow with the light-colored, shaggy hair gave a short laugh. "What? Them clothes was so dirty they fell apart when you washed them! I figgered that'd happen."

Martha couldn't help giving him a little smile. Then she shook her head. "They didn't fall apart. They totally disappeared." Seeing their surprise, she went on. "I had to wash them at the creek because they were so dirty and took so much water. I washed them twice the day I got them then left them soaking overnight on the creek bank and when I went back the next morning they were gone. . .and I don't know what to do." She took a long deep breath.

The horses moved a little in the silence that followed Martha's outburst. She could see sympathy in the younger man's eyes. Maybe the older one, too.

"I'm sorry to hear that," the older man said. "You got any plans to find the clothes? And what ya gonna do if you can't find 'em?"

Martha found some strength and stood beside the man's horse. "I don't know yet, sir. I don't have any money. That's why I was washing clothes."

The man turned his horse. "We'll be back in a few days to see what you figgered out. When someone goes into business, 'e usually knows what 'e's doin'." He touched his horse's sides and they tore off toward the street.

Martha released Josie's collar. "Well, what's going to happen to us?" she asked the shaggy dog. "I guess they still don't have a jail." She went inside the wagon and looked at the calendar she'd made. She checked off today. *Thanks for being with me, God. I was purely scared. Are you watching over Aunt Mandy and Uncle Cleve, Lord? They should be here by now, and I'm getting into a worse mess all the time. Please bring them soon. I need them, and Jackson, too.* She didn't know if Jackson, her older brother, had met the wagon train her uncle, aunt, and cousin were with. He should have by now. He really should have, and they should be coming down off the Blue Mountains already.

That night, rain splattering on the wagon canopy woke Martha. She snuggled deeper into her covers. Hopefully the top would keep her dry. It had before during a light rain. Then she remembered the times every wagon had to be emptied so everything could be set out to dry. What a mess! She dropped her arm over Josie who slept beside her, and fell back to sleep.

But she awakened again sometime later, cold and wet. She couldn't do anything in the dark and had no place to go where she'd be out of the rain. She pulled Josie into her bed and put Josie's rug over them. The dog helped warm her some, and the rug helped a little, but before long both dog and girl were thoroughly chilled. As she lay holding the dog close, she wondered what she'd do in the morning.

She must have fallen asleep, for she awakened with a start to face daylight. A moment later she noticed she didn't hear rain anymore. "What are we going to do, Josie?" she asked her wet but warm pet. "At least you don't have to put on cold, wet clothes. Well, you don't, because you're wearing them."

"Are you in there, Miss Lawford?" Mr. Noble's soft voice called through the soaked cloth wagon top.

Oh, oh. Now she not only had to get into wet clothes but she had to do it in a hurry. "I'm here," she called. "I'll be out in a minute." Josie didn't have anything holding her back so she jumped down, eager to greet her new friend.

Martha could hardly bear to take off her warm wet nightgown and put on her cold, wet clothes. Everything stuck to her but she finally got changed. Then she brushed her hair, braided it, and put it up.

Martha jumped to the ground to find it had turned to mud during the downpour. After a quick feeling of defeat she looked up to find Mr. Noble watching her.

"I knew you'd get soaked," he said. "You can't stay out here much longer you know. It's going to rain a few times, then it'll turn to snow." He had a rabbit in his hand but didn't offer it to her. "You're freezing right now, aren't you? Come to the boardinghouse with me before you catch pneumonia."

She couldn't do that! She couldn't get more indebted to this man than she already was. She'd been writing down all the meat he brought and what she thought it would be worth if she'd bought it. But she'd never be able to pay a boardinghouse bill. Never!

"I'll be just fine," she said, trying to smile through chattering teeth. "As soon as I get a fire going I'll get warm." She pointed toward the east. "The sun's going to shine, too. Just you wait and see."

"Let me help you get the fire started then." He jumped into the wagon, returning a moment later with a handful of buffalo chips. After Abe worked for some time, the chips caught fire. Wordlessly, he picked the rabbit off the box he'd laid it on and handed it to her.

She washed the rabbit and cut it up, then dumped it into the kettle to cook.

"Do you get tired of eating the same thing all the time?"

She flashed a nice smile. "When I'm not so impoverished I'll worry about getting tired of something. Right now I'm happy to have anything for Josie and me to eat." She sat down on the box, hoping the fire would dry her clothes.

He sat down on the other box. "I hate to bring this up, Miss Lawford, but it seems to me your kin should be here by now. Anytime now the Blue Mountains will be blocked with snow, lots of snow. It might have snowed up there last night."

Martha's heart shrank a little in her chest. She knew, even better than he did, what a terrible position she was in. She couldn't hold back a strong burst of shivering. "I don't know where they are, but they have to come soon. They just have to." She blinked hard. She wouldn't cry. Not in front of Mr. Noble.

He got to his feet. "I'm leaving for a while. I'll be back." He stood quietly, just looking at her for a moment. "You have to face the facts, Miss Lawford. If you insist on staying here in the wagon, I'll come out here some morning and find you with pneumonia or worse. As if you aren't in enough trouble, you're out of chips." He turned and strode toward his boardinghouse.

Chapter 8

Abe slammed up to his room, hardly seeing Nellie and not speaking as he passed her. He tipped up one side of the chiffonier and grabbed his money pouch from under it. Dropping to the bed, he dumped the contents on the smooth quilt. Barely noticing the gold pieces, Abe's mind was filled with the vision of Miss Lawford's delicate but cold form. He'd never seen anyone so brave—man, woman, or child. Those brilliant blue eyes had sparkled with unshed tears this morning but she'd held them back.

His eyes clouded as he wondered if she were crying now with no one but Josie to see and comfort her. He simply couldn't handle the way things were going for Martha Lawford. Something had to be done. Now!

He sat up and stacked his $100 gold pieces in piles of ten. He hadn't used any of them since he got here so he still had thirty. Then his $50 nuggets. Nine of those. His paper money and coins added up to $337. He pulled out a piece of paper and pencil and added his figures–$3,787. And then there was the $490 he kept in the top drawer as a decoy. He gave all the pieces an angry shove, jumbling them together. He had plenty of money to last until he could begin making more. Why couldn't he use some of it to help Miss Lawford? Ever since he'd met the girl he'd thought of almost nothing else. She was everything he'd ever wanted in a woman, so why was she sitting outside in the cold and rain while he had a warm dry room?

"Show me how, Lord," he cried. "I don't want her to suffer or get sick and die! You don't, either, Lord. I know You don't! Please show me how to help her."

Sadly shoving his money back into the pouch, he once again lifted the chiffonier and laid the bag under so it didn't show. He sat on the edge of the bed, his chin cupped in his hands and his elbows on his knees, deep in thought.

You could marry her, Abe. He could marry her! He could marry her and take care of her! In his elation, he jumped to his feet.

Then he sank back to the bed. What made him think she'd ever have him? She was scared to death of men—the sex to which he had to claim membership. More than once she'd shrunk away from him when he'd accidentally touched her. And she'd never given him the slightest reason to think she felt anything for him, other than gratitude.

"That's not it, Lord. She'd never do it. Even if she wasn't fearful, she's plenty proud. She'd call it charity." He shook his head thinking about it. There had to be another way.

You really could marry her. He shook his head again.

Then a new thought popped up. The I and R building wasn't occupied. Maybe he could rent that for her and fix it up. "Yeah!" he said out loud, finally wearing a wide smile. "Thanks, Lord," he said, not realizing the Lord hadn't said anything about renting a building for her.

But the owner of the building planned to open his own business in it almost immediately.

Abe left, dejected. As he crossed back to his place he decided he might as well check on Miss Lawford to see if he could do anything to help her dry out her wagon and things.

When he turned west, he thought his eyes were playing tricks on him— three wagons stood where only one had this morning. Probably her kinfolks! He tore off to the wagons at top speed, trying to decide if he really was all that happy they'd come. Would she decide she didn't need him anymore?

Arriving, he found several children playing around the wagons, ten oxen grazing on the nearly dried grass and weeds, and four adults talking to Miss Lawford. Several substantial pieces of wood lay on the ground beside the blazing fire. Every sturdy weed in the area supported some article of clothing or bedding.

"Hello, Mr. Noble," Miss Lawford called. "Come meet my new friends."

He soon learned Miss Lawford hadn't known them until an hour or two ago. "Where you headin'?" he asked after a while.

The men laughed cheerfully. "We ain't heading nowheres," the short one said. "We just found it. Ain't this what they call the land of many waters?"

Abe nodded. "Reckon as how some do. Got several streams running around the place. It's also called Steptoeville or Waiilapptu."

"We're collecting us some donation land claims," Wilford, the tall one said. "Miss Martha tells us we can get three hundred twenty acres each. That's enough for us."

"Did you folks get wet last night?" Abe asked.

The women shook their heads. "We spent the night near the burned out mission. Nary a drop did it rain." She smiled at Miss Lawford and patted her arm. "Sure got Martha, though."

Unkind thoughts skittered around in Abe's mind. *These people just arrived this morning. How did they have the right to call Miss Lawford by her Christian name already? Did she invite them to? She sure hadn't told him he could.* He forced his mind back to the company. "I see you got your things drying, Miss Lawford," he said. "Sure hope it don't rain again until your kin gets here." He turned to the standing men again. "I guess you folks don't know anything about her kinfolk's wagon train."

They both shook their heads. "No," Wilford said. "We just come from the Willamette Valley. I reckon we'll be finding us some claims and moving onto 'em purty soon. Gonna have to work fast to get cabins built before bad weather comes."

Abe nodded. "Sure are. I'm doing the same thing. Gotta quit messing around and get busy myself." He started away from the wagon. "See you again, Miss Lawford. Glad you're getting dried out."

"Thanks again, Mr. Noble," Miss Lawford said. She giggled softly. "I'd likely be dead if you hadn't helped me so much."

—∞—

Those people would no doubt be telling Miss Lawford right now to watch out for him, he thought, rushing back to his room. He sat in the rickety rocking chair in the corner of the room, thinking.

He really should go ahead and get his claim settled and build his own cabin.

Marry her, Abe. Abe thoroughly liked the idea. That would solve all their joint problems. She'd be able to get a claim now while they were still available. She wouldn't be out in the cold and rain with nothing to eat. He'd be able to care for her as he longed to do. It hurt him deep inside to see her suffering so. Then with a shock he realized he loved her! He'd loved her almost since they first met.

He looked up and discovered he'd been rocking furiously. Slowing to a sensible pace, he smiled. He loved Martha! What a beautiful name for a beautiful girl, inside and out. A girl with plenty of pluck. He shook his head. He couldn't file his claim without her. He'd talk to her the first time he got her alone.

Then he remembered he'd promised to take her to the spot he'd found for the claim. Maybe he could get her away from the others to go look. He grabbed his hat, tore down the stairs, and ran out the door.

"I just remembered inviting you to go see a purty parcel of land," he said when she came to meet him. They'd stopped a few feet from the others. "Think you could get away for a little while to see it?"

She glanced toward the others and shook her head. "I don't know. What do you think?"

He smiled into her sincere blue eyes. "I dunno," he said. "Are you entertaining them? Or are they just waiting to file their claims?"

She grabbed his arm. "Can we go right now?" He nodded. "I'll be back in a little while," she called to the people around her wagon. "Come on, Josie."

He led her south of the buildings, then east behind them. "It's right on Mill Creek," he said, cutting back southeast.

In a few minutes they stood on the bank of the small stream. Trees lined the creek bank almost until it reached the street. Probably people had cut those in the way of the street. He turned south and held his arms out to his sides, his hands facing the property. His heart thrilled every time he stood in that spot. "Well, what do you think?" he asked.

She looked. She looked up and down the creek, then her eyes moved over the large expanse of land. "It's the most beautiful piece of land I've ever laid eyes on," she said quietly. "I purely wish I could get a piece right beside you. Oh, how I wish I were twenty-one!"

Abe wanted more than anything in the world to ask her to marry him. And she'd made it so easy. He could tell her she could have her one hundred sixty acres right now. He could tell her he'd take care of her forever. He could tell her he loved her! Her deep blue eyes gazed into his, her full lips slightly parted, waiting. But he couldn't get the words past the mountain-sized lump in his throat. He tried several times but nothing came out.

"Come on," he finally croaked. "Let's get you back to your friends."

Leaving her just before they reached the other people, Abe decided he might as well look around some more; at least he'd be giving Charity some exercise.

Chapter 9

Martha stood where Mr. Noble had left her and watched him stride down the street. He'd been in a strange mood. First he'd been jolly and talkative, then he hushed right up. She hoped she hadn't offended him in some way. Well, she'd better get back to her new friends.

"Say, is that fellow more than a friend?" Mr. Tynnon asked. He shoved his stringy blond hair back and grinned at Martha.

She shook her head. "Just a friend, but the best friend anyone could have. Why do you ask?"

Mrs. Tynnon stepped over to Martha. "Honey, didn't you see how he looked at you? That man had stars in his eyes."

Martha shrugged. "You misread him, Mrs. Tynnon. He's just a really good man."

"Why did he have to take you off alone then?" Mrs. Nelson asked. "He's sweet on you, young lady, and a mighty fine looking man he is, too. You won't find any better in a small place like this. Maybe not anywhere."

"Mind if we stay the night here with you?" Mr. Tynnon asked. "Tomorrow we can find our claims and get out of your way."

"That would be nice," Mrs. Tynnon added. "We could get—Timothy, drop those clothes!"

Martha looked to see the little boy dragging across the muddy grass most of her clothes as well as her bedding with Josie on the other end. She jumped up and rescued them. She put them away before they got dirtier. Shoving them into the wagon, she decided she could fold them later.

"I'm sorry I can't invite you for supper," she told the visitors. "I have only a wee bit of flour to eat. I mix it with water and call it trail bread, but I have only about a quart left."

Mrs. Nelson made a face. "That's all right," she said too quickly. "We'll just share the fire. You go ahead first, child, and when you're through we'll cook our meal."

Embarrassed, Martha mixed some water into half her flour and cooked it in her pot.

"That stuff smells funny," one of the children said as it cooked; his mother told him to hush.

When the bread was ready, Martha divided it with Josie, who gulped it down without complaint. Just as Martha had finished eating, the two men whose clothes she'd lost rode up.

"Howdy," the older one said, tipping his ragged, filthy hat. "Your kin-folks finally got here, I see."

Martha shook her head. "No, these folks came from Oregon City. My aunt and uncle will be here in a few days."

Mrs. Tynnon smiled again. "In the morning we're going to find ourselves some donation land claims."

"Congratulations, I'm sure." He reined his horse around until he faced Martha again. "What have you figured out, Miss Lawford?"

Martha shook her head. "I didn't find the clothes. . .and I still don't have any money." Suddenly, she remembered her father's clothes in the wagon. Although she felt sentimental about them, she certainly didn't need them. She looked up at the big dark-haired man and smiled. "I have some clothes in the wagon you might be able to use."

Not a flicker of emotion crossed his face as he said, "Get them."

Martha clambered into the wagon, shoved aside the bunch of clothes and bedding she'd just put in, and opened the tattered black trunk. Her throat clogged as she pulled out two pairs of dress pants, three dress shirts, underwear, and five pairs of black dress socks. Hugging the garments to her chest, she realized once again that Papa would never again be with her in this world. *I needed him so much, Lord,* she cried silently. *When am I going to see some signs of the love I know You have for me?* She swallowed, secured a tighter grip on the clothes, and jumped to the ground.

The young blond man hadn't said a word, just sat quietly on his nervously moving horse. But when she handed the clothes to the older man the younger one burst into loud laughter. "I can just see you in that stuff," he howled through his glee.

The big man said nothing until he'd sorted through each and every garment. When he finished, he shoved the clothes back toward Martha. "Ain't a thing there a man'd wear," he growled. "Looks like preacher clothes."

Martha shook her head. "They're not," she whispered. "Those were my father's clothes. He was a farmer and these were his Sunday clothes. Don't you wear Sunday clothes sometimes?"

"Not like that stuff!" the younger man said, still laughing.

The older man glared at her for a moment, then his face softened. "I see you got the tubs back." She nodded. "The clothes weren't in them no more?"

Martha swallowed hard. "We found the tubs in a man's tent but the clothes weren't there. We'd have taken them if we'd found them."

"Know the man's name?"

She nodded again, then wondered if she should tell. Why not? She couldn't think of any reason to protect Slick. No reason at all. "He's called Slick. That's all I know. I think Mr. Noble knows his name, though. He lives at Martin's Boardinghouse." She pointed south. "Slick's living in a tent out that way."

The man wheeled his horse away from the group. "Thanks," he grunted as the horse burst into a gallop. The younger man touched his horse's sides and took off after his friend, or father, or whatever he was. Martha shuddered as they headed south.

Martha carried the clothes back into the wagon and repacked them in the trunk. She could tell that her friends wanted to know what the men wanted but she said nothing.

Noticing the women preparing food, she climbed back into her wagon and put away her clothes and bedding. She fervently hoped she'd not have to endure another rainy night like she had last night while she still lived in the wagon. She jumped to the ground and saw a kettle on the fire, boiling briskly and starting to fill the area with a tantalizing fragrance. She asked what they were cooking.

"It's just a soup," Mrs. Tynnon said. "We put in some wild onions we gathered near The Dalles, some potatoes we brought from Oregon City, and dried meat and salt. Nothing special."

A little while later they called the four children and began serving up the soup, the most delicious food Martha had ever smelled in her entire life. When she decided they weren't going to offer her any, and Josie began running from one to another, begging, she called the dog and took off down the street. Just smelling the food wasn't very satisfying for either of them. She put her arm around her faithful friend's neck as they walked. "I'm sorry, Josie, but those people didn't want us to have any. You just wait. One of these days you'll have all you want."

She turned right, walked past the empty building on the end of the street, and followed the creek as it turned east to the spot where she and Mr. Noble had stood earlier today. Yes! This was exactly where she'd want her farm. Exactly here. She'd put her house right over there on that little mound where it would be high and the grass would never grow brown. She looked in every direction, trying to imagine how far one hundred sixty acres would go. A long, long way.

Facing the creek, the only thing she didn't like was the sight to her left of the old abandoned Fort Walla Walla buildings. What would happen to those buildings, anyway?

She sighed and turned back to face the land Abe had shown her. How could the Garden of Eden have been more beautiful? She'd love to have this piece of ground. But it would surely be taken before she turned twenty-one. Then she laughed out loud. This place already belonged to Mr. Noble. He'd shown it to her in the first place. She cast her eyes eastward. The next place would be just as good. She'd be perfectly satisfied with it. She'd enjoy being Mr. Noble's neighbor, too. But all the good places would be taken within four years.

"You like it?"

Martha jerked around to find Mr. Noble standing behind her, looking over her shoulder at the land spreading before them. She nodded. "I even figured where to put my house before I remembered this is your piece of Washington Territory."

He swallowed and looked at her as if he were in pain. . .just as he had this afternoon. He didn't reply.

"Are you all right, sir?"

He still didn't answer but stood looking across the expanse of grass, weeds, and the few trees along the stream, his Adam's apple jiggling spasmodically. Finally, he met her eyes and smiled. "Show me where you'd build your cabin."

She laughed, a happy tinkling sound. "I said I'd build a house, sir, not a cabin." She laughed again, joyously, and ran to the small rolling knoll she'd thought to build on. "Right here," she called, standing in the middle. "Don't you think this is a good place?"

He nodded but said nothing.

"You don't like it, do you?" she asked, realizing she felt unreasonably disappointed. What difference did it make to her where he built his house . . .cabin?

After hesitating, he nodded again. "I do like it, Miss Lawford, but I thought I'd build a couple hundred feet farther up the creek." He beckoned with his hand and she followed him, feeling nice and warm in the autumn sun and realizing the luxury of the feeling.

He finally stopped on another small rise. "How's this?" he asked, his soft brown eyes boring into hers.

She nodded. "Fine, except there aren't any trees."

"I'll plant some," he said, his eyes starting to get their usual sparkle again. "Fruit trees, shade trees, and whatever else you. . . I mean I want."

Martha couldn't be sure but she thought Mr. Noble's tanned face turned rosy. "I don't know much about trees," she said, "but I like these that our Lord planted. They look just right."

He nodded. "I think they're locust trees. I could probably find some small ones and bring them over here and replant them. I'd have to do it a little later when they're sleeping."

"That sounds good. Well, Josie and I'd better be getting back to the wagon." She met his soft brown eyes again. "I'm not sure why but I like it alone better than with those folks."

"They leaving soon?"

"Tomorrow they say."

"All right. I'll probably see you then." He hesitated a moment, then turned to follow her. "I might as well see you get back to the wagon safe."

Neither talked as they walked behind the buildings, Josie running circles around them. Martha's thoughts kept going back to one pint of flour and no buffalo chips. And those people knew it and didn't offer her anything at all. But they had a lot of people to feed, and maybe they didn't have much food either. Maybe.

Mr. Noble stopped before they reached the wagons. "I'll go back now," he said. "I hope you'll enjoy your guests tonight."

"Thanks," she said. "Goodbye." She turned, dreading to have to spend the evening with the Nelsons and Tynnons. Maybe she'd go to bed early. Last night had been bad and she hadn't gotten much sleep.

"Well," Mrs. Nelson said with apparent glee, "look who brought you home."

"What did he do, take you out for an ice cream?" Mr. Tynnon asked.

Martha laughed. "I'm afraid you won't find any ice cream in Steptoeville. This is just a little western settlement. Maybe some day you'll find fancy things, but not yet." She stretched. "I hope you won't mind if I go to bed early. I didn't get much sleep last night and I'm tired. Come on, Josie."

The next morning Martha built a fire with the newcomers' wood and made the last of her flour into trail bread, trying to forget the lovely smells from last night. As always, she shared her meager meal with Josie, who swallowed the small bit and begged for Martha's half. Martha chucked it down as quickly as she could. "I'd give it to you, Josie," she whispered, "but I'm already weak from not eating."

The occupants from the other wagons still slept, so Martha and Josie walked to the creek again, following it south then east for some distance. The bright sun on her shoulders made her feel good even though she literally didn't know from where her next meal would come.

They walked farther east than she and Mr. Noble had last night and she found trees bordering the creek again. Trying to see everything, she decided this land was even prettier than Mr. Noble's.

After she felt completely alone, she knelt by the bubbling stream.

"Thank You for the warm sunshine, Lord," she said out loud. Josie came and sat beside her, licking her closest cheek. "Two days ago I didn't appreciate it but now I realize what a precious blessing it is. Six months ago I didn't even appreciate good food, but I do now. Oh, I really do now. Lord, You know how it is with me and I know You have something planned so Josie and I won't starve, but we're both hungry now. We'll try our best to be patient if that's what You want, and if we're doing something to displease You, show us, Lord, so we can stop. I love You, God, and purely want to please You. Thank You for Your past care, and Your future care, too. We pray in Jesus' name. Amen."

She sat on the bank of the creek, her arms wrapped around her knees, enjoying the busy sound of the stream rushing over the rocks, the bird calls from the meadow floor, and the warm sun on her back.

Somehow her mind went back to the long, long trip over the Oregon Trail. She thought of the times when they traveled several days without water, without either water or feed for the stock. And the times the oxen dropped in their harnesses and died on the spot. And the crossings of the Snake River. They'd thought that some of the other streams were hard, but they didn't know hard until they crossed the mighty Snake.

They'd lost a yoke of oxen when it had been swept down the wild stream, and one wagon had been turned over and destroyed. But worst of all was that a little five-year-old boy had drowned. A little boy she'd played with and helped care for during the entire trip.

Just before that, Mama had sickened, and then Papa had come down with it the day before Mama had died. He'd never known she died. In fact, he'd thought Martha had been Mama the last day of his life.

Martha bowed her head into the circle of her arms as they lay on her knees. *It's been hard, Lord. And it's still bad. What should I do? Even out here in nowhere land there has to be a way to get food for Josie and me. I'm willing to work hard. Just show me, Lord, and I'll do it. Anything.*

She sat quietly until Josie nuzzled her arm and made a sound half between a bark and a growl. Martha lifted her head and laughed. "You're telling me to get up and get going, aren't you, Josie? Well, let's go." She scrambled to her feet, giving the big dog several pats in passing, then pulled up her skirts and took off running back toward town. She'd stop at every business and ask for work.

She found rough men in every building. The two whose clothes she'd lost seemed to own the tin shop. They, as well as all the rest acted like gentlemen, and expressed sorrow over having to decline her application for work. Most of them ran their own businesses and barely made a living without hiring anyone.

The barkeeps told her they'd be afraid to hire her for her own safety, that there weren't half a dozen women in town. When she left the last building, feeling depressed, she noticed her wagon stood alone.

"Josie," she said, taking off running, "they're gone." She stopped running and stood looking at her wagon. "I didn't think I'd ever be happy to be alone, but I am." She hurried to the wagon. Then she remembered she had nothing to eat and no way to make a fire even if Mr. Noble brought her something. "At least we'll be alone so we can starve in peace, won't we, Josie?" she asked, still feeling lighthearted for some strange reason. She had no food, she'd just learned there was no work for her in Steptoeville, and she felt happy? She remembered reading in the Bible how the birds didn't work, nor the lilies of the field, but God took care of them. Then it went on to say how much more valuable people are than birds or flowers. That meant her. God loved her more than the birds or lilies.

She sat down on one of the dynamite boxes to rest, feeling she'd had a busy morning although she'd done nothing but learn there was no work for her. . .and remember the awful trip west. She fell deep into her thoughts again and didn't hear the horses until they almost reached her.

"Whoa, Charity," Mr. Noble's soft voice murmured. "You got no call to be skittish with Sampson." He stepped down from the saddle and led the two horses up to the wagon.

Martha met him. "You have another horse, Mr. Noble. It's beautiful just like Charity."

Mr. Noble smiled. "Nah, he ain't like Charity. She's a lady through and through. He's just an old nag I picked up."

Chapter 10

In his excitement, Abe's legs barely held him up. In the few days he'd been looking, he'd been lucky to find another horse of Charity's quality. Darker than Charity and with a creamy mane, tail, and socks, the horse made a pretty sight. Martha had to like him. He stood two hands taller than Charity and, though spirited, he'd be easy for her to ride.

"Come ride with me," he said, holding his breath for fear she'd refuse. He'd made up his mind that today he'd ask her to marry him. No matter what, he'd do it this time.

She shook her head. "I don't know if I should," she said. "Besides, you don't have a sidesaddle."

"A sidesaddle? Come on, Miss Lawford. No one out here uses a sidesaddle. Don't you know they're dangerous? That dress you have on is plenty full to be perfectly modest."

Miss Lawford's clear blue eyes looked questioning as though it might not be proper.

"I have something important to do," he said, hoping to tempt her. "Somebody beat Slick Collier almost to death. I found him in front of the saloon this morning and hauled him out to Fort Walla Walla. I need to see if he's still alive."

Miss Lawford's eyes opened wide, her face paled, then her hand flew to her mouth.

"Why do you act like that?" he asked.

She opened her mouth to speak then shook her head. "I better come with you," she said. "Will you teach me to ride straddle?"

Abe laughed. "You'll know how right off, and wonder how you ever stayed on that sidesaddle. After one ride you'll never sit one of them crazy things again."

"Let's get me on then. Is the horse friendly?"

"Yeah, he's great." He met her eyes for just a second. "Don't think I'd let you ride him if he wasn't, do you? Here, put your left foot in the stirrup and I'll boost you as you swing up." She did as he instructed and sat in the saddle as if she'd been riding straddle forever.

Sampson danced a little but quieted when she gently firmed the reins and talked to him. "I feel as if I'm on top of the world," she said to Abe. "He's awfully big."

Feeling secure in the way she handled the big chestnut, Abe mounted Charity. "How you doing? Want to take it easy for a while?" he called over his shoulder to Miss Lawford.

"Oh, Mr. Noble, I love him. I purely love him. We're doing fine and we're ready to do whatever you do."

Abe touched Charity's sides with his knees. "Come on, girl, let's hurry," he said softly. The sleek horse stretched her front feet forward into a long lope that covered the ground in a hurry. Behind him, Miss Lawford called Josie to come along. The less than two miles would have been a nice run for the horses, but after a half-mile Abe reigned Charity in and Miss Lawford and Sampson slowed beside him.

"I love Sampson," she said, "and I love the speed, but I'm glad we slowed because Josie's not strong enough right now to run very far."

In a few minutes the dog caught up and trotted beside Miss Lawford and Sampson, her tongue hanging out the side of her mouth. No need to mention that Josie was the reason Abe had slowed to a walk.

"How far out is Fort Walla Walla?" Miss Lawford asked.

"We're almost there," Abe replied.

"Do you have any idea what happened to Slick?" she asked.

He shook his head. "Someone beat him to a bloody mess. Beyond that, not a hunch. Do you know something?" She didn't answer, but he had a gut feeling she did. Why didn't she tell him?

As they rode quietly along, he stole quick peeks at her. Just the curve of her chin and neck left him breathless, as did the long dark lashes over her bright eyes. "You ride like you been riding straddle forever," he said. "How d'you like it?"

"You're right. It's the way to ride." She looked behind them. "Come on, Josie, just a little farther."

Abe saw the Fort Walla Walla buildings and pointed. "There's the fort. We're here already."

In a few minutes someone invited them into one of the log buildings and called a doctor to talk to them. They waited on a rough bench in a big room with tables, probably the eating hall. Several braided rugs covered most of the unfinished wooden floor.

Finally, a very tall man dressed in buckskins and having long brown hair that curled on the ends, a full beard, and a thick mustache approached. "You related to Slick Collier?"

"No, I'm the one who found him and brought him out here. Didn't know what else to do with him. How is he?"

The doctor shook his head. "I didn't find any broken bones, but he's barely breathing. I guess we'll just have to let him rest and see what happens." He stopped and drew a couple of breaths. "Learn anything about what happened?"

Abe shook his head then glanced at Martha. . .Miss Lawford. Why did he keep using her Christian name in his mind? Pretty soon he'd do it to her face and that might mess things up. And why didn't she tell the man what she knew?

She said nothing.

"How long before you have an idea whether he'll make it?" Abe asked.

The doctor shrugged. "Dunno. Maybe tomorrow, maybe a week."

Abe got to his feet and shook hands with the doctor again. "We'll probably be back tomorrow."

—⁂—

As Martha and Abe took their time returning to the wagon, Josie, who had recovered some, trotted beside the horses. "Think Josie'd stay at the wagon if we went for a longer ride?" Abe asked when they neared Steptoeville.

She shook her head. "Not unless we tied her or something. She thinks she's my guard."

When they reached Miss Lawford's wagon, Abe looped the horses' reins over the tongue of the wagon. "I got a couple of things to ask you about," he said. "You got time to talk?"

She laughed. "No, I'm sorry, sir, but I have a formal ball to attend tonight. Would you like to make an appointment for next week?"

He grinned back at her, turned the boxes upright, and shoved one toward her. "Sassy little thing, ain't you? Well, I need to hear what you know about Slick's accident."

She sighed, hesitated a moment, then answered. "I thought you'd ask me before the day ended." She wound her hands around each other then released them. "I don't know for sure, but I have an idea." She told him about the men whose clothes Slick had stolen, and about her telling them who'd taken them and where he lived. "It looks like they beat him, don't you think?"

"No!" Abe said, louder than he meant to. "Those boys are tough but they'd never hurt anyone." But even as he denied it, he came to feel she was right. "Well, what do we do about it?" he asked.

"I don't know what happened," Miss Lawford said. "Why don't you talk to the men?"

Abe thought a moment, then shook his head. After all, he'd given Slick a licking, too. Slick seemed to provoke a man to do that. First and foremost

177

in his mind was what he wanted to ask Miss Lawford. He grinned. "Maybe I'll just let it alone. Slick kind of affects people that way. If a chap has only two sets of clothes it might not set all that well to have someone steal one of them."

She nodded, looking as though she were a million miles away. He got up. "Reckon we could go for a walk?" he asked.

"Sure. Where?"

"I don't care."

She hopped from her box and took off south; after passing the buildings, she veered east.

Abe followed and Josie trailed after him. A few minutes later, they reached Mill Creek. She followed it south until it turned east and then followed it some more.

Finally, she stopped. "This is where I want my claim," she announced. "Right beside yours."

Abe felt his heart give an extra thump, then sat down on some clean rocks. He patted the rocks beside him. "Come, sit down. I need to talk to you."

She complied, then looked into his eyes. "Sounds serious."

He shook his head. "It's a serious subject, but that doesn't mean bad. In fact, it's good. The nicest thing I've thought about for a long time. No, it's the nicest thing I've thought about. . .ever." He stopped for breath hoping she'd say something to help him, but she didn't.

"I've kinda grown used to you in the last little while," he started out. He stopped. That sounded like getting used to new shoes. Maybe shoes that hurt his feet at first. He'd better tell her how he felt about her or she'd never accept him.

He cleared his throat and started over again. "I mean, Miss Lawford, that I. . .do I have to keep calling you Miss Lawford forever? What's wrong with Martha and Abe?"

She giggled and tossed a small rock. "Martha and Abe are good. I like them just fine." The rock disappeared into a deep pool, sending out ripples to both banks.

Hope spread through his chest like the ripples from the stone. Maybe this wouldn't be so hard after all. He'd just spit out the plain words and see how she took them. He cleared his throat again. What if she said no? What if she hated the thought of it? What if she hated him?

Well, he'd never know until he asked. He pulled in an extra deep breath and rubbed a shiny circle on a round, whitish stone. "I've been thinking about you a lot lately," he finally managed. "I've been wondering . . .I've been. . . What are you planning to eat now that your food is gone and your buffalo chips, too?" As soon as the words left his mouth he hated himself for them. That could completely cloud the issue. He wasn't asking her to marry him because she was going to starve. He loved her and wanted to care for her the rest of their lives.

Her ivory complexion lightened almost to white, and she shook her head slowly. Picking up a head of dry grass, she tossed it into the water. After a time that seemed forever, her brilliant eyes met his. After a serious moment, she smiled and a twinkle crept back into her eyes. "I guess I'm going out somewhere and starve to death. Josie will go with me. She's hungrier and skinnier and weaker than I am." She reached both hands behind her and leaned on them, thinking. "Truly what am I going to do? I don't know. My uncle and aunt are way, way overdue. Maybe they'll come this afternoon."

Abe wanted to lay his large brown hand over her small white one, on the smooth rock. But he resisted the temptation. "You can't spend your life watching down the Trail for your kinfolks." He wiped the sweat from his forehead, knowing the day wasn't that warm. This was the time for him to ask her, but he didn't want her to think his proposal came from sympathy. *Good going, Noble. You just demolished the most important moment of your life.* He raised his eyes to find her looking at him with a question mark in hers.

"Martha," he spluttered. Then he rushed on before he had a chance to think up any more stupid ideas. "I want to marry you," he blurted, so quickly she probably couldn't even understand his words.

Chapter 11

Martha couldn't believe her ears. It had sounded as though Abe wanted to marry her! She watched a large brown bird, probably an eagle, circling in the clear blue sky above them. Abram Noble would never ask her to marry him! Never! Yes, she'd misunderstood his garbled words. She met his eyes. "I'm sorry," she said softly. "I'm afraid I didn't hear your last words."

Mr. Noble sighed, then hesitated, as though unable to repeat it. Terror shot through Martha's veins like boiling water. He had! She'd heard him right the first time. He'd asked her to marry him!

"Uh, I asked you to marry me," he mumbled again. He jerked in a quick breath and went on. "I love you, Miss. . .I love you, Martha. I've loved you since I first laid eyes on you. Marry me and we'll build a house right here on the creek."

For some reason, she had to struggle for each breath. She'd never known a nicer man in her life, and she purely liked Abram Noble a whole lot. But she'd read lots of books. When she fell in love, she expected to see fireworks, hear bells ring, trumpets blare, flutes trill; then she'd feel a pink cloud wrap tightly around her. But right now she heard only a donkey braying down the street, and saw a puff of dust blowing across the creek.

Finally, she lifted her eyes to discover his kindly brown ones staring at her, apprehension etched in his entire face. How could she hurt him? He'd been so good to her. "I'm so shocked I don't know what to say," she whispered. "I had no idea. I had no idea at all. Could I have a little while to think about it?"

A small degree of relief relaxed his face. "Sure. You think as long as you want." He struggled to his feet and gave her a hand up. Neither said a word as they strolled back to her wagon; both hearts were too full.

As they reached their destination, he turned to leave. "See you later," he said in a muted voice as he walked off.

Martha dropped heavily to one of the dynamite boxes. Josie crowded against Martha, leaning her big head in Martha's lap. "What do you think of that?" Martha asked the big dog. She waited a moment then went on. "There never was a nicer man. But I have to be in love before I marry, so

180

don't go getting excited about it." She sat staring off into the blue, wondering how she could tell him without hurting him, her hands idly caressing Josie's rough fur.

Then an entire new line of thought came to her. If she married Mr. Noble she wouldn't have a thing to worry about anymore. She'd have plenty to eat, a nice home. Josie would have enough to eat, too, the first time in a long time. She'd probably have a horse of her own. . . .Sampson. As she thought about it she realized that Mr. Noble had no doubt bought Sampson mostly for her. Oh, what a nice man!

But she didn't love him! She'd read books about girls that married men for their money. She'd never do that to any man but especially not to Mr. . . . Abe. He was too fine a man to treat that way. *Oh, Lord,* she cried silently, *help me tell him without hurting him. I know you wouldn't want me to marry him for convenience, and I don't want to. But Lord, I'm in about as bad a position as a girl can get into. You know of course, but I'll tell You anyway. I don't have any food or fire to cook it with if I had it. Won't You help me get something to eat? Thank You, in Jesus' Name. Amen.*

After praying, she felt really hungry. Before, she'd been able to put it from her mind somehow, but now her stomach rumbled and she felt ravenous. Almost instantly she thought of the gun in the wagon. She didn't know how to shoot it but maybe she could learn. But, if she managed to kill something, how would she cook it? Her eyes fell on the myriad of large weeds surrounding her. Maybe they'd burn! She laughed. They'd probably burn like paper and be gone almost instantly.

Well, she might as well give it a try. Dragging the gun from the wagon, she sat down on a box and examined it. She had to put a shell in it but had no idea where. After looking at it for a while, she put it back in the wagon. She'd never figure it out alone. Maybe she could go ahead and gather up some of the weeds and see how they burned.

Show me what to do, Lord. Thank You for caring for Josie and me. Before she said "Amen," she saw a figure coming toward the wagon. Nellie Martin! And she held something in her hand. "Thank You, Lord," she said aloud. "I know You've answered my need as soon as I asked." She hurried to meet Nellie. "Hello," she called. "You don't know how glad I am to see you."

Nellie took a couple of skips and held out a brown package. "Mama made a loaf of bread for you," she said. "It's still warm, and she even sent some butter. I hope you're hungry."

"Oh, Nellie, you just don't know." When Martha took the bread, the smell made her so hungry she plopped down on a box, feeling weak. She'd been wishing Nellie would come see her again, but suddenly she desperately wanted her friend to leave so she could eat. She felt so hungry her legs actually shook. Then her eyes fell on Josie and her heart fell. The dog could eat the whole loaf in two gulps and still be hungry.

Nellie's voice brought Martha back. "I have to go back now, but I'll come see you tomorrow if that's all right."

Martha nodded, clutching the aromatic package in her hands. "Yes, come back, Nellie. We can take another walk."

Nellie barely turned away when Abe arrived, a rabbit in his hands. "I got a rabbit for Josie," he said, laying it in front of the skinny dog, who snatched it into her teeth and ran under the wagon with it. "Sorry I didn't find any firewood. I will, though, by tomorrow." He left immediately, too.

Finally, at long last, Martha pulled the golden loaf of bread from the brown paper. A loaf of real bread! It looked as good as it smelled. She'd had her last real bread the first few days after they had left Independence nearly seven months ago.

"Thank You, Lord," she said out loud. "I've never been more thankful than I am now, and You provided for both Josie and me almost before I asked. Thank You again. Amen." She tore the end off the bread and took a big bite without waiting to spread the butter. It tasted like manna from God. And it was.

Sinking onto the box, she concentrated on eating slowly. If she didn't, she'd eat the whole loaf without a thought for tomorrow, just like Josie. When she finished the first piece, she forced herself to put butter on the next one, and the next. When she'd eaten almost half the loaf, she wrapped it back up in the brown paper, even though she wanted more in the worst way. Would she ever again have all the food she wanted?

Josie chose that time to come out from under the wagon, licking her lips. The dog hadn't saved any for tomorrow, Martha noticed. When her pet started sniffing toward the brown paper, Martha took it into the wagon and put it inside the trunk. That bread would at least be a few bites for them tomorrow.

—⁂—

Later, when she lay on her featherbed, she thought about Abe's kind offer of marriage. It would be so nice to have someone to care for her, to know she'd have plenty of food every day, and a warm dry place to sleep. It wasn't as if Mr. Noble. . .Abe were mean or unkind. He wasn't. He'd even thought of Josie tonight when Martha couldn't cook.

Wait! He brought food for Josie at almost the time Mrs. Martin sent Nellie with food for her. Could that have been coincidence? Hardly! Mr. Noble had arranged it all. Yes, no doubt about it. She looked skyward and folded her hands. "Lord, is Abe my raven? I know You're sending me food through him as You did Elijah through the ravens. Thank You, God. And thank You for Abe. I've never met a nicer person, Lord. Do You think I should go ahead and marry him?" She almost felt she should.

Then she remembered. They could get three hundred twenty acres! Twice as much as either could get alone. Besides that, the land would probably all be claimed before she turned twenty-one. Yes, she'd better forget her silly romantic ideas and get on with life the best way she knew. But she couldn't do it. That would be the meanest trick in the world to play on Abe.

—⁓—

Early the next morning, she awakened to find frost on the ground. She took her morning sponge bath in cold water. Brrrr. It had been so much nicer when she could heat the water. She pulled on a clean brown dress that looked as if she'd walked across the country in it. She giggled because that's exactly what she'd done.

"Shall we divide the bread now or wait?" she asked Josie. The plumy tail wagged several times.

Before Martha could decide, Abe brought another loaf of bread, warm from the oven as the last one had been. Josie sniffed and grew restless.

Abe sat on one of the dynamite boxes and looked at her in a strange way. "Will you marry me, my little Martha? I'll be so good to you and care for you and love you with all my heart."

She couldn't do it. She owed him too much to hurt him by pretending something she didn't feel. Through almost unbearable pain, she shook her head. "I'm sorry, Mr. Noble. . .Abe. Josie, get back from this bread. I owe my very life to you and, more than words can say, I appreciate what you've done. But I would only hurt you if I married you, because although I consider you the best friend I've ever had, and purely know you're the kindest man I've ever met and I respect you more than anyone I've ever known, I don't love you as a woman should love a man she marries."

He flinched as if she'd given him a hard right to the chin and then he sort of wilted into a crumpled heap. He didn't say a word nor did he move. He just sat there, leaning forward, his elbows on his knees.

Seeing the pain in his eyes, Martha leaned over and put her hand on his arm. "I'm so sorry," she said. "I almost said yes, but I realized I'd be marrying you for the wrong reasons and that I'd hurt you more if I married you than if I didn't." She pushed back Josie's inquisitive face from the warm bread she still held. "You're a true friend, Abe, and it's hard for friends to hurt each other."

He shuddered and stood to his feet, smiling down at her. "It's all right. I had no reason to believe you cared for me. I—"

"Oh, but I do care for you, Mr. . . .Abe. I care for you very, very much, as a dear friend."

He smiled again, a tight smile that came out almost a grimace. "It's all right, Miss Lawford, don't give it another thought. I'll probably see you tomorrow." That was it. He rushed down the street without a backward look, his shoulders hunched.

Somehow, Martha no longer felt hungry for the bread she held in her lap. Josie had been trying to get her attention ever since Mr. . . .Abe had given her the bread. "Come on, Josie," Martha said wearily, "I'll get you the rest of yesterday's loaf." She patted the faithful head and climbed into the wagon to exchange the new loaf for the old. When she climbed down, she held out the bread. "You need it more than I do," she said.

She sat back on the dynamite box, watching Josie eat the bread in three quick bites, chewing each only a few times. "Well, our problems are still alive and healthy," she told the dog. "We still don't know where our next meal is coming from. . .and it's getting colder every night."

Chapter 12

As Abe walked back to his boardinghouse, he decided he knew how a bullet in his heart would feel. He'd never known such pain in his life. Could he live without Martha? Would he actually die from the pain as he would a bullet?

He rushed straight to his room, avoiding talking to or even meeting anyone. Easing down to his bed, he closed his eyes. "I tried, God," he prayed aloud. "Is this the way You want it? How long will I hurt. . .forever? I don't think I can handle this that long." He rested a few moments while a single tear ran from his right eye, across his cheek, past his ear, and onto the coarse muslin sheet. "She'd starve if I didn't take her food. I'm not sure I can stand the pain of seeing her. But You know I can't let her get too hungry." He lay quietly thinking for a while. And the pain continued. "Could You just take away the pain, God? I'd be thanking You a long time if You'd just do that for me." But the pain continued.

He fell asleep. When he awakened, his mouth tasted awful and he felt blacker than his shaded room. How could he live in the same world with Martha and not be able to call her his own? He pushed open the faded denim curtains to find the sun had moved into the western sky. Abe had the distinct feeling God had been talking to him while he slept. He sat up and thought hard, unable to remember.

Dropping his feet to the floor, he tried to think but couldn't get past his pain. He grabbed his hat and jacket and went out to check on the horses. Even though the sun still shone most of the time on these early November days, it didn't have enough strength to warm the air much.

When Charity saw him coming, she nickered and trotted to the fence. Sampson followed, almost reluctantly. "You're my best girl, aren't you?" Abe said to the horse, rubbing her neck and shoulders. Sampson shoved his big head against Abe's hand. "Oh, you want some, too, eh?" Abe said, pleased to know the big horse was beginning to care.

Abe gave both horses some oats and headed for the saloon.

"Heard about Slick?" the barkeep asked when Abe settled onto the stool.

Abe shook his head, reaching for the coffee he'd been served. He'd forgotten all about Slick. The man might be dead—small loss.

"Well, he got beat up the other night," the barkeep announced. "Someone hauled him out to Fort Walla Walla, more dead than alive. But I hear he's about well now. Purty hard to get rid of a skunk like that."

So, the old geezer lived. Abe couldn't tell whether he felt relief or disappointment. His own intense pain crowded out all other emotions.

Abe ate a roast meat sandwich without tasting it, then wondered what Martha had eaten that day. Sure would be a lot easier to feed her if the poor dog wasn't always twice as hungry. After ordering another sandwich wrapped, he hurried to the meat shop where he ordered a rabbit. Upon being told the rabbit was for a dog, the butcher offered him a bunch of meat scraps at no charge, adding that he could pick up scraps every day.

Abe, carrying the sandwich in one hand and the big bag of scraps in the other, headed for Martha and Josie. He straightened his shoulders. He'd act as if he'd forgotten all about the proposal and rejection. He'd just be a casual friend again. But how could he do that? He just would, that's all there was to it. He would.

She walked to meet him, a worried look on her face. But why should she feel bad? She's the one who said no. He forced a big smile to his lips. "I just learned you can get free meat scraps for Josie every day at the meat shop," he said in a superficially cheerful voice. He handed her the sandwich and dumped the scraps onto the grassy ground for Josie, who snatched up a meaty bone and retreated to her special spot under the wagon.

"Come sit down for a while," she invited.

He complied. "Have you been noticing how cold it's getting at night? Not too warm in the daytime, either."

She nodded. "I know I can't live in the wagon all winter. Thankfully my uncle and aunt are coming. I've been having a feeling it will be real soon."

He nodded. "It better be." He pointed east at the bluish, snow-capped mountains. "Have you noticed we get new snow in the Blues about once a week now? They may be impassable already, and it's going to get worse in a hurry."

"I know. They'll be here soon," she said with a weak giggle. "I just have a feeling in my bones it'll be soon." She swallowed. "I guess I'm not very grown-up, not being able to care for myself and all," she added in a tight murmur.

"It's hard for a woman," he said. "How can a woman earn money here? The only possibility I see would be working in one of the saloons, and you let me know you weren't interested in that."

She hung her head, her face pink. "But I did try," she whispered as if confessing to something indecent. "I tried both of them and they said no." She sniffed. "I tried all the businesses. No one wanted me."

He felt another stab. This time for her pain. She'd tried her best, done everything she could, and still she sat here helpless and hopeless. He draped another smile across his face. "Good thing your kinfolks are coming soon," he said, getting up. "I better be getting back. Mrs. Martin wants her guests to be on time for supper. Guess I don't blame her much." He took a few steps and turned back. "You eat that sandwich yourself, see? Josie still has some meat scraps." He smiled a genuine smile. "How long has it been since she walked off and left food?"

Martha laughed softly and shook her head. "I can't even remember. Thanks, Abe, you're the best friend I ever had. Josie, too."

—◊—

He hurried to his room where he washed up, then rushed on to the dining room.

"You ain't looking so good," Nellie said when she sat down across the table from him.

"I'm all right, Nellie, just hungry." He didn't feel hungry at all, but he had already made up his mind to eat all he could force down to keep up his strength.

When he finished eating, he went out to see the horses again. "I should take each of you out for a ride," he told them, "but I don't seem to have the hankering right now." He lumbered back to his room and flopped down onto his bed. Martha didn't look any happier than he felt. Well, she had plenty of problems, even if a broken heart wasn't among them. How would it feel to be a girl in this country with nothing, not even food, and unable to find work? It would be awful, no doubt, but would it hurt as bad as what was hurting him? Finally, he shook his head. Probably as bad but different.

Abe, I want you to marry her.

"I tried, God," he cried out loud. "You heard me. What are You talking about?"

Your broken heart will heal when you stop feeling sorry for yourself and think of her problems. Marry her. You can save her the pain she's enduring now.

"Do You have it all figured out how I can do that, God, since she doesn't want me?"

I do. Now you figure it out and marry her.

That stopped Abe. Completely stopped him. *How do you marry someone when she tells you in plain words she doesn't love you?*

Suddenly, he had a feeling he should take the horses out for a ride. Getting up from the bed, he shoved his hat onto his head, put on his jacket again, and headed for the corral. Both horses greeted him eagerly this time. "Should I saddle you both or ride you, Charity, and lead Sampson?" The

187

horses both danced eagerly and followed him on the other side of the fence until he went into the roomreferred to as the tack room. He saddled both horses, hopped up into Charity's saddle, and, with Sampson's reino in his left hand, headed west. He'd just give them a little run before it got dark.

Before he realized it, he found himself approaching Martha's covered wagon. He started to rein Charity south but then he thought, why not, and moved up to the wagon and stopped the horses. "Anyone home?" he called. "Quiet," he said softly to the eagerly prancing horses who weren't ready to stop.

Her dark head appeared between the dirty white curtains of the top of the wagon, then she hopped down.

"Want to take a little ride?" he asked. "The horses are needing some exercise."

"I'd enjoy that. Just let me get a coat." A moment later, she appeared, wrapped in a man's coat many sizes too large. "Don't laugh," she said. "This was Papa's coat. I don't have anything warm except blankets."

His heart felt a new pain. She didn't have warm clothes, living out here in the cold. "Come on, your horse can't wait."

After helping her mount, he climbed aboard Charity, and they headed southeast.

He noticed several new rough buildings. "Where do they all come from?" Martha asked, almost reading his mind.

"People are drifting in from all over, now that the Indian wars are over and the area's opened up for settling. I predict this place will look totally different a year from now." He swept his arm over the panoramic scene before them. "People and houses will be everywhere." Charity could hardly handle walking, and Sampson didn't do much better. Both horses added many quick steps to the slow pace. Abe reined Charity in. Martha did the same with Sampson. Abe looked down at Josie, dashing around, sniffing all the smells. He pointed a thumb at the dog. "Think we could give the horses a little run? Maybe we could tie her up for a while?"

Martha thought a moment. "Let's give the horses their head for a little while. If she falls behind, maybe she'll wait." She shrugged and gave him a smile that turned his stomach inside out. "I don't think I could tie her. It would break her heart."

Abe wouldn't push. He knew all about broken hearts. He touched Charity with his heels. "Come on, girl, let's give that big loafer something to complain about." She stretched into a long lope and, with Martha's experienced guidance, Sampson stayed at her side. Abe glanced back for Josie who hadn't given up yet. She tore along beside Sampson, her tongue hanging out the side of her mouth. As he watched she slowed, and the hurt in her eyes seemed to match that hurt burning a hole in his heart. He pulled the slack from the reins. "Sorry, girl," he said quietly, "we can't leave our faithful buddy behind." Josie's grateful eyes told him thank you. The dog dropped to the grass, panting hard.

A moment later, Martha and Sampson returned. "Anything wrong?" she asked.

Abe pointed to the dog. "That dog would run until she dropped," he said. "I don't run horses too hard, and I guess that goes for dogs, too. Why don't you and Sampson go on and have a good time? Then you can stay with Josie while Charity and I take a run."

—⁂—

An hour later, Abe told Martha good-bye amidst her sincere thanks. He took his time rubbing the horses down, then gave them some hay and carried thirteen buckets of fresh water from the creek for their tank.

Sometime after he fell asleep, he awakened, feeling that Someone had been talking to him. He knew now what he had to do. He had to get Martha to agree to marry him in name only. In name only! Now, how could a man marry a woman like Martha in name only? Every minute he spent with her he longed to hold her in his arms and love and kiss her. He could do that—marry her in name only—if he didn't love her so much. Things being as they were, that foolish thought was out. Completely out! He dropped his head back onto the pillow and fell asleep.

When he awakened again, darkness still filled his bedroom and he felt as if Someone had spoken to him another time. Oh, no! He had to marry Martha—in name only!

All right, just for the sake of argument, say he did marry her. How would that be accomplished? He knew! He knew all the answers! He'd simply build the house exactly on the line between her one hundred sixty acres and his. And the house would be built with a bedroom on each end with the living area between. And he wouldn't set foot past the living area. Never! Not once!

He sat up again. "God," he called, "are You doing this to me, or am I having an awful nightmare?"

I'm here, Abe. You can do it. Then you'll be blessed as my first Abram was. You'll have more cattle than you can count. You'll be rich in worldly goods as well as heavenly.

"Look, God, You made me the way I am. I won't be able to stay in my end of the house and You know it. I'll mess this up something fierce. Then what?"

You won't mess it up. You'll keep your promise one hundred and ten percent,

189

Abram. You can and you will. You have more strength than you realize.

Abe jumped from his bed and marched around the room several times. Maybe if he thoroughly awakened himself, the dream would be gone for good. He sure didn't want it returning again. Twice was more than enough. Finally, thoroughly chilled, he tumbled back into his bed.

Chapter 13

Martha awakened in the night, shivering. Every blanket she owned already lay over her. "Come closer, Josie," she whispered into the darkness. Josie didn't move, so Martha leaned over and began tugging on the dog who, upon understanding the invitation, gladly crawled into the warm nest. Martha pulled Josie's rug atop the pile of blankets. That should do it.

She felt warmer, whether from the dog or the old rug or both, she didn't care. Cold was a totally miserable feeling. She soon fell asleep, her arms wrapped tightly around the elated dog.

It seemed she scarcely closed her eyes when Josie piled out of the bed and also the wagon. The sun shone brightly. Somebody must be coming, otherwise Josie would have been happy to cuddle until the sun warmed them a little. Martha pulled the blankets over herself for another moment. She simply hated getting out of bed these cold mornings. In a moment, she threw the covers back and hopped out, gritted her teeth, and poured some water into her wash bowl. For the first time ice chips edged the bucket of water. She almost cried out at the touch of the water, but she continued to wash herself. One thing that didn't cost money was cleanliness and she'd be clean. Even if it killed her.

Josie stood, looking south. Martha looked for a long time but didn't see anything. "Nothing there, Josie," she said. She looked at Josie's meat and saw several pieces left. Climbing into the wagon, she pulled the remaining loaf of bread from the trunk. Some good food would probably warm them both up. Spreading half of the butter liberally on half the bread, she put the other half of the loaf back into the trunk so it wouldn't tempt either her or Josie. After giving Josie her half, Martha sat down on a dynamite box. "Thank You, Father," she said, "not only for the food but for loving me so much. I love You too, Father." She ate her bread, taking tiny bites and chewing until the bread turned to liquid in her mouth. When the last crumb disappeared, she called Josie to take a walk to the creek for water.

Ten minutes later, she found herself standing beside Mill Creek on the property Abe planned to claim. She pivoted in a complete circle. What a beautiful world! Warm sunshine everywhere and bright blue sky in the west.

Fresh snow covered the top third of the Blue Mountains, making them look like blueberry ice cream covered with whipped cream. Then a black shadow darkened her world. What about her uncle and aunt? Her cousin and brother? They had to get over those mountains before they became impassable. They simply had to.

Her happiness gone, she scooped up the bucket of water and carried it back to the wagon.

Abe waited for them, sitting on one of the boxes. He had another loaf of bread and a bowl of butter. Martha's heart swelled almost to bursting with gratitude. She'd spurned his generous offer of marriage and here he was, faithfully bringing her food—her raven from God.

Then she noticed his face. "You look as if you didn't get much sleep last night," she said. "I hope you weren't cold."

"No, I wasn't cold." He gave her the bread. "Would you like for me to leave so you can eat?"

She shook her head. "We ate before we went after water. I don't know how to thank you, Abe. You're definitely the kindest man in the world." She climbed into the wagon to put the bread into the trunk.

He still sat on the box, looking at her in a strange way. What was he thinking? Was her hair coming out? He definitely had something on his mind. She sat down on the other box and waited for him to speak his thoughts.

"I still want to marry you."

Oh, no! She thought she'd made her feelings clear. She couldn't find any words. She simply shook her head slowly.

"Don't say anything until I explain. I already know that you think I'm a great friend, so that's what we'll be. We'll get our three hundred twenty acres and build our house right on the line, yours on the east and mine on the west." He chuckled softly. "Or vice versa if you prefer. The house will have a bedroom at each end with the living area in between. Neither one of us will set foot on the other's private territory. We'll work together turning the place into a farm and ranch, dividing the profits in half." He stopped for a moment, watching her. "You can see that we'll both be better off with the arrangement, can't you?" he asked as if any fool could see the wisdom of his plan.

"You stayed up all night figuring this out, didn't you?" she finally asked.

He barked out a hoarse laugh. "I guess you might say I did just that."

She sat silent for a moment, thinking. She could see how a plan like this would work between friends, but he'd said he loved her. "The arrangement still wouldn't be fair to you," she finally said. "You said you...you said you...uh..."

"I said I loved you? Why don't you just forget that? I have." He grinned and snapped his fingers. "It's all over, just like that." His face became serious again. "I don't mean to push, but you have to do something right away. One morning you're going to wake up and have to shovel your way out of the wagon."

"You're the nicest person in the entire world."

His eyes brightened. "But you still don't love me?"

"I do love you, a whole lot. You're the best friend I've ever had."

He slumped a tiny bit. "All right, I'll never mention it to you again. From here on out, we're best friends. How's that?"

Martha laughed out loud. "Good."

"Then you'll marry me?"

"I don't know about that. I just don't know, Abe. Marriage is forever and that's a long time."

Suddenly, Josie began to bark and Martha followed her gaze south. Covered wagons! A whole line of covered wagons! She pointed and Abe looked, too. They must have been five miles away, but they were winding toward them.

"That's my aunt and uncle!" she shouted. "They're finally here. Abe, they're almost here!" She felt like grabbing him and dancing right off to meet the wagons. She should make them a big meal! Then she flopped back to earth. They were much too far to run to meet yet—she didn't have a thing to feed them. Maybe they'd have something for her.

Abe smiled. "Well, I guess they got through the Blues. I'm glad for you, Martha. I guess you won't be needing me anymore." He got up and stretched.

She pushed him back onto the dynamite box. "You're not going anywhere, Abram Noble. You just sit right there and meet my kin." She shivered with delight. "Oh, Abe, my brother's with them. You'll get to meet Jackson!" She simply couldn't sit still. She jumped up and walked around the wagon, came back and sat down, then jumped up again. Finally, she held her hand to him. "Come on, let's go meet them. I can't sit here and wait."

He laughed but got up. "They're two or three hours away, Martha, by wagon or foot. If Josie would stay here we could take the horses and meet them in less than an hour. The horses would like that."

"Let's get the horses, Abe. I have to see my family! I can't wait one hour, let alone three."

Abe looked at Josie. "What about her, Martha? Since you're getting meat scraps for her she's strengthening, but she can't go that far. Are you willing to tie her up?"

Martha met Josie's sad brown eyes. The plumy tail wagged twice over the dog's back. It seemed as if the big dog understood their conversation.

Could she do that to Josie? Her excitement waned some. "I don't have a rope," she said.

"I do. Want me to get it? And the horses?"

Martha vacillated. She simply had to see her family. She couldn't desert her faithful dog, and Josie really couldn't run all that way. Her eyes met Abe's. "What should we do?"

"I'll get her some more scraps to eat while we're gone. It won't hurt her a bit." He took off toward the meat market, returning shortly with a big bag of bloody scraps. "Don't let her have any now," he said, trotting off toward the horses' corral.

Ten minutes later, he came back astride Charity, leading Sampson and swinging a long rope as if it were a lariat. Jumping to the ground, he fastened one end of the rope to the wagon tongue so Josie could get on either side or under the wagon. "Bring the meat over," he said, "and let's make our getaway while she's eating."

Martha ran to Sampson's side, put her left foot into the stirrup, swung up, and adjusted her skirts so she felt modest.

"Let's go," Abe said, taking off in the general direction of the wagon train. The horses, eager for a good run, stretched into smooth gallops.

Martha felt a tremendous exhilaration. Although she'd learned to love Sampson a lot and thrilled in his long comfortable gait, her excitement came from knowing that in a little while she'd be reunited with her uncle, aunt, cousin, and brother. "I just can't believe it's all over," she called to Abe, only about twenty feet away on Charity.

After some time, Abe reined Charity in to a trot. Sampson slowed, too. "They haven't had much exercise lately," he explained at her questioning look. He grinned. "After a while we'll let them go again if they want." The wagon train still looked a long way off, maybe miles for all she knew.

They walked the horses and talked quietly. Martha noticed that neither of them mentioned the terribly important subject they'd been discussing when they'd discovered the wagon train. What's more, she didn't know whether she'd marry him or not. He might withdraw the offer anyway, now that she had her kinfolk.

"Exciting, isn't it?" His smile looked tired. "Your life will undergo a quick and definite change now."

She nodded. One way or the other it would. If she married Abe it would. If she lived with her kin it would change, too. Oh, why didn't the wagon train hurry? Or why didn't they? "Abe, if we don't let the horses run some more, I'm getting off and running myself."

He grinned. "I think they're rested." He nudged Charity with his knees. "Want to go again, girl?" The horse took off at full speed. Sampson fell behind but soon caught her.

Martha felt the exhilaration again. "They really like to run, don't they?"

"I see you do, too," he returned.

This time Abe let Charity go until they met the first wagon. "Hello there," he called, turning Charity to walk beside the man, going north now, back the way they'd come. "You headed for Steptoeville?"

"Walla Walla," the man answered.

Abe nodded. "Steptoeville's in Walla Walla County," he said, pointing north. "Dead ahead."

Martha sat quietly on Sampson as long as she could. Finally, she cleared her throat so only Abe could hear.

"Could you direct us to the Strange wagon?" Abe asked.

The man grinned. "All our wagons are strange," he said as if joining in a joke.

Abe laughed. "I mean the Cleveland Strange wagon." He motioned to Martha. "This is Martha Lawford, and they're her kinfolk. Her brother, Jackson, is with them."

The man wrinkled his forehead. "Nobody on this train named Strange," he finally said. "Everybody'd of knowed 'em with that name." He thought a moment then shook his head. "No Lawfords, neither."

Martha couldn't keep quiet any longer. "They have to be on this train, sir. I got here about a month ago, and they were on the next train. I know they're here." A big lump formed in her stomach. "I'm going to check every wagon."

Abe came to her. "Want me to come with you?"

Unable to speak, she nodded.

She did exactly as she'd said, asking at every single wagon. No one had so much as heard of anyone named Strange or Lawford. When she'd questioned the last wagon, she nudged Sampson with her heels, flew several hundred feet away from the train, reined in, slid from the saddle, and dropped onto the ground, unable to support her own weight.

Chapter 14

Martha'd barely fallen to the ground, still holding Sampson's reins in her hand, when she heard Charity arrive, then felt strong arms surrounding her.

"I'm sorry, Martha," Abe said. "I wish your family had been there." He held her close, patting her back. "I'm sorry. I'm so sorry," he kept murmuring against her hair. In the background she heard the wagons creaking, oxen bawling, children crying, people yelling, all the sounds she'd listened to for six long months. The sounds, along with the knowledge that she had no one, made her physically ill. Jumping from Abe's arms, she handed him Sampson's reins, ran about thirty feet away, pulled her skirts back, leaned over, and retched until she had nothing in her stomach.

She straightened her skirts, took several deep breaths, and scolded herself for being immature. Her eyes swept east until she found Abe, sitting where she'd left him. When their eyes met, he jumped to his feet and trotted to her. She met him halfway. "Thank you for leaving me alone while I acted the part of a baby," she whispered.

He shook his head briskly. "You're no baby. Anyone would be upset." For a full minute he stood on one foot then the other watching her closely. "Ready to head back?"

"Might as well." The wagon train had moved a little ahead of them. "Did you ask where they're headed?"

"Yes. They're headed for donation claims in Steptoeville."

"Did you ask if there were any trains behind them?"

He shook his head. "Why don't we ask them, then give the horses their heads? We'll get home long before the train arrives."

"No one else is goin' through those mountains till the snow melts," the man replied to Abe's questions. "If I had it to do over again I'd wait at Fort Hall until spring. We like ta kilt our oxen goin' up and almost lost our wagons comin' down. Snow's two feet deep up there already."

Martha's last hope plummeted with the man's words. As Sampson plodded along and Abe talked to the man, she remembered her situation—not a bite of food for her or Josie, no way she could think of to get any, and the cold weather upon her.

Abe caught up with her. "I guess you heard."

She nodded.

"Let's get back to Josie." He touched Charity with his foot, and she stretched out in long smooth strides with Sampson moving alongside.

The horses raced most of the way back, slowing to a trot once for fifteen minutes. When they stopped beside the wagon, Josie greeted Martha as though they'd been apart for three months. Sitting on the dried grass, Martha let the dog wallow over her, realizing Josie was all she had now. As Josie crowded close, licking her hands, she gave the dog lots of hugs and pats.

Abe said nothing as he sat on a dynamite box watching the emotional greetings. Finally, Martha managed to get her feet under her. Josie shoved her body against Martha and tried to get to her face, obviously not finished with the greeting. "That's enough, Josie," Martha said in a flat voice. "Lie down." With a long, sad look, the dog crumpled beside Abe. When Martha sat on the other box, Josie crept over to lie beside her.

No one said anything for some time. Martha wanted to but she couldn't think of a thing. At this point she felt empty, as though she had no beginning and no end. And she didn't care what happened. But when her eyes fell on the dog at her feet, she discovered she did care. She owed Josie. She owed her a good home and enough food.

"What you thinking about?" Abe's soft voice asked. "Or dare I ask?"

Her eyes met his and the care she saw made her smile. "You can ask anything you want, Abe. I'm sure you have a good idea what I was thinking."

He wrapped his tanned hands together. "You were deciding to marry me?"

Martha almost jumped. That was the one thing she hadn't been thinking about. "I'm not sure what I was thinking," she said, "but here's what crossed my mind just now. Do you think Josie and I should try to get to The Dalles? There might be some work I could do there."

His eyes opened wide. "Why would you think about that? Does marrying me sound that awful? Anyway, I doubt you could get there until spring. There won't be much traffic this winter."

He got up. "I'm going now. You'll have to decide your own fate. If I could, I'd stir up your brain a little." He walked over to Charity and got on her, then turned back to Martha. "I'll be around." He took off toward the back of the boardinghouse with Sampson in tow.

—⁓—

When Abe disappeared from Martha's sight, she felt totally alone. She turned her attention to Josie. "And now it's just you and me," she said. "We could go get you some bones, but Abe already did that. Are you hungry for some bread?" Making no move to get the bread, her mind sped in circles. Abe still wanted to marry her. If she refused, he'd keep bringing food to her, but how fair was that to him? Besides, she had to get out of the wagon and soon. It could snow at any time. She could feel it in the night air lately. While it had been fun living in the wagon when they first started west, and it hadn't been all that bad other than for the loneliness she felt when she got parked here, it was just plain miserable now.

She dropped to her knees beside the box. "You have to help me, Lord," she cried. "Would You want me to marry Abe for convenience? It seems to me that would be sacrilegious, making marriage vows that I wouldn't mean to keep. Show me, Lord. I'm at the end, the very end." She rested quietly on her knees for a while, then looked up toward the bright blue sky, halfway noticing the sun almost directly overhead. "Lord, You promised to be with us always and to hear our prayers. Well, where are my aunt and uncle? And my brother? It feels to me You've deserted me just as all my earthly kin have." She lowered her face to the box and let the tears flow freely. Josie inched as close as she could and licked Martha's cheeks where the tears rolled over them.

Martha felt desperately tired and crawled into the wagon to rest. Josie followed and snuggled close. They fell asleep together and awakened to a lot of commotion as the wagon train rolled to a stop a half-mile south.

Two young men on horses galloped to her wagon. "Any place to get supplies?" the older of the two asked Martha as she stepped down from her wagon.

She pointed toward the street. "There's a general store, two saloons, a boardinghouse, and a trader. I'm sure someone will be able to help."

The young man tipped his hat and turned his horse into the street. "Those places will always help if you have money," she told Josie. "Come on, let's go see Nellie." Martha had never gone after Nellie, but she needed someone to be with this afternoon.

—◊◊◊—

As they walked, Nellie took several quick peeks at Martha. They reached Mill Creek and stopped to watch it gurgle over the stones.

Nellie sat on the clean rocks and Martha followed. Josie ran into the cold water, back and forth from side to side, cavorting first in the water then the grass. "You've been crying," Nellie said softly. "What's the matter, Martha? Does it have something to do with the wagon train?"

Martha nodded. "Yes. I thought my kinfolk would be with it, but they aren't. They say the snow is bad in the Blues and no one else can. . . ," she stopped and swallowed hard. The lump stayed in her throat, so she swallowed twice more. "No one else can get through till spring," she finally choked out. Leaning her head on her hands, she swallowed again, her eyes shut tight.

Nellie put her arm over Martha's shoulders. "I'm sorry," she murmured into Martha's ear. "I'm really sorry. Have you figured what you're going to do?"

Martha shook her head as it still rested in her hands.

"You could stay with me, but my sister sleeps with me and the room is so tiny. My two other sisters have a tiny room just like ours." She thought a moment. "I don't know what Mama would say, but you can't spend the winter in that wagon."

Martha didn't lift her head, but her mind kept busy. She wanted to tell Nellie about Abe's proposal but didn't know whether it would be right. She didn't tell. After a few minutes she lifted her head and smiled at Nellie. "Please, don't worry about me. Your mother can't take in every stray that comes along. If she did you'd all starve." She giggled as she watched Josie wallowing in the grass on the other side of the creek. "And she definitely wouldn't want Josie in her nice clean house." She giggled again as she thought about the rough boards from which the boardinghouse was built. Her farm house in Missouri had had hardwood floors with beautiful rugs on them.

Just at that time the big dog decided to share the nice cold water with the girls. Splashing up from the creek, she shook vigorously. Screaming, both girls jumped from their comfortable seats and ran back toward the wagon.

Nellie hurried back to the boardinghouse to help with supper, and Martha pulled out the fresh loaf of bread, tore it in half, put one half back, and shared the other half with Josie.

After she ate she crawled into the wagon to think. She couldn't think of any other way than to marry Abe. And it really didn't sound so bad. Especially the way he described it to her the last time. A business arrangement. She knew he'd keep his agreement, too. The more she thought about it the better it sounded. She'd have her one hundred sixty acres, too, right away. She'd have a house and a garden and all the food she and Josie needed. Thinking about Josie reminded her how kind Abe was. She could count on him to be good to Josie as well as her. She jumped down from the wagon. "Come on, Josie, let's go look at our homesite again."

They stayed for half an hour and came back. For some reason, Martha felt a little disappointed. Then she realized why. She'd hoped to meet Abe there—and that he'd beg her to marry him again.

They hadn't been back at the wagon long when Nellie came with a loaf of bread and some hot sliced meat. Martha's mouth watered at the smell and so did Josie's. She knew that God's raven, Abe, had arranged this fantastic meal. She asked Nellie.

Nellie colored. "I'm not sure. . .uh. . .I'm not supposed to tell." She looked at her friend. "You never asked before. I didn't think you would. Well, I'm not saying. My word is bound."

Martha gave her friend a little shove. "You told me already, Nellie. Can you tell him thanks for me?"

Nellie's red head shook back and forth. "Then he'd know I told." Nellie soon left and Josie let Martha know she was ready for her meal. "I wish I could cook your meat," she told the dog. "Then you'd know you had a meal." She started to go put the bread in the trunk and get the other loaf but changed her mind. "Let's have a real banquet," she told Josie. She wrapped a thin slice of meat in a big piece of bread and offered it to the dog, who swallowed it in one gulp.

Martha felt disappointed. "That's not fair," she told her pet. "Now you're going to want my piece, too." She broke off another piece of bread, tossed it under the wagon, and kicked several meaty bones over it. "Now you go eat and let me eat in peace," she told Josie who ran under and lay down to her meal.

Martha didn't eat slowly. In fact she tried to eat all she wanted while the dog busied herself with the things under the wagon. The bread and meat tasted better than anything she remembered, and she ate much of it. For the first time in months she felt stuffed.

After she finished, she waited in camp hoping Abe would come. She hoped he'd come and insist on marrying her. But he didn't come. She spent the longest evening of her life waiting and watching for the tall, spare man to step from the boardinghouse and stride to the wagon.

Chapter 15

Abe dropped to his bed to think. He'd managed to force down a little food at supper, though it had tasted like dried grass. He longed to run down to Martha at the wagon to see how she was now. After what she'd been through today she needed him. He knew full well she did. But something or Someone held him back as if it weren't the right thing to do.

By now he'd decided he'd be glad to marry her on any terms. Just to be near her and know she was all right. How could he ask for more? Yes, he'd go ask her again. He got up, put on his hat, and opened the door. But he shut it again and sat back on the bed. What was this, anyway?

As he sat there wondering why he'd come back, he saw clearly that she would feel pushed if he went to her now, that he'd have to be patient until she came to him. As that thought came, a peace fell over him, and he knew she would come. *Thank you, God,* he thought. *I should have known You were showing me what to do.* He pulled off his clothes, tumbled into bed, and fell into a sound sleep.

—⁂—

The next morning, he awakened feeling great. Pulling back his coarse denim curtains, he saw a cloudless blue sky. "God is in His heaven and all's right with the world," he said out loud. He opened his door, retrieved a pitcher of warm water, poured it into his wash bowl, and proceeded to give himself a good cleaning. After dressing, he poured the water into a large can in the hall and stepped outside.

Buttoning his jacket against the cold, he couldn't help glancing west. Martha and Josie moved around the wagon, but he couldn't tell what they were doing. Resolutely, he turned away and strode east down the street to the creek, then south, then east again as the creek made another turn. He followed the creek for about two hundred feet and stopped. What a place for a claim! And they'd do it together. Somehow he'd been assured of it. They'd do it together, and he'd be satisfied just to be with her. He took off his hat and bowed his head. *Thank You, God,* he said silently. *You were right, it will be enough. And I can do it with Your help.* He replaced his hat and stood looking over the sun-drenched acres before him.

"Hello, Abe. Is this a private meeting? Or am I welcome?" Martha looked as happy as he felt this morning.

Abe couldn't believe the relief he felt at seeing her radiant smile. "Welcome, Martha. I was just looking the place over one more time. Guess I'll make my claim today before some of that new bunch on the wagon train gets it." He hadn't really thought about making his claim today but it sounded good. He walked a little ways up the creek. "Do you think I could ever be sorry if I made the claim here?" he asked.

"No. How could you, Abe? There's no prettier piece of land in Washington Territory."

He met her blue eyes. They reached right inside him, almost to his toes. "All right, I'll see you later," he said, turning to leave. Who was driving him, anyway? He hadn't wanted to leave yet. After all, the whole day lay before him. He strode off toward the street.

But her feet patted the soft ground until she caught up with him. "Could we talk before you make your claim?" she asked breathlessly.

He stopped. "Sure. Where?"

She looked back up the creek. "Back on the place? Or we could go to the wagon."

Wordlessly, he turned and hurried back to where they'd come from. "Want to sit on the creek bank?" he asked. She sat. "Now," he said after they both got comfortable and Josie disappeared up the creek someplace, "what did you have in mind to talk about?"

She turned a rosy red under her faded blue sunbonnet. "Whatever you'd like to talk about," she said quietly.

He wanted desperately to ask her again to marry him but something held him back. He looked down at her and his heart turned over in his chest. He shook his head. "I don't have nothin' special in mind," he said. "You just go ahead with whatever's botherin' you. Is something wrong? Are you all right? I have to say you look good this morning. I'm right proud of you after the disappointment you had yesterday."

She seemed to wilt, then straightened up, her shoulders back. "Are you taking a claim for one hundred sixty acres?" she finally asked.

He nodded. "That's the law, Martha. It's a fair bit more land than I ever owned before."

"Would you like to have more?" she asked very quietly.

He laughed softly. "Most men want more no matter what they got. Sure, I'd like more but I'd also be happy with a lot less." He thought a moment. "Gotta get going on it, too, so I can get a cabin built before it gets much colder."

They sat together for several minutes, neither of them talking, both thinking private thoughts. Josie came back with a small fish in her mouth. After giving a few pitiful twists, the fish quieted, and the dog swallowed it whole.

Finally, Martha met Abe's eyes again. "You know you could have more, don't you?"

He shook his head. "Not according to the present law."

Another long silence. *I know what she's doing, God. Why do I have to let her sit in such pain and embarrassment?* He didn't say anything more.

"What if we were to marry?" she asked almost in a whisper.

He almost sprang around to face her. "You want to? You want to marry me?" he asked.

She hung her head. "Well, you suggested something, Abe!" she said louder. "Don't you remember all the things we talked about? About a private room at each end of the house?"

He felt a small disappointment, then happiness. "Sure, I remember. Want to do it?"

"I want you to understand everything if we do, Abe. I'm in a terrible situation, and I can't think of any other way. If I don't marry you, you'll keep buying food for me and Josie, and that isn't fair, either. I can't think of any way that'll be fair to you, Abe, but if you want to marry me, you can at least have my one hundred sixty acres."

He shook his head. "No, Martha, we'll have three hundred twenty acres. The whole place will be ours, unless you want to keep it divided. . .like our bedrooms."

They sat in silence for several minutes, Abe wondering what she was thinking. All he wanted to do was get married—quickly and now.

Finally, she looked into his eyes again. "Who would do it?"

"Do what? Oh, you mean marry us. Well, there's the Catholic priest. He has that little pole building south of the street. You know, they just built it."

She thought a moment. "Oh, that shacky thing we step around when we come to the property."

"Yeah. And the Methodists just organized a church here. They don't have a building yet, but I'll bet they have a priest around somewhere."

She laughed. "Minister, Abe. Methodists don't have priests."

He laughed, too. "Could one of those fellows do the job?"

She fell silent again, drawing a line in the dust between two stones. "What if one of us gets tired of this arrangement?" she finally asked.

Was she thinking she might fall in love with someone else? That thought was too horrible to even consider. "I'm not plannin' to," he said. "Are you?"

She continued drawing the dusty line downward toward the creek. Then, shaking her dark head, she lifted her eyes to his. "It would more likely be you, Abe. I realize this arrangement isn't fair for you." Her eyes dipped to her finger in the dust as though it were the most important thing in the world. Then she giggled. "You'd have been a lot better off if you weren't so nice. Know that?"

He shook his head. "If I hadn't helped you I'd have missed out on the nicest, prettiest woman I've ever known." He stopped, hoping he hadn't said too much. "Well, shall we go find someone to hitch us? Then we can get our claim." He laughed out loud. "All three hundred twenty acres of it, Martha." He got to his feet and pulled her up. "Which man should we get, a Catholic? Or a Methodist?"

She hesitated. "I'd. . .uh. . .I'd rather have a civil ceremony seeing as how it isn't a real marriage, but I guess there's no one around to do it that way."

"We could ask the claims man," he said. "If he can't, then there's no one else around here to do a civil ceremony."

Abe led Martha to the trader's building where the claims people had an office in the back. "We was wondering if you could marry us," Abe said, embarrassed. "Then we want to take out a donation claim."

"Sorry," the short round man said. "You better let the priest or minister do that, then we'll talk about the claim."

Back outside, Abe met Martha's eyes. "Want to let the priest do it?" He hesitated with his next thought for he desperately wanted this marriage to be *until death do us part*. But in fairness to her he had to say it. "I hear a marriage can be annulled if it isn't consummated."

She raised her eyebrows in question, then shrugged. "Fine with me. Let's go."

They walked between the meat market and Galbraith's Saloon to the shack that people called a church. Without a doubt the poorest building in the settlement, the poles didn't begin to cover the walls. When they went inside, Abe saw lots of daylight through the roof, and dirt made up the dusty floor. One shaky bench was the only furniture in sight.

"May I help you?" a man wearing a clerical collar over rough worn clothes asked with a noticeably French accent.

Abe cleared the clog from his throat. "I hope so, Father. The young woman and I wish to be married."

"All right. I can do that for you. Let me go get a witness." He glanced down at Josie. "Think the dog should go outside?"

Abe chuckled. "Josie's going to be my stepdaughter, Father. She'd better stay for the wedding." Martha mouthed a "Thank you" to him as they took their places.

The short ceremony ended almost before it began. "You may kiss the bride," the man intoned after he said the last prayer.

Sudden terror swept through Abe. Why hadn't he thought about that? Should he just grab her and kiss her as if it were natural? No, that would be breaking her trust. "I'm sorry, Father, I can't do that. My bride's very shy."

The man nodded.

Abe pulled out a generous donation and placed it in the man's hand, an act that brought a grateful smile. "Thank you, thank you," the man said. "May you live long and happy lives together."

"Do we need a marriage certificate?" Abe asked.

"Oh, yes, yes, you do." He pulled one from a small box in the corner, and they all signed it.

Then the priest wished them well and ushered them through the place where the door should have been.

"Now, back to the claims office," Abe said, walking down the street.

Chapter 16

Martha felt a big letdown as Abe led her to the claims office. But what had she expected? She'd made it plenty clear to him that he would be only a friend. If he so much as pecked her on the cheek, she'd probably take off into parts unknown. He knew that, and she had to admit the truth of it. Why the disappointment then?

"Here we are," Abe said, sounding a little excited. "Are you ready to become a landowner?"

"Yes," she murmured. "Let's go in."

As they entered the office, Josie stayed at Martha's side. Half an hour later, they emerged with a piece of paper worth more than gold. "We did it," Abe said, looking as though he'd like to dance a jig.

She met his happy eyes. "Almost," she corrected. "Didn't he say we have to move up the creek a little farther?"

He nodded. "We don't care though, do we? That's better than getting kicked out when they survey the town. . .in a couple of weeks, didn't he say?"

"Yes." Suddenly, she needed to see if their new place was as nice as the one they'd picked out. "Let's go look at it."

"I was about to suggest the same thing." His brown eyes twinkled brightly. "You know what they say about married people. . .that they even think alike."

Martha gave him a small push. "That means after they've been married a hundred years. Come on, let's see if we like our claim."

They walked east until they passed the place where they'd sat earlier while she'd proposed to him. As she thought about that, her face grew hot way back to her ears. He'd probably never let her forget that she'd been the one to propose.

"He said the two trees leaning over the creek are the first trees on our land," Abe said as they hurried along. "There they are!" They walked on until he stopped dead. "We're on our own land, Martha!" he shouted. "This is our claim." Josie stopped short, looked to see if something was wrong, gave her plumy tail one wag, and splashed into the creek.

Martha looked down the creek and the several more trees beside it. Then she swung her gaze away from the creek. Beautiful, gently rolling land with several small knolls suitable for building. She glanced toward Abe to find him watching her.

"Is it all right?" he asked softly.

"It's perfect, Abe, even better than the other." She turned around to face the creek. "Look, you can't see the old Fort Walla Walla buildings from here. I like that a lot better." She whirled around to face the large area of land. "Come show me where we'll build. Am I going to help build our house?"

He laughed, looking pleased. "It'll be a big help. . .if you really want to. It'll go up a lot quicker. You tell me where you'd like it."

She shook her head. "Almost everywhere looks good to me."

When Abe's eyes kept straying to Martha's hand, she knew he wanted to take it, but he didn't. "Come on," he said, "let's walk until we see a spot just screaming for a house." He laughed again and met her eyes. "I noticed you didn't call it a cabin."

It didn't take them long to agree on a small rise about one hundred feet back from the creek. "We don't want to be too close to the creek," Abe said, "because someone else will get the property on the other side. We wouldn't want someone else in our front yard."

Martha agreed. "Let's scratch the house on the ground," she suggested after they'd walked and talked for more than an hour.

"We have to make some plans first. Draw it out on paper. Want to go do that now?"

She did, so they hurried back to town. When they reached the boarding-house, he started to go in.

"Let's draw it out at the wagon," she said. "I feel strange in there."

"You won't after I tell her we're married."

"You can't do that, Abe! We have to keep it secret until we get the house built."

He looked puzzled. "Why do we have to do that?"

He knew. Why did he want to make her explain it?

"You know, Abe. People might think it's funny."

Recognition jerked into his eyes. "Oh, I understand. But you're my wife now, Martha, and I don't want you out there alone. It's dangerous. I didn't marry you to let some no-good cur come along and hurt you."

She felt her face growing hot again. "But they'd expect us to sleep in the same room, Abe. I don't think they even have a spare room."

He sighed. "All right, let's go to the wagon to draw out the plans. We'll figure this out later." They walked a few feet when he stopped. "Got any paper at the wagon?"

"Just that torn piece I've been keeping track of my bills to you on."

He grinned. "I guess you can forget those bills now. Let's go get some paper. You been inside the store?"

She shook her head. "Only to ask for work. I haven't had any money." She felt excited to be going in at last. She'd been tempted to explore the place on several occasions when she'd been bored and lonely. But with so few people around they'd know she was the girl in the wagon with no money. She couldn't handle that.

Abe opened the door and stood back to let her in first. She stepped in. Several tables, built from long, half-logs and laying on blocks, stood on the dirt floor. Clothes, pots and pans, garden tools, and other exciting-looking things nearly hid the boards. Abe led the way to a half-log table holding tablets, separate sheets of paper, pencils, pens, both quills and fountain pens, and bottles of ink. It all looked fascinating to Martha. She'd like one of everything.

He chose a large writing pad with the words *Pencil Tablet* on the front. "You do have a pencil?" he asked.

"Yes," she whispered, then wondered why. "It's not very good, but it writes."

He picked up a pencil. "See anything else you need?" he asked.

See anything else she needed? Only everything. But she couldn't tell him that. "Do you need a ruler?" she asked. "You know, for the walls and things?"

He smiled and nodded. "Good thinking, wife."

Martha jerked her head around to see if anyone else had heard, but they were the only customers at the time. He picked up a twelve-inch ruler, and they carried the things to the man at the front of the store.

"Figgerin' to do some writin'?" the man asked with a grin as he added the amounts. "That'll be forty-five cents," he said. "Need somethin' to put that in?"

"Nah," Abe said. "We got four hands." He handed the pencil and ruler to Martha, and they left the store.

"That store wasn't nearly as grand as the ones I used to shop in," she said, "but it was fun. I haven't been in a store for almost nine months."

"Well, it won't be that long before you go again." They reached the wagon, and Josie rushed under the wagon and closed her eyes. Abe sat on one dynamite box and shoved the other one to Martha. "You got something hard we can put under this here paper?"

Martha could think only of the big Bible, and it was too special to use for that. "I don't think so. Sorry." Then her eyes fell on the box she was about to sit on. "What if we turned the box over, put the tablet on it, and sat on the ground beside it?" A moment later they sat side by side with the tablet before them, the pencil in Abe's right hand.

"Draw," Martha urged. "I can't wait to see our new house."

Abe laughed into her eyes. "It isn't that simple. We have to decide how big it will be and what we need in it."

She extended her arms, her fingers bent forward. "Big. We want it big. It'll have a fireplace, won't it?"

He nodded. "It'll have to." He leaned over the paper a moment, making several dots along the edges. "Thirty feet by twelve looks good to me. What do you think?"

She shrugged. "I have no idea what thirty feet would look like."

For a moment, he checked distances on the ruler then drew a ten-inch line, then a right angle and four inches, then another ten-inch line and a four-inch connecting line at the beginning end. He grinned at his drawing. "That's purty good if I do say so myself. Now, we need a bedroom on each end, nine feet by twelve." He cut off three inches at each end, leaving a large four-inch—really twelve-foot—room in the middle. "This is the kitchen and main room. We'll put a fireplace in the middle so we can cook on it and it'll heat the whole house." He looked up. "What do you think, wife?"

"I love it. And it seems huge. Are you sure we can afford such a fine house?"

"I think we can. If it'll make you happy, I know we can. Well, I'd better ride up Mill Creek to the sawmill and order the lumber. I don't know how long it'll take them to get it made up." He got up from the ground and flexed his legs, limbering them up from sitting on the ground. "Hey, I'm hungry. Let's go have some supper at one of the saloons."

She twisted her head back and forth. "You know I don't go to saloons."

He reached for her arm. "Come on. I go to them all the time and never have alcoholic drinks. They serve meals, too, you know. There's nothing inside that would shock or hurt you, especially with me beside you." He watched her for a moment then laughed. "I suppose I can keep buying bread for you if that's what you'd rather eat. How about a brimming bowl of hot stew? Doesn't that sound better?"

It did sound good. "All right, I'll go. Just once to see how it is."

When they stepped into the saloon, Josie tried to slip in between their feet. "The dog can't come in," the barkeep called.

Abe took her collar and led her out. "I'll bring you something when I come out," he promised in a whisper.

Abe bought Martha a big bowl of hot vegetable stew and a sandwich with a cup of coffee. She stuffed herself again. Before they left, Abe bought another large roast meat sandwich that he held until they reached the wagon. Then he slipped it to Josie who eagerly accepted it and carried it under the wagon.

"Well, what are we doing about tonight?" he asked Martha.

"I don't understand," she said. "We'll do as we always do, won't we?"

"No, we won't do as we always do. I have a wife now, and I intend to protect her. Are you coming to Martin's Boardinghouse, or am I staying here?"

Chapter 17

Martha drew in a deep breath. What did he mean? He'd promised her they'd be friends. "I can't go to Martin's," she said in a quavering voice, "and you can't stay here." She took several more deep breaths and felt a little better. "You promised, Abe."

His eyes hardened, his mouth thinned into a straight narrow line, and the cords in his neck stood out. "I don't remember promising to let you take unnecessary chances." He met her eyes with defiance, then his shoulders slumped. "I'll sleep on the ground here." He looked around, hesitated a moment, then grinned. "In fact, if I freeze, that may hurry the house along."

Martha wanted to protest his sleeping on the ground, but where else was there? "I can let you have a couple of blankets," she whispered in a stricken voice.

"I have plenty of blankets," he said. "I didn't get paid half the time in the army, but I got a little bedding out of it."

He marched off, returning ten minutes later with a half-dozen dark wool blankets and a fat pillow. He arranged the bedding on the grass behind the wagon. "Now, Miss Prim," he said, "I doubt anyone will know I'm here. I know you don't want me to touch you, but would you consider praying together each evening?"

"Yes, I'd purely like that." So they prayed together for the first time, each thanking God for the other and asking Him to bless their marriage. Then each fell into their own bed to ponder the many happenings of the day.

Martha admitted to herself that she'd married a true gentleman who would never break a promise to her or anyone else. She thanked God again for Abe, then asked His protection on them both. She told Him that now she knew how much He loved her and thanked Him for leading her into this marriage where she'd be purely happy. She fell into a deep sleep, her arm around Josie.

—⁓—

A beautiful baritone version of "Amazing Grace" awakened Martha in the morning. Josie didn't flick an ear. "You're getting used to my new husband already," she whispered to the relaxed dog.

"Hey, anyone in there?" he called after finishing the third verse.

Martha threw the covers back and reached for her clothes. She bathed every single day before dressing, but she felt embarrassed this chilly morning.

"Don't get up," he called. "I just wanted to tell you I'm going to Martin's to get cleaned up. I'll be back in a half-hour."

As she heard his footsteps fade away, Martha slumped back into her warm nest. Then she jumped out, grabbed her wash bowl, poured ice cold water into it, and proceeded to get herself as clean as possible. Pretty clean, too, she told herself through chattering teeth.

When Abe returned, Martha and Josie were playing tag around the wagon in the sunshine. "Let's go get some breakfast," he said. "We can get Josie's bones while we're out. Then I have to ride up Mill Creek to the sawmill."

Martha wanted to go in the worst way. Was it proper for wives to tell their husbands when they wanted something? She didn't know but she had to anyway. "If you'd let me ride Sampson again, I'd love to go with you," she asked, almost afraid to hear his answer.

A smile broke over his face. "I forgot to tell you Sampson is my wedding present to you."

Sampson! Abe was giving the horse to her? Martha wanted to throw her arms around his neck to show her appreciation. But he'd never understand.

"What a lovely gift! But I have nothing for you, Abe. What can I give you?"

He smiled and his arms twitched as if wanting to be somewhere they weren't. "You already have," he told her. "Marrying me was the best gift in the world. And I'd love to have you ride up Mill Creek with me. But what about Josie? She'd never make it, Martha. But right now let's go eat."

After eating stacks of pancakes and bacon smothered in maple syrup, they went to the meat shop for Josie's bones and hurried back to the wagon. "Did anyone know you didn't sleep in your room last night?" Martha asked, resting on a box while Josie chewed the bones noisily.

He sat on the other box and sighed. "I'm stuffed. How about you, wife? No, as far as I know, no one knows where I slept except you two girls." He chuckled. "If you don't tell, I won't." After a short silence and while Josie crunched bones, Abe looked at Martha again. "But someone will get suspicious when I do it every night. Why don't we go ahead and tell people we're married? No one's going to come out here in the middle of the night to check on newlyweds."

After thinking a bit, Martha nodded. "You're right. My mother always told me to tell the truth, and it's still best."

"All right!" Abe said with a relieved look. "Now, what did you decide about riding up Mill Creek with me?" He grinned. "You could ride your new horse."

Martha could hardly wait to see her new horse, let alone ride him. He'd surely seem different now that he was hers. All hers. "I want to go really bad," she said. "Do you think it would be all right to tie Josie up for so long?"

Abe nodded. "Those bones will last her a long time. If we get out of here quick we'll be back sooner." He put the rope he'd used before around the wagon tongue again and tied it to Josie's collar. "Let's get out of here," Abe said softly, giving Josie a few strokes.

Abe handed Martha some money with instructions to get some sandwiches while he saddled the horses. This time she didn't hesitate before going into the saloon, and she returned with four roast meat sandwiches. The barkeep didn't mention what kind the meat was and as far as Martha could tell no one ever asked. She didn't either.

A half-hour later, the two horses walked up the slowly climbing path beside Mill Creek. Martha noticed the creek had more water here than down by their place where it crossed the street. Soon they came to the sawmill and Martha thrilled as Abe ordered the lumber for their house. As she watched and listened to the transaction she noticed that other men respected and listened to Abe. What a truly good man. She felt proud of him and was overjoyed to be building a home with him. Maybe if she tried hard she could fall in love with him. But, rather than the glow of love, she felt unbelievable gratitude for what he'd done for her, the excitement of not being alone or destitute anymore, and of having property, and lastly, of building a home.

On their way home again, she wondered why the horses couldn't have pulled a wagon with the lumber.

"That would be horribly hard for them, even if I didn't haul much at a time," he explained. "I'd rather pay for the hauling and save the horses' good health. We'll be able to start building sooner, too. It would have taken dozens of trips with the saddle horses. They'll do it in about four with the big wagons and horses."

Martha again felt thankful for having such a kind man. And, as for the house, she knew they'd be in before too many weeks had passed. She could already see it in her mind.

When they reached the wagon, Josie greeted them eagerly, forgiving them for having left her.

—⚞—

The next day Martha decided to do her washing while Abe prepared the site for the house. Abe still had his things washed at the boardinghouse so she didn't have much to do. "When I finish, I'll come over and help," she called as he trudged off toward their place.

It didn't take her long to get her few things washed, rinsed, carried back to the wagon, and hung on the large weeds. When she hung the last garment, she saw the three Indians coming across the expanse of grass. *Abe*, she thought, *why aren't you here?* But she went forward to greet the tall men, a smile pasted tightly on her face. Their stench reached her before they did; she swallowed and became determined to be cordial.

They greeted her and walked toward her wagon. One of them held a bunch of wild onions in his hand. Another held something she couldn't make out, and the last had a large piece of meat. When they reached the wagon they held their offerings to her. "Food," one said, gesturing toward the cook pots.

"I don't have anything to make fire," she said but saw immediately they didn't understand. She made motions of starting a fire then shook her head. "No fire," she repeated one time after another.

"No fire," one finally repeated. Then he held up his wild onions. "Soup," he said plainly. Oh, she was supposed to make soup.

She shook her head, put the kettle on, and stuck her hand into the cold ashes. "No fire," she repeated. Then she searched over the ground a little and repeated, "No fire."

One of the Indians nodded. "No fire." He started off at a slow gait and the other two followed. She dropped to one of the dynamite boxes and heaved a big sigh. At least she was rid of them for one more day. Tomorrow could worry about itself. But before she could collect her clothes and go to help Abe, they returned, stink and all.

One knelt before the fire pit arranging various pieces of wood he'd brought, another handed her two hands full of potatoes. *"Wapatoes,"* he said, pointing to the potatoes. "Soup."

A small wisp of smoke told Martha she might as well get busy and make a big kettle of soup. She washed the meat, cut it up, and dumped it into the water, then added the potatoes and wild onions. That stuff would take a long time to cook so, though barely able to stand not knowing what was happening at the place, she might as well forget about helping Abe.

The Indians sat on the ground around Martha and watched the pot begin to steam. "Food," one said. "Cook," the second one added.

"Fire," Martha said giggling, pointing to the flames.

"Fire," they all repeated.

"Box," Martha said clearly, touching her seat.

They all smiled as they repeated the word.

She pulled off a few blades of grass and said the word, which they all repeated several times, each pulling pieces of grass. They wanted to learn English! So, all the while the soup cooked, she told them words while showing them what it was, and they repeated it. Every once in a while she'd say a word they'd just said and one of them would point at the object. They weren't dumb.

Martha became so involved in their word game she forgot all about going to the place. And the Indians forgot about eating. The fire maker kept the fire going as Martha worked with them.

Finally, she remembered the soup and discovered it was all cooked. She filled three mugs with the soup and offered it to them. One of them pointed to Martha, saying, "Soup." Why not? she thought.

She'd just filled a mug for herself when Abe hurried toward her from the street. "Are you all right?" he called, reaching her before she could answer.

"I'm fine," she said. "I just got invited to cook some soup. Want some?"

He did, so she gave him some, wondering if the Indians would be upset. But they weren't. Each ate another cupful, thanked her in English, and drifted across the prairie.

"I'm sorry I wasn't here for you," he said. "Were you frightened?"

"Not too much. I was mostly disappointed not to go see what you were doing. But you know what? They wanted to learn English. I taught them a bunch of words."

He laughed and patted her on the head. "Good little teacher," he said. "They'll be back."

Martha's blue eyes twinkled. "Maybe we can be in our new house first and they won't be able to find us."

"They'd find us if we moved to California," he said, laughing. "They're part of the price we pay for living here." He ate another cup of soup. "Not too bad if a person doesn't like salt," he said. "I happen to like it very much. I'll get you some salt at the store before they come again."

Three days later the wagons of lumber arrived. "We're ready to build a house," Abe said. "Think we can do it alone?"

Martha shrugged. What did she know about building a house? They worked the rest of the day trying to get the logs set up under the floor. When they quit they both cleaned up, then bought supper and walked back to the wagon.

"Would you mind if I hired someone to help with the house?" he asked as they sat and dreamed about their new house.

She shook her head, surprised he'd bothered to ask. "Not if you think it's necessary. . .and we have enough money."

"If you'll come to my room at the boardinghouse sometime, we'll count our money together. Then we'll both know exactly how much we have left, and how careful we need to be." He got up. "I'll go find someone to work a couple of weeks." He lingered a moment as if he'd left something undone, but he made no move to touch her before striding down the path toward the street.

Chapter 18

Walking toward the saloon, Abe felt completely out of sorts. What kind of a marriage did he have, anyway? Well, he'd known how it would be. He walked into Galbraith's. "Anyone want a few weeks of hard work?" he asked loudly enough for everyone to hear, before settling onto a stool at the bar.

"What kinda work?" "Good pay?" "Who for?" all came at him immediately.

"For me, building my house," he announced to the room in general.

"What you wanna house for?" a tall blond-haired young man asked. "You ain't got no woman."

"Oh, he's sparkin' the little gal with the wagon," another answered.

Abe sipped the coffee the barkeep had set before him. "I took out a claim and now I'm building a house. Anyone want a few weeks' work let me hear."

The blond fellow moved to the stool beside Abe. "I might," he said. "I ain't got much goin' right now. If the price was right."

"I'll give you a fifty-dollar nugget if you help as long as I need you, somewheres around three weeks."

The man stuck out a white hand. "I'll be there in the morning at daybreak."

Abe paid the barkeep for two cups of coffee and hurried back to the wagon. While they relaxed on their boxes, he told Martha of the saloon talk. "It's a good thing we decided to tell people we're married," he said. "I didn't say anything, but people'll find out I've been stayin' here."

She thought a moment and nodded. "You're right. You just go ahead and tell anyone you want. Will you still keep your room at Martin's?"

He nodded slowly. "Nowhere else to put things."

Abe soon decided to hitch the horses to the wagon and pull it to the place.

"It'll be nice to have all our things on our own place," Martha said, her cheeks flushed with excitement.

She looked so pretty and happy Abe wanted to snatch her and give her a kiss on the cheek. But his reply revealed none of his inner turmoil. "My things aren't here yet," he answered. "But it'll be nice to have the wagon and the horses there." He winked at her. "A little more privacy for the newly-weds, too."

—w—

For the next two weeks, Abe worked hard, and so did Emil, his helper. Martha did any light work Abe assigned her and brought them tools, small items, and lunch from the stores and saloons so they could spend more time on the house. Her excitement grew as the house did.

One day as Martha and Josie brought hot roast meat sandwiches to the men, she realized her house looked like a real log house. The steep shake roof would keep out all rain and snow forever. Martha had been chinking the logs on the inside. She had more to do but not too much. Abe had built a rough, very rough, table and sideboard for the kitchen from half-logs. At least it would provide a place to eat and to store the few kitchen items Martha had in the wagon. The dynamite boxes would substitute for chairs for a while.

The main room had not one piece of furniture; the only thing in the room was the stone fireplace in the center, for which she'd gathered rocks from Mill Creek. The big fireplace would easily heat the whole house. The kitchen and main room would each have two small windows to admit light; each of the bedrooms would have three windows. At the moment, although they had nothing inside, but they both had doors with locks, as did the main room. She'd braid some rugs to cover the rough floorboards.

"How long before it's finished?" she asked after giving them their lunch.

Abe wiped the sweat from his forehead. "Not too long. We still have to put the windows in. I've been holding out for glass windows but all I find in the stores are made of isinglass. Think you could handle them for a while?"

"You mentioned once that my. . .our. . .wagon doesn't even have doors. I can handle anything. I just want to move in. Could we do that without windows?"

He grinned, shoved in the last bite of sandwich, washed it down with coffee, and struggled to his feet. "I should say no," he said lightly, "but why would I? We're sleeping in the open, and I don't know about you but I'm waking up with a coating of frost every morning."

Martha looked as if he'd slapped her. "I'm sorry," she said softly. "I haven't been frosted, and I didn't even think about you being colder than I. You've never complained once." She giggled. "But you had a perfectly good bed at Martin's."

She'd never understand that, even if he froze to death, he wanted to be at least near her until she learned to love him—if she ever did. He picked up his hammer and went back to work.

That evening, after Emil left, they moved the things from the wagon into the house. Abe let Martha have her choice of the two identical bedrooms, and she chose the one on the east end of the house. They carried in all the clothes—hers, her mother's, father's, and Jackson's. Josie followed at their heels each time they carried a load from the wagon.

Then they put her few dishes, pans, and silverware on the sideboard shelves. Abe thoroughly enjoyed the work; he loved doing it together with Martha and hoped she did, too. She put the dishrags and towels on shelves, then turned to him, laughing.

"We're all moved in, Abe. We just lack one thing. The food." She burst into merry laughter again.

Her happy sounds and looks clutched at Abe's stomach. How was he supposed to do this? But he joined her laughter. "Want to go get some things so we can start eating at home?"

She nodded gaily, then her face sobered. "What about wood for a fire? We can't cut down our precious trees, can we? We'll save them for shade along the creek, all right?"

She was very young and not at all pushy, but she sure knew how to press a point if it was important to her. He nodded. "Sure. I won't cut a single tree until you ask me to." Her sigh of relief was audible to him across the room.

It seemed she'd forgotten all about his things at Martin's, but he wanted them here in their home. Even with them, he still wouldn't feel married, but at least he'd feel he lived here. "Uh, I think I'll go clear out my room at Martin's."

"I'm sorry again, Abe. I'm thinking only of myself, as you can see. I forgot all about your things. Let me go help you carry them."

"Sure. We can fill the saddlebags and let the horses carry the stuff." They walked over, saddled the horses, put the saddlebags on, and led the horses to the boardinghouse door. Then they carried everything from Abe's room and loaded it into the saddlebags. Abe brought out seven more army blankets and draped them over Charity's back behind the saddle. "Looks like we're ready to go," he said, swinging into the saddle.

Martha swung into her saddle, and they walked the horses the half-mile to their house where they unloaded the saddlebags and transferred the things into Abe's room at the west end of the building.

Later, Abe spread the seven blankets on the hard floor, feeling disgruntled and alone. He stormed into the living area and a moment later Martha came out, Josie so close behind that she almost walked on Martha's heels.

Abe pointed at the dog. "Don't you think the dog belongs outside?" he asked.

Martha's face turned white. "Why, Abe? What did she do?"

219

"Nothing, but dogs belong outside. Houses are for people."

She shook her still-pale face. "I don't feel that way, Abe. Josie belongs with me. Always."

Why should she get every single thing she wanted? And do nothing his way? Nothing at all! He started toward the front door. "Come on, Josie," he said gruffly as he opened it and pointed out. "Go on out. You can bark at the moon or something." Josie stood undecided, looking over her shoulder at Martha. "Go!" Abe said much louder. The dog gave Martha one more look and slunk through the door.

"Good night, Martha," Abe said in a crisp voice and turned back to his own room. He lifted his covers on his floor bed and crawled in. Before long he pushed some of the blankets off. This room kept out a lot of the cold even without windows.

When he felt settled down, he had his usual talk with God. "You think things are going all right?" he asked after he'd thanked Him for allowing them the nice house and, for the sixty-ninth time, the beautiful lot the house sat on. His usual peaceful feeling didn't come. "You saw what I did just now, didn't You?" he asked. "Not only was I mean to Martha, but I took my frustration out on an innocent animal. You know I don't want to be like that, God. I want to make her happy. The dog, too."

I understand, Abe. You'll do better tomorrow.

"But how is this arrangement fair to me?" he asked. "She's so sweet and beautiful that I ache for her, God. How long can I endure the pain?"

You're doing fine, Abe. I'm well-pleased with you.

"That's just great, but I ain't so pleased. You ever heard about unrequited love, God? It's something us mortals have to live through sometimes, and it hurts something awful. Livin' with her, I'll never be able to forget it. That's what made me act like I did tonight. And I didn't even mean what I said."

I saw, Abe. I was with you. It'll be easier if you can get it through your head that you're to be her friend and nothing more. Try hard to make your friend happy. Concentrate on making your place flourish, helping your town develop, and changing the wrongs into rights.

"You're the boss, God, but what I want is for my wife to love me as I love her." He received no answer, and after turning over on the hard floor several times, he fell asleep.

Chapter 19

M artha couldn't believe her ears. Abe couldn't be ordering Josie out of the house. Not Abe! She'd been terribly impressed with his kind attitude to animals as well as people. But she stood there and watched him order her dog from the house. Josie hadn't been separated from her since long before they left Missouri, and neither she nor Josie intended ever to be separated again.

She laid out her featherbed in shock. What happened? Hadn't she known Abe well enough? Was he going to be this way with the new house? She'd thought things were going perfectly, their new house nearly finished. Life was looking good. Sometimes she hoped she'd feel a twinge of something special for Abe. But, oh, she felt something special for him all the time. Just as she would feel to her very best friend in the whole world. She loved him as a friend more than she could say. He'd been so good to her and Josie. She'd felt something. Something more than appreciation. But she'd hoped for something romantic.

She crawled into her warm nest, pulling the covers around her shoulders. "Dear Lord," she whispered into the dark room, "thank You for all the blessings You just keep pouring out on me. Help me to dwell on my blessings and forget my sorrows. Help me to be what You want me to be. . .especially to Abe. What happened tonight, Lord? How should I handle—"

As she prayed, a small whine outside her unfinished window interrupted. "Should I bring her back in, Lord?" She waited quietly for the Lord to show her but she felt nothing. Then another idea presented itself to her. "Or should I sleep with her in the wagon?"

Immediately she felt she should, that she could do that without defying Abe. She gathered up her featherbed and blankets and slipped out the front door where Josie met her, dancing with joy. She hurried out to the wagon.

Martha put her finger to her lips. "We can't make any noise," she told the jubilant dog who beat her into the wagon. In a few minutes they lay together as they had for these many months. Martha breathed a silent *Thank You, I love You* prayer and fell into a deep sleep.

Martha pressed closer to Josie, realizing the cold even in her sleep. When she wakened in the morning she felt cold in spite of her blankets. She wished they could have a fire in the fireplace, but they had to let the mortar set for a week or so. Besides, they didn't have any wood.

Snuggling closer to Josie, she soon felt warm and cozy. She should get up and go into the house, but a few more minutes in her warm nest wouldn't hurt anything. "A little extra warmth never hurt anyone, did it?" she whispered into Josie's ear.

A few minutes later she heard the front door open and close firmly, then she noticed Abe walking toward the creek. When he reached the creek he looked east, then west, and returned to the house, circling it once before calling her name.

Then she realized he didn't know she'd come to the wagon, and probably felt uneasy. "We're all right, Abe," she called. "Over here, in the wagon."

He hurried over and looked at them. "I've been waiting for you to come out of your bedroom," he said. "Finally I called. . .and you didn't answer."

Martha giggled. "Only because I didn't hear you," she said.

"I thought something had happened to you," he went on as though she hadn't spoken. He stood quietly looking at them for a long minute. "Why did you sleep out here?" he finally asked.

"Josie cried."

"Oh." He looked sadder than she'd ever seen him. Maybe he was sorry he'd been so harsh.

"If it means that much to you, Josie can live in the house."

She jumped from her warm bed before remembering she wore only a nightgown. Oh well, it covered her as well as a dress. She felt like hugging Abe for saying Josie could come inside. But she didn't. "Thank you," she said. "It does mean that much to me. I thought you felt the same way about her, Abe."

A strange look darkened his brown eyes. "You'd better go inside and get changed before you catch pneumonia," he answered in a froggy voice. Martha wondered if he'd caught a cold.

Martha wrapped the blankets around herself then dashed through the grass to the front door and into the house, Josie at her side. The house actually felt warm, even with no heat and the windows unfinished! She couldn't believe the difference! Keeping Josie with her, she went into her room and shut the door, only to discover she needed water. She snatched her little bucket and ran to the creek then came back and washed up in the icy water as she had been doing ever since she had run out of buffalo chips. When she finished, she dressed, then carried the water out.

"You really bathed in that creek water?" Abe asked.

She laughed. "I do it every morning. You've been using Martin's warm water. Are you brave enough to do it like I did?"

He looked almost sick. "I'm not sure I want to be clean that bad. Not until the sun warms us up a little, anyway. Are you ready to go get some breakfast?"

They'd talked about buying food yesterday but hadn't done it. "Why don't you get some food to cook here?" she asked. "Could we cook it outside? Or would you rather wait for the fireplace to cure?"

"Let's go eat first then buy some food. Know what else I have to do today?" he asked with an embarrassed grin.

She shook her head.

"Build an outhouse. We have just about enough logs left for that. And I guess nothing could be more important."

"An outhouse! Oh Abe, that will be wonderful! I will appreciate that more than you'll ever know."

So, before the sun dropped behind the horizon that night, a new outhouse stood about fifty feet southeast of the house. Martha put her second newest Montgomery Ward catalog inside.

Martha didn't feel as comfortable in the new house as she'd expected, and she kept Josie right with her all the time. She certainly didn't want her dog bothering Abe.

When bedtime came, Abe asked if they could read the Bible together before they prayed, and that delighted Martha. There was only one thing she wanted more than that. "Could we find out more about the Methodist church?" she asked after their prayers. "Where it meets and if they'd let us start going there?"

Abe laughed. "Churches are public places, Martha. Anyone can attend. I'd really like to find a church to attend, too. It's been too long. I'll see what I can learn. Now, we better go to bed so we can get up in the morning. Good night."

Martha felt sorry for Abe when Josie followed her into her room and he went into his alone.

Chapter 20

Abe jerked off his outer clothing and fell into his hard bed, thoroughly disgusted with himself. Why had he been so cruel to Martha and Josie? He knew the answer to that question almost before he asked it, and it certainly wasn't their fault. He'd been frustrated by finally realizing that their marriage truly was in name only.

But that was no excuse! He'd been the one to push this sham of a marriage, and now he'd have to learn to live with it. He angrily turned over to discover he didn't feel any more comfortable on his left side. "I'm sorry, God," he whispered. "Will You forgive me? I'm a poor excuse for a man."

You're my child, and I love you. Don't be discouraged. I'm going to bless you in ways you can't even imagine. And I'll forgive you for being unkind, but only after you ask the same question of Martha. You hurt and confused her, Abe.

Abe jumped up from his uncomfortable blankets. He didn't want God's nebulous blessings. He wanted Martha to love him as he loved her! Then he remembered he'd also been told he hurt and confused her. He nodded. He'd done that all right. How could he make it up to her?

First off, he'd better let her know Josie had nothing to do with it. As he paced in his room, deep in thought, he noticed once again how barren it looked. Realizing Martha's looked the same, he wondered if he could make her some furniture. He laughed aloud at the thought. He'd never seen such a mess as the table and sideboard he'd built. Well, he'd make her a bed and armoire, and he'd do a good job. Maybe he could make some plans before he started, sort of figure it out like he did the house. The house had turned out all right, even if he did say so himself.

He pulled on his clothes, lit a candle, opened his bedroom door, and slipped into the living area. He'd just find that paper and see if he could come up with something better. But he couldn't see well enough by the candlelight. Knowing he couldn't fall asleep yet, he quietly opened the outside door and stepped into the much colder night air.

Hunching against the cold, he headed toward the street, thinking how Martha must have suffered last night, as well as all the other recent nights in the wagon. Both saloons were still brightly lit and loud voices could be heard as Abe walked past. Although tempted to go inside for the company, he

walked to the end of the street, turned south until he passed the buildings, then turned east and walked briskly back to his house. He smiled. It wasn't a cabin but a house. Martha said so. Thinking of Martha and how much he loved her helped Abe feel better. Somehow he'd reach into her heart, he thought as he undressed for the second time that night. He crawled into bed telling himself that being unkind to her and Josie wouldn't win her love very fast. He'd do better in the future. Feeling more relaxed and less angry with himself, he dropped off to sleep.

—ɯ—

"I can't wait to be able to cook here," Martha said the next morning. "That's when it will seem like home. Think the fireplace will be cured in another week?"

He thought so and wondered how he'd get firewood, but didn't mention it to her. "I was just thinking," he said, "that I should get some good lumber and try making you a bed and armoire. Don't laugh."

Martha's blue eyes twinkled merrily. "I'm not laughing, Abe. I think that would be purely nice. I could put my featherbed on it and be as cozy as I was back home."

Abe felt gratified that she'd acted as though she'd forgotten his little fit. But he still had to apologize and ask her to forgive him. Of course, she would. She'd never hold a grudge. But, as the day progressed, he didn't apologize and things still seemed all right. About midmorning he took Charity and rode out to the Mill Creek lumber mill to order lumber and to check around for wood supplies. On the way he found plenty of downed trees, but he realized he'd need a saw and a way to haul the wood down to the place.

After ordering the lumber, he headed Charity back home. When they reached the village, he decided to check into a bar just to see what had been going on.

"Been missin' you," the barkeep said, pouring Abe a cup of coffee. "Ya heard the town's got a new name?"

"No. You mean newer'n Waiilapptu?"

"Yep, it's Walla Walla and, from what I hear, that's what it's gonna stay."

Abe took a long swig of the strong brew, swallowed, and exhaled the hot steam. He nodded. "Walla Walla. Where many waters meet. Good. It shoulda been Walla Walla all the time."

The barkeep had something else trying to pop out of him, so Ab patiently waited.

"Now they're thinkin' on namin' the state Walla Walla," he said eage "Wouldn't that be somethin'?"

"Yeah, that sure would be something. Think there's much chance?"

The barkeep scrubbed the shiny wooden bar top. "Some think so. Guess we'll know sometime next year."

"You know what else they're doin'?" the barkeep asked almost immediately. "They're layin' out the town right away. Ain't that a scream? What's to lay out? One street. One dinky street built on an Indian trail. You and I could do that, Abe. Save hirin' the hi' falutin' surveyor they got comin' in."

Abe couldn't wait to relay the news to Martha.

"I'm purely thrilled with our town's new name," she said. "Walla Walla. Many waters. That's so nice the Indians will even be happy about it."

—⁓—

Together they checked the street every day for the surveyor. Sure enough one day they found a man with his three-legged instrument in the middle of the street, peering first in one direction, then another. After keeping at it for more than a week, word got around that four of the eight buildings on the main street—the trading post, the tin shop, the vacant store, and Galbraith's Saloon—stood in the way of the proposed cross streets and would have to be either razed or moved.

What an uproar that caused!

"They can just get someone else to survey the town," Galbraith said one day while Abe and Martha ate dinner in his saloon. "They ain't tearin' my place down fer some street that ain't even there yet."

Abe worked most of every day on Martha's bed, but in the evenings, he always put his ear to the ground. Finally, when a full-fledged revolution seemed ready to erupt, he called the men of the town together.

"Do we or don't we want our town to grow?" Abe asked. "We'll all be better off financially, and we'll be more comfortable, too, when it's a little bigger. Why don't we all get together and move the buildings off the streets? It won't take long if we all help."

"Ain't a one of them buildings won't fall apart if we try to move 'em," Rackett, the owner of the tin shop said.

"Yeah," Galbraith added, "and I've already built the inside of mine. Cain't move that."

"Sure we can," Abe said. "What we can't move, we'll tear down and rebuild." He laughed softly. "We're only talkin' about four buildings. I built my house in a couple of weeks, and there's a lot more to it than any of these here stores. If we all help, we can do each one in less than a week, and they'll be better'n they were before. But we better get on it before it gets any colder."

Finally, with no real choice, the men agreed, and they set the next day

to start on Reece's vacant store on the bank of Mill Creek.

It, as well as most of the other buildings didn't have a floor to support the walls in a move so they ended up tearing it apart and rebuilding it on the spot the surveyor had designated. It took three days and ended up sturdier than before. The next day they started on the tin shop.

As Sunday neared, Martha asked Abe if he'd learned anything about where the Methodists were meeting.

Abe laughed. "Sure did, but I doubt there'll be a meetin' this week. It's been meeting in Galbraith's Saloon, but he's gettin' ready to move. He was the most upset of any of the fellows, so I'm guessin' he's not about to be bothered with anything this week. Maybe we'll have him all moved and happy by next Sunday."

So Abe and Martha had their private Bible study together as they had been doing since they'd been married.

Early the next morning Abe decided it was time to get some wood and get the fireplace going. "Think we could take the top off the wagon and whatever else we could to lighten it?" he asked Martha.

She thought a moment. "I guess we could, but why?"

"So I can haul some wood down from the mountains. It's going to be hard for the horses, and any weight I can dump will save them."

Her sudden smile brightened her entire face, almost the whole room. "Yes, Abe, take everything off but the wheels if you want, just get that wood."

Together they removed every bit possible without disabling the wagon. After Martha went inside to do something, Abe checked the wagon once more for anything removable. When his eyes hit the wagon floor again, he noticed the double floor. If he could get that first layer of boards off it would lighten the wagon a lot. Using his pry bar, he finally got the first board off. Then the second. When he lifted the third board he noticed a small pouch between the third and fourth boards. Curious, he pulled off the rest of the boards, picked up the pouch, and hurried inside the house. "See what I found between the two floors of the wagon?"

Martha peered at the pouch. "That's Papa's money pouch," she said. "I wonder how it got in there?"

Abe grinned. "It got in there when he put it there and nailed the second floor on. He hid it there, Martha. Open it up."

She opened it and pulled out money. Lots of money. They counted it out on the table. "Twelve hundred dollars?" Martha asked incredulously. "And you've been feeding me!"

"I like feeding you," Abe said. "Didn't you say your folks sold a farm just before you started west?" She nodded. "Well, that's the money. It was supposed to get your family started here." Suddenly, he hoped she wouldn't decide she didn't need him anymore.

Martha nodded, looking sad. "The money's yours," she told Abe. "You've been paying for everything forever."

Abe shook his head. "It isn't mine. It isn't all yours, either. Some of it would be for your two brothers. But you'll still have enough left to care for yourself a long, long time. . .if you decide you don't need me anymore."

Her blue eyes opened wide. "Are you trying to get rid of me?"

"No. That's the last thing I'll ever want."

She relaxed. And smiled. "Good. I'm here to stay then. Now, may I go with you after wood?"

"I'd like that more than you know," he said, "but you'd better stay here. I may walk all the way back if I get too much wood. I'll just have to see how it goes. Anyway, I'll be back by dark."

—m—

A little while later, after stopping at the general store for a large saw, he took off. He didn't hurry the horses but they reached the timber in a couple of hours. The spicy smell of the woods together with his new saw made him eager to start cutting logs. He soon found a large pine tree that had blown down. That single tree would fill the wagon to capacity. After four hours of backbreaking labor, he had the wagon stacked with wood—and he hadn't used the entire tree. If he ever got rested up from this, he'd come back and get the rest of the tree. And more.

The horses struggled with the loaded wagon but managed to drag it home.

Darkness had cloaked the town for less than an hour when he finally reached home. The horses nickered joyfully, as happy to be finished with their labor as Abe.

He unharnessed them and rubbed them down, took them to the creek to drink, then fed them their oats and staked them out in the grass.

He knocked on the door in order not to startle Martha, but when he went in he found Nellie Martin there.

"You look tired and dirty," Martha said, laughing.

"I am tired and dirty," Abe agreed. "So are the horses."

Nellie edged toward the door. "I'll go now, Martha. You come over and see me, hear?" She turned to Abe. "You sure have built a nice place here, Mr. Noble."

"Thanks," Abe said with a pleasant smile. "We're enjoying it." He poured a basin of water and washed his face and arms while Nellie left. "Ready to go eat?" he asked as soon as the door closed behind the girl. "I'm starved."

An hour later they both carried a big load of groceries. Martha put the things on the table, then into the sideboard. Potatoes, cabbage, carrots, onions, salt pork, bacon, coffee, sugar, salt, beans, dried apples, flour, lard, dried corn, and cornmeal. They'd also found a little honey, for which they'd paid dearly.

"I never saw so much food in my life," Martha said. "I doubt we'll ever have to buy food again."

Abe grinned. "You'll be surprised how fast that goes." He winked at her. "I'm counting on you making some good meals now."

—m—

The next morning Abe worked on Martha's bed before going to the village to help move the buildings. After a while he came home and finished the bed. Martha laid her featherbed on top of it and the blankets over that.

"Thank you," she said sincerely. "It's nicer than I hoped."

He felt his face grow warm under her compliments. "If you like it well enough, I'll make you an armoire next."

"I do. I'll love the armoire, Abe."

He then left to go downtown to move more buildings.

By the following Sunday, two more buildings stood in their new homes, leaving only Galbraith's Saloon left to move. Galbraith had put his off until last, maybe hoping it wouldn't really happen.

"If we knew who the Methodists are, we could invite them here for a week or two," Martha said.

Abe shook his head. "They'll be meetin' soon enough. Then we can go and see how things are."

After their own little Sunday school, Martha and Abe went riding, with the much stronger and fatter Josie running along beside them. When they returned, Abe rubbed the horses down while Martha prepared their supper. "You two are looking good," he said to Charity. "You're both shiny and fat. How do you like our new home?" He took them down to the creek, then out to a new spot of grass and staked them. He walked out a little farther, wondering if he should make a barn before winter. Everyone said it was so mild here that animals didn't need protection, but he wasn't sure. Charity had always had protection. Finally, he told the horses good night and went into the house.

Something smelled so good it made his mouth water. "All right, what is it?" he asked Martha.

Tendrils of her dark hair curled around her face that had turned pink from the fire. And her bright blue eyes sparkled with joy. "I made a dried apple pie," she said, pushing a curl behind her ear. "Come on, Abe, it's all ready."

The sight of his beautiful wife who wasn't his wife thwarted his appetite and made his heart beat so loudly he thought she'd hear it.

Chapter 21

"Come on, Abe, let's eat," Martha said, but Abe didn't move. Standing there, looking at her, an expression of pain crossed his face. What could he be thinking? "Abe, are you all right?"

He jumped as if startled and moved to the table where he sat on one of the dynamite boxes from the wagon. After asking God to bless their food and them, he began reaching for food and serving her, then himself. "How did you make a pie?" he asked. "I thought you had to have an oven."

She laughed. "Papa brought a dutch oven from Missouri. You can bake over a fire in one, but it doesn't work nearly as easy or as well as an oven. Maybe I made a mistake baking the pie." She laughed again. "I wasn't going to mention it yet, Abe, but I purely want a stove. Mrs. Martin has one so I know they can be had. Do you think we could get one someday?"

At last Abe laughed, and laid down his fork. "I'm sure we will someday, Martha, but I'm not sure when. I don't know how to get one or how much it might cost." He sat quietly for a few seconds then retrieved his fork and continued eating the roast they'd gotten at Shaffer's last night. Finally, his eyes met hers. "I have something to show you after we finish. Do you have time?"

What could he have to show her that would take time? "I have the rest of my life," she finally said, trying to read his eyes. His appreciative smile looked so beautiful she almost had to catch her breath.

"It won't take that long," he said in breathy softness. "In fact, it won't take long at all. Maybe a half-hour."

They finished eating in almost silence as Martha tried to figure out what he was going to show her. He'd been outside for quite a while taking care of the horses. He must have seen something out there. Maybe a late-blooming wildflower. She noticed his empty plate. "Ready to try the pie?" she asked. Then she pulled the pie from the end of the table, cut it, and served the first piece to Abe.

"Heavenly," he breathed after the first bite. "When have we eaten anything to compare with this at the saloons?"

Martha shrugged and smiled. It tasted good to her, too, but she couldn't say that.

Abe's eyes twinkled. "If you can make things like this without a stove, I guess you don't really need one." He pushed his box back from the table. "I'm eager to show you what I mentioned," he said. "If you have the time, could we do it now?"

"I have the time, Abe. I'll get my coat."

"No, it's in my room. Shall I bring it out here on the table?" A minute or two later he returned and carefully emptied his pouch of gold on the opposite end of the table from where they'd eaten.

Martha had never seen so much money in her life. "Oh, Abe!" she cried, "we're rich."

"Get your dynamite box," he said, dropping to his own, chuckling. "We're far from rich, Martha, but let's see how much we have left." He separated the one-hundred-dollar nuggets from the smaller fifty-dollar pieces and counted them. "We have twenty of the big ones," he said, looking into Martha's eyes. "How much money is that?"

She thought a moment. "That's two thousand dollars."

He nodded. "Right. I knew I had a smart wife. Now, let's see, we have fifteen of the smaller nuggets. What's that?"

"You're testing me, Abram Noble. Well, it's about. . .seven hundred fifty dollars."

They counted out the paper money and what he had in his small pouch. "All right, tell me how much we have altogether."

"Looks to be about three thousand three hundred dollars." Her shining eyes met Abe's. "We are rich, Abe. We are."

He shook his light brown head. "Let me put it this way. Before we were married it was about four thousand three hundred dollars. We've used one thousand dollars, Martha. That's a fourth of it. We used most of it for lumber to build the house and furniture. Let's get our paper and decide what we'll do with the rest of it." He moved to his bedroom and brought back the tablet he'd bought the day they married.

He handed her the paper and pencil. "As we decide, you write it down. Now, first, do you have any idea how much a stove costs?"

She shook her head. "No, but I'll bet you do."

"I don't. So let's go to the next item. I'd like to buy some cows. Maybe about ten."

Her eyes widened. That sounded wonderful to her. She wanted nothing more than to have their own farm. She poised the pencil over the paper. "I love it, Abe. How much?"

"Something less than fifty dollars each, but let's say fifty dollars. How much, my little secretary?"

"Five hundred dollars. Oh, Abe, it does go fast doesn't it? We really aren't all that rich. But could we have just a few chickens?"

He smiled and his eyes darted to her hand lying on the table. Martha tucked it down beside her. For a moment he looked cross but quickly recovered and continued. "People have cows for sale," he answered, "but I haven't seen any chickens. As soon as some arrive we'll be able to buy some chicks and raise them ourselves. We'll probably find some in the spring." His eyes sought hers again, but she noticed he kept them away from her hands. "Is there anything else you want?"

"Not that I can think of, but even buying groceries will eat up our money, won't it?"

"Not very fast. I promise you, we'll be able to eat and so will Josie and the horses. I'll also check at the store about a stove. See what they can do."

"I'd like a garden in the spring. That would help, wouldn't it?" she asked.

"Yes, we'll have a garden. We'll also send for some fruit trees early in the year." He pointed at the paper. "I don't know how much they'll cost, but write them down, anyway."

Martha felt thrilled from her nose to her toes. "Isn't it exciting, Abe? I love for us to talk like this. You know, about fixing up our place just like we want it. We're going to have a bit of heaven right here in Walla Walla County, aren't we?"

Once again an unhappy look crossed his face. She thought he was going to get up and leave, but he didn't. A forced smile appeared. "Yes," he said. "That's what we're going to have. A little bit of heaven right here." Then he did get up. "Want to take a walk along the creek?" He whistled for Josie, who struggled to her feet from her rug beside the fireplace, and the three took a long walk east along the creek.

—⚬—

The next morning Abe worked on Martha's armoire for a little while then went downtown to help move Galbraith's Saloon, the last building to be moved. "It'll be the toughest, too," Abe said before leaving. "Galbraith will be watching everything we do to make sure we don't scratch a single board."

After he left, Martha cleaned up her little house, a job she considered pure bliss. Then she carried water, heated it, and washed their clothes, hanging them on big weeds when she'd finished. Josie followed her from weed to weed. "Washing our clothes sure isn't like those filthy things I washed at the creek, is it?" she asked Josie as they ran back to the house.

Inside, she started some bread. It would take all day to rise twice and bake in her dutch oven, but she had enough from the last batch for dinner. Abe always came home at noon to eat.

She sat down to mend another of her dresses, all of which seemed to be falling apart. One of these days she'd be repairing repairs. As she threaded the needle wishing she had a rocking chair to sit in while she worked, Josie started barking wildly, then the three Indians opened the door and walked in.

And so did the sickening smell! She jumped up and opened the front door and also the back door as wide as they'd go. Better to have the cool air than such a horrible smell—not that opening the doors would fix it.

They seemed to be wearing the same clothes as last time, the older one in buckskins and moccasins and the other two in white man's clothing, ragged and dirty. The older one looked into her eyes. "Food," he said.

Oh well, she'd better fix them something and get rid of them quickly so the place could be aired out before Abe came. She forced a smile to her lips and nodded. "Food," she repeated. She pulled out the last loaf of bread, cut it into thick slices, smeared lots of butter over them, then sliced the left-over roast from last night and put it over half the slices. Putting the sandwiches together, she laid each on a plate and handed it to the Indians who accepted the treat with happy smiles.

Just as one of the youngest started to take a bite, she told them to wait. "We have to thank the Great Spirit for giving us the food," she said, then proceeded to bow her head, close her eyes, and ask God to bless the food, the Indians, and her. When she opened her eyes, all three were gazing at her in awe. "Go ahead and eat," she said with a smile, making motions as though shoving a sandwich into her mouth.

The Indians looked at their sandwiches, and the older one lifted the top slice and started to put it to his mouth.

"No," Martha told him, "eat it all together." She put the top slice of bread back on and held the whole thing to his mouth. "Open wide, like this," she said, opening her mouth as wide as she could. When the Indian opened his mouth, she shoved the sandwich in and told him to bite off a piece—and he did!

That was all it took. They all sat on the floor and ate the sandwiches as she'd showed them. As they ate, one of the younger ones tapped the floor and looked at Martha with a question in his eyes. She tapped it as he had and said, "floor." They all repeated the word, tapping the floor.

They wanted to learn more words! Martha moved to the table, touched it, and said the word, after which they all repeated it. She went around the room pointing at things—fireplace, fire, window, sideboard, her own dress and shoes. The Indians became so engrossed in learning the words they nearly forgot to eat. She went through the list several times, then pointed to the objects while they said the words. They did much better than she'd expected. Finally, she told them to eat, simulating eating a sandwich, and they began eating again. When they finished their sandwiches they got up.

Martha told them to say, "Thank you," which they did.

"Good-bye," Martha said as they left. They all smiled and repeated it, followed by something she didn't understand. Next time they came she'd start learning their language.

Abe didn't feel as excited about the visit as Martha did. "I need to be here all the time to protect you," he growled.

"No, you don't. Those men wouldn't hurt me. They're learning our language, and I'm going to learn theirs. Besides, Josie's always here."

Abe gave her a grudging smile. "You know what? We've never put that dog to the test. We don't know if she'd really protect you."

"Want to try beating me up?"

He stepped to the still-open door. "Nope. Gotta go though." He hurried off toward the village.

———✳———

That evening Abe wanted Martha to go see how the town was getting laid out. They rode the horses as they did most evenings and wandered onto the street where small yellow flags had been attached to bars drilled into the ground at all four corners of each planned intersection. She saw many yellow flags but nothing north of the street except the Indian tepees.

"Those flags show the streets and their names," Abe said, pointing. "The north and south streets start at the creek with First Street. He's surveyed up to Fourth out about to where your wagon was."

"What about the east-west streets?" Martha asked. "Do they have names or are they numbered, too?"

Charity moved around as though she'd like to get going; Sampson stayed as near to Charity as he could. "They have names," Abe said. "I understand they haven't decided whether the street will be Main Street or Nez Percé Street. The next one south is Alder, then Poplar, then Birch."

Martha laughed. "I like the tree names. But why are the markers so far apart?"

"The east-west streets are one hundred feet wide and the north-south streets are eighty feet." He laughed. "That's wider than the streets in Iowa where I came from. They think Walla Walla will be a huge metropolis."

Martha touched Sampson's sides with her heels. "Let's have a good ride tonight." Sampson took off without checking on Charity for once. After they'd ridden for a while they slowed. "I didn't see anything north of the street," she said.

He shook his head. "I think they decided not to bother the Indians. Although they have no legal claim to the land, they might feel put out."

Later, when Abe came in from caring for the horses, he sat down on his box across the table from where Martha mended by candlelight. "I just remembered the lots on the street are for sale. Five dollars each, sixty feet wide and one hundred twenty feet deep. Should we buy some? They said we could buy two." She looked puzzled so he grinned and shrugged. "Who knows? Maybe we'll open a business someday."

She stabbed her needle through the fabric several times and laid it down. "Sounds good. I might even be able to help."

"Good. I'll do it tomorrow after we finish Galbraith's Saloon. Did I tell you it'll be finished tomorrow? Better than before, including the bar and stuff inside. Even Galbraith's pleased."

They had their Bible reading and prayer together and fell into their own beds at opposite ends of the house.

—◊—

Abe came home the next day wearing a wide smile. "I got the lots," he said. "I bought the second and third one, other than the businesses already established. Want to go see them?"

Martha laid down her dress that seemed to be more rips and tears than dress, and reached for her coat, Papa's coat, really. After a brisk walk, she learned their lots were #2 and #3 on the south side of the street between Reece's unoccupied building and the meat market. And a stone's throw from the creek.

"Oh, Abe, this is wonderful," she said. "We can start two businesses, each on our own lot."

He looked at her as if in shock. "So you want to keep our business lives as separated as our personal lives," he said. "Do you really dislike me that much?"

Chapter 22

A be wished right off that he hadn't said anything. He knew, almost knew, that Martha hadn't meant anything by her remark.

Her face blanched as she faced him. "I'm sorry," she said, the words rushing out together. She turned her back to him for a few seconds, then asked in a muffled voice if he was ready to go home.

They read their Bibles and prayed together before she broke down and cried. "I'm trying to be a good wife," she said when he pressed her to explain her tears.

"You're not trying to be a wife at all," he corrected, "but that was the agreement so I can't complain. You're being a good maid and cook, though. I couldn't ask for better."

Her blue eyes, bright with tears, met his. "Am I being a good friend?" she choked out.

He nodded. "Yes. You're definitely my best friend. Thank you for reminding me of that, Martha. I do appreciate you."

They fell into a routine with Abe working on her armoire most of the day while she did her housework, after which they spent at least an hour riding and exercising the horses. Then he went downtown to catch up on the news while she made supper.

One day he decided to look around in the general store and he found two things: a tool called a plane that McClinchey told him would smooth boards, and an envelope of plans to build furniture—tables, chairs, benches, beds, armoires, chiffoniers, and even cradles.

Excited, he bought both and couldn't wait to show the plans to Martha, which he did as soon as he walked through the front door. Unfolding it, he laid them on the table. After they'd enjoyed looking at the plans for several pieces of furniture, he pointed at the cradle. "See, there's even a plan for a cradle. Isn't it cute?"

Her face brightened until it looked almost sunburned. "I guess we won't need that."

He hadn't expected her to ask him to make a cradle right away, but her words felt like icicles piercing his heart. He swallowed hard. "Never?" he whispered.

The cords in her throat tightened, and she didn't answer for a moment. "Never's a long time," she finally whispered back. After a moment she squared her shoulders. "I'm so glad you got that piece of paper, Abe," she said gaily. "By the time this winter passes we'll have the best furniture in town."

———※———

When Sunday came, Martha and Abe put on their best clothes, she a dark blue muslin dress that hadn't been mended much, he a pair of dark cord pants and a light shirt. He didn't have a tie. She had to wear Papa's old coat over her dress as they walked to Galbraith's Saloon for church. The place had been cleaned up and four eight-foot-long half-log benches had been put in against the east wall. A tall table in front would serve as a pulpit. After they found their seats, Abe happened to glance at Martha's face. He saw a disappointment he didn't understand, but a moment later it came to him. The only people there besides themselves were seven roughly dressed men and two Indians who made their presence known by their smell.

The service was simple. A pump organ had been brought in and placed against a wall, but no one played it as they sang several old hymns with gusto. Then Abe remembered that Martha played the piano. "Can you play that thing?" he whispered to her, gesturing toward the organ with his face.

She smiled and shrugged. "I don't know," she whispered back, "I've never tried."

The minister preached an impressive sermon about the shepherd leaving the ninety-nine sheep and searching for the one that was lost. "So you see," he finished, "we may think we're a long way from God way out here in the West, but He's right here with us. And He'd be much obliged if we'd do our part to help find his lost sheep. There are plenty out here."

After the service the men eagerly greeted Abe and Martha, telling them how much difference they made in the singing. Then the minister, Reverend Miller, welcomed them and asked them to be sure to return the following week.

"I'm sure we will," Abe said. "And I might be able to help you find someone to play that organ over there. My wife plays a piano. Maybe you'd let her give it a try?"

Reverend Miller wasted no time showing Martha to the instrument and how it worked. "Just pedal it a moment to get the feel," he suggested.

After a few pedals Martha tried the keyboard, which worked just fine, though sounding tinny.

"Say!" Abe said proudly, "that sounds as if you've been playing it forever."

Reverend Miller agreed. "It would be a great help if you'd play for us, Mrs. Noble."

Mrs. Noble! No one had ever called her that. Abe was a husband to be proud of. Besides being so good to her, he'd saved the town a lot of trouble when he'd gotten the men to rebuild the business buildings, and she'd heard them thank him several times. She agreed to play, and they went home to dinner and, later, a ride up into the mountains.

—꩜—

The days drifted past one after another as Abe built furniture, each piece looking better than the last, hauling wood from the mountains, and building a log barn and corral from small logs he brought down in the wagon.

Martha cleaned the house, washed and mended their clothes, and prepared good food for them. She played the organ each Sunday. Abe soon realized that her playing made them both enjoy the service more, giving them the feeling that they were a necessary part of the group.

Together, with Charity and Sampson, they'd driven home the ten, worn-out, skinny cows they'd bought from a man who'd just driven them up from Mexico. Abe, using wire from the store, had fenced in about twenty acres to make sure the cows got plenty of water and feed before the winter storms came.

Martha had been beside him helping him at every possibility. Her sweet disposition and helpful ways increased his love for her. Sometimes, the feeling of a one-way love caused him to be less than sweet to her, but her prompt and complete forgiveness only made him love her more.

The first snow flurries came early in December. At first it didn't stick, but then it came down in earnest and was a foot deep on the ground, the temperature hovering in the teens. Abe went out several times a day to feed the cattle and horses and to make sure the creek hadn't frozen, which it never did.

"Brrrr, it's plenty cold out there," he said one morning, setting the bucket of fresh milk on the floor beside the table. He held out his arms to the crackling fire. "Feels good in here."

She stood beside him. "You built us a fine house," she said. "I don't like to seem a snob, Abe, but we have by far the nicest home in Walla Walla. It's even warm and snug in this cold weather."

He couldn't hold back a wide smile. "You can say that anytime you want to. Don't you know it makes me feel good?"

Her bright blue eyes softened. "I thought it might." She quieted and looked thoughtful for a moment. "I really appreciate you," she went on. "Sometimes I wonder what would have happened to me if you hadn't come along."

A picture appeared in Abe's mind of his little Martha, sitting in the snow beside her wagon, snow sagging the canopy almost to the box. She wore her father's old coat as she tried to light a fire that only spit and smoked. "Let's just thank the good Lord we're together in this nice warm house," he finally said in a soft voice.

That night, after Abe went to bed, he thought about their lives. They'd been married nearly three months, and he loved Martha even more now than he had before. Martha couldn't be sweeter. Neither could she be a better help to him. But he wanted to touch her. Just pat her cheek, or hold her hand.

"What about it, God?" he asked. "Is this all there is?"

Isn't it enough, Abe?

"I don't know. What do You think?"

I think you have a lot more than most of the men in the area.

Abe nodded his head in the dark. He sure did have more than most. He grinned in the dark. "You're right, Lord. I have plenty of food and the best woman in the world to prepare it for me. I have a warm place to live and the best woman in the world to keep it nice for me. Thanks, Lord, I should be more than satisfied. . .and I am. I'm plenty grateful for what You've given me. Maybe my marriage is a little different, but it's good. Thanks again, God. From now on I'll try hard to be satisfied with my lot in life. Help me, Lord. Help me be really satisfied."

You've learned a lot, Abe. I'm pleased with you. You're learning to be satisfied with what you have. But don't get too satisfied. Remember, Abe, I made you, I love you, and I plan the very best for you.

"Thanks, Lord. . . ." Abe rolled over, completely trusting, and fell asleep before he could tell God what he was thanking Him for.

ABRAM MY LOVE

For you, Perri.
I loved you before you were born.
Today I love you more.
My love will keep growing tomorrow and for all eternity.
May God bless you always.

Chapter 1

Early December, 1859

Martha Noble stood back and gazed at the six-foot-tall fir tree. As she took long sniffs she closed her eyes and imagined herself in the middle of the fragrant woods the tree had come from. Her husband, Abram, had just put it on its homemade stand beside the isinglass window in the main room of their log house. It was definitely a house, not a cabin; Martha had said so from the first. The cozy twelve-by-twelve-foot room had a rough table and sideboard along its back wall. A fireplace almost in the middle warmed the whole house. Another isinglass window in the back wall let in more light.

"Thank you, Abe," she said, thrilled to her toes. "I had no idea we'd have our own tree for our first Christmas. Now we'll have to pop some corn and string it."

The young couple had just made a trip on their saddle horses, Sampson and Charity, into the Blue Mountains for the tree. Their homestead in Walla Walla in the Walla Walla Valley of Washington Territory had hardly any trees and no evergreens.

Abe took a long look at his seventeen-year-old bride, started to say something, then bolted into his bedroom, closing the door behind him.

What was that all about? Martha wondered. They'd had so much fun finding the tree, cutting it, and bringing it home. "Abe," she called. "What's the matter? Did I do something?" She waited a moment. "Come out and tell me if I did something," she said calmly. Abe was the very best husband in the entire world, not given to fits of pique. After another minute passed, she tried again. "Come tell me what I did," she called. "You know I'd never purposely do anything to hurt you. Come out and tell me, Abe, so I can tell you I'm sorry and I won't do it again."

Josie, their black, white, and gray shepherd-type dog, struggled to her feet from her cozy rug beside the fireplace. She gave Martha a glance, ran to Abe's bedroom door, and barked three small yips.

Martha couldn't help laughing. "Josie says come out," she called through the closed door. "I'll pop the corn." Still no answer.

She got out the corn and put a cupful into the wire popper Abe had bought at the general store. As the popcorn popped its merry tune, Martha felt herself growing warmer. Surely she wasn't getting upset with Abe. No, it was the heat from the fire. She couldn't remember ever being angry at him. He was too nice to get riled at. She popped three cups of popcorn and threaded two needles with very long, heavy threads before she called again.

"Come on, Abe," she called merrily. "I need you."

That brought him stomping out, his face looking as red as the fire had made hers. "You need me?" His voice had an edge on it, unlike his usual quiet manner. "You don't need me, Martha. You don't even know what it's like to need me."

Martha jerked around to face him. His clear brown eyes showed pain rather than anger and his clean-shaven face tensed. His light brown hair fell over his ears and his square chin jutted forward. A dark feeling came into Martha's heart. "I've done something really awful, haven't I? But you'll have to tell me what it is so I can make it right."

He looked into her eyes a long time again, then slumped into a chair. "You really don't know, do you?"

"I have no idea. But I'm sorry it hurt you so much. Please, tell me what it was."

Dropping his head into his hands, he sat silent. Martha waited quietly, almost afraid to hear his next words. Abe wasn't touchy and he'd never been upset like this before. Josie tried to nose his hands away from his face. Unable to do that, she settled for giving the back of his hands a few tender licks.

Help us, Lord, Martha prayed silently. *Don't let anything destroy our happiness. Thank you, God, in Jesus' precious name.*

Finally, Abe lifted his red-rimmed eyes to hers then got to his feet. "Have you any idea how beautiful you are, Martha? When you look at me with stars in your eyes, as you did when I put the tree down, it's more than I can take." He watched her a moment then shook his head. "You really don't know, do you?"

She shook her head once more. "What can I do, Abe? Please, tell me."

He opened his mouth but nothing came out. He tried once more. Then he shook his head. "Forget it," he finally said. "It's me, not you. You've lived up to our agreement just fine. You've been a perfect maid, cook, laundress, general helper, and even a great companion. How could I complain?" With that he grabbed his coat and hurried through the door into the cold afternoon.

Suddenly, Martha knew what he meant. That she might be all the things he'd mentioned, but she wasn't a wife.

She'd been left alone with Josie and her family's covered wagon with only a little flour, a few buffalo chips, and no money. She'd managed to live in it until the weather turned cold. By then she'd run out of food and anything with which to make a fire. Abe had brought her and Josie food for some time. Martha had felt terrible to put him out so much, but she'd failed in the laundry business. She tried to get a job in all eight businesses in the town. No one had work for her. She'd been so alone, so alone.

One day he'd asked her to marry him. But she couldn't because, although she loved him dearly as a friend, she didn't hear bells ring, see fireworks, and feel a pink cloud wrap around her when he was near. She'd read books and knew that when she fell in love she'd hear and see these things.

A few days after she gently refused his generous offer of marriage, he'd asked her to marry him in name only. He'd given her a reasonable sounding string of reasons why it would be good for them both, a three hundred twenty acre donation land claim topping the list. She'd asked for time to think it over. But she couldn't think of any other way to live through the winter so she'd decided to say yes the next time he asked. But he hadn't asked! Finally, she'd had to do the asking.

They'd married and built their nice log house—with a bedroom for each of them at each end of the house. Martha sighed, remembering. Abe must be sorry he'd married her now. What a terrible development. What could she do? "Oh, dear Father in heaven," she cried. "Please help us. I care so much about him that I can't bear the thought of being without him. And I still don't have any money or a way to care for myself so I guess I purely need him. Tell me what to do, God." She listened but heard nothing. "Please tell me, Father," she pleaded then sat silently waiting. A feeling came to her that she needed to talk straight with Abe to be sure they understood each other.

She didn't have to wait long, for Abe soon came puffing in, his nose red and hair white with frost. "Everybody out there's all fed and put to bed," he said, indicating the barn with his thumb pointing back over his shoulder.

He looked and sounded his usual cheery self, but Martha knew they had to talk. He'd been too upset to pretend it didn't happen. Besides, God had told her to talk it out. But He didn't say it had to be this minute.

"Good," she said with a cheerful smile. "I have supper almost ready. I hope you're hungry because I really filled up the dutch oven this time. Roast meat, potatoes, carrots, onions. And I baked fresh bread today, too."

"Sounds good," he said, washing his hands and face in the basin on the small table. "I'm starved. Bet you are, too."

Martha felt far from hungry but didn't mention it.

After they finished eating, Martha sat down to string the popcorn, much less excited than she'd been earlier. Abe worked on his bedroom furniture.

He'd made hers first, which actually looked decent, a far cry from the table and sideboard, the first stuff he'd made. An hour later, she finished the last string of popcorn. After winding them around the tree, she stepped back. "What else does it need?" she asked Abe.

He looked up from his work and shook his head. "Seems like I remember stringing cranberries," he said.

Martha laughed. "Have you seen any cranberries running around loose?"

He laughed with her. "Not lately." He shook his head again. "How about some more popcorn? Then you'll need a little color."

Another hour passed while Martha popped and strung several more long strings, then twined them around the tree. While stringing the corn, Martha tried hard to think of something else with which to decorate the tree but she simply didn't have a thing.

"Abe," she called softly, "do you think they'd have anything at the store? Maybe some bright material or paper?"

He thought for a moment. "I doubt it, but we can check in the morning."

A strong feeling came over Martha that this was the time to talk to Abe. *Not yet,* she thought. *How can I ruin this nice evening?* The feeling came again, but stronger. *Now! Talk to him now.*

"Abe," she said. "Do you think we could talk?"

He laid down the plane and moved to one of the two dynamite boxes they used for chairs. Martha sat on the other one. "I'm here," he said. "What shall we talk about?"

She shuddered inside but forced herself to say it. "This afternoon, Abe. Are you so terribly unhappy living with me?"

He tossed his head and laughed. "Not at all. Everything's fine. Just as we planned it, in fact. It's just me, Martha. Once in a while I get to thinking how it would be if we had a real marriage. Haven't you heard, everyone needs a hug sometimes? We never even touch each other." He pushed his hair back. "But that's not your problem. It's mine, strictly mine. So why don't you let me handle it? I'll try hard to do better."

His contrite look made Martha long to hug him and make it better. But she couldn't do that.

"I'm so sorry, Abe," she said softly. "Many times I've wanted a hug or to give you a pat but I held back because I was afraid that would make it harder for you."

His shoulders slumped. "Probably so," he muttered. Then he went back to pushing the plane over the already smooth board.

—◆—

The next morning everything seemed normal. Abe did the outside chores

246

while Martha made breakfast. "Want to go to the store to see if we can find something to dress up the tree a little?" he asked when they finished eating.

When they got to the store they didn't find any bright ribbon or material but Martha couldn't believe her eyes when they saw several boxes of painted wooden tree ornaments—a top, a ball, a star, a wooden soldier, and a Santa Claus. "Could we afford a few?" she asked.

He grinned. "I think we can. You get whatever you need."

She felt a rush of tenderness for him. He was so good to her. "You choose then," she said. "But don't get a Santa Claus, all right?"

"Sure, but why not?"

Suddenly, she felt foolish. "Well, I always get the feeling that Santa Claus is trying to be Jesus. You know, he brings presents to the good little boys and girls and switches to the bad ones as if he knew all about everything and everybody. And he doesn't. He purely doesn't. I wish people wouldn't teach their children about him at all. I call him an impostor."

"Good enough reason for me." He picked out two of each of the other trinkets and McMorris wrapped them separately in brown paper "so they won't scratch each other up," the kindly storekeeper said.

Martha couldn't wait to get home and hang the new ornaments. They gave the tree just the color it needed, making it truly look like Christmas. "Now I can't wait for Christmas," she told Abe.

"It'll be here before you know it," he said. "Just enough time for you to cook up a lot of candy and cakes and whatever else you can think of."

"I will, Abe. I'll make you a nice Christmas. I don't want you to be sorry you married me. I don't, Abe."

He grinned and she sensed him about to chuck her under the chin but he didn't. "Don't worry about it. I have it better than most of the fellows around here. . .a whole lot better. Most of them don't have a woman at all, let alone one who's kind and hard working and is easy to get along with and talented and creative."

Martha felt her ears go red. "Tell me how I'm talented or creative."

"The last I knew, you played a pretty mean organ at the saloon and you've fixed this place up right nice." The Methodist church met temporarily in Galbraith's Saloon and Martha played the pump organ for the eight to ten men who attended the services.

"Well, thank you, kind sir. I appreciate your nice words. Did you know I have a terribly kind husband? One who takes better care of his animals than many take of their wives. And extra clever, too. He makes all kinds of furniture. One of these days people will be lining up at the door just for a piece of Abram Noble furniture. But tell me, Abe, are you glad you married me? I mean with things as they are, do you wish you hadn't?"

He grinned lazily. "How could I wish that? If I didn't have you I'd be doin' my own cooking and it wouldn't be so good either." He leaned back in his chair. "I'm real glad we're married, Martha. I truly am."

Chapter 2

Later, Abe hiked to the store to see what was going on and to find something for Martha for Christmas. About the time he got off his homestead, he heard The Voice.

You really messed it up that time, didn't you, Abe?

Abe had heard The Voice many times. In fact, he'd carried on numerous conversations with it. "I sure did, Lord," he said into the cold air. "How can I make it up to her?"

Don't worry about it; she understands. Just be good to her.

"I try. Lord, You just don't realize how hard this is for me. I love her so much I ache for her. And I can't even touch her. Not even a simple little pat on the hand."

I don't realize? I might. Remember I made you and know exactly how you are. I want you to keep so busy making Martha happy, you forget all about poor Abe. Do it, Abe. Hear?

"I hear. I been keepin' busy, but maybe I can do more." By that time Abe had reached the main street in town. "I better stop this talkin', God," he said, grinning. "Someone'll hear me and think I'm a mite crazy."

He walked into McClinchey and McMorris's General Store and looked around. The tables holding the merchandise were hewn half-logs resting on sawhorses. Some had cloths over them to protect the goods from the rough wood.

After picking up several small items, Abe told McMorris he wanted a nice present for Martha. "Maybe I could get her a couple of pieces of material for dresses."

McMorris nodded. "She'd like that. I been noticin' she needs some new clothes right bad." He showed his small assortment of goods to Abe, four bolts of muslin, each with a different flower pattern on a contrasting background. Suddenly, he turned to Abe and snapped his fingers. "I know what she'd like. Only I ain't got any yet. I heard about a new machine they got for sewing clothes. Zips 'em up in nothin' flat. . .and the sewing don't come out."

Abe felt himself come alive. Just the thing to let Martha see how much he really loved her. Maybe make up a little for the shameful way he'd treated her today, too. "That's it, Lew," he said. "Think you could get one? How long would it take?"

"I could write back East to find out. I figger if they're sellin' 'em I might get one late summer."

A disappointed sigh escaped Abe. Then he remembered the cookstove he'd asked about. "Heard anything about a cookstove yet?" he asked.

The man nodded. "I talked to Miz Martin. She hauled hers here from Oregon. I think she hauled it from Missouri afore that. I'll ask about a stove in the letter, too. Sorry, it's the best I can do," he added, noting Abe's disappointment.

Abe bought a dress length's worth of each of the four patterns of muslin and managed to slip the package into his bedroom without Martha seeing it. He grinned to himself as he took one last look at the dress material. She'd truly be surprised to receive his gift. If they'd been sharing a bedroom it would have been much harder to keep her from discovering it. He smiled grimly. At last he'd found something positive about their unusual living arrangement.

"How about a ride?" he asked Martha after they'd eaten hot bowls of beans with bacon, thick slices of homemade bread with butter, plus tall glasses of cold foamy milk for dinner. "We can bundle up and the horses will help keep us warm."

The horses danced eagerly while Abe saddled them. "Let's go out past tepee town," Martha suggested. "I'd like to see how the Indians are handling the cold weather."

They could hardly hold the horses back. Abe looked down at the dog beside him, jumping high through the snow at each step. "Why don't we leave Josie in the house?" he asked before they'd gotten off the place. "She's only going to get cold and snowy." He turned Charity back as he spoke. "I'll put her in." To his surprise the dog eagerly went inside and lay down by the fireplace. "You just enjoy the heat," Abe said, "we'll be back in a little while."

"Now we can let the horses go," he said, his breath rolling from his mouth in long, white clouds.

When they arrived at tepee town, smoke poured from the tops of the tepees but no Indians appeared outside. "I guess they're inside keeping warm," Martha said.

"I heard they dig out under the tepees," Abe said. "Sort of build a cellar with rooms, and it keeps them pretty warm."

"Oh. I'm glad they have more than just those little tents." She turned from the tepees. "Where do you want to go now?"

"Let's let the horses decide." He touched Charity's sides with his heels. "Come on, girl, it's your time. Go!" She took off on a rolling gallop with Sampson at her heels. After a few minutes the horses turned west and ran easily as if they both enjoyed it immensely.

"Looks like we might be going out to Fort Walla Walla," Abe said, grinning. Fifteen minutes later they passed the fort that had housed many soldiers during the years of the Indian Wars. Now that the fighting had ceased, the personnel at the fort had been cut considerably.

The horses continued across the gently rolling snow-covered land, then Charity led Sampson in a wide southward turn that finally became eastward.

"I think they're heading home," Martha said. "They aren't as adventurous as I thought. Maybe they're getting cold."

"I don't think so," Abe said. "They're expending a lot of energy." In a few minutes Abe saw the scraggly buildings that made up the village of Walla Walla, the new name of their infant city. The name meant *many waters* because several rivers met in the area. The town's name had been Steptoeville, after a military man who'd led many soldiers against the Indians. But the horses didn't head straight for the Nez Percé trail, euphemistically called The Street, where eight ramshackle buildings stood. Rather, they slowed to a gentle lope and cut across the prairie, where Abe and Martha had talked to the settlers some time ago. The few shacks had been strengthened and were closed up tightly against the cold. White smoke spiraled from most of the chimneys. A few minutes later, Abe recognized Slick's old tent. Slick was the miscreant who'd helped Abe get acquainted with Martha. The first day after Martha had come to Walla Walla, Slick, in a drunken fog, had grabbed her, and Abe had punched Slick out, telling him that if he ever touched another woman he'd be sorry he'd been born.

"Say, I haven't thought of Slick for a long time," he said, slowing Charity to a walk. "I wonder if he's around anymore. I hope he isn't living in his tent in this weather. Why don't we take a look." But they didn't reach the tent. A suspicious looking pile of clothing a hundred feet west attracted Abe's attention. As Charity closed the distance to the clothing, Abe distinguished a human form and slid from the saddle to inspect it.

"It's Slick," he called to Martha. "He's alive, but he feels pretty cold."

Martha guided Sampson close beside Abe. "What can we do? Where can we take him?"

Abe shook his head. "I dunno, unless out to Fort Walla Walla again." They'd taken Slick there after someone had beaten him up a few months ago. "Let's get him across Sampson, behind you. Sampson's stronger than Charity and you're lighter than me." He snatched the rope from his saddle, handed it to Martha, then gathered up Slick and shoved him over Sampson's rump. Retrieving the rope from Martha, he made the man secure behind her. "That oughta do it," he said, huffing great white clouds into the air. He rested another moment then swung into Charity's saddle. "Let's get him out there before he dies."

Sampson walked briskly along with his odd-shaped load. "He wants to trot," Martha said, holding him back. "Now I know why he's called Sampson."

Abe nodded. "I can tell it's a lot easier on him than it would be on Charity. I'm sure glad I bought that horse."

"So am I!" Martha agreed patting Sampson's strong neck. Sampson had been her wedding present from Abe. "I love my horse," she said. They rode in silence for a while, enjoying the snow, the horses, and each other. "Oh, there it is," she said, pointing at the large snow-covered wooden structure. "It looks pretty in the snow, doesn't it? Everything looks pretty, almost as if God covered all the sins and blemishes of our little world."

Abe nodded. "Isn't that what the song says? Whiter than snow? He covers the earth with snow only temporarily, but if we accept His sacrifice for us, His blood makes our sins whiter than snow forever."

Soon they arrived at the front door of the large building they'd been in before. Abe slid from his saddle, dropping Charity's reins over a post. "I hope we can find a doctor." He untied Slick from Sampson's back. Martha dropped from Sampson's side, helped Abe heft the unconscious man over his shoulder, and they walked to the front door. Abe banged on the door as hard as he could. A soldier opened it almost immediately. "I brought him back," Abe said with a grin. "Got a doctor around today?"

The soldier looked at Slick. "That the guy who got beat up a while back?"

"The one and only," Abe said. "He's pretty heavy, too. Where can I dump him?"

The soldier pulled the door half-closed and blocked the opening. "You aren't leaving him here," he said. "That devil isn't going to cause us any more trouble."

Chapter 3

W e have to leave him here," Abe said, his voice showing surprise. "There's no other place for him."

"This is a government military post," the man said. "We don't have to take in anyone we don't want. And believe me, we don't want Slick Collier."

"What did Slick do that got him the death sentence?" Martha asked.

"The man's subhuman," he said. "He cussed out every man who helped him, slugged a couple of soldiers when they tried to dress him, attempted to attack every woman who came into his room, and we have some cats and a dog living here. If we take him back, they'll all leave. Is that sufficient?"

"Not to let him die!"

"It is to us here at the fort. We try to live a decent life together and this man managed to turn everyone against the other and even made us hate ourselves. If you want him to have care, take him to your own place. I'll even tell you how to care for him. I think he's just cold. His body temperature has gone far lower than normal and if it isn't brought up soon, he'll die. Might be too late already. Anyway, if you want to save him, put him into a tub of warm water for some time. Long enough to really warm him up. Do anything you have to but get him warm and keep him that way. Good day." He shut the door and only the click of his footsteps walking away came through the door.

Abe pounded on the door until the man opened it again. "You've put quite a burden on me," Abe said, "but I'm giving it right back to you." With that he laid Slick onto the porch floor. "He's all yours," he said to the man in the doorway.

"Leave him there if you want," the man said. "Someone will find him tomorrow, I suppose. Or the next day."

"Let's go," Abe said. "It's getting late. This afternoon ride sure didn't turn out as I'd planned."

Martha looked at Abe, then down at Slick. "Aren't you going to put him back on Sampson?"

"I am not. You heard the man. And we already knew what Slick is."

She couldn't go off and leave a man to die, not even Slick. She shook her head. "We can't do it, Abe. We have to do what we can."

He slowly shook his head. "Get on your horse, Martha. We don't need the problems Slick will add to our house. That guy will haul him in as soon as we leave, anyway."

"What if he doesn't?"

"Then he'll be guilty of letting the man die."

Martha felt sick to her stomach. She'd been so proud of Abe. How could he take this attitude? To leave the man would not only be cruel, but surely illegal. Anyway, Jesus said, "If you do it for the least of these, you've done it for Me."

"I'm not going, Abe. I can't walk off and leave a helpless human being to die." She slid from her saddle and leaned over Slick.

Abe soon stood beside her. She'd never seen him look so furious. "If we take him to our place I'll have to spend every minute protecting you and Josie from him. And I'll probably have to fight him just to get him well. Come on, Martha, you heard the man. They're a lot better equipped to care for him than we are."

She couldn't bear having Abe so angry with her, but neither could she walk off and let the man die. She shook her head. "Jesus loves him, Abe, and died for him. He did, Abe, as much as He did for you and me."

Abe's face lost none of its tenseness but he scooped Slick into his arms and threw him across Sampson's back. "Give me the rope," he snapped. She handed it to him and in a few minutes they headed for home again.

Abe stopped the horses beside the front door and carried the still unconscious Slick into the main room and dropped him on the floor, a little more roughly than might have been necessary. "Now what do you have in mind?" he snapped at her.

"A hot bath I guess." She put more wood on the fire, filled the large pail, and put it on to heat.

"While the water heats I'll go take care of the horses. If he wakes up, you take Josie and get out of the house." He still sounded very angry. His anger made Martha feel upset at him.

When the water heated she poured it into the tub and added some cold. Then she went to the creek and got more water and started to heat it. At least they were trying to help Slick. One day, especially if he didn't make it, they'd both be glad they'd tried. Of course, if he did live and caused a lot of trouble. . . She tried not to think about that.

The door opened and Abe came in, ice frosting his hair. "Is the water warm enough?" he asked in a low growl.

She nodded. "I think so. Why don't you check it?"

"I really don't care. I'll get him undressed and put him in," Abe said.

Martha left and kept herself busy in the kitchen until she heard Abe lower him into the water.

"This isn't easy," he said. "He isn't helping at all." He let Slick slump in the water, bothering only to keep his head out. After a time that seemed forever, he called Martha. "The water's cold," he said. "Is there more?"

"Yes. You'll have to get him out so it won't burn him while you pour it in."

They repeated the procedure several times until Slick looked as if he had a bad sunburn all over. "Get me something to dry him with and I'll put him in bed," Abe said.

Martha handed him an old blanket. "Do you want me to go into your bedroom to make a bed on the floor for Slick?" she asked.

Abe looked at her as if she'd lost her mind. "I do not!" he roared. "If he sleeps on the floor, the first thing we know he'll be in your room, bothering you or Josie. I have to sleep with him so I can keep him where he belongs."

Oh. This was turning out to be mostly work for Abe. She hadn't meant for it to be that way but she could hardly give the man a bath or dress him.

Abe dried Slick then shoved some of his own long johns onto the inert figure. Cradling the man in his arms, Abe carried him into his bedroom and laid him on the bed he'd made after having finished Martha's bed, armoire, and chiffonier.

When Abe didn't return, Martha wondered what he could be doing. Suddenly, Slick's strident voice startled her almost off her dynamite box. "What's goin' on?" he bellowed.

"I'm getting you warm," Abe's soft voice replied. "You just lie still and let me put some more covers over you."

Then it became silent again. Until, "Are you hungry, Slick?" in the same quietly concerned voice. Martha heaved a sigh. Abe might be furious with her, but he'd be kind to the helpless man she'd forced him to bring home. She should have known.

Martha carried out the used water, a bucketful at a time. Then she made a big pot of potato soup with lots of fresh cream. While it cooked she sliced thick slabs of fresh homemade bread and slathered on lots of butter. Her growling stomach reminded her how hungry she felt, too. They'd all enjoy the hot soup, including Slick if he was still awake.

Then Abe stood beside her. "Well, I don't believe it," he said in a voice reminiscent of a bawling bull. "You mean to say you're actually doing something for *your* house guest? I thought that was all supposed to be my part in *your* plan."

Martha's mouth opened of its own volition. "I've been working as long and hard as you, Abe," she said quietly. "I carried all the water in and out.

I've also made hot soup for us all." As she talked her voice grew louder. "I don't appreciate the way you've been acting, either. You should be ashamed to admit that I forced you to use a little compassion. Do you remember the Good Samaritan? I'd always thought that was you."

His eyes opened wide with surprise and he opened his mouth to say something but Martha stuck her chin in the air, flounced past him, and went into her bedroom. Shutting the door, she crumpled to the featherbed and fumed.

How dare he act as if she hadn't done anything since they came home? And how dare he not do all he could to save a man's life? Even if it was a really bad man. Well, he was taking care of Slick now, but he didn't want to at first.

When it got dark she crawled into the bed to keep warm. Both she and Abe had been leaving their doors open to keep warm, but she wouldn't do that tonight. Not this time! Not if she froze to death! Or even if she starved. If he wanted her to come out he could just come in and ask her nicely. Or if he wanted her to open the door so she wouldn't be cold, he could open it himself. She wasn't the one who'd started this big fight anyway.

In fact, she felt very disappointed that Abe would act this way. And all because she'd insisted on treating a human being like a human being. That's all she'd asked, that they not let Slick lie in the snow and die. She'd only wanted to treat him as a human being. If he died anyway, their consciences would be clear.

She began to shiver. Slick's voice had reached through the walls much better than the heat. She wished Abe would come after her. No, she didn't either! She didn't want to have anything to do with that man. Maybe never!

Chapter 4

Abe stood in shocked silence, staring at Martha's closed door. Then he jerked his head away. Idealist! That's what she was, an idealist. Well, things were different out here in Washington Territory. Nothing was ideal and before they got through with this mess, Slick would cause them a bundle of trouble. He shrugged. Seemed like it was up to him to see that nothing out of the way happened. "Watch over us, Lord, okay? Don't let anything bad come from Martha's good deed." He had to admit Martha had been right. They couldn't let a man lie in the snow and die. Even if he was barely human.

I'm here, Abe. You know together we can do it.

He looked into the kettle that Martha had been stirring. Mmmm, potato soup. With globs of cream floating in it. That should warm anyone's bones, even his. But he'd better see if he could get some of the stuff down Slick first.

His eyes wandered back to Martha's door. She'd soon get cold and come out or at least open the door. He picked up a mug from the sideboard and filled it with soup. Would Slick want some of that bread Martha had prepared? He shook his head. Not yet. Maybe tomorrow. He carried the mug of soup into the bedroom. Slick appeared to be sleeping. "Want some potato soup?" he asked quietly.

Slick didn't respond.

"It has cream and butter floating in it," he added.

Slick moved a little but still didn't respond.

Abe sat on the edge of the bed, actually a wooden platform with blankets over it, lifted Slick's head, and spooned in a bit. Slick swallowed in a hurry and stirred. Abe shoved in some more. Slick swallowed and opened his eyes. "I'll take some more of that," he grunted.

"Can you hold the mug?"

"I can try." But his hands wobbled and sank to the bed.

Abe retrieved the cup and fed the rest to the weakened man. "Want some more?"

Slick ate another full mug before settling back down. Abe pulled the covers around the man's neck. "I'm goin' out there to eat some of this myself.

You go back to sleep, hear?"

As Abe spooned the steaming soup into his mouth, he felt lonely. Why, he wondered, with two other people in the house? He grinned. He'd always heard that three was a crowd. Actually, he knew why he was lonely. Because Martha had closed her door. And because she was mad at him. He shoved in a big bite of the soft, buttered bread. Mmmmm. She could cook circles around the saloons. For that matter she could outcook his own mother. He ate another mug of soup and two more thick slices of butter-slathered bread before quitting.

Martha's door remained closed. Why didn't she open it? Why didn't she come out for some soup? She had to be hungry. He shrugged. He'd better leave her alone. She'd come out when she felt like eating.

He peeked into his bedroom and Slick appeared to be sleeping, so he quietly returned to the kitchen table. Martha had put a nice cloth on it that somewhat covered the roughness of the half-logs from which he'd built it. Remembering the plane he'd discovered at the store some time ago, he got it, pulled back the cloth, and smoothed the rough surface from the boards. He smiled to himself. Martha would like that. While he'd been smoothing the boards he'd also made firestarting chips. Then he noticed all the dishes he'd dirtied feeding Slick and himself, and washed them. That would surprise and please her. Unable to think of anything more to do, he took his bedroom door down and sawed it in two, making a dutch door out of it. When he rehung it, he felt pleased. Now, they could open the top half to let heat in but keep the bottom half closed and Slick inside. After that he couldn't think of anything else to do.

The evening lasted forever. When bedtime finally came he couldn't force himself to get into the same bed with Slick, even though they'd given him that bath a few hours earlier.

He unfolded the blankets Martha had brought in, laid them on the floor near the fireplace, and crawled in under them.

Finding the floor even harder than his bed, he turned over every ten minutes. Why had he let Martha force him to bring Slick into their home? Their relationship, already fragile, didn't need any complications. He continued turning and thinking, turning and thinking, until late in the night when fatigue helped him sleep.

—⁂—

"Abe, what are you doing out here?" Martha's soft voice jerked Abe into sudden wakefulness. The brightly illuminated room told him the day had started without him.

He sat up, pulling the blankets under his chin, every muscle he owned screaming from his night on the floor; most of his joints complained, too. "I couldn't quite sleep in the same bed with Slick," he replied, grinning with embarrassment. "Glad you left the blankets out here."

"I'll go back to my room for a while," she said, closing the door behind her.

Abe jumped from his hard bed and climbed into his overalls. He'd better check to see if Slick was still alive. The man awakened at Abe's touch. "How do you feel?" Abe asked.

"Hungry," Slick growled in a hoarse voice. "Ya got anything?"

"Not yet. Is your throat sore?"

"Naw. I'm always hoarse when I wake up."

Abe felt more relief than he'd expected. Must be because Slick would be able to get out faster if he didn't have any complications. "I'll run down some food," he told Slick as he went out.

Martha already had a fire going and a kettle of water almost boiling. "I'll have some oatmeal ready in a little while," she said.

Almost before she finished, Josie erupted into a snarling barking thunderstorm. Martha grabbed the dog as she charged toward Abe's bedroom. "Josie, stop!" Martha ordered. The dog continued her uproar, trying to escape Martha's arms.

Abe looked behind him to see Slick in the main room, standing against the far wall and looking terrified. "Better get back in the bedroom," he said quietly. "I can't guarantee your safety outside that room."

Slick didn't need to be told twice. Abe followed him into the room. "Ya better git that dog outside," Slick said.

Abe shook his head. "Josie lives here. You're only here because Martha felt sorry for you. So sit down and I'll bring your breakfast."

Martha looked thoroughly alarmed. "What are we going to do?" she asked. "Josie's never been that upset in her life."

Abe shook his head, grinning. "You can't imagine how she's relieved my mind. If she'll keep Slick in the bedroom, half our worries are over."

Slick didn't appreciate the oatmeal very much. "Ain't you got anything else?" he whined. "I et that stuff every day of my life until I left home. It about turns my stomach."

Abe didn't feel a bit sorry. "Your mother never made it like my wife. This is swimming in cream with a mountain of sugar. Eat it or I'll throw it out," he said. "It don't make any difference to me."

Slick ate the cereal without complaining anymore.

Deciding he'd better keep Slick halfway clean in self-defense, Abe brought in a bowl of warm water. "Don't bother me with that stuff," Slick growled. So Abe used the water for his own bath, putting on fresh clothes when he finished.

"I need to go feed the horses and make sure the creek isn't frozen," he told Martha when he returned to the main room. "But I'm afraid to leave you with Slick, even with Josie here."

"Josie and I already fed the stock," Martha said. "We had fun in the snow. And the creek's running just fine."

That afternoon Slick slipped into the main room again and Josie pinned him against the wall before Martha could stop her. When she finally got Josie to come away, Slick wobbled a bit and slumped to the floor. Abe grabbed him, carried him back into the bedroom, and shoved him on the bed.

"You gonna stay here this time?" Abe growled. "Josie's not the only one who don't want you out there, Slick. If she wasn't on duty I'd still be, so you might as well just stay put." He pointed at the two-part door. "Did you see how I fixed the door so you'd be warm?"

"Yeah. But I never knowed anyone who'd take a dog's side against a man," Slick whined. "I ain't even got a gun. Where's my gun, anyway?"

Abe shrugged. "You didn't have one, Slick, and if you did, I'd 'a' took it from you. So why don't you sleep and get well?"

Slick stayed where he belonged that day, eating everything Abe brought him, and begging for more.

"How's he doing?" Martha asked the next morning.

"Doing great except for a bad case of cabin fever. He hates havin' to stay in there. I like it a lot though."

After breakfast Abe decided Josie had everything under control and went out to feed the livestock. He hurried, doing what he had to, and rushed back to the warm house. Before he reached the door he heard Josie making a lot of noise. When he stepped inside he found the dog beside the fallen man, her front feet on his chest. Her lips, opened in a deep snarl, revealed her long white fangs. Slick wasn't moving a muscle.

Abe moved to his side. "What did he do, Josie?" he asked the dog in a calm voice.

"Are you crazy?" Slick yelled. "Get that dog off me. I'm telling you, Noble, if that dog bites me it'll be the last person it gets."

Abe burst out laughing. "Seems to me it's pretty much up to Josie who she bites right now, Slick. Why aren't you in the bedroom where you belong?"

"If you'll git this beast off me, I'll leave and you'll never see me again, Abe. I can't stand bein' in this zoo no more."

"Is that a promise?"

"Get this dog off me!"

"Where's Martha, Slick?"

"How do I know? She went outdoors right after you did."

260

"So what were you doing? Trying to find something to take with you?"

"No, I was hungry."

Just then Martha came into the house. "Josie!" she yelled. "What are you doing?" She rushed to the dog and started pulling her off the sick man.

Abe pinned Martha's arms to her sides and lifted her to her feet. "Take it easy," he murmured in her ear. "Josie was busy saving the family silver. When we both left, Slick decided it was time to go through our things."

Between the three of them—Abe, Martha, and Josie—they managed to keep Slick in the bedroom for several more days. He showed no appreciation for the warm food, warm room, or the company.

Finally, he appeared in the open half of his door. "Noble, I'm gettin' out of here. Where's my clothes? Or do I wear yours?"

"Where you goin', Slick?"

"Anywhere. Somewheres where they ain't got dogs." He stopped a moment to think. "I'm gonna get that one, too, Noble. Just you wait and see."

Abe scratched his ear. "Didn't happen to tell Martha how much you've enjoyed the food she's fixed for you, did you?"

Slick looked a little confused but didn't answer.

"Did you mention all the clothes she's washed so you could keep clean? She also washed the rags you came in, Slick. She's worked hard to make you comfortable. We hauled you out to Fort Walla Walla, but one time was enough for them. We coulda left you to die, but God wouldn't let us do that."

Slick turned around, walked over to the bed, and sat down.

Abe motioned Martha to the table. "Think you and Josie could watch the place a little while? I got me someone I need to see."

Martha smiled. "I think Josie could do it alone as long as Slick has no clubs or guns."

Abe pulled on his heavy boots and headed toward town through the slushy snow. When he reached Galbraith's Saloon he stomped off the mess from his boots as well as he could and went in.

"Where you been keepin' yourself?" Galbraith asked, pouring a tall mug of coffee for Abe.

Abe shook his head. "Martha and I've been havin' ourselves a house guest. We've got Slick Collier over there. Found him frozen on the ground. The fellows at the fort didn't want him again so we took him home." He looked up from his steaming brew and laughed into the barkeep's eyes. "Martha's dog don't like Slick much. Been keepin' him in the bedroom when she isn't chewing on him." He took a long sip. "Thing is, I'm gettin' real tired of havin' him around. And he feels the same. Know where the preacher lives? Maybe he'd take him in."

Galbraith shook his head. "Lives at Martin's Boardinghouse," he said. "He might have an idea though."

Chapter 5

M artha washed the breakfast dishes and swept the floor. Then she started some bread. Slick would enjoy warm bread. Now what made her think of what would please Slick? Or care?

"Come 'ere, you rotten cur," she heard from Abe's bedroom. Why would Slick be calling Josie? She stepped around the table and looked toward the half open door to see Slick hanging his left hand down to Josie, snapping his fingers and whispering for her to come. In his right hand he held a heavy board he'd torn from Abe's bed. A board! She'd better get that quick!

But before she moved, Josie emitted a loud growl, a snarl, and a low bark, then hurled herself through the open top half of the door, knocking Slick across the hard bed onto the floor on the other side. A loud mixture of yells, curses, growls, and snapping sounds, together with the noises of bodies rolling around, came from the bedroom.

Martha flew into the room half a second later. "Josie," she yelled, "keep him down. Just don't hurt him." She shook her head. What did she think Josie was, an out-of-control human? Josie kept up the wild commotion, so Martha grabbed the big board and tossed it into the main room.

"The. . .dog. . .is. . . ," Slick said, gasping for air. Josie's racket precluded Martha's hearing any more. Slick lay on the floor now, offering no more resistance.

"Stop!" Martha demanded firmly. She grabbed the dog's shoulders and jerked her back. Josie's plumy tail gave one wag as she looked over her shoulder at Martha, then she backed away from Slick and marched into the main room.

Just then the door opened and Abe came in. Seconds later he appeared in the open bedroom doorway. "What's going on?" he asked. "Slick been bothering you?"

Martha shook her head. "He and Josie had another set to."

Slick tried to regain his feet, but gave up, returning to a prone position on the floor. "I gotta git outa here afore that animal kills me," he murmured. Then he relaxed and closed his eyes.

Abe met Martha's eyes. "Josie go too far?"

She shook her head but didn't say more. Slick might be tired but he'd hear anything they said in there. "I have to go mix up bread," she said. "Want to help?"

Abe started to follow, then looked back at Slick, still on the floor. He returned, lifted him to the bed, and left the room, shutting both halves of the door. "What happened?" he asked, dropping onto a dynamite box.

Martha shook her head. "You won't believe it," she said. "Slick tore a big board from your bed and was trying to lure Josie into your room. He'd have closed the door and killed her, Abe. I know he would have. Then I'd have been purely sorry we saved his life. I really would have, Abe."

Abe grinned. "I noticed Josie had the upper hand. It must not have worked."

"Oh. That's right. Before I could move, Josie jumped right through that open door half and attacked Slick. Abe, I'm so wicked. At first I wanted Josie to hurt him really bad."

Abe's caring eyes filled with so much love that Martha thought he would take her into his arms. But he didn't. "You could never be wicked, Martha," he said. "Slick scared you. That's all." His eyes left Martha's for a moment and when they met hers again that soft expression had disappeared. "I may have found a place for Slick. The preacher lives at Martin's and he says the church will put him up at the boardinghouse until he can handle it on his own."

Martha felt a great peace wash over her. She hadn't realized how much she loved living with Josie and Abe—alone. "Good," she whispered. "I hope he'll behave himself. Did you tell the minister he's a bad man?"

Abe nodded. "He'll take it upon himself to watch him. After all, four young girls live at the Martin place."

Martha fixed soup and roast venison sandwiches for dinner before Abe put Slick on Sampson and took him the short distance. While Abe was gone, Martha warmed water and washed all of Abe's bedding and hung it outside in the bright cold sunshine. It might not dry in one afternoon but at least it was clean.

Abe returned in a half-hour acting as happy as Martha felt. He carried a small magazine. "Come sit at the table with me," he said. "I have something to show you."

The magazine turned out to be a nursery catalog from back East. "Let's order our seeds and trees for next spring," he said, eagerly.

As they looked through the pages, Martha wanted everything she read about. Abe turned to the apple trees. "Let's see," he said, running his finger down the column. "There's transparent, Gravenstein, king, and winter banana." His sparkling brown eyes met hers. "Which kinds do you want?"

They all sounded so wonderful. "Could we have one of each?"

He laughed. "How about two of each? And a few cherry, peach, and plum, and some nuts. What do you think?"

"Oh, yes! Maybe we could buy a few shade trees, too. The locusts along the creek are nice but several kinds would be even better."

He filled in some more spaces on the order blank. "I'd like to raise a lot of oats and some hay. People have stock and will be getting more. Fort Walla Walla will need some. They'll use a lot of produce, too. Think we could raise some to sell?"

When they finished, they'd ordered many pounds of oats and Timothy grass seed for the hay, as well as tomato, bean, corn, cucumber, and squash seed, and several kinds of melon seeds. They'd decided they could buy potatoes at the store, let the eyes sprout, and plant them.

"I'm so excited," Martha said. "I want to go right out and work up a garden now."

Abe smiled into her eyes. "It does sound fun, and the time will be here before we know it. But Christmas will come first. What would you like for Christmas, my little Marty? I mean Martha."

Christmas? She had everything anyone could ever want right now. She shook her head. "I don't need one thing more. You've made me so happy, Abe. But what would you like?"

He chuckled. "I've been thinking. We should get a pair of work horses one of these days. Think you could come up with that?"

"I'm afraid I wouldn't have the slightest idea how or where, even if you put the money in my hand." But she'd been knitting him some blue and green mittens, a scarf, and a warm hat. If she had time, she planned to make him a sweater, too.

—⁂—

As the weather warmed and the snow melted, Martha confessed that she was hoping for a white Christmas. But the dry ground made it easier for them to reach the saloon for church each week. Martha played the organ and soon Abe led the singing. Following his true baritone, the others gathered enough courage to sing out and soon the small group made a loud and joyful noise to the Lord.

One day when Nellie came to visit, Martha invited her to the rough little church. "You'll be disappointed the first time," Martha said, "but then you'll like it a lot." To her surprise Nellie accepted her offer; having another woman there made it much more pleasant for Martha.

Before long the Indians came to the house again. Martha fixed them steak sandwiches and tall glasses of milk. As they ate, Martha taught them English words and they taught her the Indian equivalents. Finally, Martha pointed to her chest and said, "Martha." Then she pointed to the older one. He looked at his chest and repeated, "Martha." She couldn't help bursting out laughing but kept working with them until they understood she was Martha. The older one told her in simple words and signs that his name was "Gray Wolf" because he'd killed a large wolf that had tried to steal his baby sister. Of the younger ones, the chunkier one's name was "Pony Boy" because he'd captured seven ponies when only twelve years old. The last one, tall and thin, was named "Camas" because he loved to eat camas roots more than anything else.

In spite of the dreadful smell, Martha could truly say she enjoyed the Indian visits now. When they left she opened the doors and windows and let it air out until it felt as cold inside as outside. So far none but the original three ever came and she hoped it would remain that way.

Christmas Day finally came and Abe read the Christmas Story from Matthew and Luke to Martha. "I wondered if we could have a special prayer for Christmas?" he asked, almost timidly.

"I'd purely love that," Martha said. "Let's kneel and everything."

"Dear Heavenly Father," Abram began, "we thank You for sending Your precious only Son into this sin-filled world to pay the price of our sins, to die in our place. We can't even imagine the anguish that unselfish gift caused You." He raised his eyes and nodded at Martha.

"Dear Sweet Father God," she continued. "Thank You for loving us so terribly much. . .enough to make the supreme sacrifice for us. We love You, too, Father, though we don't know how to love at all compared to Your great Heavenly love. Help us to find the needy in spirit and body and to do all we can to help them. Help us to live our lives completely for You, Lord. We ask these special favors in Jesus' precious name and thank You for hearing and answering our prayers."

"Amen," they quietly said together.

Then Abram hurried to his bedroom, brought out the four dress lengths of material, and placed them in Martha's arms.

"Oh, Abe," she whispered, "they're purely beautiful. And I needed them so bad." She held each piece to her cheek. "I'll make them up right away. Which shall I make first?"

"The pink one," he said. "It brings out the color in your cheeks."

Then Martha gave Abe the articles she'd knitted.

He tried them on at once. "Perfect," he assured her though one sweater sleeve came down half an inch farther onto his hand than the other.

In her joy of the day, their closeness to God, and the emotion of the moment, Martha wanted to throw herself into his arms. But she felt afraid.

That night, as Martha pulled her covers under her chin, she thanked her Lord once again for her nice warm home and especially for Abe, the most wonderful husband in the world. "I'll never need to ask You for anything again," she finished.

Before she fell asleep, an image of a big black cookstove popped into her mind. Well, she might like one more thing. A cookstove so she could bake several loaves of bread at the same time. Maybe someday.

Chapter 6

As Abe crawled into his warm bed, he thought about the cookstove he'd tried so hard to get for Martha. That would have made her so happy, no telling what she'd have done. Maybe she'd have lost her head and kissed him. As he thought of Martha, he got all agitated. Sometimes he felt disappointed with his marriage. Oh, he loved Martha with all his heart and he appreciated having her around, all right. In fact, the thought of being without her left him cold. He pulled the covers more tightly around his neck and thanked God for His loving care, the warm house, and good food. He nodded in the dark. He had to thank Martha for making his food so special. "But how am I supposed to keep on like this?" he grumbled. "I love her so much I can hardly stand not touching her. I want her to be my wife, God."

I understand, Abram. And I want your complete happiness even more than you do. Trust Me. I have great plans for you if you can just be patient.

"There must be something I can do to help. What should I do? Hug her a little? She'd like it, God. I know she would."

Don't touch her, Abe. She has to come to you, not run from you.

Abe turned over repeatedly that night, inconsolable, impatient, and unable to sleep. On top of all that, his bed hurt his back. But the next morning he gathered himself together and hurried out to feed the horses and cows, with Josie, as usual, bouncing along with him. The warm winter sun improved his spirits. By the time he returned to the house with his pail of steaming milk he sang a few lines of "This Is My Father's World." Well, if it was his Father's world, he'd better trust Him to take care of an unimportant little part of it—Abram Noble.

"I just thought of what I'm going to do for the next month," he told Martha. "I'm going to rebuild the poor excuses for furniture I made. I can do better than the mess of stuff here. I'm embarrassed to admit I made it."

Using the instructions and plane, fine saw, and lacquer he'd gotten at the general store and bundles of sandpaper, he started his project. By the end of the year, nicely finished furniture graced Martha's bedroom. "This time I'm not ashamed to call this bedroom furniture," he told Martha, lovingly running his hand down the end of her chiffonier.

She pulled out the top drawer then gently closed it. "You'd better not be ashamed, Abram Noble. This is fine work. You should go into business making and selling furniture. No one in Walla Walla has nice things. . .and many would like to."

Abe felt as if she'd given him a birthday present. "That sounds like a great idea." He thought a moment, wondering if anyone would actually pay for quality stuff like this. He'd spent many hours building the three pieces and he wasn't about to give his time away. He noticed his hand quietly stroking the shining armoire. Yes, it was nice. He nodded, meeting her eyes again. "I'll finish making what we need and if it goes good, I might give it a whirl. You may have just figured out a way to feed us."

That afternoon, after having carried a day's worth of firewood into the house, Abe strolled downtown to see what was going on.

"We'll soon know now," Galbraith said, sliding Abe's coffee mug to him. Abe grinned and sipped his drink. "What're we gonna know?"

Galbraith wiped his hands on his apron, pulled a stool opposite Abe, and sat down. "We'll soon know if the state's goin' to be Walla Walla, too. It's comin' up in Olympia soon. In January, I think."

Abe grinned. "That'll be pretty good, won't it? Walla Walla City in Walla Walla County in Walla Walla State. Yeah, I like that. Think it'll happen?"

"I dunno. Lots of agitation for it."

Abe's mind flipped to the man he'd taken into his home not long ago. "Seen Slick?"

"Yeah, he's been in, but I heard he had another setback. Still at Martin's as far as I know."

Abe hurried home to catch Martha up on the news. Then he sat down with paper and pencil to figure out how much Martha's furniture had cost and what he could get for it. After a bit, he looked across the table where Martha worked on one of her Christmas dresses. "First thing we need is a couple of work horses. I'd never ask Charity and Sampson to pull that heavy wagon in the mud."

When Martha looked up and met his eyes, his stomach constricted. Her huge blue eyes smiled along with her full lips—lips made to be kissed. "Are there any around?" she asked.

"Any what?"

Her laugh raised goosebumps on his arms. "Horses, Abe. Isn't that what you mentioned?"

He got up and walked over to the front window. The isinglass let light in, but he couldn't see the creek flowing on the other side. He forced himself to concentrate on the creek, the gurgling water rushing over the smooth stones. It had much more water now than it had had last fall. If they ever had a child they'd have to put up a fence to keep it away from the water.

He jerked around and stormed into his bedroom. What a thought! If they ever had a child! He sat in his bedroom until supper. Most of the time he managed to concentrate on furniture he wanted to build. His plans included kitchen chairs and living room furniture; hopefully he would be able to build them.

"I've been figuring all the things I can make," he told Martha at the supper table. He grinned and mentioned the things he'd try. "I might as well find out what I can make. If we go into this, at first people will come here to see your things. Sure that's all right?"

She nodded, smiling. "Of course, it's all right and you can make anything you want to. I'm purely proud of you, Abe. I have the best husband in the world. Josie thinks so, too."

—⚹—

The next morning Abe decided to go look for some horses. "I'm completely out of lumber," he told Martha. "Even though the snow's gone and the ground's dry I don't want to make the saddle horses do what they weren't bred for. Why don't you come with me to look for some work horses?"

She put her nearly finished dress back into the basket. "Sure, I'd love a ride this morning. Do you know where there are some?"

He shook his head. "Not for sure. But Fort Walla Walla has work horses. They're sort of gearing down and might be glad to get rid of some."

Josie followed them so they held the horses to trotting. Even at the comparatively slow pace, they arrived at the military installation within a half-hour.

After Abe explained their needs, the uniformed man took them to an open corral. He pointed to the far side. "See those big chestnuts over there? They're not only the strongest horses we have but the gentlest. Since things have quieted down here, and we're through building, we don't need so many horses."

Abe couldn't believe the horses the man pointed out. He mentally added most beautiful to the man's description of the pair. They looked nearly alike with light brown, almost tan, coats and creamy manes, feet, and tails. A glance at Martha told him she felt as entranced as he.

"What do you think?" he asked quietly.

She nodded. "They're majestic," she breathed. "What kind are they?"

The soldier smiled. "They are good looking, aren't they? They're Belgians, both nine years old. Luke weighs two thousand fifty pounds and John weighs twenty-two hundred pounds."

Abe feared to ask the big question, but he'd never get the horses if he

269

didn't. "How much?" he asked, then found himself holding his breath. He wanted those horses almost more than he'd wanted his donation land claim.

"Four hundred dollars for the pair."

Abe swallowed. He'd figured $250 in his wildest imaginings. He'd never heard of horses costing more than that. He looked at Martha. "What do you think?"

A clear tinkly laugh escaped her lips. "What do you think, Abe? I don't know whether that's a steal or a robbery."

The soldier smiled and turned his attention to Abe.

Abe cleared his throat. "I need them to haul lumber down from the Blues. And to plow in the spring."

"They can do that all right."

Abe stood on one foot, then the other. What if he couldn't sell his furniture? Then he'd need good horses to work up the place more than ever. But surely he could get some good horses for half that much. But suddenly he didn't want good horses for half that much. He wanted Luke and John. He shook his head. "I'm not sure. I think we'll talk it over and get back to you."

The man readily agreed. Abe, Martha, Charity, Sampson, and Josie went home. Abe curried the horses and fed them, thinking about the Belgian team. He milked the cows and fed them all, Luke and John not leaving his mind for long. Then he looked at the cows, really looked at them. They were all supposed to freshen in the spring and most of them looked pretty round. But cows always looked round. Pretty hard to tell. With any luck they'd have five or six heifers. A good beginning. He took the milk and hurried back to the house.

Martha had prepared a nice venison stew for supper. "What did you decide?" she asked while they ate.

He shook his head. "It'll take a big hunk out of our savings. I'm just not sure."

"Will you be happy with another team?"

He grinned. His wife was very perceptive. "I'm afraid not. It was love at first sight."

Martha spread a thick layer of butter over her bread, laid it in her plate, and spread stew over it. Then her gentle blue eyes met his. "I could tell. I think you should get them, Abe. You'll make it up with your furniture before you know it."

He felt a rush of gladness inside as if he'd been waiting for her benediction. Maybe they'd go after them in the morning.

When they prayed together that night, they both asked the Lord to show them if they should buy the big Belgian work team.

270

—⁂—

The next morning they both felt the Lord wanted them to buy the Belgians, so they rode out to Fort Walla Walla. Abe had four of the larger nuggets in his pouch. He couldn't wait to take the big horses home. When he handed over the nuggets, he had a moment's doubt but his exhilaration pushed it away. The soldier hooked leads onto the big horses' halters. "You want to lead one?" Abe asked Martha.

She laughed with delight. "Sure. Give me the smaller one. Or can't you tell?"

Abe handed her Luke's lead. "I can't even tell them apart, let alone which is bigger," he said, feeling as he'd felt on his tenth birthday when he'd gotten his first horse, a small chestnut Morgan.

The soldier pointed to one of their ears. "Luke has a cream-colored ear," he said. "Pretty soon they won't look alike to you, but until then remember: lukewarm milk. . .cream ear."

They made quite a procession going home. "I didn't think Sampson would ever seem small," Martha said as the animals trotted along.

Abe compared Martha's mount to the one she led. "He looks about half the size of Luke," he said. "And so dainty he could break a leg without trying."

"I know," she agreed, laughing. "And Charity looks like a baby horse. These big guys will be able to pull a wagonful of lumber or wood, won't they?"

Suddenly, he really didn't know what they could pull. "I guess we'll have to experiment," he said. "Just because they're big doesn't mean I'm going to abuse them."

—⁂—

The next day Abe took the team and wagon after trees for furniture. The wagon had been Martha's family's covered wagon. Abe had stripped it as much as possible to make it easier to pull into the mountains for lumber. On the way into the mountains Abe learned the team was well trained and willing. He piled trees onto the wagon until it settled down some. The horses acted as if they weren't pulling anything so he put more on. Finally, he loaded all the wagon would comfortably hold. He climbed on and spoke to the big team. If they struggled, he'd shove some off. But they started the wagon with no strain and pulled it down the hill and home in an hour and a half.

"Makes me feel awful for making Charity and Sampson work so hard," Abe said that evening.

Martha looked up from threading her needle. "Don't give it another thought," she said. She stuck the thread into her mouth to get it wet, then

271

shoved it at the eye of the needle. She missed but got it through on the next try. "You've never mistreated a horse in your life, Abe Noble," she said, evening up the ends of the thread. "I'd swear it in court."

He nodded. He hadn't pushed them at all, not at all. He let Josie outside while they read their Bibles and prayed together, then called her in and they all went to bed.

"I'll bet Martha never even thinks of me in this bed alone and lonely," he said out loud after he'd said his private prayers.

Chapter 7

After Martha finished her private talk with the Lord, she reached over the side of her bed to give Josie a good-night hug. "Are you as happy as I am?" she asked the sleepy dog. "It makes me happy to see Abe so happy, too. It purely does. He's so nice he deserves it."

Abe spent the next day outside sawing up trees, making rough boards and firewood at the same time. Martha interrupted her sewing several times to check on him. Finally she finished her first dress and sunbonnet, a pale pink with red and darker pink flowers. She folded it and put it away in order to surprise him when she wore it on Sunday.

During the next three weeks Abe made a rocking chair, a settle, an easy chair, and several small tables for the main room. Martha padded them with heavy denim stuffed with feathers and down she bought at the general store. She also bought enough material and feathers to make Abe a featherbed somewhat like hers.

Nellie came over one day when Martha had nearly finished making her dresses. "It looks so beautiful," the red-headed girl said. "All I know how to do is wash clothes after filthy men. I hate it."

Martha looked up from her stitching and nodded. "I know what you mean. It's worse than awful." *Thank You, Lord, for my good husband who got me out of that kind of awful stuff. Thank you, too, Abe.* "I could teach you to sew if you'd like, Nellie."

Nellie wanted to learn, so that day Martha started teaching her how to cut out and sew a dress, using Martha's last piece of Christmas material. Nellie came for three days until they finished the brown, full-skirted dress with a fitted bodice and long tapered sleeves. Martha made the twenty-four tiny buttonholes but told Nellie she'd teach her when they made a dress for her—if her mother would buy the material.

—⁂—

One day at the end of January, Martha walked to the village to buy some candles and a bar of soap.

"Say," Mr. McClinchey said, "I suppose you heard there ain't goin' to be no state named Walla Walla."

273

"No, I didn't. What's it going to be?"

He shook his gray head. "Only heard they rejected our name. Don't rightly care what they name it now."

When Martha told Abe, they decided it would no doubt be Washington as that's what the territory was called.

"Well, what do you think?" Abe asked about the living room furniture he had just finished.

"I love it. I spend my nights in my room thanking the Lord for you. Well, not just for making furniture, but it's good, Abe. It's purely good." She looked around the room where all the pieces wore matching clothes—the denim she'd stuffed to make the furniture comfortable. Just looking at it gave her a warm feeling. "I do like it," she finally added.

"Would you mind if I put up a sign at the saloons and the general store?"

"I'd love it. Maybe I'll get to show off my beautiful house. I might even make a friend or two."

Sure enough, two couples came to see Abe's work. Martha proudly showed them the bedroom furniture, the kitchen sideboard, table, and chairs, and the living room things. One of them ordered a complete set, just like those he'd already made. They didn't force Abe into giving them a completion date but told him their house was almost finished.

When the door closed behind the couple, Abe gave a little shout and grabbed Martha. Then he released her. "Sorry," he mumbled. "Guess I got carried away in my excitement." Martha couldn't tell whether he looked more embarrassed or disappointed. But he recovered quickly. "Do you know how much profit we'll make on all that furniture?" he asked. Then, not waiting for her answer, continued, "Almost enough to pay for Luke and John. I'll work day and night and have the things finished in a month."

"And I'll take care of the livestock," Martha added, wanting to do her share.

The schedule worked out almost as Abe had planned. Martha did most of the household work, including carrying all the water for drinking, cooking, and washing clothes. She also did the shopping, made the cloth parts of the living room furniture, and helped Abe when she could.

Before Abe finished the furniture, spring arrived with balmy weather, and people began to drift into Walla Walla from Oregon City, the Dalles, and even western Washington Territory. When Martha walked to the store, she passed through the front yards of several new cabins that had been built in the warm weather.

Abe told Martha he'd have to get the crops in before he did any more furniture. With the new settlers he knew he'd have a market for whatever he could grow or build. "All of a sudden I need to be two people," he told Martha over supper one evening with a satisfied smile. "Things are goin' good."

The people who'd ordered the furniture were more than pleased as they hauled away three wagonloads of things to make their house a home.

"I'd like to buy ten more cows," Abe told Martha after the people had gone. "The first ten are ready to calve so our herd's goin' to grow."

Of course Martha trusted his judgment. Whatever he thought was best, she believed wholeheartedly.

Abe brought out the plow and disk he'd bought last fall and began working the ground from morning until evening. He always took the horses to the creek at noon and Martha noticed he took them once during the morning and in the afternoon, too. She smiled, proud of her caring husband.

—⁓—

One morning in late March, Nellie tore into Martha's house without knocking, something she'd never done before. "Martha, they're here!" she yelled. "They're here! Come and see."

Martha, washing clothes in the kitchen end of the main room, lifted her eyes from the tub. "Who's where?" she asked.

"The big wagon train. Come on."

As Martha tore out the door, she wiped her hands on her dress; Josie was so close she stumbled on Martha's feet. Abe, far out in the field would have to find out later. In a few minutes they ran west on Main Street toward a large number of covered wagons. People seemed to be climbing or jumping down from all the wagons.

Martha hadn't said a word to Nellie since they'd left the house. In fact, Nellie had fallen far behind. But Martha couldn't help that. She had to see if her family was in the train.

"Is there a Cleveland Strange family with this train?" she asked the first person she came to, a woman who looked about ready to have a baby.

The woman nodded. "Yes, thank heavens. They've been a big bles—"

"Thank You, God!" Martha yelled as she took off, running among the wagons, unable to wait while the woman finished talking. Dashing wildly from wagon to wagon, she searched for a familiar face. Finally, she spotted a shiny bald head and heard him laughing loudly at something. "Uncle Cleve!" she shrieked, running to him and throwing herself into his arms.

He pulled her close and laid his head over hers. "My little Martha," he said, softly for him, but everyone in the wagon train could have heard him. He stroked her back as tears ran from both their eyes. "I'm so sorry," he said, again loudly. "Did you get through the winter all right?"

Then Martha felt herself being jerked from Uncle Cleve's arms and into some softer ones. "My baby girl," Aunt Mandy whispered into Martha's

275

hair. "I've been crying for you all winter, being here alone and all." She pushed Martha back and looked at her. "You look fine, baby. Are you?"

Martha couldn't let go of her aunt, who'd been round as a dumpling the last time Martha had seen her. She still didn't look exactly thin. "I'm fine, but you lost a lot of weight on the trip. You look tiny, Aunt Mandy."

Her aunt nodded. "The trip was no picnic. But I regained a lot sitting around all winter." She smiled. "I looked half decent for a while."

Martha looked at her aunt. The short woman had sparkling dark blue eyes and dark hair like Mama's and hers. "Auntie," she said, "you're far more than half decent looking now. You're the most beautiful sight I've seen since I got here."

Uncle Cleve's wide mouth turned up in a happy laugh. "She's the most beautiful sight I've seen in my entire life," he bellowed, "but you're a close second."

"Where's your wagon? Where are you staying? Can we get a donation land claim and get going on our log cabin?" Aunt Mandy asked.

Martha decided not to tell them about Abe yet. "Can you bring your wagon and come with me now?" she asked. "I'll take you to the place I'm staying."

Uncle Cleve told his tired oxen to get up. "We have to go a bit farther," he yelled at anyone who happened to be listening. "I'll come back and talk to you folks again tomorrow and tell you what I've learned." Then he walked beside the oxen as Martha steered them down the street to Mill Creek and south until the creek turned east. The two horses tied to the wagon looked in better shape than the oxen pulling it.

"Just a little farther," she said. Suddenly remembering her brother and cousin, she lost every ounce of strength she possessed. She stopped. "Where are Jackson and Riley?" she whimpered, feeling clouds gathering on her private horizon. If something had happened to her brother Jackson she'd never be able to handle it.

Aunt Mandy, seeing Martha's terror, put her arm around her. "They're all right," she said. "Another wagon train followed us a day behind out of Fort Hall. Jackson and Riley stayed to help them get the wagons down the Blue Mountains." She shook her head. "Quite an experience, coming down that mountain."

Martha's blood began to warm and flow again. She gave her aunt a dazzling smile. "I'll never forget," she said, laughing happily. "It was just awful." At the moment her joy made her forget anything sad or hard that had ever happened to her. "Come on, Uncle Cleve, let's get these oxen some water and rest. The horses, too."

A few moments later they came to Martha and Abe's place. "This is it,"

Martha said, feeling happier than she ever had in her entire life. She steered Uncle Cleve to the side of the house where the wagon wouldn't be in the way. She felt a thrill of pride as she looked at the place from a stranger's viewpoint. Everything looked neat and well-cared for. "Take them out of the yokes, Uncle Cleve, and lead them through that open gate. They can get to the creek and anywhere they want for a lot of acres." When the six oxen were put inside the fenced area, they headed for the creek, running right into it with the horses following. Martha silently thanked Abe for his foresight in building the house above the pastures.

"Whose place is this?" Aunt Mandy asked when Martha opened the door and invited them in.

Martha didn't answer right away. She wished Abe would happen to come to the house. She checked the clock—eleven-thirty. He would be in soon but she couldn't keep her aunt and uncle waiting that long. "Would you like some cold milk?" she asked in a delaying tactic.

"Sounds great," Uncle Cleve said. "We haven't had any milk since we left Fort Hall."

Martha ran out to the creek where she kept the milk in waterproof containers.

"This is a lovely home," Aunt Mandy said when Martha reappeared. "I didn't expect to have anything this nice for years."

Just then the door opened again and Abe stepped in. "Looks like we got company," he said.

Martha noticed he'd stopped at the creek, too, and had washed his face and arms, which caused the rest of him and his clothes to look even dustier. But Martha didn't care. He still looked beautiful and kind and caring.

Finally, she noticed everyone staring at each other and no one talking.

Chapter 8

A be looked at all the strangers and felt as though he'd come into the wrong house. Then Martha met his eyes. He'd never seen such elation in those beautiful eyes. Happiness, yes, but this was more. Suddenly, he knew. This was her family! Was this the end of their half-marriage? When faced with the possibility, he realized that what he had was much better than nothing. He tried to read Martha to learn what she'd told them.

Then she laughed her joyous tinkle that made birds sing inside him. "These people just got here," she explained. "They're my family, my Uncle Cleve and my Aunt Mandy." She turned to her aunt and uncle and laughed again. "And this man is my dear, sweet, wonderful husband, Abram Noble."

Abe felt a rush a relief. She'd just let him know she'd told them nothing. He felt so good he almost forgot to be a good host. "Welcome," he finally said. "I'll bet you're thirsty and hungry. You came to the right place. My wife is a fantastic cook."

"I'll have dinner on the table in just a little while," Martha said.

Martha's relatives still appeared to be in shock, but Abe could see them trying to shake themselves out of it.

"Let me help," Aunt Mandy said, hurrying to the sideboard from which Martha pulled food items and carried them to the table. She chuckled. "It's not polite to arrive at someone's place at mealtime, you know."

Martha hugged her aunt again. "But you aren't company, Aunt Mandy. You're my family." Tears ran down her cheeks. "You can come any time you want," she choked. "And you'd better, too." She swiped the tears away with her hand, then gave a big knife to her aunt. "Here, you make the sandwiches while I finish the soup. Then we'll put it all on the table."

They soon settled into Abe's freshly made chairs. Abe thanked God for their safe trip and asked Him to be with each of them through the afternoon. Then he remembered Martha's brother but was afraid to ask. *Oh, God. Please help her brother to be safe. Don't let Martha be hurt any more.*

"Your dried pea soup is delicious," Aunt Mandy said, her eyes twinkling. "Similar to what we ate on the Trail. . .and ate. . .and ate. . .and ate." She laughed. "I'm just kidding, Martha. You've put some other things in this that make it just delicious. And the sandwiches are like manna from heaven. We didn't get yeast bread, even at Fort Hall, except for a couple of times."

"The milk's fair to middlin', too," Uncle Cleve boomed out, "but that's not what we're needin' to be talkin' about." He looked from Martha at one end of the table to Abe at the other. "Which of you's going to tell us how this all came about?"

Martha glanced at Abe so he guessed it was up to him to start. "Well, I met Martha when the town drunk tried to haul her off. After that we just sort of kept seeing each other until we got married and took out a donation claim."

Martha shook her head. "He's too modest. He saved me from the town drunk; he saved me from starving; he saved me from freezing; he saved me from loneliness. And he's always doing things for everyone. He's a real western hero, Uncle Cleve."

No one said anything until Aunt Mandy reached her arm around Martha's shoulders. "Pretty rough, huh? I was afraid it would be. I want to thank you for saving our girl, Abe. We love her a whole lot."

Abe felt his tan cheeks turn red. "I did it for my own personal reasons," he said quietly. "I love her a whole lot, too." He noticed everyone had finished eating, so he stood up. "Is there anything I can do for you folks this afternoon? If not, I need to get back to my plowing." He felt better discussing an impersonal subject. "We're planning to harvest enough oats to feed all the animals in Walla Walla County as well as the people."

Uncle Cleve laughed loudly. "Well, son, you'd better get to work. That's a mighty high goal you've set for yourselves. We can talk more tonight. We want to know all about donation claims and the beautiful little valley here."

Abe hurried out and harnessed up Luke and John for the afternoon's work. He'd likely quit at supper time tonight. He'd been working until dark but that might seem inhospitable. The gentle giants of horses he'd bought were willing and hard workers. Abe took them to the creek at four o'clock and worked two more hours. Then, able to think only of what Martha and her kinfolks were doing, he eagerly put the horses in the corral and joined the others in the house.

"Well, did you get another hundred acres plowed?" Uncle Cleve asked loudly. "I always appreciate a good worker, whether it's a horse, a man, or a boy."

Abe laughed, nodding. "I know what you mean. But you forgot to mention a woman. I suppose you know my little Martha works like my Belgians."

After supper Uncle Cleve had to go talk to the people in the wagon train, so they all went along. When they approached the group of wagons,

Martha pointed out a new building on the north side of the street. "I haven't seen this before, Abe. When did it come up?"

"A man named James McAuliff built it a couple of weeks ago," Abe said. "It's going to be another general store." Noting Martha's doubtful look, he continued. "Oh, there'll be enough business for two. More people comin' in all the time." He chuckled. "There seems to be enough business for two saloons already."

Uncle Cleve told the men from the wagon train that he hadn't learned much yet but he'd be back in the morning to see them again. The four walked north a couple of blocks to Mill Creek where it wandered on its way west.

Aunt Mandy pointed to the several tepees scattered in the area just east. "Do Indians live in those things? Or are they leftovers from times past?"

Abe smiled. "Indians live in each and every one. If you want to know about Indians, ask Martha. Some of her best friends are Indians."

Martha colored and shrugged. Then she told about the Indians refusing her trail bread, and their later visits where she and they exchanged bits of language.

By unspoken agreement the group wandered back toward Main Street and east toward Martha and Abe's place.

"Are they all friendly?" Uncle Cleve asked as they strolled along in the warm evening twilight.

"We haven't seen any trouble since we've been here," Abe said. "They've signed a treaty that says they'll stay on the areas set aside for them and not bother the white people. The treaty also says white people will leave them alone and stay away from their places called reservations."

Aunt Mandy pointed toward the tepees. "Is that their reservation?"

Martha laughed merrily. "That's supposed to be part of our town but no one bothers them. They walk into everyones' houses without knocking, demanding food. They stink like you wouldn't believe from fish oil they smear all over their bodies." She giggled. "They think it keeps them warm. I don't know what they'd do if a person locked their doors or told them to get out when they walk in. As far as I know no one does that."

They arrived at the house and went inside where they had their usual Bible reading and prayer. Everyone thanked God for bringing the folks here safely.

"Now," Uncle Cleve said, "could we talk about donation claims?"

"Sure." Abe accepted the big bowl of cream-smothered rice pudding that Martha handed him and took a big bite. Mmmm. That stuff was good as the ice cream he'd had back in Iowa. "Thanks. This hits the spot." He returned his attention to Uncle Cleve. "You can have three hundred twenty acres. I'd suggest you spend tomorrow looking over the area for a place you like. You can take the saddle horses if Martha doesn't mind." He smiled at Martha. "The big one's hers. Anyway, Martha can show you where to file for the claim. Then you just build yourselves a cabin—" He glanced at Martha again and chuckled. "I mean a house, and live on the property."

"That's it?" Uncle Cleve sounded incredulous.

"I think so. We filed our claim in November but I doubt it's changed much. Anyway, the agent will tell you."

Soon Martha's relatives returned to the wagon to sleep.

"I like them," Abe told Martha. "And I'm especially glad they're here for you." Then he remembered her brother. Surely everyone wouldn't have been so joyous if anything had happened. Anyway, he'd better ask. "Uh, Martha, I expected your brother to be with them."

She nodded. "He was, Abe. He and my cousin Riley. But they stayed to help another wagon train over the Blues. It's pretty awful coming down that steep mountain," she said. "But they'll be here in a few days."

They soon went to bed at opposite ends of the little house. As Abe tried to fall asleep he thought about his marriage. He really should have talked to Martha about how they'd handle things with other people in the house so much. "You take care of it, God," he mumbled when his mind became too fuzzy to think.

—⁊⁊⁊—

The next morning Abe finished breakfast and tried to harness the horses as quietly as possible. But Luke couldn't suppress his noisy greeting, which the other three horses took up with alacrity. Abe grinned to himself as he followed the big Belgians off to the far field. He'd guess no one within a half-mile slept after what he'd just caused.

Well, he wondered, would the coming of Martha's kin be helpful or harmful in his relationship with Martha? He rightly hoped it would be good as they could sure use a positive influence for once.

"What about it, Lord?" he asked. "I don't rightly see how they could hurt anything, do you?"

They aren't going to hurt anything, Abe. They'll be a blessing to both you and Martha. You just keep treating Martha as you have. She's a special woman, Abe. Now get to work. You have lots to do.

Chapter 9

"That was quite a meal," Uncle Cleve said the next morning, sipping his second cup of coffee. I may be too full to go look for our spread." His twinkling eyes challenged Aunt Mandy. They'd just finished their breakfast of fried potatoes, bacon, toast, and coffee.

"Oh yes, you will go look," the round little woman replied. "What do you think we came all this way for? What we're doing today is the reward for all our suffering in the past year." She turned to Martha. "I'm so excited I can hardly stand it. You'll go with us, won't you?"

"I'd love to," Martha said. Then she shook her head. "But I'd better not. Abe doesn't like to ride our horses double. Did you know a horse isn't supposed to carry more than ten percent of its own weight? Abe says Sampson weighs about sixteen hundred pounds and Charity one thousand three hundred fifty pounds. We should trade horses, but we're each attached to our own. I'm so proud of my husband, Aunt Mandy. He's the kindest person I've ever known. He doesn't even overwork his animals."

Uncle Cleve grunted. "He'd have had some great fun on the Trail." Then his twinkling eyes met Martha's again. "We can ride our own horses, Martha. Didn't you notice we brought them? Speaking of great, I agree, that's some man you managed to trap. You'd never have found one that good in Missouri."

"Yes," Aunt Mandy agreed, "but you're both far too shy around us. You act almost like strangers. We'd like to see you acting like newlyweds."

Uncle Cleve looked wise. "Just give them a couple of days to get used to us," he told his wife, "and they'll never know we're here. I know how it is with these kids with stars in their eyes. Don't worry about them."

After they'd gone off to saddle their horses, Martha looked down at Josie. "What do you think? Are you glad they're here? They're going to wonder why Abe and I aren't all gooey, all right." She headed into the house to start a double batch of bread. She usually made one loaf every day because she could bake only one at a time in her dutch oven. When she got a stove she would be able to make several loaves at once and not have to do it every day.

Uncle Cleve and Aunt Mandy returned with the horses just when

Martha finished setting the bread. "I'll let you two go find your new home," she said. "I'll be fixing a good dinner for you."

—∞—

Aunt Mandy and Uncle Cleve returned just in time for dinner. "What's the soil like around here?" Uncle Cleve asked when Abe came home to eat.

"It's the best," Abe answered. "Topsoil goes down ten feet in some places. Seems to be at least partly ash from the volcanoes in the Cascade Mountains. Anyway the soil's friable early in the year and anything will grow here. Did you find a place you can't live without?"

Uncle Cleve laughed loudly. "The whole valley's so purty we'd take any of it. But you'll be surprised what we got to thinking. We wondered about the place across the creek from yours. Or is that part of the Indian Territory?"

Abe shook his head. "There's no reservation around here but I'm not sure why no one's claimed anything north of the creek. Probably because of the Indians but they aren't this far east. Why don't you go ask the agent?"

After her guests ate a nice dinner, Martha and her aunt cleaned up the house. Then Martha took them to the land agent's office in the back of the trading post. Martha and Josie waited in the trading post for them, as the agent's office was small.

"It's all right," Uncle Cleve bellowed when they came out. Both of the newcomers looked happy.

"I guess we can move our wagon over there this afternoon," Aunt Mandy reported. "He said they might get around to surveying the places this year. We won't know exactly where we live until then."

In spite of Martha's insistence that they stay right where they were, Uncle Cleve hooked the oxen up and pulled the wagon across the creek. "This may be the last river we have to ford," he joked in his stentorian voice. He shook his head. "I'll bet the oxen hope so. They've had a miserable life this last year."

Martha had no doubt of that. Her trip over the Oregon Trail hadn't faded from her memory yet. She remembered oxen lying down and dying in their yokes while men whipped strips of hide from their bodies trying to get them going. She shuddered, then forced herself to think about something else. "You'll eat with us until you get your house built, won't you?"

Aunt Mandy giggled. "We can build a fire just like you, darlin'. Why should we intrude on the newlyweds? We'll just go to the store, restock our barrels, and be independent again." She flashed a joyous smile at Martha. "I can't believe we'll be in our own home again in just a few weeks."

—∞—

That night the new arrivals came for information again. "Where did you get all those nice logs to build your house?" Uncle Cleve asked.

Abe pointed east. "Up in the foothills of the Blue Mountains. I had the logs sawed and brought down because we had only the saddle horses at the time. You can save a lot of money hauling the logs with your oxen. You can use our wagon since you're living in yours."

At the end of the week an enormous pile of logs lay on the ground across the creek, ready to be converted into a house. The group planned to start it on Monday.

Martha's uncle and aunt attended the Methodist church in Galbraith's Saloon with Abe and Martha. Then they ate with Martha and Abe and spent the day talking, catching up on each other's activities for the past year.

"When do you think Jackson and Riley will be here?" Martha asked. "I can't wait to see them."

Uncle Cleve shrugged; Martha giggled. Uncle Cleve was the only person she knew that she could hear shrugging. "They should be along any day," he said. I guess the people in town would know where to send them if they should ask."

Abe grinned. " 'Fraid so. We just rebuilt the town so we know each other pretty well."

At their insistence Abe explained how the town survey placed half the buildings in the intersections so they tore them down and rebuilt.

"We bought two lots on Main Street," Martha added. "We might build a furniture store on one of them."

"I'd like to place an order already," Aunt Mandy said. "These pieces are nice."

Abe explained that he had to be a farmer right now, which the older folks completely understood. After a while Aunt Mandy and Uncle Cleve walked across the rock stepping stones they'd built.

"I could plow a few acres for the produce gardens tomorrow if you have time to start planting," Abe told Martha later. "I have this hunch that we can sell all we can grow."

"Do. I'm eager to plant. The seeds I planted in February are ready to set out, too."

The following afternoon found Martha busily planting seeds and plants in the soft earth Abe had plowed and disked for her. Josie ran through the prepared ground, rolled in it, and dug in it. "Calm down, Josie," Martha called to her exuberant pet. Josie pulled her dirt-covered nose from the hole she'd been digging, looked at Martha, wagged her plumy tail, and poked her nose back into the hole.

The following day Martha planted seed potatoes while enjoying Josie's capers. Suddenly, the dog's ears jerked erect; a half-moment later the big dog began barking wildly. Martha looked up to see two riders approaching, then recognized Jackson and Riley. Both young men had grown beards and mustaches, Jackson's nearly black and Riley's nearly blond. Their hair had grown long but both boys looked clean.

Dropping potatoes everywhere, Martha tore to the end of the row about the same time they slid from their saddles. Josie beat Martha to Jackson and jumped at him as though she wanted to be in his arms. He squatted and hugged the dog until Martha reached him.

"Jackson, Jackson, I can't believe it," she kept repeating, tears running down her cheeks. Then she noticed Riley standing to one side, looking embarrassed, and hugged him, too. "Come in and have some cold milk," she invited when she got her mind together. "I keep it in the creek so it'll be good." She got the milk, then led the young men into the house.

They talked a few minutes over roast meat sandwiches, then Jackson cleared his throat. "Uh. . .where's. . .is William all right? Where is he?"

Oh, yes. He didn't know. "The people in the wagon train wouldn't let me keep him. The Butlers. Remember them? They were right, too, Jackson. I almost starved to death and froze to death, too."

His gaze dropped to his glass of milk. Finally, he lifted his eyes to hers. "I know. I shouldn't have gone back. You two needed me." He took another long swallow, wiped away the white mustache, and continued. "I think the folks' death hurt me so bad I had to go find out if we had anyone left at all. I know that's no excuse."

"Do you know where my folks are?" Riley asked.

Oh, dear. Here she'd been rambling on, forgetting all about Aunt Mandy and Uncle Cleve. "Come on," she said, taking his hand. "They've taken out a claim already." She ran him across the rock path, over the creek, and to the wagon sitting in the sunshine behind the trees lining the creek. "This is it," she said. "They're somewhere around." They found Riley's parents combing the creek bank for bits of wood to burn. "Come over to our place and use some of our wood. We've brought a lot down from the Blues."

Sitting on the edge of the creek, they all talked. Martha soon learned that Riley and Jackson planned to take donation claims, too.

"But what if you get married?" Martha asked. "I'll bet you can't go back and get another donation claim after you get married."

"I heard there aren't any women out here anyway," Riley said. His grin almost said he didn't care but Martha knew better. Her cousin's and brother's favorite subject for years had been girls.

"Abe says there are going to be a lot of new settlers this year. Some of them will be girls I bet."

"Who cares what Abe says," Jackson said, roaring with laughter. Then he stopped. "Who's Abe?"

"He's Martha's handsome, smart, rich husband," Aunt Mandy said. "You'll have to meet him."

"Oh, he will," Martha said. "In fact, it's about time for him to come for supper." She jumped up. "Come on, Jackson." He followed her back to the house.

About the time Martha finished fixing a quick meal, Abe came in. After she introduced the two young men, they spent a pleasant hour getting acquainted. Abe reluctantly returned to work for a couple more hours, promising to continue their discussion that evening.

"Aunt Mandy was right," Jackson said. "You caught a good one. I can tell we're going to be good friends."

Martha decided to plant a few more rows of potatoes and Jackson found his way across the stream to the Strange place. When Abe came home just before dark, he asked where Jackson was.

"He's across the creek," Martha said. They'd been referring to the Strange place as "across the creek."

He walked to where Martha had been working. "Looks like my little work horse has been busy, even with her long-lost brother here."

Martha hurried Abe into the house. "Come in, Abe, we have to talk."

"What about? Jackson? I thought he'd be with us since he is your brother."

They sat down across the table from each other. "That's what I wanted to talk to you about." She whispered as though Jackson were in the next room. "We don't have a place for him, Abe. We built it for two."

He smiled. "He's your brother, Martha. You don't tell your brother you forgot to make a place for him. We'll build on another room if we have to."

She could barely put her deepest concern into words, but she had to. "If he stays here, he'll find out about us," she said.

He nodded. "Yes, he'll find out. Is that so bad?"

Martha nodded. She couldn't explain it even to herself, but she simply didn't want anyone knowing.

His brown eyes drilled into hers. "I've been upset with you a few times, Martha, but this is the first time I've been disappointed in you. Remember how you watched, day by day from the wagon, hoping and praying for them to come. Remember your bitter disappointment when they weren't in that final wagon train last year? I didn't think you'd ever in this world neglect a relative, Martha, no matter what the reason. And if we've gotten ourselves into such a mess that we can't do our duty to our kin, it's a sorry shame."

Chapter 10

When Abe spoke sharply to Martha, her face blanched and her blue eyes expressed such shock that he wished desperately that he could recall the words. But what he'd said had been true. Sure, Jackson planned to take a claim, but he needed a place to live until he got his cabin built.

Even though Abe knew he'd been right, he couldn't handle seeing the pain in Martha's eyes. If only he could take her in his arms and kiss her hurt away. But he couldn't.

"I'm sorry," he murmured. "I'm really sorry, Martha, but where's your brother going to stay?"

"He's been staying with my aunt and uncle."

"But he's here now, and he's always lived with you. Don't you think he'll expect to live here?"

She shrugged. "What'll he think when he sees us sleeping in different rooms?"

A perfectly sensible thought crossed Abe's mind. They'd have plenty of room if he moved into Martha's room. They could give his to Jackson. He opened his mouth to suggest it but that's not what came out. "More important is what'll he think if we don't invite him to live with us. I guess I could sleep in the main room on the floor," he said. "Slick never figured it out. Maybe Jackson wouldn't either."

"Jackson would."

Abe decided to end the conversation, though he felt strongly about it. He shrugged. "He's your brother. I guess you can treat him however you please." He strode out of the house, then on out to the barn. A little time with the horses would soothe him. He curried all four horses and rubbed them down, talking to them all the time. Then he milked the cows and carried the milk into the house.

"Maybe we should share our milk with your family," he said. "We don't need it all and I'm sure they'd enjoy it."

"I'd like that," Martha said in a small voice. She strained the milk and poured it into shallow pans to let the cream rise. "Oh," she said as she washed the pail, "I may as well give them the milk right away. They can let

287

the cream rise if they want to." She poured it into a small milk can, put the lid on, and handed it to Abe. "Your idea, you should get to take it to them." Her voice still trembled from their fight.

"I'm sorry, Martha," he whispered. "I didn't want to hurt you. Why don't we both take the milk over? We could visit for a few minutes."

Dusk had nearly given way to darkness when they crossed the creek to the cheerful fire encircled by four people sitting on short pieces of log that Uncle Cleve had obviously hauled down from the Blues.

"Well," Cleve's voice boomed out when he saw them. He jumped up and sat Martha on his makeshift seat. "The lovebirds managed to come out of the nest."

"Cleve, hush," Aunt Mandy said, laughing.

Knowing they'd embarrassed Martha even more, Abe longed to squeeze her hand. "We just came out long enough to bring you some milk," he said instead. "Everyone's cows will soon freshen but right now there's not much milk in our little village so we're sharing."

"Oh, thank you," Aunt Mandy said. "We'll all appreciate some fresh milk."

"We're just talking about the boys' donation claims," Uncle Cleve said. "They'd like to file them as soon as possible."

Abe nodded in the firelight. "Makes sense." He met Jackson's eyes. "Find the right place already?"

"Nah. Anyplace looks good to me."

"But that's half the fun," Abe insisted. "I can't tell you how much fun Martha and I had choosing our spot."

"Well, morning comes pretty early," Abe said later. "Ready to go, Martha?" This was the time to invite Jackson but he couldn't do it after their quarrel. He desperately hoped she would.

She rose from her log chair and took several steps toward the creek with Abe. Then she turned back. "Are you about ready to come home, Jackson?" she asked. Abe felt certain no one but he heard the slight tremor in her voice.

After a moment's silence, Jackson cleared his throat. "I thought I'd just sleep here on the ground with Riley since you two have each other."

"Come on and enjoy a good bed for a change," Abe urged.

Jackson shook his head. "How about if I come over for breakfast?"

"We'll be looking for you," Abe said. As they hurried across the creek he heard Martha suck in a long breath and emit a giant sigh.

When they reached the cabin, she took a drink of water then handed the dipper to Abe. Then, as if in supplication, she put her hand on his arm. "Thank you for forcing me to ask him," she said almost whispering. She giggled nervously. "At least we're saved for now."

After they read the Bible and prayed together, Abe lay in his comfortable featherbed, thinking about the mess he and Martha had created for themselves. "Look at it, God," Abe whispered into the darkness. "Never mind how it makes me feel; I knew this farce wouldn't work."

It's working, Abram. You're developing a homestead and beginning a life together.

"You know what I mean, God. She's going to be mortified when her kin find out. And they will."

You're doing fine. You do your part and don't worry about things you can't help. Just be happy she's with you rather than in a wagon across the creek.

Abe had to nod at that. "I am glad. Thanks, God. You have no idea how much I love her."

I don't?

Suddenly, Abe's face felt hot—even in the dark. He'd dared tell God He didn't know something?

—⟨⟨⟨—

The next morning Abe lay in bed, thinking about his visits with God. He had no idea whether they were dreams or what, but they meant everything to him. "Forgive me for having even a passing thought that You don't know everything about me," he whispered, "and please never stop talking to me." He hurried into his clothes to spend his day "developing a homestead."

Martha looked pale, as if she hadn't slept well, and Jackson didn't appear before Abe harnessed up the horses and went to the far fields.

Abe followed the horses and plow down the long fields, enjoying the sight and smell of the soft earth turning over before him and the sweet sound of the meadowlarks around him. Soon, his thoughts turned to Martha. He'd been feeling sorry only for himself in the marriage but it couldn't be easy for her, either. He remembered back when they first met and she'd tried to lie to him about where she was staying. He grinned. Not being a deceptive person, she soon had to tell him the truth. This duplicity wasn't easy for either of them.

Before he knew it, twelve o'clock and dinnertime came. He turned Luke and John into the corral and, after washing up in the outside bowl, went inside.

"Hello," he greeted Martha and Jackson. "I hope everyone's as hungry as I am."

"I am," Martha said. "I finished planting the potatoes and most of the lima beans." She set a big plate of sandwiches on the table, then a bowl of fried potatoes and bacon. "I truly hope it will rain soon and start the things growing."

"Not yet," Abe said. "Let me get the hay and oats in first. What did you do this morning, Jackson?"

Jackson shrugged. "Not much. Sort of resting up, I guess."

When Abe came in for supper, Jackson wasn't there and Martha seemed upset.

"I thought he might help me," she fretted, "but he sat around with Riley all day. They didn't even go out looking for claims."

"They may be worn out," Abe said. "Give them some time."

—⁂—

The following Sunday afternoon the two families enjoyed dinner at Abe and Martha's again, then relaxed talking. Sometime later, Nellie Martin arrived and, after being introduced to the newcomers, settled herself in for a visit. Abe smiled to himself as the two young men came alive, vying for her attention, which she quite obviously enjoyed. Before the afternoon ended, Abe decided Jackson had won the race.

After that, Jackson seemed to spend most of his time with Nellie. Both looked happy, and happiest, when together. Jackson stayed with Riley every night so Martha's secret remained undiscovered.

By the time May Day arrived, Abe and Martha had everything planted—the produce gardens, which included several kinds of melons, and the oats and the hayfields. The Stranges moved into their new house and Uncle Cleve and Riley each used a yoke of oxen and Abe's disk and plow to prepare ground for hay and their own personal vegetable garden.

The cows had calved with four heifers, five little bulls; one, who was too small, hadn't lived. Adding to his work, Abe hauled three cans of milk as well as a smaller one of cream to McClinchy and McMorris's General Store each morning. McAuliff wanted some for his store, too but Abe didn't have enough yet. They talked about buying ten more cows as soon as they had time. Abe didn't mind the extra work. He and Martha reveled in their little homestead's growth.

Abe soon learned there were no cows to be had in the area. So he put in an order for ten of them with a man who was about ready to go to California after some cows.

Still, Riley and Jackson hadn't gotten around to finding places for themselves, let alone filing claims.

One evening, Jackson and Nellie told Abe and Martha they planned to marry soon. After the hugging slowed down, Martha told Nellie how glad she'd be to have a sister at last.

"I'm glad you waited to file your claim," Abe said, "but you'd better get with it now. We'll help you put up a cabin. . .oops." He looked at Martha and grinned. "I suppose it'll be a house. Anyway, let's get it up while we're having this break between planting and harvesting."

After they left, Abe sat thinking about the two who'd just left. One of them was touching the other most of the time, patting an arm, smoothing hair, or outright putting their arms around each other. They obviously could hardly stand it when they weren't touching.

"What are all those deep thoughts?" Martha asked, slipping into the chair across from where he sat on the settle.

He shook his head, wondering if he should tell. "Well," he said, "I was just thinking how much Jackson and Nellie are in love and how they love to touch each other."

She nodded but said nothing.

"Know how that makes me feel?" he asked.

"I know. I'm sorry." She looked sad for a moment then brightened. "At least I'm trying to do my share on the place. Does that help any?"

He wanted to shout at her but swallowed it. He knew she couldn't help it if she didn't want to touch him. . .or be touched. And he'd been the one to suggest this "friends only" marriage. "Yes," he said softly, "it helps. Of course, it helps."

Chapter 11

Martha felt crushed at Abe's pain. She knew full well she was causing the pain. She knew that. But she couldn't pretend something she didn't feel. Could she? Yet, she really did feel a lot for Abe. Never in her life had anyone been so dear to her. He was so easy to live with, so kind and good, not only to her but to everyone. She'd never respected anyone as she did him. It made her feel especially good that everyone else in town thought highly of him, too.

But that wasn't like seeing fireworks and hearing bells ring and feeling a beautiful soft cloud wrap around you when a person came near or spoke to you. Oh, how she wished she could feel that way about him.

She couldn't force herself to feel that way, nor could she pretend she did, but she could do her very best to make him happy in other ways. She'd cook his favorite foods, keep his house in order, keep his clothes clean and mended, do all she could in the gardens, and always be cheerful to him. She sighed. What a large promise to fulfill. But she'd do it.

As time went on, Martha thought more and more about her baby brother, William. One day she mentioned it to Aunt Mandy. "I'd like to go after him," she said. "Those people aren't going to bring him back. It's a long trip from the Willamette Valley to here."

"We could take care of your place if you go. Why don't you ask Abe?"

But Abe didn't take to the idea. "The Willamette Valley is many times bigger than Walla Walla County," he said. "We could wander all summer and never find them. The best thing we can do is wait here, since they know where you are." His kind eyes twinkled mischievously. "If he came, he'd discover we have separate bedrooms."

"But he's too little to think about it," she said, hoping she spoke the truth.

Abe's head swung back and forth. "Not too little to tell, though," he said with a wry smile.

Martha didn't say anymore but she thought about her little brother a lot, hoping he was happy and well-cared for.

—ɷ—

Jackson and Nellie married one Sunday after church services in the saloon.

Aunt Mandy laughed afterwards. "I never expected my kin to marry in a saloon, but I expect you'll be forgiven." Both families helped Jackson and Nellie build their cabin on their claim near Fort Walla Walla.

One afternoon Martha felt hot and tired. She'd been working in the produce gardens since six-thirty in the morning. She felt dirty and thirsty, and her back hurt. Maybe she'd go in and get a drink. The short walk might get the kinks out, too.

As she came back out, a strange, yet familiar-looking, horse approached. She waited to see who the man was looking for. When he stopped fifty feet from her she approached him. "Are you looking for someone?"

He tipped his hat, touched his horse's sides with his boots, and slowly approached. "Miss Martha Lawford?"

She'd heard that voice before. But where? Who was he? Then it came to her. Dan Barlow! One of the young men with her wagon train, who'd ridden horses from Missouri to Oregon City. She'd last seen him on the Oregon Trail at the Umatilla River when Mr. Butler, whose oxen she'd been using, left to travel on to the Willamette Valley and she had turned off to come here.

"Dan Barlow! What are you doing here? I thought you'd be settled in Oregon City by now."

The young man slid from his horse and ran the few feet to Martha. "You're a sight for sore eyes, Miss Lawford. How's it going for you?"

Martha hardly knew how to greet the young man. Should she invite him in? She'd better see what he wanted. "I'm fine, Mr. Barlow. But what brings you so far from home?"

He grinned and pushed his hair back. "Well, a lot has happened. First off, Julia Tate and I married right after we got there. Then her folks drowned in a ferry accident on the Willamette River. You probably remember her folks?"

She remembered them all right. People who cared nothing for animals or people, including their own daughter, Julia. She nodded. "I remember them. I'm sorry. What a shame to make it all the way to Oregon then have something happen."

He nodded. "Yes. Anyway, when we went through their things we found they had a lot of money hidden away in a money pouch. We used enough to get us through the winter, which we hated." He grinned into her eyes. "Do you know it's rained there nearly every day since we arrived? Seven months of continual gray skies and rain. Finally, it got too depressing, so we decided to try a new 'Garden of Eden' for a while. So, here we are with plenty of money to get started."

What! They were moving to Walla Walla? She'd better invite him in and give him a drink. He gladly accepted her offer.

After fixing him a roast meat sandwich and a glass of milk, she sat down across the table from him. "But if you're moving here, where's Julia? Did you just come to look the place over?"

He shook his head. "No, I came to find you without her because we brought someone you may like to see. Julia's been taking care of your little brother a lot, Miss Lawford, because she needed someone when her parents died." He shrugged. "I can't explain it, but he comforted her a lot."

Willie! What was he saying? She couldn't stay in her chair any longer. "Do you have Willie with you?" she screeched, standing over him, almost jumping up and down over him. "Where is he? Go get him, Mr. Barlow. I need him, too. Do you have him? Is he with—"

He stood up, too, laughing. "Wait, and I'll explain. We do have him but we didn't know if you'd be able to take him yet so Julia stayed with him and the wagon west of town. We thought we shouldn't get him excited if he can't be with you. Julia would be happy to keep him if it's going to be hard for you."

Martha started out the door. "Come on, Josie, let's go get them."

Dan Barlow followed Martha out the door and west. She ran all the way through town and then on west, Josie at her heels and Dan Barlow ten feet behind. "Where are they?" she puffed, refusing to slow down.

Unable to spare enough breath to speak, Barlow pointed southwest. Then Martha saw a covered wagon with six oxen lying on the ground, still in harness. "Julia! Willie!" she screamed, still running.

When she reached the wagon she found Julia and Willie behind it, picking wildflowers. "Willie!" she yelled, holding out her arms.

The little blond-headed boy looked at her strangely for a moment, then threw himself into her arms. "Martha," he said, "where's Mama and Papa?"

Just then Julia threw her arms around both of them. "How are you, Martha?" she asked. "We were afraid you'd starve or freeze last winter. Rachel Butler kept praying for God to send someone to help you right away. She said He told her He did send someone."

Martha kept hugging Willie and Julia, thankful for the confusion so she didn't have to answer Willie's question. Surely the Butlers or Julia helped him remember that Mama and Papa had died on the Trail from cholera.

Finally, she remembered her manners. "Bring your wagon to our place," she said. "We can talk there, and your oxen can drink and eat."

Mr. Barlow got his oxen up and guided them up the creek to Martha's and Abe's place.

"Put them in that corral," Martha instructed, pointing. "They can get to the creek and there's lots of good grass." After Dan cared for the oxen, Martha invited them in again.

"Who lives here?" Willie asked. Martha sat on the rocker and he climbed into her lap.

Martha smiled into the beautiful blue eyes. "I do, love. You do, too, now." She glanced at the clock and discovered Abe would be in for supper in a half-hour. "You know what I have to do?" she asked the little boy, easing him onto his feet. "I have to make some supper. Are you hungry?" She put a big skillet on the stove. "I guess you don't know I'm married," she said to Julia and Dan. "Rachel's prayers were surely answered because the first day I came here the dearest man saved me from a bad man. Then he visited and brought me food until we married." Martha couldn't understand why they didn't look surprised.

Julia nodded. "We asked about you in the general store and the man sent us to Galbraith's Saloon. Galbraith told us you'd married, and where you live. That's how we found you."

"We were glad to hear you married," Dan Barlow said. "Everyone on the wagon train worried about you. Are you happy now?"

Martha finished peeling a potato and cut it into the bacon grease in the hot skillet, then nodded. "God has been so good to me. He sent me the nicest man in the world. Purely the most wonderful husband alive." She cut up a large onion, then several chunks of bacon and put them into the skillet with the potatoes.

"I'm hungry," Willie said. "Can I have some of that?"

"You sure can," Martha said. "You can have all you want. I'll cut up some radishes, too, and some greens I picked this morning." She started preparing the raw vegetables quickly. "I have to hurry," she said. "My husband will be in right away for supper."

"I'm hungry now," Willie said.

Martha hugged her little brother. "The food isn't quite ready yet, love. Can you wait just another few minutes?"

Just then Abe walked in, obviously looking around for the owner of the wagon in the front yard. Martha smiled at him. "Here he is, the best husband in the whole world. Abram Noble, these people came west with me. Dan and Julia Barlow." She giggled. "Only they weren't married then."

Abe thrust out his hand to Dan. "Welcome to our home." He turned back to Martha. "I thought everyone else went to Oregon. And who's the little boy?"

Martha gasped. "Oh, Abe, I purely forgot. They brought William. Willie, can you say hello to Abe? He's going to be very important in your life now."

Abe hurried to William, kneeled before him, and pulled him close. "We'll be all right, won't we Willie? Do you like to ride horses? We'll have to get you a pony. Would you like that?"

Willie looked up at Martha then back to Abe, nodding soberly.

Martha quickly set the table and put the potatoes on, together with the bowl of radishes and greens. "You can all wash up in the bowl on the small table," she said. "Supper's almost ready." She cut a loaf of fluffy homemade bread and put it on the table along with a dish of butter and glasses of milk.

Abe asked the Lord to bless the food and also their guests before they dug into the tempting food. "Are you folks here to stay, or did you just bring William?" Abe asked as he buttered his second thick slice of bread.

"We're here to stay," Dan said. He laid his fork down and leaned eagerly toward Abe. "We'd like to get a donation land claim if they're still available."

"They're giving them away faster than anyone can keep up with them," Abe said. "No one seems to know when the land will be gone, but I'm glad you're here now rather than next year. Why don't you rest up tonight and look around tomorrow. You should be able to find something you like by dinner time. After dinner Martha can take you to the claims office."

Dan wiped the milk mustache from his lip. "Is it too late to plant?" he wanted to know.

Abe shook his head. "Not too late, but I'm not sure you can find seed in time. We can give you some we had left over."

Julia giggled. "We brought lots of seed. I guess we'll be planting in a few days. That won't be so bad with such pretty weather. Nothing's fun in Oregon because it's always raining."

"You can probably start planting tomorrow," Abe suggested. "Unless you build a cabin first."

Dan took a bite of bread and butter and shook his head as he chewed. "We can live in the wagon for a while. I want to get a lot of food planted."

"I want some more 'tatoes," William said, still chewing his slice of bread. Abe served him another big spoonful.

Later, Martha made a gingerbread and served it heaped with sweet whipped cream. Finally, the guests went to the wagon to sleep. William had fallen asleep on the settle.

Abe grinned. "What you gonna do with Willie? Want him to sleep with me?"

"Why would I want him to sleep with you?"

"I don't know. I just remembered how much you didn't want Jackson to stay overnight with us."

Martha remembered, too—to her shame. "Well, I want Willie. Can you carry him into my bed?"

Abe grinned. "It's not fair, Martha. You get both Willie and Josie. Which can I have?"

Martha knew he was playing with her. But, secretly, did he really feel that way? She hurried into her bedroom and folded back the quilts. "Put him right here, Abe, and I'll undress him."

After she'd tucked Willie in, she went back to the main room to read the Bible and say her prayers with Abe. She always looked forward to that.

—⁓—

The next morning Martha prepared a hot, filling breakfast for Abe, then a little later for Willie and Julia and Dan Barlow. Then they left to look for a donation claim.

"Well, did you find anything you like?" Abe asked as they ate dinner together.

Julia and Dan looked at each other and laughed. "We looked everywhere," Dan said. "There's so much nice land around it's impossible to choose. So we wondered how close we could get to you folks. . .and if you'd mind. Julia could help you a lot with Willie."

"We don't mind," Abe said. "You'll just have to check around nearby. If you want on the creek you could just follow it east until you find something vacant that you like."

Willie needed a nap so Martha stayed with him while Dan and Julia went looking again. But this time they returned in less than an hour. "We found it," Julia said. "It's just a half-mile up the creek on the same side. Can you come help us make the claim?"

When Willie awakened about an hour later they all walked to the trading post where the claims office was located. In twenty minutes Dan and Julia Barlow were the proud owners of three hundred and twenty acres of fertile soil. They moved their wagon right onto their claim but returned to Abe and Martha's for supper.

That night Martha's relatives came over and met the Barlows. They all celebrated with rice pudding swimming in thick, cold cream. Abe told Dan he could use his plow and disk, as he and Uncle Cleve had finished with them.

After everyone left, Martha told Willie some Bible stories, sang some little songs with him, and prayed with him. Then she put him to bed and returned to the main room.

"I like the way you take care of your little brother," Abe said. "Are you going to want to pray again with me? Or would you rather I read my Bible alone?"

"I want to read with you," Martha said. "That's purely my favorite time of day, the time we read and pray together."

"Thanks," he said. "It means everything to me, too."

—⚏—

In the days that followed, the Barlows worked from dawn to dusk getting their crops planted; Martha and Abe didn't see much of them.

One day, while Martha and Abe ate supper, Riley came tearing across the creek. "Gold!" he yelled. "There's a gold strike at Orofino!"

Abe dropped his fork into his plate with a clatter. "Who said?"

"Walk down Main Street. Everyone's saying it."

Riley soon went on his way to spread the word. When Martha, Willie, and Abe finished eating, they hurried to Galbraith's Saloon. "What's this I hear about gold in Orofino?" Abe asked after putting Willie on a stool and ordering chocolate cake for them all.

"It ain't all that certain, but the rumors're flyin'," Galbraith replied. "It's come through the Indians so don't hold your breath." He poured the coffees and milk that Abe had ordered to go with the cake. Pouring himself a coffee, he pulled a stool to the other side of the bar and sat down. "Seems some Indians camped up there somewhere and during the night they seen somethin' glowin' in the dark. Scared them about to death, superstitious fools. But the next morning they got curious and started looking for whatever it was.

"They soon found it, as the story goes, a big shiny stone, more'n likely a diamond. They worked all day trying to chip it out of the rock but couldn't so they left it. One of them happened to go clear down in Californy where he told someone. This guy he told, he come right back here, took the Indian with him, and tried hard to find it. They didn't find it but he decided to check for gold whilst there and that's the beginning of the gold strike, so they tell me."

No sooner had they returned home and shut their front door when all their relatives burst in.

"We're goin' mining!" Riley said. "I plan to be in on the first of this here thing."

Abe felt a big lump form in the bottom of his stomach. "Who's we?" he asked.

"Riley and me, of course," Jackson said. "If anyone's going to get rich, it might as well be us. Why don't you come, too, Abe?"

"Just wait a minute," Abe said. "I'm not interested in running off from my wife already," he said.

Martha hoped Jackson would catch the suggestion. He didn't seem to but she felt something inside she'd never felt before. Maybe it was gratitude for Abe's consideration. She could never ask for more in a man. No one said a word, though Nellie's face looked ashen.

Then Abe related the story Galbraith had told them, emphasizing the part about it possibly being rumors. "Now," he continued when he finished, "you boys aren't doing anything until we find out if it's true. And you, Jackson, have a wife and a place to think about."

Uncle Cleve and Aunt Mandy hadn't said a word. The boys fidgeted but didn't say anything, either.

"Here's how I got it figured," Abe continued. "Orofino's about a hundred miles away and there's not much there. Walla Walla will be the closest place for miners to stock up with food and supplies. If this thing's for real, this town will go wild. Let's all stay together and cash in on the need for produce, hay, and equipment. If it's not real, we'll be better off here than running off to nowhere."

"He's right, boys," Uncle Cleve said in a quiet-for-him voice. His eyes whipped to meet Martha's. "I don't know how you caught him, girl," he said, returning to his normally loud voice, "but you'd better keep him. He's got a good head on those broad shoulders."

Riley and Jackson finally calmed down and Martha cooked some taffy that they pulled outside in the warm evening air so Willie wouldn't drop it all over the floor. Then they sat around, eating the candy and dreaming about getting rich from the gold mines.

—∞—

In the following days, Martha kept busy hoeing weeds from the produce gardens. The plants could have used more water but it rained enough to keep them going. She carried water from the creek to hurry those new green peppers along, noticing the extra beautiful plants; she couldn't wait to see what kind of vegetable they produced.

Rumors of a big gold strike kept flying around. No one seemed to know much more than they had at first and no one knew anyone firsthand who'd gone. Soon, people began drifting into town, some to buy supplies before continuing on to Orofino, some to settle in Walla Walla, thinking the tiny town would prosper from the gold, and others who Abe and Martha couldn't figure out. They squatted wherever they chose, put up tents, and seemed to have no intentions of doing anything.

One day, Aunt Mandy asked Abe about making them some furniture. As soon as he found time, he took Luke and John into the Blue Mountains. Uncle Cleve went with him and helped cut and load the hardwood trees.

In the days following the trip, Abe worked two jobs, caring for the stock and fields, then working on the furniture. As he completed each piece, Uncle Cleve and Aunt Mandy carried it across the creek into their house. With the new curtains Martha's aunt had made, the place began to look like home.

Martha's three Indian friends continued to visit her. By this time they could communicate using a combination of words and gestures. They made her understand they weren't happy with the white man's invasion of their reservation where the gold had been found. Then they went on to show her they really didn't care because whoever stayed up there through the winter would freeze to death.

When Martha repeated the forecast of freezing to death, Jackson and Riley agreed that next spring would definitely be a better time to go.

More people arrived daily and Abe fussed about the growing population almost that often. "I'm glad for the settlers to come in," he said one Sunday afternoon when the family gathered in the Nobles' main room. "It's those who squat and don't make any attempt to start a life that bother me. I'm afraid they're up to no good."

"You worry about everything," Jackson said. "You'd worry about me if I weren't Martha's brother. Those people may have so much money they don't have to worry about working or mining."

Abe grinned. "Or living in a house. Have you noticed the people I worry about mostly live in tents?"

Nellie, Martha, and Aunt Mandy sat around the big table exchanging recipes, but Martha took in every word the men said. Abe's concern caused her to worry, too. "What can we do about this thing you're talking about?" she asked.

Abe shook his head. "Hard to say, but I count my fifteen cattle every morning."

"Glad to hear you can count that far," Riley said with a chuckle, "but what'll you do when one disappears?"

"I'll go find it and bring it back." Abe said, his brown eyes twinkling. "Then I'll make the man who took it sorry he did. After that I'll make him sorry he was ever born."

—m—

The following week Abe finished all the furniture that Uncle Cleve and Aunt Mandy had ordered. Uncle Cleve brought over a large pouch and started pulling nuggets from it.

Abe shook his head. "I wouldn't think of taking money from kinfolk," he said. "You helped me get the wood and the rest don't cost enough to worry about. Martha and I are so glad to have you all here we'd do most anything for you."

Martha knew the hours Abe had worked and the sleep he'd sacrificed to furnish her family's house. "You're the kindest man in the entire world," she told him when the others left. "I know how hard you worked on their things and I appreciate you more than I can say."

Abe gave her a long strange look and walked off. That was a strange reaction. Usually he let her know how much he liked her kind words. He'd thank her and tell her he did it for her, that one of these days he'd have time to make her some more furniture, or something like that.

"Dear Father," she said, "thank You for bringing Abe to me. He's purely the kindest and most considerate man in the whole world. Bless him, Father. He's truly Your child. Help him to be happy. He deserves it."

Martha had a strong feeling in her heart that it was her responsibility to make Abe happy. "I'll try, Lord. Truly, I'll do my very best."

Chapter 12

When Martha began telling Abe how wonderful he was, he couldn't sit and listen. If he stayed he'd soon be asking her how she could think he was so wonderful and still act as if they were just friends. He walked out the door and began the evening chores. It took him much longer to milk now that all the cows had freshened. Martha usually helped, milking some while he milked the others. This time she came out in time to milk three of the cows, which was a huge help. After they finished milking, she strained the milk, then he hauled it to the general store.

One morning Abe decided the time had come to get Willie a horse. "Want to go for a ride?" he asked them at the breakfast table.

"Where?" Willie asked. The little boy was always eager for something different.

Abe grinned and said nothing. "Will you have time before dinner?" he asked Martha.

She nodded. "Aren't you going to tell us where we're going?" she asked. "We're purely curious."

Abe shook his head. "Not yet. Willie can ride with you on the way out."

A half-hour later, the two horses stopped at Fort Walla Walla. "What's here?" Martha asked.

"Horses," Abe said with a smile. They walked together to the front door. "Got any small horses or ponies?" Abe asked when someone opened the door.

The man took them out to the same corral in which they'd found Luke and John. He pointed toward the back where a small cream-colored mare watched them. "There's the nicest little mare we have on the place."

Abe squatted beside Willie and pointed to the horse. "What do you think of that pretty horse?" he asked. "It's almost white."

Willie shook his head. "It's not pretty," he said.

Abe looked at the man and shrugged. Then he winked at the man. "Don't you have anything pretty?"

The man shook his head and thought for a moment. Then he snapped his fingers. "I just remembered a real pretty one we got out here." Willie ran behind the man; Martha and Abe followed behind.

"We got a really pretty little gelding in this here corral," the man said. "Here, boy, let me boost you onto the fence so you can see it better."

Abe followed Martha to a spot beside Willie and the man. He couldn't believe his eyes. A whole yard of Indian ponies, some with brown and white spots, a few with black and white spots, and several with brown, black, and white spots.

"Where'd you get these?" Abe asked. "I'd be afraid to take one of these critters home. Some Indian would soon relieve me of it."

The man shook his head. "We got bills of sale for each one. Don't you know Indians are trying to sell ponies all the time?"

"I know," Martha said. "Indians were everywhere on the Oregon Trail trying to trade ponies for something." She laughed out loud. "One old man wanted to trade some ponies for three of us girls. I remember one who wanted to trade his squaw for a horse or cow."

"I'm convinced," Abe said. He moved beside Willie, who still sat on the top rail of the fence. "See anything in there you like?" he asked.

"Yes!" Willie yelled at the top of his lungs. "These horses are pretty." He pointed at one halfway across the corral—white with large black spots. "I want that one."

Abe looked at the man. "Is that a good one for him?"

The man nodded. "Sure is. One of the best. It's a five-year-old gelding, about nine hundred pounds, lively but gentle. He'll like that little guy and be able to ride him for a long time. We'll throw in the saddle."

Abe gave the man a nugget. The man brought the pony, saddled him, and boosted Willie onto his back. "Do you know how to ride a horse?" he asked Willie.

Willie nodded. "Uh-huh. I rode a horse once in Oregon."

The man spent a half-hour teaching the little boy how to make the horse stop and go and how to turn it. Finally, he turned to Abe. "I think he's ready to go," he said.

"Yippee," Willie yelled. "Come on, Speckle, let's go fast."

Willie had no trouble getting Speckle, as he insisted on calling the horse, home. Josie stayed beside Speckle and Willie all the way, as if wanting to make sure the boy and horse were all right.

That night Martha made sure Willie thanked God for his nice horse. "All good gifts come from God," she told him, "so we have to thank Him for everything good."

Willie couldn't stop thanking God or Abe. "Speckle's the nicest toy I ever had," he told Abe.

"Speckle isn't a toy," Abe gently reminded him. "Speckle is one of God's special creatures, just like you, Willie. He gets tired and hungry, and hot and cold, so we have to take good care of him for God, don't we?"

Willie helped care for Speckle the best he could and insisted on riding every day.

—ᴍ—

Two weeks passed. Abe and Martha worked hard, making their place look better all the time. One morning Martha's uncle came tearing across the creek. "Someone stole Riley's mare," he yelled even louder than usual. "Riley's mare's gone!"

Abe ran from the barn where he'd been milking. "You sure the horse isn't around someplace?"

Uncle Cleve shook his shiny head. " 'Tween us, we been over the whole place. She's gone, Abe. One of those tent bums got her."

Abe almost smiled to himself. He didn't know who took the mare but the entire town knew it was gone now. "Well," he said, "I gotta finish milking and deliver the milk. Then I reckon we'd better go get the horse. Either you or Riley best go with me."

"I'll help you, Abe," Willie yelled with delight. "I have my own horse to ride now."

Abe scooped the child into his arms. "You have to stay home and take care of Martha and Josie, Willie. Maybe we'll all go for a ride this afternoon."

A half-hour later Abe, Uncle Cleve, and Riley took off toward tent city south of the street. Riley, looking slight as ever, rode Aunt Mandy's big black gelding. They rode around the many tattered tents, tipping their hats and speaking to anyone they saw but saying no more. When they didn't see Riley's light bay mare, Abe led them west toward Fort Walla Walla. Tents had been thrown up here and there over much of the land that hadn't been claimed. The men casually rode around all the tents they could see but didn't find the horse.

Abe shook his head. "Must be farther out, or on the way to the mines. We'll do this again this afternoon just to be sure." As Abe started to turn Charity toward home, he saw a pair of horsemen riding hard from the south. He took the slack from the reins and Charity stopped. "Might as well see who's comin'," he muttered.

As the riders drew near, Abe recognized one of the horses. He jerked to attention. "There's your mare," he said quietly. "You come but let me do the talkin'." He touched Charity's sides and the horse took off. They met the horsemen a ways from the settlement. "Hold it," Abe called in a soft calm voice.

The two young men stopped their horses. "What you want?" the one who wasn't riding Riley's mare asked.

Abe pointed at the horse with his thumb. "We want the horse." He peered into the eyes of the rider. "We're all armed so don't try to leave. You know the penalty for rustlin' horses, don't you?"

Neither rider said a word.

"Well, in case you don't know I'll tell you. You get invited to a necktie party. . .as the honored guest. If this is your first offense a one-hundred-dollar fine will do the job this time." *Forgive me for makin' my own laws, Lord. If someone don't do somethin' this town's goin' to be too dangerous to live in. These boys deserve a little pushin'. Don't You think so, God?*

The one on Riley's bay looked terrified. "We ain't got a hunnert dollars."

Abe nodded quietly. "Well, we got a good tree and some rope. We don't cotton to horse thieves in this here town. A few people like you could ruin our perfectly good town." Then his eyes jerked toward the one on Riley's horse as if he'd just had a thought. "Got any friends you could borrow the money from? We'd be glad to ride with you to get it. 'Course, after that we'll see you out of town."

The men talked a few minutes and nodded. "We'll get the money. You wait here."

All three horses moved closer, in a half-surrounding movement. "We'll go with you," Abe said. The men walked their horses in front of Abe, Uncle Cleve, and Riley, until they came to a ragged brown tent shaped like a tepee.

"We have some money in there," the smaller one said. "Can we get it?"

Abe slid from his saddle. "One of you can. I'll help."

In two minutes the man opened a pouch with several nuggets, handed two of them to Abe, and put the rest back into the pouch. He gave a big sigh. "There, we're even," he said.

Abe motioned with his gun. "Not quite. We'll wait while you tear down your tent and get out of town. You got enough nuggets there to buy a good horse. Want us to take you to some?"

In response to the men's request, Abe took them to Fort Walla Walla where they bought a sorrel mare. Then they went back, loaded their gear on the horses, and headed west toward the Dalles.

"We patrol this area pretty close," Abe said as they rode off. "You'd best remember this town's off limits to you boys." The three followed the other two a few miles west of Fort Walla Walla, then reined in and watched until they became specks on the horizon.

Abe couldn't help grinning. "Reckon they won't be back. People like that don't like a town that enforces their laws so much."

Riley, riding his mare and leading his mother's gelding, threw back his head. "Yeow!" he yelled, sounding like an echo of Uncle Cleve. "My cousin-in-law's a one-man posse. Those fellers thought he was the law for sure.

Wasn't he somethin, Dad?"

Uncle Cleve agreed. "Let's get on home and get to work. Thanks, Abe. You wasn't just ajawin' when you said what you'd do if somethin' got stolen."

"You're welcome, Cleve. You'd 'a' done the same for me." Abe rode with his relatives until they nearly reached Main Street. "I'll be leaving you boys here," Abe said. "I got somethin' for the sheriff."

"How you be, Abe?" Sheriff Jackson asked when Abe walked into his new office on Main Street beside Martin's Boardinghouse.

Abe handed the two nuggets to the sheriff who looked at them, then back to Abe. Abe grinned. "I sorta made a few laws this mornin'. Seems a couple fellers stole my cousin's mare. When we took the mare back I fined them one hundred dollars."

The sheriff looked shocked. "And they paid? How'd you ever do that, Abe?"

Abe shuffled a little and hung his head. "Well, I gave 'em a choice of paying and getting out of town, or a noose party. They paid up real quick, and we escorted them out of town."

Sheriff Jackson shoved the nuggets into his pocket, shaking his shaggy black head. "I figgered 'tweren't no use tryin to do nuthin' the way things are around here. Maybe a feller could do a little now and then."

"Wouldn't hurt to try," Abe said with a big grin. "See you around." He went out, hopped into Charity's saddle, and rode home thinking about the first ever genuine Walla Walla County election coming up the first of July. The way he figured it, Sheriff Jackson didn't stand a chance to be reelected since he hadn't done much at all. Nothin' would better describe Sheriff Jackson's activities.

When Abe got home, he found Nellie visiting Martha. Both women greeted him enthusiastically. "We heard what you did," Nellie said. "Martha's married to a hero now."

Abe's face began to burn, pleasantly. "Hardly," he said. "We just did what had to be done."

Martha looked so proud he wanted to grab her and give her a big hug. "Uncle Cleve said you did it all by yourself," she said. "First thing you know you'll be sheriff."

Abe shook his head. "I have more'n I can handle running this place. As it is you have to work like a man and that don't please me much. Thanks for the faith, though. How're you and Jackson doing on your place, Nellie? Getting it going?"

Nellie giggled. "Not so's you'd notice. Jack says it's too late this year. We'll be all ready for next year's planting though."

Abe didn't say anymore but he wondered what the young couple planned to live on. He almost wished Martha hadn't given Jackson his share of the money they'd found in the wagon floor. He and Nellie might need it bad during the coming winter. Those two young people just didn't care to plant. Aunt Mandy and Uncle Cleve were still planting fast maturing crops. He hadn't heard them say it was too late. Martha fed him and Nellie a nice venison roast for dinner, cooked with potatoes, carrots, and onions. Then he hurried out to the produce fields to try to get a day's work finished before dark.

—⫘—

As Abe and Martha's radishes, lettuce, and onions matured, McClinchey from the store and both saloons wanted all that he could furnish. He divided his produce among the three.

Every evening he worked on a piece of furniture for the church. Sometimes Riley helped him. Between the two, they built a pulpit, some tables, and several pews. The church would be finished in a few months, and Abe wanted to be ready to furnish it when they moved into it.

When election day came Abe, Uncle Cleve, Riley, and Jackson all went to the Catholic building on Alder Street and proudly cast their ballots. Walla Walla's new sheriff was James A. Buckley; Galbraith was elected auditor and recorder. Abe didn't know the others who'd been elected. He could hardly believe it, as just a few months earlier he'd known everyone in town.

People kept coming into the little town. The ones taking claims made them south of town; the ones squatting set up their tents in the surveyed area, following the yellow markers and lining the streets with their tents. Abe and Martha kept busy from dawn to dusk and sold everything they could produce.

One day a large, well-dressed man found Abe in his potato field. "I'm W. F. Basset," he said. "I've just returned from Orofino. We built a sluice out of cedar bark up in them mountains," he told Abe. "It wasn't much at all but we took out eighty dollars worth of gold in nothing flat. I hear you're a straight arrow. How about going into this thing with me? We'll be almost first at the gold and rich in no time at all."

"Thanks for the invitation," Abe said, "but I have a wife and livestock here." He grinned. "We'll be growin' things for you and your men to eat and feed your horses."

Abe heard the man then went directly to a fellow called Sergeant Smith, who decided to put everything he had into the venture. One day Smith found Abe in the tomato field. "I'm settin up and equipping a fifteen-man crew to head for the gold mines. I'm invitin' all the merchants to donate something to our expedition," he said. "Sort of contribute to the business what's goin' to be good to you."

Abe straightened, rubbing his back. "I'm not putting any of my hard-earned money into a pipe dream," he said. "Is everyone else putting out?"

Smith grinned. "No, only just Simms. He gave us one thousand pounds of flour, and Kyger and Reese lent us eight hundred dollars for supplies. Otherwise, I'm footing the bill. I'm spending my life savings on this, Noble. You're missing the chance of a lifetime."

Abe leaned on his hoe, a smile playing across his face. "I figgered this here claim was my chance of a lifetime and I don't aim to mess it up. Good luck to you though." He extended his hand and Smith shook it vigorously.

Riley and Abe continued working on the church furniture each night until they had twelve pews made and decided that would have to do for now. Each pew would easily hold six people and they had fewer than ten attending in the saloon.

People seemed to be coming into the area from everywhere. Stores and other business establishments opened on Main Street so fast that Martha and Abe couldn't keep up with them. The city boasted several doctors and attorneys now, though Abe hoped they'd have no need of either. Houses of one sort or another blossomed on the side streets and on donation claims.

One noon Abe felt so tired and hungry he could hardly wait to put the horses into the corral and feed them before going in for his own dinner. But when he opened the door the smell nearly forced him back out. Indians! He stormed on into the house, leaving the door wide open. He quickly opened all the windows then turned to Martha and her guests.

"What do you think you're doing wasting the day with these savages who stink worse than skunks?"

Chapter 13

Willie began crying when Abe yelled. Martha took the little boy into her arms, unable to believe her ears. Abe shouting at her and the Indians. Especially the Indians! And saying right before them that they stank! She hoped they hadn't recognized the words but they understood a lot now. Before she could think what to do, the Indians got up, told her goodbye, and filed out through the open front door.

"I'm starved," Abe growled, "but I'm not sure I can eat in this stench. I don't know why you put up with them all the time."

"But Abe, you're the one who told me to feed them if it was the last bit of food I owned."

Hearing her kind words, his face softened. "I'm sorry," he said. "I was just so hungry I could hardly feed the horses before coming in."

Martha took a good sniff but couldn't smell anything. Maybe she was getting used to it. "Can you eat now? Or is the smell still too strong?" She gave Willie an extra big squeeze and released him. "Do you smell something awful?" she asked the little boy.

He sniffed long and hard, then nodded his head.

Abe sniffed too. Then he pulled Willie to him, hugging him tightly. "I'm sorry I made you feel bad," he told Willie. "I'm so hungry everything makes me mad. But I was still bad to yell. Should I tell Martha I'm sorry, too?" Willie nodded his blond head, crowding close to Abe. "I'm sorry, Martha," Abe said. "I'll try to be better. Now, let's eat before I get bad again. Besides, I have to get back to work."

Martha put the prepared meal on the table.

"It seems to me they come around pretty often," Abe said while they ate. "What's drawing them, do you know?" He grinned. "I suppose it could be your good food."

She shook her head. "I don't think so. We're learning each other's languages, Abe. We're doing good, but I never could get them to understand Willie's my brother. I tried so hard to tell them, Abe. I just love to try to talk to them. It's so much fun I forget all about their smell. Next time I'll try to remember to open up the place when I see them coming."

"Thanks. That'll help." He finished his rice pudding. "You are a good cook, Martha. I'm proud of you and it makes me look forward to meals."

She felt herself growing pink at his unexpected compliment. "Thank you, Abe. I'm going to work in the produce gardens this afternoon. Anything special you want me to do?"

He shook his head. "You have enough to do without farming, but I appreciate everything you do, believe me."

"I believe you, Abe. Now, you get to work and I'll be right out."

Willie loved being with Martha and had to help with everything she did, from hoeing the gardens to setting the bread.

—⁕—

As time passed, peas, tomatoes, corn, green beans, lima beans, onions, several kinds of squash, and Martha's amazing green peppers ripened. They had lots of several kinds of melons, too. Abe hauled many wagonloads of vegetables to the stores, saloons, and Fort Walla Walla.

"We're almost prosperous farmers," he said one day when he returned with an empty wagon and a pouch full of nuggets. "I have a notion to have Johanson bring us back twenty rather than ten cows. What do you think?"

Martha felt extra tired that afternoon. It seemed that as the different gardens matured, the work days kept getting longer. "Will we have to milk them all?"

Abe laughed. "I guess we could let the calves run with them. But we could sell more milk right now. Maybe we could milk some. Or maybe we need a man to help. What do you think?"

Martha wiped the sweat from her forehead. "I'd rather not think right now. You do what you have to do."

So Abe asked the man to change his order to twenty cows.

Finally, the potatoes were ready to dig. They alone filled many, many wagons. Abe delivered them all to Fort Walla Walla. Uncle Cleve hauled many wagonloads of produce and finally potatoes to the general stores on Main Street.

October arrived, and with it rose the excitement of the new church on Alder Street reaching completion. Abe bought oil at the general store for the last of the church furniture.

One day Abe and Riley carefully stacked the remaining pieces of furniture onto Abe's wagon and hauled them to the church and positioned them in the nicely finished thirty-by-thirty-foot building.

Martha brought along an old piece of long johns to dust the furniture. "Doesn't it look beautiful?" she asked when they finished. The inside of the building looked rustic but finished. Not one stick of rough wood could she see. Two large windows on each wall filled the room with light and two steps in the east end led to a rostrum, where Abe's pulpit stood. Three chairs sat behind the pulpit and a small table sat in front of it, all Abe's creations.

"Sure does," Abe said. "Makes me feel proud that I helped."

"The place is going to look empty," Riley said. "We ain't going to fill more'n two or three of those pews, you know."

Abe shrugged. "Who knows? Maybe people'll start coming once we get away from the saloon."

Galbraith put up signs so everyone would know where to find the new church. The week before the first service in the new church, he personally invited everyone who came into the saloon.

On that Sunday, Abe and Martha hurried to church so Martha could play soft music on the organ during the half-hour prior to the service. When Reverend Miller started the service, about half the pews were filled. Abe led several hymns while Martha played, then, following prayer, the minister spoke to the people.

As Martha listened, she felt as if the Lord were surely speaking to her heart. The minister reminded the congregation that God loved each one of them so much He allowed His precious only Son to die in their place. "Do you realize that our heavenly Father loves you much more than you can possibly love your children? Or even your mate? What do you say? Oh, you think you love your children and mate as much as is humanly possible?" He nodded his head enthusiastically. "I'm sure you do. But God loves us far more than's humanly possible. He can do that because His is perfect love, unmarred by the selfishness, jealousy, and other sins we must battle."

Then he asked if they had expected to have such a beautiful church in which to worship, in this undeveloped land. Most hadn't expected such a nice church so soon. He said everyone can count on receiving God's blessings just as they had in the building and furnishing of their own church.

"The Lord's eager to help and bless each of his children, then He loves the praise true believers give. Know why He wants us to thank and praise Him?" Reverend Miller shook his shaggy head. "No, it isn't because our Lord is vain. It's because thanking and praising Him helps us to remember His love and draws us closer to Him." He ended his sermon with a reminder that when a person doesn't let the Lord lead in his daily life, he's not only hurting himself, but he's also hurting His Lord.

Martha kept the new thoughts in her heart and determined she'd not shut the Lord out ever, whether she needed something or just wanted to thank Him for what He'd done for her.

—⟋⟋⟋—

Two days later, Abe came rushing home after hauling the milk to the store.

"Come quick, Martha, and see what I have on the wagon. You'll never believe it until you see it with your own eyes."

She started to rush out but he stopped her. "This is so special you have to close your eyes until you get there."

She closed her eyes, laughing. "But I can't see if I do that."

"Close your eyes and put your hands over them. I'll lead you out." He took her elbow and led her down the one step to the ground and around the house to the spot where he kept the wagon and then he carefully positioned her.

"Now, take your hands away and open your eyes!" he shouted.

She removed her hands and looked up into the wagon. And she truly couldn't believe her eyes! She leaped onto the wagon and stood beside a huge beautiful cookstove. It had six shiny black lids, an oven beneath, and piles of black stovepipe on the wagon floor. For a moment she felt breathless. Jumping to the ground, she threw her arms around Abe's neck—then jerked back. She couldn't be doing that! She'd get him all mixed up. Jumping back on the wagon, she opened the oven door. That huge oven would hold many loaves of bread or several pies. Wait! What was that leaning between the stove and the edge of the wagon? It looked like glass. She pointed at it.

"Those are your new windows," Abe said. "I'll put them in for you right away, maybe tonight."

"Oh, Abe, this is too much. Real windows. Windows that we can see out of. Thank you, Abe. Thank you a million times."

"Like the stove?" Abe asked.

"I love it! I purely love it. Oh, Abe, how did you get it?"

His grin reached almost to both ears. "I ordered it for you last fall, hoping to get it for last Christmas." He chuckled. "Living in the wild west isn't exactly like living in Independence, Missouri. I ordered the windows at the same time."

"Oh, Abe, I'll cook you anything in the whole world. You just name it and I'll cook it."

"I'm glad you like it so much, but the first thing we have to do is get it off that wagon and into the house. I guess we'll have to wait until Riley and Uncle Cleve get in from delivering their produce."

Martha went into the house to move the table so they could put the stove in with the pipe out the window. Her heart kept singing in her chest. She didn't have to cook over a fireplace anymore. It would hardly be any work at all, cooking on a real stove, and her food would be better, too. She'd almost feel guilty cooking on such a wonderful stove while Aunt Mandy had to use a fireplace. Well, she'd let her aunt use her oven for baking. That would help the older woman a lot.

312

After dark that night the three men and two women tried to move the stove from the wagon. After a few moments Abe shook his head. "We need another man," he said.

"I'll go get Dan Barlow," Martha said, taking off eastward. Josie followed and Willie yelled for her to wait for him. Eventually they got to the Barlows' and returned.

The larger group managed to get the heavy stove into position and the pipe all hooked up and through the window.

"When the work's all done this fall I'll build another chimney for the stove," Abe said. "I guess we can't put the glass window in there until then. Hey, I'll bet Martha would cook up a cake for us all tonight."

Martha couldn't wait and Aunt Mandy helped her.

About the time the cake came from the oven, Jackson and Nellie happened along. Martha couldn't bear to cover the evenly browned spice cake with frosting, so she served it with piles of cold whipped cream.

Jackson and Nellie sat on the small settle poking each other, tickling each other, and giggling. When Nellie tasted the cake she sighed. "This is so good, Martha. I've never learned to cook on a fireplace. Tell Jackson how to get a stove for me, will you?"

Abe laughed. "First thing you gotta do is give McClinchey a big nugget. You still got one of those?"

Jackson shook his head. "Not anymore. We need to be getting some money purty bad."

"Dad and I been piling up the money," Riley said. "We sure ought to get Ma a stove."

Uncle Cleve agreed and Aunt Mandy looked as if she'd struck her own gold mine until Abe mentioned how long it took to get Martha's.

"I'd like one, too," Julia said shyly. "Some day you'll get me one, won't you, Dan?"

Dan smiled into the young woman's eyes. "We've been working like slaves," he said. "I have a nugget for McClinchey. I'll order one tomorrow with Riley and Uncle Cleve."

"Maybe one of you could lend Jack some money to get me one," Nellie said. "I know he'd enjoy his food a lot more."

"Jack needs to get to work," Abe said with a chuckle. "I've never seen anyone have such a long honeymoon." Martha noticed he didn't offer to lend the money.

After everyone left, Abe had another piece of cake. "I thought you'd been doin' just fine with the dutch oven," he told Martha. "But this cake does beat all."

Martha thanked him while thinking about her brother. "Abe, do you think Jackson's lazy?" she asked.

He grinned and she thought he was going to drop his arm over her shoulder. He didn't. "Did I say that?" he asked. "I have noticed, though, that he's not preparing much for the winter."

—⟋⟋⟋—

Each week a few more of the seats Abe had built for the church were filled. He received several requests for furniture each week. He took the orders to work on during the winter when he couldn't be outside.

One day Martha noticed they'd finished harvesting most of the produce and that the weather had turned colder. The twenty new cows had been delivered and Abe had them in the pasture, fattening them after their long trek. The oats had been cut and sold for threshing.

One evening Abe took out all the isinglass windows except the one with stovepipe through it. He installed the glass windows and Martha and Willie ran from one to the other to see what they could see outside. Josie followed them to each window, eager to join the excitement.

Thanksgiving came and Martha cooked the entire dinner for the four families; they'd invited Dan and Julia Barlow to join them. Martha made pumpkin pies with rich cream and spices, mince pies made from dried apples, venison, and spices, hot rolls, and many goodies from their own gardens.

Then Christmas came and went with a repeat of the family dinner. Martha gave Abe several flannel shirts she'd made and he gave her a dressy wool coat so she wouldn't have to use her father's old, much-too-large one.

As the new year, 1861, came in, the weather remained cold and dry. With only a couple of light snowfalls that didn't stick, the couple rode Charity and Sampson throughout the winter. Willie, riding Speckle, kept right up with them. That pony could outrun Josie and Abe thought that was plenty fast.

Abe worked hard on furniture and made good money on the pieces he sold; each piece looked just a little nicer than the last. Due to the good weather, he hauled trees down from the Blues all winter. Martha made dresses and shirts and sold them to McClinchey; though working hard, she never managed to make enough to satisfy the store owner.

One morning Martha hurried outside and discovered the air felt warm, really warm. She'd been so busy she hadn't taken time to notice the mild winter slowly warming into spring. Redwings called from the trees bordering the creek and meadowlarks trilled their melodies over the fields. The spicy smells of spring clung in the air while the sun sailed high in a China-blue sky. Martha's heart sailed high, too. She needed to get going on the produce gardens. The thought made her want to get down on the soft ground and start digging.

The Indians hadn't come during the winter but they'd soon start again. She'd faithfully drilled herself on the words they'd taught her and she could hardly wait to learn more.

She ran into the house. "Time to start the outside work," she called to Abe. "It's purely warm out there."

Abe laid down his plane and the board he'd been smoothing, got up, and stretched. "Sounds like a lot of work, doesn't it?"

She laughed. "I have seven hundred fifty-three needle holes in my fingers and I'm ready for a change."

"I have at least that many blisters from working on my furniture," Abe said, chuckling quietly.

When Abe smiled, the sun released some of its sparkle into his eyes. As Martha gazed at his handsome face she realized how dear he was, how much she really cared about him. Not that way of course, but he was terribly special.

Chapter 14

A be started to joke around with Martha, but when she got that look in her eyes he walked outside and followed the creek to Main Street. Martha! She had no idea what she did to him. Most of the time she acted like a normal wife, as if she thought he was the greatest. Oh, she didn't act like Nellie with Jackson, but she sure kept Abe reeling. Sometimes he wondered just how much longer he could take it. Was this really better than being without her?

When he reached Main Street, he turned west and passed two dozen men, women, and children milling from business to business. Pushing into Galbraith's Saloon, he hopped onto a stool and ordered a coffee.

"Just heard some news about another Abe," Galbraith said, pouring the steaming mug of brew. "Lincoln got hisself elected president late last year. And the country back there's about to break in two. I guess the southern states're seceding one after another. I for one am glad I'm out here in the wild west where nuthin' ever happens."

Abe swallowed. "I guess we all are, but maybe that's not God's will. Are we supposed to be back there helping?"

Galbraith laughed. "Helping them kill each other? I seriously doubt it, Abe. That's not how I read the Good Book."

"Well then, helping them stop—"

The door opened and a short, fat, middle-aged man stepped inside. "Anyone wanta bet on a dog race?" he yelled.

Abe hopped off the bar stool. "Where's this dog race?" he asked.

The man pointed toward the front of the saloon. "About a block north of Main Street."

Abe didn't ask any more questions but trotted between the trading post and Rackett's Tin Shop. He immediately saw a group of men gathered around a large oval lane surrounded by chicken fencing and walked over to join them. As he stood there, sizing up the situation, he felt something touch his pocket and slammed his hand against it. Hanging tightly to the hand he'd captured, he followed the arm to the person at the other end. He masked his shock at finding a slight young woman, probably younger than Martha, glaring at him as she tried to jerk away.

"This town don't like pickpockets," he said softly. "Think you can quit? Or do you need a ride out of town?" He still held her hand.

She gave a few unproductive jerks then relaxed. "Who do you think you are anyway, St. Peter?"

Abe grinned. "I'm his little helper. Are you ready for me to let go? If you get caught doing this again, you may be treated awfully rough. This town has hard laws. How'd you like to spend the next two years in jail? Without much food."

Her eyes grew large. "I'll quit," she said. "Turn me loose."

"All right. Just remember you've had your warning. The next time it'll be cell city for you." He released her.

Rubbing her wrist, she moved away from the dog racing area.

Forgive me, God, for not telling it exactly how it is. I realize she could probably pick pockets without getting caught until You return but I was trying to help her as much as the town. "Who's been training the dogs?" he asked a man who'd moved closer to listen to his confrontation with the girl.

"What training they need?" the man asked. "Just drop a rabbit inside the fence. Them dogs know what to do."

"Who's in charge?" Abe asked.

The man indicated a tall skinny man with a scraggly beard and pointed nose. Abe walked over to the man. "How you training the dogs?" he asked.

"They're already trained," the man said. "Guess their owners do it."

"You can't have them chasing rabbits," Abe said. "You'll get a big fine if you're caught doin' that. You can't whip up the dogs, neither."

"Who says?" the man asked, somewhat less pleasantly.

"The law says. . .and I'll see you pay." Abe turned and walked back to Sheriff Buckley's office and reported what was going on.

"Why not let 'em have their fun?" the sheriff asked. "It ain't like they was out robbing or killing people."

"Animals feel pain as much as people," Abe said. "It isn't right to abuse them. Besides, mistreating animals makes barbarians of men. You'd best stop them before they get started."

—⁂—

By the time Abe returned home, disgust at the entire human race had replaced his irritation with Martha. After all, Martha couldn't help it if she didn't fall in love with him. Maybe it was his fault. Maybe he wasn't trying hard enough. He shook his head. No, that wasn't it. When they married, he'd agreed to leave her alone.

"Lord, is this how it's goin' to be? You might as well tell me if it is so I can start gettin' used to it."

Just do the best you can, Abe. Try to be happy, make Martha happy, and keep up the good work. Remember a long time ago I told you to help your town develop and right as many wrongs as you can? You're doing well, Abe. I'm proud of you.

As the days went by, the dog racing didn't stop and soon many people raced horses, too. Lots of money changed hands as the result of gambling, which upset Abe more than he cared to admit. Men gambled with money that their families sorely needed and, in their desperation to win, beat their animals unmercifully. He couldn't get the sheriff interested in mounting a strong program against the activities.

Then people began to report burglaries and armed robberies. Citizens feared going out on the streets alone or after dark. Very seldom did the offender come to justice.

Still, more people flocked into Walla Walla as a result of the gold mining at Orofino. By July many small and even some major incidents of violence became regular occurrences. Abe spent considerable time trying to figure out a way to bring law and order to the area. The increasing and shifting population caused control to be almost impossible.

One morning the Indians arrived before Abe left to deliver milk and produce to the markets and they still sat in his house, stinking it up with their fish oil, when he returned. Even though Martha had opened every window and door, the stench turned his stomach. He determined to be pleasant and get out as quickly as possible. Holding his hand in the air, he smiled. "How," he said in his best Indian dialect.

Martha's tinkling laugh sounded out. "Oh, Abe, just say hello to them. They understand a lot of our words now."

The old Indian held out his right hand to Abe. "Good morning," he said, obviously proud of himself. "I'm Gray Wolf."

Abe grasped the wrinkled hand. "Good morning," he repeated. "I'm Abe. How are you this morning?"

The old man nodded. "Indian's good."

The young chunky man reached for Abe's hand, too. "Me Pony Boy," he said.

Then the last one, tall and skinny, repeated the action. "Camas," he said.

"Well, I don't want to interrupt your lessons," Abe said after shaking hands with everyone but Martha, "so I'll go on out to the gardens and get to work."

Nearly two hours later, the Indians filed out the door. From where Abe worked he heard them telling Martha goodbye and thanking her for the food and "talk-talk."

Soon Martha squatted beside him as he pulled spent lettuce plants from the ground and dropped them into his bucket. "I'm sorry, Abe. Would you like for me to stop studying with them?"

His eyes jerked to hers. He hadn't meant to give her that impression. "It's all right," he assured her. "If you enjoy being with them I want you to continue. It's good for you to learn other cultures."

The next morning, when Abe delivered his milk, McClinchey told him there'd been a killing the morning before. "Seems an Indian, name of Long Nose, got hisself axed to death," the merchant said. "Good thing Sheriff Buckley was handy and on his toes."

Abe grunted to himself. He hadn't seen the sheriff do anything that impressed him. "So I suppose he has his man already?" he asked, not believing that for a second.

McClinchey nodded vigorously as he wiped the dust from a table of galvanized buckets. "Yep, he does." He raised his eyes to meet Abe's. "Seems this other Indian, Pony Boy, wasn't too happy when his girl friend decided she liked Long Nose better. Buckley has that fat Indian in a cougar cage right now."

Abe could hardly keep his mouth shut when McClinchey mentioned the name Pony Boy. That Indian was one of Martha's friends. He took several breaths to calm himself. "When and where did you say this thing happened?"

McClinchey tossed his wet cloth into a box, pulled up two stools, and sat down facing Abe. "It happened north of Main Street on the bank of Mill Creek yesterday morning at the same time you delivered your milk to me."

Abe fairly jumped off his stool. "See you later," he called as the door closed behind him. He had to find Sheriff Buckley right away. Pony Boy couldn't have done it. He'd been with Martha at the time of the incident.

"He done it before he went to your place," Sheriff Buckley insisted when Abe explained the situation.

"Did he confess?"

"How could the savage confess? He don't talk our language and I don't talk his."

Martha! Abe had to get Martha. "My wife has been teaching them our language and she's been learning theirs," Abe said. "You wait right here while I get her."

When Abe explained what had happened, Martha dropped her hoe, grabbed Willie's hand, and eagerly left with Abe. With Josie following, they returned to the sheriff in ten minutes.

"Please take me to him," Martha said. "We'll get this all straightened out in a few minutes." A few minutes later Martha faced the sheriff. "What made you think Pony Boy did it, Sheriff?"

"A man saw him, Miz Noble. Is that proof enough?"

She shook her head no. "He was with me all morning. We were studying each other's languages."

The older man spit on the floor near Martha's feet. Abe wanted to belt him in the teeth but constrained himself. He wouldn't help Pony Boy much if he shared the cage with him.

"You must take me to him," Martha insisted. "This is all a big mistake, and the sooner you start looking for the real murderer, the more likely you'll be to catch him."

Sheriff Buckley cast his eyes skyward and shook his head as if Martha were a fool who knew almost nothing. "Come on then," he grunted. A moment later he walked through the door and turned west.

As they neared the small cougar cage standing in the blazing sun, Abe couldn't believe a man could be inside. Then he saw Pony Boy sitting at one side of the steel-barred box, his head bent to avoid the low overhead bars.

Martha dropped to the dust beside the cage. "What have they done to you, Pony Boy? Do you know anything about this Long Nose person?"

Before he understood her, she had to repeat her statement several times together with some Indian words and lots of hand motions. It took some doing for them to converse but, after about a half-hour, Martha looked up at the sheriff.

"He says he barely knows Long Nose and the girl not at all. He lives out past the fort and has never associated with the group here."

The sheriff scoffed and spit again. "Ain't that exactly what you'd expect him to say? He done it all right. Mulrooney seen him."

Martha jumped to her feet and stared up into Sheriff Buckley's eyes with fire shooting from hers. "Pony Boy didn't do this dreadful thing, Mr. Buckley. I know that absolutely for certain. You need to punish someone, but it's important that you get the right person."

Sheriff Buckley grinned down at Martha insolently. "I do need to punish someone, Miz Noble, and I got the right man. In fact, I'm so sure I may hang him before the sun goes down tonight."

Abe felt as if the sheriff had slammed a board across his chest; he pulled hard to get some air. The next breath came easier. "I don't see any need for the haste," he said softly. "You might cause an Indian uprising if you hanged the wrong man."

Sheriff Buckley's eyes snapped. "We ain't got the wrong man, Noble. Now why don't you take your excitable woman on home and let me get on with my business? I'm about to call a jury here to see if the savage's guilty."

"We'll stay," Abe said.

"I'll get him some water," Martha said, taking off toward home with

Josie behind her. Abe felt Willie's little hand groping for his. Holding the hand tightly, they both watched Martha hurrying away. Abe felt proud to be her husband. She had as strong feelings about right and wrong as he did. Turning around, he found the other two Indians who'd been at his house.

The old man recognized him and said several unintelligible words. Abe shook his head, and the man said, "Martha?"

Abe pointed east toward their place. "She went after a drink for Pony Boy." Seeing the man didn't understand he pointed toward his place again, then made drinking motions, pointing to Pony Boy.

The man understood and nodded. He kneeled on the ground and talked to the man in the cage for a few minutes.

Then Martha returned. She shoved a big bowl of cold water through the bars. The parched man drank deeply, took several breaths, then emptied the bowl.

"Any voters here today?" the sheriff asked.

A chorus of bass voices let him know the men were all voters.

"All right, who'd like to be jurors for this here thing?"

Seven men stepped forward.

"Come on," Sheriff Buckley yelled, "we need five more honest men."

Several more men responded.

"You have to be on that jury," Martha whispered to Abe. Strange, he'd been thinking exactly the same thing, though he didn't relish the idea.

He stepped over with the others. "I'll do it," he said softly.

The sheriff looked upset. "You can't be on no jury, Noble. You're half Indian yourself."

Abe had to smile at that. "I believe the man is entitled to a jury of his peers, Sheriff. The way I understand that, he needs a few full-blooded Indians on the jury."

Sheriff Buckley laughed out loud. "That would be a fine idea if they understood anything we said. Or we understood them."

Martha jumped in front of the sheriff. "I understand them just fine and they understand me. I'm volunteering right now to interpret for this trial."

Abe couldn't believe his ears when half the crowd cheered for Martha.

Chapter 15

Martha felt the dark curtain in her heart open just a little. The people wanted her to translate this thing. They wanted to know the truth of the matter.

But the sheriff smirked in her face. "I don't think we need no hysterical woman translating for us. Why don't you just go on home and take a nap?"

Gray Wolf took Martha's arm and pointed to Abe. "Talk for Pony Boy," he said.

Martha nodded. "He's going to be on the jury who decides if Pony Boy did it," she said.

The tall dark man shook his long matted braids. "No," he said with finality. He pointed to Abe again. "Talk for Pony Boy."

For a moment Martha couldn't figure what the man meant. Then it popped into her head. He wanted Abe to defend Pony Boy. What a wonderful idea! Abe knew where Pony Boy was at the time of the killing. Besides that he was completely unprejudiced.

"Sheriff," she said softly, "Pony Boy wants Abe to defend him."

Sheriff Buckley laughed raucously. "Nobody's goin' to defend that animal," he said. "Guilty is guilty."

"Right," Abe said, stepping back up to the sheriff. "And Pony Boy's not guilty. I'm doing it." *Help me, Lord. Pony Boy couldn't have done it, but You know I'm not a lawyer. Please, God, You speak through me, all right?*

I'm here, Abe.

Thanks, Lord. I knew I could count on You.

The group quickly set up a "courtroom" in the street. The jury stood to the judge's left, and the sheriff and Abe and Pony Boy stood to the right, Pony Boy shackled to Abe. Crowds of onlookers stood on every side, even between the judge and his courtroom personnel.

With everything in order, the judge banged his makeshift gavel, a hammer, on a shovel blade. "Let the court come to order! Bring on your first witness," he told the sheriff.

The sheriff called Mr. Mulrooney, the man who claimed to have witnessed the act, and the judge had him swear to tell the truth. "Just tell us what you seen," Sheriff Buckley said to the man.

The man appeared to think hard for a few moments. "Well, I seen that there savage sneak up behind the other Injun with an ax and bust his head wide open. That's what I seen."

"Why didn't you stop him?" Sheriff Buckley asked.

"He was a hunnert yards away. How could I get over there as quick as he could swing an ax?"

The sheriff nodded. "You couldn't have, Mulrooney. I can see that." Sheriff Buckley turned to the judge. "I guess that about does it, Your Honor,"

"Not quite," Abe said, moving in front of Mulrooney. "I have a few questions for you."

Panic distorted Mulrooney's features as he turned to Sheriff Buckley. "You didn't say nothing about this," he whimpered.

"Exactly where did this thing happen?" Abe asked.

The man pointed north. "There. . .beside the creek."

"At what time?"

"Early mornin'. . .about eight o'clock."

"Are you sure of that?"

The man nodded, then caught Sheriff Buckley's eye. "Well, it was sometime around there," he amended.

Abe nodded and smiled slightly. "How did you identify the man as Pony Boy?"

Mulrooney looked terrified again. For sixty long seconds he didn't answer. "You ever see another fat Injun?" he finally asked Abe.

Abe laughed out loud. "I'll bet I can find several if that's what it takes. Why do you think it was over a girl?"

Mulrooney looked desperately at Sheriff Buckley. "Don'tcha think this has gone on about long enough?" the sheriff asked. "I proved it was the right savage right off. We're jest standin' here wastin' these people's time."

The judge banged his hammer on the shovel blade again. "Shut up, Buckley and get out of my way so I can see." He turned to Mulrooney. "Answer the man's question," he said.

"I forgot it," Mulrooney whined.

"Did you see them fighting over a girl?" Abe repeated.

"Someone said something like that," Mulrooney said after thinking a while.

"That's all my questions right now," Abe said.

Sheriff Buckley didn't have any more witnesses so the judge asked for Abe's. Abe called Pony Boy, free now from the shackles, to the front between the judge and jury. The judge asked Pony Boy to swear to tell the truth and, after some translating by Martha, he agreed.

"Where were you this morning?" Abe asked.

Pony Boy pointed at Abe. "Your house."

"What time did you get there?" Martha translated and hand signaled until he understood.

He shook his head. "Not know." Then his face brightened. "You know."

"Yes, I know," Abe said. "You got there before seven and left after ten. All right, did you know Long Nose?"

Pony Boy talked to Martha for a moment. "He says he's talked to Long Nose a few times," she said. "But he doesn't really know him."

"Does Pony Boy have a girl friend?"

"Yes," Martha replied after talking to Pony Boy again. "He says his girl friend lives out by Fort Walla Walla. The dead man told him his girl friend lives right here by Main Street. Pony Boy doesn't know her at all."

"Thank you, Pony Boy," Abe said. "Why don't you come over here and stand by me?" Then he asked Martha to step into the invisible witness stand where the judge accepted her promise to tell the truth.

"What time did the Indians come to your house that day?" he asked Martha.

"They came before you left with the produce and milk, between six-thirty and seven," she answered.

"And when did they leave?"

"Almost eleven. We had a good time, and all three seemed more relaxed than they ever have. We're teaching and learning each other's language."

Abe nodded. "I can't think of any more questions."

The judge turned to Sheriff Buckley. "Let's hear your closing statement."

"Well," the sheriff began, "if an eyewitness ain't good enough to convict a man, I don't know what is." He looked directly at the men who composed the jury. "If you seen someone split someone else's head open with an ax would you be shore you saw it? That'd be purty hard to forget, wouldn't it?" He nodded to the judge and backed out of the area in front of the jury.

The judge nodded to Abe who moved into the place Sheriff Buckley had vacated. "You have Pony Boy's word that he didn't even know the girl he's supposed to have killed Long Nose over. Then you have my wife's testimony that the man was with her during the time the murder was committed. I happen to have been there when the Indians came and again when they left so you also have my word that it couldn't have been this man. The sooner we decide he didn't do it the sooner we can get our sheriff interested in finding the one who did. Thank you."

He walked back beside Pony Boy and Martha and wiped the sweat from his forehead. Martha guessed the sweat hadn't all come from the hot day. Abe had worked hard for Pony Boy and had done a tremendous job. She felt proud to be his wife. She patted his arm. "You sounded like a real lawyer," she whispered. "Really good."

The judge told the men in the jury to walk over to the Methodist church and deliberate until they came to a decision. The crowd moved restlessly about but, as far as Martha could tell, no one made any move to leave.

Pony Boy leaned to Martha's ear. "What happen?" he asked.

Suddenly Martha realized how confusing this whole thing must be for the Indian who didn't understand half the words that had been spoken. "Men talking," she said, motioning "talking" with her lips. "We wait."

Several people came by to talk to her and Abe. About a half-hour later, Dan and Julia Barlow appeared. "Well, what do you think?" Dan asked. "Was that Indian really at your place all morning yesterday?"

"He and his father and brother were," Martha said. "Pony Boy didn't do it. But how have you two been?"

"I've been helping Dan harvest our produce and whatever needs doing," Julia said. "We love the nice weather here."

"Better drop by and see us," Abe said. "Don't wait for something special."

Before Dan could answer, the men from the jury hurried back to the spot they'd left. The crowd quieted and Martha feared to whisper for fear all the people standing around would hear.

The judge turned to face the jury. "You've reached a verdict?"

One of the men stepped forward. "We have, Your Honor. We find the defendant innocent of all charges." A roar of applause and shouting went up from the people.

"Congratulations, Pony Boy," the judge said kindly. "You're free to go." Then he turned to Sheriff Buckley. "I hope you'll seek the perpetrator of this heinous deed," he said. "Court adjourned."

Martha hugged Pony Boy. "You can go home now," she said happily. "They know you didn't do it." Gray Wolf and Camas approached and asked her what was happening and she repeated her words, signaling that they could go off to the west toward Fort Walla Walla. They all smiled widely and thanked her profusely. After congratulating Abe, the Barlows walked with Abe and Martha as far as their property, then continued east toward their own claim.

Martha had never felt so proud of Abe. "You saved Pony Boy from being hanged," she said. "You're so good you should study to be a real lawyer."

He shook his head. "I have more than I can do with our place and cattle. But thanks anyway."

—◆—

After the trial, things calmed down a little, although as far as Martha could tell, Sheriff Buckley made little effort to apprehend Long Nose's killer. People kept coming in and taking out donation claims or building business establishments. Some stayed a few days, then continued on to the mines at Orofino. The stores sold everything they could get in— food, supplies, whatever.

One day while Martha and Abe looked for stove polish in McClinchey's General Store, she noticed some lightweight rope and asked what it was for.

"It's clothesline rope," the man said. "You hook it to posts, then hang your clean clothes on it to dry. Keeps the clothes a lot cleaner than the bushes. Easier on the back, too."

Abe insisted on buying Martha some. "I'll put it up for you one of these days and you'll like it a lot."

When the first of September rolled around and most of the crops had been harvested, Abe decided he definitely must go after a lot of cattle. "We're having to depend on grain and meat from Oregon City," he told Martha. "We'll be able to sell however many I can bring home. I'm thinking of maybe a hundred head. . .or even more."

He looked so young and serious that Martha's heart turned over. How could she stand being without him for the several months it would take him to drive the cattle all the way from California? "You have to do what you have to do," she said, trying to sound calm.

"Can you handle the place here with Jackson's help?" Jackson had been working for Abe for several months, whenever he could tear himself away from Nellie.

Martha felt like collapsing, just thinking about getting along without Abe. If she could only depend on Jackson it would help. She forced a smile. "Of course, I can get along. What do you take me for, a lady?"

Abe felt such a surge of love for Martha, he desperately wanted to snatch her into his arms and tell her she was the most wondrous lady he'd ever seen. But he forced his hands to his sides. "I think you'd work yourself to death," he said, "if that's what the farm required. I'll make sure you have enough help. And I have to find a bunch of men to go with me," he said. "Got any ideas?"

She nodded. "How about Uncle Cleve and Riley? Their work's almost finished, too, and I'll bet they'd like a bunch of cattle as much as you."

"Good idea. But I need some more. We need a half-dozen or more men in the party to be safe, and also to handle the cattle."

Just then Jackson showed up. He'd been expected early in the morning, but Abe and Martha were used to his showing up hours late or not at all. When he discovered what they had been talking about, he insisted he should go along.

326

"How many cattle can you afford to buy?" Abe asked.

"That's not fair," Jackson said. "You know I have only what you pay me and it takes that to live on."

Abe nodded. "Don't you think you'd better stay home with your wife then and help Martha? That way you'd be earning money rather than wasting your time."

Abe hated the thought of being away from Martha for two months; she'd probably forget all about him in that length of time. The night before he left, he lay in his lonely bed wondering if it would be a mistake to go. "Should I forget the trip, Lord?" he asked out loud. "Is this one of my big mistakes?"

Go, Abram. This will enrich your life more than you expect. You'll be glad you did.

Abe nodded, satisfied. He had complete faith in God Who'd communicated with him for as long as he could remember. He grinned. People would think he was crazy if they knew about these talks. They'd think he was irreverent, too. No one talked to God as if He were a friend but Abe's visits made him feel much closer to his Father in heaven. He lay in bed quietly wondering how his going would enrich his life. Must be he'd make a big fortune on the cattle he brought back.

Chapter 16

Jackson stayed, though he didn't like it much.

Uncle Cleve, Riley, and seven other men who also planned to buy cattle left early the next morning. Abe took both Charity and Sampson so he could ride one for a while, then the other so neither horse would have to work so hard. The horses pranced, eager to be on the way.

Martha wished she felt half that excited about the adventure. Then she smiled to herself. If she were going, no doubt she, too, would be excited.

—⁂—

The next day Willie wanted to ride Speckle. "I'm sorry," Martha said, "but I don't have a horse to ride with you."

"I can ride alone," Willie said. "Speckle and I can do anything together."

After a little more urging, Martha saddled up the horse and turned them loose on their own place. "Stay where you can see the house," she said. "I love you, and I'll worry if I can't see you." Every little while she checked out her real glass windows and she always saw the boy and his horse, even though sometimes they'd gone quite a distance.

Jackson came more regularly than he ever had. "Why don't you let me take Willie for a while?" he asked one afternoon as he was about to go home.

Martha's heart did a double beat. How would she get along without Willie while Abe was gone? "He'd better stay with me, Jackson. I'd be purely lonely without him." But, at Jackson's insistence, she told Willie he could go for a few days if he wanted. He chose to stay with Martha.

For about two weeks things went smoothly. One morning, just after Martha returned home from delivering milk to the stores, Josie raised a big ruckus, looking toward the back of the house. When Martha checked she discovered a young girl gazing at her through the kitchen window. Startled but not frightened, Martha hurried outside to see what the girl wanted. As she stepped through the door, the girl turned to run.

"Don't be afraid," Martha called. "Come back and have lunch with me."

The girl stopped, looked, and listened but didn't move.

Martha motioned for her to come. "I'm just about to make some creamy potato soup," she called. "Come help me eat it."

After a long moment the girl slowly moved toward Martha. Tiny, thin, and dark with oversized brown eyes, Martha thought the girl to be about fourteen. She hadn't seen her before but that wasn't strange considering all the people coming and going nowadays.

She held out her hand toward the girl. "Hurry," she called. "I'm hungry. I'll bet you are, too."

The girl kept coming, dragging her feet as though they were too heavy to pick up.

Finally, when the stranger almost reached her, Martha smiled. "Hi, I'm Martha Noble. Come on in." She turned and went inside, hoping the girl would follow.

She did, very hesitantly, and Martha decided to go ahead with the soup. Maybe when the girl discovered they were alone she'd feel more secure. Martha peeled and cut up four potatoes and one onion and put them in a pot of water on the stove to cook. Pulling some bread from the sideboard, she cut four slices and put them on the table along with dishes, silverware, butter, and wild strawberry jam she'd made last spring.

"Come and eat," she finally said to the girl who hadn't said one word but hadn't missed a motion Martha had made. When the girl sat down Martha quickly asked God to bless the food and also Abe. She made sure the girl got plenty of bread and jam as well as soup and cold milk. Finally Martha laughed nervously. "You aren't much of a talker," she said. "You know my name but I haven't the faintest idea what to call you. Would you mind?"

After studying Martha for what seemed forever the girl smiled ever so slightly. "I'm Melissa Ladd." She said no more, but continued shoving the food in.

"When did you last eat, Melissa?" Martha asked softly.

Melissa laid her fork down on the edge of her plate, a sign to Martha that she'd had some refining somewhere at sometime in her life. She thought a moment and smiled impishly. "I guess I swiped some corn from you yesterday."

Martha chose to overlook the confession. "Where did you cook it?"

Melissa laughed outright. "I ate it raw. Corn's good raw."

Martha's heart ached for the tiny little person who obviously had no home. "How old are you, Melissa?"

"Seventeen. I'll pay for the corn when I get some money. Honest."

Now Martha laughed. "I'm not worried about the corn, Melissa. We have plenty and are happy to share. But are you alone? Where's your family?"

The relaxed look on Melissa's face disappeared. "I don't want to talk about it."

"All right. How would you like to stay with me for a while? My husband's in California and I'm lonely. We even have a spare bedroom for you."

Melissa stayed and eagerly took over most of the housework while Martha and Jackson worked outside. They harvested sweet corn every day and took it to the merchants and restaurants that now lined the main street. They also harvested the late potatoes and winter squash. After giving Jackson all he'd need for the winter and saving an equal amount for Abe and Martha, they sold the rest to McClinchey and Fort Walla Walla.

As Martha and Melissa got better acquainted, Martha learned that Melissa's mother died on the Oregon Trail. Her stepfather, who'd abused both Melissa and her mother, had whipped Melissa continually after her mother's death, until she'd run away. Her scars, covering her entire back and legs, still looked red and angry. Melissa explained that most of the marks had been from the man's using a heavy chain for a whip, his usual instrument of torture. Her stepfather had taken out a claim in Walla Walla and, as far as Melissa knew, he was somewhere around. She refused to go to the store or leave the place for any reason.

Martha taught Melissa to make light bread and other good food. Melissa taught Martha what it was to fear someone so much it controlled a person's every thought.

Though Martha kept very busy, she missed Abe so much she could hardly stand it. She worried that something had happened to him on the trail and wondered how she'd live without him. "Lord, please take good care of him. I purely couldn't live without him. Thank You, Lord. I know he'll be safe with You." Martha enjoyed having Melissa with her but the girl didn't replace Abe.

One evening the girls popped corn and made popcorn balls which they ate until they could hardly wobble to the settle for Bible reading and prayer. Martha shared her love of God with Melissa but couldn't tell by the girl's response whether she enjoyed it or put up with it as part of living with Martha. She attended church with Martha every week and after fearfully checking all the people in the congregation, her clear soprano voice reached Martha's ears as she played the organ.

Martha had been wakeful after eating so much popcorn but had finally fallen asleep when something awakened her. Josie, close beside her, growled deep in her throat. "What is it, girl?" Martha whispered. "Shhh. We don't want to wake Willie." The dog growled again.

Then a slight tapping on a window somewhere nearly took the breath from Martha's throat. "Help me, Lord," she whispered in the blackness. "Protect us from whatever's out there. Thank You, Lord. I love You." She jumped from the bed without waking her little brother, pulled her robe around her, and stepped into the main room. In the dark she still saw nothing and the sound had stopped, too. Josie stayed beside her, the hair on her backbone standing in a wide stiff ridge.

After a moment the tapping began again. It seemed to be at the front window. "You be still," Martha whispered to Josie while creeping toward the window, concentrating intently. A slight noise at her side, then a light touch brought a scream from Martha's throat.

"Martha, be still! Someone's out there," Melissa whispered.

Loud footsteps running away from the house, then Josie's wild barking turned Martha's blood to jelly. She sank to the floor, her arms around her faithful dog's neck. A moment later, soft light illuminated the room as Melissa brought a candle from the kitchen. "Don't be afraid now," she said in a sensible voice. "You and Josie got rid of him."

They each had a cup of coffee before having a short praise and thank You meeting with God, then returning to bed. "Could I sleep in your room the rest of the night?" Melissa asked in a tiny voice.

Martha wondered how Melissa could fit in the bed with her and Willie, but couldn't think of anything she'd like better—except for Abe to be here.

The next morning they found large footprints beside the window and a long cut in the glass. Someone had been trying hard to get in all right. Why? They didn't have anything anyone would want. Martha gulped. Not even much money. Abe had taken most of it with him to buy cattle. He'd laughed as he tucked it into a secret seam in his overalls. "We're using all we have to buy the big pearl in the field," he'd said. "But just wait until we fatten and sell all the cattle I bring back. You'll be able to have anything you want after that."

Although Melissa slept with Martha and Willie again the next night, they barely slept. "We ain't got nothing to worry about," Melissa said. "Your dog will wake us if anyone comes near."

No one came that night, and the following day Martha told Aunt Mandy about it. She assured the two of them that they were safe in the locked house. But shortly after dark, the older woman appeared at the door. "Now you have me all aflutter," she said. "Can I sleep on the floor somewhere?"

Martha gladly put her aunt into Abe's bed. By now she felt so frightened she didn't care all that much who found out that she and Abe had separate bedrooms. Melissa seemed not to be very frightened; somehow Willie hadn't learned about the would-be intruder.

Nothing happened that night and Aunt Mandy hurried across the creek the next morning to do the chores over there. Every night thereafter Aunt Mandy slept at Martha's. After two weeks with nothing happening, Martha relaxed. It was probably someone wanting food or some easy money and was long gone by now.

—⁂—

September turned into October and still Martha hadn't heard from Abe.

She'd realized that he'd probably beat his letter if he did write but she stopped at the post office every day hoping and then feeling disappointed when nothing came. If she only knew he was all right she'd manage to live until he got back.

Just before dawn one morning Josie erupted into a frenzy of barking and Martha tumbled from her bed even before awakening. Rushing into the main room with Josie beside her, Martha nearly ran into a tall, thin, squinty looking man who stood brazenly in the middle of the room. A glance at the window told Martha he'd cut the glass. This was the same man who'd been here before! He didn't back one inch from the dog, either. By that time Aunt Mandy poured from the other room and Melissa started through Martha's door. But before she closed the door she turned and backed out of the main room into Martha's bedroom, slamming the door behind her, then locking it.

"Get her out of there!" the man commanded, indicating Martha's bedroom.

"Don't do it," Aunt Mandy said to Martha. "This must be the stepfather."

"You bet I am and I came after that ungrateful wench. She ain't gettin' away from me."

"You get out of my house right now," Martha said. "We know how you treated Melissa and she's never going back to you."

"Get out or we'll throw you out," Aunt Mandy added.

"I came after that girl and I don't go till I got her," he growled. "Just get her and we'll leave."

"This is your last warning," Martha said in an even tone. "Melissa isn't going with you now or ever. Start moving toward the door right now!"

Rather than move toward the outside door, the man took two steps and put his hand on Martha's bedroom door where Melissa hid.

"Get him, Josie!" Martha yelled, grabbing a frying pan from the stove. The dog lunged at the man's chest as Martha rapped him on the head with the pan. Aunt Mandy took a long swing at the man's chest just as he lifted his hand and knocked both Martha and Aunt Mandy to the floor. At that moment the bedroom door flew open and Melissa threw a large wooden block that had been used to keep the window from falling down. The block struck the man on the side of the head and he went down like a tree in a hurricane.

"Hurry!" Melissa yelled. "Get a rope."

Martha rushed outside and brought in the clothesline that Abe hadn't put up yet. She unwound the lightweight rope and the three women wound up the man like a mummy, his arms at his sides.

About the time the women had the man immobilized, he regained consciousness and started yelling for the sheriff.

Martha laughed. "Are you sure you want the sheriff? You cut a window to break into our house. We're only defending ourselves."

"Leave him there," Aunt Mandy said. "It's time we all got busy with our chores." So they all went about their business, getting the day off to a start.

Martha took her milk pails and started out but before she opened the door, Melissa barred the way. "I'll milk, Martha. I'll do anything, but I won't stay in here alone with him. He's wicked and I'm afraid."

So they both did the outside chores while the man lay on the floor in his own mummy bag. They came in together and prepared a breakfast of sausages, bacon, and fried potatoes.

"I'm pretty hungry," the man said. "Make me a plate of that stuff."

Melissa acted as if he hadn't spoken. Martha hurriedly finished her breakfast and ran the distance to the sheriff's office. Grumbling, the sheriff followed her back to her house. When he saw the man all trussed up, his grumbles changed to a loud laugh. "You mean to tell me you let these two little girls do this to you?" he asked the man.

"Them and more women and that dog," he answered. "Undo these ropes and get me out of here."

But the sheriff accepted the women's story and told the man he'd have to pay a $125 fine for breaking into a house of helpless women. After the man produced three nuggets, the sheriff gave him a stern talk about the results of crime. "And if you ever bother any of these women again I'll lock you up and lose the key," he finished. The man didn't bother to answer but ran out the door and south across Abe and Martha's pasture.

"I better go somewhere else," Melissa said after Sheriff Buckley left. "My stepfather'll keep coming back until he gets me. I know he will."

Martha and Aunt Mandy laughed. "You'll do no such thing," Aunt Mandy said. "That was the most excitement we've had since the men left. You just stick around and we'll protect you."

"Yes," Martha added. "If you leave I'll be purely scared." So Melissa stayed, Aunt Mandy stayed, and the man didn't return.

—◆◆◆—

October passed into history and Martha thought of little other than Abe's return. He'd said it would be about two months and that had passed. Each day she thought more and more about the possibility of something happening to him and never seeing him again, never talking to him, laughing with him, even working with him. "Bring him home safely, Lord," she prayed over and over. "Bring him home and I'll never complain to You again."

Immediately she realized you don't bargain with the Lord. He knows best.

The weather cooled and many cold nights brought frost on the grass and spent plants. Martha and Jackson kept busy milking the cows and hauling the milk to market. Melissa and Aunt Mandy did lots of cooking.

And the town kept growing.

One night Martha, Melissa, and Aunt Mandy sat around making a dress for Melissa when Josie, with deep growling, announced the presence of intruders. The women looked at each other, then each quietly picked up the weapon she'd laid aside for that purpose. Martha grabbed the frying pan, Melissa a piece of wood, and Aunt Mandy picked up the rolling pin she'd brought from across the creek.

Josie started barking at almost the same instant Martha heard men's voices and horses tramping and snuffling. "It's the men!" Martha screamed, heading for the door. Aunt Mandy followed her out to meet three horses with three riders. Martha easily picked out Abe in the moonlight and ran to him. "Abe," she cried, "I thought something had happened to you. I thought you were dead!"

Abe slid from his saddle and stood quietly. Even in the moonlight he looked so beautiful, so young—and so whiskery. She threw herself against him, her arms winding tightly around his neck, sobbing. "I missed you, Abe, I love you so much. Oh, Abe, I love you."

Finally, his arms wrapped tenderly around her and his head bent over hers. The two were so literally wound up in each other they didn't hear Aunt Mandy tell Uncle Cleve and Riley to go put Abe's horse away, then they should all go home and talk.

"Let's go inside," Abe whispered. "I'll take care of the stock later."

Martha tried to tell him Melissa was in the house but she didn't have a chance. He simply took her arm and led her inside. When they stepped into the candlelit room, Melissa looked up from the hem she was sewing.

"What?" "You!" Melissa and Abe exclaimed at the same time. Melissa jumped up and looked as if she might run out into the night.

Martha grabbed her new friend's arm and pushed her back into the chair. "It's all right," she told Melissa. "You don't have to leave."

Abe stepped back and tipped his dusty hat back on his head. "What's she doing here?"

Martha didn't understand the problem at all. Why did she see fear in Melissa and animosity in Abe? "What's going on?" she asked Abe, still hanging on to him. "Do you two know each other?"

Abe pulled Martha close again, and didn't say anything. Martha turned her eyes to Melissa. "Do you know him?"

Melissa's eyes studied the floor. "He caught me picking a pocket," she whispered.

Martha couldn't put it together. She shook her head.

"All right!" Melissa yelled. "I picked his pocket. And he chased me out of town." She stopped a moment and took a deep breath. "Only I didn't go." She spoke so softly Martha wasn't sure she heard the words.

"Why not?" Abe demanded.

Melissa's head bent low and rested in her hands as she sat in the chair. "Where could I go?" she whispered without raising her head. Only her trembling shoulders indicated to the watchers that she was crying.

Martha leaned over the girl and hugged her to her. "Please, Melissa," she sobbed, "I can't bear it when you cry. Everything's going to be all right." She raised her eyes to Abe. "Could you please tell me what happened? I guess you never mentioned it to me."

He shook his head. "Never saw any need. Nothing much to it. I just caught her with her hand in my pocket and told her to get out of town before I caused her a lot of trouble."

Chapter 17

A be felt a lot of mixed emotions. He could hardly believe the way Martha had greeted him—and that she'd said right out that she loved him! He'd spent a lot of time thinking about his homecoming and wondering how it would be. But in his wildest dreams he'd never expected her to be so eager, so full and running over with love.

Then the pickpocket girl. How did she get into his house and why did she have to be here this particular night? And if Martha was so excited to see him and if she truly loved him, why did she insist the girl stay? Of all the times in their life together, they needed to be alone now.

"Abe," Martha said softly, "could we go for a walk? We could walk down the creek a ways and sit and talk, couldn't we?"

Melissa jumped to her feet. "You don't have to do that. I'm leaving right now."

Martha grabbed her arm again. "You can't do that. I won't even go for a walk with my husband if you don't promise to be here when we get back. You can go to bed if you want but you have to stay. Promise?"

Melissa's eyes darted to Abe's. He nodded. "You stay here at least until we get this all straightened out."

She slumped into the chair and picked up the abandoned dress. "I'll be here and watch in case Willie wakes up. Go on and have your talk about me."

Martha spun toward the girl for the third time. "Melissa, I haven't seen my husband for over two months. We may talk about you a little but we have fourteen million things to discuss. Now you just be patient and get to work on that dress." She took Abe's hand. "Come on."

They walked, hand in hand, up the creek for five full minutes before either spoke. Finally, they came to a place along the creek where the trees separated and moonlight reached the water's edge. Abe led Martha halfway down the rocks and sat down, gently pulling her beside him. She looked so beautiful and vulnerable in the moonlight. What if she heard his heart beating? He didn't know what to expect. Would she go back to being his best friend? *Please, God, no! Help her to love me as I've loved her for so long.*

He eased his arm around her and she snuggled against him. Putting his other arm around her and pulling her close, he lowered his mouth to hers and their first gentle kiss sent electricity racing through his entire body into his very toes.

When he heard her quick intake of breath, he knew it had affected her the same way. How he wished that the girl wouldn't be waiting when they went back into the house.

Wait a minute, Noble! You have what you've been fervently praying for, so why all these complaints about little things? Things that will go away.

Right! Thanks, Lord. I needed that. He pulled her cheek against his and tried to simmer down. He'd have to get to the bottom of this Melissa thing before they could get rid of her.

"I love you so much," he whispered into Martha's ear. "For the last two months I thought of you every minute I wasn't chasing cows. I spent hours thinking about getting home but I never once imagined it would be like this."

"I found out how much I purely love you," she whispered back. "I thought I might lose you and you'd never know how truly much I do love you. I prayed and prayed and prayed for you, Abe."

His hands smoothed the hair on the back of her neck. Finally, he couldn't help it. He pulled the pins from her hair, allowing it to tumble around her face and shoulders. Pulling in a long breath of fresh air, he marveled silently at her exquisite beauty.

Then he remembered she'd said she'd prayed for him. And that she waited for an answer. He grinned in the moonlight. "We had some close calls," he said softly. "And some near miracles. I'll bet that's when you were praying for me." He kissed her again and again, holding her close. He'd kissed a few women in his life but this was a new experience. He simply couldn't get close enough to her.

After a moment she pulled back, giggling. "Know what I just saw and heard?" she asked. He shook his head. "I just heard bells ring and birds sing and saw fireworks! And a pink cloud just wrapped around us. Oh, Abe, that means I purely do love you."

"Thank you, Marty. Oh, thank you! You have no idea how much I love you but I'll spend the rest of my life showing you."

"But we need to talk about Melissa, Abe. Her mother died on the Trail just like mine did. And her stepfather abused her something fierce. I saw the marks where he beat her with a chain. Then he came here after her and broke into the house. I don't know what to do with her, Abe, but we can't shove her out in the cold by herself. She's the age I was when we married, and I know how hard it would have been for me if you hadn't taken care of me."

Abe relaxed his grip on Martha. Whew! What a mouthful! He'd

expected a hard luck story but nothing like this. One thing was certain. He couldn't send the girl out of his house any more than Martha could. "I should have known you had a good reason for keeping her here," he said. "Of course, she can stay as long as she needs to." He nibbled her ear. "Even though the timing couldn't be worse. We'll make it work out somehow."

She pulled his head to hers for another kiss that shook them both and lasted longer than he'd intended. He jumped to his feet and pulled her up. As they walked home, she leaned her head on his shoulder. His arm around her kept her close.

Abe began to think about the real world. He desperately needed a bath and shave. Martha and Melissa would go into their rooms while he did that.

—⁂—

The next morning Abe whistled as he hurried out to milk and feed the cows and horses. He had to be the happiest man in the world. Martha truly loved him and he loved her even more than he thought possible. She was his very own, to have and to hold, from now on, forever. No matter what happened now, they could handle it together.

When he finished caring for the home animals, he saddled Sampson and went out to check on the three hundred head of cattle he'd brought back from California. It had been a hard trip—hard on the men and also the cattle. He found the cows huddled in the far corner of the pasture and knew he'd better drive them to the creek so they could drink and he could give them some hay. It took him several hours to drive those wild animals one mile but he managed to get them where he could handle them better. He decided he should start teaching Josie to be a cattle dog.

When he returned to the house, he found Uncle Cleve and Aunt Mandy there talking to Martha. "Your little bride seems pretty happy to have you home," Uncle Cleve shouted in his usual fashion. "I can't even remember when mine felt that way about me."

Aunt Mandy whacked him on the arm. "I missed you a lot, you old goat, and you know it. You have no idea how much we all wanted you to come back. But we had our own little excitement and danger." She went on to tell about Melissa's stepfather breaking in and how they captured him.

About that time, Melissa opened her bedroom door. When she saw all the people she started to shut it, but Martha called for her to come join them.

Uncle Cleve took a long look at Melissa and whistled. "This girl's going to be a real beauty when she grows up," he said. He winked at Martha. "If you're planning to keep her around you'd better watch that husband of yours."

Melissa's frightened eyes turned merry and she laughed. "She doesn't have to worry about him. He hates me really bad."

The older couple's eyes flashed to Abe. "How could you dislike that child already?" Aunt Mandy asked.

Abe dropped an arm over Martha's shoulders and smiled at Melissa. "I don't hate her at all. Maybe I was just a tiny bit disappointed not to be alone with my wife, but it's all right."

Later at dinner, Melissa asked Abe why he hadn't told about her pocket picking. He shrugged. "I guess I forgot all about it. Why don't you do the same?"

The day hurried past as everyone did his job and tried to catch up on the news. Martha invited her relatives over for gingerbread after supper. When they walked in, Riley was talking and laughing with his mother but, catching sight of Melissa, he stopped in the middle of a sentence, his eyes growing large.

Abe noticed Riley's shock and made them acquainted with each other. "Melissa's going to be with us for a while," he ended up saying. "Why don't you tell her some of the exciting adventures we just experienced?" He thought a moment. "And maybe she'll tell you about the excitement the women had while we were gone."

Jackson and Nellie soon came and Abe helped Martha serve huge slabs of the spicy smelling treat smothered in piles of soft sweet whipped cream. Everyone went on about how good it was and how much they all needed a stove like Martha's.

Riley and Melissa sat together all evening and no one heard much out of either one.

For the first time ever, Abe watched Jackson and Nellie giggle, tickle, and tease each other without being envious of them. He had the dearest, sweetest, bravest, and most beautiful woman of all. He wouldn't trade one hair of her head for both Nellie and Melissa. Melissa. He grinned as he watched her and Riley. He'd be surprised if something didn't develop between those two—and it couldn't happen soon enough to suit him.

Every time Martha came near Abe, he touched her—her arm, her hair, her back—just anything to be touching her. *Thank You, God. This is the moment I've been waiting for all my life. You knew it would be worth waiting for, didn't You? Thanks again, Lord. Maybe I can do something for You sometime.*

"Say," Aunt Mandy said later in the evening, "did you men know there's going to be a ball in our little town next weekend? A real genuine ball?" No one knew anything about it. "I noticed a sign telling about it," the woman continued, "and asked McClinchey. He says the firemen of all the different companies far and near are sponsoring it in the Walla Walla Hotel. It's supposed to be formal; it's the talk of the town."

"I want to go," Nellie said quickly. "Can we go, Jackson?"

"Sure. I'm always ready for some fun."

Aunt Mandy encouraged Uncle Cleve to go, and Abe asked Martha who eagerly accepted. He snatched her and held her close. "I love you so much," he whispered against her lips.

Uncle Cleve slapped his knee. "Now that's what I've been wanting to see those two do," he roared. "Guess we just had to get them apart a while."

Abe laughed softly, nodding. "I guess that's what you had to do, Uncle Cleve."

After everyone left, Melissa said that Riley had asked her to go to the ball with him. "Would it be all right with you if I went?" she asked Martha and Abe.

"I'd like nothing better," Martha said. "Say, we'll have to make us each a dress. The fanciest dresses we can dream up."

—⁂—

The next day Martha told Abe she'd really missed the horses and asked if they could take a ride. "Willie's been real good to stay where I can see him when he rides Speckle. But I bet he'll enjoy a nice long ride with us."

An enormous lump jumped into Abe's throat and his eyes burned as if he'd been crying. "I have something to tell you, Martha," he said. "I brought only Sampson back." He swallowed but still he couldn't talk.

She walked into his arms and they held each other for a long time. Abe wanted to tell Martha how much he appreciated her quiet sympathy, but he couldn't say a word. He began to think how he should be so happy to have Martha, to have her heart and soul, and he was. So happy that he shouldn't feel badly about losing a horse—even Charity. Well, Charity didn't compare to Martha, but he'd been through a lot with that mare. She'd been unbelievably loyal, a true friend, with a heart as big as a mountain. He'd loved the horse more than a man should ever love an animal.

He swallowed again. He'd just say it and be done with the subject. Then he could think about more pleasant things—like Martha. "I put her into a corral one night in California and the next morning she was gone. Sampson and I searched all day for her. Finally, I found her tracks along with a man's, and followed them to an Indian settlement." He swallowed again, determined to finish. "They sold her for food, Martha," he choked out. He swallowed a sob then took a deep breath. He wanted to tell Martha he'd have killed the Indians if there hadn't been so many of them. He couldn't get another word out. Maybe she didn't have to know that, anyway. He wasn't proud of his feelings at that time.

She held him close, saying nothing at all, giving deep comfort as he'd never felt from another human being.

—∞—

That Saturday night Abe, Martha, Uncle Cleve, Aunt Mandy, Riley, Melissa, Jackson, and Nellie all strolled to the Walla Walla Hotel where the first city ball would be held.

"You look so beautiful I'm going to be jealous," Abe said to Martha. "I may not let you dance with anyone else."

"Why would I even think of dancing with anyone else?" Martha asked, her arm through his as they hurried along.

"Because I'm getting my name in for at least one dance," Uncle Cleve bellowed.

"I may be jealous, too," Abe heard Riley whisper to Melissa.

Melissa laughed. "Don't worry; no one else will even ask me to dance."

When they arrived, Abe noticed right off that Martha's and Melissa's gowns were some of the prettiest there. Martha's dress was a lustrous sky blue with lots of matching lace. Melissa's was a pale yellow, shiny as satin, with yards of sunshiny lace. Nellie wore her best lavender house dress and looked nice, but Martha and Melissa looked as if they could be at a ball in Missouri rather than in the wild west. They had done each other's hair, fixing them nearly alike, piled high on their heads, with wispy tendrils curling down on their cheeks and necks.

Several white-clothed tables held large punch bowls running over with a heavenly-looking liquid. Bouquets of colorful dried flowers made the tables look completely festive.

Abe looked around the large room to see crepe paper streamers everywhere. Bright posters covering most of the wall space displayed the various fire department's mottoes. *We Destroy To Save,* Union Hook and Ladder Company. *Conquer We Must,* Willamette No. 1. *Small But Around,* Vigilance Hook and Ladder Company. *We Raze To Save,* The Dalles Hook and Ladder Company. *Always Willing,* Columbian No. 3. *On Hand,* Multnomah No. 2. He smiled as he finished reading the posters. He'd had no idea there were so many fire departments in the entire territory.

Returning his attention to Martha, her flushed cheeks and starry eyes caused his breath to catch in his throat. How thankful he felt that he had his sweet Marty—where did that name keep coming from? He just loved her so much that he had to say the most precious things he could, and the name Marty seemed to be one of them. *Thank You again, Lord, for teaching her to love me. How can I ever repay You?*

Just say Thank You, Abe.

At that moment the violinist tuned his instrument with the piano, then a beautiful waltz filled the room.

Abe met Martha's eyes and she floated into his arms. He hoped he could do this well enough to please her; he'd danced very little in his life and that had been before he joined the army six years ago. She followed his slightest movement and in a few minutes he relaxed to the music and enjoyed the feel of the woman he loved more than he'd dreamed possible—more than life itself.

The music stopped; Martha stepped back and looked into his eyes. "You're a good dancer, Mr. Noble." Her tinkly laugh started music afresh in his heart. When the music started, she melted into his arms again. He'd never been so happy. Then someone tapped his shoulder and he unwillingly relinquished his beautiful dream to Uncle Cleve.

"Didn't think I'd let that young upstart keep you to himself all evening, did you?" he bellowed at Martha as they danced away.

Deciding he'd better be gallant, Abe found Aunt Mandy and danced with her. As they danced, he realized how very much he'd come to love these two kin of Martha's. Jackson and Nellie swooped past them, then Riley and Melissa.

"What do you think about those two?" Aunt Mandy asked.

Abe swirled the older woman around. "I think we may as well be prepared for something because I see fireworks ahead," he said, grinning. "I've never seen Riley looking so happy." He hesitated a moment. "I've never seen Melissa much at all. But I'm happy for both of them."

Aunt Mandy searched Abe's eyes. "I'm happy for you and Martha, too. You know, Abe, I always worried about you and Martha for some reason. Not anymore. These days you act like two lovers very much in love."

He nodded. "That's exactly what we are, Aunt Mandy. I thank God every day for Martha. She's more than I could have ever asked for."

The music ended and Uncle Cleve brought Martha back. "She's some dancer," he said loudly. "I'm not sure you deserve her, but here she is anyway."

Before dancing more, Abe took his sparkling wife for some of the sandwiches and punch.

When they finally walked home, lazy snowflakes drifted from a low white canopy of clouds. "Looks like it could really let loose," Uncle Cleve said in his stentorian voice.

"I hope not," Martha said. "We purely aren't ready for winter yet."

"No," Abe agreed. "I still have to bring down our winter's supply of wood from the Blues. Also whatever wood I'm planning to turn into furniture. We probably won't have another winter like last year where we could get wood most anytime."

When they got home, Martha made a pot of coffee even though it was past their bedtime.

"What do you think of Riley?" Melissa asked Martha as they sipped the hot brew.

Abe laughed. "Don't ask her. She has to like him; he's her first cousin. I have a better question. What do you think of Riley?"

Melissa smiled pensively and nodded. "I like him. I hope he likes me."

Martha's tinkling laugh brightened the candlelit room. "Don't worry about that. He doesn't even know what hit him."

"Right," Abe said. "Time will tell whether you two belong together. You just be his friend and see what happens. And now I think it's time for all of us to get to bed if we plan to get up in time to feed the animals."

—⚉—

The next morning, snow still drifted lazily down. While Martha and Abe did the chores, several inches whitened the landscape. Fortunately it wasn't so cold that they had to worry about ice on the creek.

When they came in, Melissa had breakfast ready—a contribution that had become a habit. Before the day ended, Riley came over to ask Melissa to have supper with him at one of the new restaurants in town, a request she eagerly accepted. Before she left with Riley, she helped Martha fix supper for the two of them.

That evening, before Abe finished milking the cows, Martha took part of the milk and went to the house. Abe seized the opportunity to have a talk with God. "Now I know what You meant by being enriched by going away," he said. "Thank You, Lord, from the bottom of my heart for helping Martha love me. I love her more than life itself."

I know you do, Abe. Your love will only grow sweeter as time passes, so you take good care of her, hear?

"I promise, God. And I'll never complain about anything again. It don't matter what happens now that I have her."

You remember that, Abe. I plan to. We'll both remember that your happiness depends only on having Martha by your side. She'll be there for you, Abe.

"Thanks, Lord. I could thank You all day for the rest of my life and still not thank You enough for my bride."

You go ahead and do that Abe. I don't mind. Now you get into the house to her.

"Well, now, this is exactly what I've been waiting for," Abe said when he found Melissa gone. He wanted to talk to Martha about all his new feelings for her and explain exactly how much he loved her. How, though he hadn't thought it possible, he loved her so much more than he had before.

How could he ever expect to put into words the way he felt about her? He'd do it. Somehow he'd do it because he really wanted her to know.

But when she sat in the rocker across from him, her eyes expectant, he suddenly felt shy.

Chapter 18

Martha sat beside Abe on the settle and snuggled close. She felt happy to be alone with him for a while, too. She'd longed to be alone with her love a lot all the time. "What did you want to say?" she asked, lifting her lips for a kiss.

He looked embarrassed a moment then kissed her, a kiss that rattled her right into her soul. "I just wanted to tell you. . . I wanted you to know what you've. . ." He hesitated then pulled in a deep breath. "I love you more than I thought I could," he said quickly, panting as if he'd been running.

"Abe, you're embarrassed," she said, laughing. Her heart felt it would overflow with her love for him at that moment. "Well, I love you more than I thought anyone could love. I purely do, Abe."

He ran his finger down her nose, then cupped his fingers around her neck beneath her ear. "I just discovered there aren't any words to explain the way I love you," he whispered in a gruff voice. "So I guess I won't try."

He held her close, his right hand tracing her face, her arm, her body. She raked her hands through his hair, down his cheeks, and around his neck. Perfect. Her life had become perfect since Abe came home. Why had she waited so long? Maybe it took his absence and her worry to force her to grow up.

The next morning the snow had mostly melted and the pristine landscape turned to mud. Martha and Abe spent most of the day hauling a large wagonload of firewood from the Blues. "We'll need to do this only a dozen more times," he laughingly told the women as they ate the delicious supper Melissa had prepared.

—⁂—

On November twenty-ninth, the first edition of the first newspaper in Walla Walla, *The Washington Statesman*, rolled off the press. Abe brought two copies of the four-page paper home for them to read.

"Look," Martha said right off. "It says thirty-three hundred dollars worth of gold was taken out at Orofino on the twenty-first and another twenty-six hundred dollars worth on the twenty-second. Does that make you want to go mining?"

Abe shook his head. "We have too much to do here."

"Well, I'd like to go," Melissa said. "If I had someone to go with, I'd be gone tomorrow."

Martha felt surprised. She'd had the idea Melissa wouldn't go far at all without Riley. She mentioned that fact.

Melissa laughed. "I said if I had someone to go with, didn't I?"

"Look here," Abe said, looking up from the paper. "A man named Charles Bussell has been contracted to build a county jail. How about that? Now we'll have more choices then to either hang a man or turn him loose. That should be a big help."

They talked about the several doctors and dentists that had arrived in town, as well an attorney and a photographer. An ad said that the photographer, E.M. Samms, could take pictures on cloudy days as well as sunny, getting an accurate likeness. Abe thought they should try the new process.

"Hey," Melissa cried. "A theater is going to open in Walla Walla next week. Maybe Riley'll take me to see a play."

Martha laughed. "Yes, and maybe Abe will take me."

Riley did and Abe did, too. And they all enjoyed the production, *Hernani,* by Victor Hugo, a love story with lots of verse. Martha thought she'd never seen such a wonderful play, even with the relatively inexperienced performers.

The next Friday when *The Washington Statesman* came out, Martha and Melissa hurried to see what the Robinson Theatrical Troupe would be putting on, but found the same play running.

"I guess that since it takes the players so long to learn their parts, they have to show it a while," Melissa said. "Maybe we can see it again some time."

Later, Abe found an interesting article about their area. It said the climate is wonderful for cattle or sheep, that the cattle have to stay close to the rivers during the dry season but that in the fall, after it rains, they can go higher and find grass that is still green. It went on to say the area is so temperate and lush that the cattle need no feed nor winter protection at any time of the year. It also recommended that news about the unusually livable area should be sent out to people looking for a place to settle. In a short story on slavery, a minister said slavery would go to hell where it came from.

—∞—

One afternoon, after Abe and Martha had finished hauling wood down from the mountains, Abe decided to stop at Galbraith's Saloon to see what was going on. It had been a long time since he'd been there.

After ordering a cup of coffee, he rested and watched the customers, most of whom he didn't know, going in and out. Just a few months ago he knew every person in town. One thing he noticed that he hadn't seen before was that Galbraith served each man a whisk broom along with the drink he ordered. After watching a few minutes, Abe saw a man take a sip of his drink, jump straight into the air, drop to the dirty floor, and quickly sweep the spot where his head was about to fall. When he recovered, he picked himself off the floor, returned the broom to Galbraith, and left the saloon.

"You must be serving pretty strong stuff these days," Abe said to Galbraith.

"That's what they tell me, " Galbraith said. "Personally I never taste the stuff. I just sell what comes in."

When Abe got home he told Martha and Melissa about the men sweeping the spot where they would fall.

"I wish I could have a taste of that stuff," Melissa said only half jokingly.

"No, you don't," Martha said. "Melissa, don't you know alcohol is bad for you and the Lord asks us not to use it? Aren't you listening at church or when we have our little Bible studies here? Do you know that the our Lord Jesus loves you so much He died for your sins—and mine—so that you and I can live forever with Him in a place where no one will be trying to hurt us? No one will die or feel sad or be sick. Oh, Melissa, I'm so thankful to Him that I'd never do anything He asks me not to."

Melissa acted almost surprised at the things Martha told her. "I didn't realize exactly how it is," she said. "Maybe you'll have to tell me more about it."

"I'd love to," Martha said. "Any time you want."

—⁂—

Finally, Martha and Abe hauled the last load of wood from the Blues. "There," Abe said, stacking the wood at the north end of the house. "even if it gets down to zero and stays there all winter we'll be plenty warm."

"Abe," Martha said, laughing. "Don't even joke about such a thing. Besides, you know it doesn't do that here."

"I know. One big reason I like it here so much is that we know it won't get very cold." He reached for her. "Come here, my favorite little wood hauler. I haven't had a hug in the last hour and I'm getting desperate for one."

—⁂—

As time went by, Abe and Martha saw less of Melissa or more of Riley, they couldn't quite decide which. Anyway, it seemed that either both were sitting at the supper table or neither was there. Martha and Abe had lots of time alone and they enjoyed every minute of it.

Christmas came and Martha had a dinner for the entire family, including Jackson and Nellie, who kept to themselves more than the others.

"Riley and Melissa may take off alone after they're married," Abe told Martha one day.

She nodded. She'd been thinking of something else she wanted to talk to him about. "I hope they don't go too far for too long," she said. "Which reminds me, Abe, do you think it's important that Riley know about her trying to pick your pocket?"

He chuckled. "Nah. If she'd known anything about it I wouldn't have caught her. I think she was just a desperate kid. Probably hungry. I try not to think about how she got along after I threatened her and walked off without helping her."

A few days later, the temperature plummeted to ten degrees and the snow came down like a blizzard. Abe went out several times a day to check for ice in the creek. The snow kept coming and the temperature kept dropping until a week later it was twenty degrees below zero in the middle of the day.

Martha kept the stove and fireplace full of wood and that kept the house not warm but far from freezing. Abe took the big ax and chopped holes in the iced up creek until it froze solid. Then he spent hours each day melting snow for the animals. When his fingers grew numb he went into the house for a while and was back out as soon as he warmed up. He couldn't begin to melt enough snow for the animals but it helped. Eating snow is a hard way to get moisture and most animals don't get enough. Often, Martha went out to be with him but the bitter cold drove her in almost immediately.

"We're going to lose some of the new cattle if it doesn't warm up soon," he told Martha one night two weeks later. "It's just too cold. The horses and most of the close up cattle can get into the barn but no way can I get three hundred head of half-wild stock inside that small building."

But it didn't warm up. As each day passed, the house seemed to grow damper and colder; as the rooms grew colder, tempers grew warmer. All the time, day and night, Melissa insisted on wearing everything she had. Martha didn't like that because it made for more washing and she had to hang it in the main room as her hands would have literally frozen if she'd tried to hang the things outside.

Martha scolded Abe when he tracked snow into the house where it melted and made a big mess. Abe got impatient with Josie for crowding so close to the fireplace.

Each Friday Abe managed to get down to the newspaper office so they had a paper to read. They read the ads to each other again, noticing that a druggist now practiced on Main Street. He sold gargling oil, pain killer, mustang liniment, and rheumatic lotions. The Bank Exchange Saloon announced that it was now fixed up for baths. "Probably ice water baths," Melissa grumbled. "I've heard tell they're supposed to be good for you."

A news item told about a shooting at one of the saloons. "I hope it wasn't Galbraith's," Abe said. "That would hurt him a lot."

Another news item said southern planters were destroying their crops to prevent them from falling into the hands of the North. It added that two Unionists were hung by Rebels for bridge burning.

Still, the bitter cold continued. It dropped to minus twenty-nine degrees; for a two-week-period it was minus twenty degrees at noon. The people suffered terribly and the animals began to die.

Martha completely gave up washing clothes and both she and Melissa stopped trying to cook fine meals, settling for something simple but warm to satisfy their hunger. Abe kept the wood boxes full and cared for the livestock. No one thought of fancy balls, going to the theater, or even doing something for enjoyment at home. They did what they could to stay alive and sat around the fire keeping as warm as possible.

When Martha's flour ran low, Abe discovered that flour and most other foodstuffs had disappeared from the merchants' shelves. The Noble family wasn't in danger of going hungry yet but they decided to be frugal in their cooking.

Whenever Martha's spirit's got low, Abe pulled her into his arms. "Remember," he whispered into her ear, "we have each other. No matter what happens, we have each other."

She eagerly returned the hugs and kisses. "And it has to warm up soon," she whispered against his lips. "It's never done this before and it's been purely cold for over three weeks already."

Willie and Josie spent most of their time sitting together, close beside the fireplace, trying to keep warm. Neither complained, even when the food became much more plain, or when the quantity diminished. They just wrapped themselves in the blankets Martha had given them and tried to keep warm.

Almost every day Riley made it over to see Melissa but it took him most of the time he stayed to warm up from the short walk across the creek. He walked on the frozen creek. Aunt Mandy and Uncle Cleve had all they could do to keep themselves warm and their animals alive without putting out the extra effort to come over. Martha didn't see or hear from Jackson and Nellie during the cold. She just hoped they were all right.

Christmas came and went with very little notice. Abe read the Christmas story from Matthew and Luke for Martha and Melissa and they offered a thank You prayer for God's unfathomable gift, sending His precious only

Son to live in this world and to die for our sins.

Other than a feeble "Merry Christmas" offered a few times, no one had the time or inclination to do a lot of celebrating.

No one considered going to church during those times but every night Abe read to his little family from the Bible and they prayed together.

"What do you think about your God letting this happen?" Melissa asked one night after prayers.

Abe shook his head. "I don't understand it, Melissa, but I still trust Him. Here's the way it might be. When man sinned, God told him he'd have to die. Otherwise sin would go on forever. Men in general are getting worse, not better. We can see that right here, as our little town keeps getting more violent. Death and catastrophes are results of sin. So, the way I see it, all the terrible things that happen aren't God's fault, but man's and Satan's.

"I thought Jesus died so people could live forever with Him," Melissa said.

Abe nodded. "That's what He did. If everyone accepted that sacrifice, even life on this earth would get lots better. But one day He's coming again to take His followers to homes He's prepared."

"And it'll never get cold there," Melissa murmured.

"That's right, it won't," Martha agreed. "So let's get to bed right now and try to sleep away the cold night." They all went after their feather mattresses and blankets to line them up beside the fireplace. They'd long ago given up trying to sleep in the bedrooms.

As the weeks continued to creep past with the temperature not reaching zero, Martha and Melissa rationed the food they cooked. Most of the potatoes had frozen as well as the squash and anything stored in the barn. They had lots of rice, dried corn, oatmeal, dried peas, and some flour. The cows had dried up early in the cold spell so they had no butter or cottage cheese as well as no milk.

The newspaper's coming out faithfully each week was the bright spot for the little family. The January 10, 1862 edition said that many cattle were being found dead and that people must care for their animals. The editors complained bitterly about the cold and said that if this was normal, anyone thinking of coming to this area should be warned and that everyone already here should seriously consider migrating to more temperate climates. The paper for January 25 said that half to two-thirds of the stock in the valley had died.

The weather warmed a little but still hung around zero or a little above.

The newspaper dated February 22 said that out of the 35,000 cattle in the valley it was doubtful that five hundred would survive. If the bad weather continued for two more weeks, it added, none would survive. And if the cold continued, more people would be starving.

Chapter 19

Early in March, 1862, the sun came out, the temperature rose, and the snow melted. Not only had it been the longest, coldest winter Abe had ever lived through but when he looked around and figured his losses, he felt stunned. Cattle lay everywhere, starting to decompose. He'd lost every one he'd driven from California but had managed to save four of the heifers he'd bought a year ago. The calves had all died and so had Sampson and Luke, even though they'd been in the barn.

He sat on the woodpile with Josie licking his fingers. He patted her head. "Yes, I'm thankful we still have you," he said softly. "If you'd been out- side you'd be gone, too." He pulled the big dog onto his lap and held her close, tears swimming in his eyes. "You and I are just lucky dogs," he whis- pered. "We had a fireplace to huddle beside." After a little more cuddling, he put Josie down and went back inside. He'd have to tell Martha. During the cold he'd tried not to think about his losses. He'd just done his best to care for the living stock.

After breakfast Martha wanted to go outside with him and see how the place looked. Instead, he pulled her onto his lap on the settle. "We've lost a lot," he told her, "but we can rebuild. We still have our snug little house, Willie, Josie, and each other."

She jumped from his lap and stood beside him. "You aren't trying to tell me all our livestock died?" Her lip quivered but she didn't cry.

He stood and pulled her into his arms again. "That's about it," he said into the top of her head. "We have four heifers, Speckle, and John. At least two of the heifers are pregnant."

"What about Sampson?"

Looking into her stricken eyes, Abe couldn't answer. He simply shook his head. They dropped back into the settle together and quietly held each other for a long time. Finally, Abe leaned forward and stroked the big gray head in front of them. "We still have Josie and Willie," he repeated. "And most important of all, we have each other." He lifted her chin and turned her face to his. "We can handle whatever comes and do anything as long as we're together. Can't we?"

She swallowed, then nodded.

Hand in hand, they walked over many acres of their place, observing the horrible remains of the unprecedented cold weather. They also saw signs of spring, new green things poking their heads through the soft earth.

"What about our fruit trees?" Martha asked.

"I don't know, but I'm afraid," he said. "They were young and I doubt they're hardy at that temperature. We'll just have to wait and see."

After they finished looking their place over, they crossed the creek to learn how Martha's uncle and aunt had fared. They found two sad-faced people.

"We lost all six oxen, six of the ten cows we had, and all of the new stock. Plus Mandy's gelding died." Uncle Cleve's usually stentorian voice sounded almost muted. After a moment of silence the big man smiled. "But all three of us are alive and well. After what we've been through that seems almost a miracle, so we're praising God for that." His bright blue eyes twinkled. "And I do believe spring will bring lots of things, including a new daughter for us. What do you think, Martha?"

Martha nodded. "I think so, Uncle. At least it'll be easier for them to court now."

That evening, Jackson and Nellie walked in the door, looking pale from all the weeks indoors but otherwise healthy. "We lived on cornmeal muffins, corn bread, grits, and whatever else you do with cornmeal," Jackson said with an impish grin. Then he glanced over to Nellie. "And love," he added. "We lived mostly on love."

Jackson had hardly worked since his marriage, Abe thought, and right now he had about the same amount of worldly goods that Abe and Martha had—after losing all the dollars they'd worked so hard to earn. Sometimes life seemed strange indeed.

When Abe went downtown to Galbraith's, he learned that many people had died from the cold, too, and that it wasn't at all unusual right now to find human remains as well as various animals' anywhere a person happened to walk.

"I wonder where Slick Collier spent the winter. . .and if he's all right," Martha said one afternoon.

Abe shrugged. "I suppose we'll know one of these days." He grinned. "You sure you want to know?"

"No, but I hope he's all right."

The men all worked together, with the animals that still lived, to drag the many carcasses to large piles away from town. Then they built huge fires with dry wood and lard, which they kept burning for days, finally reducing the remains to ashes. Abe noticed the unusual silence as the men did the unpleasant but necessary work.

After two weeks of cleaning up and getting used to the tragic loss, Abe realized they had another serious problem. "We can't work the farm with only John, and we haven't money to buy another work horse until we work the farm."

"Speckle will help John pull the plow," Willie offered.

Martha's eyes met Abe's. They both smiled at the little boy's innocence.

Abe put an arm around Willie and pulled him close. "Thanks, Willie. You can tell Speckle thanks, too, but I'm afraid he's too small. Did you thank God for keeping your horse safe during the bad cold?"

"Yes. Martha helped me."

"We have to think of something," Martha mused. "We purely have to. It's time to start plowing. Praise the Lord, we have each other." After a moment she brightened. "Abe! Remember the money from my folks? You refused to take it and I forgot all about it. It's enough to buy a horse." She ran into their bedroom to get it, returning with the envelope. "Here it is, four hundred dollars," she said, eagerly handing it to him.

"I can't use your money," he said, keeping his hands at his sides.

Martha laughed. "What are we saving it for? For when I have the marriage annulled and go start my own farm?"

He realized once again why he loved that woman so much. Reaching out toward the envelope, his hand shot past it and caught her arm, pulling her to him. "You're the very best wife I've ever had," he murmured, kissing her. "And not just because you're rich, either. Do you know how much I love to touch you? I used to be so jealous of Jackson and Nellie. But, back to the money. Let's think about it a few days before we do anything."

"Guess what?" Melissa asked, bursting through the door, interrupting their special moment. "Riley has something to ask you."

Riley, right behind the tiny woman, had been laughing but at her words his face reddened and he quieted. He drew two deep breaths then grinned at Melissa. "Don't rush me, woman," he said gently. "Well, Abe, Melissa tells me I have to ask you if I can marry her."

Abe almost jumped in surprise but managed to hide it. After all, Melissa must consider him at least a little special to do this. Then he wondered if she considered him old enough to be her father. Naw. She just looked up to him. "Well," he began, trying to think of something intelligent to say. "Melissa's a very special person, but I can't say we haven't been expecting it. Have you prayed about this?"

"Yes, we have," Melissa said. "I made sure we prayed together the first time he asked. We waited a long time, and we both feel God wants us together."

Abe nodded. "Very good, Melissa. I'm proud of you." He turned to

Riley. "Do you feel certain you can support her?"

Riley smiled all over his face. "Yeah. We're gonna get a donation claim as soon as we're married. And I have enough money to last a year."

Abe reached for Riley's hand. "Sounds good to me. Congratulations. May you have a long and happy life together."

Martha hugged Melissa and promised to help her with the wedding and whatever else she could do. Then the excited pair went across the creek to tell Riley's parents the good news.

Several days later, the Indians arrived. Abe invited them in and since it was almost noon invited them to eat with Martha and him, wondering all the while how Martha stood the smell of fish oil.

The meal turned out even worse than he'd imagined. The Indians' table manners were nonexistent. They hardly touched their silverware, apparently not having had much experience with it. They shoved the food in as though they'd never had any before in their lives.

Abe did his best to appear to be enjoying himself as he pushed the food around on his plate but, as soon as possible, he excused himself and escaped into the glorious fresh air. He felt only a little guilty leaving Martha laughing and communicating with them in a happy mixture of words and signs.

As he checked the fences of his quiet pastures, Josie walked around with him. Then they turned east and followed the creek that hurried past, carrying lots of water. Several people had taken claims upstream from them now. He hurried on to the Barlow claim. Dan met him outside the snug-looking cabin. "Been wondering how you made it through the cold," Dan said, shaking Abe's hand.

"We did all right," Abe said, "but we lost most everything else." He pulled his shoulders back and grinned. "But we're thankin' the Lord that we still have each other, and Willie and Josie."

Julia came out the front door looking very plump in the front. After talking awhile, Abe turned around and followed Mill Creek west back to his place. As he walked, he thought about Julia, which caused him to think about Martha. Suddenly he had a thought that sent him into spasms of delight. One day maybe he and Martha would have a little baby of their own!

As he moved along, he noticed all the places upstream from them. One of the first things he needed to figure out was a way to be certain his water was pure. He'd thought about digging a well and nodded. That's probably what he should do all right. And he should do it right away.

Just then Martha and the Indians came upon him, causing him to temporarily forget the water problems. His other thoughts, too.

"Come talk with us," Martha said. "They've been telling me something exciting."

They all sat on the rocks beside the creek in a half-circle. "I told them about losing everything we had and they told me a secret," she said. Turning to Gray Wolf, she asked him a question, using words Abe didn't understand. After the man answered, Martha turned back to Abe. "He says they know where there's a big cave with lots and lots of gold," she said.

Abe's eyes opened wider. "Ask him where it is."

After another conversation, she translated again. "It's near Orofino and no one besides these three knows where it is."

"What's that to us?" Abe wanted to know.

As Abe listened to Martha talking to the Indians, he realized how much she'd learned from them and how really well she understood and spoke their language.

"We can have all we want if we go with them," she said. Gray Wolf talked some more. "He says it's easy to find and we could get all we wanted in just a few days."

Abe, who considered himself unflusterable, felt his heart beating harder. "What does he want out of it?"

Shortly, Martha turned back to him. "He wants to give it to you because you saved his son's life. And he thinks you're a good and honest paleface." She giggled. "He didn't say paleface. I just threw that word in for fun."

Abe didn't know what to say. He suddenly understood how the men felt who'd gone off to mine gold. They had the hope of getting rich quickly and that was the feeling he had right now. "Tell them we'll talk about it, and ask them to come back in a few days."

After another round of talk that Abe couldn't understand, the Indians got to their feet. Abe hopped up, too, and so did Martha. Gray Wolf reached for Abe's hand. "Thank you, food," he said plainly. "And talk-talk," he added.

Before Abe managed a thank you to them, they filed away down the stream as quietly as deer.

—⚏—

That night Abe asked Martha to sit with him on the settle and talk about what the Indians had said. "I wonder if we have enough money to set our-selves up for Orofino if we decided to go," he said.

"What do we need?" Martha asked. "We have the wagon and John. We have enough money to buy another horse. . .if we can find one."

"And if the price hasn't risen ten times," Abe said. "Would you like for me to do this?" he asked. "Would you want to stay here alone?"

Martha snatched his hand from around her neck and stroked the back of it. "Yes, I'd like to do this," she said softly, "and no, I don't want to stay here. I want to go with you."

Riley and Melissa burst in, laughing and arguing about the donation land claim they'd take. "And just where would you find a better spot?" he asked, spinning her through the room by her hand.

"Do you really want my parents watching us all the time? Seeing what we do wrong?"

"Say, where is this claim you're talking about?" Abe couldn't resist asking.

"Across the creek, next to his parents'," Melissa answered, her eyes shining.

"But I thought you said your parents would be watching you," Martha said.

Melissa's eyes and cheeks fairly shone with happiness. "I did," she said, laughing joyfully. "His folks won't bother us but you two'll be over there all the time, telling me how to set the bread. . .or something else. We should go off like Jackson and Nellie if we want to be alone."

Abe knew by her face and tone that she didn't mean a word of what she said. She just wanted him and Martha to know she considered them folks—even though Martha and she were only about two years apart. "Yes," he agreed. "You should if you want to be alone. But we'd like for you to be nearby so we can tell you how to do things. We might even do something nice for you now and then."

"But we have something else to talk about right now," Martha said. She met Abe's eyes. "Can't we tell them?"

Abe wasn't sure the Indians would want the whole family in on this big secret. "I'm not sure they'd be welcome, if we should decide to try it," he said, "but go ahead and tell if you want to."

After Martha explained the plan, they insisted they wanted to go, too.

"We don't know if we're going," Abe said, "and if we do we'd have to talk to the Indians before we could include you." He grinned at Martha. "Guess who else will want to go?"

"Jackson and Nellie. Oh, Abe, this is sounding more and more exciting all the time." The little group talked about it until Riley left at bedtime. Abe, Martha, and even Melissa prayed about it after Bible study, asking the Lord to work it out the way He knew best.

Later in bed, Martha and Abe whispered about the Indians' story. "We'll get by somehow, if we don't go," Abe said. "I was telling myself I could make plenty of money making furniture, but no one has money to buy anything anymore. But God will take care of us. We know He will. And we still have each other."

"I know," Martha whispered back. "But if we do this we'll have each other and a chance at the gold, too. And we know it won't work if the Lord doesn't want us to go because we put it in His hands when we prayed."

Abe held her tightly and kissed her to sleep. He relaxed, knowing he could fall asleep right away. Whatever happened, he and Martha could handle it together—the two of them and God.

"Good night, God," he whispered over Martha's soft little snuffling sounds. "You make sure whatever we do is according to Your will, all right?"

I will. You just fall asleep now while I take care of the rest of your life. Good night, Abram.

A NEW
LOVE

This is the final book of the "Forerunners Series." I find it fitting to dedicte it to its author, VeraLee Wiggins, who passed away on December 24, 1995, at the age of sixty-seven. She was my beloved wife and constant companion for over fifty years.

I wish to thank Stephen Reginald and all those at Heartsong Presents who made this series possible. God bless all of you.

Leroy Wiggins

Chapter 1

Abram Noble and his wife Martha stood in the early April sunshine in their greening vegetable garden, hugging each other. "We'll be all right as long as we have God and each other," Martha assured him. "What else do we need?"

Abe grinned and pulled her close again. She referred to the horrifying winter they'd just endured. The temperature had plummeted to 29 degrees below zero in December and hadn't risen to zero until a month ago, March 1862. They had lost almost all their livestock—two horses and nearly two hundred cattle, in which they'd invested their entire fortune.

Everyone in Walla Walla Valley, Washington Territory, had suffered similar losses. The newspaper, *The Washington Statesman,* had said fewer than 500 of the 35,000 head of livestock in the valley had survived the horrendous winter. Many people had lost their lives too.

Abe hugged Martha tightly. "You're right. God and each other are all we need. But it feels purty good to have something to eat once in awhile." He released her and looked over their place, a 320-acre donation land claim. Last year it had produced abundantly, enough to almost make them rich. Then they'd spent the money on the cattle that had died.

"The garden won't produce for a couple of months," he said with a sigh. "I could make some more furniture to sell, but no one has any money left to buy it." He lifted her face and kissed her soundly.

A loud pretended vomit interrupted Martha and Abe. "You're making me sick," Willie said. "Can I go for a ride? Speckle says he wants to."

Martha wiggled out of Abe's arms and hurried to Willie, her seven-year-old brother. "You're just jealous," she said, hugging him. "We purely love you too, but you won't let us hug you much." Martha and Willie's parents had died on the Oregon Trail, which they'd learned to call Heartbreak Trail.

Abe took Willie's hand, and they walked together to the barn to saddle Willie's pony Speckle, who'd somehow made it through the winter.

"Come on, Josie," Martha said to her gray, white, and black shepherd, hurrying toward the log house. "We'll start some bread and beans for supper."

She had the beans boiling on her bright-black wood cookstove, and half the flour in the bread when Abe came in and plopped into a chair beside the table. "I'm thankful Willie's horse made it," he said. "Willie might not have been able to understand what had happened." He raised his eyebrows. "For that matter I don't understand either."

Martha pummeled the bread, then began kneading it vigorously. "We don't. But we're better able to—"

The front door opened, interrupting her words. Three tall Indians marched in, straight as young trees, two dressed in white man's worn clothes and one in Indian buckskins. All wore moccasins.

Indians walked into any house in the valley, asking for food. Settlers always complied, rather than have a confrontation. The government had recently set aside reservations, but many Indians didn't believe that white men had the right to tell them where to live. These who had just walked in lived in a little community of tepees west of Walla Walla. Others lived in tepees south of the Street, the Nez Percé trail the town seemed to be building around.

"Food," the older man said.

"Gray Wolf!" Martha squealed. "Pony Boy! Camas! I'm so glad to see you." Then she pulled chairs out across the table from Abe. "Come sit down while I find something for you to eat."

Abe stood up. The fish oil the Indians smeared over themselves, thinking it would keep them warm, bothered Abe much more than it did Martha. "Sorry," Abe said, "I have to go out and see what I can do."

When Abe went out he left the door open. Pony Boy watched him leave. "Abe mad?"

Martha laughed and shook her dark head. "No, he's just afraid we're going to starve to death." She laughed again. "Not really. But he is worried. We have nothing left." She sliced the last loaf of bread and spread it with wild strawberry jam she'd made last summer. Putting the slices on small plates, she pushed them to the Indians, then asked the Lord to bless the food and the Indians. "Sorry I don't have any meat," she said. "No one does right now."

While the Indians ate, Martha finished kneading her bread and put it to rise. "Shall we work on our languages awhile?" she asked when each finished his second slice. For two years Martha had been teaching these Indians her language and learning theirs. They understood each other well now, using bits of both English and Nez Percé.

Gray Wolf, the other two Indians' father, shook his head. "We talk gold."

"Yes." Martha remembered. The Indians had told her and Abe that they knew where there was lots of easy-to-get gold, and had offered to take them there. "We don't know whether our God wants us to go after it," she said. "We have to wait until He tells us."

"How God talk?" Camas asked.

Martha thought a moment. "He talks to Abe," she said. "He and Abe carry on conversations. With me, He talks to my heart and helps me to understand what He wants."

"When God say?" Pony Boy wanted to know.

Martha shook her head. "I don't know. We're waiting."

Gray Wolf moved close to Martha. He pointed at the ceiling, then patted his chest. "Martha God talk Gray Wolf. Now."

If he'd sounded that determined the first time they met, Martha would have been terrified, but now she knew these Nez Percé men were kind and friendly.

She shook her head. "He talks when He wants to talk, Gray Wolf. We don't tell Him to do things."

"No talk Gray Wolf?"

Martha put her hand on his arm. "He does, Gray Wolf. He talks to everyone in the world but sometimes people don't listen. Most people don't listen." She cupped her hand behind her ear. "You listen. Maybe you'll hear Him."

The graying Indian shook his head. "No like Indians."

"Yes, He does, Gray Wolf. He loves everyone. He loves you as much as He loves me."

Soon the Indians filed through the open door. "Martha God say go, get much gold." As they marched proudly across the prairie, Martha opened the other door and all the windows. She always tried to get rid of the smell before Abe came in.

Martha cleaned the house and had the beans and bread ready when Abe came back with Willie following him.

As they eagerly ate the beans and bread, Martha reminded Abe of the Indians' offer to get them some gold. "We purely need it bad," she said.

Abe shoved half a thick heel of warm bread into his mouth. "We do," he said. "It would help us get on our feet again." After eating silently for a few more minutes he raised his eyes to Martha. "Thing is we don't want that gold unless God wants us to have it. He may have a better plan." An impish grin spread across his face. "Haven't you heard hard times draw us closer to God? That's really what we want, Martha. To be close to God."

"Of course we do," Martha replied. "But we are close to Him, Abe. And I want what He wants just as much as you do. But we don't know what He wants yet. Maybe you could talk to Him tonight."

Abe nodded. "I'll try to do that if I don't fall asleep first. Or if He don't."

Willie burst out laughing. "Abe! God doesn't sleep."

As Martha prepared to serve a rice pudding, someone pounded on the front door.

Abe grinned. "We know it isn't the Indians." He opened the door to Martha's aunt and uncle who lived across the creek.

"We got lonely so here we are," Aunt Mandy said. She pulled Willie to her. "How's my boy tonight?"

Martha served everyone rice pudding. "I want cream on mine," Willie said.

Abe chuckled. "You know we don't have that stuff anymore, Willie. If it'd help, we'd all fuss for some."

"How are Riley and Melissa?" Martha asked. The two were Mandy and Cleve's son and his wife, both dear to Martha and Abe.

"They're fine," Uncle Cleve said. "Got through the cold better'n most. Mostly 'cause they didn't have any cattle to worry with. What about Jackson and Nellie?"

"They made it too," Abe said. "Those two seem to live on love no matter what the weather." Jackson and Nellie were Martha's brother and wife. Abe referred to Jackson's obvious preference for enjoying his wife rather than working.

"How does Luke like the new work horse you bought?" Uncle Cleve wanted to know. The unprecedented winter had killed John, one of Abe's prized Belgian team. He'd bought another work horse with money they'd found in Martha's covered wagon—money that had belonged to her parents. "You getting your place worked up with them?"

"Work together almost as well as Luke and John did," Abe said. "Got the place all plowed and most of it disked. We're about ready to plant. How about you?"

"Doin' fine. The new oxen're young but catchin' on. Riley's eager to use 'em. Soon's some more animals come in he's plannin' to buy his own." Uncle Cleve pushed back his chair. "Seen the last paper?" he asked. "Says thousands of miners're waitin' in the Dalles fer the river to get low enough for the steamboats to navigate. That'll be right soon now. Says they'll be hoofin' it to Walla Walla where they 'spect to find animals, food, and gear fer minin'. Wonder what we're gonna feed 'em."

Abe shook his head. "This'd be a real bonanza if we hadn't all been froze out. Well, we'll just do the best we can." He thought a moment and a frown crossed his face. "Crime's been gettin' pretty awful. No tellin' what it'll be like as more people crowd in. Town may not be fit to live in."

The next morning Abe awakened looking radiant. "What happened to you?" Martha asked. "You look like a plate of fried sunshine."

"I feel like one too," Abe answered. "We're plantin' hay this year so we can go after some gold! We'll leave as soon as it's in the ground."

A thrill ripped through Martha that brought out a gasp. "He told you it's all right! Didn't He Abe?"

"Yep. And to get the hay in the ground quick. He knew we needed the gold right bad."

"How long will it take to plant the hay?"

Abe thought a moment. "Three weeks if we work from dawn to dusk. Think the Indians'll be back by then?"

She nodded. The Indians were eager to get going. "Long before that, Abe. Do you think they'll let Jackson and Nellie, and Riley and Melissa go too?"

They hurried to the fields and didn't come home until after dark. As Martha warmed up beans and split peas for supper, a thought crossed her mind. "How are we going, Abe? We don't have horses."

"We'll take the wagon and work horses. That way we can carry plenty of beans and side meat."

Three days later the Indians returned. When Martha saw them, she ran in from the field. "Food," Gray Wolf said.

Martha smiled. No matter how good of friends they became she still always had to feed them. She gave them bread and strawberry jam again.

"Martha man talk God?" Gray Wolf asked while they ate.

"Yes!" Martha said with joy. "We're going after the gold, Gray Wolf. But we have to finish planting the hay first."

"When?"

"About three weeks. Can we take some of our family with us, Gray Wolf?"

He swung his head back and forth. "Abe, Martha, Indians. Martha, Abe, Indians."

Martha felt strong disappointment. She'd have felt much safer with a larger group. A larger group of her own people. But maybe the Indians felt safer when they had a majority.

The Indians returned one evening about a week before they planned to leave. "Have horses?" Pony Boy asked.

Abe grinned and pointed toward the barn. "Out there, Pony Boy. We'll take the big horses and the wagon."

Gray Wolf nearly jumped into the air. "No wagon! Too much loud."

Abe looked surprise. "We need a wagon, Gray Wolf, to haul our supplies. Besides we don't have saddle horses. Ours are all dead."

Gray Wolf settled back down. "No wagon," he repeated softly. "Ride Indians' horses."

"What about food?" Martha asked.

"Indians get food," Camas said. "Good food."

Martha looked at Abe. He smiled. "I think if we want to go on this expedition, we do it their way. All right, Gray Wolf. We'll ride your horses and eat your food."

Gray Wolf nodded. "Good." He grinned at Martha. "Long time eat Martha food."

"Yes," Martha said, "but I didn't mind. We've gained some good friends." Then Martha remembered Josie. "Can I bring my dog?" she asked.

Pony Boy grinned broadly, then the grin left. "No eat dog," he said.

"Dog much loud," Camas said. "No eat dog."

Martha wondered what they meant. Then she remembered the first time they'd asked for food. She'd lived in her wagon then. All she'd had was flour and water. When she'd cooked that for them they'd become angry and offered to eat her dog. She raised her eyes to Pony Boy's. "No, I'd never eat my dog. Josie's my good friend. I'll leave her home."

Martha asked Aunt Mandy if she'd keep Willie and Josie while they went with the Indians. She didn't say any more and her aunt didn't ask.

The first day on the road Martha felt strange. After all, what did she know about these three Indians? Only that they came for food and English lessons. She also knew they felt extremely grateful for Abe's saving Pony Boy's life when he'd been accused of a murder he didn't commit. That's why the Indians offered to help them.

Noon came and the Indians let the horses drink but didn't stop for a meal for the people.

As it grew dark that evening, the Indians led them to a protected place to spend the night, and staked the horses to graze. The Indians left for a little while and returned with several kinds of leaves and roots. Also five fish. Martha noticed the Indians didn't disturb a leaf, stick, or stone while they walked. She didn't even hear them return until they appeared in the clearing.

Camas made a fire while Pony Boy cleaned the fish and Gray Wolf fixed the roots and leaves. "Why can't I help?" Martha asked.

"Indians cook," Gray Wolf said.

A short time later the Indians offered Abe and Martha a fine banquet, everything served on the stick they'd cooked it on. Abe asked to thank His God for the food and the Indians agreed. Martha ate all she could hold and noticed Abe ate even more. As Martha wondered what she would do with a delicious root, a squirrel ventured near. She held out her hand to the shy little animal. It backed away. Then it crept nearer. Finally it reached Martha's hand. Snatching the food, it turned and raced off through the forest.

Only a few moments later a large bird swooped down from a tree, caught the screaming squirrel in its talons and flew back to the same bough.

Everyone watched in shocked silence. Finally Camas spoke. "Sign. Bad luck." He shook his head.

"Not good," Gray Wolf agreed.

"Wait a minute," Abe said. "We don't have to depend on luck. Our God takes care of us." He asked Martha to pray with him and they both thanked God for being with them through the day and asked His protection during the night.

When they finished, Martha opened her eyes to find all the Indians staring at them.

"White man God live in sky?" Camas asked.

"Yes," Abe said. Then he patted his chest. "Our God lives right here too, in Abe's heart where He hears our prayers."

Gray Wolf nodded.

"Luck good," Pony Boy said.

"Abe God make luck good," Camas said. "Good God."

The next day they met several groups of white men heading for Walla Walla. "Any luck in the mines?" Abe asked several times.

Chapter 2

B ut no one wanted to talk about gold. Everyone seemed to be looking over his shoulder, fearful of who might be following. Abe thought he understood. If a person could get away with anything in Walla Walla, who would protect a man from thieves on this long lonely trail?

Every night they camped beside some sort of stream and every night the Indians somehow found a fish for everyone. For breakfast they each had another fish and more roots. They didn't eat anything between.

When the Sabbath Day came, Abe wondered if they'd be able to stop and rest. He should have settled that important point before they started. "Forgive me, Father," he said softly, "for overlooking Your special day when we planned this trip. Soften their hearts and help us teach them about You."

Start planning your lesson, Abe.

Abe grinned. "Thanks, Lord. I knew You would help us."

When Abe asked the Indians if they could stop and worship the Great Spirit, they agreed so quickly that Abe could only silently thank God again for preparing the way.

Abe told them how much God loves them. "Do you know how far away the stars are?" he asked them.

"Long way," Camas replied.

"Far," Pony Boy agreed.

Abe showed them his Bible as he had many times before. "My God's book says He loves us as much as the stars are high. And as deep as the sea. He loves us much. He loves every one of us that much and it makes Him feel bad when we hurt each other."

The Indians seemed happy to listen to Abe talk about his God.

One evening after they'd been traveling eight days they came to what the Indians called "Big Water."

"I think this is the Snake River," Martha told Abe. "Remember I told you about the little boy, Pete, who drowned in the Snake? It looked like this."

They followed the river and that evening Abe and Martha went with the Indians to get some fish. The Indians didn't use poles, but just put worms or flies on hooks attached to some kind of cord and dropped it into the water. Soon they started pulling fish from the water, some too big for one person to eat.

"We're having a feast tonight," Abe said. "We won't need anything else."

After awhile Abe and Martha walked on down the river a ways watching the ducks and geese. Suddenly Abe saw something swimming lazily a few feet beneath the surface. He'd never seen a creature like it. He leaned over the water, pointing. "Look, Martha, I see an alligator! There, swimming under the water."

Martha searched through the murky water for a minute. "Yes! I see it, Abe. Isn't it the strangest looking thing you've ever seen?" She watched it another moment. "But it isn't an alligator, Abe. Alligators have legs. I think it's a sturgeon! That's a prehistoric fish with scales like an alligator. I read about them in a book. How long is it?"

Abe peered into the water. "Looks to be about ten feet to me." He raised his eyes to hers. "All right, how long is a sturgeon?"

"The book said they grow to fourteen feet and weigh three thousand pounds in the Great Lakes. I don't know if they grow bigger or smaller here."

"Well, they aren't much smaller."

Martha put her arm around his waist. "Know what else it said about the big ones? By the time they get really big they're two or three hundred years old. That's purely older than we are, Abe."

After watching the sturgeon awhile, they went back to the Indians and told them about the great fish. The Indians wanted to see it, but it was gone.

After they followed the Snake River another day, the Indians showed them a place where the river flowed shallow and wide. "We cross," Gray Wolf said pointing across the river.

Martha's face turned white and her hands clenched her horse's reins. Abe knew she remembered the horrible crossing where the little boy drowned. He rode as close to her as his horse would go. "It's nothing," he said softly. "The horses won't even have to swim."

Pony Boy overheard and nodded. "Horses swim."

Oh. Abe tried again. "Well, it won't be bad. Nothing like where you crossed in the wagons." He turned to Gray Wolf. "Could you go first? Martha's pretty nervous. She saw a little boy drown in this river."

Gray Wolf nodded and motioned for his two sons to follow him. Abe moved a little closer to Martha and leaned across the two horses for her hand. The Indians rode single file and almost reached the other side before the water deepened enough to force the horses into a swim. With hardly any current, the horses didn't even struggle but hit the bank straight across.

"Ready?" Abe asked Martha. Silently, he asked God to be with her and strengthen her.

She urged her horse into the stream, lips straight and tense, her back like a piece of wood. As the horse moved across, Martha seemed to relax some. Abe rode behind. "I'm right here," he called. "You're doin' great but I'm watching every move just in case." Martha reached the deep place and her horse started swimming. Abe felt the cold for her as her horse dropped deeper into the water until it came to Martha's waist. She said nothing.

Then they stood in the sun on the east side of the river. Martha slid off her horse laughing happily. "Abe, I told you it wasn't anything." She laughed again at her absurdity.

They followed the Clearwater River and the next day Abe showed Martha and the Indians where the Spalding Mission stood a ways off the trail. "The Spaldings and the Whitmans came from far away to teach you Indians about our Great God," he said.

Gray Wolf grunted. "Poison Indians. Give Indians food. Make sick. Give medicine sick papooses. Papooses die."

Martha and Abe looked at each other in shock. "I've never heard that," Abe said after recovering somewhat. The horses plodded on.

"Hear Indians kill missionary?" Pony Boy asked.

Martha glanced at Abe. "He means the horrible massacre in '47."

"Yes, we heard," Abe said. "Do you know anything about that?"

Gray Wolf nodded. "White papooses sick. Red spots.

Indians get spots too. White doctor give medicine. White papooses get well. Indians die."

"I don't know, Gray Wolf," Abe said. "I've never heard that at all."

Gray Wolf's back straightened even more than usual. "True. Know watermelons?"

Abe grinned. "We sure do," he said. "We been raising a lot to sell. Muskmelons too."

Gray Wolf nodded. "Doctor put medicine in watermelons make Indians sick. Bad sick."

Abe could hardly take this in. "You mean he gave Indians watermelons with poison?" He met Martha's eyes. "Why would he do that?" The horses had taken advantage of the intense conversation by slowing almost to a stop.

Martha shook her head no.

Gray Wolf gave a little hoot and nudged his horse with his heels. His horse picked up its speed and the others followed. Then he grinned at Abe. "Indians take watermelons. Doctor not like."

Oh. Now Abe saw. The Indians had been stealing Whitman's watermelons and the missionary put something in them to make the thieves sorry. Anyway, if this farfetched story was accurate that was probably what happened. "I see," he told Gray Wolf, "but that doesn't explain why he'd poison Indian babies who were sick."

Gray Wolf shook his head. "Not like Indians. Not want papooses grow up."

Three days later the Indians led Martha and Abe off the trail through dense trees and brush.

"How do you know where you're going?" Martha asked when they camped beside a small stream that night.

"How long does this go on?" Abe added.

"To gold," Camas said.

"Two, three days," Pony Boy said.

The next day they wound through the thick woods, around small and larger hills, until Abe had no idea where they were. He chuckled to himself. Probably exactly what the Indians had in mind. As they meandered east and south, all the trees looked alike to Abe and so did the hills covered with more trees.

Two days later the Indians spread out single file and rode close to one of the larger hills. In the afternoon they stopped and unsaddled the horses, then tethered them so they could graze. "Walk," Camas said. "Horses make loud."

Abe took Martha's hand and they followed the three Indians, who seemed to make no sound at all as they neared a steep hill. As he listened to the silence ahead, he thought he and Martha must have stepped on every brittle stick in the woods. "Why do we have to be quiet, anyhow?" he asked. "We're the only living beings in these hills."

Gray Wolf dropped back beside them. "Much living things," he whispered. "Indian Reservation. Nez Percé. Indians living. Bears living too."

Abe pulled Martha closer to him. "You better stay close to me," he murmured. "I might be able to save you from an Indian." He chuckled. "Of course, I'll run from a bear. But I'll drag you along if I can."

The Indians led them ever closer to the steep hill. Finally they disappeared behind some tall bushes. It seemed the bushes grew right against the hill but Abe kept walking. When he reached the spot where he'd last seen the Indians, he found the trees tight against the hill just as he'd thought. But as he forced his way under the trees, he found a small opening in the mountain. "So—they went in here," he said. Putting his arm around Martha, he stood with her in the opening and looked in. "It gets dark pretty fast," he said. "Wonder how they can see in there."

"I don't know," Martha said, "but I don't think they wanted us to follow."

Abe grinned. "I'll bet they hoped we wouldn't even find the opening. That's how come they hurried on ahead."

Taking Martha's arm he led her away from the cave, out from the thick trees to an opening. Sun shone brightly where the trees weren't so close together. "We may as well sit down and rest. No telling how long they'll be in there."

"I hope they find something," Martha said. "The trip's been fun, but it'll be more fun if we have some gold to help the others and buy things we need when we get home."

Abe lay on the fresh green grass beside her in the warm sunshine, leaning up on his left arm. He traced over her nose, over her mouth, and around her chin with his right index finger. "Did I ever tell you how completely beautiful you are?" he asked quietly. "And how much I love you? This trip will still be perfect if we don't find a penny's worth of gold. Think of all the time we got to spend together. Not working. Not running somewhere doing something. Just riding along together." He leaned over her and kissed her gently, sweetly. "And this," he finished.

"You're making me blush, Abram Noble. You're really noble." She giggled. "I mean it, Abe. You're truly good. Which reminds me. I've been wanting to tell you how sorry I am for waiting so long to be a real wife to you. I know now how unfair it was for you."

Their love had been so special that Abe hadn't thought of their unreal marriage for a long time. "It was kinda hard," he admitted. Then he remembered God's part in it. Martha had lived in a covered wagon. Her food had run out, she didn't have any money and the snow was starting to fly. "But hey! It was all God's idea. He told me to do it. He not only told me to do it, He insisted. And kept on insisting until I asked you. He told me I would be blessed more than I could imagine. He knew how it would all end up." Abe couldn't help it. He gathered her close and held her tightly for a long time.

They both fell asleep. When Abe opened his eyes the stars twinkled overhead. No moon appeared to send silver beams into their quiet world. He shook Martha gently. "Are you ready to wake up?" he whispered.

She jerked and sat up, looking around. "Aren't they back yet?" she whispered. "Haven't you seen them at all?"

Abe grinned in the dark and shook his head. "Not a glimpse. You know what that means don't you? They're getting lots and lots of gold for us."

Martha giggled. "Or they can't find any—and now they can't find their way out. I'm hungry, Abe. How about you?"

"My stomach's been rumblin' for hours." After a quiet moment he laughed. "You got somethin' to eat tucked in a pocket somewhere?" He felt her shaking her head.

They talked quietly for another hour, waiting for their three friends to appear. "What if they don't come back?" Martha finally asked.

Abe thought that over. "Well, I reckon we'll take the horses and go home. I'm not sure we'll be able to find food but we'll get home somehow."

Abe began to pray softly, "Dear Father in heaven, we thank You for being so close to us. And for loving us so much You gave Your only Son to die for our sins so we can live forever with You. We thank You for blessing our trip so far and we pray You'll keep right on blessing it real good. Be with the Indians, God, and bring them safely out of that dark hole in the mountain. Thank You, Father, in Jesus' name."

Pretty soon Martha fell asleep again. As she slept, Abe gently rubbed her back and arms. "Thank You, God, for giving me this best woman in the world."

There's none better, Abe. You take good care of her.

"I will, Father. Thanks." He crowded close to Martha and fell asleep.

—⁓—

"Abe, wake up." Abe stirred at Martha's voice. He discovered the sun shining brightly and Martha bending over him.

He jumped up beside her. "Are they back?"

She shook her head. "No. Do you think we should do something?"

"Yeah. We better find something to eat. My stomach's stickin' to my back right now."

They searched around, finding several weeds they knew were edible. After about an hour of hunting food Abe grinned at Martha. "Now I know why cows eat all day long."

"Why?"

"Because it takes them that long to get filled up." They laughed together as they continued finding and eating weeds. "Maybe we should be eating the roots," Abe said. They stacked up a pile of weeds for the Indians as they picked and ate.

A little before noon something touched Abe's arm as he pulled an extra tough weed. He jerked around to find

Camas. Pony Boy and Gray Wolf followed several feet behind. All three carried burlap bags that looked heavy. Abe laughed out loud. "Where'd you get the bags?" he asked Camas.

"White man. Wapotatoes. Ready go?"

"Yeah. We're ready. What'd you find? How come it took so long?"

Gray Wolf set his bag on the ground. "Plenty gold. Got lost."

Abe couldn't help laughing. "Martha," he said, "our guides got lost. Do you believe that?"

"Gold long way," Gray Wolf said. "Dark. Find gold. Much tunnels. Lost." He opened his bag and motioned Abe to look inside. When Abe complied, he couldn't believe what he saw. Lots of large chunks. Maybe ten pounds altogether. But it didn't look very gold.

He raised his eyes to Gray Wolf's. "You sure this is gold?"

Gray Wolf smiled and nodded. "Gold. Look other sacks."

Abe took Martha's hand and led her to the other two bags. They looked the same but held more gold then Gray Wolf's.

"How much of this is ours?" Martha asked Abe softly.

Before he could tell her he didn't know, Pony Boy answered. "Gold Abe's," he said. "Save Pony Boy hang."

Abe shook his head. "You don't owe me anything, Pony Boy. I just happened along at the right time." He wondered how much the gold was worth and decided to ask.

"Not know," Gray Wolf answered. "Much money." He met Abe's gaze. "More in cave."

Abe smiled to himself. The Indians were generous to give Martha and him some of their gold but their secret remained a secret. He had no idea how to get it. When they reached the trail again he wouldn't even be able to find the cave. Anyway, he had a strong feeling the Indians had stashed that gold in the cave, that it had come from somewhere else.

After the Indians ate the pile of weeds, Camas led the way to the horses where they put the gold in the saddle bags, saddled the horses, and secured the bags behind the saddles so they didn't appear very full. They took off the way they'd come, with only a few weeds in their stomachs since yesterday morning. But Abe felt great anyway. There was more to a man than food in his stomach.

"Thank You, God," he whispered as they followed the Indians through the trees and brush. He still felt completely lost.

They stopped early that evening and enjoyed the bounty the Indians provided. Two fish each and several kinds of roots baked in the fire.

Two days later they reached the trail and Abe heaved a sigh. Now he could find his way home. Not that he'd need to with the Indians guiding them.

The Indians seemed happy and contented as they rode homeward. They stopped again for the Sabbath Day. Abe and Martha taught the Indians several songs during their little service. Abe could hardly keep a straight face as they tried to sing the hymns in their broken English.

He asked Martha to talk to them.

"We already told you God made the people and the world," she said. "He loved them because He made them, and He came and walked with them each day in the beautiful garden home He made for them. He gave them many kinds of luscious fruit to eat from the trees. He told them they could eat all they wanted from any tree in the garden except one. He said they couldn't eat from that tree because it wasn't good for them and they'd die if they ate that fruit.

"Adam and Eve loved their garden home and didn't think anything of that tree until the devil disguised himself as a snake and talked to Eve. He told her the fruit of that tree was good to eat and they wouldn't die if they ate it. And that they'd become like God if they did. So Eve tried it and found it tasted good. She gave Adam some of it too, and they began to grow old right then. People have died ever since.

"But God loved His people and didn't want them to die. He made a plan to stop people from dying. I'll tell you about that next Sabbath if we're still on the trail." She giggled. "I'll tell you about it anyway if you'd like to hear."

"Indians hear," Pony Boy said.

They started on the trail early the next morning, their stomachs full of the good things the Indians had found for them. A few hours later they neared the Spalding Mission again. Abe wondered if they'd get into a discussion about the missionaries again.

As he thought about what he'd tell the Indians, two riders approached from behind, riding hard. "Stop!" one of them yelled. "Stop right there or we'll shoot you dead!"

"Come!" Gray Wolf said, kicking his horse hard. "Hurry!"

"Hurry, Martha," Abe said. "They don't mean us any good."

In less than a minute the four horses stretched their legs in long galloping strides. "Maybe we can get to the Spalding Mission," Martha puffed.

Chapter 3

Martha thought she'd never felt such fear in her life. "Help us, Father!" she called loudly. The men yelled, the horses hooves beat the ground, but she knew God heard anyway. "Thank You, Lord," she added.

As they cut the distance between them and the mission, she began to think they might get away. The men fired several shots but didn't hit anyone. Finally Martha saw the mission and heaved a big sigh of relief. When the men noticed that, they'd leave. She hoped.

But suddenly two more men appeared in the trail ahead of them, masked and mounted on big horses. Martha glanced at Gray Wolf, wondering where they could go. Surely he'd cut off through the woods.

"Stop them nags right now or we'll shoot 'em out from under you!" someone yelled. Gray Wolf pulled his horse to a stop and everyone followed his lead.

One of the other men moved his horse beside Martha while looking at Abe. "We know you got gold so git it. Now!"

Abe looked at Gray Wolf, who nodded almost imperceptibly. Abe slid off his horse, unfastened his saddle bag, pulled out the burlap bag of gold and handed it to one of the men. "How'd you know we had gold?" he asked almost civilly.

"We watch everyone goin' through. Ain't hard to tell." He turned to Gray Wolf, aiming his rifle at the Indian's head. "Get off that horse, redskin, and get the rest." Martha glanced around and found guns pointed at them from every direction.

Gray Wolf dismounted, pulled out his burlap bag and handed it to the man. "Take part, leave part," he said sullenly.

The man laughed nastily. "Why would I do that, you savage? Now get the rest."

Gray Wolf looked directly where the man's eyes slitted through the mask. "Gray Wolf no have more."

The man cracked Gray Wolf over the head with the butt of his gun. "Get it, redskin. Before I lose my patience!"

Gray Wolf marched over to Martha's horse and looked into her saddle bag, then shook his head. "No."

A shot rang out and Martha thought Gray Wolf had been hit. But he didn't fall. She looked at the other men to find one of them lowering his rifle. He'd shot into the air.

"The next one's fer you, Injun!" the man called out.

Gray Wolf ambled to Pony Boy and took his saddle bag. He pulled out the last bag of gold and threw it at the man. Then he turned and mounted his horse. "Go," he said and started down the path. His two sons followed, then Abe and Martha fell in behind. Martha expected to hear shots but only an eerie silence shrouded the area.

A few moments later the four thieves passed them at full gallup.

"Well," Abe said dropping back beside her. "I guess we all get to live. That's somethin'." He turned his face upward. "Thanks, God. Money would have been nice but life and health are necessary." He grinned at Martha. "And someone to love."

The Indians didn't say a word for hours. Neither did they hurry their horses. They said a few words in their own language, but Martha couldn't hear well enough to understand.

That night they stopped early. Martha and Abe waited at the campsite for their friends. "I'd like to help," Abe said, "but they seem to want to be alone while they fish and hunt roots."

Martha had been wanting to talk to Abe. They sat on a downed tree trunk. "Well, what do you think, Abe? Are you terribly disappointed?"

He looked thoughtful, then shook his head and grinned. "We aren't any worse off than when we started. We've had a nice trip and learned to know the Indians better. All we have to do now is figure out how we're goin' to live until our crops give us some money."

Martha smiled at him. "What you're trying to say is you are purely disappointed but won't let it get you down."

Abe hugged her close. "I guess that's about it." He pointed his thumb upward. "With Him up there takin' care of us we'll be just fine. It won't hurt us to depend on Him for our food."

The Indians soon came back with fish, roots, and some kind of berries. After the good meal Camas told Abe and Martha to come. They followed through some brush to a clearing where a beautiful little blue lake sparkled before them. "Fish here," Pony Boy said.

They sat on some rocks on the shore and enjoyed the lake for a couple of hours, talking quietly. Martha wished Abe would talk to them about the gold, but he didn't. The Indians didn't say anything either. When the sun turned the sky to gold and orange, they went back to camp. Abe had started having a little worship service each night and the Indians seemed to enjoy it.

This night he asked Martha to talk to them so she continued the story she'd started last Sabbath. "Remember how Adam and Eve ate the bad tree? Well, God felt really bad about that because He loved Adam and Eve and He didn't want them to die. God couldn't tell them it was all right this one time because no one would believe Him anymore. So many years later He sent His only Son to die for men, to take the punishment man deserved, so they could live again. He did that, Gray Wolf, so you and I can live forever with Him. He did it for you, too, Pony Boy and Camas." She turned to Abe. "He did it for you too, Abe. He loves you even more than I do. I don't see how there could be more love than I have for you, but He loves you more.

"All we have to do is to accept the big sacrifice He made for us and love Him with all our hearts and our minds and our strength and our soul. That's all."

The Indians said nothing but looked very thoughtful. When Abe asked them to bow for prayer they all did.

"Gray Wolf talk God," Gray Wolf said. Then he began: "Gray Wolf want love God. Want live God. God, come love Gray Wolf."

Abe moved quickly to Gray Wolf's side. "You're now a child of God," he said. "God loves you and will take you to live with Him forever." He grinned at Gray Wolf. "Think you can put up with us forever? That's a long time."

Gray Wolf nodded. "Abe, Gray Wolf brother."

—⁂—

Martha rejoiced over Gray Wolf as she and Abe lay side by side in the dark night. "Are you awake?" she whispered to him.

"I am now," he answered, pulling her close. "Somethin' wrong?"

"No. Now I know why we came. We're to make Christians of these wonderful men." She waited for Abe to answer but she heard only a quiet little snore. "Well, teaching them to love God's more important than gold," she told him even while he slept.

The next morning after they ate, Gray Wolf seemed agitated. "Is anything wrong?" Abe asked.

"Abe go gold?" Gray Wolf asked.

Abe looked at Martha. She shook her head. If they got more those men would probably take it away again. Why not go home and figure a way to get food.

"I guess we'd just like to go on home," Abe said grinning. "If we don't have something, they can't take it away."

The Indians didn't hurry at all that day. In fact Martha would have said they dawdled. She couldn't figure why and she couldn't ask Abe. The

Indians understood too much English now for them to say anything they didn't want to share.

Two nights later Abe asked Martha to talk to them again. She'd been hoping he would, as she had something she wanted to say bad.

"You all know now that our big God will let you live with Him forever. But I want to tell you He's with you all the time right here." She put her hand over her heart. "If we love Him as much as we know how to love He'll live in our heart and help us and guide us."

The three Indians put their right hands over their hearts. "God here. God help," Pony Boy said. "Love God. Help us."

Martha noticed Abe put his hand over his heart too.

"God talk Pony Boy?" the young Indian asked.

Martha nodded. "God does talk to us. But He doesn't talk to everyone the same way. He talks to Abe like a friend. He talks to me by feelings. You listen, Pony Boy, and He'll talk to you somehow."

"Gray Wolf wonder," the big Indian said, "big God not help. Men take gold."

Oh. "He kept the men from hurting us," she said. "We'll get along somehow without the gold. Maybe we'll be better off this way. Maybe He didn't really send us to get the gold, Gray Wolf. I think He loved you men so much He sent us so we could teach you about Him."

Gray Wolf didn't say anymore but went off to bed with a serious look on his face.

The next morning the Indians were gone when Abe and Martha woke up. They soon appeared with fish, roots, and berries. After they ate they dawdled around camp awhile. Martha couldn't understand why they were so relaxed, as they'd hurried off every morning before.

When they finally started, the Indians actually let the horses graze along the way. Martha wished she could get a chance to see what Abe thought about it.

Two mornings later when she woke up to find the Indians gone, she let Abe sleep a little longer. The three hadn't returned by the time he finally got up. They still hadn't returned an hour later. "Must be having trouble finding fish or roots," Abe said. "I wish they'd let me fish. They could teach me a lot. I wouldn't mind knowing how to find food in the forest too." He grinned at her. "When we get lost, we'll just have to find weeds and eat all day."

They decided to do that now, so they found all the weeds they recognized and piled them beside the coals from last night's fire. "They may not even eat this stuff," Martha said. "But at least we tried."

Two hours later, about mid-morning, the Indians returned with not a sound. "What's this?" Abe asked.

The Indians rode three strange horses and led a fourth. A moment later they pulled the saddle bags from the horses. "Look," Camas said. Then he pulled out of his saddle bag a burlap bag that looked familiar Camas opened it to reveal a bunch of gold. The others each had a bag too.

"What happened?" Abe asked. "How did you get these?"

Gray Wolf looked pleased. "Find bad men. Drink fire water. Sleep."

Camas couldn't wait for Gray Wolf to finish. He cut right in. "Take horses. Guns. Gold. No take saddles. Bad men carry saddles."

"Horses call," Pony Boy continued. "Men sleep. Men wake up. Walk."

Abe burst into loud laughter. "You really got them. But what will they really do when they wake up?"

"Walk," Gray Wolf said with a rare smile. "Walk and walk and walk."

The Indians didn't want to take time to cook breakfast, so they all grabbed handfuls of the weeds Martha and Abe had gathered.

The Indians didn't let the horses dally anymore. They traveled late and got up early. And hurried the horses all day.

One evening they saw a flock of grouse. "Get guns," Camas said. "Eat birds."

"No, let's not," Martha said. "Let's just look at them. Aren't they pretty? They're a family, Camas, like we are."

They ate fish that night but the next night the Indians took their guns when they left. After awhile they heard a report. Martha shuddered, wondering what poor animal just lost its life.

Soon the Indians appeared with a dressed bird, much larger than a grouse. They started a fire, put a long limb through the bird, and barbecued it. Though somewhat tough, it didn't taste too bad. Wild, but definitely edible.

"What color was this bird?" Abe asked.

"Black," Camas said. "Red on head."

Martha felt her meal trying to come back up. Camas had just described a vulture, birds which ate only old rotten meat. After a few minutes she felt better and realized the Indians had shot the vulture because she didn't want them shooting pretty birds.

Several days later, they reached Walla Walla. Martha had never felt so happy to be home in her life. Home and safe! And with gold. *Thank You, God,* she said silently. The Indians would go west, out by Fort Walla Walla; Martha and Abe would go east to their farm.

The Indians reined in their horses. "Abe," Pony Boy said. Abe stopped his horse too. "Take horses," Pony Boy said, pointing to the thieves' horses. "Abe's horses."

Abe shook his head. "No, Pony Boy, I can't take them. They're yours.

You earned them. I'll take Martha home, then bring back the horses we rode." He held a hand out to Pony Boy. "How do we ever thank you for the gold? It'll help us and our families get a new start." After shaking hands with Pony Boy, Abe repeated the action with Gray Wolf and Camas.

"Brother," Gray Wolf said when Abe shook hands with him. "Big God make brothers."

"Right," Abe said. "And don't you forget it. You come eat our food anytime." He laughed. "As soon as we get some. It won't take long, so you come, hear?"

Pony Boy drew near. "Indians go Abe's tepee. Take horses." Gray Wolf liked the idea, and they rode with them so Abe wouldn't have to return the horses and walk home.

Martha couldn't wait to see Willie. She'd been his mother for a long time, and she'd worried a little about him while they were gone.

They stopped the horses by the door, took the saddle bags with the burlap bags inside, and hid them in their bedroom.

The front door slammed hard, and Willie grabbed Martha around the waist. "I thought something happened, Martha. Why were you gone so long?"

Martha sat on the bed and pulled her seven-year-old brother onto her lap. "We went a long way, Willie. We hurried." She leaned to his ear. "We got some gold too." She resumed her normal voice. "Now we can buy food. And one of these days we'll buy horses. Then I'll be able to ride with you and Speckle."

"Tomorrow? Can you buy a horse tomorrow so I can ride a long ways?"

Uncle Cleve and Aunt Mandy came in then. "You look like you're all in one piece!" Uncle Cleve said in his usual stentorian voice. He and Mandy both hugged Martha and Willie in her lap.

Abe came out of the other bedroom. "We're fine. And had a great trip. Those Indians are faithful friends." He hugged Aunt Mandy and Willie and shook Uncle Cleve's hand. "Got a little gold too," he said. "I guess we'll have to find out what it's worth before we share it."

"We don't need any," Aunt Mandy said. "We didn't have all our money in livestock like you did. We still got plenty."

Aunt Mandy invited Abe and Martha for supper, an invitation Martha appreciated as she didn't have much in the house to eat.

The next morning after a breakfast of oatmeal, Abe turned to Martha. "How about going to the traders with me this morning? We can take a couple of pieces of gold and see what they think about it."

Martha hurried to put the dishes away, combed Willie's hair, and headed toward the Street with Abe, bubbling over with excitement. Josie followed, running all over the Street in her exuberance.

"Well," Edgar Baldwin, a thin dark-haired man said looking at the pieces Abe had laid on the counter. "I ain't never seen nothing like this called gold afore."

Chapter 4

Abe took in a long breath. When he'd thought the gold was gone he'd felt maybe that was how it was supposed to be. Now that he had it in his hands it had to be gold. Real gold.

Are You there God? he asked silently.

I'm here, Abe.

You'll make sure this is the way You want it, won't You?

Count on it, Abe. And trust Me to know best.

Abe relaxed. Whatever God had in mind was all right with him.

Baldwin looked at the pieces again and shook his head. Finally he called his brother from somewhere in the back. "Waddaya make of this stuff?" he asked.

The bearded man picked up the biggest piece and turned it over several times. "Looks like gold to me. Feels like it too." He set the stone down and looked at Abe. "Where'd you get this stuff?"

Abe grinned. "It came from Idaho but I didn't get it. Some Indians gave it to us. Thought I did 'em a big favor. They think it's gold."

Edgar Baldwin nodded. "I ain't the gold expert in the family. If Dan thinks it's gold, then it's gold." He extended his hand across the counter. "Congratulations, Abe."

"Thanks," Abe said, shaking the hand. "But we want to know how much this stuff's worth."

Dan Baldwin looked over the gold again. "Looks to me like that chunk'd make ten big nuggets. Looks like good stuff too. Might be worth a thousand dollars but I'm not a gold trader."

Abe almost quit breathing. That rock on the counter was only one of dozens they'd brought home. "Where'll I find out for sure? How do we turn this stuff into somethin' we can use?"

Baldwin pointed east. "There's a gold trader on the other side of the Street down about six buildin's. He can help you."

People milled all over the Street, making it hard for Abe and Martha to find the building they sought. Abe had thought the town grew a lot last year, but now the mass of people utterly amazed him. Still all the buildings looked like shacks.

"This here's good gold," the roughly dressed gold expert told them when they found him. "I'll just cut it into small and large nuggets for you. All's I have to do is make all the nuggets weigh the same. If'n you want you can trade the smaller pieces on nuggets."

Abe felt as if he were glowing. "Sounds great. How much you planning to charge for all this?"

The man shrugged. "I can take ten percent. Or I can take the stuff that's too small to weigh. Whatever you say."

Abe looked at Martha, who just smiled at him. "What do I know about these things?" she asked.

"I guess we'll think a little on it," Abe said, turning toward the rough wood door. "We'll be back soon."

———~m~———

When they closed their own door at home, Abe grabbed Martha high in his arms and twirled her around. "We're rich!" he shouted. "Positively, absolutely rich! And so are all our kin."

After they collected Willie from Aunt Mandy and ate dinner, they sat on the settle and talked. "Let's count the pieces of gold and see if we can tell how much we have," Abe said. They hauled the three heavy sacks of gold from their hiding places and counted the big pieces, guessing how many big nuggets could be cut from each. They did the same with the smaller pieces. When they finished, Abe looked at Martha. Her eyes reflected his shock. They'd tried to be conservative with their estimates, but they figured they'd have more than fifty thousand dollars.

"We don't need that much money," Abe said. "With all the new people comin' in I can make a good living makin' furniture. And we can make a living from our farm too."

"We do need it, Abe," Martha said quietly. "We purely do. We can do a lot of good with it. I hear they're trying to get a school going right away. We can help that. And all kinds of other things too." She giggled. "We might even help my brother a little."

Abe laughed with her. "We'll help him a little, but he has to learn to work like other men. We'll also help your aunt and uncle. And Riley and Melissa." Martha's cousin, Riley, had married Melissa, who'd lived with Martha and Abe since Martha had found her hungry and frightened, looking in the window. Although scarcely a year younger than Martha, Melissa considered Martha and Abe her parents. "We mustn't forget God, either," Abe added. "The Good Book says to give Him a tenth of our increase. But that ain't enough. We'll give more like we always have." He chuckled. "That much gold may puzzle our church brothers a bit."

"Will we take all the money to the gold trader? Or a little at a time?"

Abe took her hand in his. "I don't think we'll do exactly either. Let's take several pieces right away and share with your kin, the school, the church, and whatever. Then we can get it fixed up as we or someone needs it."

That afternoon they took a bag of larger pieces to the gold man who cut them into nuggets. He kept the small pieces he cut off for his payment.

They took ten big nuggets to Aunt Mandy and Uncle Cleve. "Oh, honey," Uncle Cleve said in his usual bellow. "We don't need them. We have plenty left to live until our crops mature. Riley and Melissa won't need any either. He had several big nuggets just the other day. And they put in lots of crops."

"Well," Abe said as they crossed the creek toward their place, "we didn't get rid of even one nugget." He grinned. "Jackson won't turn us down. But right now why don't we take this bag of nuggets to the new school? I hear they're plannin' to open next month. I'm thinkin' they could use the money now. Then let's walk out to Fort Walla Walla and buy us each a saddle horse. We might even find a cow. People been drivin' them in from California already."

Willie rode Speckle along as they walked first to the school, then the two miles to the fort. "What kind of horse you gonna get, Martha?" he asked.

Martha laughed. "I don't know, Willie. Whatever they have, I guess." She sobered. "I can't expect another Sampson. Or even close. He was one of a kind." Her beloved chestnut gelding, Sampson, had frozen in the cold last winter.

Abe took her hand. He knew how she felt. He'd lost his treasured mare, Charity, just before the cold. When he'd gone to California to buy and drive cattle home, Indians had stolen Charity and eaten her. It still made his stomach churn to remember.

Soon they reached the fort and a soldier took them to the log corral where they kept the horses they wanted to sell.

Abe spotted *the horse* before he'd looked at half the herd, a huge black stallion with a perfect star in its forehead. White covered all four feet like knee stockings.

Whaddaya say, Father? he asked silently. *Would You be for me havin' that one?*

He looks good, Abe.

All right! Thanks, Pard.

But Abe wouldn't say anything until Martha chose. She came first and Sampson had been big. She might choose that big black beauty by the fence. He tried to look at the other horses before him but his eyes seemed stuck on the black.

"Oh, Abe," Martha said, clutching his arm. "See that pretty little chestnut mare? She looks nearly like Charity. Do you want her?"

Abe shook his head. "Not this time. I wouldn't like being reminded of Charity every day. Have you found one you like?"

"Not yet," Martha said, her eyes shining with excitement and love. "But I'm not choosing until you do."

Abe laughed. "I hope we won't be standin' here all night but you're choosin' first."

Martha laughed too. "All right, Abe, if you're sure." Her eyes turned toward the corral. "See that big big boy over there? That cream-colored gelding?" She turned raptured eyes on Abe. "Oh, Abe, isn't he wondrous?"

"Yeah!" Willie said. "That 'n's just right for a girl." Then he pointed into the middle of the herd. "You gotta take that black one over there, Abe."

Abe ruffled the little boy's blond hair. "Hey, you've been so quiet I thought you'd gone away somewhere." He turned his eyes back to the big black. "You like that one, do you? Well, I might take him—just for you."

When Abe pointed out the cream and black horses, the soldier grinned. "I bin wantin' that black myself," he said. "I bet he'll give you a ride you'll remember." He looked through the sheets of paper he held in his hands. A moment later he looked up. "The black's seven years old and two hundred and twenty-five dollars. Name's Lucifer."

Abe's eyes quickly met Martha's. She grinned. He didn't. That name definitely had to go. "How hard you reckon it is on a horse to have his name changed?" Abe asked.

The man shrugged. "Reckon it won't matter none. The horse'll soon come to whatever you call it. Prolly think their name's a call to food anyways." Then he looked up Martha's horse on his paper. "Yer horse is four years old, Ma'am. Prolly got more energy than a tornado. Two hundred and forty-five dollars. Name's Thunder. 'Course you can change it if you want."

Responding to Abe's question about a cow, the man shook his head. "We ain't got any extra milking right now, but I hear they're coming in by the hunnerds."

As they rode home Abe touched his heels to Lucifer's sides. The horse moved into a nice trot. He touched them again and the horse took off on a rolling canter. He took the slack from the reins and the horse slowed. He leaned over and petted the powerful black neck. "We'll do all right, won't we, boy?" he asked the shiny horse. "I've never seen a more responsive animal. And I'll be buildin' you a good tight barn before winter."

When they neared home, Abe asked Martha, "What do you think?

Think you'll get along with Thunder?"

"I love him, Abe. I purely love him. I'm going to find some sugar cubes for him right away."

"I gotta give Speckle some too," Willie said. "You know what, Martha? Speckle looks a lot smaller than he did before you and Abe got your horses."

Martha laughed. "He may be small but he's a good faithful friend. Now we can take long rides, Willie. When we're together, we won't have to stay in sight of the house."

That night Riley and Melissa stopped by. Abe wandered into his bedroom, returning with a bag of nuggets. "Got somethin' here might help you out some," Abe said, handing the bag to Riley.

Riley opened the bag and looked inside. His gaze jerked to Abe's over the top of the bag. "What's that all about?" he asked.

Abe grinned and sat down across from Riley and Melissa. "We been prospectin'—well, in a way. The Indians took us after some gold and we figgered that was about your share."

Riley closed the bag and shoved it back toward Abe. "Reckon we don't need it, Abe. Thanks for thinkin' on us anyway. We planted a lot of garden stuff and we're sellin' it as fast as we can haul it to the Street. We got more'n enough to last another year already. And we got over two months left." He looked as if he'd done something mean and felt sorry. Then his lips lifted into a grin. "Reckon Jackson and Nellie could use some though."

Abe grinned back. "That's what I been hearin'. Did they put in any crops? Or anything?"

Riley shook his head. "Not to notice. I think Jackson's been helping build some cabins though."

Martha joined Abe on the settle. "Think he'd keep working if we gave him something?" she asked the men.

"I guess he deserves a chance to show us," Abe said. "We'll have to go give them their share tomorrow."

They decided to go that evening after Riley and Melissa left so they could catch Jackson at home. Besides it would be a good chance to ride the new horses. Abe had been thinking about a name for his horse. "What do you think of Midnight for my horse?" he asked Martha and Willie. "I realize it isn't very original, but he's black."

Martha hesitated. "He's black all right. Would you rather have a name that's a little different? I was thinking about King Ebony. Ebony's black, you know. You could call him King. But Midnight's good too, Abe. I was just thinking."

King Ebony. That sounded pretty good. And there wouldn't be half a dozen other horses around with that name. He grinned. "I think I like that name, Martha. 'Course there' probably a lot of Kings around. Yeah. It's King Ebony. And I'll call him Ebb. Purty classy, huh, Willie?"

"Yeah!" Willie yelled at the top of his lungs. "I like it! Best of all I like for you to have horses again so you can ride with me."

Before they knew it, they reached Jackson and Nellie's place. Jackson gladly accepted the nuggets. "How come you didn't invite us to go?" he asked. "We could have gotten enough to last the rest of our lives."

"The Good Lord knows workin's good for us, Jackson," Abe said kindly. "It strengthens our muscles, our minds, and our morals."

Later, when they crawled into their warm feather bed, Abe held Martha close. "Thanks for thinkin' up Ebb's name," he said. "I love everything about you, includin' your good mind."

Two days later Gray Wolf came to their house alone. And he didn't say "food."

Abe thought Martha's face paled. "What's wrong?" she asked.

"Come talk Indian," he said. "New jail—steal three cows. Not steal cows."

Abe moved over and put his arm over Martha's shoulder. "Let's go," he said quietly. "Want to come, Gray Wolf?"

The Indian followed them to the Street, then west to the building housing the jail. "We'd like to see the Indian who's charged with stealing the cows," Abe said politely.

"Ya mean the Indian what did steal the cows—three of 'em," Sheriff Buckley said smugly. "Guess I can let you see the savage. Don't talk nuthin' but gibberish though." He led the way down a dirty rough-wood walkway, stopping at a big steel cage. "That's him, sittin' on that box." The sheriff turned and hurried back.

Abe turned to Gray Wolf. "You know him?"

Gray Wolf shook his head. "Heard him."

"How do you know he didn't do it?"

"Say so."

Abe grinned. That might be a good enough reason for Gray Wolf, but he doubted the jury would agree. Especially a white jury. "Can you talk to him?" he asked the tall bronze man.

"What say?"

Abe grinned again. "Ask if he took the cows."

The Indian said some Nez Percé words Abe didn't understand and the other one answered.

"Not take cows," Gray Wolf told Abe.

"Do you know when this happened?" Abe asked.

Gray Wolf didn't. Abe went after the sheriff. "We all need to talk this out," he explained. The sheriff came back reluctantly. "When did this happen?" Abe asked.

"Three or four days ago."

"Why do you think the Indian did it?" Abe asked. "Did he have the cows?"

Buckley spit on the floor. "You know better'n that. Them Indians ate the cows right off."

"Tell me about it."

"Them cows disappeart 'bout soon's they arrived from California. They weren't nowhere. If'n a white man got 'em he'd a hung on to 'em for breeding. Only a dumb redskin woulda et 'em when cows're so scarce around here."

Abe began to feel they didn't have a case against the Indian at all. He looked at his boot and wiped it on the back of his overalls leg. "But—uh—why do you think it's this particular one?"

For a moment Sheriff Buckley looked concerned. Then he met Abe's eyes and grinned. "Well, I figgered we'd make an example of 'im. Lots a' cows disappearin' lately. We gotta stop it somehow, Abe. After we string up that Injun, won't have much rustlin' no more."

"You know better'n that, Sheriff. You gotta find the guilty man or it'll never stop. If it's a white man he'll be tickled to death for you to keep on throwin' Indians in jail. They'll like it even better if you hang 'em."

The sheriff didn't argue, but led Abe and Gray Wolf to the outside door. "Good-bye," the sheriff said. "See you in court."

"What happen?" Gray Wolf asked.

"You can expect your friend to be released before the day's over," Abe said.

Gray Wolf smiled, something very rare for him. "Thank you, Abe. Need gold?"

Abe held his hand to Gray Wolf, who snatched it and shook hard. "We'll never need more gold," he told his Indian friend. "You gave us enough to last all our lives."

Later that afternoon Abe returned to the sheriff and demanded he release the Indian. Finally the reluctant man unlocked the door and ushered the surprised Indian outside.

—⁂—

"Let's take the horses and ride until we find some cows," Abe suggested to Martha and Willie the next day. "A lot of cattle have been brought in from California, and we have gold—so let's get as many as we can."

As they rode, Abe noticed how settled the area was becoming. Houses were coming up blocks south of the Street, which had expanded east over Mill Creek all the way past their place. Out past the houses, tents littered the landscape.

As they headed west, Willie yelled, "I see lots of cows. Over there by those trees."

Abe followed Willie's finger and sure enough, hundreds of cows grazed on a low hill. "You're right, Willie. No one wants that many cows for himself. Let's go talk to the man."

The cows had arrived from California less than a week earlier and the man was ready to sell. Abe bought two hundred cows, twenty milking, sixty due to freshen in the next two months, and the rest not bred yet.

"What are we going to do with all that milk?" Martha asked as they rode home.

"Haven't you noticed all the people milling around?" Abe asked, grinning happily. "We'll sell the milk. I just had a thought, though. Remember my little wife a few years ago? And Melissa a little later? I'll bet there's lots of hungry people around. Maybe we could figure out a way to find them and give them food. With the crowd we have around now it might not be so easy."

"I'd love to, Abe," Martha said. "I'd purely love to. I'd be happy to use all our gold feeding hungry people. I remember how awful it is. But how are you going to get those cows out of that herd and drive them home?"

"I was thinkin' about gettin' Riley and Jackson to help me."

"Abram Noble! You have Willie and me. We're two people on two horses. Why can't we help?"

Abe's heart grew large. What a woman. She'd do anything for him, whether she could or not. But maybe she could. He took the slack from Ebb's reins. "Want to try it now? The pasture fences are still good."

Martha wanted to and Willie *really* wanted to, so they turned around and went back. With the help of the rancher and his sons they got the cattle separated from the herd and started theirs back to their farm. The rancher and his sons rode along with them.

About halfway home the cattle decided to break away, running in all directions. "Hup!" the rancher yelled. "We're losing 'em all!"

Chapter 5

Each one turned his horse to head off the cattle nearest him. The rancher and his sons regrouped the majority, Martha and Thunder got their share, and Willie gathered in several too. Abe and Ebb raced around and turned the remaining few back southeast. Finally the cows quieted down and plodded along within the ring of riders on three sides of them.

"Hey, Willie," Abe called, "you're a natural born cowboy. You did almost better'n anyone. Next to Martha, of course."

"Yippee!" Willie yelled, "I'm gonna be a cowboy. Speckle's gonna be my horse too."

They got the cows into the pasture with no more trouble.

Martha went into the house while Abe and Willie took care of the horses. She felt exhilarated too. Bringing the cows home seemed like a great accomplishment. Giggling to herself, she decided maybe she'd be a cowboy too when she grew up. Her heart grew almost too big for her chest as she thought about Abe. He always knew just the right thing to say to make Willie proud. She hurried to get supper ready for her boys.

Later the Indians came and ate some of Martha's fresh bread while she taught them about Jesus' love.

The next morning Abe went out to check on the new cattle and make sure they found the creek, while Martha did the washing and started bread. She'd just filled the tub with hot water when Abe came rushing in.

"Fifty of the cows are gone," he said. "Can you get Thunder and help me look for them?"

Martha dropped the clothes she'd been sorting, called Willie, and went out with Abe.

"You and Willie go east and I'll go west," he said. "They can't be far."

They searched fruitlessly most of the day, then met back at their place. "I'm afraid they didn't wander off," Abe said. "They'd never go that far."

"What do you mean?" Martha asked. "You don't think someone took them!"

Abe grinned with only a trace of sadness in his face. "I'm afraid we just lost a big hunk of yesterday's investment." He went to finish caring for the remaining livestock, the two big work horses, and the three saddle horses.

Martha returned to her ruined bread and unwashed clothes. *Oh well,* she told herself, *there's always tomorrow.* She made baking powder biscuits and split pea soup.

The next day Abe had to go to the Street so Martha set bread again and heated water for washing. She'd finished with the bread, put it in the warming oven to rise, and was scrubbing sheets when he came back excited.

"Two stores were burglarized last night and they tell me it's happening all the time."

Martha straightened from the scrub board and rubbed her back. "What does Sheriff Buckley think about it?"

Abe grimaced. "The same thing he always does. Says an Indian did it. That might be true, but it might not." He dropped into a chair beside the table. "Somethin's gotta be done, Martha. It's gettin' so nuthin' and nobody's safe around here." He bowed his head. "Lord, You gotta show me what to do. All right?"

He sat with his head bowed awhile, then looked at Martha with a grin. "He says if the law won't stop it the rest of us got to."

Two days later the man they had bought the cattle from appeared at their door. Martha invited him in and gave him a glass of cool milk and some oatmeal cookies while Willie ran to get Abe from the barn.

After Abe washed up a little he shook the man's hand. "Glad to see you. Maybe you heard I need some more cows?"

The man shook his grizzled gray head. "I didn't. In fact, I came to see if you'd come after some while I wasn't lookin'."

Abe looked shocked. "You don't mean you wondered if I stole 'em? I didn't, sir. How many'd you lose?"

"About as many as you bought as near as I can figger. It looked like I had a lot of cattle, but I spent everthin' I had on them critters and I needed the money bad."

Abe looked pained. "Know of anyone else who's lost animals?"

The man laughed mirthlessly. "Yeah. Everone you talk to. Sometimes stuff disappears. Other times masked robbers get it with guns. 'Pears to me this town's getting outta control."

"Me too," Abe agreed. "I lost a bunch too. Let's watch close-like awhile and try to get Buckley interested in cleanin' up Walla Walla. Used to be you could leave a nugget in the street and it'd be there when you got back."

Abe checked his cattle often and cared for them carefully to be sure they got plenty of food and water. He hired three men to help milk and sold twenty-five gallons of milk every day. He gave away about the same amount. He'd put up a sign on McMorris's general store for anyone who couldn't buy milk and needed it to come to their place. Martha gave milk to everyone who came. All they had to bring was their own bottles, jugs, or cans.

Soon people began getting robbed on the Street. Many times the robbers injured their victims and sometimes killed them. No one was safe, not even the strongest of men. Even the merchants weren't safe. Several of the newer businesses gave up after numerous robberies.

Fifty more of Abe's cows disappeared one night, leaving him with half what he'd bought. The same thing happened to all the settlers, and discontent increased to a crescendo. When they tried to talk to Sheriff Buckley, he simply shrugged. "You seen all those people milling up and down the street? And the hunnerds of tents nearby? I got two marshals 'n' that's all. What's three men gonna do in that mess? I'll tell you what they're gonna do. They're gonna get 'emselves killed. That's what." So he sat in his office and listened to complaints.

A month later seven more businesses folded. Others hired armed men to watch over them while they continued serving the public. Several people died defending their goods or themselves.

Late one night Josie erupted like a spring from the floor where she'd been sleeping. The hair on the back of her neck stood up and a low growl rumbled deep in her throat. "Shhhh," Martha whispered to the big dog. "What do you hear, Josie?" Then Martha heard a loud buzz, like many people talking and stomping around. A loud pounding on the door brought both her and Abe to their feet.

"Are you going to open the door?" Martha asked, feeling herself start to shake. "They're going to wake Willie in a minute."

Abe, who'd been reading *The Statesman* with Martha, grinned. "As many as 're out there, they'll knock the door down if we don't."

Martha peered around him as he threw open the door. She couldn't believe how many men stood out there. Maybe a hundred. "Come on out, Abe," McMorris yelled. "We're forming a vigilance committee to clean up this town and we need you."

"I better see what's happening," he told Martha. "Lock the door behind me." He stepped out into the black night, and she turned the block of wood to lock the door.

Martha sat back down and tried to read the paper but after reading a shocking article about people selling babies, she couldn't remember one thing she'd read. "Please take care of Abe, God," she prayed out loud. "He's so good and can do so much good for You. And I purely love him, Lord." She giggled ever so quietly. "But You love him even more, don't You? Thank You, Father. I could never get by one day without You."

She mended some overalls for Willie, hugged and petted Josie because the men had made her nervous, swept the floor, hugged and encouraged Josie, prayed for Abe's safety, hugged and loved Josie. "I'm getting tired," she told the faithful dog, "but I'm not going to bed until Abe comes home safely."

Sometime after midnight a soft knock on the door awakened Martha from the settle where she'd fallen asleep. She crept to the door. "Who is it?" she whispered, hoping if it wasn't Abe, the person wouldn't be able to tell she was a woman.

"It's me," Abe's dear voice called. "I promise not to eat you alive."

When she fumbled the lock open, he came in looking excited. "We're going to stop this lawlessness," he said. Then he chuckled. "Looks like my job is to keep anyone from gettin' killed. I mean the thieves 'n rustlers. Those boys are right mad."

A cold fear stabbed Martha. "How can a bunch of you stop them when the sheriff can't?"

Abe took her hand. "You just said it, Martha. That was a big bunch here tonight. We're gonna meet again tomorrow night to get organized. Then we'll divide up and watch this town day and night. We won't take the bounders to Buckley. We'll just figger out our own justice, somethin' that'll make 'em sorry fer what they did."

Martha felt fear again. "You aren't going to be a criminal in order to catch criminals, are you, Abe?"

He grinned and shook his head. "I told you that's my job. Somehow we gotta get the job done but I gotta keep 'em under control. Let's go to bed, Martha. I have a strong feelin' tomorrow's gonna be a big day."

Willie woke at dawn next morning and wanted Martha to ride with him. They quietly left the house in order not to awaken Abe, saddled Speckle and Thunder, and took off. Somehow, before the sun came over the Blue Mountains, they ended up several miles south of town, over some rolling hills.

Suddenly Willie pointed south. "Look, Martha. Look at those men herding all those cows. Are they cowboys like me, Martha? Are they?"

When Martha saw the six or eight men driving a large herd of cattle toward the mountains, her heart jumped into her throat. Were those men legally moving the cattle?

"I'm not sure, sweet," she answered calmly. "Say, I'll bet Abe's awake and hungry. I'll race you home, Willie."

She loosened Thunder's reins but didn't give him his head. The big horse would leave Willie and Speckle in the dust and she'd never do that. Better for Willie to think he and Speckle at least had a chance.

The horses took off in a fast canter which Speckle soon turned into a gallop. That little horse really ran fast for his size. Thunder idled along just ahead of Speckle. Martha let them go for awhile, then slowed Thunder to rest Speckle.

After a little while they galloped again, then trotted.

Finally they reached their place. "Let's get the horses rubbed down fast, Willie," Martha said. "Then you can give them some oats while I fix breakfast."

Abe was up and dressed when Martha rushed through the door—thankfully without Willie. "I might have bad news," she burst out as he greeted her with a hug and kiss. She told him about the cattle and riders heading toward the Blues.

"Were they pushing the cattle hard?" Abe asked.

"I don't know, Abe. I just hurried back to tell you."

"I'll gather up whoever I can and go after them," he said. "This may be exactly what we're hopin' for. Can you get breakfast ready while I'm gone?" He took off out the door without waiting for an answer.

Martha put some potatoes on to fry with bacon cut through them. Then she made hot biscuits. The least she could do would be to send him away with a full stomach. He might not get any dinner.

Abe returned and while he ate, he told Martha as much of his plans as he could with Willie sitting there.

"I got Cleve, Riley, Jackson, and six of the men who came after me last night. We're goin' for a ride." He chuckled. "I got our kin cause I figgered they won't lose their heads."

Abe kissed Martha good-bye and tousled Willie's soft hair. "I'll hurry back," he said. "Quick as we can." He pulled Martha tight to him. "Say a couple of prayers," he whispered against her ear.

Then they disappeared behind the house, heading south. Martha and Willie spent the morning weeding the vegetables. Martha prayed every time she could clear her head from Willie's chattering.

As the afternoon wore on Martha became more concerned over Abe. She sent Willie off on several errands so she could pray uninterrupted.

Just as Martha started preparing supper she heard a great commotion in the yard. "Martha, Abe's here," Willie called.

She dropped a potato on the table and ran outside. One look at Abe's dejected face told her things hadn't gone well. "What happened?" she asked.

He talked as he rubbed Ebb down. "This here's some horse," he said. "He's all heart. Really worked him today. Never found 'em, Martha. We found a lot of tracks but they sort of disappeared in the grass."

Martha hurt for him. "Are you convinced they were stolen cattle?"

He nodded. "Tomorrow I'll try to find the owner. He might be a big help to us."

Abe disappeared to care for the livestock. Martha finished supper.

The next day Abe invited Martha and Willie to ride to the far out places with him. They left right after breakfast and Abe stopped at every place that looked as if it had or could handle cattle. Most said they had cattle coming from California, Texas, or Mexico. Some had lost all their cattle in the cold and didn't want any more.

Finally they found their man. His anger spilled over Abe, Martha, and Willie when they approached him. "Yes, I lost a lot of cattle. Night before last. What do you know about it, young man? Are you looking for more?"

Abe didn't blink. "No sir, I'm trying to find the men who're rustlin' and bring them to justice. How long had you had your cattle, sir?"

"Three days. Not even long enough to get them settled down. Just brung 'em from Texas. Fine bunch of cattle. Disappeared the second night we had 'em. If I find the perpetrators I'll take the law into my own hands. They don't deserve no pussyfoot handlin' like the sheriff hands out."

"We've just formed a vigilance committee, sir. Would you like to join?"

For the first time the man appeared interested in Abe. He looked him over. "Who are you, anyway, son? Are you from the law?"

Abe grinned. "Not so's you'd notice. A bunch of us decided to forget the law and clean up our part of the world. Get rid of the rustlers, and the sticky fingers in town."

"You bet! I'd like to help do that."

"All right! We're meeting at my place tonight at dusk. Be there." Abe told the man how to get to his place, took the man's name, and the little group rode off. "I wish we'd found the man's cattle," Abe said.

That night ninety-three people gathered at Abe's place and they sat on the bank of the creek to talk. Martha sat with Abe but didn't take part in the discussion. Feelings ran high as most of the men had lost something personally to the lawless segment. They divided the men into ten groups of nine each and decided where each would guard. Then they discussed how to handle the thieves when they apprehended them.

"I say we shoot 'em on the spot," one young man shouted.

"What we gonna do, help the situation or add to the violence?" Abe asked quietly.

"We gotta give 'em a reason not to do it again," someone else offered.

"Maybe 'pends on what they did," a voice called out. "Flog 'em on the Street for stealin' somethin' worth less than one hundred dollars. Hang 'em for stealin' cattle or horses or killin' people."

"What about stealin' somethin' worth five hundred dollars?" a high voice asked.

"Ain't nothin' worth that much but cattle," someone answered.

"Isn't there some way other than hanging?" Abe asked.

Ninety-three jeers told Abe what they thought of his gentle ideas. "If you don't want to restore law and order to this town, why don't you go help the sheriff?" someone called.

"Yeah," someone else added, "we're gonna get rid of this thievin', rustlin', and killin', now, 'stead of after a bunch more of their kind comes in."

"Yeah! We'll let the varmints know this here town's off limits to the likes of them."

The meeting ended with each group starting their watch. Part sleeping the other watching.

As Abe and Martha prepared for their Bible reading and prayer they talked about the meeting. "Guess I was right about havin' to keep things under control," he said. "Some of these boys could end up as honored guest in a necktie party themselves if they don't watch out."

Chapter 6

A be fell into bed, dead tired. His group had chosen four men to watch the south side of the Street. Abe volunteered, but they'd informed him they'd start out with real men. Men who really wanted to stop crime.

He turned over in bed, then turned over again. Why did he feel so agitated? Maybe he should get up and check on the men so they wouldn't do something they'd regret.

Sleep, Abe. You can't save the West single-handed. You've done a good work getting this thing started so forget it for tonight. Sometimes drastic sins demand drastic measures. Remember Sodom and Gomorrah? Good night, Abe.

"Thanks, Lord," Abe whispered, feeling a huge load leave his heart. Why hadn't he handed it over to God in the beginning? "Thanks again, Father," he whispered. "You'll be doin' a better job watchin' than I would, won't You? And You don't need sleep. Good night, Father." He leaned over and kissed Martha's sweet sleeping lips, and fell into a sound sleep.

The next morning Abe told Martha what the Lord had said to him.

"Do you think that means there's going to be bloodshed over this?" Martha asked.

"I'm sure," Abe said. "When men find an easy way to get rich quick they don't quit just because someone asks them to."

As soon as Abe and his three helpers got through with his chores he headed for the Street to see if anything had happened. Not seeing anything, he hurried to the home of one of the men who'd been on duty. "Hey, Abe, come on in," the man said. "Wait'll you hear what happened. Someone caught some cattle rustlers red-handed. If you ride out south a ways you might see four varmints swingin' in a tree. Now, I ain't no idee who could a done it, but those boys won't be doin' nuthin' again fer a long long time."

Abe felt his breakfast coming up and tore out the door. Outside, he fell to his knees, then sat on the ground, feeling a little better. "Lord, is this the way You want it to happen?" he asked.

You're all right Abe. Get up and go home.

Abe didn't wait to ask the man if anything had happened on the Street.

He and Martha walked downtown later in the day and everyone had heard about the hanging. All were shocked, but most rejoiced, hoping this would slow the violence that seemed to escalate every day.

Abe worked with Martha in the vegetable gardens that day.

That night Abe joined the group watching the Street. They'd decided to have all nine men working together in each group for safety. Four patrolled each end of the Street and one watched near the center. They walked and talked quietly for hours, taking turns waiting in the center. Just before dawn all Abe could think about was getting through and hitting the bed for a couple of hours.

Abe, you need to be alert. Look around.

Suddenly Abe didn't feel even a little sleepy. "Come on," he said softly to the others, "let's pick up our pace a little. No telling what'll happen around here before mornin'."

Less than fifteen minutes later Abe saw a movement at the side of the gold expert's place. He pointed silently and all four moved toward the building. The man seemed to be leaving the place. Abe and another man dashed around the building so they could corner him between the buildings, two on each side.

"Stop right where you are!" Abe yelled when they were all in place. "We're a posse and we're armed. Don't move or reach for anything!"

The man's hands flew into the air.

Slowly the group of men closed in until they circled him, just out of reach. "State your name and what your business is here at this time of night."

"I'm Joseph Winieke. I own this place and decided to check on it. What do you think you're doing?"

Abe peered through the near-darkness. Sure enough, it was the man who'd taken care of their gold. "He's right, boys," Abe said. "Relax." He turned to Winieke. "Sorry, sir. We're a group of men who've decided to watch the town and try to curb the violence. Do you realize it's not safe for you to come to the Street alone in the night?"

"I know. That's why I'm here checking my place."

With unspoken agreement, the men rushed away from the man's place of business and headed off down the street. "That was purty embarrassin'," one of the men said.

Nothing more happened so when day broke they all went home. As Abe hurried home, he grumbled. "Now why did You tell me to wake up, God? You figger I needed to be embarrassed a little?"

No, Abe, I figgered if you were wide awake you could prevent a terrible accident—and you did.

Abe felt properly chastised for scolding God. "Sorry, Father. I had no call to holler at You. I know you don't make mistakes." He grinned. "But I sure do."

As far as Abe could find, nothing had happened in any of the patrols that night. He slept until about ten o'clock, got up, and helped Martha in the vegetable gardens.

Just before they quit working for dinner, Jackson and Nellie rode in from the back. "We got lots of news," Jackson said. "Nellie gets to tell hers first."

Nellie blushed and her hand fluttered to her stomach. "Well, Jackson and I are going to have a baby early next year." Her eyes flitted from Abe to Martha and back. "I hope you're glad."

Martha jumped up and hugged her. "Of course we're glad. I'm purely thrilled to death, Nellie."

Abe put his arm over her shoulder. "I'm glad too, Nellie. Maybe a little jealous." He dropped his other arm over Martha and pulled her close. "I'm just a hopin' we'll be next."

Nellie laughed out loud and threw her arms around both Martha and Abe. "Oh, thank you, thank you," she said.

"I was scared you'd be mad about the baby, 'cause Jackson doesn't work like he should."

Abe laughed. "That's between the two of you, Nellie. Maybe the baby will make him feel more responsible and he'll get to work."

"I'm goin' to," Jackson said. "I'm goin' to even before it's born." He chuckled. " 'Course them nuggets you gave us'll last a long time."

Abe shook his head. "Not as long as you might think. Better save them for emergencies."

Martha fixed potato soup for everyone before going back to work. Abe felt proud of her. He'd been wanting bad to start their family but hesitated to mention it to her for fear she'd think he was complaining. He sighed. It would just have to happen when it happened.

After supper that evening, Martha and Abe read *The Statesman* for a little while before Abe had to leave. They laughed at an announcement that said the men at the mines who subscribed to the paper shouldn't dilute their gold dust with sand when they paid. It also said that the school opened July 10 with fifty-seven pupils and, due to a generous benefactor, was doing exceptionally well.

When darkness covered the world again, Abe kissed Martha and Willie good-bye and headed for the Street. The night passed quietly and Abe hurried home. He'd eat breakfast, take care of the animals, and go to bed for awhile.

After feeding the horses, he hurried out to the cows in the pasture. But they weren't there! He walked around awhile searching, then admitted the cows had disappeared. A hundred and fifty cows rustled while he watched the Street! That was not only a big loss but a huge insult. Now he was mad enough to string up the rustlers himself—well maybe not. He hoped not anyway.

"What do I do now, Lord? Go after those vermin?"

You're doing fine, Abe. Keep up the good work.

"I don't feel like I'm doing fine, Lord. What are we supposed to do for milk now? And those cows were going to start a big herd for us. I sort of pictured a large Noble dairy in a couple of years."

Don't worry about tomorrow, Abe. Why don't you get one cow to provide your milk right now? You take care of Martha and Willie today. I'll worry about your tomorrows.

"Thanks, Lord," Abe said. Then he wondered if that thanks had been a tiny bit sarcastic. He'd better go tell Martha what happened. She had to find out.

"You men will get this town all straightened out soon," Martha said when he told her. "Then we can have all the cows we want."

That afternoon Abe rode around looking for anyone with cows. Seemed there weren't very many anymore. When he came to a place with seven cows he stopped to ask.

"Last week I got home from drivin' three hundred head of cattle from California," the man said. "Long hard trip. Two nights ago someone walked off with the whole herd. I can tell you I was mighty glad to see those rustlers swinging on the end of a rope, even though they weren't the ones got mine. Hope whoever strung 'em up gets the ones got mine."

Abe almost told the man he thoroughly agreed with his thinking. *Better not.* "Would you like to join a group of citizens trying to cut out crime?"

The man wanted to, so Abe told him to come to his house at dusk.

That night nearly one hundred and fifty men showed up at the meeting. Abe stood before the group. "You all here to stamp out crime?" he called.

A mighty roar answered him so they divided into fifteen groups, hoping to completely cover the near area. As dark descended, each group went to its assigned post.

That night Abe's group apprehended two youths hauling booze out of Galbraith's saloon. Part of the group detained the young men, while the rest put back the dozen bottles of whiskey and nailed the place shut for security.

"Know what happens to people like you?" Abe asked the boys. They both shook their heads, barely visible in the dark. "You get a public beating tomorrow morning at ten o'clock." Even in the dark he saw the youngest one wilt.

The committee didn't turn the boys over to the sheriff, but held them themselves. And promptly at ten o'clock Galbraith himself administered seven lashes with an ox whip to each one. "Yer lucky you ain't on that tree south of town," someone yelled as the victims limped away. "I seen three more carcasses on it this mornin'."

Abe hurried to his friend, one of the group who watched the farms south of town. "Yeah, we got another batch," the man said. "Caught 'em with couple hunnerd cattle headed fer the Blues. Almost made it too. If'n we was to go up there we might find a lot more'n we expect."

"Let's go," Abe said. "Let's get a lot of men and go after them."

They didn't go at that time so Abe went home for a little sleep. About the time he woke up, Sheriff Buckley arrived looking upset. "I want to know what's going on," he told Abe. "Looks to me like things are gettin' out of hand."

Abe grinned. " 'Pears to me things've been out of hand for some time now. Everyone who's gotten cattle this summer's lost it again."

The sheriff fidgeted from one foot to the other. "However that may be, I was wonderin' if you know who's taking the law into their own hands."

"Would you like to sit, Sheriff? Right there on that chair." Abe thought for a moment. He'd never tell Buckley anything, yet he didn't want to appear rude. "If I knew for sure, I'd have to thank them. Those varmints got two hundred cattle from me and I didn't like that too much. What you plannin' to do about all this?"

The big whiskery man shook his head. "It's tough, Abe. I ain't got no help—only the city marshals. No tellin' how many people 're out there wreckin' our town. What can one man do?"

Abe rubbed his clean-shaven chin. "Well, you might find out who's workin' for you and join 'em."

After muttering a few more excuses, the man left. Abe felt so good he jumped into the air, stretching his arms high. They'd clean this town up whether the sheriff liked it or not. He cut three thick slices of fresh home-made bread and spread strawberry jam over them. Ummmm. He'd never tasted better bread—or jam. What would he ever do without his own little Martha? She was everything any man could want and more.

He hurried out to tell her about the sheriff's visit.

—∭—

In the next weeks thirty-three more bodies appeared on the "Hanging Tree" south of Walla Walla, and two hundred and seventeen people received beatings. Three were young girls and no one complained when Galbraith gave them only two light lashes each with the ox whip.

Not one of the patrols caught anyone for over a week. Abe found and bought fifty cows, ten milking and the others not yet bred. He hired only one man to help milk the ten. The new livestock stayed where they belonged and no one reported anything missing. Abe began to feel pretty good. "Whattaya think, Lord? We about got it licked? How much longer should we keep our vigilance committee on duty?"

Always be vigilant, Abe. About everything.

"What does that mean, Lord? Shall we still watch the town every night? That's purty hard work, Y'know. Missing sleep and all."

Abe didn't receive an answer to his question so decided to let the men decide when to quit.

One afternoon a man and woman walked up to Abe as he helped Martha weed the vegetables. "Hello," he said. "Something I can do for you?"

"I hope so," the friendly-looking man said. "Someone in one of the stores said you're Abram Noble."

Abe grinned and stuck out his hand. "I reckon someone's right. But no one told me who you are."

The man grinned and his eyes showed a love that few do. "I'm Thomas Dorland and this is my wife, Rachel."

Somehow those names sounded familiar, but Abe couldn't figure out how.

The red-headed woman stepped closer to Abe. "I'm Martha's good friend and I can't wait to see her. Can you tell me where she is right now?"

Abe turned to look down toward the end of the garden to find Martha hurrying toward them. The other woman held out her arms and so did Martha. Abe thought they'd never turn loose of each other.

Thomas Dorland must have thought so too, for he stepped to the women's side. "Martha, remember me? I'm Tom."

Martha and Rachel pulled apart, and Martha held her hand to Tom. "I'm so glad to see you both," she said. "I can't tell you how many times I've dreamed about you, Rachel. I've missed you terribly. But whatever are you doing here?"

Tom laughed. "We're looking for a place to live—and set up business. Got any ideas?"

Chapter 7

Y ou mean here?" Martha asked, her eyes large with surprise. "I
thought you settled in Oregon City." Then her eyes glowed with
understanding. She threw her arms around Rachel again. "Yes! You
have to settle right here in Walla Walla and doctor our people." Martha
couldn't believe her eyes and ears. Rachel was going to be near and be her
friend again. She hugged Rachel again. "I can't remember ever being so
happy to see anyone before. I purely can't." Then her eyes met Abe's. He
looked amused.

"Except when Abe went to California. I'm sorry, Abe. I must make you
acquainted. Rachel this is the most perfect, wonderful, handsome husband
in the world—mine. Abe meet my dearest friend, Rachel Butler—I guess it's
Dorland now. And her husband, Tom. He's a doctor, Abe. A doctor who
really cares."

Abe and Tom shook hands. "You lookin' for a donation land claim, Dr.
Dorland?" Abe asked.

Tom shook his head. "I never seem to have time to work ground, Abe.
And call me Tom. Everyone else does." He shifted his weight from one foot
to another and pulled Rachel close. "We just need a little place to build a
house with room for an office." He looked around. "Where's Josie, Martha?
She's one of my favorite patients. I hope you still have her."

Martha looked around. "She's fine, probably sleeping in the shade of the
house. We'll see her soon." Then Martha remembered their lots on the
Street. "They could have one of our lots, couldn't they, Abe? Seems we're
never going to use them." Her heart felt so light it might lift her from the
ground. "I guess you don't have any children?" she asked Rachel.

Rachel and Tom both laughed. "I guess we do," Tom said. "We have a
little boy twenty-one months old and nine-month-old twin boys." He nodded meaningfully. "Yes, Martha, we have children."

"What about you two?" Rachel asked. "I'll bet you can't beat our record."

Martha shook her head, feeling embarrassed. "We don't have any yet.
We're just waiting for the Lord to start sending them."

"Yes," Abe agreed. "We'll take all we can get." Suddenly he looked at
Martha. "What are we doin', keeping these people out here in the hot sun?

404

You folks come on in and we'll give you a cold drink of water—or milk."

Neither Rachel nor Tom moved to follow Abe and Martha. "Come on," Martha called. "You must be thirsty—or hungry."

"Truth is," Tom said, "we have quite a crew with us.

Not only our three young'uns, but Rachel's father. Do you remember Nate Butler, Martha?"

"Of course I do." Martha felt a strange lump in her throat. Tom hadn't mentioned Rachel's mother. "Bring him along. He's probably thirsty too. What about your mother, Rachel?"

"She died when we first got to Oregon City. But we also have a woman with two children and an older woman who insisted on coming too."

This began to sound like a bunch of people. "Oh. . .well, bring them all. We have lots of milk right now. I can make sandwiches, too, if you're hungry."

After asking if Martha was sure, the two left to bring back everyone. They arrived with several wagons and tired oxen an hour later. Abe hurried to help put the wagons in a convenient place and to care for the oxen.

Tom and Josie found each other, both acting as if they'd finally found their dearest friend. Tom had saved Josie's life on the Trail when coyotes tore her stomach open and her intestines nearly out.

Martha invited them in and took the oldest baby, Tommy. She loved the three babies on sight. She'd just love Rachel's babies until God sent her one of her own. Two larger children raced around as if they'd been confined for a long time. Martha knew better, for she'd walked all the way across the country with Willie.

"These two are Joel and Evie," Rachel told Martha. "Joel's six and Evie's three. They've been our best travelers." A dark, plump, pretty woman approached and stood beside Rachel. "And this is their mother, Melissa Witlow. Her husband was killed in an accident so she lives with us. She's been my lifesaver on the trip and several months before."

Mr. Butler looked just as he'd looked on the Trail, but much happier than Martha expected. She rushed into his arms and he held her tight. "Little Martha," he said softly. He turned to Abe. "I hope you know what a wonderful person this little girl is. She brightened our long hard pilgrimage more than anyone else."

"I know," Abe said. "She brightens my life all day every day." He raised his eyes upward. *Thank You again, God. Only You could have given me a wife like Martha.*

Mr. Butler started, looking around. "Where's Cindy?" he asked Rachel. "Martha has to meet her."

"I'm here, Nate." A petite, gray-haired woman dashed up to Mr. Butler, slid under his arm as if she belonged there, and held a hand to Martha. "I'm

Cynthia Buchanan—I mean Butler." She looked up at Nate with eyes filled with love. "We're newlyweds," she explained. "We got married on the way. We stopped in the Dalles to rest after that horrible Barlow Road—" She giggled like a young girl. "And ended up married." The woman looked so happy and sweet that Martha couldn't resist hugging her.

After giving them all milk to drink, she started fixing supper. They must be hungry.

"Why don't we walk over to the Street and have a look at our lots?" Abe suggested when he returned from caring for the animals. "If you're interested in one of them, we might as well get going on your house and office. We can build a log buildin' or outta boards, whatever you want. We have a sash factory now and several lumber companies. I 'spect we can have your home and office built in three weeks."

Martha decided supper could wait. She hadn't started anything cooking yet so it wouldn't burn.

Tom didn't seem too excited about the lots on the Street.

"I guess those lots weren't what you had in mind," Abe said as they started back to the house.

Tom grinned ruefully and shook his head. "We thought Walla Walla would be primitive and in a way it is, but I can't believe all the people! More people crowd the Street than we had on our main street in Oregon City."

The group walked on. "The gold frenzy in Orofino caused the population explosion here," Martha explained. "They're all here to cash in on that in one way or another."

When they reached home, Rachel and Melissa helped Martha cook some steaks, potatoes, gravy, beets, and beet greens, with applesauce for dessert. She also served thick slices of homemade bread with lots of butter.

After they finished they talked in the main room. "Do you have many doctors here?" Tom asked. "And do you know anything about their practices?"

Abe shook his head. "We know there are some because they advertise in *The Statesman*, our newspaper, but we've never gone to a doctor. We never needed one—thanks, Lord." He got up, picked up a newspaper and handed it to Tom. "This might help you know what's out there. You can keep it if you'd like."

After a bit the newcomers returned to their wagons for the night.

The next morning, Abe and Martha both milked and cared for the cows, and Abe hauled milk to the Street where he sold it. Then the people began coming for free milk. Martha had given away twelve gallons when Rachel came into the house.

"Are you selling milk from your house?" she asked.

"No, we're giving it away. What we can't give away, we sell."

Rachel seemed unable to understand. "How can you afford to do that?" she asked. "Isn't that the way you make your living?"

Martha felt really good about what they were doing, but felt it better not to tell anyone about the gold. "We've had some wonderful blessings so we're sharing. That's all."

As the group ate breakfast, Tom looked at Rachel. She cleared her throat. "Tom's trying to get me to ask something for him. We talked last night and we'd like a little more land than the lot you showed us. We'd also like a little more quiet. We wondered if you could sell us an acre of your land somewhere near the front?"

Martha looked at Abe who shook his head. "Sorry, Tom. This is a donation land claim and we can't sell any until we've lived on it long enough to satisfy the government." He thought a moment. "We might be able to build you a house and office though. We could fence it off so it would be separate, but it would still have to be in our name."

"Hey! That sounds great to me. We could rent it. What do you think, Angel?" Tom asked Rachel.

She nodded. "I don't care, just so I get to be close to Martha."

"Let's get to work then," Abe said. "But you won't rent it. It'll just be yours. I guess we can help our new doctor that much."

The men left to start planning the new building project and the women cleaned up the dishes and children.

When they'd nearly finished, Nate Butler appeared. "Are you about through with my wife?" he asked. "I'm missing her."

Cynthia rushed into his arms. She giggled softly. "Aren't you embarrassed to act like this in front of the ladies?"

As he shook his dark but graying head, Martha thought his soft blue eyes looked terribly kind, even more than she remembered. "How can I be ashamed?" he asked his new little wife, "when I'm so proud to call you mine?" Holding Cynthia close he turned to Martha. "Cindy and I decided we'd like to take out a donation claim. Think we'd be eligible?"

Martha assured him they would. "Would you like me to take you to the office? But that's getting it backwards. First you find the place you want, then go in. It takes only a few minutes and the place will be yours."

The two hurried away, arm in arm.

"Where did your father ever find someone like that? So sweet? And also so healthy?" Martha asked.

Rachel and Melissa broke into laughter. "You're looking at the world's best fool for God," Melissa said. "Cynthia was brought to Tom and Rachel to care for while she was sick. She was the last straw in a big haystack of people Rachel and Tom took in." Melissa laughed merrily. "They decided to leave to get away from all of us, but Cynthia and I refused to be left behind."

Rachel laughed with her. "She's not quite right. We waited to go until the rest of the children left us and until Tom's patients got well. We didn't leave anyone needing us—except Mrs. Gump." At that name the girls both burst into laughter again.

"Mrs. Gump is a human vulture," Melissa said. "When you see her coming, get out of the way. Rachel had a sewing machine and that woman brought her a trunk of cloth to sew into clothes every week. Even the week the twins were born."

When they had finished the dishes and swept the floor, they sat down in the main room to watch the babies.

Josie insisted on staying beside the little ones, licking their faces and keeping them in the back of the room. When Gabriel and Jesse grabbed her fur and pulled up beside her, she stood still as if she knew they weren't steady on their feet.

Soon Tom and Abe came in. "We have it all staked out, Angel," Tom said. "We'll have a house of our own soon."

Then Nate and Cynthia returned. "The places close in are all taken," Nate said. "We need to be near. Besides we wanted to be close to all of you."

Abe nodded. "Nothin' left close in all right. Any special reason you need close in?"

"Yes. I'm a blacksmith and need to be where people can find me. We was wondering if you want to sell that lot or was it just to Tom and Rachel?"

"Funny, I was thinkin' on the same thing," Abe said. He looked at Martha. "What do you think?"

"We'll still have one left," Martha said. "Why not let them have it?"

"All right!" Abe said. "We'll build your place too."

The next weeks were busy for everyone. They decided to build Nate and Cynthia's first, as it would be a quicker job. The children spent their days playing outside with Josie and each other. The women kept food cooked for the men who worked hard on Nate's place.

One afternoon a strange Indian walked into Martha's house. For a moment she felt frightened, then remembered her friends, Gray Wolf and his sons. No one could be nicer or truer. She met the tall bronze man in the middle of the room. "May I help you? Do you need some food?"

"Come," the Indian said. Then he added a bunch of Nez Percé words Martha couldn't understand. She managed to sort out the Indian word for hurt. "Is someone hurt?" she asked.

The Indian nodded and repeated his only English word. "Come."

"I think I better go with him," she told Melissa who was helping her do the washing. "Can you take over here?"

Martha walked one step and ran two to keep up with the tall Indian who hurried toward the Street. She tried to learn more from him but he didn't understand any of her words. She'd thought she understood Nez Percé a little but couldn't make out his words at all.

Following the Indian, Martha ended up at the new jail and went in behind him. The marshall met them. "Stop right there, redskin," the man said gruffly.

The Indian stopped. So did Martha. "What's going on?" she asked the man.

The marshall grinned. "You're the ones who just came in. Whaddaya want?"

Martha looked at the Indian and decided there'd be no help from him. "Have you just brought in an Indian?" she asked.

"We've always just brought in an Indian," the man growled. "This here place is full of 'em. Too bad all they can do is grunt like an animal."

"Let this man take me to the one he knows," Martha pleaded.

The guard stepped back. "Ain't no skin off my nose. Make yerself t' home."

The Indian's black eyes met Martha's. She nodded and he took off down the dark hall. He hurried as if he knew where he was going. Suddenly he stopped in front of one of the steel cages and faced it, standing tall and straight. The person inside could barely be called a man—he wasn't more than fourteen or fifteen years old.

"Hello," Martha ventured. The boy inside said nothing. His eyes looked like those of a trapped animal. She couldn't tell if he didn't understand her or was too frightened to talk. "Can I help you?" she asked. Still nothing. She'd have to try something else. She said hello in the Nez Percé language.

His eyes brightened ever so slightly and he said a few soft words. Martha listened closely and understood two words. *Brave hurt.* Did he hurt someone? She held her hand out in a stay motion to the Indian who had sought her help. Then she ran to the guard. "Come tell me what this boy is accused of," she said, then ran back.

"Well, that'n's been drinking a lot of firewater—if you know what that is."

"I know," Martha said. "Is that a crime?"

" 'Tis with them savages. They go plumb wild."

"What did this one do?" Martha asked.

"Well, some feller who just arrived from California got knocked on the head and his nuggets all stoled. This Injun done it. He soon walked into Ball and Stone Saloon flashing the money around. Soon's the man feels better he can identify the savage."

Martha couldn't believe the man calling this justice. "That's not even circumstantial evidence, sir. Lots of people have nuggets—or money."

The man stood tall and looked down on Martha. "It ain't evidence? Well, how come is it your bunch of vigilantes don't even wait to identify the perpetrator? Just string 'em up without waitin' fer nothing."

For a second Martha felt cornered. Then she remembered what those men did wasn't her responsibility. She smiled at the rough-looking man. "They aren't my vigilantes," she said. "But from what I hear they only do that when they catch the men actually herding the stolen cattle out of the valley."

"I don't see no difference, ma'am."

"Well, I do. Mind if I go back and try to talk to the man again?"

The man dropped to a nearby chair. "Go ahead. It's a free country."

Martha hurried back to the cage, the free Indian following her. "Can you talk to me?" she asked the boy in the cell. He didn't answer. Suddenly she had an idea. "Are you Nez Percé?" she asked. He shrugged and looked confused.

"Help me help this boy, Father," she prayed out loud. "Help me to understand him before something awful happens to him. Thank You in Jesus' name. I love You. Amen." Suddenly she felt lighter and freer than since she'd come. She turned back to the frightened boy. "Cayuse?" The boy nodded his face, showing joy at this bit of communication.

But she didn't feel very relieved. "Lord, how am I going to understand him when I don't know his language at all?"

Then the boy said something to her. And she understood some of it! Somehow she knew they took his nuggets—his only three nuggets. She smiled at him, held up three fingers, and motioned with both hands for him to keep talking.

He said several more guttural words. He said them over and over. Then somehow she knew he hadn't hurt the man but had seen the man who did. "Thank You, Lord," she cried. "You purely are helping me understand this boy." She reached through the cage and patted him on the arm. "I'll be right back," she said and ran after the jailer again. "This boy didn't do it," she said. "But he saw it happen. He didn't take the nuggets, either, and you'd better give his back to him." She almost added that the man who did it was white, but she couldn't say something she wasn't sure about.

The burly man looked surprised. "You really bin talkin' to 'im, ain't you? How you learn all that Injun stuff, anyhow?"

Martha shook her head. "He's Cayuse and I don't understand their language. You have to turn this boy loose, Mr. Gilliam. I asked God to help, and He wouldn't let me understand something untrue."

The man sneered and shook his head. "Too bad God don't stop all the crime around here. But since He don't, I guess we'll have to figger out who done it all by ourselves."

Martha decided to go get Abe from down the street where he was working on Nate Butler's house and blacksmith shop. Men listened to him much better. When she told him what happened, he asked if Gray Wolf would understand the Cayuse boy.

"I'm not sure. Should I get Thunder and go find Gray Wolf?" Abe told her to do that while he went on over to the jail.

Chapter 8

As Abe hurried to the jail he shook his head. This town would straighten out a lot sooner if everyone didn't try to lay everything on the Indians. He had no doubt the Indians did some of the things the law accused them of, but it seemed the white men couldn't wait to blame every crime on them.

When Abe entered the rough wood building, the marshall grumbled at him. "That little woman a' yours keeps purty busy, don't she? What she think she can do about this here redskin?"

"Hello. How are you, Marshall Gilliam? Beautiful summer day, don't you think?" Abe ambled down the dark aisle toward the cages where they kept the prisoners. The jailer followed. Soon Abe spotted a tall Indian outside a cell occupied by a very young boy. Looked like it could be father and son. This must be the one.

He turned back to the officer. "Martha tells me you have no reason to hold this young man. She also tells me he didn't do it but knows who did. Why don't we get him to help us find the guilty man?"

A dark scowl passed over the man's face. "Abe, you've been around the barn a few times. Don't ya know what he's doin'? 'Course he ain't gonna say he done it when there's redskin lovers around. Let him out to help us find the one who done it, he'll be gone, just like that."

Abe forced the man to meet his gaze. "Martha's right, then. You don't know who did it."

The man insisted the boy turned up with the exact number of nuggets immediately after the attack and robbery.

"How many people were on the Street at that same hour, do you suppose, had three nuggets? Did you check them all out? Turn him loose now."

Before the man figured out an answer, Martha rushed down the dark hall to the cell. "I couldn't find Gray Wolf or the others," she puffed. "But let's go talk to him." She approached the cell again.

The boy came as close as he could. He said something, and a moment later Martha understood enough to realize he'd asked if he could go home. She turned to Abe. "He wants to go home."

Abe turned to the marshall. "Better set him loose, 'fore the U.S. Government finds out you're holdin' an Indian without cause."

The man looked angry for a second, then shrugged. He pulled a long key chain from his pocket, unlocked the cage door, jerked the boy from the cell, and shoved him down the hall. The boy took off running and disappeared out the front door.

The jailer looked at Abe. "See? He done just what I said."

Abe hurried to the door and looked both ways. Then he saw the boy halfway down the block, still running. He stepped outside and gave a long loud whistle. The boy looked over his shoulder and kept going. "Hey! You! Wait up!" Abe motioned for the boy to come back. He didn't wait to see what the boy would do but ran toward him as fast as he could. And the boy waited! Abe could hardly believe his eyes. What would he do when he got there? He couldn't talk to the boy. A few moments later he reached the boy and stopped beside him. He held his hand out as if to shake hands but the boy didn't reciprocate. Then Abe heard Martha puffing up beside them.

The boy looked at her and smiled broadly. He said a whole paragraph of something. A moment later, Martha turned radiant eyes to Abe. "His name's Little Rain, and he can help us find the man who hurt and robbed the man."

Abe felt so excited he could hardly talk. "How's he going to do that?"

Martha said something to the boy but he only shook his head. "He doesn't understand me," she told Abe.

The boy said something else to Martha, pointed east down the Street, and started walking briskly. "He's taking us to the man who did the robbery," Martha told Abe as they followed him.

When they reached the building of the gold expert, the boy led them inside and pointed at the man who stood at the rough wood counter talking to a young couple.

Martha looked shocked. "He's saying Joseph Winieke did it," she said. "Do you believe it, Abe?"

Abe pointed at the man while looking at the boy. The boy nodded and motioned for Abe to go to the man. Abe moved over a bit and waited for the couple to finish and leave.

The couple didn't leave but the gold expert looked up. "C'n I help you folks? I'm jest talkin' to these people."

Abe put his hand on the boy's back and urged him to the counter. Martha followed. "Do you know this boy?" Abe asked Joseph Winieke.

The man looked at the Indian boy a moment. "Can't be sure. Might. Most everyone comes in here sooner or later. Hey! Ain't you the one brought in a big bag of nuggets?"

"Yes, but this isn't about that. The law picked up this boy for beating up and robbing a man of three nuggets this morning. The boy says you did it."

The man didn't bat an eyelash. "Yeah, I did it. Hope that's the last time too. Third time he walked off with my nuggets. If he does it a hunnerd times I'll get 'em back a hunnerd times. Might get rough one of these days too. A feller gets kinda tired of everthin' he has gettin' stoled."

Martha gave a little cry and hugged the boy tight. The boy said something and she nodded. Then she pointed at Joseph Winieke. "The man took it from him," she told the boy speaking clearly. "He just got it back."

The boy said something else and Martha nodded, then gave him a little push, smiling tenderly.

Abe watched, thinking what a fine mother she'd make one day soon. He took Martha's hand. "Let's go back to that officer and tell him what happened."

The man hardly commented when they told him what had happened. "Maybe you should ought to find the man who got beat and make him an example," Abe said as they walked out the door.

They walked over to where they were building Nate and Cynthia Butler's home and blacksmith shop. "See?" Abe said, proudly showing Martha. "Coming right along. I guess they'll be moving into the house in a week. Said they want me to build 'em some furniture."

He steered Martha toward their place. "Guess I could make us a good living now making furniture with all the new people in town. Hard to know whether to try farmin' and buildin' furniture both or to spend all my time on one 'er the other."

"You should do whatever you purely enjoy the most," Martha said.

They approached their place, which Abe knew would be full of people. He grinned and returned to the subject. "Trouble is I don't know which I like best. I enjoy 'most everything I do, my little Martha."

Josie met them before they reached the house, delighted to see them. "I suppose you got too rambunctious and they threw you out of the house," Martha said, petting the big dog as they hurried on.

Melissa opened the door as Abe reached for it. "It must have been some big emergency," she said. "I have supper ready and everyone else is here. Hurry and get washed."

Abe told them what happened as they ate. "It's not the first time we've rescued the Indians from them," he said. "They don't seem to care who did it, just so they can catch someone, preferably not white."

Tom shook his light brown head. "They all forget the Indians were here first and we're the intruders, don't they?"

"Oh!" Martha's face looked animated. "I just remembered something purely important. That Indian boy is Cayuse and I don't understand much of their language. So I asked God to help me understand him—and He did! He really did. I didn't understand it all and it took me a bit to figure it out but I understood enough to get him out. He's with his family now, wherever they are. Thank You, Lord."

Abe grinned. "And the sheriff and marshall are disliking us more all the time."

Nate and Cynthia moved into their bare house a week later. The men spent another week building Nate's blacksmith shop, then started on Tom and Rachel's place. Melissa would live with Tom and Rachel for awhile at least.

Abe and his hired man milked the cows each morning, and Melissa helped Martha strain and give away many gallons of the milk. Abe hauled a lot to the general stores and saloons. The hay was ripening and looked good.

Abe joined the crew building Tom and Rachel's house each morning as soon as he could. Cleve and Riley worked every minute they could. Jackson worked most of each day, after arriving late, and was the only person working for wages. The Dorland house was going to be similar to the one they had in Oregon City, only larger. They used narrow boards, called clapboards, on the outside. The house looked colonial with two stories and large round pillars in the front.

About three weeks later, they'd nearly finished the roof. One day as the men shingled the steep roof, Jackson started to slide down. "Help!" he screamed. "I'm goin' down."

Riley dropped his hammer, ran the twenty feet to Jackson, and dove on top of him. Jackson nearly stopped, then both young men began to slide. Abe watched a moment in horror, then ran the thirty feet and threw himself on Jackson who was closer to the edge. Jackson stopped, but somehow Abe's jump flipped Riley around and he disappeared over the edge of the roof, eighteen feet above the ground.

Jackson struggled. "Lie still," Abe commanded looking around for something to anchor to. Cleve tossed Abe a rope and nailed the other end to the other side of the roof. Then he dropped his hammer and followed Tom down the ladder, barely touching the steps.

Abe maneuvered Jackson around. "Grab that rope," he said. Jackson did. "Now walk up the rope to the ridge, then to the end to the ladder." Jackson did as Abe told him and climbed down the ladder.

Abe couldn't wait to get on the ground before talking to God. "Lord, please, You gotta help Riley," he pleaded. "He's a real man, Lord, loves his wife and family, works hard, and he loves You too. Remember how he helped me build furniture for the church? Thanks, Lord. Thanks for caring for Riley."

Abe pulled himself to the ridge and down the ladder.

Racing to the front of the house, he found Tom bending over Riley. Riley seemed very still.

"Do you know anything?" Abe whispered into Tom's ear.

"He's alive with a strong pulse and breathing well," Tom said. Then seeming to forget anyone was there he continued examining Riley.

Abe stood with his hands clenched into fists. "Thank You, Lord," he whispered quietly. "When we put ourselves in Your hands we know we'll be all right."

"Think you'd be able to help me, Abe?" Tom asked a moment later. "All I can find wrong is a broken leg and a big bump on the left side of his head."

Abe dropped to his knees beside Riley. "Just tell me what to do. I'm strong and steady."

Cleve stood watching the doctor work on his son. Watching his lips move slightly, Abe knew he was praying. Jackson seemed to have disappeared. Tom's eyes met Cleve's. "We're going to need some soft cloths and strong straight boards for splints. Could you get them, Cleve? Maybe at the general store?"

Cleve looked delighted. "I'll be back in a few minutes," he said over his shoulder as he hurried off.

Tom grinned. "I guess that's what you call doing two jobs at once. I thought it would be easier on him if he didn't watch us trying to get the bone back. Can you hold his body perfectly still while I work on his leg?"

Abe, on his knees, leaned over Riley and grabbed him under the arms and tightened his muscles. "I got him." As Abe looked up to see what Tom would do next he noticed a ring of people around them watching. He started to tell them to move on but held his tongue. Maybe at least part of the people were genuinely concerned. Besides it wouldn't do any good to tell them to leave. At least the people weren't making any noise, not even talking.

"All right," Tom said, "hang on—tight." Abe tightened his grip on Riley. Tom pulled and twisted until Abe could hardly keep Riley still. Tom rested a moment. He grinned at Abe. "Just as well Riley's sleeping through this, wouldn't you say?" Abe nodded but he also wished Riley would wake up. It just didn't seem right, him being unconscious like this.

Tom kept wrenching on Riley while Abe did his best to keep the young man from moving. After a time that seemed forever, Abe heard a popping sound, then Tom relaxed. "We did it, Pard. I never had a better helper. You must have iron muscles."

Abe grinned. "Been working purty hard for a long time. Guess that helps. Think Riley'll be all right now? I'd like to see him wake up purty soon." Abe looked up to see Cleve standing nearby, his arms full of things and a big smile across his face.

He handed the things to Tom. "It felt like McMorris took forever, but seems I made it just right."

Tom began wrapping the leg with the cloth. With Abe's help they soon had it well padded. Then the young doctor fastened the small but strong planed poles around the leg with twine Cleve had brought.

Tom jumped to his feet and Abe did the same. "Let's get him home," Tom said. "Where's that?"

"We'll take him to my place," Cleve said. "It's a little closer'n theirs. If he wants to go on we'll take him." He looked closely at his quiet son. "He's gonna be all right, ain't he, Doc?"

Tom nodded. "The swelling is receding already, but I want to stay with him until he's awake and doing better." He looked around. "Is there a carriage or something to take him to your place?"

Cleve snorted. "Not many carriages around this town. Most everyone uses wagons."

"I have a wagon down the street," an older man said from the watching crowd. "It has springs and we can fix up a bed in a couple minutes."

Cleve nodded.

"Thanks," Tom said, "that'll be great."

Abe thanked God as he walked behind the wagon. *Life would be pretty scary without You,* he said silently. *You're mighty good to us puny little creatures.*

Twenty minutes later Tom, Cleve, and Abe laid Riley on a feather bed in Cleve and Mandy's cabin across the creek from Abe and Martha's place. "You go on with whatever you need to do," Tom said. "Mandy and I'll watch Riley. I expect him to come around anytime now. Certainly before supper."

Abe hurried across the creek to Martha. After her hug and kiss, Abe pushed her back. "Heard about Riley?" he asked.

"No!" She looked as if she might get hysterical but settled down. "Has something happened to him?"

Abe nodded and quickly went on. "Broke his leg, but he's goin' to be all right. Fell off Tom's roof awhile ago. We took him to Cleve and Mandy's just now." Should he tell her the rest?

Yes, Abe, the truth is always best.

"Hurt his head some too. Tom says it's better already and thinks he'll be wakin' up right away now."

Martha's eyes grew big, then she nodded. "If Tom says he's better, then he's better. What about Cleve and Jackson and Mr. Butler?"

"Nate's at home finishing up the last things on his shop. Jackson took off after Riley fell. Probably went home to Nellie. He almost fell too, Martha. Riley fell tryin' to save Jackson." How much should he tell Martha? If he didn't someone else would. "I tried to save them both and it almost seems I pushed Riley off while I grabbed Jackson." He shook his head. "I sure feel bad about my part in it."

Martha hugged him close again. "You didn't do any such thing, Abe Noble. You're always saving someone, one way or another." She shoved him back. "How did I ever get so lucky, getting you? Oops! It wasn't luck. You are my most precious gift from God. After Jesus, of course. Thank You, God."

She led Abe into the house and fed him some vegetable soup with a big slice of soft homemade bread. "Are you going to be glad when we're alone again?" she asked.

He shook his head. "Well, I s'pose it'll be nice, but those babies are sure fun." A dark cloud tried to cover his personal little sky, but he chased it away. "I can tell how much we'll enjoy ours by watching them," he added to cheer them both up.

"Yes," she said quietly. "I purely want us to have a baby of our own."

Abe got up from the table. "Think we ought to go see if Jackson's all right?"

They were glad for the chance for a ride on the new horses with Willie and Speckle. Since they weren't going far they let Josie run beside them. They found Jackson and Nellie taking a nap but all right. "Think you'll be able to come back to work tomorrow?" Abe asked Jackson. "Tom and Rachel are eager to get their house finished."

"I'm not letting him go up on that steep roof anymore," Nellie said. "He nearly fell too, you know."

"I know," Abe said. "Riley fell saving Jackson. I guess that makes him a hero."

Neither Nellie nor Jackson replied.

Later in the afternoon, Tom appeared at his new house where Abe and Cleve were putting on shingles. He climbed the ladder and sat on the ridge at the top. "You'll both be glad to know Riley's awake, seeing straight, and talking." He chuckled. "I wouldn't say he's very happy to be on his back for a month or two though."

Cleve laughed out loud—and when he laughed loud everyone nearby heard. "I guess he'll live through it. He better be thankful he's gonna get well. Coulda kilt him, you know."

Tom nodded. "It could have. But it didn't, so let's just be thankful. Now, what can I do here?"

Abe put him to work, and before the sun set they had one side of the roof shingled. Abe figured it would take two more days to finish the other side. The next day they found a young man eager to earn some money, so the four finished the roof.

During the following week they plastered the inside. Abe watched as they applied the whitish stuff to the inside of the walls. "Better not let Martha see this," he said. "When we built our house, there wasn't much to be had. It's a different world already."

After painting the plaster, they put hardwood floors down, sanded them smooth as glass, and rubbed oil into them until the boards shone. *What a house,* Abe thought. Maybe it was time for him and Martha to build a new one.

They finished Tom's house, then built a much smaller replica of it for his office. Then Tom and Rachel moved in. "I'm sure goin' to miss those babies," Abe said, as they carried in the few things that the Dorlands had hauled from Oregon City.

Rachel laughed. "You won't miss them, Abe. We're right here on your place so we'll be seeing you a lot."

Abe stopped in to see Riley nearly every day. Riley didn't take to his idle life well at all. Melissa read to him a lot and they played games, but Riley couldn't handle what he called wasting his time.

One day Abe noticed they hadn't seen Jackson and Nellie for a while. "Why don't we ride over and see 'em tonight?" he asked Martha at supper. "A good ride would be fun for all of us, and maybe we could take them a pie or gingerbread."

Martha hurried a gingerbread into the oven. As soon as she took it out she called Willie. "Can you go help Abe saddle the horses? We're going over to see Jackson and Nellie. We're taking a gingerbread and cream to eat too."

The last part got Willie into the mood. Almost as soon as Martha had poured some cream into a quart bottle, the horses stamped and nickered at the door.

"Race you!" Willie called as they rode toward the back of their place. He nudged Speckle into a gallop before Abe and Martha had time to register his challenge.

"Come on, Ebb," Abe murmured leaning over the shiny, black mane. "You going to take that?" The big horse leaned forward and burst into a moderate canter. Even in the relaxed pace he gained on Willie and Speckle. Abe slowed him just a bit. "We don't want to ruin their fun," he told Ebb. "Just a little behind is just right."

Martha and Thunder tore up beside Abe and passed. Ebb voluntarily sped up until he ran beside Thunder. Abe signaled to Martha to wait. "Let Speckle and Willie win," he said. "How'd you feel if you always lost to the big people?"

Before any of them wanted to quit, they reached Jackson and Nellie's cabin, which looked more like a shack. They'd never planted grass and Jackson had scattered junk all around the cabin. Abe shook his head. Least a man could do was keep his place tidy.

When they knocked on the door no one answered. Abe knocked again. Sounded like he heard some kind of sound inside. Could something be wrong? He pulled the latch to see if the door was locked. It opened. Though dark inside, Abe saw Nellie lying on the settle. "Hello, Nellie," he called. "Can we come in?"

She looked up, then back down but didn't answer. "You better go see what's wrong," he whispered to Martha. "Willie and I'll wait here."

Martha went in. "Goodness, Nellie, it's dark in here." She pulled open the curtains and fastened them. "Is something wrong, Nellie?" she asked when she finished. Nellie didn't answer. "Are you sick?" Martha finally asked.

Nellie shook her head no, then handed Martha a piece of paper. Martha read it. "Abe, you better come in here," Martha said.

Abe stepped through the door and Martha handed him the letter. He read:

Dear Nellie,

  It ain't that I don't love you 'cause I do. But I'm thinkin' I'm not cut out for family life. When you find this I'll be a long way toward the east coast. I'm aimin' to get into the Union Army and clear out all them slaves. I won't worry about you 'cause Abe and Martha will take care of you. Good-bye. Wish me good luck in the military.

  Jackson Lawford

Chapter 9

Martha felt faint. Jackson had run off and left Nellie! And her expecting. How could any man do that? Then she remembered how he'd run off and left her and Willie when their parents had died. What was the matter with her brother anyway?

"When did you find this note, Nellie?" she asked.

"Yester—" Nellie swallowed a hiccup. "Yesterday mornin' when I got up."

"Did he go to bed with you the night before?" Abe asked.

Nellie nodded and burst into tears. "He. . .he was so loving. I can't believe he did this." She threw herself into Martha's arms. "Martha, could someone have taken him and made him write that note?"

Martha looked over Nellie's shoulder at Abe. He shook his head. She pulled Nellie closer. "Gather up your things, Nellie. We're taking you home with us." Suddenly Martha had a positively horrible thought. "Nellie! Did Jackson take the nuggets we gave you?"

Nellie shrugged. "I can't find them." She burst into tears again. Martha looked at Abe, shook her head, and waited until Nellie calmed. "I think he did," Nellie finally said.

"I think he took the nuggets. Every one of them."

Abe put his hand on Nellie's back. "Don't worry about the nuggets, Nellie. We have some more we can give you if Jackson doesn't come back."

"He won't come back. I been waiting all yesterday and all today. He won't come back. I'll never see him again."

Another rush of sobs shook her round body.

When Nellie quieted, Martha helped her gather her things. Then she went out after Nellie's horse. But it was gone too. Abe looked shaken. "Do you think something else could have happened to Jackson?" he asked softly.

Martha shook her head. "The first thing I remembered was how horrible I felt when he left Willie and me on the Trail when Mama and Papa died. Being without him was awful, but the worst part was knowing he hadn't cared enough to help Willie and me when we needed him so desperately. I didn't know how to handle the oxen or anything. And I felt as bad about losing our parents as he did. It was purely awful, Abe."

Oh thank You, God, for my wonderful Abe. And bless Nellie. She needs Your love and assurance badly right now. Thank You, Father.

"I'm sure he left her, Abe. He's too lazy and weak to be responsible." They returned to the house to get Nellie.

Nellie struggled with a large bundle. "I forgot to tell you my horse is gone," she said.

"It's all right," Martha said. "You can ride with me on Thunder. I don't like to ride double but we're both small and we'll walk him. He's big and it isn't far."

"I can walk," Nellie whimpered.

Abe had walked up behind her. "You get on that horse, Nellie. I'll help you up." He helped her up, then hurried to Ebb carrying Nellie's big bag.

"Race you!" Willie screamed touching Speckle's sides with his heels. Martha smiled as the two raced off ahead. "Are you all right back there, Nellie?" she asked.

Nellie didn't answer, but Martha felt Nellie's chin bump her back as she nodded her head. Thunder didn't like plodding home so far behind the other horses. Every little while he pranced and turned nervously.

"He doesn't like me on here," Nellie said after Martha had soothed and quieted him a few times. "Let me walk, Martha. It isn't far."

Martha's tinkly laugh rang in the air. "He doesn't mind you at all, Nellie. What he hates is me holding him back. He knows he could beat the other two even with both of us on him." She giggled, "But it's good for him to be humbled a little."

When they reached the house, Abe had already put Nellie's things into Willie's room—the room Abe had slept in when they first married.

"Willie can sleep in our room for now," Abe said softly to Martha.

"Please, can he sleep with me?" Nellie whined. "I hate being alone."

Abe looked at Martha and she shook her head. "Ask him," she mouthed.

He grinned. "We'll see, Nellie. If he thinks it would be good fun to sleep with you he probably will."

Martha could tell Abe worked extra hard to keep everyone laughing at supper that evening. Willie took it up, and even Nellie laughed a few times.

Nellie also ate a big meal. "I didn't eat anything after Jackson left," she said. "At first I kept waiting for him to come back so we could eat together, then I couldn't seem to get hungry."

Nellie put on a brave front, helping Martha and playing with Willie all evening. When they finished worship and Nellie invited him to share her bedroom, he willingly went.

After Abe kissed Martha goodnight, she couldn't fall asleep but lay very still. The house creaked. Two men far away yelled, and several dogs barked. Josie, on a rug at the foot of their bed, didn't make a sound.

Suddenly Abe leaned on his elbow. "Have you noticed how nice Tom and Rachel's house is?" he whispered.

Martha burst out laughing. "How did you know I'm awake?"

He put an arm around her and pulled her close, her back to his chest. "With all that sighing, how I could I not know? Well, have you noticed?"

She turned to face him in the dark. "Yes. It's going to be just right for a doctor and his family."

"But would you like a new house—something like theirs?"

"Abe! Why would we need a fine house like that?"

He chuckled. "Seems we already need an extra bedroom—for Willie. And no tellin' how long Nellie'll be with us. In a year or two her babe'll be needin' a room."

Long silence.

"Well, I think you deserve a nice house, Martha. You've done without long enough."

Martha couldn't believe her ears. But she should have known. Abe would do anything for her. That was just how he was. "I don't know, Abe. Let's sleep on it. If you still think it's a good idea, we'll ask God in the morning. I purely don't want anything in the whole world if He doesn't think it's best."

"Right. Are you sleepy now?"

The next morning Nellie slept until after the animals were cared for, the milk given away and sold, breakfast was ready, and Martha awakened her.

"Can I help you?" Nellie asked.

Martha hadn't been sure Nellie would ask but she'd given it some thought. Nellie would be happier keeping busy.

Besides she really could help. She smiled at her pudgy sister-in-law. "Of course you can, Nellie. Would you rather cook? Or clean and wash clothes? That's most of the indoor work. I won't ask you to work outside."

"I can't cook much," Nellie said. "Jackson didn't care whether I cooked or not. We usually ate meat sandwiches. I can clean and wash clothes though. I bet I can do that nearly as good as you, Martha."

Jackson didn't have any right to expect Nellie to do anything, Martha thought. He hardly worked. "I was hoping you'd say that," she said out loud. "I love cooking and baking. I can do that and have more time to do my outside work too." She hugged Nellie. "Oh Nellie, I'm so sorry my brother is such a cad, but I'm excited to have you here. It's going to be fun."

"I don't know what's going to be fun about it, but we'll be all right," Nellie sniffed. Then her eyes brightened. "Remember when you lived in your wagon at the end of the Street and we waded in the creek—and fell down?"

Martha remembered. "You didn't care a bit. You just danced around until you dried, then went home to help your ma as if nothing happened."

Nellie looked pensive. Martha thought she might burst into tears. "How was it, living with Jackson?" Martha asked. "Was he kind and thoughtful? Or a selfish pig like he's acting now? This is just what he did when our parents died on the Trail, you know. He went off and left me to care for Willie and also the oxen and everything."

Nellie smiled. "He treated me like his own queen, Martha. Really he did. That's why I'm so surprised—and why it's so hard."

Martha nodded, happy that at least Jackson was a good enough man to treat his wife well.

That night, when they finally found themselves alone, Abe asked her again if she'd like to have a house like Rachel's. Martha giggled. "I don't know what I'd do with a fine house like that," she said. "Isn't this one good enough, Abe?"

He grinned. "Well, seems to be gettin' smaller all the time. Tom and Rachel just moved into their own house. Now Nellie's here. Soon her little babe will be too. We're goin' to be crowded."

"Could we build another room? Or even two?"

Abe shook his head. "You're just a simple girl, aren't you? Maybe that's part of why I love you so much. But you'd love a nice house, Martha, after you lived in it awhile."

"Maybe we better ask God what He wants us to do, Abe. If He wants us to have a bigger and better house, I'll go along with it." She giggled. "If we do build a fine new house I want a room in it that even Rachel doesn't have."

He looked surprised. "What room would that be?"

"A bathroom, Abe. I read in *The Statesman* that everyone's building bathrooms in their houses back East."

"What's a bathroom?"

"Abe! Just what it says. A nice room with a tub and towels and everything you need to take a bath. Think how nice it would be to take a bath anytime you want, no matter who's in the kitchen. I think that would be purely heaven, Abe. You'd never believe how fancy the bathrooms are in some places. In some of them you just pull a plug and the water runs out the bottom of the tub. And—"

Abe looked as if he'd seen a bright light. "Yeah!" he interrupted. "You're right, as usual, my little Martha. I say we build a house with a bathroom."

She shook her head. "Not until we talk to God about it."

So they knelt, held hands, and asked God to guide them in every little thing, and especially right now to let them know if they should build a house.

"All right," Abe said when they finished. "Let's both be listenin'." He tweaked her ear. "I got a little pushy, I know, but I really want to do what my Pard up there wants."

Martha listened—as she set bread; as she put a roast surrounded by potatoes, carrots, and onions into the oven; and as she picked bugs from the potato plants and put them in a tall jar with a small neck. When she finished, she would pour boiling water into the jar. She had to do this every week. If she didn't they'd lay eggs on the underside of the potato leaves. When the larvae hatched, they would make short work of the potato plants. Seemed like every kind of bug thrived here. Even more so than in Missouri. She smiled to herself. She really didn't blame the bugs for settling in Walla Walla. They couldn't choose a nicer place to live.

After she finished with the bugs, she hoed the potatoes, still listening for God. *Well, He'll speak to Abe. He always speaks to Abe.* As she worked, waited, and thought, she began to get excited about the house. How wonderful to be able to take a bath without chasing everyone out of the house.

At dinner, Nellie and Willie teased each other, seeming to have great fun. Nellie had the washing hanging on the line and the house looked neat. Abe and Martha talked quietly together, comparing what they'd accomplished that morning.

When they finished eating, Martha started to wash the dishes. "That's my job," Nellie said. "It's cleaning, isn't it?"

"No, it's finishing the cooking," Martha explained. The girls ended up doing the dishes together.

As Martha hurried out to feed the cows, Abe met her. "Hear anything from upstairs?" he asked.

She shook her head. "No. I thought for sure you would."

He helped her wash windows during the afternoon. "How's Nellie doing?" he asked while they mixed vinegar and water to make more window cleaner.

Martha straightened up and rubbed her lower back.

"Better than I expected. I thought she might not know how to do anything in the house. She's trying to be cheerful, too. It must be hard, expecting a baby without a man to help."

As they talked Nellie approached. "Martha," she called, "I can't find anything more to do in the house. Can I help you out here?"

Abe handed her his washing rags and headed for the barns.

"Do you know how to do this?" Martha asked, "or do I need to show you?"

Nellie grinned. "Just show me which windows need cleaned. I'll get them clean one way or another."

As the sun sank toward the west, Martha knew she'd better get supper going for her family. "Come on, Nellie," she invited. "You've done well today and must be tired." Josie, who had been lying in the soft warm earth, followed them into the house.

Later that night, after Nellie and Willie had gone to bed, Martha and Abe sat across the table talking as they drank coffee. "Still didn't hear anything?" he asked.

She shook her head, hardly believing he hadn't either. "Do you think He'll want us to build?" she asked.

Abe nodded. "Sure. Why would He care? I don't mind tellin' you I like your bathroom idea a whole lot. Why didn't I think of that a long time ago?"

Martha felt relieved. "I'm getting purely excited about it too. A big house with lots of room for everyone and everything would be real nice." She giggled. "Who knows? We may have half a dozen babies a few years from now. Might as well get ready for them, don't you think?"

Abe jumped from his chair, ran around the table, and pulled her close. "Thank you, Martha my own," he whispered. "This is the first time you said right out that you want a lot of children. I do too."

Her heart felt as if it would beat right through her chest. She turned her face up to his kiss. Ummmm. How she loved him! How could it possibly have taken so long for her to find out. "Yes, I want lots of children, Abe. And I'm ready right now."

They finished their coffee and oatmeal cookies, and went to bed, arm in arm.

The next morning everyone did what they had to do to get the day going: milk the cows, give and sell the milk, make breakfast, and whatever. When they finished and before they went to the fields, Abe invited Martha to go buy groceries with him. As they passed the new Dorland home and medical office Abe suggested they stop a minute to see how the family was getting along.

After Rachel squealed her pleasure and invited them in, Martha looked at everything with new eyes. She would no doubt soon have a house similar to this one. Except hers would have a bathroom. The large living room, painted a soft green, looked inviting with colorful area rugs covering the hardwood floors.

"Come into the kitchen," Rachel said, "and we'll have a cup of coffee while we talk. Tom's in his office. He's had a couple of patients already. Oh, Martha, we're so glad we've come here."

As they talked, two horses thundered up to the house, stopping so quickly dirt flew from under their hooves. The riders jumped down and beat on the door.

"Where's the doc?" one of the whiskered men asked. "We're with the wagon train that's comin'. It'll be in town in a few days, maybe tomorrow. Thing is, we left two wagons in the Blue Mountains. An axle broke on one and the other'n turned over comin' down the steep grade. Broke all to pieces and fell on one of the men helpin'. Pro'ly broke a leg. Had to leave 'im up there. His wife stayed to care for 'im."

The other man broke in. "Couple doctors in town told us you're new here and probly don't have nuthing to do. Could the doc come back with us?"

Rachel called Tom and explained what had happened. He grinned and held his hand out to first one of the men, then the other. "I have a few patients, boys, maybe five. But they aren't very sick. I think I can go." He turned to Abe. Could you go get Rachel's father?" He turned to the men. "He's a blacksmith and may be able to get the wagon fixed."

Abe and Martha hurried to the Street, to Nate's shop that they had built on the lot they'd sold to him. He said he would be ready to go in a half hour. Cynthia asked Martha to tell Rachel she would come down and stay with her while the men were gone and help her. She giggled when she said it, so Martha knew she needed Rachel.

As they walked back, Abe seemed quiet. "What's wrong? Are you worried about that trip into the Blues?"

Abe grinned. "Not exactly. But I thought maybe I'd go and help."

Chapter 10

As Abe hurried getting things ready, he wished they'd had an answer about the house. Never mind. When God wanted them to know, they'd know.

Tom banged on the door and came in. "I need a horse, Abe, and so does Nate. Where can we get some in a hurry?"

Abe let them ride Thunder and Ebb to Fort Walla Walla. They soon found horses they liked and rode them back home, leading Abe and Martha's horses. The men from the wagon train said they'd buy supplies while the others got horses. They showed up about the same time Abe, Tom, and Nate did.

"How long do you think it'll take us to get there?" Abe asked Wally, the younger of the men.

"It's about eighty miles. We left there day before yesterday. Rode purty hard. Stopped and rested about four or five hours each night. Ate bread as we rode."

"Ebb's a good mover," Abe said, "but when he's tired I rest him no matter what."

Tom nodded. "Me too. I haven't had Thor long but I don't intend to override him, either. That all right, boys?"

The taller one, Irv, said it was all right but they needed to make as good time as they could.

When Abe kissed Martha good-bye he wished he hadn't decided to go. No, he couldn't wish that. Someone needed him. The five riders took off south at a gentle canter.

Starting out like this reminded Abe of the gold hunting expedition. An important element was missing from this group. Martha. He leaned forward and petted Ebb's shiny black neck. "We'll just make the trip as quick as possible, won't we?" he asked the huge horse.

They stopped several hours after dark, watered the horses, then let them graze. The men ate meat sandwiches Martha had made. "Better enjoy this meal," Tom said. "I think all we have after this is bread and dried apples."

When Abe dropped onto his blanket, he turned his eyes toward the starry sky. So starry he couldn't separate the stars. "You up there, Lord?" he asked. "I hope You agree with what we're doin'."

You're doing what's right, Abe.

Abe wanted to talk to Him some more. Abe knew he had something to talk about, but he fell asleep trying to remember.

Darkness still hid the world when Irv shook him awake. "Wally says we gotta go," he said loudly. "Them people in the mountains may need us right bad."

The other man, Wally, woke Tom and Nate. The men grabbed some dry bread and ate it as they hurried toward the Blues. The horses all seemed eager to go, even though the sun hadn't risen yet. "It's cause it's cool," Irv said. "Horses don't much like hot weather. Neither do I."

They made good time most of that day, stopping late at night again, this time in the Blue Mountains. About mid-morning the next day they reached the wagon with the broken axle and the injured man. A young woman ran to meet them. "I'm so glad you got here," she said. "Ray's sicker. Now he doesn't even know what happened or where he is."

Tom leapt off Thor before she finished talking. "Where is he?" Tom asked quietly.

"Over here," the woman said, leading the way to the wagon. As Abe watched the two, his admiration for Tom grew. If something ever happened to him—*please no, Lord*—he'd sure like Tom to be nearby.

The man lay on a folded blanket on the ground behind the disabled wagon. Tom dropped to his knees beside him. "Hello, Ray. I'm Tom Dorland and I've come to help you. I'm a doctor. Where are you hurt?"

The man looked at Tom as though seeing through a deep fog. "You a doc?" He sighed loudly. "Good." He relaxed and closed his eyes.

"Hurt pretty bad?" Tom asked. The man nodded without opening his eyes. Tom didn't force the man to try to talk anymore but began going over his arms, legs, and body. After several minutes of examining and reexamining, he turned back to the woman. "The men were right. He has a broken leg. His right arm's also broken. How long's it been since this happened?"

The woman thought a moment and shook her head. "I'm not sure. Four, five days—maybe a week." Her lips turned up in a tiny smile. "It's been a long, long time."

Nate, Irv, and Wally turned away from Ray and began working on the wagon.

Tom leaned back over the man, running his fingers over the right leg and arm. Then he met Abe's eyes. "I'm not sure we can set them now. Depends how much they've healed." He shook his head. "Sure would have been easier when it first happened."

"Let's get it over," Abe said. "We both know what we gotta do." He grinned at Tom. "Remember, I'm experienced at this stuff now. Ready for me to hold him?"

Tom shook his head. "Not yet. I have a tiny bit of something new in my bag, and I doubt we'll ever need it more."He pulled out a tiny bottle, unscrewed the top, took a small cloth, and poured a few drops on it. "I have something here for you to smell, Ray," he said softly to the man. "It won't smell too good, but it'll help the pain a whole lot. Do you understand?"

Ray nodded and reached for the cloth. Tom didn't release it to him but looked to the woman. "Could you hold this over his nose until I tell you to stop?"

She quickly took the cloth and did as Tom asked.

When Ray relaxed, Tom nodded. "Hold him, Abe. This isn't going to be easy. I'll start on the arm—it'll probably go better than the leg."

Abe held with all his strength as Tom pushed, pulled, and twisted. The man didn't seem to feel anything. After a few minutes Tom told the woman to take the cloth away. "When he starts hurting, put it back," he instructed. The woman nodded.

Abe thought the ordeal would go on forever, with Tom repeating the hard thrusts and twists. Finally when Abe thought he couldn't hold the man any longer he heard a loud pop.

"There," Tom said with a relieved sigh. "It just rebroke. Now it'll set easily." Only a few minutes later another small snap told Abe the bone had slipped into place.

"Can I let go now?" he asked, lifting his eyes to Tom's.

Abe could hardly believe his eyes. Sweat covered Tom's entire face. He looked red and tired, and breathed hard. He dropped to the ground. "Yeah, let go. Next thing we gotta do is wrap it." He retrieved the three lighter wooden dowels he'd brought and the lengths of soft material. After wrapping the arm and securing it firmly, he turned to Abe. "How was that for a day's work?"

"Tough," Abe said. "Harder for you than me, though." He glanced at the man whose eyes rested on Tom. "Probably hardest of all on Ray."

"I'm going to let Ray rest awhile before we set his leg," Tom said. He glanced at the woman. "Don't want to push too much chloroform at him too fast. I guess he hasn't eaten for awhile. The chloroform upsets the stomach sometimes if it's full."

Abe walked over to the men at the wagon. "How you doin'?" he asked. "Think you'll have it fixed today?"

Nate grinned but shook his head. "We're workin' as fast as we can, Abe, but this is slow, hard work. Maybe tomorrow afternoon."

Abe returned to Tom and his patient. Tom asked the man, Ray, how he got hurt. "Helpin' a wagon down a steep hill. Thing turned over on me. Hurt oxen—had to shoot 'em." He attempted a chuckle. "Lucky they didn't shoot me too."

"Well, you're lucky," Tom said. "We won't have to shoot you this time. You're going to be just fine. Are you ready to do the leg now?"

The man nodded. "Be glad when it's over."

Tom poured a bit more chloroform into the cloth and handed it to the woman. After doing a few more preparations and bowing his head a moment, Tom tensed up. "All right, use the chloroform. Be sure to take it away when he relaxes and use it again when he feels pain. Abe, hold him absolutely still." After five minutes Abe decided Tom wasn't going to be able to rebreak the leg.

"Think we oughta get one of those boys to hold him so I could help you?" Abe asked.

Tom didn't answer but shook his head. Abe still held the man in a grip of iron. After a bit Ray began moving and moaning. "Give him the cloth," Tom commanded. A moment later the man quieted. Then Abe heard a loud snap and "Thank You, Lord," in a quiet whisper. "All right, Abe, hold him while I put the bone together." A few minutes later a much smaller pop was followed by a huge sigh from Tom. "It's all over," he said. "Thank You, God. I could never have done it without You." He turned to the woman. "Take away the cloth."

Tom and Abe sat on a low log for a few minutes. The woman sat on another one nearby. "You fellows hungry?" she asked. "Before the train left, they cut a back leg off one of the oxen and I've been frying slices of that. I have flour and things to make trail bread too."

Tom nodded. "Thanks—uh, you know we never have gotten your name."

"I'm Ray's wife, Sandra. Call me, Sandy."

Tom smiled. "Thanks for your good help, Sandy. We couldn't have done it without you. We still have to finish with Ray, then I'll bet everyone would like some of that meat." He smiled. "I feel as though I've done a big day's work. How about you, Abe?"

Abe nodded. He didn't feel as hungry as he did tired at the moment, but he knew he'd soon be hungry enough.

The woman put her hand on Tom's arm. "I can't thank you enough, Doctor. Do you think my husband will be all right now?"

"As right as rain, Sandy. It'll take a while to heal but after that, he won't even limp. Come on, Abe. Let's finish fixing that leg."

Sure enough after they finished the leg, Abe felt ravenous and hardly able to wait until Sandy had everything fixed. Tom told her to boil a piece of meat until it fell apart and feed Ray the meat with the juice.

The men fixing the wagon washed up in the nearby creek with Tom and Abe.

"Comin' along all right," Nate volunteered after they had prayed and filled the tin pans Sandy had provided. "We should have it ready to roll by noon tomorrow."

"Will Ray be ready to go by then?" Abe asked Tom.

"I think so." Tom turned to Sandy. "Can we haul him in the wagon? It'll be bumpy but he'll be all right."

She nodded. "Yes. They took our wagon on and left us only the one with the broken axle so we won't have so many wagons to worry with when we get going. But there are plenty of blankets in this one to make him a bed."

By noon the next day Ray was much better and eager to go on. Sandy had fed him beef broth and well-boiled meat almost continually since Tom had told her to.

Nate and the men put the finishing touches on the wagon about three o'clock in the afternoon. "May as well start," Abe said. "Nothing here to keep us until mornin'—or even one hour longer."

Everyone agreed so Sandy put all but one blanket under Ray and the men lifted him in as gently as possible. They gathered the horses and oxen and started the slow procession home.

"Don't worry," Ray said. "Don't hurt nuthin' like it did before Doc fixed it."

They traveled for several hours, before stopping to eat sandwiches Sandy had made from her meat and Abe's bread. Ray ate a sandwich with the rest of them. "I'm nigh well already, Doc. Hardly feel a twinge, even ridin' in that wagon."

Tom gripped the man's shoulder. "You're doing great, Ray, but you aren't even started healing yet. You realize I had to rebreak both your arm and leg don't you?" Ray reluctantly admitted he knew.

They hadn't gone far when Abe heard some kind of ruckus in the bushes south of the trail. He listened, nudged Ebb toward the sound, until through the brushes he saw three doe deer, one fawn with barely visible spots, and two gray animals that looked like large dogs. Wolves! He would bet those animals were wolves, and no doubt trying to get the fawn.

He hurried Ebb back to the trail. "Come on," he called softly. "Somethin's goin' on over here I don't like much."

Nate, Tom, and Irv quickly joined Abe where they could see the animals. Suddenly Tom pointed. "Look!" he said. "The fawn's tangled in something and the wolves are going to get it."

"No, they ain't," Nate yelled. "We're stoppin' those things."

"I'll get my gun," Irv said. "I'll fix them."

"You aren't goin' to shoot 'em," Abe said. "Martha would disown me."

"And Rachel would shoot me," Tom said. "Go ahead and get the gun anyway. Maybe we can scare them away."

"You'll scare the does away too," Nate said. "Then what'll the little one do?"

While they tried to decide what to do, the animals became aware of their presence. The wolves took off through the brush, the doe deer gracefully leapt over a few logs and out of sight too. The fawn struggled but didn't go anywhere.

"I'm goin' over there," Abe said. "You fellows watch for them wolves. You know they're watchin' us." He slid off Ebb's back and walked softly toward the fawn. It didn't move an eyelash. *It's hopin' I don't see it,* Abe thought.

"Lord, I'm tryin' to help Your little creature here. You help me do it without anyone or anything gettin' hurt, all right?"

You're doing fine, Abe.

When he reached the fawn, he saw it had thoroughly tangled itself in a kind of cord the Indians used for fishing. *Those buzzards,* Abe thought. *I'd a thought they'd know better.* As he examined the cord, he realized he could never untangle it from the terrified animal—even if it continued holding still.

He hurried back to the others. "It's Indian fishin' cord," he said, "and it's really tangled up. I ain't got a knife, either. I need a knife and someone to hold the fawn while I cut that stuff off."

Nate handed him a knife and Irv followed him to the fawn. "You wanta hold it or cut?" Abe asked. The man felt more secure holding than trying to cut off the tight cords.

Abe opened the knife. "You hold still, little one," he said softly. "We're trying to help you."

The fawn barely breathed while Abe pulled the cord loose from its body, stuck the knife in, and cut. He repeated the action innumerable times while the little animal held perfectly still. "We got to be careful not to let you get away when I got the cords only partway off," he murmured, cutting, pulling out, cutting. Finally the last loop fell to the ground. "You can go now," he said, lifting the fawn to its feet and giving it a little push. "Go find your mama, baby."

When the fawn discovered itself free, it took off like a big jack rabbit through the bushes. Abe smiled, closed the knife, and returned to the men. "Hope it finds its mama," he said.

Abe felt real good the rest of the day. They stopped hours after dark, released the animals to graze, and threw down their blankets.

They started the next morning before sunrise and traveled hard all day. By the next day they had nothing to eat but Sandy's trail bread and side meat. No one refused the simple fare.

They arose before sunrise every day, ate dry bread on the trail and rode long days. The travel wasn't hard on either the people or the animals, not even the oxen, as the trail was good and mostly flat.

Ray grew better each day and his happy spirit encouraged everyone, especially Sandy. One day Abe asked him where his wagon train was headed.

"Oregon City," Ray said with a mischievous grin. "Sandy 'n' I ain't, though. I ain't gettin' away from Doc for a long time. Or never."

"I've been in Oregon City," Tom said. "Take my word for it, Walla Walla's a better place to settle. Better medical care too."

Finally, Abe stood on a hill overlooking the Walla Walla Valley. A day later, they arrived home. After greeting Martha and Willie, Abe asked where Nellie was.

"She's doing poorly," Martha said. "I have her in bed." She looked concerned. "She's been having pains nearly all the time since you left. I'd like Tom to look at her."

"Too bad to interrupt his homecoming, but I'll go get him," Abe said, heading out the door.

"The Indians came for food and another Bible story. They're always eager to hear more. You heard anything from your Pard since you left?" Martha called.

"He was with us," Abe called back.

He returned with Tom a half hour later and went out to check the livestock. Martha followed. "What did He say?" she asked.

"Nothing. He just came along with me. He's always glad to help someone."

"No, Abe. I don't mean Tom. I mean your Pard."

Oh, she meant the Lord. "I don't remember exactly, Martha. He just let me know He was with us."

"Abe! Don't you remember what you were going to ask Him?"

Abe thought. And thought. Finally it popped into his head. The house! Did God want them to build a new house? He laughed. "I plumb forgot all about that big problem, Martha. Didn't think about it once while we traveled."

Chapter 11

Martha couldn't believe her ears! They'd thought of little else for the last few days before he left. How could he possibly forget all about it? "Abram Noble, I don't think you even want a new house!"

He grinned again. "I do if the Lord wants us to, Martha. You taught me to feel that way. But we were purty busy up there in the mountains. First we fixed the man and the wagon which kept all our thinkin' real busy. Then we had to go slow since we had a wagon and a hurt man." Then he remembered the deer and the wolves, so he told her about that.

"Abe, you're the world's best man. No one else would have taken the time to help a little animal."

Abe held her tight for a moment, then released her so he could look into her beautiful gray eyes. "You're wrong, Martha. Everyone wanted to help the deer. Tom said Rachel would scalp him if he didn't help."

Oh yes, Martha remembered how much Rachel loved animals. Almost a passion. She nodded. "True, Abe. Rachel purely loves animals. Maybe more than I do."

"Well, I just want you to know all of the men were in there fighting for the little fawn's life. What did Tom say when he saw Nellie?"

"I left, Abe. I wanted to know about the house. I've asked many times every day but haven't an inkling what He wants us to do."

Abe put his arm over her shoulders and steered her toward the house. "We'll know, Martha. He'll tell us what to do."

Soon after they reached the house, Tom appeared from Nellie's bedroom. "She's definitely having contractions. Better keep her in bed until they quit and for awhile after. The baby could never live. Not possible at six months." He pulled up a chair and plopped down astraddle, leaning his elbows across the back. "She says her husband left her. Do you think he'd come back to save the baby?"

Martha felt her heart lurch. "We think he went back East. He left a note saying he was going to join the military and free the slaves." She sniffed. "He doesn't like responsibility and may have gone because of the baby. He's a cad."

Tom sighed and got to his feet. "Do anything you can to make her happier. Maybe you can get her excited about the baby."

Martha went into Nellie's room. "You don't want to lose your baby, do you?" she asked kindly.

Nellie shook her head. "No, but how can I take care of a baby by myself?"

Martha sat on the bed beside Nellie and stroked her hair. "You're not by yourself. You know that, Nellie. We're here for you. Your ma's just down at the Street too."

"Ma told me Jackson wasn't any good, Martha. She'd never help me after I married him anyway."

"Well, we will. Don't worry about a thing." She thought of something that might cheer Nellie. "I'll tell you a secret," she whispered, though no one else could possibly hear. "We're thinking about building a new house. Not for sure, but we're thinking. If we do we'll be sure to make lots of room for you and the baby."

Nellie didn't look impressed.

"Look, Nellie," Martha said, "I've been wanting a baby so bad it hurts. But so far I'm not having one. Now, I'm thrilled about yours and can't wait to help you take care of it. What do you want, Nellie? A boy or a girl?"

Nellie stiffened just a little. Martha knew she was having another pain. "I'd love for you to have a beautiful, dainty little girl just like you," Martha said. "We can make gorgeous little frilly clothes for her. Won't that be fun?"

"How can I talk about clothes when I'm hurting so bad?" Nellie cried.

"You're right, Nellie. I'm sorry. I have a better idea. Let's ask God to stop the pains so you can enjoy waiting for your little girl."

Without waiting for Nellie's answer she dropped to her knees beside the bed. "Dear Father, we thank You for blessing us so much. We especially thank You for one of Your biggest blessings—Nellie's baby. It's not time for it to be born, Father." She giggled softly. "You knew that, didn't You? Father, we're asking You to stop her pains and help her baby grow big enough. We pray in Jesus' name and thank You so much for hearing and answering our prayers. Amen."

Martha got up. "Everything's all right now, Nellie. You won't have even one more pain. I just know you won't."

"Everything's not all right, Martha. Maybe it is for you, but it's not for me. Now I can't even work to earn my food. I'm not a bit sure I want this baby, Martha. And God doesn't want me to have it either."

Martha tinkled her sweet laugh. "God does want you to have it, Nellie. And you're going to, so why don't you start wanting it too?"

Nellie's next pain was lighter, the next one lighter yet—and the pains ended.

That night after they thanked God for ending Nellie's pains, they asked Him to help them know whether they should build a new house or live in the old one. When they finished, Martha gave Abe instructions to listen carefully for God to answer.

"I will, little Martha," Abe said. "You listen too."

The next morning neither knew His will. "Let's not get impatient," Abe said. "As long as we don't hear, we know it isn't time to build a new house yet."

Martha kept Nellie in bed for several days after the pains quit, though Nellie insisted she should be helping. She let Nellie get up for the first time to go to church that weekend.

With Abe and Martha's generous gifts, the church had been enlarged to accommodate the more than a hundred regular attenders. Riley had helped Abe build the needed pews as he had done when the church first began. Abe always said the people who went to church probably weren't out rustling cattle or hurting their fellow men.

Martha started sewing for the baby in earnest and tried to get Nellie to help. Nellie stitched a few diapers but usually found something else to do.

After Nellie went a month without pains, Martha and Abe bought her a little sorrel mare. "Not for you to ride now," Martha said. "We just wanted you to have something to look forward to later."

When the hay ripened, Rachel helped Nellie and Martha prepare food for the harvesters. Nellie did her part willingly without complaint but never seemed to get over Jackson's leaving. And she had never heard from him or about him.

—⁂—

About the first of December Nellie's pains started up again. Tom came. "It's still a little early," he said after examining her, "but I think the baby will be all right. And I don't think we'll be able to stop the pains."

He guessed right. That night, about eighteen hours later, Nellie had a healthy little girl. Martha noticed she didn't get very excited about the baby, but then she'd had a hard afternoon and evening.

Martha couldn't contain her excitement. "Look, Abe," she said, pulling the little quilt back so he could see the tiny face and fists waving aimlessly. "Isn't that the most perfect little thing you ever saw?"

Abe's face expressed the awe Martha felt in the presence of God's little miracle of life. "Know what I want even worse than a house?" he whispered.

Martha nodded. "I purely do too, Abe. I do. Maybe soon."

Nellie nursed her baby but didn't take much interest in its care. Martha brought her to Nellie often and always bathed the baby in Nellie's room so she could watch.

"See how clear her eyes are getting?" Martha asked one day. "She may be able to see your face now, Nellie. Smile at her so she knows how much you love her."

Although a week had passed since the baby's birth, Nellie hadn't offered to get out of bed. Neither had she named the baby. One afternoon when Martha finished her work early, she plopped down on Nellie's bed. "Let's think of the prettiest names we know. This perfect baby has to have the most beautiful name in the whole world."

"I don't know any pretty names."

"Nellie! You do too. How do you like Elizabeth? You could call her Beth or Lizzie or Betty. Or how about Susan? Susie. Or Kathleen? That's extra pretty."

"Do we really have to do this right now, Martha? I'm tired."

Martha gave up and prepared supper. What could she do to make Nellie feel better? She would feel awful if Abe left her and she had a baby alone. She knew she would, so she couldn't blame Nellie.

Melissa, Riley's wife, came to sit with Nellie often. Martha didn't have time to stay while they visited, but it looked to her is if Nellie didn't welcome their old friend very much.

Martha talked to Tom. "She's doing fine physically," he said, "but she seems to have lost interest in any and everything. I thought the baby would cheer her up but so far it hasn't."

"Maybe she needs to get to work," Martha suggested.

Tom nodded. "An interest in something would be fine. But she feels she and the baby are a huge imposition on you and Abe. I'm afraid she'd take it wrong if you tried to involve her in the work."

Martha tried to excite Nellie about buying Christmas presents for Babykins, as Martha had started calling the nameless baby. Nellie performed her responsibilities like a trained animal, doing well whatever she attempted, but without enthusiasm. She took no interest at all in spending Martha and Abe's money for Christmas presents or anything else.

Abe made the baby a beautiful cradle for Christmas and Martha made her a soft blanket, frilly dress, and heavy matching coat. They gave Nellie a nice church dress and heavy coat. Nellie didn't even try them on and barely thanked them for the gifts.

Martha finally became indignant. "Even if I could get Jackson to come back, I wouldn't!" she said to Abe. "He doesn't deserve this beautiful family after the way he's broken Nellie's heart. And if it weren't for us, that baby wouldn't know what love is."

The winter progressed with some snow and cold weather but nothing unbearable. Still they didn't have an answer about the new house.

Abe made furniture and had more orders than he could fill. "I could make us a good livin' doin' this," he said. "But it's so much fun gettin' outside in the spring and helpin' God start things growin'."

Martha loved him so much and felt terribly proud of him. "Why don't you keep on making furniture in the winter and farming in the summer?"

He nodded. "I guess I'll do that for now at least. One of these days a good furniture maker will show up and I'll be finished."

"No you won't, Abe Noble. No one's going to beat your furniture."

One day in February the sun came out and shone like a warm spring day. Abe and Willie invited Martha to go riding with them. "Nellie," Martha called. "Come go for our first spring ride. I'll carry Babykins so you'll be free to ride on the wings of the wind. Did you know God does that? Rides on the wings of the wind? In His chariot, a cloud." Nellie didn't know—nor did she want to go riding. They locked Josie in the house with Nellie.

"Where shall we go?" Willie asked as they rode out of the corral and Abe shut the gate. "I want to go a long long ways."

Abe appeared to give it much thought. "We could wander over to the Blues and on up Tiger Canyon. We'd get a good view of our town and see how it looks now."

"Yeah!" Willie yelled. "Martha, go make some sandwiches so we can stay a long time."

She returned with the sandwiches in a few minutes. They took their time, stopping to enjoy everything they saw.

They ate their sandwiches sitting on an overhang at Tiger Canyon, a huge canyon with trees growing all the way down the steep banks, making a lovely view. They stopped at a gurgling creek to quench their thirst and headed home.

"What a way to welcome spring," Abe said. "I'm ready to start the spring plowing. Are you, Willie?"

"Can I, Abe? I can make those horses go."

As they rambled toward home Abe and Willie figured how he could help drive the big horses. They arrived home just after the warm sunshine turned pink and the sun melted into the horizon.

"We're home, Nellie," Martha called as she hurried into the main room. "We had a great day. You should have come with us. It was warm and smelled of pine needles."

Nellie didn't respond.

"Nellie, where are you?" Martha called, hurrying into Nellie's room. The room looked strangely empty. Then Martha noticed all of Nellie's things were gone from the pegs on the wall. The baby! Martha rushed to the cradle, leaned over, and looked in. The breath she had been holding returned in a whoosh. Babykins lay sleeping soundly in the cradle.

Martha ran back to the main room. "Abe, for a moment I thought Nellie had gone somewhere, but Babykins is asleep in there." Then she remembered Nellie's things missing from the nails. "I wonder where she went," she said.

Abe went outside and returned in five minutes. "Her mare's gone," he said. "And I haven't seen Josie. I guess they're all together. I can't believe she left Babykins alone, even for a little while." He peered into Martha's eyes. "She shouldn't have done that, should she?"

Martha shook her head. "No, you never leave babies alone, even for a few minutes. Bad things can happen to babies in a hurry."

Babykins stirred, then almost instantly burst into full blown wailing, screaming at the top of her lungs. Martha headed for the bedroom. "Something's wrong," she said. "Babykins has never cried like that before. She barely fusses." When she picked up the baby she seemed all right but searched frantically for something to eat. Martha carried her into the main room.

"She's starved. Abe, how long do you suppose Nellie's been gone?" She jiggled the baby, changing her from one arm to the other. Then she changed the soaked diaper, but that didn't help either.

"I'll go look for Nellie," Abe said. "This is not the way a responsible mother treats her baby. Or the people she's staying with."

Martha walked the baby, rocked the baby, and talked to the baby. She did everything she could think of to get the baby's attention, but Babykins wasn't interested in anything in the world except filling her stomach with warm milk.

Abe returned in half an hour. "She's not close around," he said, talking loudly so Martha could hear him over Babykins' screaming. "It's pitch dark, not even a moon. But I covered the town and a few miles out on each side." He plopped onto the settle. His face looked positively haggard. "You. . .you don't think she's taken off, do you?"

Instantly Martha saw in her mind the empty nails in Nellie's room. Surely she hadn't gone after Jackson! Her terrified eyes met Abe's. She nodded. "I'll bet she has. Abe! What are we going to do with the baby? I can't nurse her!"

After waiting and listening to Babykins scream for another hour, Martha dissolved some sugar in a little warm water. Then she dipped a clean cloth in it and put the cloth in the baby's mouth. The baby clamped onto it and sucked as if she'd never had anything to eat in her life. After she'd sucked the cloth dry, Martha dipped it again and offered it to the frantic baby.

"Abe, would you go ask Tom what we should do?" she asked while the baby emptied the cloth again.

Abe left and Martha noticed the blessed quiet. She'd had no idea the baby could cry like that. She had always cared for her at the first fuss. "You poor little girl," she cooed to the wildly sucking baby. She fed the child three more clothfuls of sugar water before Abe returned. Tom and Rachel came with him.

"Too bad I don't have a baby," Rachel said. "I nursed all three of mine at once for awhile." she sighed. "But maybe that's why I lost my milk so soon. I'd like to still be nursing the twins."

"You'll have to give her cow's milk if Nellie doesn't come back," Tom said. "Do you think she's really gone?"

"I don't know where she'd be around here," Martha said. "Or how she could go off and leave her baby alone." She shook her head, still holding the cloth for the baby to suck. Finally she nodded. "Yes, I do think she's gone."

"Well, cow's milk is wonderful—for baby cows," Tom said. Then he grinned. "But Babykins won't be the first baby to make do with it. Do you have a baby bottle?" When Martha said no, he sent Abe to the store after one. "Now, you'd better write this down. Put one cup milk, one cup water, and two teaspoons sugar in a small kettle. Bring to boil, cool, and use. Right now that recipe will last her most of the day. It'll keep for a day if it isn't too hot. Later you can double the recipe." He ran his finger down Babykins' soft little cheek. "She'll probably do all right on it. Of course she'll do better on her mother's milk. Let's hope she comes home later tonight."

After Tom and Rachel left, Martha fixed some milk for the baby. Suddenly she missed Josie. Josie wouldn't go off, even if Nellie did—would she? "Abe, are you sure Josie's not around here somewhere?"

Chapter 12

Abe came into the room carrying Babykins over his shoulder. "I haven't seen her, Martha."

Martha dropped her spoon in the milk. "I haven't either, Abe. If she were here, she'd have been jumping all over when the baby cried." Her eyes filled with tears. "Abe, Josie's gone. Something's happened to her. Whatever went on here while we were gone today?"

Abe put one arm around her, still holding the baby over his shoulder. "Nothing really terrible happened, Martha, like something happening to Nellie. We'd have seen signs if it had. Josie went with Nellie, Martha. She didn't know Nellie wasn't coming back."

A smile spread across Martha's gentle, beautiful face. "You're right, Abe. She went with Nellie." Then the smile disappeared. "But she'll never come back, Abe! My Josie, who walked clear across the country with me. I'll never see her again."

"Never's a long time, Martha." He'd better be careful what he said. He would never tell Martha a lie, but he had to make her feel better. "They'll both come back one of these days. You tell me. How could a mother stay away from this beautiful baby?"

Martha didn't look so very convinced, but she put on a brave smile. "Yes. Well, let's try this bottle. I purely hope she'll drink from it." When she took Babykins from Abe, she discovered the baby had fallen asleep. "We better wait until she wakes up," she said. "You're a pretty good father," she added.

Abe barely knew what to think. "That may be what I am," he said, nodding. "I can't believe she really did it. Ran off and left her very own flesh and blood to the mercy of—whoever chooses to take her."

When the baby wakened, she knew exactly what to do to get milk from the bottle and did it with zest. But she fell asleep before she emptied it. Martha had filled it up, not knowing how much Babykins took each time.

Martha and Abe went to bed, still in shock. Were they to be the parents of that little baby forever? Abe couldn't fall asleep. "How about it, Lord?" he asked. "Is Nellie really gone? Is she coming back?"

You're doing fine, Abe.

"Thank You, Lord, but You didn't tell me anything." Abe fell asleep waiting for God to answer.

———∿∿∿———

"Abe, wake up." Abe struggled to open his eyes to a laughing Martha, holding the tiny baby. He sat up and reached for them both. "You don't know how pretty you look with that baby in your arms," he said, hugging them both.

"The baby didn't wake all night," Martha said. "Usually I take her to Nellie twice each night and last night she slept all night. Abe, she's going to do all right on cow's milk."

That afternoon a young woman came to the door with a tiny baby, much younger than Babykins, in her arms. Martha invited her in, then offered coffee. "Would you like some too, Abe?"

Abe looked up from the drawer he was fitting together. "Sure. Why not?"

Martha brought the coffee with cookies. As they ate they talked about the possible early spring, their homesteads, and how wild the Street was getting.

Finally the young woman cleared her throat. "I heard someone ran off and left her baby with you," she said.

"Yes," Martha said, "my sister-in-law. We're still in shock."

"Well, you can see I have a baby." She looked hard at Martha. "I was wondering if you'd like for me to take the baby and nurse it for a few months? I have way too much milk for one."

Abe felt himself take in a breath. He hadn't been ready for this. Surely Martha wouldn't give up her kin to a stranger to raise.

Martha smiled. "How sweet of you," she said softly.

The woman relaxed. "I couldn't waste my milk while a baby goes hungry, you know."

Martha glanced at Abe, then leaned forward. "But we had a doctor in last night and he told us how to fix cow's milk for the baby. She slept all night. How would it be if we wait and see if she can get along on cow's milk? If she can't handle it, we'll be happy to work out something."

The women went on talking about the babies and their little problems. Abe noticed the woman's baby didn't look nearly as clean as Babykins. He didn't want her taking care of their baby. He just didn't.

After awhile the woman went home. As far as Abe knew Martha hadn't even learned where the woman lived. He nodded his head. Good. They didn't need to know.

When Martha closed the door, Abe pulled her into his arms. "You're a much better mother than that woman. You wouldn't give our baby away, would you?"

Martha shook her head. "Only to save her life," she said. "Then I'd take Babykins to her for each feeding and bring her back. Even if it took every minute of my day."

Abe knew that. Why had he let himself get so worried? "I'm glad, my little Martha. I wouldn't have liked to put her into that woman's care. Or anyone's care but yours."

The baby slept all night again. "I'm sure she's going to be all right," Martha said. "I'm so happy, Abe." She searched his eyes. "How do you feel about all my kin expecting you to care for them? First Willie. We know he'll be with us until he grows up. Now this little baby. Do you feel pushed, Abe?"

How could he explain how he felt? "I'm the luckiest man in the world, Martha. I never think of Willie as your kin. He's as much mine as yours. And I already love this baby.

"I can see it's going to be hard keeping a baby and loving it like our own, never knowing when its parents might take it away from us. But that problem isn't just mine. We share it, Martha."

The baby seemed perfectly contented on her new formula and was much too young to miss her mother. Besides, Martha had always done everything for her except nurse her.

The next morning when the baby fussed, Martha heated the bottle while Abe rocked her. As he held her, talking to her, she watched him intently. A moment later her mouth turned up in a beautiful baby smile. "Martha! Come quick!"

Martha tore into the bedroom. "What happened? Is she all right?"

Abe pulled her to him. "Watch this." He began talking quietly to the little girl who listened carefully, her eyes never leaving his. But he couldn't coax another smile from her. He looked up at Martha. "She smiled at me, Martha. A real smile."

"Don't worry, Abe," Martha said. "She'll do it again."

She smiled again the next day and then often and easily.

—⚹—

A few days later Abe heard a strange sound at the door. Almost like the baby whimpering. He went to see what was out there.

When he opened the door a thin, scraggly dog struggled to its feet. "Josie!" Abe yelled. He threw the door open. "Come in, girl. Martha! Josie's here!"

Martha came running with the baby in her arms. When she saw Josie, she handed the baby to Abe and threw herself to the floor, hugging the dog.

Tears ran down her cheeks as she talked to Josie. "Where have you been, baby? Oh, Josie, you don't know how I've missed you." Josie licked Martha's face and lay down on the floor. Martha looked up at Abe. "Where did you find her? Where's she been? What happened, Abe?"

Watching Josie flop down to the floor, Abe thought she looked weak. Bad weak. "I think Josie's hungry, Martha," he said. "She just came to the door. That's all I know, but you better get something for her to eat. She's come a long way."

Martha soon set a plate of meat, potatoes, and gravy before the dog. Josie opened her mouth and inhaled the food in a few gulps. Then she wagged her dirty tail and lay back down. She would probably be all right, but right now she didn't look so good.

"She looks near as bad as when I first met the two of you," he said. "I wish she could tell us where she's been."

"Yes," Martha said. "Then we'd know what happened to Nellie too."

—⁂—

Martha spent the next week caring for the baby and feeding Josie back into strength and health. Every day Martha and Abe talked about Nellie, wondering if she'd show up and take the baby. Abe told Martha that Nellie had gone far away. He knew because Josie had obviously gone far too.

As Abe worked on his furniture he thought what a precious family he had. Martha must be the best woman in town. Josie was getting stronger each day. Willie was growing to quite a young man, almost eight now. And then there was Babykins. *Babykins! What a thing to call a beautiful baby girl. We'd better give her a name before she thinks she's Babykins.*

"Martha?"

Martha scurried in from their bedroom where she'd been bathing the baby. She held the tiny girl in her arms, wrapped in a large yellow towel. "Did you call, Abe?"

He got up from the floor where he'd been working. "Yes, I was just thinking we need to name Babykins, proper—like."

Martha laughed. "You interrupted her bath for that? Don't you think she could get along without a name for another ten minutes?"

Oh. He hadn't thought. He pulled Martha to him for a quick kiss. "Sure. You go finish the bath. But you might be thinkin' about a name. It's gotta be sweet and pure and beautiful just like her."

Martha sat on the rocker and wrapped the towel tighter around the baby. "I was just joking, Abe. I'd finished her bath and was drying her when you called. Your timing was perfect. I bet you have a name in mind."

He shook his head. "Not really. But she does need a name. Have you been thinkin' on it, Martha?"

She wiped a drop of water from the tip of Babykins' dark hair with the corner of the towel. "Not really Abe. Well, a little bit. I think Kathleen's really pretty. Or Rebecca or Elizabeth or Nellie."

Abe thought a moment. He liked all of them except Nellie. *What is this, Lord? Do I dislike the name Nellie because I don't want to remember Babykins has any parents besides us?*

Be careful, Abe. Nellie and Jackson are real.

We don't have to name the baby Nellie, do we, Lord?

Rebecca's a nice name.

Abe couldn't believe his ears—or his heart—wherever it was he heard God's voice. God had just named the baby! Better get that other question in real quick. *Lord, do You want us to build a new house? We'll need a bigger one with our family growin' like it is.*

"Abe! You started this conversation. Now you're daydreaming so bad you don't even hear me," Martha scolded.

Abe turned his attention to Martha with a start. Then a big grin covered his face. "The Lord just named the baby. Think Rebecca's all right?"

A lovely sweet look came over Martha as she smiled.

"I love the name, Abe. I purely love it." She raised her eyes. "Thank You, Lord for naming our baby. Rebecca's the prettiest name of all. Help us take the best care of her, Lord, and teach her to love You as we do. We ask in Jesus' name and thank You. Amen."

Abe moved beside Martha, then dropped to his knees beside the rocker and touched the baby's hair. "Hello, little Rebecca," he said softly. "You really look like a Rebecca."

Martha put her hand on Abe's as he touched the baby. Suddenly her eyes opened wide. "Abe! What's her last name? Does it have to be Lawford? Or can it be Noble?"

Abe hadn't thought that far. Lawford. Noble. Finally he grinned. "We could say she was born to us."

Martha returned his grin. "We could—but we couldn't. You know where the Good Book says all liars end up."

"Yeah. I didn't mean it. I wonder if Tom would know."

They hurried over to Tom and Rachel's place, Martha carrying the baby and Abe watching Willie and Josie race around them. They found Rachel busy making a cake. Two cakes.

"I was just going to send Melissa over to invite you to the twins' first birthday party," she said. "We'll have cake and rice pudding with whipped cream. I made one chocolate cake and one white so they can make a great mess at the party. Tommy will too, for that matter."

"I suppose Tom's busy," Abe said.

"He's out in the office, I think," Rachel said. "Unless someone's dragged him off to see a patient." Then her eyes became concerned. "Is Babykins all right?"

"She's fine," Martha said. "But her name's not Babykins anymore. The Lord just named her Rebecca. We were wondering if Tom would know what her last name would be, ours or Nellie and Jackson's?"

Rachel smiled and shoved a red curl behind her ear with a chocolaty finger. "He might know, but if he does it's not because he's a doctor. Let's go see if he's in the office."

Martha, Abe, Willie, and Rebecca followed Rachel to the office. Josie stayed beside the door. They found two people sitting in the entry room who told them the doctor was with someone else right now.

They all sat down on a leather davenport to wait. Just then someone banged hard on the office door. Rachel ran and opened it. Tommy came in. "Mama come. Jesse cry. Fa' down."

Rachel turned to Martha, grinning. "Gotta go. My little keepers keep close tabs on me. Come back to the house after you see Tom."

—ᴍ—

Tom didn't know much about things like Abe and Martha were dealing with. "Why don't you find a lawyer? If you can't you might look up the judge. They ought to know what the law says about it."

They thanked him, stuck their heads in the door, and told Rachel good-bye, then headed for the Street. They knew there were lawyers in town because they'd advertised in *The Statesman*, but they hadn't had occasion to need one.

They walked west on the Street until Abe spotted a sign, ADAM JENSEN, ATTORNEY AT LAW. "Isn't that a lawyer?" he asked.

Martha smiled. "I think so. Why don't they all call themselves the same thing?"

On going in, they found a thin blond man with a bushy mustache sitting at a small round table writing on a tablet. He stood and nodded. "Adam Jensen, at your service." He motioned to chairs on the other side of the table, which they took.

"We've some questions about our baby here," Abe said. He told the man exactly what had happened and what they wanted to know.

"How long's the mother been gone?" Jensen asked. They told him a month. He shook his head. "Not long enough. The only way you can legally change the baby's name is to adopt her. If the mother doesn't come back in five more months I'd go ahead and draw up adoption papers. 'Course you can call her by your name now. Won't matter 'tall."

"I want my name to be Noble, too," Willie cried.

Abe nearly jumped at Willie's outburst. He'd had no idea the boy even listened to the discussion. Suddenly he recognized how Willie felt. He would be the only one in the family with a different name. No one wants to be different. He turned back to the lawyer. "Well, let's let Willie's name be Noble. Isn't anyone to object to that. His parents are dead."

The attorney started asking questions and writing on the pad. When he'd asked about nearly every iota of their private life, he smiled. "Sounds good. Won't really make any difference whether you adopt him, he's yours anyway. Could just change his name."

"No! I want Abe to 'dopt me!"

Abe grinned. "Let's go for the adoption."

The attorney wrote up several papers while Abe and Martha waited, Rebecca rested, and Willie wiggled.

When he finished, Jensen reached out a hand to Willie. Willie put his hand in the big one. "Congratulations, Willie," the attorney said. "You're legally Mr. and Mrs. Noble's son. You can call them Papa and Mama now."

Willie burst out laughing. "No! They're Martha and Abe. Is my name Noble now?"

Jensen assured him it was.

Abe paid the man and the family started out the door. "Come back in a few months if the mother doesn't show up," Jensen said.

—◆—

Martha laughed out loud as they walked toward home. "That didn't turn out the way we expected, did it?"

"No," Abe said, "but it turned out great. Don't you think? We have a happy boy, who won't be on the outside now if we do adopt Rebecca."

Everyone fussed for food when they got home, and Rebecca got her tummy filled first. She always took her bottle with joy and excitement, thinking it was the perfect food.

After dinner, Abe worked on a table and chair set for an eager family, while Martha cleaned the house and did a washing. The baby slept.

Later in the afternoon Abe grew restless. He needed to do something different. Something to take his mind off Nellie, and what she might do. Martha looked as if she had finished her heavy work. She sat in a chair mending Willie's pants.

Suddenly a ride sounded good to him. Out in the fresh air. He sat down in the chair across from Martha. "Are you tired of that?" he asked.

She looked up with a question in her eyes, then joy.

"Of what, Abe? I'm never tired of doing for my family."

"Well, the horses need some exercise. And so do I."

She laid her work aside, got up, and started to get her coat. Then she stopped and looked at Abe. "How am I going to ride? We have a baby now."

Abe had forgotten all about that. Nellie had been here before when they rode, so she watched the baby. "You're going to ride, Martha. We'll think of something. Think someone could keep the baby?"

Martha shook her head. "Everyone's busy, Abe. We better figure it out ourselves. I wonder if I could make some sort of papoose board."

Abe thought that a great idea. "Martha, you said it! Let's go get one from the Indians. They must have an extra one around somewhere."

Willie and Abe soon had the horses saddled, warm coats on everyone, and Rebecca wrapped in a heavy blanket. Abe helped Martha up, then handed the baby to her. "This'll work just fine until we get the papoose board," Martha said. "I suppose I shouldn't do anything too reckless though."

"When we get the papoose board can we go for a good ride?" Willie asked.

"You bet," Abe agreed. "We'll let the horses go as fast as they want." The three turned the horses west toward Fort Walla Walla and the little Indian village, and plodded sedately along. After a half hour Abe saw the trees and large buildings at the Fort. A moment later they drew near the little tepee village.

But three horses standing impatiently by the trail ahead caught Abe's interest. As they neared he saw several people rolling around on the ground. He nudged Ebb who understood exactly and sped up his walk. When they got close, Abe saw two white men beating an Indian with big clubs. He jumped off Ebb, dropped the reins, and ran behind the white men. "Drop the clubs," he yelled loudly, as he slipped his right hand in his pocket. "Now! I have three bullets for each of you, and I'll deliver as soon as I get this said!"

The clubs dropped to the ground, the men looked around, and the Indian tried to struggle to his feet. As Abe picked up the clubs, he recognized Camas. "What's goin' on here?" he asked the white men.

Camas made a small sound, and Abe looked at him. Blood dripped from the young Indian's nose and a wound on his forehead. Those men hadn't been playing a game. The Indian pointed to the white men. "Take gold," he said. Abe didn't understand. Camas tried again. "Take Abe's gold!"

Chapter 13

Martha heard and understood. These were two of the men who'd taken their gold, the men the Indians had stolen the gold back from—as well as the thieves' horses and guns. She started to yell at Abe, to explain what happened, when she could tell he also understood.

He snapped to attention, keeping his right hand in his coat pocket. "All right, you two, throw down your firearms. Now! We been stringin' up vermin like you around here. Lots of 'em. My finger's mighty nervous, dealin' with the likes of you."

"We ain't got no guns. Why'd you think we was usin' clubs on that savage? Them sneaks took our guns too."

Abe seemed to accept that. "All right, get on your horses with no funny stuff." The men moved toward their horses. "Martha, you cover the one on the brown horse. I'll watch the white horse."

Martha almost giggled. Neither of them had a gun. Abe didn't believe in carrying one. Said some innocent person was more apt to get hurt than the one breaking the law. "All right, Abe," she answered. "I've got him."

"Head toward the Street," Abe ordered. "The law's about halfway down. You're on your way to jail. You boys don't know how lucky you are. Most people around are dishing out their own justice when they come across the likes of you."

The men didn't say a word, just turned their horses in a northeast direction. Abe, Martha, and Willie rode behind them.

When they reached the Street the men turned east, went a few blocks, and stopped beside the sheriff's building and jail. Abe bailed off Ebb in a hurry. "Get off those horses. Easy-like." The men did, their hands raised.

"Get movin' right through that door," Abe instructed. The men started toward the door, but the sheriff met them before they reached it.

"What's goin' on, Abe?" he asked.

"Caught these boys killin' an Indian," Abe ground through his teeth.

"Where's the Injun?" the sheriff wanted to know.

Martha inhaled hard. She'd forgotten all about Camas. She looked at Abe to find him staring at her. He'd forgotten too. *Please, Lord, help Camas to be all right. Thank You in Jesus' name, Father. Amen.*

Abe flashed a sickly grin at the sheriff. "Guess we forgot all about him. He was bleedin' from the nose and also a cut on his head where these varmints tried to beat him to death with clubs. Two on one, even."

The sheriff waved his gun at the men. "Go on in there." When they got inside, the sheriff told them to sit on some chairs near a table. When they got settled, he sat in a chair in front of them. "Wha'd that redskin do to you boys?" he asked softly.

One of the men took a deep breath and gave Abe a long look. "They stole our gold and our horses," he said. "We seen this savage on one of our horses so we decided to take it back. We'd 'a' gotten it too, if that fool who thinks he's God's little helper hadn't 'a' come along."

The sheriff looked at Abe, his eyebrows up.

Oh, God, Martha prayed silently, *show Abe what to say. Thank You, Father. In Jesus' name.*

Abe moved to the table the men sat around. "I reckon the good Lord brought us to that spot today. Fact is, we happened to be with the Indians when those two with two others robbed the Indians' gold last spring. A couple days later the Indians found them in a drunken stupor and took their gold back. They took the horses too, for self-protection. We'd 'a' all been shot dead before we got home if they hadn't taken the horses." Abe held up his right hand. "As God is my witness, that's exactly what happened."

The sheriff turned back to the men. "That what happened?"

The men spit out a few curse words before one answered. "No, that ain't what happened. They just came upon us whilst we was sleepin' and took the horses. We had to walk a hunnert miles. Carried the saddles half that way, then dumped 'em."

"No gold involved?" Abe asked the men.

The men looked at each other for several seconds, their eyes wide. "No gold," the man answered. "Just horses." He turned back to the sheriff. "I hear you punish horse thieves quick and harsh in this town. You best go get the Indian before his kin rescue him."

The sheriff appeared to study the matter. Then he turned to Abe. "I don't rightly know what to do, Abe. The men deny your charges."

"Look, Sheriff," Abe said. "They've admitted enough for you to know they're the ones involved. You heard him say the Indians took their gold and horses. When I asked him point blank if there was gold involved he denied it. He's lyin' through his teeth. And they can't deny tryin' to kill the Indian today. Lock 'em up. Take 'em to court to find out if they're guilty. That's what trials are for."

Thank You, Lord, Martha said silently. *You gave Abe all he needed.*

The sheriff lumbered to his feet and waved a gun at the two men.

"Well, I guess you got free room and board fer tonight. We'll sort through this tomorrow."

Abe turned to Martha. "Let's go get Tom and take him to check Camas."

A half hour later they discovered Camas gone. "Someone hauled him off to a tepee," Abe said. "Right over here, Tom."

Gray Wolf met them before they reached the tepees. He held his hand out to Abe. "Abe good," he said.

"Thanks, Gray Wolf. Camas?" He pointed to Tom. "Doctor."

Gray Wolf, looking relieved, turned and led them to a tepee behind his. He pointed, turned, and returned to his own home.

Abe called Camas' name. A pretty Indian woman opened the flap and motioned them in. Martha and Willie went in first, then Abe and Tom brought up the rear. Camas, who'd been cleaned up, lay on a pallet on the floor of the smoky tent. The place smelled like fish-oil mixed with food and smoke. Martha remembered Willie beside her and Rebecca in her arms. "Abe," she said softly. "We'll wait outside for you." He nodded to show he had heard, so she led Willie out.

"Doesn't it smell good out here?" Willie asked right away.

"Yes. That's why I brought you out. But since we're out, let's see if Gray Wolf knows anything about papoose boards."

Gray Wolf responded to her first soft call. "Camas?" he asked.

She shook her head. "I don't know, Gray Wolf. They're looking at him now."

"Doctor fix Camas?"

"He'll try." How could she change the subject to something as frivolous as papoose boards?

But Gray Wolf did it for her. He pointed at the sleeping baby. "Martha papoose?"

Martha laughed to herself. Gray Wolf and his sons came often for food, English lessons, and Bible lessons. He must know tummies get big before little ones come along. "No. Martha keep papoose." Now was the time. "Martha need papoose board," she said. Seeing he didn't understand she said, "Papoose board." She motioned to her back, as if putting the baby back there. Gray Wolf looked carefully at her back but didn't seem to understand. "Put papoose there," she said, leaning over and forming a board on her back.

Suddenly Gray Wolf's eyes brightened. "Papoose Martha back," he patted Martha's back.

Maybe he was getting it! "Martha need papoose on back," she said. "Gray Wolf help?"

Gray Wolf thought a moment. "Gray Wolf help?" he repeated. Martha nodded yes.

"Come Gray Wolf." Martha followed the tall Indian toward another tepee.

He stopped at a dark-colored one and called softly. His usually coarse voice sounded almost like a bird. A tall Indian woman came out and Gray Wolf pointed to Martha and the baby, then said a few words in the Nez Percé language. Martha understood some of them. One was "give." He must be planning to give it to her. Oh well, how do you pay an Indian who has a whole cave full of gold?

The Indian woman ran lightly between the tepees until she disappeared. Gray Wolf turned back to Martha. "Come back," he said.

The woman did come back in a few minutes. She held exactly what Martha needed. A pretty papoose case made from light and dark leather. The woman handed it to Martha. "Thank you," Martha told the woman. She repeated it to Gray Wolf two or three times. Then she handed it to him and pointed to her back. He took it and laid it on the ground. Then he took the baby, put her into it, and laced it up tight so she wouldn't slump down. Rebecca didn't awaken. Not even when Gray Wolf strapped it on Martha's back. It felt good to Martha, and her tired arms rejoiced. She turned this way and that, jumping just a little. Rebecca slept on. Martha thanked Gray Wolf again and again.

"Abe fix Camas," he said every time she thanked him. She had prayed for Camas to be all right, but she decided to do it again with Gray Wolf. She pointed up. "Abe's God fix Camas."

She kneeled on the ground and pulled him down beside her. Willie dropped to the ground on her other side. Martha put her arm over Willie's shoulders. "Dear Father," she said. "We thank You for Your great love for us and for forgiving our sins. Because You love us so very much, we love You, too, Father, more than life. Now, Father, we ask You in Jesus' name to help Camas get well right away. Thank You, Father. Amen."

In less than a minute, Abe came out of the tent. "How is he?" Martha asked.

"He's hurt bad, but we asked God to help. He'll be all right."

Gray Wolf hadn't understood much. "Camas?"

Abe pointed upward. "Big God help Camas get well."

Gray Wolf understood that. He nodded. "Camas get well."

A grin spread over Abe's face. Martha wondered what he'd thought of. He pointed into the sky again. "Big God bring Abe and Martha here today. So we help Camas."

Gray Wolf thought a moment, then he relaxed and nodded. "Big God bring Abe." He peered at Abe. "Gray Wolf thank big God."

Abe looked at Martha. She nodded. "Let's kneel before our big God,"

Abe said, "and thank Him for bringing Abe and Martha here. And for helping Camas get well." They did, then got to their feet. Martha saw Gray Wolf wipe a tear from his eye. Either he loved God a lot or he still feared for Camas' life.

Abe noticed the papoose board on Martha's back and moved over to have a look. "That looks pretty good," he said. "Now you won't drop her when you ride. Hey, you'll be able to work in the garden too."

"Yes. That's partly why I needed it so bad. She likes it too."

Abe pulled some money from his pocket and turned to Gray Wolf. "Let me pay you for the papoose board."

Gray Wolf backed up. "Abe God make Camas well."

Tom came from Camas's tent. "Is he going to be all right?" Martha asked.

Tom looked tired but peaceful. "When I first saw him I wasn't sure, but something happened since then. He's much better." He grinned. "Could have something to do with our great God." He turned to Martha. "Would you stop and tell Rachel I'm staying with him tonight? At least for a while, just in case.

Martha, Abe, Willie, and Rebecca on Martha's back mounted their horses and prepared to leave. Gray Wolf seemed unwilling for them to go, hanging around even when they wanted to start.

Suddenly Abe jumped from his horse. "Something wrong, Gray Wolf?" he asked the older man.

Gray Wolf turned to face Camas's tent. "Doctor?" he said with a question in his voice. "Doctor big God man?"

"Yes!" Abe nearly bellowed. "The doctor is our big God's man. Our big God will help Tom, Gray Wolf."

Gray Wolf reached out an arm and patted Abe's back. "Good. Abe go."

"Thank you for the papoose board," Martha called as they rode away.

They stopped and told Rachel that Tom wouldn't be home for a while, maybe not until morning, and went home weary but happy.

The next morning Martha gave away many gallons of milk. More people seemed to hear about it, for more came every day. Then Abe took the rest to the Street to sell. He couldn't bring enough to satisfy the merchants with the expanded population.

After they finished the necessary tasks, Abe asked Martha if she would like to try out her papoose board on a walk to the jail. "I want to see what's going on," he said. "I wouldn't be surprised if they turned those two loose and arrested Camas."

But they hadn't been turned loose. "I really ain't got much reason to keep 'em," the sheriff said. "Seems to be one person's word against the other's. Knowing them redskins like I do, I'd likely believe the two we got here."

Martha felt fear, then remembered God. *Make this turn out right, Father,* she prayed silently. Peace filled her being.

Abe looked as serene as Rebecca on Martha's back. "You know me too, Sheriff. Ever known me to tell something that isn't true?"

The man spit on the floor. "Well, can't say as I have, but you ain't God. You could be mistaken."

"Buckley! You heard them change their story last night when I asked about gold. When people tell the truth they don't have to do that. You'd better start working up a case against them. If you turn them loose, I'm gonna make you more trouble 'n you ever saw. Come on, Martha."

As they walked back home, Martha thanked God again for Abe. *He's purely your man, Father,* she ended.

"Let's get the horses," Abe said. "I can't wait to see how Camas is. We owe Willie a good ride, too."

"Yea!" Willie said. "Let's take sandwiches."

"You just want an excuse to eat," Martha told him.

After feeding Rebecca and making sandwiches, they saddled the horses and headed west. As they dismounted, Martha noticed an Indian limping toward them. Camas!

She ran and hugged him carefully. "Tom made you better!" she said.

Camas shook his head and pointed a finger skyward. "Big God make well."

"You're right," she said, laughing. "People can't make you well, but our big God can."

Gray Wolf came out, so they all thanked the big God together. Then Abe led his little family on a nice ride in the early spring sunshine. As they rode Martha kept thinking how nice the papoose board was. Why didn't white people make something like that to use? They stopped to eat sandwiches, then returned home.

Abe began sanding on a chair to go with the table he'd just finished for a new family in town. "How many chairs do you have to make?" Martha asked, thinking chairs looked harder than tables to make, with all those small pieces to cut, shape, sand, and finish.

Abe looked up at her and grinned. "Only seven more after this one. If I'd stay home and work, I'd get them done in a few days."

Martha fed the baby, put her to bed, and started mixing up bread. When she had everything in it and was kneading the big batch of dough, she decided to ask something she'd been thinking about. "When can we start working outside?" she asked. "We've been outside a lot lately. Looks like we're having an early spring—and we had a glorious winter. Abe, isn't God truly good to us?"

"He is, Martha." Abe chuckled. "I been thanking Him a lot for that baby in there. I think He arranged for us to have her, knowin' how much we both wanted a baby."

Martha smiled. "I been thinking about that too, Abe. But He could have given us one of our very own just as easily. He'd never cause all the heartache involved for us to have Rebecca." She shook her head as she turned dough and pushed it and turned it again. "Never, Abe. He's a God of love."

"You're right, Martha, but He can make good come out of bad things. I reckon I'll just keep thankin' Him."

"Me too, Abe. Me too." She gathered up the lively mass of dough and dumped it back into the bowl, spread a cloth over it, and put it on a shelf over the cook stove to rise.

Later that afternoon Willie came running into the house where Martha scrubbed baby clothes. "Martha, a man just rode by on a horse. He asked me if Nellie Lawford is my kin. I said yes, and he said he saw her yesterday."

Martha dropped the diaper she held. "Where did he see her?" she asked. Willie shook his head. "I don't know. He didn't tell me that."

She grabbed Willie by his shoulders. "Where's the man, Willie? I have to talk to him."

"He's gone, Martha. I told you he was riding a horse—a big gray horse with brown spots. He stopped only a minute to talk to me. Then he just kept going."

Martha dropped her hands from Willie's shoulders and raced outside. She looked east, then west. Not a horse and man in sight—not even a horse or a man. She ran back inside. "Willie, tell me what the man looked like."

"I don't know, Martha," Willie said. "I saw the horse though. I told you what the horse looked like."

Chapter 14

Get hold of yourself, Martha, she told herself. She took a deep breath. And another. Willie had done everything right. He couldn't have done more, even if he had noticed what the man looked like. She pulled Willie onto her lap. "I'm sorry I got so excited," she whispered into his ear. "You did everything exactly right."

Abe walked into the house. "Abe!" Willie yelled, "a man went by and told me he saw Nellie."

Abe dropped to his knees before Willie, still on Martha's lap. "Where is she?" he asked.

"The man's gone. He had a gray horse with brown spots."

Abe looked at Martha. He had never seen her looking so stricken. "What happened?"

She shook her head. "That's all we know, Abe. The man stopped just long enough to tell Willie. I ran out but didn't see a thing." Her lips formed a shaky grin. "At least the horse was unusual. If we ever see a horse like that we could ask."

"Yeah." Abe got up. "Come on, Willie. Let's get the horses saddled. We're goin' for a ride." He lifted his eyes to Martha. "Get Rebecca ready." Then he took Willie's hand and together they went outside.

As they saddled the horses, Abe noticed how much real help Willie was becoming. He felt as though just yesterday he'd made Willie think he was helping, but now the boy grabbed cinches and tightened them, put on bridles and most anything.

When they finished, they led the horses to the house. Martha waited in front of the house with Rebecca strapped on her back.

Abe jumped from his saddle and helped Martha and Rebecca up. Martha gave him a radiant smile. "Where are we going, Abe?"

Her words surprised Abe. He'd figured she would know. "We're headed for Jackson's place. Maybe she just went home—and forgot to get Rebecca."

When they rode up to the house it didn't look very lived in. But he wasn't going to leave until he knew for sure. He slid from the saddle, moved to Thunder's side, and held his arms to Martha. "Come on, we're goin' in." He turned to Willie. "You comin'? Let's go see what's goin' on."

As they approached the door, Abe wondered why he'd pushed this confrontation. Maybe if they had just left it alone, Nellie would never have come after Rebecca. Willie banged his fist loudly on the door when they stood in front of it. No one answered. Abe knocked. Still no response. Abe noticed his breathing had nearly stopped as they waited in silence.

After another minute he drew in a deep breath. "I'm goin' in," he said, pulling the latch. "It's locked. Now what? Are we givin' up?" He looked to Martha for her response. She shrugged. "I'm for breakin' in," he said. "Nellie could be in there sick or worse."

Willie ran around the house and returned almost immediately. "The back doors hangin' open, Abe. Come on."

Abe grinned. "Why didn't I think of goin' in the back, Willie?" He held a hand to Martha. "Come on. We're goin' to see if she's here or if she's been here." He studied her face. "Think we can tell if she's been here?"

"I'm not sure. I didn't look around much when we took her home."

"Well, come on," Willie said. "If we go in we'll soon find out."

Willie led the way into the kitchen part of the main room. Abe noticed how clean and neat it looked. He met Martha's eyes. "Did it look this neat when we left with Nellie?"

She shook her head. "I haven't the faintest idea. Let's look through the house a little."

They found a few of Nellie's clothes in the bedroom and also a pair of Jackson's overalls. None of them knew if they'd been there before. Abe checked the fireplace. It was cold with hardly any ashes. He had no idea how long it had been since it held a fire.

They closed the back door as they left, knowing little more than when they came.

"Let's go ask at Fort Walla Walla about the horse," Abe suggested. Letting the horses have their heads, they turned west.

—⟶

The soldier nodded at Abe's question. "Yes, we sold a horse like that. It's been over six months, probably near a year now. I have no idea who bought it."

Abe leaned toward the man. "This is important, sir. Do you have records you could check?"

The man invited them in and offered them chairs while he searched for the information. After a long fifteen-minute wait an army officer approached. "We found the information you're looking for," he said. "But you'd better tell us why you want to find the man."

Abe looked at Martha. She smiled. "Sure," Abe said. "I don't mind at all." He explained about Jackson and Nellie disappearing. He pointed at Rebecca on Martha's back and explained they had left the baby. And that a man riding that horse had told Willie he had seen Nellie.

The man nodded. "Just wanted to be sure everything was all right. The man's name is Wallace Dugan. That's all I have. He didn't have an address at the time. Says here he was taking out a donation land claim."

"Wallace Dugan," Abe repeated. "That oughta be some help. Much obliged, sir."

When they reached the thriving little town of Walla Walla, Abe said, "I'm gonna check on the Street."

"I have to go home, Abe," Martha said. "Rebecca's starting to wiggle. She's overtime for her feeding so in a minute she'll let the whole world know."

"You go on," Abe said. "I'll just ask around a little."

When Abe entered Galbraith's Saloon, the owner looked surprised. "Ain't seen you for a while, Abe. Thought maybe you was too good fer me nowadays."

Abe grinned and sat down at the counter. "You know better'n that. If you had a wife could cook like mine you wouldn't eat out much either. Bring me a coffee and sandwich."

While he ate, Abe asked Galbraith, his faithful old friend, if he knew the man, Wallace Dugan. Galbraith shook his head. "He's been in but not for awhile. Probably got a wife. Them women beat me out of a lot of business."

"Know where he lives?"

Galbraith grinned. "I barely know where you live. Only reason I have any idea atall is 'cause you came when there weren't nobody here yet." He whistled. "So many people here now, can't even tell which ones're your friends."

"You're right," Abe said, shoving in the last bite of sandwich. He got up. "Gotta find that man one way or another. See you later."

His next stop was at the sheriff's office. "I hoped I wouldn't have to look at your face today," the man said. "I still got 'em locked up. Got a lawyer goin' over the facts too, to see if we need to take these boys to trial."

"Sounds like you're doing good," Abe said. "Right now I wonder if you know a Wallace Dugan."

The sheriff squinted his face as he thought. "Can't remember the name, anyway. What's up? He beat up some savages, too?"

Abe laughed as he brushed his hair back. "Not that I know of. I just wanted to talk to him on some business. Thanks."

Abe tried several more stores and businesses but finally gave up and went home. After rubbing Ebb down and releasing him in the corral, he went inside. Maybe he could finish that chair today.

"Why were we looking so hard for that man?" Martha asked when he went in.

Suddenly Abe didn't really know. He grinned sheepishly. "I'm not sure. I know it's not because we want to get rid of Rebecca. Could it be that we're terrified for Nellie to be in town?"

Martha touched Rebecca's soft little cheek as the baby sucked vigorously on her bottle. "I'm purely in love with her already, Abe. I don't think I want to know any more about Nellie. Ever. I could hardly stand it when we went looking for her."

Abe nodded. He understood the feeling. "I know. I really didn't want to, but I thought we had to. You know, face the enemy. Never let him sneak up behind you."

"Maybe we should move away, Abe. Somewhere where they could never find us."

For a second Abe thought that was a great idea. But he shook his head. "We have to do the right thing, Martha. I'd like to do that too, but that's almost running from the law. We'd be looking over our shoulder the rest of our lives."

Martha looked sad. "We're going to be doing that anyway, Abe."

"No. Remember that attorney, Jensen, said we could adopt her in six months? Then she'll be ours, Martha. Forever. And we won't have to hide."

Relief flooded her eyes. "That's right. So we won't run. We'll just live through it."

Willie had moved to the settle beside Martha. "I'm yours, Martha. I'm yours forever, and you don't have to hide from anyone."

Willie! What did he think about their wild talk about running with Rebecca? Abe sprang to the couch, grabbed Willie and held him tight. "You bet you're ours, Willie. I thank God every day for you too. Today when we were saddling the horses I noticed how you're growin' and gettin' stronger. We're mighty proud of you, Willie."

Martha took it up where Abe left off, telling Willie how proud of him they felt and how much they loved him. The little boy marched off with his head high and his back straight.

The next day someone came with a message for Abe. He took the rumpled piece of paper and read:

Abe,

We're havin' a trial for them boys you brung in. Tomorrow afternoon in the courtroom. Figured you'd want to be there—and cause a lot of trouble.

James A. Buckley
Sheriff, Walla Walla County

"I guess I won't be workin' on chairs tomorrow," Abe said. "I gotta go and make sure they don't turn it around and put the Indians on trial."

Martha put the last pin in Rebecca's diaper. "I want to be there too, Abe. Think that would be all right?"

"Sure, if Willie can sit still that long." Abe thought a moment. "I think I'll go on down there now and see what they've done."

The sheriff greeted Abe. "Figured you'd never wait 'til tomorrow to get here," he said. "Shoulda waited 'til tomorrow to tell you."

"I'll bet you wish you'd done that, don't you? Well, I was just wondering who the attorneys are."

"Abraham Donovan's prosecutin' them. Got Adam Jensen to defend. That suit ya?"

Abe nodded. "Sounds good. I don't know Donovan, but Jensen seems pretty fair. Did you give him all the information I gave you? Are you callin' any witnesses?"

The sheriff gave Abe a smug look. "You wanta know, come and see." Somehow Abe wasn't quite satisfied with the sheriff's answers. He decided to get Ebb and go see the Indians. They should be at the trial for sure.

The next morning Martha and Abe hurried to get everything done to free up the afternoon. Abe could hardly wait. He expected almost anything to happen, and not necessarily honest things.

Aunt Mandy offered to keep Willie and Rebecca for the afternoon so Abe and Martha could both watch the proceedings carefully. They hurried into the courtroom at a quarter to one. People filled the four rows of five chairs each. Twenty people laughing and talking created quite a buzz. The judge, attorneys, sheriff, and prisoners weren't there yet. Neither were the Indians.

Abe and Martha found a place to stand against the west wall. "Good thing we didn't bring Willie and Rebecca," Abe said.

Then the door in the front of the room opened and the prisoners came in with Adam Jensen. The sheriff and Abraham Donovan came in next, and finally the judge. The Indians came in the front door, spotted Abe and Martha along the wall, and joined them.

Sheriff Buckley called the court to order and asked for twelve "staunch law-abiding men" to serve on the jury. Men from all around stood up and marched to the special seats that had been saved for them. When they all sat down, they lacked one juror. Abe suggested Gray Wolf go but he didn't. A roughly-dressed, middle-aged white man meandered to the last seat.

The judge called the prisoners to the front. "You are charged with beating an Indian with a blunt instrument and inflicting bodily harm. The attorneys will give their talks."

Abraham Donovan opened the case with his speech. "These men were caught in the act of beating a single Indian man severely with clubs. The Indian lay on the ground helpless, but the two prisoners didn't stop. No, they continued beating him with their huge clubs as though surely trying to kill the savage."

The sheriff stood. "The defending lawyer will talk now."

Adam Jensen stood up. "These men have been totally misunderstood, friends. They're the victims in this case. They were merely trying to retrieve their own horse that the Indian had stolen earlier. The man refused to give them their horse, though not denying it to be theirs. Watch and see how it really happened."

"I think Abraham Donovan goes first," the judge said.

Donovan stood and walked to the front again. "The case is pure and simple," he said, "just like I already said. Abram Noble and his wife came upon the scene and saved the redskin's life. That's all there is to it, gentlemen of the jury. It's your civic duty to find them guilty." He sat down.

Adam Jensen walked to the front. "This is the part of the story you didn't know. The redskin and two of his friends stole four horses from the defendants last summer, leaving the defendants to walk a hundred miles. When they recognized one of their horses they went after it. Wouldn't you? When the savage refused to give it to them they fought for it. Wouldn't you?"

He sat down. Donovan hurried to the front. "I'm sorry, Mr. Jensen. I didn't know about that. I want to drop my case against the gentlemen. I'll move that we—"

Abe tore to the front of the room, interrupting Donovan's motion. "You still don't know what happened, any of you." He scowled at the sheriff. "Except Buckley. I happened to be with the Indians last spring when these men, along with two others attacked. They robbed my good friends, Gray Wolf, Pony Boy, and Camas of all of their gold, lots of gold. They were armed and masked, like any common bandits. A few days later, the Indians luckily found the robbers in a drunken stupor and retrieved their gold. They took the robbers' horses to protect their lives until they got home. The men could have had their horses anytime.

"When they recognized their horse, they didn't demand their horse. They wanted revenge so they tried to kill Camas. They nearly did too. The Indians are here. So is my wife. Ask any of them. Their stories will match mine because mine's true. As God is my witness I swear today that everything I've said here is true."

Abe strode over and stood beside Martha against the wall. Deep silence shrouded the courtroom. Martha patted Abe's leg. Still no one said anything.

Finally Adam Jensen walked to the front. "Gentlemen," he said, "I feel I've made a grave mistake. Am I correct that Mr. and Mrs. Abram Noble are pillars in our society? The very epitome of integrity? I've heard some of the things they've done to promote honesty and fair play in our town as it grows and develops. I've also talked to the prisoners at length and felt something not quite right. I couldn't put my finger on it, so I decided I was being prejudiced. But I feel deeply that Abe Noble has just told us the real story as it really happened. I've never knowingly defended guilty men, so I'm withdrawing my services to them immediately."

Chapter 15

The judge jumped to his feet. "You can't do that, Jensen. The law says everyone gets legal representation. You jest be thinkin' on how you can best do that without crossin' your morals."

Abraham Donovan strode forward. "I think what we need here is to find out exactly what happened. I'm callin' that Injun what got beat to the stand."

Camas didn't move. Martha realized he didn't understand, so she leaned over and told him in simple English mixed with Nez Percé. He looked toward Donovan and shook his head no. Martha smiled. "You have to," she said. Then she took his arm and led him to the front. "Martha stay," she whispered, easing him toward the witness chair.

When Camas stood beside the chair, Marshall Gilliam held up his right hand. "You swear to tell the truth, the whole truth and nuthin' but the truth, so help you God?" he droned.

Camas looked at Martha. She smiled and nodded. "Say yes," she whispered.

Camas looked as though he feared another beating but he met the judge's eyes. "Yes," he said.

The judge looked to Abraham Donovan. "Your witness," he said.

Donovan moved toward Camas. The Indian shrank back into the chair. "It's all right," Martha whispered. "Listen. Maybe you can tell what he says."

"Did you steal that horse from these gentlemen?" Donovan asked.

Camas looked puzzled. Martha stood straight. "Camas take horse?" She pointed toward the accused men.

Camas nodded. "Yes," he said loud and clear. "Camas, Gray Wolf, Pony Boy take four horses."

The corporate gasp nearly made Martha collapse. Camas had just freed the robbers! No! He'd done exactly right. She smiled and nodded at Camas to show him he'd done right.

Donovan strutted before his audience. "I guess we owe our mistakenly arrested friends an apology," he said.

Again Abe bounded to the front. "Wait a minute! This man just told you the truth. Now be a lawyer and get to the bottom of it!"

Donovan looked angry for a moment, then smiled. "I can do that, Mr.

464

Noble, if it'll satisfy you." He faced Camas again. "When did you take the four horses?"

Martha watched Camas and realized he understood. "After men take Indian gold. Much gold. Indians take gold, horses, guns."

Donovan looked at Martha. "You have this savage well-trained, Mrs. Noble. Like a dog doing tricks."

Martha felt her face flush. "Mr. Donovan, why don't you want to learn the truth and deal justice to everyone? These Indian men are totally honest. Ask him anything, but do it in real simple language. I promise he understands your language better than you do his." Several laughs around the court room gave Martha hope.

Abraham Donovan simmered down and worked with Camas. When Camas understood, he answered every question, and none of Donovan's tricks fooled him.

When Donovan quit, the judge asked Jensen if he wanted to question Camas.

"I think they've pretty well answered everyone's questions," Jensen said.

The judge instructed the jury, and the men went into the small room the judge indicated.

An hour later, at six o'clock, the jury hadn't come out, so the judge instructed everyone to go home. Most did. Martha and Abe waited with the Indians.

At eight o'clock the judge said the verdict would be announced the next morning at eight o'clock. The sheriff took the prisoners back to their cells. The Indians headed west toward their tepee homes.

Martha felt hungry, tired, and eager to see Willie and Rebecca. "Come on, Abe."

Willie hugged both Martha and Abe and couldn't quit talking. Rebecca, now three months old, smiled big, toothless smiles. "I think she missed us," Martha told Abe.

The next morning Martha and Abe got up earlier than their usual five o'clock to do the chores and to give away and sell the milk. Abe hadn't even gone to the barn yet when Josie announced intruders. Almost at once, several men arrived on horses, demanding to talk to Abe.

"Ya heard what happened in the night?" one of Abe's vigilance committee brothers asked. "I'll tell you what happened. A bunch of thugs broke into the jail, beat up the marshall, and took off with them vermin what robbed your Injun friends."

Martha couldn't believe her ears. "You mean the men on trial are gone? Escaped?"

The big bearded man nodded. "That's right. That ain't such good news fer your Indian friends, neither."

Abe sprang to life. "I gotta milk the cows and feed the cattle," he said. "Go round up whoever you can find. Let's catch those cutthroats and make 'em wish they'd stayed in jail."

The men roared approval and took off, pushing their horses hard.

Martha helped the men milk, strained it, set aside the many gallons she would give away, and poured the rest into cans to be delivered downtown.

"What about the Indians?" she asked while Abe loaded the big cans onto the wagon. "They need to know."

"I plan to go by their places soon's I get rid of the milk," Abe said. "I'll be back after that."

Martha tried to keep her mind on the two children, while preparing for the washing and baking, but it wasn't easy. She took Rebecca and Willie and hurried across the creek to tell Cleve and Mandy. "I'll be ready to go as soon as I get my own chores done," Cleve said. "Don't let 'em go without me."

Martha went home and looked at the clock. Six minutes after six. Seemed it should be about noon, so much had happened already.

The men returned before Abe. Cleve rode across the creek and joined them. Martha couldn't count them but she thought there must be more than a hundred men and horses. The loud talk made Martha realize how unhappy the community felt at the early morning jail break.

When Abe finally came, Martha hurried to him, hoping for a moment alone with him. "How did the Indians take the news?" she asked in a hushed voice.

He grinned. "Silently. Like everything else. But you can believe they'll be on their toes."

The men rode off in a big cloud of dust, nickering horses, and masculine voices yelling and laughing.

Martha returned to the house to bake bread, scrub clothes, and wait. Six hours later she had baked the bread and fastened the clothes on the line, but she still waited. Strapping Rebecca onto her back, she helped Willie saddle the horses, and they went for a long ride, keeping their eyes wide open.

Back home again, Martha prepared supper. Surely Abe would soon be home, hopefully with the criminals all captured.

But it was not to be. Abe returned two hours later, after Martha and Willie had struggled to milk all the cows while keeping Rebecca happy. Abe said they hadn't caught sight of the men.

"Like they dropped into a crack in the ground," Abe said. "We checked every crevice in a twenty-five mile radius." A smile pushed the disappointment temporarily from his face. "At least the Indians don't have to be afraid. I stopped and told them."

Abe had had a hard day with no rest, no food, and no water. Ebb had had only water from a dirty slough. "Know what kept me going?" he asked Martha.

Martha shook her head. "I'm not sure, Abe. Was it knowing you were saving the Indians?"

"No, Martha my own. It was knowing you were here waiting for me. We all got discouraged, but no one had you to come home to but me." He kissed her tenderly. "God gave me the greatest blessing, when He gave me you."

Martha felt all warm and bubbly inside. She had been waiting all day for Abe too. "I purely love you, too, Abram my love. Thank You, God, for making us for each other."

—⚬—

Life slowly slipped back into its usual grind. The vegetable gardens came up with vigor and so did the weeds. Martha strapped Rebecca to her back and worked as much as she could.

The next week *The Washington Statesman* said the jury had found the defendants guilty. "They must have known, to stage that dangerous jail break," Abe said, sipping coffee as they read the paper Friday evening.

One evening Adam Jensen, the attorney, stopped by. After they visited awhile about the jail break and other things, he looked at Rebecca in Abe's arms. "You heard anything from the baby's mother or father?" he asked.

Abe pursed his lips as he shook his head. "Not a word. We've done a little looking too. We really don't know whether they're both gone back East or if one or both are still in town. We're keepin' our eyes open, though."

The lawyer got up. "Well, I must go. Keep in touch. If you're still after adopting, we might be able to push it through one of these days."

"What did he mean?" Martha asked after Jensen left.

"Is one of these days sooner or later than six months?"

Abe handed Rebecca to her and pulled them both into his arms. "I don't know," he said, "but if I was a bettin' man I'd bet it's less than six months."

—⚬—

One day Martha realized she couldn't keep Rebecca on her back all the time anymore. The baby wanted to play. She also wanted to be able to see Martha.

"Abe," she asked one evening after supper, "you're so good with your hands, I wonder if you could make me a cart for Rebecca."

"What do you have in mind?" he asked.

"Well, could you get someone to make you some wheels, something like wagon wheels, only smaller and lighter? You could make a cart for Rebecca to ride in. Maybe one I could push."

"Maybe Nate Butler could make us some wheels."

A week later Abe brought home two lightweight wheels smaller than those on a wagon. He used light lumber and built a little chair with sides on it as well as a back. He fastened the seat on a little frame over the wheels, put a strap across the front of the chair to keep Rebecca from falling out. "There! Get that girl!" Abe said proudly.

Martha put a blanket into the cart first, then gently put the baby in. Abe fastened the strap around her so she couldn't fall out. Martha pushed the cart back and forth a little ways. "It's good, Abe. I think this'll work a lot better now that she's older. I'll try it tomorrow while I work in the vegetable gardens."

The next morning, before Martha had a chance to go outside to hoe weeds, Gray Wolf, Pony Boy, and Camas walked into her house. "Food," they all said.

Martha knew them so well by now, she could have told them she didn't have time. But she felt glad to see them and welcomed a chance to visit with them a bit. "You men just sit down and I'll make you some sandwiches," she said, knowing they understand most of what she said. Slicing some meat she had roasted last night, she made three huge sandwiches, put them on plates, and pushed them in front of the Indians. She asked God to bless the food and also each Indian. Then she put a tall glass of milk in front of each.

She sat down across the table from them while they ate.

"I guess you haven't had any trouble with those bad men," she said, knowing the men were far away.

Gray Wolf swallowed a big bite. "Indians know where bad men. Cows too."

Chapter 16

Looking up from the harness he worked on, Abe saw the three Indians and Martha approaching from the back yard. Martha usually didn't interrupt his work unless it was important. Curious, he laid down the leather strap and went to meet them.

"Hello," he called.

"Good morning, Abe," Gray Wolf said, enunciating carefully.

"Hurry, Abe," Martha called. "These men have something important to tell you."

Abe shook each Indian's hand, giving them the respect they deserved. "What is it, friends?"

"Let's go back to the house so we can sit down," Martha said.

When they all sat in the main room, Abe met Gray Wolf's eyes. "I gather something's happened. Is everyone all right?"

Gray Wolf leaned forward, his face almost excited. Now Abe knew something had happened. Gray Wolf hardly ever showed expression, seldom even smiled. "Indians know men take gold. Know cows. Mountains."

Abe took in a big gulp of air. "Did you see the men who took our gold?"

All three black heads jerked up and down. "See in mountains," Pony Boy said.

"Cows too," Camas finished.

"What cows?" Abe asked.

Gray Wolf looked patient. "Cows men take."

Abe couldn't sit still. He jumped to his feet. "You mean the cows rustled here this year?" Three black heads nodded.

"Who are the men? How many are there?"

Camas held up seven fingers. "Men took gold. Three more."

"Where are they?"

Through much talking, and with Martha's help, the Indians made them understand the men were holding lots of cattle in a box canyon, a valley with mountains on three sides. The men had built a fence on the fourth side to keep the cattle in the canyon.

The Indians offered to lead Abe to the place. "Tryin' to capture that many men in a spot like that'd be way too dangerous," Abe said. "They'd shoot us like ducks on a pond."

The Indians shook their heads. "Drink much firewater," Gray Wolf said. "Sleep long sleep. Cows make much sound. Not hear Indians."

"How do you know all this?" Abe asked.

"Indians watch. Not shoot Indians. Not see Indians. Not shoot Abe. Not see Abe."

Abe looked at Martha whose laughing gray eyes indicated she thought the whole thing hilarious. "Tell me how this is funny," he asked, truly curious.

She burst out laughing. "Oh, Abe, it purely is. Here we've been fretting about where those men went while the Indians have been watching them. You can tell they've been watching a lot too."

"How many times you men been in there?" Abe asked.

Gray Wolf looked at his sons. They all shrugged. "Much times," Gray Wolf said. "Not see Gray Wolf. Drink firewater—sleep."

"Well," Abe said, "I don't know how to proceed, but the men have to be captured. I think we'll have to share this with the vigilance committee." He turned to the Indians.

"Is it all right if I talk to white men about this? When we get a bunch of men together we'll get you to help us."

Gray Wolf got to his feet. His sons followed. "Gray Wolf help catch bad men. Soon?"

Abe grasped each hand again as the men left. "Real soon," he assured them. He held up one, then two fingers. "In one or two days."

Gray Wolf nodded. "Indians go first. See drink firewater. See sleep."

Abe called the group together in his yard that night and told him what the Indians had said. At first the men thought it would be a suicide mission, but when Abe explained the Indians had been there many times at night and the men were always in a drunken stupor, they wanted to go that night. Abe told them they would have to take the Indians with them and that the Indians would scout ahead.

They decided to make the raid the next night. Besides the Indians, they would take fourteen men, seven pairs. Each pair would approach and apprehend one of the drunken men.

"Better take a few extra—in case those savages counted wrong," someone called.

"They aren't savages," Abe said. "And they count as well as you. But it's still a good idea. Anyone could make a mistake in a place like that. Or friends might drop in that night. We'll take three more pairs."

—◊◊◊—

The next night about nine o'clock Abe kissed Martha good-bye. "I'll be praying for you every single minute," she promised.

Abe told her he would be praying too. Then he mounted Ebb and headed southeast with the group of men. The three Indians rode with Abe.

After riding two hours, they began climbing into the mountains. After another hour the Indians told the men to wait there.

Abe took advantage of the time to pray. "You know what we're doin' here," he said. "Thanks for carin' about us, God, and please go with us tonight so there won't be any bloodshed. Thanks, Lord."

You're welcome, Abe. Go, without fear.

Abe felt a tremendous relief. "Thanks, Lord. I'll bet You knew I was terrified, didn't You? Of course You did."

Over an hour later, Gray Wolf returned alone. "Men sleep," he said. "Come."

"How many are there?" Abe whispered into the dark.

"Men take gold. Three more."

They rode the horses another mile, then Gray Wolf insisted they leave them. Almost immediately Abe noticed a fence on his right. A large gate lay wide open. When the men all passed the gate, Gray Wolf closed it. As they moved into the canyon, Abe heard cattle lowing. The sound grew louder as they progressed.

After another half mile they reached a campsite with burning lanterns hanging in the trees. The barely-glowing coals from a campfire told Abe the men had been sleeping awhile. Then he saw the men. Some half-sat on logs, hunched over with their heads on their knees. Others lay on the ground, seeming to be sound asleep, an eerie sight in the light of the flickering lantern light.

Abe signaled the men to come in. Each team chose a man and they all reached the men at once. The extra men served as scouts watching for anyone else who might be around.

Abe and his partner gently took their man's hands, put them together behind him, and tied them securely. The man stirred but didn't awaken. Then they tied his feet tightly and attached the rope to the one holding the man's hands. "Now he won't do any kickin'," Abe whispered.

When they finished, Abe looked around. Everyone else finished soon. One man awakened, screaming and yelling as if he were being physically tortured. Abe heard the vigilante tell him to shut up but the man kept yelling.

"A little unnerving," Abe's partner said. "Seems he's yelling to someone to come help him."

Abe smiled in the dark. "Yeah. These other guys who slept through the whole thing." Slowly it dawned on Abe that they had forgotten one thing. How were they going to haul seven drunken men more than a mile to the horses?

Eventually the vigilantes went after the horses and tied the rustlers over the horses behind the saddles. *Should have brought extra horses,* Abe thought. Well, they'd take it real easy.

Before they reached Walla Walla, several of the men had awakened and yelled loudly the rest of the way.

"What we gonna do with these vermin?" someone asked.

"That there tree's still standin' south o' town," several answered.

"Let's take them to the jail," Abe said. "And finish what was started last week. Seems only right. I think we got them all but let's take turns guardin' the jail anyway."

When they reached the jail, Abe ran inside to see if anyone was on guard. He found one man sound asleep. "Wake up!" he yelled. "We got a whole jail full of varmints for you."

After a lot of confusion, all the men stood behind bars. Several men took their positions to guard. "We don't need none of you around here," the jail guard said. "You can see those cages're tighter'n a new shoe."

"Yeah, that's what we heard last week," someone said. "We'll just help out a little, while these boys're in there."

The next day the men were still caged, awake, and screaming obscenities at anyone who came near. Abe didn't hang around long.

A large group of men on horses went to the canyon and herded the cattle back, disappointed to find only about one hundred and fifty head.

Abe went back to the jail. The men had yelled themselves hoarse, so the place seemed quiet. "Where's the rest of the cattle?" Abe asked one of the men who had beaten Camas. "There was near a thousand rustled last summer. That's not counting the ones the varmints already hanged took. Those cattle went back to the rightful owners."

The man spit at Abe. "Think I'd tell you if I knew? We never had no thousand."

Abe moved down to the other end of the cages, hoping the men there hadn't heard his discussion with the spitter. "How many cattle did you boys get?" Abe asked a man who looked to be in his late teens.

The boy looked frightened. "Ain't got no idea," he said quietly.

Abe thought a moment. "Been selling 'em off?" he asked.

The boy nodded. "Sellin' 'em to miners for meat."

Abe took a good look at the boy. "You look like a decent young man. How'd you get stuck with this bunch?"

The boy's eyes grew red as though he were about to cry. "I didn't have any money or food. No one would help me or give me a job. These men fed me, then made me help take cattle. I did it, knowing it wasn't right. My ma would cry in her grave if she knew what I did." He paused a moment. "So would Pa."

Abe believed the boy. His grammar indicated he'd been raised in a genteel family, and so did his fine-featured face. "How old are you?" Abe asked.

"Tomorrow I'll be seventeen." The boy's entire body trembled. "If I live that long."

Abe reached through the bars and patted the boy. "You just rest and pray to God for help. You commit your life a hundred percent to Him and He'll figger out somethin'."

Abe talked to the other five, finding them hard, cruel men, not caring what they had done and seeming to care less what happened to them. Abe then asked the sheriff when the trial would be held.

"Why you need a trial?" the sheriff replied. "Ain't a one of 'em denies takin' them cattle. I heard the vigilantes're out gettin' the tree ready."

Abe remembered the seventeen-year-old boy. "They may not deny doing it, but one is a young boy those other ruffians saved from starving, then forced into the gang."

The big man shrugged. "May be. Ain't none of my problem, er yours neither."

"But it is our problem. Would you want something like this to happen to your son? The boy's innocent, Buckley. That's what trials are for."

Abe wandered down the street to the office of Jensen, the attorney's. "Heard anything about a trial for the gang we brought in?" he asked Jensen.

Jensen shook his head. "I haven't been invited to participate anyway."

Abe told him about the boy and left.

—⁊⁊—

When Abe told Martha about the young boy, she demanded they do something. "Will they take them and hang them today?" she cried. "We purely can't let them do that, Abe. Remember Melissa? She could have been punished for picking your pocket. And she was hungry just like that boy.

"I think God's telling us we have to do more to feed starving people, Abe."

Abe sat down at the table. "I agree. Something we gotta take up right soon. Let's go see what's happening."

Abe put Rebecca into her cart, fastened the strap, and yelled for Willie. Before they got out the door Jensen arrived. Martha poured coffee for the men.

"There's going to be some sort of a trial," the attorney said. "They asked me to defend the accused. Good thing you stopped by, Abe, or I'd have refused. I won't try to turn guilty men free, but I'll do my best for the boy. The thing'll be this afternoon at two o'clock. Thought you'd want to know."

—⚏—

Abe and Martha arrived early enough to find seats this time. The hardened criminals didn't deny their guilt and didn't show any remorse or respect for anyone talking to them.

Jed, the seventeen-year-old, acted like a different kind of person. Abe could tell he impressed Jensen and also the judge. Jensen called Abe to the witness chair, giving Abe a chance to say he thought the boy would prove to be a blessing to the community if they released him. The jury returned a verdict after a fifteen minute discussion, finding all but Jed guilty. They ordered the guilty men to be "hanged by the neck until dead" that afternoon at sunset. They made Abe guardian of the boy, Jed.

Then Adam Jensen stood up. "I'd like to speak for most everyone here and thank our Indian brothers for locating these men and helping us apprehend them. Would Gray Wolf please come to the front so I can shake his hand?"

Martha gave the tall Indian a small shove. He walked straight and tall to the front of the courtroom. Jensen and Gray Wolf reached out together and shook hands heartily. "We're fortunate to have you men in our community," Jensen said. "Would you like to say something?"

Gray Wolf nodded. "Firewater bad." Many people laughed and audibly agreed. Someone started clapping and soon the whole crowd clapped and stomped their feet. The Indians marched out the door, straight, solemn, and tall.

Abe and Martha took Jed home with them.

Jensen arrived a little later. "I brought some adoption papers," he said. "If you still want to adopt that baby, I say let's do it now."

Martha gasped. "Would that mean no one could ever take her from us?"

Jensen nodded. "That's about it. And she's a mighty lucky baby too. I figure you folks are going to be a great asset to this town and the people in it for a long time."

They wasted no time getting the adoption taken care of. Now Rebecca Ann Noble was theirs for always—and William Robert Noble's little sister. Abe thought of Jed, also an orphan. Well, he wasn't going to even think of that at the moment.

That night as Abe started falling to sleep, God spoke to him. *You did well, Abe. You're My precious son. But you'd better build some rooms onto your house. Several of them. And don't forget the bathroom.*

A Letter to Our Readers

Dear Readers:

In order that we might better contribute to your reading enjoyment, we would appreciate your taking a few minutes to respond to the following questions. When completed, please return to the following: Fiction Editor, Barbour Publishing, Inc., P.O. Box 719, Uhrichsville, OH 44683.

1. Did you enjoy reading *Northwest?*
   ❑ Very much, I would like to see more books like this.
   ❑ Moderately—I would have enjoyed it more if _____
   _____
   _____

2. What influenced your decision to purchase this book? (Check those that apply.)
   ❑ Cover   ❑ Back cover copy   ❑ Title   ❑ Price
   ❑ Friends   ❑ Publicity   ❑ Other _____

3. Which story was your favorite?
   ❑ *Heartbreak Trail*   ❑ *Abram My Love*
   ❑ *Martha My Love*   ❑ *A New Love*

4. Please check your age range:
   ❑ Under 18   ❑ 18–24   ❑ 25–34
   ❑ 35–45   ❑ 46–55   ❑ Over 55 _____

5. How many hours per week do you read?

Name _____

Occupation _____

Address _____

City_____ State_____ Zip_____